The Game of Lies

by

Karen A. Lynch

This book is a work of fiction. Places, events, and situations in this story are purely fictional. Any resemblance to actual persons, living or dead, is coincidental.

ISBN: 1-4107-9883-6 (e-book)
ISBN: 1-4107-9881-X (Paperback)
ISBN: 1-4107-9882-8 (Dust Jacket)

This book is printed on acid free paper.

1stBooks – rev. 10/14/03

Dedication

This book is dedicated to the women of the clandestine service, who, along with their male counterpart, are the unsung heroes of America's pursuit of peace in a most dangerous world.

And to my husband, and my hero, Grayston L. Lynch, whose three Purple Hearts, two Silver Stars, Bronze Star with V for Valor, and the Intelligence Star, serve as eloquent testimony to his bravery, courage, devotion to duty and his country, and to his contribution, both as a career Army officer and CIA Intelligence Officer, to preserving the freedom we all cherish.

Acknowledgements

Writing a novel is a solitary endeavor. It requires authors to spend countless hours pounding their keyboards and racking their brains for that illusive idea, that spellbinding tale, that just-right melding of action, drama and romance that eventually results in a satisfying read for their audiences.

My novel, *The Game of Lies*, was no exception, but without the support, dedication and input of many generous and knowledgeable souls to flesh out the characters, create the vivid scenes, and lend authenticity and realism to a fictitious world, this novel could never have been written.

And so, my grateful thanks go, first, to my husband, and my real life hero, Grayston L. Lynch. Gray was career military, retiring as an officer from the U.S. Army Special Forces. He is also a retired CIA Intelligence Officer, whose own exploits would rival those of James Bond. To him, I owe the fine-tuning of the intelligence work in this book. Then to Jerry Gross of Gerald Gross Associates LLC, a genius of a freelance editor, and a kind man, who never let me waver in my determination to finish this novel. Next, to my oldest (25 years and counting), and dearest friend, John Piesen, a great journalist, and the first and last person to ever lay eyes, and an editor's pen, on this manuscript, and who is to this day, my staunchest supporter.

Others include Shaolin Master Sin The, and his protégés, and my teachers in the Shaolin martial arts, Eric Smith and Bill Leonard, who taught me not just the fighting ways of Shaolin, but also the spirituality of this great art. Robert Plomski, retired Army and police officer, whose expertise with all manner of weapons he graciously passed on to me. LTC (Ret.) Thomas Quisenberry USA for his help with the Huey helicopter scenes. Peter and Wendy Reynolds, my Irish horsy friends, who lent the Irish flavor to this book. The University of Kentucky, whose school of architecture, provided the detailed plans for what is now the Renaissance Museum in France, and which serves as the setting for the book's main action scenes. Victor Dobrov for his help with Russian and Ukrainian logistics and intelligence.

A special mention for my friend, retired CIA Intelligence Officer Tom Poole, who after finally realizing writing a work of fiction was not the same as writing an after action report, lent his expertise. And to Patricia Farnum and MAJ (RET) Al Farnum, USASF, just the best of people, who read this manuscript until they ferreted out the last of the editorial bugs.

As for the book's cover, thanks go to the very creative and insightful, Judy Walker, of Judy Walker Designs and Illustrations. To Paul Burt and Regina Ransford of 1stBooks Library thanks are in order for leading me through the publication process. They were always available to answer questions, provide helpful advice, and encouragement.

And, of course, a warm thanks to my family; my daughter, Elizabeth Ann Haynes, granddaughter, Amy Elizabeth Haynes, and my son-in-law Douglas Haynes for their loving support. Most of my family is now gone, but they were warm, generous, caring people, who encouraged me to follow my every dream. I am most grateful to them, for they are to whom I owe my many successes in life and everything I am today.

There were many others along the road to this books completion that made invaluable contributions, but because of who they are, they must remain nameless.

Prologue

LEXINGTON, KENTUCKY

Alanna Reynolds stood in the stable door and watched as the horse transport carrying the last load of her Thoroughbred yearlings rolled down the tree-lined drive and out the of Wicklow Stud's main entrance headed for Keeneland Race Course's Lexington sales facility.

The departing yearlings were a splendid group. They represented many months of careful, loving preparation, along with a considerable monetary investment. She would miss them, for all of them had been born on the farm and hand raised. But she understood it was their sale and, hopefully, their future success on the track that would insure the future of her farm and her involvement in the world of Thoroughbred racing and breeding which she loved.

The preliminaries completed, she headed to her car.

As Alanna approached her black Volvo station wagon, parked at an angle to the barn door, a loud noise coming from inside the barn stopped her and made her turn around.

Inside the door, a man stood in the shadows, his arm raised as in a greeting.

"Jake. What a surprise," she called, to what appeared to be the familiar figure of Jake Carter, her best friend, protector, mentor, and comrade in arms through many a dangerous moment in her life.

Leaving the car, she started back to the barn, first at a walk, then at a run, as the figure seemed to move backward into the aisle.

"Jake. Jake, wait! Where are you going?" she called to the retreating figure.

As she entered the barn, all that met her was a long empty barn aisle, and dead silence. Slowly, she walked to the end of the aisle and back, nothing. No one was there. A sense of foreboding came over her, for there could be no mistaking that the man she had seen was Jake. But, Jake, she knew, at this moment should be in France, thousands of miles away.

"Jake!" she shouted into the emptiness, urgent and fearful.

But, only the chirping of a nesting bird answered her call. Its melody echoed in the sound coming from the crazy bird clock a stable hand had hung on the barn wall to her right as it struck 5 p.m.

She noted the time, then turned slowly and walked back to her car, stopping half way there to give the barn one more backward glance, then continued on, the bright luster of the day now tinged with melancholy.

You'd better stop missing lunch, she thought again, trying to dispel her uneasiness at the strange occurrence.

Getting into her car, Alanna drove around the side of the barn to the main house. Parking near the side door, she entered at a run, taking the stairs to her room two at a time. Somewhere in the background, she heard Angela, the housekeeper, conversing with her son, Danny.

Since it was already after 5:00, there was barely time for her afternoon ritual before she would need to make an appearance at Keeneland's pre-sale cocktail party. However, after her haunting experience in the barn, she felt a great need for its power to recenter her thoughts and emotions.

Slipping out of her barn clothes, she donned a black Gi, securing it around her waist with a black belt.

Barefoot, she walked quickly across the hardwood floor to the second floor gym. It was a large square room with a well-padded floor, high ceilings and mirrored walls. Skylights let in light, while the silently turning blades of a ceiling fan cooled the room.

Dario De Santes, her friend, lover and partner in what sometimes seemed another life, had spent many hours honing her Shaolin martial arts skills. Though dead for five years, and while never actually having spent time in this room, his spirit nevertheless filled it, and, in it, they were one again.

Alanna bowed deeply before entering the room as a sign of respect. Then, entered and slid back the mirrored panel, directly to the right of the door. The panel held an assortment of oriental weaponry, exercise gear and a stereo system.

She chose from the weapons a pair of Octagon Sais; an intricately carved Tai Chi sword; a pair of Kamas, a sickle-shaped blade mounted on 16 inch tear-shaped hickory handles; and a pair of Nunchakus, made of two 12 inch long oak dowels connected by a length of chain, which she laid in a line on the floor several feet from the wall.

She pressed the play button on the stereo, and moved to the center of the room.

The opening refrains of Kitaro's Asian melody Silk Road were very soft. As they filled the room, she knelt and then sat back on her heels. Bending from the waist, she touched her head and fists to the floor in ceremonial greeting. Rising, she again bowed slightly from the waist.

Her opening moves were from the Pa Qua system. She started slowly, stretching each muscle as she let the music carry her through the moves of the Pa Qua kata. As her body loosened and warmed, the moves became more powerful and dynamic. Kicks, strikes, blocks, and leaps joined together to form a routine of beauty, grace and strength. Each move was done with lightning speed and perfect form. The sound of the stiff, cotton fabric of her garment cracked like gunfire as her arms and legs lashed out. Flowing from one move to the other, she covered the entire room.

The music changed to a fiery tempo. First, she chose the Tai Chi sword, and to the rhythm of the music, she performed movements that emulated a sword-fight, slicing the air, jumping over the blade. Next, she chose the Kamas, cutting the air in intricate patterns with their blades. Then, she attacked, jabbed, and slashed an imaginary enemy with the Sais.

Finally, picking up the Nunchakus, she swung them around her, above her head, and then down low, jumping over them. She moved so fast that the Nunchakus were merely a blur to the eye.

Danny, who had been sent by his mother to tell Alanna of an awaiting phone call, let himself in through the barely opened door. Sensing this was not the time to interrupt, he watched in silent, respectful awe. Since he had become old enough to take an interest in girls at the tender age of 11, he had developed a crush on his mother's employer. Now her saw her in an entirely different light. Not as the khaki-trouser, Izod shirt-wearing horsewoman he knew, but as someone out of a fantasy.

He gasped at the speed and power of each movement, at the athletic ability that allowed Alanna to somersault, land and be airborne again. Unbeknownst to him, he was witnessing a performance never before seen by anyone other than Dar. He stood mesmerized.

Her closing move found her in the same position as the opening gesture.

The room fell silent. Danny dared not move; he felt it would break the spell, the aura, which now seemed to fill the room. He could not explain the sensation. It was electric, penetrating every pore of his body. He became frightened and started to leave. As he started out the door, he heard her call softly to him.

"Is there something I can do for you, Danny?

"I'm sorry to disturb you, Miss Reynolds," he said, turning to face her. "Mother sent me to say there was a call holding for you."

She came to the doorway where he stood.

"Thank you, I'll be right down to answer it."

She smiled as she spoke, so that he would be assured she was not angry with him and laid her hand reassuringly on his shoulder. Warmth emanated from her hand; it coursed throughout his body, relaxing him, seeming to soothe his fear. As it was the first time she had actually ever touched him, it excited him in a very sexual way.

Seeing a blush come over him at her touch, Alanna shook her head, smiled, and moved passed.

"I think I'll take that phone call now," she said, leaving him to sort out his feelings.

Who are you? How can you make me feel this way, he wondered silently.

Alanna had come to Lexington five years ago. Even then, he was old enough to understand the talk, and rumors that had surrounded her arrival. But, early on, it was obvious to all that she was a knowledgeable horsewoman. Soon, she became a great success at breeding Thoroughbred horses, and people grew to like and respect her. But many still speculated that there was much more to Alanna Reynolds than met the eye.

When she'd touched him, he decided they were right, and he wondered if he, or anyone, would ever uncover the mystery that surrounded her.

"What is called "foreknowledge" cannot be elicited from spirits, nor from gods, nor by analogy with past events, nor from calculations. It must be obtained from men who know the enemy situation."

Sun Tzu, The Art of War

FRANCE

The small, battered car wove its way through the deserted streets of Trouville. The driver slumped against its steering wheel, hoping his strength would not give out. The blood, oozing from a gunshot wound in his chest, saturated his sweater and jacket. One-handed, he turned the vehicle into a narrow alley, a difficult maneuver. He was weakening, his vision blurring.

Jake Carter had been in the intelligence business since his graduation from Georgetown. Though his achievements had, of necessity, gone unheralded publicly; he was considered by his CIA employers to be one of the best in the business. A normally unpretentious man, he, nevertheless, prided himself on his unblemished record of completed missions — a record, he knew, as dangerously close to perishing as he was.

He swore under his breath as he painfully negotiated a final turn. Even keeping his eyelids open was proving difficult now, but he had made it. The car jerked to a stop. He shouldered open the door, and, using it for support, gathered what power he had left in his limbs, and staggered to the rough-hewn back entrance of the pastry shop.

The weight of his falling body put him through the door. As he lay sprawled on the cold, brick floor, his vision clouding, Jake could just make out the figure of his contact, Jean-Louis, rushing towards him, then, kneeling beside him. Into his ear, Jake whispered, "Tell them JESTER OUT - RESURRECT CHAMELEON."

A final breath --- mission complete, agent out.

1

Chapter 2

Granton Taylor swung his black Porsche 928 into his space in the parking area of the Central Intelligence Agency's Langley headquarters. The engine growled to a halt. As he opened the door, he was assaulted by a blast of mid-July heat and humidity. Even the moderate breeze that propelled a small scrap of paper past the back of his car was hot. It would have been a good day, he thought, to play hooky and go sailing on the bay.

Dismissing the idea, Granton reached across the seat, picked up his neatly folded suit coat and slipped it on. From the floor behind the driver's seat, he retrieved his black leather briefcase. He locked the door, activating its alarm, and across the car's roof, acknowledged his armed escorts, a recent necessity, who were seated in the car that had pulled up and parked in the space next to him. Organized, he headed into the building.

As he rode the elevator up to his seventh-floor office, he wondered how long it would take for today to go wrong. Five years as deputy director of operations had taught him the only thing certain about each day in his business was the uncertainty.

In the last few days, the Middle East crisis, which had been brewing for years, had reached the borderline red alert stage. So dire had the situation become, that the Israelis, having been pushed into a corner by the demands and threats from its Middle Eastern neighbors to allow a Palestinian state amidst almost daily terrorist actions against the Israeli people by a variety of Palestinian terror groups, had openly promised nuclear retaliation on any Middle Eastern country that took military action against Israel.

The heat was on the CIA to see that that didn't happen, and Granton's department was the one charged with the responsibility. It was just one of a half dozen hot items his people were dealing with as rogue nations flexed their disruptive muscles around the globe.

Granton checked his watch. The digital display, which blinked out a sharp 7 a.m., reassured him that he was on schedule. The elevator door slid open and he exited into the main hallway, which bustled with activity. Halfway down the hall, he paused momentarily to straighten his tie, and smooth down his hair before opening the door to his outer office.

Waiting inside were Assistant Deputy Director of Operations John Dekker, Chief of Special Operations Jim Streigal, and one of Streigal's

European case officers, whose name momentarily escaped Granton, but who, he knew, normally handled operations in France.

"Good morning, gentlemen," Granton greeted the men, who rose as he entered.

Streigal was the first to return the greeting.

Then, Dekker responded, "And a good morning to you, Granton." After which, he gestured towards the short, stout man standing slightly to the left of him, and said, "You remember Andre DeGare?"

"Yes, of course. Things are going well in France I hope, Andre?" Granton said as he took the man's outstretched hand and shook it.

"That's what we're here to see you about, sir," DeGare replied hesitantly, somewhat intimidated by the stature of the man who had an arm-wrestler's grip on his hand.

DeGare had first met Taylor at an Agency function back in April. It had amazed him then, as it did now, how youthful and vigorous Taylor, at 55, appeared to be. The word at the Agency was that Taylor had come to the CIA from the Army's Green Berets, and that it was his reputation as a first-rate field agent, and para-military expert while with the Agency, that had gotten him his present job.

Despite now being desk-bound, Taylor still appeared to move with the cat-like grace of a jungle fighter. The finely tailored suit he wore emphasizing his tall, lean, physically fit figure. Only a pair of wire-rimmed glasses and slightly thinning gray hair seemed to be a concession to the passing of time.

"Well, whatever it is," Granton said, "it must be serious to require all your attention. In that case, follow me and let's get on with it."

Behind the men, he could see his long-time administrative assistant, Catherine Eller, waiting at her desk, the red folder that contained the previous night's cable traffic, in her hand.

He approached her, greeting her warmly. "And, how are you this morning, Miss Catherine? I hope you, at least, have some good news for me. How was the Boston Pops concert last night?"

The stylish, middle-aged woman smiled and replied in a voice laced with a heavy Old Virginia accent, "Why, I'm just fine this morning, Mr. Taylor, thank you. The music was wonderful, truly wonderful. I surely wish you and Ellen had been there to enjoy it with me?"

"I'm glad to hear you enjoyed it," Taylor replied, as he took the folder from her, "Actually, Ellen and I were going until, Brian, our 8-year-old, came down with a fever. You know, that's how it goes when you've got young ones."

3

"How well I know!" The mother of three responded while handing him the folder.

Tucking it under his arm, Granton turned and headed for his office, while motioning for Dekker, Streigal and DeGare to follow. Halfway through opening his office door, he paused. Turning back, he said, "Catherine, please see if you can find out what's holding up that information I requested yesterday from State? Oh, and hold all my calls until we finish this meeting."

"Certainly, sir," she replied, as she reached for her phone.

"Come on in, gentlemen," Granton said, as he preceded them into his office.

The men followed, DeGare closing the door behind them.

Granton moved behind his desk. From there, he motioned in the direction of the two chairs in front of it, inviting the men to be seated.

"Seems, we're a seat short." Pointing to a ladder back chair set against the wall, that he mostly used to hang his jacket on, he said, "Andre, grab that chair and bring it over here."

As they took their seats, he set his briefcase on the credenza behind his desk, placed the red folder on the desk, and took his seat. Once they were all settled, he gave his full attention to them, focusing mainly on Dekker, the senior member of the trio.

"What've you got, John?"

"We've word from Paris, Granton, and I'm afraid it's bad news," Dekker said. "Jake Carter is dead."

Dekker, seeing Granton's facial expression freeze in response to the announcement, and knowing that Granton and Jake went back a long way and had been close friends, paused to allow time for him to absorb the impact of the message.

After a respectful period of silence, during which Granton made no attempt to comment, Dekker continued, "I'm sorry, Granton, I hated to drop the news on you like that. I know how close you two were."

Granton simply nodded, and Dekker went on. "Andre has been handling Operation SABRE, the one Jake was running, here at headquarters. So, I think it's best if he fills you in on what we know so far."

Without any further display of emotions, Granton turned his attention to the other man. DeGare moved forward to the edge of his chair, and in an apologetic tone, began the briefing. "Unfortunately, Mr. Taylor, we know very little about what happened to Carter at the present time. What we have is a flash cable from the Paris station. The station said it had

4

received a phone call on one of their emergency numbers from a Jean-Louis, a French national who was one of Jake's sub-agents."

DeGare stopped to clear his throat, then went on. "They said the man was a little frantic, but the gist of his report was that Jake had stumbled into the back door of his pastry shop at about midnight their time. That's about 5 p.m. our time. He was badly wounded, and collapsed and died almost immediately. He said he heard Jake mumble something like, 'Tell them JESTER OUT - RESURRECT CHAMELEON.' No one has a clue what he might have meant by that."

Taylor let the room fall silent for a moment, and then in a cool, low voice he replied, "I appreciate your bringing this to my attention so quickly, Andre. Jake's death is not just a serious operational loss to the Agency, but as Dekker pointed out, also a great personal loss to me. That message was meant for me and ..."

The intercom buzzed suddenly, interrupting the meeting,

Catherine's voice responded to his lifting the receiver. "Sorry to interrupt, Mr. Taylor, but the director's office just called. The director and Admiral Porter would like to see you as soon as possible."

"Tell them I'll be there directly, Catherine" he said, and hung up the phone.

Taking their cue from his closing comments, the men rose to leave.

"Sit back down gentlemen. The powers to be will have to wait for now. This comes first," Granton said, and they resumed their conversation.

"Penta," DeGare said, referring to the Paris chief of station, Ron Penta, "arranged to have the local police find Jake's body in his car alongside the road on the outskirts of Trouville. He was hoping that word would get back to whoever did it, and that they'd assume Jake had not made contact with anyone before he died."

"Good thinking," Granton replied, then sadly inquired, "Andre, have arrangements been made to get Jake's body home?"

"Yes, Penta has made arrangements." Andre said. "We've been told Jake had no close family, so will you be handling the details of the burial?"

"Possibly. Let me know when they expect Jake's remains to arrive."

Remembering his waiting superior, Granton asked, "Anything else?"

"Not for the moment," Dekker replied.

"Then," Granton said, "I need to see what the old man wants and brief him on what's happened. In the meantime, get me all the background information on this operation you have, and as soon as I

5

have a plan, I'll get back with you. Any new information you get is to be forwarded to me immediately, day or night. Is that clear?"

"Absolutely." Dekker said, as he and the other men got up to leave. "I'll have that information on your desk today before lunch."

"Fine. Good day, gentlemen," Granton replied, as Dekker joined his associates, who were already headed for the door.

Granton rested his eyes on the red folder as the men bid their farewells and made their exit. Then he pressed the buzzer on his desk, and a few seconds later, Catherine, carrying her steno pad, entered the room.

"Please, sit down, Catherine." Taylor pointed to the chair Dekker had just vacated and she took a seat, setting the unopened pad on her lap. He paused a moment, and then, in a more personal than professional tone, said, "Catherine, we've had word from Paris this morning --- Jake is dead."

Catherine, whose relationship with Granton over the years had been friendly, yet businesslike, tried to maintain her professional facade, but slowly the tears began to fall. "Oh, God, not Jake, he can't be dead. It's got to be a mistake Mr. Taylor. Please, tell me it's a mistake."

"Lord knows, Catherine, no one wishes it were a mistake more than I," he said, walking around to the other side of his desk and handing her the handkerchief from his jacket pocket.

Granton knew that Jake and Catherine had also developed a close personal relationship over the years. During one of his and Jake's elbow-bending sessions at a jazz spot they'd frequented called Blues Alley, Jake had confided in Granton that he'd often thought about marrying Catherine. Yet Jake could never quite bring himself to do it. He claimed that the reason he'd refrained from marrying her was that his devotion to his duty came first. However, Granton had always suspected that the real reason Jake had remained single had had more to do with the freedom he so cherished than devotion to duty.

"Would you like to go home, Catherine?" Granton offered.

"I don't think so, Mr. Taylor," she said, pausing to dab a tear from her cheek with the handkerchief. Though she wanted to, she refrained from asking for the details of Jake's passing, knowing instinctively that if Granton had wanted her to know them, he would have volunteered them. Instead, she said, "I appreciate your offer, but, if you don't mind, I think I'll stay. I'd really rather not be alone right now."

When he said nothing more, she asked, "Do you need me for anything else, sir?" When he shook his head, indicating a no response,

6

she said, "Then, would you excuse me? I need a few minutes to get myself together."

"Take all the time you need," he said. "And, Catherine, if you change your mind about going home, you have my permission to leave whenever you wish.

"I know one thing," he confided in her, the sadness in his eyes revealing a side of him Catherine had never seen, "Doing without that old goat around here is going to take some getting used to."

She smiled through her tears, and nodded in agreement, then chanced asking, "You will let me know what arrangements have been made for him, won't you?"

"Of course," Granton replied, knowing full well that he wouldn't.

Clutching her pad close to her chest, she exited quietly. As Granton watched his office door close behind her, he marveled at how the ghosts that lived behind it were beginning to mount up.

Jake, code name JESTER, had been the senior member of the CROWN JEWELS, an elite unit within the Agency of which Taylor was once a member, and later, commanded. It was made up of specialized agents whose talents were aimed at the most difficult and sensitive assignments.

With Jake's passing, all of the five original agents were now gone from the unit. Two had retired. He, and another team member, had been promoted and had been assigned desk jobs. But, Jake, who had also received regular promotions, preferred working in the field, and that's where he'd stayed, his experience a valuable asset to all he'd worked with. Now, he too was gone, killed in the line of duty. Murdered.

The Agency, over the years, had added a limited number of select, new members to the group. In Granton's estimation, only three of the new recruits had ever measured up to the original group. Of these three, only one was still in the field, Jeremy Slade, code name SCAVENGER, whom Granton had recruited out of Delta Force.

Unfortunately, Jeremy's actions, after a blown mission in the Balkans had caused his value to the group and the Agency to become questionable, and had almost ruined his otherwise distinguished career.

One of the other two was Dario De Santes, code name SCORPION, an international banker by trade, and son of a former U. S. Ambassador to Brazil and China, Alesandro De Santes. Dar had been the senior member and leader of this group. He had been killed in the Balkan fiasco.

And the other was an intelligence officer recruited by Jake and De Santes, code name CHAMELEON. CHAMELEON, at Jake's urging, and because of the Balkan incident, had resigned from the Agency.

All members of the CROWN JEWELS had been issued code names, and had always referred to one another by them. Jake had made the best use of his final moments by choosing the words that he knew would mean everything to Taylor.

The assignment, which had sent Jake to France six months ago, was extremely urgent and sensitive. It involved the French Mafia, who supposedly was doing business with the Iranian-backed Hizballah. The tenuous emanations, the Agency's fancy "cover your ass" word for messages, intercepted by satellite from Hizballah's Beirut cell, then indicated that Hizballah was in the processes of securing nuclear materials, with the assistance of the French Mafia, for their terrorist activities. In order to confirm the reports, and to penetrate the Mafia organization, Jake had gone under deep cover.

Jake was skilled at living his cover, yet, obviously, it had been blown. With the tight security accorded his identity, there could only be one possibility --- a leak.

The presence of a mole had also been suspected, but never proven in the tragic debacle in the Balkans, which had cost De Santes his life and the resignation of CHAMELEON. Although an extensive investigation was conducted at the time, Security and Counter Intelligence had not succeeded in uncovering a mole. Unable himself to prove or disprove that one existed within the ranks Granton lived with the constant dread of the issue resurfacing.

Granton loved his job. It had been his just reward for a long and successful career as a field agent. His eyes took in the confines of his office with its richly paneled walls, rare paintings, fine Oriental rug, antique furniture and as its centerpiece, a hand-carved, mahogany desk imported from London that befitted his position. Sometimes, he missed his days in the field, but this was not just a desk job he'd been relegated to, but THE JOB. It was his life. Some days, however, like today, it just plain stunk!

He sat a moment longer, and reviewed in his mind the little he knew about the circumstances surrounding Jake's death, but it was Jake's last words that kept invading his thoughts.

"Tell them, JESTER OUT - RESURRECT CHAMELEON!"

If it were only that simple Jake, he thought.

Granton hit the intercom switch. "Catherine, are you there?"

"Yes, Mr. Taylor."

"Tell the director I'm on my way over," he said.

"Yes, sir," she replied.

Before heading off, he opened the folder and sorted through the cables looking for the one from Paris reporting Jake's death. Midway through, he noticed a letter addressed to him. Diverting from his search, he opened it, and read what now obviously was Jake's last communiqué.

"Jesus! Jesus! Well, Jake, poker just went up," he remarked, at its startling contents. "It's high stakes now."

Resuming his search, he found the Paris cable, and slipped it, and the letter into his jacket pocket. Then, he took a deep breath, and headed out the office door.

As Granton made his way the short distance to the director's office, it occurred to him that Admiral Porter's visit was probably not a social one. The Admiral headed the National Security Council in the White House, and felt it was his sacred duty to ride herd on what he wrongly perceived were some "loose cannons" at the CIA. He was a firm believer in the benefits of modern technology over human resources, especially, when it came to the business of gathering intelligence — an opinion he shared with his old mentor, former CIA Director Stanley Tucker.

Granton and Jake were two of the lucky few to survive multiple purges of the Clandestine Service. Tucker's purge had almost gutted the department in an attempt to reduce the Agency's reliance on human based intelligence. He'd favored shifting funds and manpower to the Technical Collection side of the agency. In a memo to the Clandestine Service, the former director had advised them that he did not want any field agents over the age of 55.

Luckily, none of the CROWN JEWELS were in that age group, but it did cause the Agency to lose the services of a great many experienced, skilled senior intelligence officers who specialized in various areas of the world, and the production of critical intelligence -- officers who had just reached their peak of proficiency. Most of them opted for early retirement, and later, when Tucker realized his mistake and tried to lure them back, only a few returned.

Though Granton had not had time to be briefed on this meeting with the Admiral, he was sure it had something to do with operation SABRE. "Watch Dog" Porter, as the Admiral was known at the Agency, had not been one of SABRE's supporters, and Granton and the Director knew sabotaging SABRE was a high priority on his agenda.

9

Granton opened the door to the Director's outer office. The security guard waved him through.

As he entered the Director's reception area, the receptionist ushered him on in, saying. "Good morning, Mr. Taylor, go right on in. The Director is expecting you."

"Good morning, Nancy." Granton returned the greeting and after knocking on the door, proceeded into the director's office.

"Good morning, Lee. Admiral," Granton said. The naval officer returned Granton's greeting with a nod.

CIA Director Lee Hawthorn interrupted his conversation with the Admiral to greet his DDO. "Granton, come in. Grab yourself a cup of coffee and join us."

"Granton, as you know, Operation SABRE comes up for review before the Special Group very shortly." Hawthorn began, as Granton filled a cup and took a seat on the director's left.

"I'm aware of that, Lee" Granton replied.

"Well, the Admiral has expressed his and the Special Group's concern that, despite the fact SABRE is six months old, it has not provided any concrete intelligence on the movement of nuclear materials out of any former Soviet Union country and into the hands of Hizballah, or any other militant Arab group for that matter," Hawthorn said. He kept his voice as neutral as possible, considering he was in total disagreement with the Admiral. "It is the Admiral's opinion that SABRE be scrapped."

"Now mind you, Granton," the Admiral interrupted, "this is no reflection on your people, but the Russians are keeping a close eye on their nuclear materials and so, I believe, are their other former member states. Hizballah has about as much chance of getting their hands on that stuff as I have of walking on the moon. So, you can understand why we feel we can't justify the manpower and the expenditure any longer."

"Admiral," Granton replied, "up until yesterday I might have had to concede that SABRE was moving a bit slow. Sometimes, sir, that's the way it is in intelligence gathering. However, I just received a cable in the latest traffic concerning SABRE, and with your permission, Lee," Granton turned and addressed the Director, "I would like you and the Admiral to read it. I think it will change the Admiral's estimation of SABRE's importance."

Hawthorn took the cable from Granton, and focused his attention on it. Without comment, he passed it to the Admiral.

10

As the Admiral's eyes lifted from the communiqué, Hawthorn said, "Porter, this changes everything. They've just killed one of our top intelligence officers. This is the man who was running SABRE."

"Well," the Admiral said, hesitantly, "I can see that, but what is this cryptic part here? Who's CHAMELEON, and also, who's JESTER?"

"Those are old cryptonyms of our CROWN JEWEL agents," replied Granton. "I headed the group at one time, so these cryptonyms are all familiar to me. JESTER is Jake Carter, the agent that was killed. CHAMELEON is no longer with the Agency. Jake was directing this message at me. 'JESTER OUT' means the obvious, that 'the opposition killed me'. In asking me to 'RESURRECT CHAMELEON' he is indicating that she has some special entry to this group."

"She!" Interrupted the Admiral. "CHAMELEON is a woman?"

"Yes, sir," Granton replied, "and, intelligence officers don't come any better than this one, Admiral!"

"Granton," Hawthorn said, "are you really sure that Jake was telling you that the French Mafia was responsible for his death?"

"Well, sir, it was one of the groups targeted by SABRE," Granton continued. "It's CROWN JEWEL jargon, meaning the opposition, either the French Mafia or Hizballah, got him."

"Well, Porter," Hawthorn, now angered, interjected. "I am extending SABRE, and if your group gets in the way, I'll take it right to the President. I'm not in the business of allowing a bunch of French gangsters or Arab terrorists to murder one of my men, and then canceling the operation because of their actions."

Porter, taken aback by the Director's intensity, could only reply, "You'll get your six months, Lee. I'll guarantee it. Your man must have been onto something important if those thugs were willing to risk incurring the U. S. Government's wrath to protect it. My sincere condolences about Carter."

The Admiral rose from his chair. "Well, gentlemen, I know you'll want to get to work on this, so I'll not hold you up any longer. I'll be briefing the President on this today, and I'll get back to you as soon as I can."

"Thank you, Admiral, we appreciate your support." Hawthorn rose to see him off.

After closing the door and allowing enough time for the Admiral to exit the area, Hawthorn turned to Granton, and shaking his head, said, "God, what an asshole that anchor clanker is! I think we've clipped his wings back a bit, but we've got to keep our eye on him."

11

Then, walking over to the cherry credenza, where he refilled his cup of coffee, Hawthorn inquired, "This CHAMELEON left before I came aboard, I take it. Who is she? Where is she? And, can we get her back?"

Granton paused for a moment, then he replied, "Her name is Alanna Reynolds, and the last we heard she was operating a Thoroughbred breeding farm in Kentucky. As to whether we can get her back ... that, quite frankly Lee, I don't know. It's been five years since she left the Agency, and, when she left, she was pretty upset with us."

"Well, whatever it was that made her unhappy with us, she's had five years to forget it," the Director concluded.

Short on the facts in the Reynolds' case, the Director had, of course, oversimplified the problem. He added, "If she's important to this mission, Granton, we have to get her back."

"I understand that, Lee," Granton replied, "I think I might have a way."

"Well, you better get moving on it," the Director urged.

"Yes, sir, I must," Granton said, "because, we may not have much time. What I didn't say in front of the Admiral was that Jake gave an envelope to one of his couriers a couple of days ago. It was addressed to me personally and it arrived this morning with the cable traffic. The information contained in this letter is probably what caused Jake's death."

Handing the letter to the Director, he said, "I think you better read this."
The Director read:

Granton,

We were slightly off base on our target's objective. Newly confirmed information shows that the French Mafia and Hizballah have made a real breakthrough with one of the Russian Mafia families.

Instead of nuclear material, the Russians say they have in their possession a backpack type nuclear device of 1/4 KT (kiloton) power. The deal is that the Russians will exchange it for American dollars and drugs. Everything else about the operation remains the same. The only problem they have now is how to get it to France. The reason I am sending this by direct letter is that this information is so sensitive I don't even trust it to the Paris station.

Granton, if anything should happen to me, I regret that I have no choice but to recommend that you try and bring CHAMELEON back in.

Because of her present occupation, she already has access to one of our major players.

God forgive me for doing this to her.

Finishing the letter, the Director rose slowly, and without comment, from his desk. He walked to his window, hands clasped behind his back, where he remained looking out for what to Granton seemed like an eternity.

Finally, turning to Granton, he said, "Fill me in on this backpack nuke thing, Granton. What is it and what can it do?"

"Well for starters, Lee, it'll take out a half a mile in all directions -- completely!" Granton said. "A 1/4 KT backpack nuke is equal in power to 500 tons of TNT. But the most insidious thing about the little bastard is that it weighs less than 40 pounds, is about the size of a soccer ball, and it can easily be carried in a large suitcase. That makes it very easy to carry into the target area.

"They don't have to build a nuclear bomb, this bomb is self contained, no assembly required. All they have to do to fire off this little package is set the timer; pull the safety pin and walk. They could set it in a target area days, or even weeks, before it went off, the timer is that precise."

"Do we have any idea what their target is?"

"No."

The shock at hearing about the bomb's capabilities, and the Agency's lack of information on its intended target, caused the Director to lapse into another pensive silence. Concluding, he said, "Well, Granton, it looks like we've been handed a full plate. This is so serious that I'm going to have to brief the President on it myself. Immediately."

"Yes, you do, Lee." Granton affirmed the necessity to alert the nation's leader. "But, other than the President, I would like to request that this operation be handled on an absolute need-to-know basis, because, on top of everything, I have a gut feeling that we have another high level leak.

"Jake didn't blow his cover," Granton continued, "I have a feeling he was sold out. We had this happen once before with the CROWN JEWELS on an operation in the Balkans. We were ambushed. They were waiting for us. We lost one of our best officers and almost lost the whole team. Security and Counter Intelligence investigated the leak for a long time, but they could never pin anything down. I felt a little more at ease when Counter Intelligence exposed Anderson and Shaw, but Jake's death makes me feel otherwise. There's another Anderson out there somewhere, and I won't risk him blowing this operation."

"Damn, Granton, are you saying we may have another mole in here?"

"It's the only logical explanation I can come up with, Lee," Granton replied. "We played Jake's cover close to the vest, and as I said before, Jake just wouldn't make stupid mistakes that would blow his cover. For that reason, I'd like to get Security and Counter Intelligence in on this. I'd also like to classify all SABRE traffic 'Eyes Only' and limit distribution to our own shop."

"I think that's a good idea," Hawthorn said. "Put it on the BIGOT list to restrict access. At least we can halt any future leaks," Then he added, "It said in the letter that the information concerning the nuclear device is confirmed. Any idea where Carter got his information?"

"It would be my guess," Granton replied, "that it came from one of his Russian contacts. Jake had very reliable contacts. He even had a high-level one in Russian intelligence. Thankfully, it was a contact neither Anderson nor Shaw managed to blow. I'm going to have our station in Moscow try to confirm that a nuclear device is missing, but if it is true, the Russian government will probably try and keep the news under wraps until they can retrieve it. They'll lose credibility if that nuke makes it out and into Hizballah's hands."

"You know, Granton," the Director commented, "if we're lucky, maybe they'll take care of the problem."

"Lee, I sure wouldn't sleep very well at night if I thought the Russians were the only ones working on this. As uncertain as the political situation is over there, no one knows how efficient, or dedicated they are at seeing to things of this nature. Hell, the ones investigating the matter could be the ones who sold them the damn thing. I don't think it's advisable to sit back and wait for them to get the job done."

"You're right, of course, Granton." the director concurred, "Do what you have to do, you've got my complete support."

"Thanks, Lee. If we're finished here, I'd like to get back to my office," Granton said, picking up the cable and the letter and returning them to his pocket. "SABRE's always been a tricky mission, and with this new development, I'm sure you can appreciate how much more complicated it's likely to become."

"Certainly, Granton, get on with it."

As he reached the door, Granton added, "If you want me to participate in your meeting with the President, Lee, give me a call. If not, I'll keep you apprised of any new developments as they happen."

"I'll expect to hear something soon," Hawthorn said, as he reached for the hot line to the President's office.

Granton was in high gear as he came through the door to his office. As he passed his assistant's desk, he said, "Catherine, get me Jenkins in Caracas on the secure line."

"Yes, sir," she said.

He seated himself at his desk, and moments later, the intercom buzzed.

"I have Jenkins on line four with a scramble, Mr. Taylor," Catherine said. "You can take it whenever you're ready."

He picked up the receiver, and then pushed the number four line.

"Jenkins," Granton's message to his Chief of Station in the Venezuelan capital was brief, "This is Taylor. I want Slade...now!"

* * *

Francois De La Croix's attention was drawn from the racehorse pedigree he was evaluating by the entrance of his personal secretary into his office.

"Monsieur La Croix."

"Yes, Phillip," he replied, letting his gaze shift from the pedigree page and over the top of his reading glasses to his secretary.

"Monsieur Shabban is returning your call."

"Thank you, Phillip," he said, putting aside the pedigree and his glasses, and picking up the receiver. "Kamal, my friend, I am sorry to report that the delivery of the package has been delayed again, but I am assured that alternate transportation arrangements are being made."

"How much time will the delay cost us?" Kamal inquired, obviously annoyed at the news.

"Only a week or two, my friend. It will be worth waiting for, I assure you," Francois responded confidently.

"This is most unacceptable, Francois," replied Kamal, frustration evident in his voice. "The conference date is already set. Hamas, Hizballah, Islamic Jihad, all of the Palestinian faction leaders have agreed to attend. The Saudis have convinced them they will be safe in Ta'If. The Americans, Israelis, British, Turks, Jordanians, everyone who counts will be there.

"You do not seem to understand, Francois, I can change the course of the Arab World forever. I can be the savior of my people. With this one move I can eradicate Israel from the face of the earth and I cannot abide a delay. I must have the weapon now."

"Calm yourself, Kamal, you will have your chance to alter history," Francois replied. "In the meantime, what news have you about our other problem?"

"Taken care of — permanently, last night in Trouville," Kamal reported. "The American put up resistance, but we found out later that he died of his wounds. I do not think anything of value was lost in the incident."

"How can you be sure?"

"Our contact at police headquarters said that they discovered his body in his car on the outskirts of Trouville. We do not believe he had time to make contact with anyone, so whatever information he discovered died with him."

Kamal paused, and when La Croix did not respond, inquired, "You disapprove, Francois?"

"Do you think that killing him was absolutely necessary?" Francois remarked.

"Yes, yes it was. He was as close to discovering the workings of our organization as we could stand. If we had left him alone, he could have destroyed us."

"In that case I have to agree with you, but you must understand that the killing of an American intelligence officer in France is not going to be well received by my government," Francois admonished, adding, "In the future, Kamal, if anything like this becomes necessary, I must insist that it not be done in France, so that it does not reflect badly on my *family*."

"There is no way they can trace this to you."

"Incidents of this nature always cause my *family* problems."

"Francois, I do what I must."

"I understand Kamal, but in the future do it somewhere else."

"I do what I must, Francois," Kamal said, and the conversation was ended with a click of the receiver.

Francois hung up his receiver, then picked it up and buzzing his secretary, said, "Phillip, get me Henri."

He resumed his appraisal of the pedigree until the ringing phone interrupted him.

"Henri."

"Oui, Monsieur La Croix," Francois' head lieutenant, replied.

"There was an unfortunate incident last night, Henri. An American intelligence officer met with an untimely end in Trouville. It, of course, was none of our doing. But, should the police become convinced otherwise, see that they are steered in the proper direction. Have I made myself clear, Henri?"

"You have indeed, monsieur."

Kamal set the receiver back on its base. He was angry that Francois had exhibited so little understanding concerning the necessity of eliminating the American. It was for sure that Francois would not have liked to see this deal come apart, as it meant a great deal of money to him. Yet, Francois had acted as if he, Kamal, had not considered the consequences carefully before ordering the man killed. The killing had been necessary, and damn Francois and the consequences. He could deal with them too.

As he raised his head, he caught sight of his image in the mirror. It was not a handsome reflection. Fate had seen fit to bless him with a less than perfect countenance at birth and an Israeli assassination attempt gone wrong had not enhanced his looks any. He was not ugly in the strictest sense of the word, just hard-featured. It was the jagged scar, a souvenir of the bomb blast that was intended to take his life that was the biggest detractor from his appearance. He thought, with some relief, that most of the women he bedded these days were more impressed with the size of his wallet, and what he had to offer in the way of sexual attributes, than in his facial features.

Turning away from the mirror, he picked up a book off his desk, and went out onto the patio of his rented house, which was located in the outskirt of Paris in Montmarte. The flagstone patio, with its small but beautiful walled garden and lily-covered pool, offered a certain serenity that Kamal required. Lying down on the cushioned, wrought iron chaise lounge, he placed his book on the table next to it.

Letting his eyes travel over the breadth of the garden, he thought about how his life had been up until now, and about what he intended to do with his future once this deal with Francois was completed.

While he was deep in thought, his houseman appeared, carrying a tray on which sat a cup of coffee. He offered it to Kamal, who took it, and placed it on the table next to the book. He nodded his thanks, and when the man left, retrieved the cup, took a sip and resumed his musing.

Kamal considered how much his life had changed over the years, but that no matter how its panorama varied, there was one constant — his

17

desire to return to his homeland, Palestine. It was there that he was born in 1934, and there he hoped to die as an old man.

Kamal thought of his boyhood as the youngest of three children. He thought about his father, who had made his living as an accountant. And his mother, a kind woman, who had encouraged him to ignore the Palestinian passion for a homeland and pursue a peaceful life, having already lost her two older sons to the cause at the hands of the Israelis. Both his parents had lived out their lives in safety, but in exile.

Kamal considered his family's wanderings after leaving Palestine, first to Egypt, then Jordan, and finally Lebanon. How, as a youth, he had been sent to America to be educated, to be Americanized — a process he never fully achieved. His education, however, had been first rate. He'd graduated from Harvard with a doctorate in mathematics, and, soon after, received a professorship at Berkeley.

Over the years, he had returned to the Middle East to visit his relatives, and had longed to stay. But, because of the political climate, he had more or less resigned himself to the probability that he would be spending the rest of his life pursuing the American dream of a job, a wife, a family, a house in the suburbs, and two cars in the garage.

At the age of 34, Kamal's life changed dramatically. After the 1967 June War, he became an activist in the Palestinian national movement. However, unlike many of his Palestinian friends, whose lives until then had mirrored his, Kamal, influenced by his mother's wishes, did not give up his job and his family to return to the Middle East and wage war on the Zionists and the rest of the world. Instead, he chose to aim his activism at more local targets, such as the students and faculty of Berkeley, and other universities and the American Congress.

It was a choice that was partially responsible for his being alive today, for those of Kamal's comrades who had chosen militancy early on now rested with Allah, sent on their immortal journey by the Israeli army or by Mossad.

Initially, Kamal believed in the Palestinian national movement because it was the first time in his people's history that Palestinian men and women had taken up arms on their own behalf. The movement's opinions were open and honest and realistic. It appeared that they had finally achieved a grassroots effort lead by popular leaders accountable to their people.

Kamal still believed he could change the world's perception of the Palestinian people and their cause by peaceful means, by educating the world rather than terrorizing it. He was sure that the world would see the

Israel's occupation of Palestine, the violence and cruelty imposed on his people by the Israelis, depriving them of their rights, as wrong. That Israeli injustice would be evident to all, if only he would lobby on the Palestinian's behalf.

Kamal knew this would not be an easy task given American influence in the world and its support of Israel both monetarily and politically. Despite these obstacles, he even, at one point, believed that it was possible for the Palestinians and the Israelis to live together in peace.

Eventually, Kamal began to feel the futility of his peaceful efforts, for then much of the world was against the Palestinians regaining their homeland, a feeling that had changed of late. But, now, as then, the Palestinian organizations, themselves, by their divisiveness, were contributing to the ever-increasing impossibility of reaching that goal.

The Israelis succeeded, with the help of the Western media, in portraying the Palestinians as terrorists. While the Palestinians, refusing to learn anything from their past, never capitalized on their strengths and potential, lost sight of their focus, which was to secure freedom and equality for the Palestinian people, and failed in achieving their real goal, which was to mobilize their best people for a common good. Instead, each faction became concerned only with its own survival.

It was this conclusion that finally convinced Kamal that he must abandon his books, and resort to the gun. He became a member of Hizballah and had, over the years, risen in the ranks until today he commanded a spot near the top of the organization.

What irritated Kamal the most was that it eventually came to the least capable of the Palestinian organizations, the Palestinian Liberation Organization, the PLO, to negotiate the Palestinian people's and Palestine's future. Amazingly, unlike their rival groups, Hizballah, Hamas, Islamic Jihad and the Popular Front, and despite their equally violent history, the PLO had achieved a certain level of popularity, and was able to gain some recognition. Nevertheless, Kamal hated and despised the PLO and their leader, Yasser Arafat.

It was fairly obvious to Kamal that Arafat's one objective in life was to promote his personal agenda, and to be the man in charge no matter the cost to the Palestinian people. It was a weakness that was played upon heavily by those anxious to negotiate a Middle East peace. To accomplish his ends, Arafat, Kamal was convinced, had sold out the Palestinian people, and their dream of an independent homeland.

Kamal knew that he could never achieve the Nasserite dream he envisioned for the Palestinians through peaceful efforts, or for that

19

matter, through the efforts of the Palestinian groups, not even Hizballah. For, despite the proliferation of the groups, their ever-increasing strength, the fear they instilled in their enemy because of their strength, and their many professions that they would never negotiate with the enemy, that the enemy must withdraw from all lands seized without condition. There simply was no really solid political organization among them to represent the Palestinian cause.

Kamal, and his splinter Hizballah group, he felt, were the Palestinians' only hope. He knew that for him to be successful in achieving his ends, to restore to his people their dignity, freedom and their homeland, and to ultimately unite the Arab people politically, he must do away with all the Arab factions, gain the respect or the fear of the world, and take command of the situation himself.

It was to that end that he now sought to gain access to the nuclear device, which Francois had assured him, could be had through Francois' Mafia connections.

If things went as planned, soon all of the Middle East's Arab forces would be his to command, the strength and unity of the Arab world would be behind him, and all of this would be accomplished at the expense of the Israelis, who, with the help of a few strategically placed bits of incredibly reliable intelligence and material proof, would become the scapegoats. So disgusted would the American people and the American Congress be with the Israeli's supposed use of one of its nuclear devices to eliminate its adversaries, along with the senseless and callous killing of thousands of innocent bystanders, including some of the world's most respected statesmen and diplomats, that in all likelihood all military support would be cut off, and the hour of their demise as a nation would be at hand.

He smiled at the thought, and returned to his reading.

* * *

The clock on the nightstand in the Washington apartment read 7:05 a.m. A large, hairy, masculine hand lifted the receiver of the ringing phone and in a groggy voice responded, "It's kind of early, don't you think?"

"Not in this part of the world." The voice with the thick middle-eastern accent replied.

"So, what's so important you need to call me at this hour?"

20

"I called to congratulate you on the accuracy of your information. We are no longer troubled by a certain problem. If you check your bank account, you should find its balance very satisfying."

"That is good news."

"I thought you'd be pleased. Keep in touch."

The line clicked off and the hand replaced the receiver.

Chet Rakeland sat up in bed. His first visual sighting was the picture on top of his dresser of his parents and him, taken when he was a toddler at the Kansas State Fair. They were standing on either side of their prize winning Black Angus steer. His mother's hands were resting on his shoulders, while her eyes were looking admiringly over at his father, who stood, chest puffed out haughtily, on the other side of the creature.

"Cocky asshole!" Rakeland spat the words at the male figure in the portrait. Shifting his gaze over to the female figure he added, "It's too bad, Ma, that you didn't know then what a drunken, wife-beaten' murderin' asshole he'd turn out to be. Might of saved us both a lot o' grief."

Rakeland looked back over his shoulder at the clock, and saw that it now read 7:20 a.m. "Shit! I might as well get to it," he groaned, as he threw off the covers and swung his feet to the cold, bare, hardwood floor. As he passed the dresser on his way to the bathroom, he stopped and picked up the photo, concentrating his attention on the slightly plump, but pretty, red-haired woman.

"I told you I'd make a bundle someday, didn't I, Ma? Well I'm doin' just that," he said in a tone that lacked a certain pride of achievement in it. "How I'm goin' about it wouldn't exactly please ya lady, but then you're not here anymore to give me any grief about it. Unfortunately."

As if she could hear him, he added, "Now don't you go thinkin' for a minute that this fortune is comin' easy. Hell no! I'm riskin' my neck and workin' my ass off for it. It takes great skill to deceive the deceivers. But, that's the beauty of my peon job in Technical Services. It opens the door to a lot of inside information, secret info, the kind worth big bucks. You'd be real impressed at how your Casper Milquetoast boy has learned to manipulate those jokers over in Operations. Yeah, real impressed!"

Rakeland set the picture back on the dresser, but continued to maintain eye contact with the female figure. "Don't feel sorry for 'em, Ma! They had their chance to reap the benefits of my genius.

"Ha!" he snarled. "Those Operations assholes wouldn't know genius if it jumped up and hit 'em square it the face. Dumb asses! I saved their necks dozens of times and they still couldn't see it. Think I ever got any credit, think it got me promoted out of this dead-end fuckin' job. Hell no! All the glory went to Special Ops."

Raising his fist in the air, he proclaimed, "Well, not any more, by the time I'm through with them, Congress will think they're the biggest bunch of bunglers under the sun."

His gaze settled briefly on his father. "Ah, I know you wouldn't be impressed, but you'll still be around to bear the shame. Like I did after you killed Ma. I don't expect that I'll get away with this charade forever, but by the time those nerds over at the Agency get the picture, I'll be sippin' vodka in my Russian dacha. I might even leave 'em a note tellin' 'em how I did it. It'll make one hell of a scandal. Ah yes, first Anderson, then Shaw, then me. Congress will think there's a fuckin' colony of moles up there. And when they get to figurin' out what I cost 'em, they'll realize that I've made those other two look like amateurs."

Laughing wickedly, he thumped the image of his father in the face with his finger, and then headed off to the shower singing the national anthem.

Chapter 3

The sound of the ceiling fan blades cut the humid tropic air, waves crashed against the rocky cliffs below the hotel's window, the scent of jasmine, the sensation of the silken skin next to his merged in a singular explosion as his passion reached its climax. Jeremy Slade relaxed as the tension drained from his limbs.

The woman's long, slender fingers slid down Jeremy's slim, muscular back. They traced the scar of an old wound and languidly glided across his firm buttocks.

"Ah…my Jeremy, you are magnifico. So, tell me again, my dearest, why it is that we can not be together like this forever?" Her full red lips assuming a passionate pout as she spoke.

Jeremy got up slowly, allowing his gaze to linger on the woman's bronze-skinned, naked body stretched enticingly on the white linens, her long black hair draped across the pillow. Her dark eyes, with their ever-present mischievous gleam, looked back at him questioningly.

While working out of the Caracas station on a regular intelligence assignment, Jeremy had become acquainted with Carla Menendez, and had pursued this mutually satisfying relationship with her. Her value to him was much more than sexual. As wife and valued confidant of General Humberto Menendez, the head of coastal security for the Venezuelan Army, she was privy to some confidential and useful information, not the least of which were the comings and goings of the various drug traffickers and international terrorists which Gen. Menendez conveniently overlooked for a staggering fee.

This discovery had prompted the Caracas station to assign him to this duty full time.

It was a shame, Jeremy thought, as he admired her beauty; that their liaison was about to come to an end. His local sources had indicated that of late the General was paying more attention to his wife's extracurricular activities. Knowing this, and continuing their relationship, was a sure way to blow his cover and the assignment.

"I am afraid," he said, smiling, his hand sliding along the length of her leg, "that, as jealous as your husband is, my sweet, the only way he'd allow us to be together forever is if we were dead. And trust me, he'd see to it."

Jeremy's attention was drawn from the woman by the sensation of the metal backing of the watch he wore turning ice cold. The sensation retreated, then returned.

Sensing the distraction, she asked, "Is something wrong?"

She paused, and then with the pout now reflected in her voice, added, "Or, could it be that I am so forgettable that you are already thinking of your next rendezvous?"

"Silly, Carla," Jeremy said, while playfully throwing the top sheet over her body. "How could you even imagine such a thing? You must know you have soured me for all others."

Then, offering his hand to her, he said, "Come on, luscious lady, you'd better get yourself together. Your driver will be here any minute."

Carla rose from the bed like a cat rising from an afternoon nap in the sun. Stretching lazily as she stood before him, she let her arms drape themselves around his neck and their lips met passionately once more.

Gently breaking the embrace, he said, "Time to go, my love."

Reluctantly, she removed herself to the bathroom, and moments later, emerged, elegantly dressed in a white suit and hat, the pout still on her lips.

"Call me soon, Jeremy," she purred, blowing him a kiss as she left the room, closing the door softly behind her.

Wrapping himself in his robe, Jeremy first locked the door, and then went to the bedside table. The signal the watch had emitted was from the Agency's Caracas station. He picked up his cell phone, and placed a call to the offices of Foxx and McCandles, an American subsidiary of an oil drilling company that employed him for cover purposes. The cover suited his education, which consisted of a degree in geological engineering from the University of Oklahoma.

"Put me through to mining," Jeremy said, to the young lady who answered. His call was immediately routed to the U.S. embassy, and the office of the CIA's Chief of Station in Caracas, Raff Jenkins.

Anticipating Jeremy's call, Jenkins picked up the line on the second ring.

"Jenkins here."

"How's business, Raff?" Jeremy responded, using the correct identifying code.

"Glad you called. We've got a critical one for you." Jenkins continued the encoded message. "It's offshore rig number 10. They're worried she might blow. Get moving on it."

"I'm on my way," Jeremy said, and terminated the connection. He waited a moment, and then placed another call.

A ringing on the line was followed by the ever-present recorded message and the usual wait. Finally ----

"Viasa, buenos dias," came the greeting delivered by a sweet-sounding, young, female voice.

"I need a reservation on your next flight to Washington, D.C., for one. That will be one way, and make it coach."

As he finalized his reservation, uneasiness, born of experience, settled upon Jeremy. What could be so important that Taylor was pulling him off this assignment? He'd been setting it up for going on two years and just when it looked like pay dirt --- this!

* * *

The knock came unexpectedly. Jeremy shoved the last of his belongings in his bag. A quick look through the peephole revealed Rodriquez, the bellboy, and one of numerous recipients of handouts by Jenkins to insure that there would be no surprises at Jeremy's hotel, looking down the hall.

Just as Rodriquez reached to knock again, Jeremy opened the door.

"Señor Slade," Rodriquez said nervously. "I have been told to warn you that Gen. Menendez and his men will be here in a few minutes. It might be wise, señor, if you let me escort you to a more discreet exit. There will be a car waiting."

Jeremy grabbed his bag, and followed Rodriquez down the narrow hall. He could hear the sound of boots hammering the hotel's ancient main staircase as his pursuers closed in. Just as he and the bellboy were about to enter the passageway to the servants' entrance, the general and his men arrived on the landing.

"There he is, get him!" Menendez shouted, ordering his men after Jeremy. "Move, move, you idiots!"

Seeing Jeremy duck into the servants' entrance, he shouted down to the man on the landing below. "Sergeant, to the servants' entrance, quickly!"

Menendez was furious! He knew his wife played around and generally turned a blind eye to it, but a tip from a reliable source had alerted him to the fact that her newest romantic interest might have more than just romance on his mind. In the course of having his wife watched, he had learned some very unnerving things about Señor Slade.

25

Menendez had a lot of questions to ask, and he meant to get some answers. Getting the answers from this gringo was going to be half the fun. The general was one of the best old style interrogators in South America. His methods for getting results would make the old English torture chamber methods look like child's play.

The self-locking knob on the door that closed behind Jeremy and Rodriquez slowed the soldiers. Jeremy could hear them shooting it off as he and the bellboy hightailed it for the servants' entrance door.

Jeremy caught sight of a laundry chute coming up on his right. Running up alongside Rodriquez, he shouted to the frightened bellboy, "Take this." And with that, he shoved his bag in the boy's arms and pushed him through the laundry chute opening.

The door behind Jeremy crashed open and a bullet whizzed by his head. His right hand moved to his opposite wrist. He jerked off his cufflink, pulled the pin on its backside and threw it in the direction of the pursuing men. It landed halfway down the hall, made a whining noise and immediately began emitting a noxious smoke screen. His pursuers stopped in their tracks, coughing and gagging. A few more shots echoed in the hall behind him, considerably off target.

As Jeremy burst through the servants' entrance door that led to a parking lot, the sun momentarily blinded him. Quickly, he ducked behind a car as a hail of bullets peppered its side, showering fragments of glass over him.

Just the other side of a low evergreen hedge was salvation in the form of a Jeep Cherokee, its driver-side door opened and its engine running. Somehow it seemed light years away as another round fired at him slammed into the side of the car he was hiding behind. He drew his gun and returned the fire while trying to figure a way to distract them long enough to traverse the distance to the waiting Jeep. He knew it would only be a matter of minutes before the general's men came around from the other side, cutting off all avenues of escape.

Suddenly, a deafening roar filled his ears. From around the corner of the building, bearing down on the soldiers, metal arms raised, cradling a dumpster to shield itself, was a huge refuse collection truck.

As it came between them, Jeremy ran, somersaulting the low hedge. Landing on his feet, he darted for the car as a trail of bullets followed behind him. He leaped into the driver's seat, shoved the car in gear and roared out of the parking lot onto the main boulevard.

Damn! That was too close. His heart was pounding. Forget the airport, the general's men would be all over it by now.

He was startled by the Jeep's radio coming alive. "Should you require transportation to a healthier climate my friend," Jenkins' familiar voice instructed, "may I suggest Saint Lucia's flight number one, leaving in one hour. Check the glove compartment for details."

Chapter 4

Granton adjusted the window blinds to block the glare from the late afternoon sun that was beginning to invade his office.

Yesterday, he'd received the bad news that his best friend, Jake Carter, had been killed; and Operation SABRE, the operation Jake had been running, one vital to America's security, had been seriously undermined. Very soon, he'd be faced with the monumental task of putting Operation SABRE back on track with the help of two of the most capable, but with out a doubt, least cooperative, people on the planet.

His secretary knocking softly, and then opening his office door interrupted his thoughts. "Mr. Taylor," Catherine said, from the doorway. "The briefing with Mr. Slade has been set up. He should be at the Farm by the time you arrive. Simon is waiting for you at the heliport."

"Thanks, Catherine. Notify the Farm that I'm on my way."

He returned to his desk, and after carefully checking the papers in his briefcase, headed for the heliport where a silver and blue Jet Ranger waited, and entered the craft.

* * *

Jeremy watched the Jet Ranger draw a lazy circle around the perimeter of the campsite. Making its approach, it swooped gracefully to the earth like a great hawk that had sighted its quarry.

Granton waited only long enough for the skids to touch the surface. Quickly, he released the seat belt, snapped open the door and stepped to the ground. With the blades still whirling around his head, he emerged from the craft, then headed across the field toward the low-slung ranch house that bore the name Colfax, and that served as Special Operations headquarters at the Farm, the CIA's training facility set in the Virginia countryside.

It had been two years since Jeremy had requested a transfer to Latin America, and at least that long since Granton had seen him. As he approached Jeremy, it seemed to Granton that nothing much had changed about the man, whose powerful 6-2, 210 pound frame now rested leisurely against one of the cabin porch's supports.

Jeremy was considered by some to be the stereotypical Agency "cowboy". It was true in more ways than one. He was a doer. When the

28

job called for a fearless, kick-ass type, Jeremy was your man, a fact that unnerved some of the Agency's more cautious members.

But as Granton mounted the porch stairs, he noticed that some things had changed. Jeremy still bore the rugged, good looks of a western hero, and the slight hump on the bridge of his nose, which bore testimony to his fondness for never dodging a fight. But, his chestnut-brown hair, which somehow always managed to look slightly askew, was now, at 44, beginning to show a peppering of gray. And, his brown eyes, recessed under a strong forehead, no longer harbored that incessant, sometimes annoying, devilish gleam, replaced now, instead, with an expression of frustration and annoyance.

Jeremy had been raised in the mountainous country outside of Redcliff, Colorado, by parents who knew and loved the outdoors. His wilderness skills had been fine honed by his Special Forces and Delta Force training, and his participation in several Delta Force covert actions, where he had distinguished himself on many occasions. It had been from Delta Force that Jeremy had come to the CIA.

His assignment to Caracas had really been a self-imposed exile. Granton had agreed to it only because it had kept Jeremy from resigning from the Agency. The Balkan mission, of which he had been one of the participants, had cost Jeremy more emotionally than he was prepared to pay.

Though Granton and Jeremy had worked together many times, and there was no doubt that they could trust one another completely, Granton, nevertheless, felt that a certain void existed between them. It wasn't the difference in their ages, Granton was sure of that, because Jeremy had been very close to Jake Carter, and Jake had been Granton's age. Most likely, it was the difference in their backgrounds, he being from the East, a West Pointer, and Jeremy, being a westerner, who'd come up through the ranks. It might even have been simply the natural reservation a field officer felt in the presence of a headquarters officer.

Granton had often meant to discuss the matter with Jeremy, but for various reasons, he hadn't. Overall, the void mattered little, but it was at a time like this, a time when a little close rapport would be helpful, that the problem might detract from their ability to communicate.

"Sorry I had to take you away from the charming Señora Menendez, but I think you might find what I have in this briefcase more important." Granton opened the conversation casually, avoiding any of the normal forms of greeting. He proceeded on through the screen door, leaving

29

Jeremy to follow at his own pace. "I could use a drink, how about you? Jack Daniels on the rocks, if I remember correctly."

Jeremy took his time. The screen door slamming shut behind him as he entered the room.

"What in the hell, Granton, could be so important that you pull me off a job I've been setting up for two blessed years?" Jeremy verbally pounced on his superior. "Nothing like blowing the operation, and doing it just when I have the bastards cornered.

"I don't get it. You have a computer full of people who could do whatever needs doing in that little black bag of yours," he ranted on, indicating with a look at Granton's briefcase, "and probably do it every bit as good as I could."

"Hmmm. I see that two years in the Southern Hemisphere have made a modest man out of you, Jeremy," Granton remarked, nonchalantly, while setting the briefcase on the dining room table and proceeding on to the large oak bar. "There was a day when you thought no one could do as good a job as you. But, in this case, you're right. There is someone who can do it better, unfortunately for both of us, you're the man I need to get them to do it."

Then, reaching for glasses, ice and a bottle of Jack Daniels, he set about making the drinks. While giving the drinks a quick stir, he added, "Oh, and as for you having Menendez cornered, I read Jenkins' report, and it looks like it was the other way around."

Their initial verbal exchange ended with Granton having made his point, and Jeremy not pursuing the matter further.

Picking the drinks up, Granton moved to a pair of tall leather chairs near the fireplace. He set Jeremy's drink on the coffee table in front of one of the chairs, and sat down in the other one.

"Sit down, Jeremy," he said, somewhat brusquely, as he indicated the chair across from him. "We have a lot to cover."

Grudgingly, Jeremy left his holdout position just inside the door and joined Granton in front of the fireplace, easing himself into the seat of the winged-back chair.

Leaning forward in his seat, Granton raised his eyes to meet Jeremy's, and in a solemn voice, said, "Jeremy, Jake was killed yesterday." He did not proceed further with his conversation, allowing time for Jeremy to comprehend fully what he'd just said.

There was no reply. Jeremy simply dropped his head into his hands and took several deep breaths.

"How?" Was the only word Jeremy could finally force his shocked body to speak.

"Jake was running an operation in France. He was right on top of a significant breakthrough when he was shot." Granton kept the explanation brief.

The room went very still. Jeremy raised his head from his hands, but his thoughts were elsewhere. Granton sipped at his drink, and let him work through the initial grief that hearing of the death of his old friend and mentor had initiated.

"I need your help, Jeremy." Granton pushed on. Further mourning would have to wait.

"I can't help you, Granton." Jeremy's voice was almost a whisper. "I'm finished with anything that has to do with Europe."

"It's... more complicated than that, Jeremy." Granton eased his way into dangerous territory.

"No. It's very simple." Jeremy's voice had found its normal tone. "Find someone else, Granton. My going to Europe won't bring Jake back and, Lord knows, every time I set foot there, all hell breaks loose."

"Before he died," Granton stepped ever further into the quagmire, "Jake had time to get a message to me. Frankly, I was quite surprised by it, because Jake asked for the one thing I know he was most reluctant to request."

"He wouldn't have asked for me. He knew how I felt," Jeremy said, suddenly sensing what was about to be said.

"He didn't, Jeremy," Granton said, shaking his head.

Both men paused, and the tension in the room was palpable.

"He wouldn't bring her back, Granton, not on a bet! He would never ask her to do that!" Jeremy voiced the words he did not want to hear or say.

Granton reached in his pocket, removed the cable and handed it to him.

"Why? Why in God's name would he do this?" Jeremy said, incredulously, at its contents. Crushing the offending message, he sent it sailing into the wall.

"Because, unfortunately, Jeremy, he knew she's our only legitimate way in," Granton replied, letting the gesture slide. "He knew there wouldn't be time to build a legend for another intelligence officer. The requirements to penetrate this group are so specific that there isn't anyone else who can come close to fitting them. Her profession is the perfect cover, and she has the knowledge and training to make this operation succeed."

Another long silence set the stage for what Granton knew would be one of the toughest moments in Jeremy's life.

"And I'm supposed to bring her back in. Right?" He finally said, the pain in his voice very real.

"There's another way to do it, Jeremy, but believe me I'd rather not use it."

"What makes you think she'll come back at my request? She hates my guts!" Jeremy was now actively caught in the dilemma. "When I left her lying wounded in that hospital in West Germany, the only thing that kept her from killing me was Jake and a healthy dose of tranquilizer."

"Hey! You may be absolutely right. Approaching her may be a complete waste of time, but like I said, Jeremy, there's no time to waste. It's really not a matter of will she come back in, but is she still capable of doing the job, and how soon can she start," Granton said, with more confidence than he felt.

Granton got up. From the black briefcase he'd set on the dining table, he removed three file folders. He crossed back over to Jeremy, and handing him the first two folders, said, "Here is your cover legend and your cover backup." Then, handing him the third file, he added, "This one has the complete file on Operation SABRE. Make yourself comfortable and give them a good going over. Security will pick these up from you before you get on the plane for Lexington."

"I haven't agreed to do this, Granton."

"You haven't, but you will." Granton again voiced his opinion, this time with more confidence. "And you'll see her through it, because that's the way it has to be, Jeremy. After you read SABRE, you'll see why neither of you can afford to walk away from this one.

"There's one other thing you should know," Granton added, trying to keep the tone of his voice from giving away his concern. "Jake's death may have been the result of another leak in the Agency. I don't have any real proof that that's a fact, just a bad feeling. So this operation is going to go down just a little differently. I'm going to run it personally. In that file are sterile, secure telephone numbers, you'll report only to me and only through one of those numbers.

"Well... I've got to get back to the office," Granton said, rising and preparing to leave. He stopped midway in securing his briefcase, and added, "Look, Jeremy, I know this isn't going to be easy for either of you, but we're talking serious consequences if this operation fails. It's already in jeopardy of doing just that with Jake's cover being blown. The opposition knows that we're on to them, so they'll be on their guard.

"And, of course, there's the extra problem of not offending the French on this one. It's common knowledge that Francois De La Croix, one of the major players in this action, is head of the French Mafia, and that he's very influential within some circles of the French government. It could cause all kinds of unpleasant international repercussions if we were caught playing in their bailiwick.

"Because of La Croix's governmental influence, and because of the suspected leak, we have not consulted with our French brethren on this as yet. As it is, we're going to have a hell of a job explaining away Jake's murder to the French authorities.

"Brief yourself well, Jeremy, and then get some rest. It's imperative you leave tomorrow morning. Your travel arrangements are outlined in the folder, along with your cover for this assignment. Keep in touch and good luck," Granton said, as he exited through the front door.

Jeremy didn't acknowledge Granton's departing remarks. He heard the whine of the Jet Ranger as it powered up, and as the sound of the helicopter faded into the distance, he considered the circumstances.

Good luck, my ass, he thought. God, if ever there was a no-win situation, this was it. Let's see, my military time combined with my Agency annuity, should provide me a decent living on some quiet Caribbean island, even taking early retirement.

Jeremy took a deep swallow of the whiskey, and, as it burned its way down his throat, he considered the future. Jake, you old bastard, he mused, you couldn't stand the thought of spending eternity alone in hell, so you had to arrange to take what's left of us along with you.

Suddenly, he felt as if his life had been drained out of him. Staring into the fireplace, he imagined flames dancing in an exotic tempo, sparks drifting up the chimney, smoke from the fire curling seductively around the sparks like an ardent lover. It reminded him of another time, of someone special, of someone lost. It had been a long time since he'd faced the nightmare. He knew that it would return tonight and that somehow he'd be living it again — soon.

He stared briefly at the folders, then, reluctantly, sealed his fate by opening them.

* * *

Karen A. Lynch

Jeremy chose the master suite. A masculine room with log poster bed, Navajo wall hangings and a large stone fireplace over which hung an imposing moose head. The room reminded him of home.

A quick shower refreshed him. Wrapping himself in a thick terry robe, he propped up the pillows on the bed, and settled in to see whose skin he would be slipping into for the duration of this operation. Christ, they were reaching on this one, he thought, as he glanced over the specifics.

Cover name: Mark Jergens.

Occupation: resort hotel owner.

Corporation name: Cheval d'Or.

The report went on to say that Cheval d'Or was owned by a friend of the Director, who had agreed to cooperate with the Agency in establishing his cover. You are a wealthy man, it said, who desires to be in the racehorse business. You will embark on fulfilling that desire tomorrow in Lexington, Kentucky, at the Keeneland Summer Yearling Sales. En route you will familiarize yourself with the sale catalogue, which will be provided. You are to establish yourself as a potential buyer. Your experience with horses growing up and college polo, should serve you well here.

Right! He laughed out loud to himself, that is if I still remember which end you feed and which end you muck after. I mean it's only been 20 years since graduation.

Ah, here's the good part! Unlimited credit, the file said, has been established with Keeneland on your behalf.

Oh, yes, big time spender! Well, if I go, at least I'll go in style, and he laughed at the irony of the thought.

Jeremy had treated his cover legend rather lightly, but the information in the operational folder, that contained the background information on SABRE, he treated with strict professionalism.

God, this is a hot one, he thought. There's no telling what those bastards might try with a tactical nuclear device in their hands. A good place for a smart man to be was far away from this job, but then knowing the safe place to be wasn't one of Jeremy's strong suits.

It was still early evening, but he felt exhausted and soon he was fast asleep.

There were enough occasions in Jeremy's past to bring on a bad dream. But, it was always the same incident that repeated itself consistently, and with breathtaking accuracy.

34

As he slipped into a deep sleep, he felt the dampness of the Serbian woodlands that surrounded him, chill him, making him draw the covers tighter to him. Then images and sounds floated back through a thick fog, the thud of bullets hitting the trees, and the ground as the vision appeared of Alanna and he stumbling and running, trying to avoid the searchlights that illuminated the thickets around them.

The sound of their breath coming in heavy gasps as they tried to get traction on a rain-soaked knoll. His one arm shouldered the H&K MP5 machine gun, his other held tightly on to her, afraid for a second to let go, knowing she would head back to try and save Dar, their partner and her lover, who had chosen to remain behind and cover for them, and, who now lay dying at the ambush site.

Alanna's voice pleaded with him. "Please, Jeremy, we have to go back. We can't leave him. Oh, God, please!"

"Don't look back," he heard himself say. "There's nothing we can do for him. I have to get you out of here!"

They could hear Dar's cries of pain, then there were no more cries, only the sounds of the men and the dogs in pursuit.

As their pursuers were about to close in on them, he woke shaking and soaking wet. Jeremy knew then for sure, however painful it would be, it was time to put this ghost to rest.

Eventually, Jeremy fell back into a fitful, dreamless sleep, and then somewhere in the distance the sound of a phone ringing forced him to open his eyes. A few moments later, the bedroom door opened, and Richards, the old houseman, entered with a tray. On it was a full breakfast, which including freshly squeezed orange juice and Jeremy's favorite French blend coffee.

"Good morning, Mr. Slade! It's good to see you again, sir." Richards greeted him warmly, and after depositing the tray on the bedside table, walked to the window and opened the shutters, allowing the brilliant sunshine to enter and warm the room.

"Oh, by the way sir," he added, when all he got was a muffled grunt to his greeting, "Bill Rice just called, and said a car would be here in an hour to pick you up. Your plane will leave at 11 a.m. Since you had to leave your last place of residency empty handed, Mr. Taylor has provided you with a new wardrobe. I took the liberty, earlier, of putting together something you might be comfortable traveling in."

35

Unable to delay the inevitable any longer, Jeremy sat up in bed, and returned the greeting, "Thanks, Richards. It's good to see you too. You're looking well, as always."

A sudden call of nature spurred Jeremy from under the covers and in the direction of the bathroom. En route, he picked up the glass of juice and noted, with approval, Richards' wardrobe selections.

"You know, Richards, this organization just doesn't properly appreciate a man of your abilities. Someday, when I retire, write my memoirs and become rich and famous, I'm going to sneak in here in the dead of night and rescue you from these turkeys."

"That's very flattering, sir," Richards replied. "But, if you write your memoirs, you may be the one who needs rescuing. I think you'd make number one on the Agency's hit list."

"Unfortunately, I think you might be," Jeremy said, the toilet flushing drowning out the last syllables of his reply, "right…"

* * *

Having studied his cover legend again on the drive to the Farm airfield, Jeremy turned the briefcase containing the files over to a security man, and headed to his waiting plane.

"Hey, Jeremiah, it's good to see you again, buddy." Bill Rice, the tall, red-haired, ex-Delta Force helicopter gunship pilot extended his hand to Jeremy as he boarded the plane idling on the tarmac. "It's been a long time."

Pausing in the doorway, Jeremy said, "Good to see you too, Bill. I see you've switched your allegiance to something a little faster than those Hueys." In reference to Bill's love for the old Vietnam era helicopter

Impressed by the quality of the plane he was in the process of boarding, Jeremy asked, "I wonder what drug lord lost this high priced bit of fancy merchandise to U.S.government coffers? What is this thing?"

The men paused long enough to allow the engines on another of the Agency's planes that had pulled up beside them to die down.

Rice chuckled at Jeremy's awe. "It's a Falcon 900-B, my man," he said. "She's a pretty swanky bird. Sure beats the hell out of that Gulfstream and those Hueys. Well, maybe not the Hueys"

Then reverting to the use of Jeremy's cover name, which he had been briefed on, he added, "But, then Mr. Jergens, a wealthy man like you would hardly be expected to settle for less. Right?"

"Absolutely! Lexington, James, and hurry!" Jeremy chided the pilot jokingly as he watched the neighboring plane's door open and its passengers emerge.

Smiling, Rice replied, "Yes, sir, Mr. Jergens."

Pausing momentarily before entering the cockpit, Rice said, "By the way you remember Tad Clark, he's flying co-pilot. He and I will be riding shotgun for you."

"My back feels safer already." Jeremy nodded in greeting to the co-pilot. His comment was genuine, and indicated his gratitude at having men of Rice and Clark's caliber to back him up. "Come on, let's see if this fancy piece of metal can fly."

"Make yourself comfortable." Rice cracked a huge smile. "We'll have you in Bluegrass country in no time."

Rice joined Clark in the cockpit, while Jeremy chose a seat on the terminal side of the plane. As he glanced out the window, Jeremy noticed one of the men, who had disembarked from the Gulfstream, in conversation with one of the flight crew. They were looking in his direction.

The Falcon 900-B's engines screamed as they gained rpms and the plane moved onto the taxiway.

"Our scheduled arrival time in Lexington is 1:10 p.m." Rice's voice came over the intercom system. "If you need anything, sorry, but you'll have to help yourself, we're the only warm bodies on this plane. After they paid for this buggy, they couldn't afford the price of a sexy stewardess. You'll just have to rough it.

"Oh, there's a sale catalogue on the bar in there, I'm supposed to see that you get it." Rice added, "No stewardess, boring reading material, oh well, at least the bar is stocked. I won't bore you with the seat belt routine, but buckle up."

The jet taxied to the main runway and took off. Once airborne, Jeremy made his way to the bar. It was too early in the day for a drink even though he could have used one. Instead he helped himself to a diet Coke, and took the sale catalogue back to his seat.

* * *

Ed Simechek was busy unloading some cargo from the Agency's Farm shuttle when he felt a tap on his shoulder.

"That's a pretty fancy plane that just headed down the runway, any idea what kind it is?" Simechek recognized the inquirer as Chet

Rakeland, one of the men from the Agency's Technical Services Division who was a frequent passenger on the shuttle.

Not wanting to answer any questions, Simechek pointed to his earmuffs, and shrugged his shoulders, hoping the man would take the hint and go away. When the man persisted, he removed the earmuffs from his head and replied, "Sorry, mister, it's hard as hell to hear anything with these things on. What'd you say?"

"I said, that's a fancy plane that just left here. What kind is it?"

"She's an expensive job, a Falcon 900-B."

"Agency own her?"

"Naw, she's hired for some operation."

"Any idea where she's headed."

"Strictly, need to know, my man, and they didn't feel I needed to know. Sorry."

Simechek tried to get back to work, but Rakeland continued.

"How about the guy that boarded her last, the brown-haired one in the designer suit? Couldn't have been Jeremy Slade, could it? I worked with him in Turkey. I could have sworn it was him."

"Can't help ya there either, mister," Simechek replied, annoyed at the intrusion into his work, and the interrogation he was undergoing evident in his voice. "I don't know no Jeremy Slade."

"Hey, hey, don't get riled, friend, I was just curious,' Rakeland said, easing away from the man. "Thanks anyway."

* * *

"Lexington approach, this is November, six, one, four, Whiskey Mike requesting permission to land." The radio crackled as Rice contacted the tower for landing instructions.

"Roger, November, six, one, four Whiskey Mike, turn left heading 240 vector, runway 22."

"Roger, 240 Vector, runway 22." Rice repeated the instructions.

"Intercept ILS, contact tower at the outer marker," the air traffic controller added. "You are cleared for approach."

"Jeremiah." Rice's voice came across the cabin's speaker. "We've been cleared to land in Lexington. Our ETA is in 10 minutes. I hope you had a good flight, sir!"

Ten minutes to touch down, Jeremy thought. Ten minutes and then what, an hour or two before he'd again be face to face with the only woman in the world who could twist his emotions inside out.

The thin hazy clouds they were descending through became a snowy, cold December afternoon in New York City as Jeremy envisioned the entrance to McGregor's Shirt Shop and the first time he'd laid eyes on Alanna Reynolds.

Jeremy had gone to the shop to meet Dar and make a pick up. Dar was a half hour late, and Jeremy and Dan McGregor, who ran the shop as a CIA cover, were beginning to worry. They had almost decided to abort the meeting when Alanna arrived.

He remembered how he'd felt as she came through the door. How he'd been struck by the intensity of her cornflower blue eyes set against her ivory complexion, and her cheeks, gently rouged by the crisp winter air. How he had considered, maybe, just maybe, this was the person he'd been waiting for. The one who he'd be willing to trade his crazy job, his crazy life in for.

Before he'd known the true purpose of her being there, he recalled trying to engage her in a little flirtatious conversation. In response, she had given him one of those warm sunny smiles he was to become so fond of, and then turned her attention to a rack of ties on the counter in front of her, gently, but successfully, avoiding his obvious come on.

Nothing that had happened to Jeremy in life so far had disappointed him so thoroughly as learning on his return to headquarters that the woman he had fallen in love with was the lover of his boss. Jeremy, angered at the danger Dar had placed Alanna in, broached the subject of the inappropriate use of the woman to him in private. Dar's response had been that it was none of Jeremy's business.

It was apparent to Jeremy that Dar was running Alanna without her knowledge. Since running an innocent had always been against Agency policy, Dar, for whatever reason he'd justified using her at the time, had put his job on the line. The fact that Dar claimed to love her didn't seemed to deter him from exposing her to the risk even that "simple" assignments entailed. Jeremy guessed that somewhere in Dar's dark, quirky nature, the one that every spy possessed, he felt the need to use whatever was necessary, or whoever was available to accomplish his mission.

A master of the old Chinese Shaolin style of martial arts, Dar had passed on his expertise to Alanna, which did offer her a certain measure of protection. And, in the process, Jeremy suspected, salved Dar's conscience, if, indeed, he had one. Jeremy knew that in Dar's eyes and heart, Alanna played second fiddle to the Agency. If she knew, she never let on that she did. If she didn't know, then Jeremy was sure it was the only long-term deception anyone had ever successfully pulled off on her.

Jeremy touched the window, as though he could reach the phantom images of 10 years past. Then he let his thoughts fade as he directed his attention to the scenery rising to meet him. He'd heard about Lexington and Bluegrass Region, but nothing had prepared him for the breathtaking view below. As far as the eye could see, there were lush pastures crisscrossed by miles of white or black board fences. The fields, dotted with mares and foals, some lying in the sun napping, others gathered together under the shade of the large trees, resembled a pastoral painting.

Planes approaching Lexington make their descent over some of the most famous Bluegrass farms, Darby Dan, the King Ranch, and most notably, the red and white barns of the legendary Calumet Farm. Farther to the right, the impressive stone grandstands of Keeneland Race Course broke the neat array of farms.

Cecil B. DeMille could not have orchestrated an opening for his multi-million dollar productions better than this air approach to Lexington gave the first-time visitor.

"Lexington approach, Four, Whiskey, Mike, over marker."

"Four, Whiskey, Mike, you are cleared to land.

The Falcon 900-B's wheels settled gently on the runway, the brakes screeched in protest as they strained to the limit to stop the jet as it roared to the end of the tarmac.

And so, thought Jeremy, the game of lies begins.

Chapter 5

"Angela, I'll be rather late tonight. Just make sure you let the dog have a run before you leave."

"Good luck," the housekeeper replied as she watched her employer head down the back porch steps and to her car. "I will leave some cold chicken and salad in the refrigerator."

The engine of the black Volvo Turbo wagon roared to life. Its tires made a soft, crunching noise on the gravel as it headed out the long drive.

Alanna stopped the car halfway down the lane, opened the door, and walked to the fence. On the other side, a beautiful dappled gray mare and her big, well-built, iron gray colt stood watching her approach.

"Take care of my Derby winner, Cariña," she said soothingly.

The mare nuzzled the foal gently as if in understanding. Smiling to herself, she headed back to the car and drove off.

The drive to the sale grounds took 20 minutes. The sun was just making its appearance to her right. Its light filtered through the trees that lined the narrow road, turning them and the fields into a fairyland of emerald and gold, while a light early morning fog hovered over the land, filling the low spots in the pastures and roads, making them appear as misty gray pools.

This was the time of the day Alanna loved best, everything at it freshest, cleansed by the night, at peace with everyone and everything. Lexington had meant a fresh start for her, a return to the passion of her youth — horses. She turned on the radio and let the soothing, sensuous sounds of jazz artist Kenny G distract her.

Reaching the Keeneland entrance, Alanna headed her car down the long tree-lined road toward the row of barns that stood behind the large pavilion in which the horses were sold. There was already a great deal of activity in the barn area.

She found a parking space close to where her group of yearlings was stabled, gathered up the eight halters from the back end of the wagon, and headed across the road to barn 11.

"Good morning, Miss Reynolds."

"How ya doin', Miss Reynolds?"

An assortment of male and female grooms greeted her warmly as she passed from barn to barn.

"Good morning, Mike. Good Morning, Susan. Your boss sure has got y'all hustling this morning," she commented to two of the River Mist Farm's crew, and winked conspiratorially at the farm's owner as she passed through his barn.

"Who's that?" inquired a European buyer of a groom, who was showing him one of River Mist's yearlings.

"That's Alanna Reynolds. She owns a place called Wicklow Stud over in Versailles. She's the best horse breeder 'round these parts. Bred two international champions, and the dam of an Arc de Triomphe winner, not to mention a ton of other good horses," the groom replied, his admiration obvious. "Pretty lady, isn't she?"

"She is that," replied the gentleman, his eyes following her until she disappeared through the next barn's passageway.

"Good morning, Julie," Alanna said, as she handed the halters to the young, dark-haired girl who was in charge of her horses. Then, moving down the shedrow, Alanna proceeded to check each yearling. "The New Dawn colt didn't colic again, did he?"

"No, m'am, he did just fine," Julie replied, and set about handing the grooms the halters to put on their charges. "I guess the shipping over here just got him a little excited. He can be a bit of an airhead every now and again.

"By the way," she added, "the Sun Star filly took some hair off her left ankle during the night. Luckily, there isn't any swelling. I had Dr. Cowden check it anyway. Otherwise, no casualties."

"Thank heaven for that," Alanna said, as she moved to the stall where the Sun Star filly stood tied, waiting to be groomed. She entered the stall, ran her hand down the filly's hind leg and gingerly avoided a cow kick the young horse let out in defiance. Alanna reprimanded her softly. "That's enough, sweetheart, I just want to have a look."

"Good girl." Alanna praised the filly as she set her leg down and allowed it to be examined.

Satisfied the injury was superficial, Alanna continued her conversation with Julie, who had joined her in her inspection tour. "Most of the major bloodstock agents and their clients were at the cocktail party last night. Hope it put them in a spending mood."

Suddenly, she stopped walking and pointed to one of the grooms, who was having trouble getting her yearling back in its stall, "Julie, would you please get Todd and give Rebecca a hand with her horse."

As her assistant rushed to the other groom's aid, Alanna walked out of the aisle, and to the walking ring directly in front of her barn, in order to give her shedrow the once over. To one side of the entrance hung a large green and white sign inscribed with the farm's name and logo. Below the sign were a half-dozen green and white directors chairs, flanked on either side by arborvitae shrubs in white wooden tubs, affording a comfortable sitting area for buyers to await the yearlings they had requested for viewing.

Satisfied that everything was in order, Alanna headed for her tack stall, and a cup of black coffee. Cup in hand, she and Julie went over the yearling's pedigree updates. Alanna then instructed the assembled grooms as to each of their yearling's particular mannerisms, and made suggestions on how to show each to his best advantage.

"It's almost 8," she said, concluding the briefing, "please give your yearlings a last going over. It will be show time before you know it."

The morning's showings had gone well. There was a short lull during the lunch hour, but traffic picked up again at 2.

Alanna called to one of the grooms. "Dave, please put a lead shank on your colt. I noticed his eye looked a little runny. I'd like to check it."

As she entered the colt's stall, she heard Julie call out the catalogue numbers of her two best yearlings, just as she had been doing all morning, a very encouraging sign.

"Miss Reynolds," Julie said, peering into the stall door. "The gentleman looking at the Sun Star colt has some questions about the pedigree updates. He wondered if you could answer them."

"Certainly." Alanna patted the shoulder of the horse she'd been working on. "Tell him I'll be there in a second.

"Dave," she said, to the young man assisting her, "the colt had a small piece of straw in the corner of his eye, which I removed. If you get a damp sponge and wipe off the eye area, he'll be fine. Don't forget to put another coat of baby oil around his eye."

Alanna stroked the colt's muzzle reassuringly. Then, headed out of the stall and towards the walking ring.

He was sitting with his back to her, on one of the benches under the green and white awning pavilions that Keeneland had set up in the middle of each walking ring to shade buyers from the intense heat of the mid-July sun. The Sun Star colt was standing on the gravel walking area in front of him still posed for his inspection.

Even seated, and from behind, Alanna recognized Jeremy. The trembling inside her grew with each step she took toward him until she thought it must be visible to everyone around.

43

Steadying the fury that was building in her as best she could, she moved in front of him and faced him. She was not prepared for the hatred that welled up inside her as he raised his head and their eyes met. The only outward hint of tension was her hesitation in addressing him.

"Alanna Reynolds," she opened, and offered her hand in greeting, as she would have to any visitor to her consignment. "I understand you need some additional information on this colt."

He rose and accepted her outstretched hand. The feeling of his hand on hers made her blood run cold, but her outward expression remained one of friendly interest and enthusiastic salesmanship.

Julie was bringing out a filly on the other side of the ring for a young couple's inspection. The Sun Star colt, his attention span having reached its limits, turned his attention to the filly.

"Mr. ---," Alanna paused. "Oh, I'm sorry, I don't believe I got your name?"

"Forgive me," Jeremy replied. "My name is Mark Jergens."

"Mr. Jergens, if you're finished inspecting this colt, may I suggest we have the groom put him up. We can walk over there," Alanna pointed to the grassy area at the far end of the walking ring, "out of the way, and I'll see if I can answer your questions."

"I'm finished with him, lead the way." Jeremy was surprised at her composure.

"Thank you, Jeff," she said to the colt's handler. "You can put him up now."

As the colt moved back to his stall, Alanna walked to the grassy knoll as far out of earshot as possible, Jeremy followed uneasily.

The five years since their last meeting now seemed like an eternity, yet, if anything, she was more beautiful then he remembered. Barely five-four, her blonde, delicate features were a facade for a woman made of iron. Her quick, graceful way of moving, which gave her a regal air, was the same movement that made her such a deadly adversary in combat.

Her most distinct feature were her eyes, a mesmerizing blue. They possessed a unique ability to change from a deep sea blue to the present ice blue. A feature that, depending on the occasion, was capable of sending either thrills or chills down a man's spine.

The cool cover vanished as she turned her back to the casual observers. Her mood shifted considerably.

"I don't know what you're doing here, Jeremy, but I suggest you leave." She glared at her once close associate, not overlooking his new

Brooks Brother look and Cartier watch. Either the Agency had upped his salary considerably, she thought, or he's made a big score on the side.

If ever there was truth to the saying "the eyes are the windows to the soul", Jeremy's eyes confirmed it. Now they reflected only grief and sadness, two emotions she was not prepared to deal with.

Fueled by painful memories, her anger returned, putting an icy edge to her words.

"Whatever purpose brought you here, I'm not interested. Get out of my life and stay out of it. Do I make myself clear?"

"Very!" He said. She started to turn and leave. He touched her arm and she recoiled from his grasp. "Please, Alanna, hear me out." His voice was soft, consoling.

"Alanna, Jake is dead."

Unlike her first reaction to him, he could see the shock and sadness register. Jake had been very close to Alanna, almost replacing the father she'd never really known.

"When did it happen?" Her voice broke for a moment.

"Yesterday, in Trouville, about 5 p.m. our time," Jeremy replied.

"Five o'clock, are you sure?" Alanna asked, stunned, the vision of Jake in her barn aisle at that very moment in time clear in her memory.

"Yes," Jeremy replied, extending his hand to offer her a white envelope. "He left a message for you."

"I don't want the message, he's dead," she said, her composure returning along with the coldness in her voice. "Jake and Dar are both gone. I have no more ties with you or your friends. Just leave."

Jeremy watched her turn and go. Without a trace of their emotional conversation in her voice, she approached the two men inspecting a yearling. She greeted them and proceeded to point out the yearling's attributes, ignoring Jeremy's presence with chilling ease.

Granton, you bastard, why me, he thought. Why was it so important I deliver Jake's obituary? Jeremy knew that Alanna was dying inside. Once he could have put his arms around her, comforted her, shared her sadness. Now she had only hate for him.

He would have liked to tell Granton to shove this assignment but, seeing her, Jeremy realized how important it was to him, personally, to carry on. He had a feeling Granton knew all along that this would be his reaction.

Jeremy walked to the director's chairs. Sitting in one of them, he pretended to make notes on the catalogue page. Alanna had given him only a cursory glance as he passed her, quickly returning her attention to the two men.

As he rose to leave, he discretely dropped a small copper-colored disk into one of the planters. It easily filtered down into the bark mulch surrounding the bottom of the shrub, and on the ground, he dropped the white envelope with her name on it.

Walking away from the barn, he switched on the receiver and confirmed that it was working properly. He smiled at no one in particular, looked at his list in the back of the sales catalogue, and then crossed the grassy strip to the shed row opposite Alanna's. He requested a yearling and proceeded to examine him.

Alanna watched Jeremy go out of the corner of her eye. She knew she hadn't seen the last of him. What in the world was happening? Jeremy wasn't here just to deliver the bad news about Jake. She was sure it would not be long before she found out. Right now, all she wanted was somewhere to go and hide, and vent her grief. Everyone she really cared about was gone.

Alanna tried to remember when she'd talked to Jake last. It had been at least three months. He said he was somewhere in France. Alanna sensed then that he was in some kind of trouble. If only he'd asked her to help, she would have gone. Alanna knew he wouldn't have asked. Jake wanted her out of the Agency, "before its too late," he'd said.

He'd made her promise not to seek revenge for Dar's death. He warned that revenge clouded the judgment, and usually caused the demise of those who sought it. Without Jake, she knew she would not have survived her physical or emotional wounds.

When Alanna had begged Jake to quit too, he'd just laughed at the suggestion and said what would an old codger like him do with a normal job. It was best to go out doing the thing you loved.

She looked up toward the heavens and whispered, "God bless you, Jake. You may be the only one of us who got what he wanted."

"Is there something wrong, my dear Alanna?" The deep sound of the French voice brought her back to the present.

She lowered her eyes and turned to see the concerned look of Comte Francois de La Croix.

"Bonjour, Francois," she said warmly, as they exchanged the traditional air kisses on both cheeks. "I'm afraid I just learned that I've lost an old and very dear friend."

"Ah, yes, reason to be sad," he said sympathetically. "Perhaps I can cheer you somewhat. My clients have shown great interest in your Sun

Star colt, and have asked me to look at him. I assure you, they are prepared to go to great lengths to own him."

He took her hand in his, and continued, "I had hoped you would do me the honor of joining me for dinner tonight, where we might discuss the matter of the colt. Ah, but with the passing of your friend..."

She smiled again, and said, "Come with me, Francois. Not only would I be happy to show you my colt, but I would be delighted to have dinner with you as well."

Jeremy raised his head from his catalogue to double check what he felt was a slightly offset knee on the colt he was inspecting, when he caught sight of Alanna and her companion. Will you look at the smooth bastard, he thought. He recognized the Frenchman conversing with her, but not from horse sales or racetracks.

Though he'd never had any dealings with operations in France, he was well aware of the Comte de La Croix's association with the French Mafia, as well as several of the European based terrorist groups, the most recent of which, as indicated in his briefing, was with the French Hizballah cell headed by Kamal Shabban.

By the way Alanna was responding to Francois, it was clear to Jeremy that they were well acquainted. Surely, Alanna knew of his reputation. If she did know, she didn't seem to care.

They were close enough to the tub Jeremy had dropped his little eavesdropper into, so he pretended to fumble with what looked like a digital pager. Instead of the usual telephone message in print, Alanna and Francois' conversation was being displayed as it was recorded. If he'd missed anything, all he had to do was play it back.

Francois once again took Alanna's hand in his. "The colt is magnificent. You will not have a problem getting a big price for him." He signaled to his veterinarian, who followed the colt into his stall for closer examination. "I will pick you up at seven this evening. Does Le Café Chantant suit you?"

"It does, indeed. How clever of you to pick my favorite restaurant?" she replied.

"Ah, clever. Perhaps. Let's just say, my dear, that I make it a point to get to know the little things about people that interest me," he said. "Until then..." He kissed her hand and moved on, his entourage following close behind.

Jeremy was beginning to hate everything about this assignment, most especially Francois. A sick, uneasiness stirred in him. He was certain Jake knew about this, this... whatever you wanted to call this relationship. Suspecting that his cover was blown, and knowing that this relationship with Francois would give Alanna the access she needed, he now understood why Jake had no choice but to bring her back in to complete the mission.

Jeremy made his way back to his rental car. After driving to a secluded part of the parking lot, he stopped and he pressed a button on his specially encoded cellular phone that Rice had provided. It patched him through to one of Granton's secure lines.

When Granton's voice responded, Jeremy said, "Our boy, Francois, is here at the sale. I need you to get me permission to put surveillance on him while he's here."

"How interesting!" Granton replied. "Well, we already have a Presidential Finding to conduct Operation SABRE, but I'll ask the Director to have the President amend it to include permission to maintain surveillance on any foreign nationals involved while they are in the United States. In the meantime, you have my permission to keep an eye on him."

"That should do it," Jeremy said. "Oh, by the way, I can see why Jake felt we needed Alanna in on this operation. She greeted Francois like a long lost relative when he showed up at her barn."

"And how were you received?"

"Like a bastard child at a family reunion."

"Am I to interpret that remark as you were not successful?"

"She doesn't want anything to do with me. She made that very plain."

"I'm sorry to hear that," Granton said, genuinely disappointed. "But, we just don't have the time to get you back in her good graces. I guess I'll have to resort to another method. I'll get back to you."

Alanna was headed into the tack room when Jeff Bigler, the head groom, called to get her attention.

"Miss Reynolds," he said, handing her a white envelope, "Did you drop this?"

Alanna took the envelope that she recognized as the one Jeremy had offered earlier, opened it and unfolded its contents slowly.

Written on it, "Tell them, JESTER OUT - RESURRECT CHAMELEON".

To Alanna, Jeremy's mission in Lexington was now abundantly clear.

Chapter 6

It had been a long day. Alanna checked her watch; it read 4:30 p.m. She'd better be heading home.

"Julie," Alanna said. "You'll have to close up this evening. I'm having dinner with Francois, and I need some time to get this body ready. The night watchman will be here at five, so you can leave then. Thanks for a great job. We've had a very productive day. I'll see you at six in the morning."

"Have a good time," Julie replied. "Tell Francois we need at least a million dollars for that colt!"

"I will." Alanna smiled at Julie's remark. She hoped that was what Francois had in mind to give for the colt, because that's what it would take to own him.

As she reached her car, she noticed that many of the other consignors and buyers were leaving. Alanna knew there'd be plenty of partying in Lexington tonight. It took a lot of bourbon to grease the monetary wheels into rolling out the big bucks for these prospective champions.

She'd received several party invitations herself, but she felt a nice quiet dinner with some interesting company seemed a better idea, especially considering the distressing news she'd received.

Alanna started the engine, adjusted her seat belt and headed out of the sales grounds. She passed the area where the horse van companies parked their rigs. After the sale tomorrow, they would be loaded up with their valuable cargo, and would head out for destinations all over this country, Canada, Mexico and to airports, where horse air transports companies would deliver them around the globe.

There was a red Cadillac behind her, and, behind that, a large, silver semi-truck, followed by a black pick-up truck. Alanna laughed to herself. She never got out of the old habits. Always check your rear view mirror, you never know when someone might think your destination interesting enough to follow you to it.

She made a right turn out of the sales grounds, and, after a half-mile, a left onto the narrow Putnams Corner Road. Then she was on her own.

Alanna waited impatiently as the electronic gate to the back entrance of the farm opened. Without waiting for it to open completely, she maneuvered through it and headed toward the road to the main house. Rick Andrews, the farm manager, intercepted her in his farm truck at the junction. Running her window down, she waited for him to pull alongside.

"Miss Reynolds, you had a call from Bob Smithers," Rick said, as he brought the truck to a stop. "He said he had some interesting new pedigree updates for you, and for you to call him as soon as you got in."

Rick's voice took on a concerned tone. "Is everything all right? You look upset."

"Everything is fine, Rick." She let a smile cross her face. "I'm just a bit tired, we had a very busy day. How were things here?"

"Everything was quiet," he replied. "I'm glad you guys had a good day. We sure need to get a good price for those yearlings."

"Don't I know it?" She confirmed his observation.

"Keep your chin up, we've got some really good horses in that group. They'll bail us out," he said, trying to ease what he suspected were pre-sale jitters. "I've got to finish my rounds of the farm, but Callie and I will be in all evening if you need anything."

"Thanks for the moral support, Rick." Alanna smiled her appreciation. "I'm having dinner with Francois De La Croix, but I shouldn't be too late getting back. We're dining at Le Cafe Chantant if you need to reach me. Keep an eye on the house, would you please?"

"Sure thing. Have a good time. Relax. I'll see you in the morning before you leave for the sales grounds." Rick put the truck in gear, and, with a wave, drove off.

Alanna had much respect for Rick. He was the best young farm manager in Kentucky. She knew how lucky she was to have him. When she'd bought the farm with a down payment from some insurance money Dar had left her, she knew running such a big operation required the best help you could afford.

Since the farm's purchase, she'd been successful as a commercial breeder of Thoroughbred racehorses, but recently the economics of the business had changed. She could barely afford Rick now, and she knew he had better offers, but he and his wife, Callie, had become her friends, and they'd stuck with her. They all knew how important a successful sale was to the farm's continued operation.

Alanna wound her way up the main drive to the back of the house, and pulled the car into the garage. As she closed the car door, a large white dog came bounding around the corner of the garage, tail wagging and barking excitedly.

"Hannibal, you rascal, you wouldn't come in for Angela, would you?" She ruffled the hair behind the Great Pyrenees' ears and accepted a big paw in greeting. "There'll be hell to pay in the morning, my boy. I suspect your treats will be cut. I can't say you don't deserve it.

"Come on, in the house with you," she said, as she opened the back door.

He preceded her through the screen door and into the kitchen, heading straight for the pantry. She followed him, took a couple of cans of dog food down from a shelf and spooned them into his dish. The animal ate hungrily.

"You're one spoiled dog, Hannibal," She said, patting him fondly on the rump. "Take it easy. You'll make yourself sick."

Alanna left the kitchen, and headed down the main hall to the den, which housed the farm office. She laughed softly when she noticed the door to the office was opened a crack.

"Blackjack," she said, as she entered the room. "Honestly, I do believe you were a cat burglar in an earlier life, and your present condition is your reward for your evil ways."

The comment was aimed at a large black cat stretched full length across the desk pad on her desk. The cat's only response was the opening of one jade green eye and a huge yawn.

"Where are your two accomplices? Ah, there you are!" She said, as she walked over to a winged back chair, where Redford, a large, longhaired orange tabby, was sprawled across his cushion, four legs pointed toward the ceiling. She gently rubbed his tummy, then moved her hand upwards to scratch the chin of Ming Tu, the regal blue point Siamese, posed on the back of the chair like a porcelain figurine.

"You guys really have it made. Next life I'm coming back as a cat," she said, as she slumped into the chair opposite the one the cats occupied. "What a day!"

Reaching over, she scooped up Redford and cuddled him close to her, her face buried in his soft, thick, orange coat. She could hear him purr in contentment at the gesture. Slowly, the tears began to fall. Redford had been a Christmas present from Jake two years ago. She could still picture Jake smiling as he lifted the small ball of orange fluff, a green ribbon tied around the kitten's neck, from the pocket of his heavy top coat.

She had named him Redford, after her favorite actor Robert Redford, because, she'd said, the handsomest cat should be named after the handsomest guy.

Feigning disappointment, Jake had said, that all along he was sure that she'd thought of him as the handsomest guy.

Jake. Gone. It was almost too much to bear; first her parents in a car accident, then her elderly grandparents who'd raised her, then Dar. Oh,

Dar. Loneliness enveloped her and the tears flowed. Redford squirmed and jumped off her lap to get away from the dampness that had begun to saturate his coat. She buried her head in her hands and let the tears flow.

Stop it, she scolded herself after letting her emotions subside, feeling sorry for yourself won't bring them back. Alanna got up from the chair and went around to the other side of the desk. She removed a couple of tissues from a box in one of the drawers, and proceeded to dry her eyes and blow her nose.

Satisfied that she had regained control of her emotions, she picked up the phone and returned Bob Smithers' call, waiting impatiently for an answer. There was no answer only a recording saying his office was closed for the day.

She hung up the phone and stood silently for a moment. Then she reached down and ruffled the black cat's coat making him jump up and assume a pose of mock indignation.

"Come on guys, I've got a very important engagement this evening and I need to get the red out of these eyes and into these cheeks." With that she headed out of the office, the three cats in pursuit.

Alanna glanced down at the foyer of the house as she climbed the long winding staircase to her room. She had loved this house, this farm at first sight. All of the farms buildings had a French country look to them, so unlike the Georgian and Southern Colonial architecture, which was the norm for the area. Still, they had an easy elegance that blended beautifully with the lush, green pastures that surrounded them.

The farm had been built in the late fifties by a rich industrialist who had spent many years in the Normandy region of France. Upon the industrialist's death, his estate had sold the property as is, furniture and all. It had been quite a buy and she had, until today, been very happy and secure here.

Alanna entered the bedroom. It was the room she loved the best. It was green and peach and white, light and airy and it opened, through French doors, onto a balcony that faced the main field into which the mares and foals were turned out.

She loved to start her mornings watching the young horses play. They'd dash across the emerald green carpet of grass, bucking and kicking, feeling the wind at their backs - future champions, losers, too soon to know, or care - to them and to her it was all just good fun.

She stripped down and wrapped herself in a terry robe. The steam rose from the sunken tub as she filled it with water and fragrant bath oil. Slipping out of her robe, she eased into the billowing froth and found herself aroused by the sensation of the water moved by the jets in the sides of the tub. The luxurious scent of the bubbles enhanced the experience. She longed for Dar to come to her. How often they had shared an erotic moment like this, secure in each other's love.

Dar would be 44 now, if he had lived? To say he was handsome was an understatement. Six foot, athletically built, tan, with thick, slightly wavy coal black hair worn stylishly, but conservatively, and eyes the color of mahogany made him fit for a Hollywood leading man role. He had been born in Venezuela to Cuban-American parents, and bore the unmistakable Latin look of his ancestors. Despite his good looks, he was not a vain man. He had been raised to be a gentleman. Kind, considerate and loving, he was easy, in return, to love.

His father had been the U. S. Ambassador to Venezuela, but, when Dar was five, his father was appointed U.S. Ambassador to China. The senior De Santes had remained in China at the end of his tenure as ambassador. With his government connections, he'd found the business possibilities in the newly emerging economic atmosphere of China too enticing to pass up.

The family had made China their home for the remainder of Dar's youth. One of Dar's interests while growing up there had been a fascination with the old Shaolin method of the martial arts. By the time he'd left for Yale and a career in international banking, he had become a master in the form.

Dar had told her that military service had never appealed to him, but like his father, he had a desire to serve his country. He'd been out of Yale three years when an old family friend, one who had been with the Agency, had put the notion of working for the CIA in his head. The rest was history.

Alanna smiled as she remembered back to how they had met. Dar had been attending the Ox Ridge Horse Show in Darien, Conn., as the guest of the U.S. ambassador and his wife, who were friends of his family. The ambassador's wife had presented the trophy for the class she had won. It was she who'd introduced them that night at the exhibitors' party.

Alanna was 20 at the time, and had just graduated from college with degrees in French and Russian. She'd promised her grandparents that she would get a college education and a degree in something useful. An excellent student, she'd managed to cram her college experience into three years, in order to pursue her real love, show jumping.

Having concentrated on horses rather than romance during her teen and college years, she remembered how naive she'd been in the ways of the heart. How totally unprepared she'd been for Dar's smooth approach, and how easily she had fallen for him.

An outstanding rider, her desire, after graduation, had been to make the Olympic Equestrian Team, and go on riding as a professional for the rest of her life. But, that dream was suddenly overshadowed by her desire to spend her life with Dar. A decision that had serious repercussions, providing her entry into a shadowy world where the line between truth and lies quickly blurred, real living was replaced by a charade, emotional attachments proved a liability and death was an ever present companion.

Sadly, she thought how Dar's dying that night they had been on the operation in the Balkans had devastated her. Even though she'd known that theirs was a dangerous business, she had never seriously contemplated losing him. When it was over, she had blamed everyone connected with the assignment for it going wrong and his death; the enemy, Jeremy, the Agency, and, especially, herself.

Now, five years had passed since Dar's death. Long ago, Jake had urged her to start dating. She laughed when she thought about Jake's remark on the subject, "If you plan on staying celibate much longer, Alanna, you might consider joining a nunnery. Dar wouldn't have expected or wanted you to put your life on hold because he died. So, get on with it, girl."

She'd realized he was right, but so far nothing serious had ever come of her dating again. It was the way she wanted it.

"Oh my gosh. It's almost six," she said, out loud, and she quickly stepped out of the tub. As she toweled off, her thoughts drifted back over the events of the day, the surprise at seeing Jeremy, the terrible news of Jake's death. Her attention was drawn to the last of the water draining from the tub. She didn't want any part of the old life, the Agency games, and yet she sensed, like the water, she was about to be drawn back in.

Jeremy, of all people, knew how she felt. He even knew that once she had vowed to kill him for not helping her save the life of the man she loved, but here he was, errand boy for Granton Taylor, putting his life on the line, for what? She was sure it wouldn't be long before she found out. Something very big was going down, and, whatever it was, they wanted her back in the fold.

Like the water now swirling around the drain, she would be pulled downward by the whirlpool, and soon, unless something unforeseen saved her, there would be no escaping their grasp. She would be sucked once more into the abyss.

The sound of a car pulling slowing into the circular drive at the front of the house brought her back to the present.

She checked her image in the full-length mirror before heading downstairs. The glass revealed a small, lithe, well-shaped young woman, skin glowing with just a hint of tan. Her hair, the color of champagne, was arranged in loose curls atop her head, small wispy tendrils gently framing a delicately featured face. The blue-green silk shantung slacks and matching sleeveless top she wore had caused her eyes to take on the color of an azure sea. An antique gold locket completed the ensemble.

She gave a curl an extra twist and hurried down the stairs in time to answer the ringing of the doorbell.

Francois was a tall man, somewhat stout, but because of his height he carried his weight well. He was a smart dresser and had a certain suave, sexy way about him that, in addition to his being a wealthy, eligible bachelor, made him very appealing to women.

Now, he stood at her front entrance, a large bouquet of yellow roses in his arm, looking more like a teenager on his first date, than the head of the French Mafia. This was a bit of intelligence Jake had provided when he'd learned that she was associating with him through the horse business. Something he'd also let slip in way of warning was that Francois was widening his criminal associations to include terrorist groups.

Instead of this knowledge causing her to distance herself from Francois, it had prompted her to cultivate their business relationship in order to provide Jake with inside information on the man, if he ever indicated to her that he needed it. Now, that Jake was dead, Francois' terrorist connections seemed a moot point.

Alanna knew that Francois' Mafia connections were not common knowledge in the horse business. As far as anyone, including Jake could prove, all of his equine clients were legitimate. His dealings with her had always been gentlemanly and honorable, and since he had access to the capital to buy her yearlings, she had decided it could do no harm to maintain the relationship awhile longer. If some might question her motives, so be it. Anyway, dangerous men and dangerous games had always intrigued her. At least in this game, she would make the rules and reap the rewards.

"Good evening, Francois," she said, smiling warmly as she opened the door, and motioned for him to enter. While exchanging air kisses on both cheeks, she continued, "Please. Come in. I have a bottle of champagne chilling on the porch. I thought we might have a toast to the start of an exciting evening."

"You look wonderful, as always, Alanna," he said, handing her the vivid yellow flowers. "They remind me of the sunshine, as do you."

"Thank you. They're really lovely," she said as she accepted the bouquet. "I'm very impressed with whoever does your background checks. How else would you have known that yellow roses are my favorite flowers?"

"Let us just say that this was less good information and more intuition." He smiled at her reference to his earlier pronouncement of his habit of checking out people. "I'm glad my intuition was correct."

"While I put these in water, would you care to do the honors and pour us a glass of champagne?" she said, pointing in the direction of the staircase. "Just go under the staircase and through the French doors, the champagne is in a cooler on the bar. I won't be but a minute."

"It would be my pleasure," Francois said, heading in the direction in which he had been pointed.

A few minutes later, Alanna entered the sun porch, the roses now arranged in a large crystal vase. She set them on a table and accepted one of the Waterford crystal glasses filled with champagne that Francois offered her.

Francois raised his glass in a toast. "To Alanna, a beautiful lady, whom I have the pleasure of dining with this evening. You have no idea, my dear," he continued, "how long I have desired to ask you to spend an evening with me, but you have always given me the impression that there already was someone special in your life. When I asked you to dinner this afternoon, I was sure that you would turn me down. I am glad my intuition there was wrong, and I hope this will be just the first of many evenings we will spend in each other's company."

"You're very kind to say so, Francois," she said, raising her glass and her eyes to meet his. "I must admit, you've fascinated me for some time as well. Now, perhaps, I'll get to find out what it is about you that fascinates me so."

His expression took on a somewhat boyish grin. "I'm flattered to hear that," he said. "I hope I will not disappoint you."

"I doubt you will," she replied.

Chapter 7

The muted sounds of conversation, and the soft tinkling of crystal and silver greeted Alanna and Francois as they entered Le Café Chantant.

"Good evening, Miss Reynolds, it's good to see you again," Roland, the maitre d', said, as he recognized one of his best customers, and rushed to greet the couple.

"We have reservations for two in the name of La Croix," interjected Francois.

"Ah, oui, monsieur," Roland replied. "Your table is ready. If you will follow me, please."

The two men struck up a conversation in French as Roland led them to their table, taking their time as they made their way though the diners and toward the balcony level. Alanna wished they would cut the reminiscing short and move along, for she had suddenly discovered Jeremy's presence directly in their path.

She was hoping he would ignore their passing, but that was not to be. As she came alongside his table, he turned from his conversation with his two male companions, and pretending surprise at seeing her, rose to greet her.

"This is a delightful surprise, Miss Reynolds. You do remember me from this afternoon?" he asked innocently. Not receiving a reply, he added, "Mark Jergens --- I looked at your Sun Star colt."

Alanna was less interested in what Jeremy was saying then in the two men with him. She did not recognize the one on his left, but the one directly across from him was Bill Rice. Rice, piloting one of the Agency's helicopters, had snatched her off a beach after one of her more successful operations.

She had been wearing a hood that had covered her face during the mission, and had not removed it until he had left, and she was well inside the safe house he had left her at, so, she was sure he had no idea who she was, yet he smiled at her as though he did. On the slim chance that he had recognized her, she returned his smile, grateful for his past assistance.

"Yes, Mr. Jergens," she said, turning her attention back to Jeremy, "I remember. I apologize for not recognizing you immediately in this dim light. How are you?"

Jeremy had also attracted Francois' attention as he sought the reason Alanna was being delayed. Francois returned to Alanna's side. She was trapped. Not to introduce them would not only have seemed unmannerly, but would have required an explanation to Francois, something Alanna would rather not have to give.

"Francois, this is Mark Jergens. Mr. Jergens, may I introduce Comte Francois de La Croix," Alanna said, hoping this encounter would be as brief as possible.

"My pleasure," Jeremy said, extending his hand to Francois, and, so as not to seem rude, introduced Bill and Tad by their aliases. "Miss Reynolds, Comte de La Croix, may I present my pilot, Bob Riker, and co-pilot, Ted Cominski."

Bill and Tad rose, and each, in turn, returned the greeting and the handshake that Alanna offered.

Francois acknowledged Bill and Tad with a nod of his head as he returned Jeremy's handshake, and said, "Did I hear you say you had looked at the Sun Star colt, Mr. Jergens? You must be planning to compete with the big money at this sale. That colt will bring a enormous price."

"If that's what it takes to get a colt of his quality, I've come prepared," Jeremy replied.

"Well, best of luck in your endeavor, Mr. Jergens." Francois' response was civil, but cool. "Do enjoy your stay in Lexington and please," he added, letting his gaze settle briefly on the other two men, "don't let us keep you and your friends from your dinner."

"Well, thank you," Jeremy replied, and unable to resist, he added, "Having met Miss Reynolds has already made my trip here a pleasure."

"I'm sure," Francois said, in a tone even cooler than his previous remark. Without further comment, he took Alanna's arm gently, and steered her in the direction of their table.

Suddenly, Jeremy's interest in the mission intensified, if for no other reason then that he was developing an intense dislike for Francois.

Arrogant bastard, he thought.

His thoughts were echoed in Rice's comment, "God, what a pompous ass." Noting Jeremy's surprise at his remark, he clarified it. "Not the lady, man! She has unforgettable blue eyes, wouldn't you say, Mr. Jergens?"

"How observant of you, Bill, on both counts," Jeremy replied.

Well, if the Agency hoped Alanna would be able to infiltrate the French Mafia, Jeremy would have to say she was off to an excellent start. But, as yet she hadn't been approached to do it, and it bothered him that she had developed such a good rapport with such a dubious character.

Roland showed Alanna and Francois to a secluded table on the upper balcony. He held the chair for Alanna. "Your waitress this evening is Claudia," he said, as he set the menus and wine list before them. "She will be with you directly. I hope you will enjoy your dinner."

Francois thanked him, and the maitre d' left them to see to another guest.

"Do you know anything about Mr. Jergens, Alanna?" Francois inquired, as he sat down across from her.

"Sorry, I don't. I'd never met him before this afternoon," she replied, as she placed her napkin on her lap. It was only half a lie, she thought, after all she'd never heard the name Mark Jergens before this afternoon.

"He seemed to be looking at all the expensive stock." She purposely made the point to see Francois' reaction. She thought it was going to be interesting to see how deep in debt the Agency was willing to put itself to establish Jeremy's cover. "He might just give your people a run for their money."

"You might be right, Alanna," Francois replied, as he had now sensed that Jergens had thrown down a challenge to him not only for the ownership of the horse, but the attentions of Alanna as well. "I guess I'll have to do a little research on Mr. Jergens."

Check all you like, Alanna thought. Knowing the Agency, she was confident all Francois would find was that Jeremy's credentials were solid gold.

All through dinner, Alanna had avoided making eye contact with Jeremy, even though they had had an unobstructed view of one another. Her demeanor with Francois was so relaxed and intimate that it made Jeremy's skin crawl. However, the thought was not lost on him, that through an act of sheer stupidity, namely making so much of his enjoying meeting Alanna, he had committed the cardinal sin of intelligence work — unnecessarily pissing off the opposition.

"If you're not going to finish that steak, you can pass it this way." Rice's inquiry intruded on Jeremy's thoughts, and implied, subtly, that maybe he was concentrating too intently on the couple seated on the balcony above them.

"Reach for it, Rice, and you'll pull back a bloody stub," Jeremy said, as he raised his fork menacingly, breaking the tension around the table with a hearty laugh.

The three men lingered over coffee and after-dinner drinks until Alanna and Francois rose to leave. As they passed Jeremy's table, the couple simply nodded their goodbyes, and then stopped momentarily at the door to offer their compliments to their host.

"Take care of the check, Bill," Jeremy said, as he got up to follow the receding couple.

"Sure, thing," Rice said. Cracking one of his signature smiles, he added under his breath. "If I had my choice, I'd lose that Frenchman, and follow those blue eyes… anywhere."

"Good thing it's not your choice," Jeremy said. "See you back at the hotel."

Jeremy exited the restaurant a discreet distance behind Alanna and Francois. He lay back in the shadows of the entrance until they had entered Francois' limousine, then made for his car, which was parked directly across the street. Following them proved more difficult then he had expected. The limousine driver took great pains to make the journey back to Alanna's farm as slow as possible. A tag was easily exposed under these conditions, so Jeremy had to use extreme caution.

Alanna sensed that Jeremy had followed them, but resisted the urge to look out the back window to confirm her suspicions. Impatient to be alone with her thoughts, she wished the driver would speed up. If he were going any slower, she was sure that they could have gotten out and walked faster. An obvious stall on Francois part, but she said nothing.

The talk en route to the farm was filled with light conversation concerning the state of the horse industry, and the well being of their many mutual friends. When Alanna and Francois finally arrived at her door, the chauffeur remained in his seat.

"I had a wonderful evening, Francois. Thank you," she said warmly, while moving to the edge of the car seat, implying that it was time for the evening to end. "You've helped me through a very difficult time."

"It was my pleasure, Alanna. I only wish I could have done more." He took her hand in his. "I am sorry the evening has to end. I want to be with you again. Soon! Perhaps we can celebrate after the sale tomorrow evening. You will have sold your colt for a fantastic price, and I will have bought a future champion."

"Yes, I'd love to, but I must say good night for now, I have a very early morning."

She squeezed his hand and then liberated it from his grip. "I hope you're right about the colt. I think he'll do very well overseas. He was bred for the European style of racing."

Francois signaled the driver, who came around the car and opened the rear door. Stepping out, Francois turned and offered his hand to Alanna, who took it and exited gracefully.

As they approached the front door, she searched her purse for her house key. Finding the key, she unlocked the door, but only let it open a crack before she turned to Francois. "Thanks again, Francois. I'll look forward to tomorrow."

Alanna turned her head, offering her cheek for the expected air kisses, but instead of a kiss on the cheek, Francois' hand caressed it, then tilting her head up slightly, he kissed her gently on the lips. "Good night, sleep well," he said.

"Good night," she said, drawing herself away from him and slipping through the opening in the door that she had allowed to widen only enough to let her through.

Francois waited until she was safely inside the house, then returned to his car and left. As they drove out the farm drive, he laughed a little at her coyness, but he thought how refreshingly gentile and ladylike that was. Most women he dated, aware of his wealth and power, were only too eager to invite him in for a late night drink and more often than not, more, even on a first date. He would not have expected less of her. She had exactly the kind of class and polish he was looking for in a woman he might choose as a wife.

A few steps inside the door Alanna's foot came in contact with an object. The force of her foot striking it sent it sliding across the vestibule floor and into the wall. She turned on the vestibule light and noticed that the object was a large manila envelope. She picked it up. It had no markings.

"Mmm, how interesting!" she said, as she carried the envelope into her office.

She kicked off her shoes as she entered and hit the switch that lit the lamp on her desk. Oooo, she thought, as she made her way over to her desk, scum bag that he is, Francois sure can raise a girl's blood pressure. Sexy, sexy, man. She laughed out loud, clucking her tongue and shaking her head in reprimand for her giddiness. Then she turned her attention to the more serious business at hand.

She took the envelope from under her arm, and let her fingers move over its sealed edge. Sooner or later, she'd told herself, the Agency would spring its ace in the hole. That was their method. First, they try the soft approach. If that doesn't get your attention, well, they usually have something in their bag of tricks that will. Granton Taylor was ruthless.

61

Alanna knew if he wanted her back in, he'd have her back in — one way or another.

"Well, Granton, why do I know that this little package is from you, and what kind of little enticement have you conjured up to lure me into your clutches - money, jewels?" She said, out loud to herself. "I guess there's only one way to find out."

She picked up a letter opener from off her desk, slipped it under the flap and giving the opener a quick pull, opened the envelope. Setting the opener down, she looked inside the envelope. There appeared to be some photos and a folder. Selecting the photos first, Alanna withdrew them and set them on the desk. The light from the desk lamp fell across the top picture.

Captured, in what appeared to be a cropped and blown-up photo taken by a security camera, was the body of a man, draped backwards over the top of a chain link fence. His eyes were wild with pain, his mouth appeared twisted in an agonizing cry, streams of blood ran from the many gaping exit wounds in his chest, down his neck and face and into his eyes and mouth. The man was Dar.

Horrified at what she saw, Alanna reeled away from the black and white nightmare as though she had been struck. Air refused to enter her lungs, she felt herself gasping. Grabbing the edge of the desk, she tried to steady her legs — legs that suddenly refused to support her. Then there was a sound coming from the depths of her, exploding, as it hit the air, into a primeval scream. She threw her head back and it rushed from her mouth and echoed in her brain. "Nooo, Noo-oo," she cried out. "Argh!!!"

Her hand swept across the desk, taking with it the carefully arranged papers and books. The brass and crystal desk lamp flew across the room into the opposite wall and shattered.

Even that release of energy did not quiet the screams that echoed and reechoed through the silent, dark halls of the empty house.

Jeremy had pulled his car off the farm drive behind a stand of large pine trees. Moving to the side of the house, he waited for Francois to leave. Watching from his vantage point, he saw nothing of any consequence happen between Alanna and Francois, unless, of course, you cared to consider the kiss he'd observed, which, disgusting as it was, she had not offered, but rather Francois had taken.

He delayed his departure waiting until the downstairs lights went out. It was then that he heard an indistinguishable cry. It had an eerie quality, like that of a mortally wounded animal. The cry was followed by the sound of shattering glass, and the thud of heavy objects.

Jeremy could think of only one reason for the sounds he had heard. In a second he was headed for the door. Reaching it, he drew his gun. Flattening his body against the wall next to the front door, he tried to determine where the sounds were coming from.

Someone must have been waiting for Alanna when she'd come in the door. He decided that the best way to handle this situation was to be direct. The intruders would probably not be aware of his presence, so the element of surprise was on his side.

Moving in front of the door, he charged it, hitting it with the full force of his shoulder. It flew open. He let his body drop to the floor and roll, a technique that minimized the target he would present to an assailant.

Just as suddenly as the noise had started, everything became deadly quiet.

Seeing no one in the hall, Jeremy rose slowly and entered the office, his pistol aimed in the direction of the lone figure standing among the disarray.

The voice coming from the figure was ragged and angry. "Well, Mr. Slade, you're just in time for the finale to this little scene."

Alanna moved out of the shadows and into the light. Jeremy didn't like what he saw. The fact that the whirlwind that had been let loose in this room was the sole result of her having an emotional outburst gave him a very bad feeling.

Alanna bent down and picked up what, to Jeremy, looked like a large manila envelope. "How much of this surprise package was your idea?" She asked, holding it up, as if for his inspection, but he was too far away to distinguish anything about the parcel. "Was Granton in such a hurry to know my reaction to this abomination that he had you park yourself outside my front door?

"That was a nice touch, crashing through the door, gun in hand. You always did know how to make a dramatic entrance."

Jeremy realized, by the way Alanna had changed her stance, that the focus of her rage was being shifted from the inanimate objects in the room to him.

She moved slowly toward him.

"Alanna, look, let's talk this over before we both do something we'll regret." Jeremy still had the automatic leveled in her direction and his old instincts told him to use it. But, for the first time in his entire career, his emotions began playing dirty tricks with his instincts. His finger froze on the trigger.

63

"Don't you want to see what's in the envelope, Jeremy?" She seemed to be moving faster. Suddenly, the envelope came whirling through the air directly at his face.

Her movements were quick and accurate. Distracting Jeremy with the envelope gave Alanna the split seconds that she needed to close the distance between them. She had gained a deadly advantage.

Except for Dar, there had been no one in the Agency who was more skilled in the martial arts then Alanna. Her job had been to penetrate the enemy's defenses unobserved, secure the objective and retreat without disturbing the dust on the tables, if possible. Weapons were too cumbersome. So in most instances, if she were detected, she had to eliminate her attackers barehanded, silently and quickly. She was very good at what she did. In fact, she was the best.

Jeremy threw up his left arm to deflect the envelope from hitting his face. His vision momentarily blocked, he could not defend himself against her first strike. The reverse smash with the outside of her leg sent his gun flying across the room.

The motion swung his body to the right, exposing his left side. The powerful side kick that followed, struck a glancing blow to his ribcage. Small as she was, Alanna was capable of summoning a great deal of force, enough to send his already off-balanced body crashing into the arm of the winged-backed chair behind him.

Losing his footing, he ricocheted off the side of the chair to the floor. He hit the floor just in time to be missed by two flying feet that connected instead with the chair, shattering it to pieces.

Rolling painfully away, Jeremy scrambled to his feet and tried to put some distance and the large oak desk between them. He turned his right side to her an attempt to protect what he knew was a very badly bruised or broken ribcage.

"God, damn it, have you gone crazy?" Excruciating pain had caused Jeremy's response to Alanna's attack to be less than diplomatic.

Alanna sensed Jeremy's attempt to shield that side. "Come on, Jeremy. Come on, hero, make a fight out of this." She taunted, and stalked him, working him into a position where she could spring across the desk at him. "You're making this too easy. Too bad that coward boss of yours isn't here. Maybe the two of you could make this more interesting." Using her right arm in a sweeping motion, like the wing of a bird, her fingers and nails forming a claw, she struck at his face. Her nails glanced off the side of his face, missing his left eye by a fraction of an inch.

"Fight? Fight? Shit!" He said, as blood from the scratch splashed in his eye. "What brought this on? Damn it, I'm not here to fight with you!"

Jeremy was utilizing every bit of the martial arts training the Agency had provided him with just to avoid a direct hit. But he was not as good as Alanna, nor as quick and with blinding speed she vaulted across the desk, striking his good side in midair with another powerful kick.

"Argh!" He screamed in pain, as the momentum of the kick hurled him back against the wall.

"You have no idea how much I've wanted an opportunity like this," she said, her fury mounting with each attack on him. "I guess I owe Granton one. Of course we both know how fond he is of letting other people do his dirty work. Ever consider that this may be his way of getting you off the payroll?"

Jeremy couldn't remember the last time he had taken a beating to equal this one. He didn't want to hurt her, but he didn't want to die, either. With her awesome arsenal of skills and techniques, his size and weight and combat training, which would have normally been an advantage, were for all practical purposes neutralized. Jeremy knew, somehow, he had to get her to the ground; there he would have the advantage. But, the way this fight was proceeding the chance of that becoming a reality was becoming slimmer with every passing second.

They had once more reached the center of the room. A misdirected blow took out the last lamp throwing the room into total darkness except for the light coming from the hall.

It was then that the fight took a deadly turn. Alanna struck Jeremy with a kick to the groin. His breath left him, and a paralyzing pain began to course through his body, causing him to double up and fall forward. He opened his mouth to scream, but nothing came out, and the world seemed to be turning black. His only link with reality was the small voice in his brain that screamed at him to do something. Even with his body failing, he knew she was about to deal the deathblow. Lacking the strength to do anything else, he took the only option available. Utilizing his downward momentum, he hit her above the knees in a rather awkwardly executed football tackle. It was a move of last resort, and the most he hoped to gain from it was time.

Alanna, surprised that her attack had been nullified, was already planning a counter move, when suddenly she felt her right shoulder strike a solid object, tipping her body slightly to the left. This was followed by a dull thud, as her head connected with the edge of a heavy oak coffee table. By the time her body hit the floor she was out cold!

Chapter 8

Jeremy was hoping that when he and Alanna hit the floor that he would have the strength to pin her there. He realized that was going to be impossible as he felt his body falling to the right of hers. In his agonized state of mind, it was unclear to him how she had managed that move. The only thing he knew for certain was that when she connected the next time, the fight would be over. It took a full two minutes before he realized fate had dealt him the winning hand.

Since the threat of imminent death had passed, his first reaction was to do nothing. He could see that his adversary was out for the count. Just to make sure it wasn't a permanent state, he reached over and checked her pulse. It was strong.

Jeremy's body began to rebel at the hardness of the floor. To his right was a leather couch. Rolling his body onto his stomach, he eased himself first to his elbows and then using his legs as little as possible, since they still lacked sufficient sensation to support him, dragged himself onto it.

It had often occurred to Jeremy that he probably was not going to die of old age in his own comfortable bed! Images of being shot trying to run a defector across hostile borders, having his brains turned to mush by some needle-happy interrogator, or even being blown to smithereens by the blast from a well-rigged bomb in some far off place -- those were the real possibilities, not here, not in this lovely house, in the quiet Lexington countryside, by this angelic-faced woman.

It was at times like these, that the reality that there might be an easier, saner way to make a living became most evident. This job took a special kind of demented mind that felt the need to live constantly on the edge, tempting fate to the limits. Maybe the fear of growing old alone, sickly, helpless, was worse than facing a firing squad or a cyanide capsule.

It was different for Alanna, he thought, with envy. She had always had other options. Like the life she was living now. It always amazed him what a mess humans were capable of making of their lives in the name of love, country or any other supposed obsession. He was certainly proof of that!

Jeremy looked down at Alanna's face, soft and innocent in its state of unconsciousness. It belied a darker side of her nature that could meet deadly force with deadly force without hesitation. The capacity to kill lay in both of them, it had, on occasion, been a necessary component of the intelligence work they had performed. But, in his wildest dreams, Jeremy had never believed Alanna could turn that killer instinct on him. As he touched his sore rib cage and moaned, he chided himself on having become such a poor judge of character.

He thought back to how her attack on him this evening had developed with same startling, reflexive ease, just like the first time she had used her awesome skill to terminate an advisory.

It was in desperation that Dar was to set up their second encounter. Two weeks after Jeremy and Alanna's first meeting in New York, Dar had acquired the name of a group of Russian agents, which the CIA had dubbed the Marcov cell. The agents were causing considerable trouble in a location through which the Agency was attempting to bring across a Russian defector.

Dar had tried twice to rendezvous with Granton Taylor, then a field agent, to deliver their names and to hopefully undermine their effectiveness. He also had a new set of papers for the "defector". Papers good enough to get him through any checkpoint the man would have to pass on his way to the freedom he'd been promised in exchange for services rendered. With the number of agents the Marcov cell was running, any meeting the two men might have hoped to arrange would have only ended in disaster.

Jeremy had been assigned to get the paper work to the Russian and get him out, but unless he did so promptly, the window of opportunity would shut with a bang!

At that time, Alanna never suspected that Dar's dealings were more for the Agency and less for the international bank he represented. He had always been careful not to draw suspicion to himself, both for her safety and because of his uncertainty as to how she would react should she discover the truth about him. But, this time he had to risk it.

A financial wizard, Dar had accumulated a considerable fortune through his own investments, and an inheritance he'd received from his parents. When he expressed interest in putting some of his money into Thoroughbred racehorses, a field Alanna had become very interested in, she was delighted. She was even more pleased and excited when he suggested she make arrangements to attend the December Sales held in Newmarket, England.

Dar had said that he'd read on the financial page that a major European breeder was dispersing some fillies of racing age, which were from his most prized bloodlines, at the December sale. He knew that

Alanna was interested in this particular European breeder, because his family had, for generations, been the breeders of some of the world's most successful racehorses. The fillies would make valuable broodmare prospects, and he knew she would like to have one or two of them. Because of this, Alanna did not need much encouragement to make the necessary arrangements.

Off-handedly, he had suggested that, while she was there, she might just do a small favor for him. It wouldn't take much time. All she had to do was deliver a small envelope, containing some figures, to one of his associates from his bank's London office who needed the information to close an important deal. Dar said that he could arrange for the man, Tom Williamson, to be in Newmarket on Saturday. He would set up an 8 o'clock dinner meeting for them at the Kings Head Inn. Just so Tom would be sure he had the right person, she should wear the antique gold locket he'd given her. Tom was a connoisseur of such items, and would have no trouble recognizing the real thing.

Dar was considerably more worried about using her this time, as operating against the Marcov cell was hardly a job for an amateur. He just didn't have a choice, she was an unknown quantity in the intelligence game, and that was precisely what he needed now. He'd just have to make sure there were no slip-ups.

Alanna arrived at Heathrow that Saturday morning. Picked up a rental car and headed for Newmarket, an hour's drive from London. On her arrival in Newmarket, she checked into the Bedford Lodge Inn, a small, quaint hotel at the edge of town. It was headquarters for the international horsy set attending the sales.

At noon, Alanna joined a group of Irish friends for lunch in the dining room. Then, she and Mark Quinn, an Irish friend who ran a stud farm in Dunboyne, just outside Dublin, spent the afternoon inspecting the horses she had selected from her catalogue. Unlike the American sales, where all of the catalogued horses are available for inspection at the sales grounds, at Newmarket, those horses advertised as in training had to be viewed at the yards where they trained. It made for a busy afternoon.

At 4 o'clock, exhausted, she took a light tea back at the hotel, and then headed to her room for a warm bath and a short nap.

Jeremy had not been told anything about his contact, other than that it was a woman wearing an antique gold locket. He had been warned to use every precaution and to reconnoiter the rendezvous point thoroughly.

At 7:30 p.m., Jeremy, sure that he had not been followed, pulled his rented Rover into the back parking lot of the Kings Head Inn at Six Mile Bottom, a small village on the outskirts of Newmarket.

The dinner crowd had not arrived as yet, so the only inhabitants of the establishment were the kitchen help, bartender and a portly, gray-haired gentleman who sat at the bar, and was engaged in a game of backgammon with the tall, pock-faced young bartender.

"Can I be of help ta ya, sir?" The bartender inquired. "Will ya be joinin' us for dinner, or perhaps it's just a little liquid libation I could interest ya in?"

"I have a dinner reservation for two. The name's Williamson." Jeremy replied. "I'll have a pint of Guinness while I'm waiting, and could you point me to the men's room."

"Sure thing." The bartender went to the end of the bar and pointed to an area beyond a curtained doorway. "The loo's right through those curtains and to your left." Then, he picked up a mug and filled it with the rich brown liquid, and set it on the bar.

Jeremy took a quick sip. Then, he slipped behind the curtain to explore the rear area of the building. The back room was set up to accommodate a large party. The restrooms and back entrance were at the far end. Satisfied that all bases were covered, he headed back to the bar.

Alanna had been to the Kings Head Inn many times with her Irish and English friends, who prided themselves on having a good time. She liked the small, intimate quality of the inn, whose fireplace gave the main room a warm, golden glow.

There was only one customer when she arrived. When he did not acknowledge her, other than with a casual greeting, she removed her coat, and took a seat at a table near the fireplace.

Jeremy, returning, noticed the new arrival. Though her head was bent, inspecting something in her purse, making her features indistinguishable, the firelight had caught the glimmer of the gold locket that hung from around her neck. He walked to the bar, picked up his tankard, walked to her table and was about to introduce himself, when she raised her head. Their eyes met and for a moment it was doubtful who was the more astonished.

No wonder Dar had demanded security precautions be so tight. He was still trying to get away with letting her play the innocent.

"How interesting!" Alanna said, regaining her composure, although like their first meeting, making eye contact with this man resulted once again in her heart skipping a few extra beats, and what she feared was a noticeable blush coming to her face. "Well, Mr. Williamson, you are Tom Williamson?"

"What? Oh, yes," Jeremy replied, not sure whether he should feel elated or worried at the identity of his contact. "That I am. I'm sorry, but you have the advantage. My associate never did tell me your name."

"Goodness, how thoughtless of him. I'm Alanna Reynolds," she replied, a trace mystified at why Dar would have made such an obvious omission. "Had I known we'd be meeting again so soon and that you would actually be an intricate part of my friend's business affairs, I wouldn't have treated our first meeting so off handily. I hope you were successful in acquiring what you came for that day?"

"I got what I came for, but I have to admit, the day still turned out a major disappointment anyway." Jeremy suddenly found himself straying from his original purpose of the meeting and not caring in the least. The banter they were exchanging had very sensuous overtones to it.

"I'm sorry to hear that," she said, seeming to understand that her reluctance to respond to his advance was key to the expressed disappointment. And feeling the electricity between them, she found herself saying, "Well, we didn't have the luxury of a proper introduction then as we do now."

Indicating the chair across from her, she added, "so why don't you join me and we can discuss our options."

He sat down, and Alanna, sensing that his interest in her was serious, decided to back off the fooling around before she was in too deep. She let her lover's name cool the emotional atmosphere that was beginning to overheat. "Dar..."

Damn, Jeremy thought, don't bring him up now, not yet.

"Dar said you were in need of this information." As she spoke, she removed a small manila envelope from her purse, and offered it to him.

"Yes, yes I am," Jeremy replied, cooling the ardor in his voice. "I really appreciate your getting it to me."

"No problem." Then there was silence, and they just simply looked at one another, neither one knowing how to proceed with what should have been simple conversation,

Finally, she said, "You know, I'd like to think this is a coincidence, but our meeting twice is quite bizarre, wouldn't you say?"

"Not really, not if you understood how bizarre my life is normally." Jeremy's answer was accompanied by a small nervous laugh, because for the first time in his life, he found himself tongue-tied. Damn, he thought, she has a numbing effect on my psyche.

"Oh, really. Care to tell me about it?" She said, keeping up the attempt to break the conversational deadlock they'd found themselves in.

"Not, especially." Jeremy replied, the uneasiness he was feeling echoed clearly in his voice. Realizing how foolish he had been to get off on this area of conversation, he attempted to back away saying, "Really, I was just kidding. Actually, my life is pretty boring, and the last thing I would ever want to do is bore you with tales of my boring existence."

Suddenly, Jeremy began to feel the uneasiness grow. But ironically, it was not his companion who was the cause of this new sensation. It was the bells and sirens of a highly tuned instinct telling him something had gone wrong, very wrong with this plan.

Hoping the feeling would go away he said, "Why don't we order dinner?"

"Yes, that's a very good idea. I'm starved," Alanna replied, but her equally attuned instincts were beginning to raise hackles on the back of her neck. Why, she didn't understand.

Jeremy, knowing better than to ignore the feeling, took her hand and said, "Look, Alanna, we have to leave."

Alanna saw the concern in her companion's eyes, and sensed it was better not to question the reason for it now. "I'm ready if you are," she said, emphatically, already reaching for her coat and purse.

God, no wonder Dar dared to use her, Jeremy thought, she had a real sense about things.

"Behind that curtain on the right is a room," he said, indicating the cloth covered doorway. "As we leave, I want you to walk nonchalantly over to it and when you get in back, stay there until I'm gone. In fact stay there a good 15 minutes after I'm gone. I can't explain why now. I just need you to do as I say."

As they started forward, the curtain moved. Alanna saw the motion the same time Jeremy did.

"Forget the back room," he said, almost under his breath, the underlying tension he was feeling evident in his voice.

Jeremy felt her hand on his arm and when he turned to look at her, he no longer saw the face of innocence; the cornflower blue eyes were now the color of ice. "I can help you, Tom, if you tell me what's wrong."

"I can't risk your getting any more involved in this, Alanna." Jeremy said, and as he held her hands tightly in his, he cursed the man who'd sent her. "It's very complicated, but there are people here, now, who want what you just gave me, and they'll kill to get it. It's me and the

71

information they're after, so if you just stay here when I leave, you should be all right.

"Don't worry about me, this is just another one of those 'boring' days in my life that I refrained from telling you about," Jeremy's voice exuded confidence as the adrenaline in his system began to flow. "I can handle this. When I'm gone, get clear of this place as fast as you can and keep going until you're safe in your bed back home. I'm really sorry about this."

Then, trying to lighten the moment a little, he added, "I owe you a dinner. Maybe you'll give me a rain check?"

"Anytime." She smiled, but the icy look in her eyes had not melted.

Alanna watched him draw his gun and release the safety. Their eyes met briefly, and then Jeremy bolted out the front door. She noticed, as the first shot hit the door jam, that the bartender and his customer always alert to an IRA attack, both dove behind the bar. As she flattened her back against the thick stonewall, her attention was drawn to the curtain, which had parted, revealing a rather large, menacing man headed in her direction.

Jeremy, having cleared the door, returned the Russian agents' fire as he weighed his options. There were three men whom Jeremy could see positioned behind various forms of cover around the front parking area, and at least one that he knew of in the rear of the building. Not good odds. But, it was the one that he hadn't seen, the one hidden behind the bush he was about to pass that was to prove his undoing. As he ran by the bush, he felt a heavy blow to the back of his head. He fell hard, dazed by the impact.

Images of interrogator lights were already forming in his mind, as through his blurred vision he made out the business end of a silencer looking him in the eye.

Jeremy tried to get up, but they shoved him back, facedown to the ground, and pulling his hands behind him, tied them with a sharp plastic cord that bit mercilessly into his wrists. Then they jerked him to his feet and pushed him in the direction of their car.

As they approached the vehicle, a man got out of the back seat, and indicated with a nod of his head that the tall, heavy set man escorting Jeremy go back into the inn.

Jeremy tried to break loose, as he realized they were going back in for Alanna, but the other man escorting him simply cranked the cord tighter around his wrist, causing Jeremy such excruciating pain that he was forced to his knees.

"Don't be a hero." The man from the back seat warned him. It was the first anyone had spoken. "Did you think we'd forget the woman?"

"She doesn't know anything." Jeremy tried to persuade him.

"Let us decide that," was the reply.

When the tall one did not return promptly, the leader sent in another and urged him to hurry. He, too, disappeared around the side of the building never to reappear.

It was very quiet now. The leader seemed annoyed and confused by the failure of his men to return. He ordered the man holding Jeremy to remain there and then started in the direction the others had gone. Suddenly, there was movement from behind a car he was about to pass. He was a big, athletic man and as his peripheral vision caught sight of the movement, he turned in its direction. Before he could utter a cry, Alanna had delivered a kick to the groin and as he pitched forward, she caught him with an upward thrust of both her fists joined, reeling his head backwards and snapping his neck.

The man guarding Jeremy raised his gun to fire. Jeremy threw his body against his arm making the shot go wild. When the Russian looked back in her direction, the only thing he saw before the blackness came, were two feet, level with his head. In a moment it was done. When his body hit the ground, the last of the Russian agents was dead, blood seeping out of the corners of his mouth.

Suddenly, Alanna, the killing machine, once again became flesh and blood. She was looking down at the bodies of her victims as if in a trance. Jeremy, while still not sure what exactly had happened, knew for certain she'd never done this, never killed anyone before. Trained to defend herself, she had responded instinctively, and now the realization of how effective she had been was beginning to sink in. He could see she was not handling it well, and he had to shake her thoughts loose or the shock would get her.

Before he could say anything, she turned to him and said, incredulously, "My God, I've killed them." The horror of the deed began to sink in.

"That's exactly what they had in mind for us. Of course, we would have suffered considerably more before they finished the job," he said, thinking it a bad choice of words, but unable to think of anything more eloquent, his head still reeling from the blow he'd taken.

Jeremy knew Alanna would never again be the same sweet innocent she'd been. It had been a long time since he'd made his first kill. The circumstances had been different. He had been in a war, bullets flying in all directions. It had been an impersonal kill. He hadn't had to look into the eyes of the man whose life he'd just taken, and so he knew he was unable to fully understand her feelings, but however it happened, taking a life changed you forever.

"Untie me, Alanna." He almost had to shout to get through the daze she was falling into. "Now. Get with it. We've got to get out of here before the police come. Move, woman!"

Her movements were slow and awkward, but she managed to untie him.

"The others," he said, taking hold of her and trying to get her thoughts moving again. "Where are the other men?"

"Dead." Was all she could say, before she ran behind a car and threw up.

Unbelievable. Well, at least there were no witnesses to identify her. The Brits in the bar would keep their mouths shut, and the Agency's liaison people would see to MI6 covering the matter up properly.

Jeremy rubbed his aching wrists, and then dragged the bodies of the two dead men out of sight. There would be a lot of explaining to do to Headquarters, but he'd have to work that out later. Putting his arm around Alanna, he steered her in the direction of his car.

"Come on, let's get out of here," he said, opening the front passenger door, easing her into the front seat. He started the engine and headed the Rover towards Newmarket. Picking up his cell phone, he put through a call, and when there was a response, he instructed them to send someone immediately to pick up a... "What are you driving?" He asked.

"A green Renault," she replied, almost in a whisper.

"A green Renault. Get it back, quietly, to the Bedford Lodge." He hung up the receiver and took hold of her hand, which was ice cold.

"I'm going to take you back to your hotel," he said. "You are unknown to those jokers, so you'll be safe."

"No," she said, her voice strong, but her eyes were filled with tears. "I'm staying with you. I couldn't stand to be alone. Please!"

Nothing had gone right yet, and this handholding job he was facing was about the last thing Jeremy wanted to do. He knew he didn't have a choice. Somehow, someone, maybe even he had botched the meet, and she'd saved his life. Now, she was his responsibility.

"Then we'll both go back to your place," he said. "They're probably on to my place by now anyway."

Alanna was silent the remainder of the ride back. Her tears had dried, but she kept an unwavering eye on some point in front of her, in an almost trance-like state.

He pulled into a dark corner of the Bedford Lodge's parking lot and parked the car.

Turning to her, he tried to persuade her to cheer up, if only not to call attention to themselves. "You better fix your makeup up a bit," He tried to sound humorous. "And try to smile. You know you're supposed to look happy when you get lucky." Then, he reached over to her and let the back of his hand gently wipe a lone tear from her cheek.

"Come on," he said, and with a sigh of resignation, he got out and helped her out. The back door of the inn turned up locked, so they were forced to use the front entrance. Putting his arm around her and drawing her close to him, he guided her through the door and into the brightly lit foyer.

The lounge, to the left of the entrance, was full of horsemen drinking, swapping stories and making deals. As Alanna and Jeremy came into view of the lounge, a short, stocky, gray-haired man approached them, a broad grin on his face.

"There you are, you gorgeous creature," he said good-naturedly. "We were all wondering when you'd get back."

It was then that he noticed how pale she was. "Good grief, girl, is anything wrong?" When Alanna failed to respond to his question, he turned his attention to Jeremy.

"I'm Packy McLaughlin, what's happened to my girl here?"

Jeremy could feel Alanna trembling against him. "She'll be fine, sir." Jeremy tried to reassure the man and still keep up their forward movement.

Packy would have none of it. "Who are you?" He asked Jeremy pointedly.

"I'm Tom Williamson. Alanna and I are old friends. We were out to dinner and I'm afraid she's eaten something that didn't quite agree with her. If you don't mind, I'd like to get her to her room so she can rest."

"Yes, by all means, do," Packy said, backing off slightly, his voice full of concern. "I certainly hope you feel better in the morning, Alanna. But, if you should happen to feel worse, Dr. Miller's in room 12, I'm sure he won't mind if you give him a call."

"Thanks, Packy." She finally found her voice and managed a weak smile. "I'll be fine."

Just speaking to a friendly familiar face seemed to give her strength.

When they reached the top of the stairs, Jeremy asked for her room key. She fumbled through her purse for a minute, then pulled it out and handed it to him.

It was a corner room with a view and a private bath, rather a luxury in these small inns. The furniture consisted of an armoire, small desk, and chair, one uncomfortable looking upholstered chair, a full-sized bed and night stand.

He sat her down on the bed and went for a glass of water. When he returned, she was holding the locket in her hand, tears streaming down her face.

"Why?" She asked. "Who is Dar, really? Who are you, really? In New York, that was no coincidence you being at that shop. I was delivering something from him to you just like I did tonight. You're some kind of drug dealer or spy, aren't you? And he is too, isn't he?"

Jeremy had lowered himself into the chair, his eyes cast down.

"Answer me! Answer me!" she shouted.

Jeremy put his finger to his lips in an effort to quiet her, but she persisted.

"I have a right to know." The disillusionment in her voice was very evident. "I've just ruined my life for some cause, and I haven't the vaguest idea what for. And I want some answers."

He got up, walked to the window and looked out in the direction of the parking lot, both to check and see if anyone had followed them, and to give himself a little time to figure out how to deal with the situation. "I can't answer your questions, I'm not authorized to," Jeremy finally replied, trying as best he could to cope with her rising anger. "All I can say is I'm truly sorry you've been caught up in this mess, and I'll see that you get home safely. When you get back, you can ask my associate to explain."

"Your associate! Your associate has a name — or maybe he doesn't." Suddenly nothing made any sense to her. She'd been living with a stranger.

The now silent room was jolted back to life by the ringing of the phone, which Alanna did not attempt to answer.

"You'd better answer it," Jeremy said. "Your friend's probably gotten word of the incident and is worried about you."

In defiance, Alanna picked up the receiver and let it drop to the floor.

"Alanna! Alanna!" They could hear Dar's desperate voice call out on the other end of the line.

Jeremy walked over, picked up the receiver and held it out to her.

"You want answers! He's got'em. Talk to him." Jeremy made the request almost an order.

Reluctantly, she took the phone from him.

"Alanna, are you there, answer me, please!" Dar's voice pleaded with her.

"I'm here, Dar," she replied, while never taking her eyes off Jeremy.

"Thank God, you're safe!" Dar said, as she held the receiver away from her so that Jeremy could hear every word. "I got word there was some trouble at the pub. A terrorist attack or something, I was worried sick. Are you all right?"

At the word terrorist, Jeremy visibly cringed. He thought Dar must be mad with concern for her safety, but most of all, he must be scared witless that the cat was finally out of the bag.

Alanna's reply was filled with a newfound confidence. "Oh, please, Dar, don't insult my intelligence. You lied to me. I loved you, believed and trusted you, and you used me. I would have died for you if it were necessary. Today, I killed for you, and I don't even know why."

"I'm sorry, Alanna, really I am." Jeremy could hear Dar pleading a useless case. "I know you'll understand if you give me a chance to explain. I guess I never figured anything would go wrong. I can't change what I've done, but I promise, it won't happen again."

Alanna and Jeremy listened as Dar continued to try to contain a deteriorating situation. "I've made arrangements to get you home. I'll meet you at the airport and everything will be fine, you'll see."

"How can you be so arrogant as to think you can make what happened tonight right?" She retorted. "Can you resurrect five people from the dead? I'm not coming back, Dar, ever." Her confidence was high. "I'll send someone for my things. Oh, and don't worry about me. I'll be safe. After all, look who I had for a teacher."

"Alanna, please, you'll feel differently in the morning." Dar couldn't avoid the business end of this deal, especially since no transmission had mentioned Jeremy's whereabouts, reluctantly he asked, "Look, sweetheart, can you tell me what did happen. What happened to the man you were to meet and the envelope?"

"Suffice to say the lessons you taught me were more than adequate to handle the situation. As for your "associate," he's right here," she said, glad for an excuse to end the conversation.

"It's your 'associate'!" She handed the phone over to Jeremy. "He'd like a word with you."

"It's Tom," Jeremy said, using his alias to identify himself.

"What the hell happened?" Dar asked, obviously irate.

'Things went a little astray. I'll fill you in later," Jeremy replied.

"And the package?" Dar inquired about the papers.

"The lady's just fine." Jeremy purposely did not answer the question he'd been asked, a little angry that Dar seemed more concerned with the papers then the woman.

"She's upset now," Dar said, too confidently and too proud, or stupid, Jeremy was not sure which it was, to admit his mistake, "but, she'll get over it when she gets home."

I wouldn't count on it, Jeremy thought. Then in answer to Dar's question about the papers, said, "I have what I need to close the deal."

"Thank God." Dar sounded relieved. "Jeremy make sure Alanna is all right tonight. I've made arrangements for JESTER to get her home. I caught up with him in London, and he said that he should be able to take care of the matter by tomorrow, mid-morning. That'll free you to take care of business. Do you need anything other than a clean up crew, which I've already taken care of?"

"No," Jeremy replied, his eyes on the woman, who sat quietly on the bed, her head in her hands.

"Good then, that's everything," Dar said. "I'll look forward to hearing how the deal went."

Dar was about to hang up when Jeremy said, "Just a minute." Putting his hand over the receiver he said to Alanna, "Any parting words?"

Her look of disgust was answer enough and he said to Dar, "Guess that's it." And he hung up the phone.

Jeremy set the phone back on the nightstand, and sat back down in the chair. The room was silent for a moment, then Alanna said, "I know you're not 'authorized' but there must be something you can tell me. Please, I feel very confused. Am I at least entitled to know whether I'm one of the 'good' guys?"

"I guess being a 'good' guy is all relative to what side you're on," he said, as he mulled over how to handle this situation. "If you mean did you do it for flag and country, the answer's yes."

"That's comforting," she said. "I'd hate to think I'd become a murderer and a traitor all in one night."

Jeremy indicated the bathroom. "Why don't you take a nice bath, you'll feel better. Then you can get a good night's sleep. It's over and done with, Alanna, you're just going to have to learn to live with it. The odds weren't in your favor tonight. Be glad he made you good enough to change them."

Alanna did as Jeremy suggested. He heard the water run, in the meantime he took off his jacket, tie and set his gun on the floor next to the chair. Then he searched the closet for an extra blanket, which he laid over the back of the chair. A little while later, she emerged from the bathroom wrapped in a powder blue silk robe.

"Hit the sack." Jeremy ordered, then indicating the uncomfortable looking chair, added, "I'll be right here if you need anything."

Alanna walked to the nightstand and turned out the light. Jeremy could hear the sound of the soft fabric of her robe as she removed it and laid it at the foot of the bed. The light from the parking lot made a gilded path through the window and along the floor. He could just make out her silhouette in it. Beautiful, he thought.

He was about to doze off when he heard her voice.

"I know you're probably not supposed to tell me this either." Alanna's voice sounded very distant. "But, I'd like to know your name, your real name!"

There was silence as Jeremy weighed the issue.

"Jeremy," he replied, quietly. "Jeremy Slade."

"Jeremy," she said the name softly, almost a whisper. "Is there someone you love, Jeremy? Someone you trust?"

"No." He lied. She wouldn't have understood, he thought.

"It's just as well," she said, with a sigh of resignation. "Love always manages to cause you pain."

How well he knew. "You'd better get some sleep," he said, as suddenly the urge to run from this room became very powerful.

"What are you afraid of, Jeremy?" She seemed to sense his uneasiness. Amazing, without having made a single sound, he realized that she was no longer in her bed, but moving slowly towards him. He rose, not sure what to expect, and then she was standing in front of him.

"Hold me, Jeremy!" Her voice was almost a caress. "Please, I need you to hold me close to you."

She let both her hands slide gently up his chest. Her head rested lightly against him. His arms moved around her, his lips kissed the top of her head. He could hear his heart pounding.

"Make love to me, Jeremy." The words rang in his ears, though she had spoken them in a whisper. "I need to feel your life in me."

"What about Dar?" He hated to chance ruining the moment, but he had to know.

"He was the only man I've ever known, until tonight. Now it's you that I want and need," she said, as her naked body closed on his.

79

"I lied when I said I didn't love anyone," Jeremy said.

"I know." She had bewitched him totally. "I saw it in your eyes in that shop in New York. Show me, Jeremy, show me how much you love me."

She unbuttoned his shirt. Jeremy felt her tongue move along his chest. Her hand traveled down to his belt and undid it. She explored the hardness that had sprung up.

Taking his hands, she led him to the bed. "Lie beside me," she said. "Take away the pain. There is a tenderness in you that I need to feel."

Jeremy had never had an experience to equal this sensation. Maybe it was because he'd never really been in love with the woman he was making love with before. She was exquisitely sensual in her lovemaking, bringing him to the edge in such a way that every fiber of his body tingled with a fiery sensation he didn't think possible. He found himself responding in kind. Experiencing a new kind of sensitivity to a woman's needs. Feeling the pleasure in her pleasure.

They slept peacefully in each other's arms.

The next morning, he was gone.

Chapter 9

A sharp pain brought Jeremy's thoughts back the present. He rose slowly from the couch, and stumbled across the debris that littered the floor until he found the manila envelope. Inside it, he found a folder, which contained a letter from Granton, and a brief recap of Operation SABRE. It was what the letter said that sent Jeremy searching frantically through the debris.

"Oh, my God," he said, as he sank to the floor, the picture of his fatally wounded partner and Alanna's lover, clutched in his hand. "My God, Granton, what were you thinking when you sent this?"

He put his head in his hands, and let out a cry of anguish, then railed at the sky, "How could you have done this?"

He waded further through the debris until he had found the remaining three pictures. One was of Jake lying on the bakery shop floor. The other two were pictures that had also been taken by the surveillance camera in that Serbian munitions plant, and they were the ones Jeremy stopped to examine closely. One was the original of the blown up shot of Dar's body hanging over the fence. In the background, you could make out the figure of a man, a man Jeremy recognized as Kamal Shabban. The second picture was an enlargement of the man, so there was no mistaking that the identity was that of Kamal, the leader of the French Hizballah cell.

Jeremy used the edge of the desk to help raise himself from the floor. He put the folder and pictures back in the envelope, and laid the envelope back on the desk. Then, using the wall for support. he made his way to the hall and found the kitchen. He felt around in the dark until his fingers located the switch, and he turned on the kitchen light.

The walls were lined with cabinets. Starting with the one closest to him, he located a glass and filled it with water. From under the sink, he got a bottle of ammonia and applied some to a piece of paper towel. Then, he headed back to the office.

He found the overhead light switch and turned it on. Alanna still lay unconscious next to the table. He set the glass of water on the table. Then, easing his tortured body down, he straddled her. Cradling her head in his hand, he held the ammonia-soaked towel under her nose.

Alanna moaned slightly, and rolled her head sideways to get away from the stinging odor. Her eyes opened slowly, and then closed again as a rush of tears, a reaction to the chemical, and a wave of dizziness accompanied her first conscious moments. Jeremy slid her body away from the table, and set her head gently back on the floor. Groaning, he moved his body alongside of hers, and sat down on the floor.

Alanna opened her eyes, and tried to focus on the face above her. It was blurred. She touched the spot on the back of her head that had struck the table. It was seriously sore, and beginning to form a goose egg.

"You'll be all right in a minute," Jeremy said. "You took a nasty blow from that table. I'd like to be able to take credit for getting the situation under control, but it beat me to it."

"Well, where do we go from here?" She inquired, in a half-daze.

"Nowhere," he said. "I want you to listen to what I have to say, Alanna. You tell that bastard Granton to forget it. Tell him you're not interested in coming back in, there's nothing he can do to make you, and to shove this mission.

"I saw the pictures," Jeremy continued. "He's playing mind games with us, Alanna. It's what he's famous for. That's why they gave him that fancy office. He's the best people manipulator the Agency's got. Please, don't fall for it. You have something worth having here, and you've buried all the dead you need to.

"Look, I just need to bid on your horse tomorrow," his voice was beginning to sound coarse and weary. "It'll establish my cover and you'll be out of this mess. I promise I'll settle the score for both of us."

"What about you, Jeremy?" Alanna asked, as she fought off a nauseous feeling that kept welling up in her stomach. "Haven't you buried enough of your friends, too? Now, do you want to join them?"

"The only thing I buried that meant anything to me were my feelings for you," he lied, a practice, he noticed, that was getting easier the longer he was in the intelligence business, "and I did that five years ago in that hospital in West Germany."

His chest was beginning to swell from the bruises, causing his voice to become raspy as his windpipe constricted. "Now the only thing I have worth keeping is my life; I don't intend to lose it. You have everything to lose, don't throw your life away for this.

"Let me help you upstairs and then I'll leave," he offered. "Just play the game tomorrow, and then you're out."

"Leave me. I'll be fine," she said, as Jeremy got painfully to his feet, and offered his hand to her. "I don't need your help, or your sympathy, and whether I do or don't come back in is my decision."

"Whatever!" Jeremy replied. "Just think about what I said when you drive out of here in the morning. Really consider whether the price of revenge is worth giving up all of this, and maybe your life!"

Looking down at her still prone figure, he said, "Well, since I can't seem to be of more assistance around here either as a Good Samaritan, or a punching bag, I'll just say good night. My sincerest hope is that you feel as lousy in the morning as I know I will."

Jeremy walked to the original place he'd been standing when this whole fiasco had begun, and surveyed the area into which his gun had flown. Finding it, he picked it up and returned it to his holster, and without another word, left.

Nauseated from the blow to her head, Alanna laid back down on the floor. The ceiling above her was making lazy circles around the fan that hung, unmoving, from it. The force of the whirlpool was pulling at her hard now. Jeremy had thrown her the lifeline she'd hoped for; if she had the sense to grab it, she'd be safe. If not, there would be no turning back, and Jeremy might have been right in saying no coming back.

Slowly, the propeller motion of the ceiling ceased. Using the edge of the table that had earlier rescinded Jeremy's death sentence, she eased herself into a standing position.

The envelope was lying on the top of the desk where Jeremy had left it, the nightmare pictures now tucked safely inside. Picking the envelope up, she made her way out of the room. It was going to be a long, sad night, she thought.

Alanna walked out to the hall, and made her way to the stairway. Using the banister for support, she climbed the stairs. As she opened the door to her bedroom, three pair of eyes greeted her, then scampered for the underside of the bed and safety.

"It's okay, boys, the fight's over," she said, softly to the cats. "Fortunately, the home team lost."

The three cats emerged slowly at the reassuring sound of her voice and resumed their vigil from assorted positions on top of the bed.

Alanna walked to the French doors that led to the balcony, opened them and stepped outside. She rested her hands on the wrought iron railing, and eased her head back, her eyes scanning the clear, star-filled sky. The soft breeze was filled with the smell of night flowers, and though she could not see them through the blackness, she could hear the soothing sounds of the horses moving about the field, the mares gently calling to their foals.

Jeremy, she knew deep down inside of her, never in their entire relationship had had anything but her best interest at heart. It was obvious again tonight that he was willing to risk his life to save hers.

But, she had never been able to bring herself to forgive him for not letting her return to Dar that night.

Their mission had been to infiltrate a Serbian munitions factory, and establish whether intelligence reports, indicating that the factory was manufacturing chemical weapons instead of arms, were true. A routine assignment for them, it was, nonetheless, dangerous, and, made more so by the fact that unbeknownst to them, the mission had been blown.

Jeremy and Dar had already returned to their point of entry. They had completed their reconnaissance of the factory's storage facilities, which were located a short distance from the entry point, and the photographing of its contents with their infra-red equipment. Her assignment to search the office files and safe had taken her deeper into the factory's interior, and had delayed her return. To save time, Jeremy had scaled the perimeter fence. He was about to catch the satchel containing the photography equipment that Dar had thrown him, when all hell broke loose.

Suddenly, sirens began to wail. Brilliant beams of light shot from their many sources on the factory's roof, and perimeter watch towers, and swept the area, illuminating great swatches of ground with their light. It was only by sheer luck, that on the first two passes they'd missed the spot in the fence where he and Dar stood, hidden in the shadows, awaiting her return. She could hear the sound of dogs barking and the guards shouting as they began to scour the area.

Just as she broke from cover, and began running an evasive course toward Jeremy and Dar, one of the searchlights zeroed in on their exit point. Seeing the light headed in their direction, the men had quickly fallen to the ground, where they lay prone, hoping they would not be detected. But the perimeter around the factory had been designed to eliminate any hiding places, and, in this case, flat on the ground was not shelter enough to keep them from being spotted.

The guards and their dogs were closing in on their point of entry fast. Seeing that the guards had the advantage, she increased her speed and changed course, making straight for Jeremy and Dar's position. To save valuable time, she had abandoned any attempt to avoid the searchlight's beam, and, in doing so, drew considerable fire from the mounted emplacements atop the factory's roof.

To give her cover, Jeremy and Dar were returning the fire with their automatic weapons. She had almost reached them unscathed, when she felt as though she'd been punched in the back with a fist. Adrenaline and shock kept her going. As she stumbled into Dar's arms, he dropped his gun, grabbed her, and lifted her to the top of the fence, while Jeremy kept up the covering fire. When Dar was sure she was over the top, he'd picked up his gun and resumed firing. Up until that point not a word had been spoken, but as she slid down the other side of the fence, she'd heard Dar yell to Jeremy, "Get out of here. I'll cover for you."

"No... No!" She'd remembered clinging to the chain link fence and screaming at him through the sound of the gunfire. "Throw me your gun, Dar. I'll cover for you. Hurry!"

He had looked at her with great sadness in his eyes, and said, "You have to go, Alanna. I'll always love you, Cariña!"

Then, he'd looked quickly over at Jeremy, and using his gun to point the way to safety, he ordered Jeremy to take her and leave.

"Take her and go, or we'll all die," he'd said, and with that he'd turned his back on them, loaded a fresh magazine into the weapon, and fired off another burst.

She remembered Jeremy grabbing her by her arm and dragging her off towards the woods that bordered the factory, ignoring completely her pleas to stop. She had been in tight spots before, but never had she felt so out of control. It was her worst nightmare come true, and it was happening before her eyes in surrealistic, slow motion.

Her attempts to free herself from Jeremy's grasp were initially hampered by the rough, slick terrain they were attempting to negotiate, and, later, by a sudden, burning pain in her chest. Despite her best efforts to ignore the pain, it soon began to sap her strength, and not long after that, to make her feel light-headed.

By then, they had heard Dar's final, agonizing cries. Knowing she no longer had any reason to go back, Jeremy released his hold on her.

"Hurry! We're almost there," he'd said, as he, unknowingly, moved off alone into the darkness ahead of them.

She had not followed him. Having been suddenly overwhelmed by a sense of well-being, she stood her ground. The pain was gone, and instead of the blackness they had been maneuvering their way through, she seemed to be engulfed in a bright, warm light. She'd felt safe, and happy. Tentatively, she'd touched the wound in her back and felt the warm, sticky blood that had saturated her clothing. It was then, that her body, weakened by the loss of blood from her wound, had allowed her legs to give way, and her to sink to the wet, forest floor.

When Jeremy had discovered her missing, he'd backtracked along the trail. She could hear him calling her name, but the sound of his voice seemed far away, and she was unable to respond. By the time he'd found her, she was unconscious. Determinedly, he had carried her the mercifully short distance to the helicopter rendezvous point, where an Agency medic had administered the trauma therapy that had saved her life.

When she regained consciousness in a military hospital in Frankfort, Germany, it was Jake who was there to reassure her. And, Jeremy, he'd been there too. He'd touched her hand lightly. Angrily, she'd rebuffed him. Without a word, he'd turned and left. It was the last she'd seen of him until this afternoon.

Yes, she'd known even then, that it would probably have been futile to attempt to save Dar's life. They were outnumbered and outgunned; as a matter of fact, she, typically, hadn't even been carrying one. But at that point, she had felt that if she couldn't save Dar, she wanted to die with him. Life, to her then, was worth nothing without him. She had been wrong about that too, and she had Jeremy to thank for not letting her make that fatal mistake.

But, the old aching pain and loss had returned when she'd first seen Jeremy. The old memories, the news of Jake's death, and the pictures of Dar had all conspired to put her over the edge. Here was a man who had saved her life. Yet, even with all the self-control she had attained through her martial arts training, she had been unable, in the end, to cope with her emotions. She had almost done the unforgivable; she had almost taken his life.

"God, Jake," she said, out loud. "I'm sure glad you weren't here to see tonight's performance. You certainly would have given me a good boot in the pants for that one, especially, since I almost wiped out your protégé. Sorry, old friend, I won't let it happen again."

Her head still feeling leaden and her mouth having acquired a sour taste, Alanna went into her bathroom for an aspirin and a glass of water. Returning to the bedroom, she removed what was left of her clothing. Reaching into the closet, she removed a long white silk robe and slipped it over her naked body.

Then she opened what looked like an ordinary wall panel. It revealed a small room, which she had added on to the original house. Oriental in décor, and completely soundproof, it was designed especially for meditation. She bowed deeply as she entered and stepped into another world. Crossing the tatami-covered floor, she lit the candle set on an ancient Chinese brass candle stand. The musky scent of incense, the tinkling sound of wind chimes set in motion by the breeze from the open door lent the room a mystical aura.

Alanna returned to the door. A switch outside it allowed her to turn out all the lights in the house. The room fell dark, the house fell silent, except for the candle and the chimes, which became muted as she closed the door and the breeze ceased blowing.

Taking a seat in the middle of the room facing the candle, she folded her legs in the classic meditation position. Focusing on the flame, she drifted into an altered state.

She pictured herself back in Jake's Washington apartment, nervously awaiting her first face-to-face meeting with Dar after the Newmarket incident.

It had been almost two months since she'd last seen Dar, and there had only been one other phone conversation between them since the one in the Bedford Lodge. It had been the one, two days ago, during which she had agreed to this meeting.

"Sit down, Alanna." Jake had advised her. "You're going to wear a hole in the floor."

"I can't do it, Jake," she said, as she made for the closet to get her coat and leave.

He followed after her, blocking her access to the closet. Taking hold of both her shoulders, he said, sternly, "Sure you can! I thought you wanted to work with me?"

"I do want to work with you," she replied, shrugging off his hands and walking back into living room, where she took up a position looking out of a window that gave her a magnificent view of the Potomac. "But... but, suddenly all that rationalizing and justifying you and I did about Dar's part in this mess. How it's just the nature of someone doing his kind of work to use what they feel they have to to get a critical job done. That in my case he didn't mean to put me in the predicament I found myself, that he just got desperate, and didn't think the matter through good enough. Well, I can't accept that. All I feel right now is a sudden urge to completely obliterate him... from my memory and this planet."

"Now, don't go losin' your cool, girl." Jake had followed her back into the room, but did not approach her. Instead, he took his pipe from off its stand on the coffee table, lit it and settled into the overstuffed sofa. "Come over here and sit by me."

"You're not going to sweet talk me out of this, Jake."

87

Slipping into his Irish brogue, he said, "Would I do a thing like that to the likes o' ya, lass."

"You'd try and con the devil himself, so why not little ol' me?"

"Because, you're my family, and I don't con family." Jake said, with sincerity and warmth in his voice. "Give him a fair chance to absolve himself. Then, if you still feel the way you do, I won't try to influence you any further. I'd like you to work with me, but your happiness comes first. Since, your relationship with him is the determining factor where both of those things are concerned, I have to let you make the final decision."

Before she could reply, there was a knock at the door.

As he rose to answer it, Jake cautioned. "Remember what I said. You have the upper hand here, so keep your cool."

When, finally, Dar was standing in front of her, pleading with her to forgive him, saying he was sorry for having used her love and naiveté selfishly, for his own ends and for taking away her innocence and betraying her, all her plans to hate him had evaporated. She had planned to hate him, tried to hate him, but in the end, improbable as it seemed at that moment, she had forgiven him.

She had been taught all her life, first by her religious grandmother, and then by the martial art she practiced, that forgiveness was the way to happiness. She had never regretted her decision to forgive Dar, for, had she not, the hate would have eaten at her soul, whereas the love they once again shared had nurtured it.

And now, here was Jeremy, back, smiling that reckless smile of his. Doing what he'd done best all these years. Always just a step behind her, keeping her safe, a shoulder to cry on, a friend to laugh with, to share impossible dreams with --- no pressure, no demands, just there for her. Could she be less forgiving of him? Was there really anything to forgive? She could see now that the answer to both her questions was a resounding, no. The only question now was would he forgive her.

As she brought herself back to a conscious state, she intoned, "Free me from negative thoughts, from hostility, from indecisiveness, let me know and follow the Way!"

Chapter 10

"What did you find out about our friend, Mr. Jergens?" Francois asked, as he entered his hotel suite.

"I'm afraid nothing out of the ordinary, or of great interest, monsieur," Phillip, his secretary, replied. "Mr. Jergens' dossier is on the table in your bed chamber.

"You have a visitor," he added, indicating the man seated at the far end of the living room.

Francois looked in the direction of his guest, then turned to Phillip, and said, "Thank you, Phillip, that will be all for tonight,"

"What time will you be having breakfast, monsieur?"

"Eight o'clock will be fine."

"Tres bien, monsieur," Phillip said, making his way to the door. "Bonne Nuit."

As Phillip bid him good night, Francois made his way into living room and to the short, dark completed, raven eyed man who had been amusing himself by paging through a magazine as he sat waiting on the couch.

As Francois approached him, the Hizballah courier rose, bowed deeply, and greeted him with the required identifying statement. "The night is filled with many stars."

"May Allah fill you life with twice as many blessings." Francois acknowledged the Arab's code with the return code.

Francois removed a leather bound book from a briefcase on a table in front of him. Handing it to the Arab, he said, "The arrangements have been made. Deliver this to my friend, I am sure he will find it interesting reading."

The courier bowed deeply again, as he accepted the book and put it into his briefcase. "I will do as you bid," he said.

Francois escorted him to the door, and said in farewell, "May Allah be with you."

"And with you," the Arab replied as he again bowed deeply, turned and disappeared down the hotel hallway.

This is going to be a very profitable deal, Francois thought, as he smiled back in satisfaction at the reflection of himself in the suite's entryway mirror. All he had to do was keep the Russians and the CIA from getting their hands on the nuke.

It made him irritated, and stung at his pride, that the CIA had infiltrated his operation. A lead provided by an old source within the

Agency blew the infiltrator's cover, permitting him to be dealt with in time. However, Kamal's disposing of the man may not have been in their best interests.

Francois thought it would have been less risky to outsmart him, limiting his access to information, rather than killing him. Intelligence agencies took it personally when you eliminated one of their own. Doing so usually confirmed what they might have already suspected, causing them to intensify their efforts.

But, since a course of action had already been exercised, Francois hoped that Kamal's people had rid them of the infiltrator before he'd had time to do any real damage. One thing Francois knew for sure was that the meddling Americans would be back. This time, he'd be ready for them.

Francois sat down on the bed and picked up the folder marked MARCUS ALLAN JERGENS.

"What is it about you, Mr. Jergens, that troubles me so?" Francois asked out loud. Nothing of interest in this dossier, Phillip had said. Maybe that's the answer. Maybe you are too perfect. Let's have a look and see.

Phillip was right, at least on the surface, Francois thought after reviewing the information. The only thing interesting about you in this file Jergens is your millions. It's what's not in this file that concerns me.

"Roberto." He paged his bodyguard on his two-way radio.

There was a knock at the bedroom door, and then a husky, slightly balding, young man entered the room.

"Roberto, I want a tag put on Mark Jergens, and have someone see to bugging his room, as well," he said to the man, who nodded casually and exited as silently as he had entered.

We'll just let you fill in the blanks Jergens, Francois thought.

Nowhere in Jergens' dossier was there any mention of a background in horses, or a horse related industry. Yet, Jergens seemed to know what bloodlines to pursue. Francois realized that the explanation for that could be as simple as Jergens having an advisor.

Also, it would be helpful to know how serious Jergens was about Alanna's Sun Star colt, and how much he was willing to spend to get him. Perhaps, paid the right sum, he could convince one of Jergens' associates to enlighten him.

The memory of his evening with Alanna intruded into his thoughts. He was politically powerful, wealthy, and for his 50 odd years, an attractive man. Sophisticated, charming and lavish with his money, he had his choice of the most attractive women in the world. Yet, he was a lonely man. His family had long since died, and not having married, he had no children. Well, at least no legitimate children he knew of.

There was this large gap in his otherwise perfect world, and it had been drawn to his attention, more and more lately, that he wasn't getting any younger.

Francois had found Alanna to be intelligent, amusing, gentle and sensitive. She had an innocent quality about her that was sensual. As he had gazed into her incredibly blue eyes, he'd had the sensation that their vivid color, like that of the sea, was due to their depth, and like the sea, that depth would forever hide her secrets beyond the reach of mere mortals. Once again, he fantasized how she might fill that gap in his life, and found the fantasy very pleasing.

It was important for him to be successful in his bidding on the Sun Star colt, not only because it would please his clients, but it also gave him another link to Alanna. He'd been given a limit for which he could bid on the colt, but he did not intend to be outbid!

Francois' interest in Jergens was also two-fold. First, he instinctively sensed that the man was dangerous. How it affected him, he did not know, as yet. Secondly, Francois perceived that Jergens' interest in the Sun Star colt, like his own, might just extend to the colt's owner as well, and that bothered him most of all.

* * *

Jeremy pulled his car into the Marriott Griffin Gate Hotel's parking lot. En route to the hotel, he had stopped at a nearby hospital emergency room where a thorough examination had revealed that nothing had been broken in the melee. He had explained away his injuries by telling the doctor he'd been involved in an overly ambitious karate sparring session. The examination revealed some serious bruising for which the doctor in charge had prescribed some muscle relaxants and painkillers, a good soaking in a hot tub, and cautioned him to lay off the karate for a few days, at least. The last bit of advice, Jeremy intended to take seriously.

As he walked from the lot to the hotel lobby entrance, he'd reflected on how he hadn't been the only one whose emotions had been swayed tonight. Alanna had beaten him good, but he'd been right in his belief that she could not kill him. She had pulled every move short of its naturally powerful conclusion. She'd never meant to kill him, because despite the size differential, she could have and would have done it with the first strike. That was her style.

This realization did not lessen the physical discomfort that seemed to grow by the minute. If some good had resulted from this excruciating encounter, it might have been worth the discomfort, but, unfortunately, working off her emotional pain by inflicting physical pain on him, hadn't seemed to improve their relationship any.

Hell, he thought, what I'd really like right now is to forget this crap, have a double, maybe even a triple Jack Daniels, a soak in a hot tub accompanied by a few Musi Mays to work out the kinks in this body, and immediate reassignment as chief of station in Honolulu.

As he walked through the lobby to the elevators, Jeremy noticed his pilot seated at the bar. Rice motioned him over.

Jeremy eased his sore body onto the bar stool next to Rice, and said, "Had an interesting evening?"

"Not until 20 minutes ago," Rice replied, taking a sip of his ginger ale. "Your friend, the Comte, had a visitor. I guess Mr. Shabban figured with all the Arabs in town for the horse sale, no one would think his boy, Fadil, would look out of place. I figure the briefcase he was carrying probably has something in it we'd be interested in."

The bartender came over to the men to take Jeremy's order, and Rice changed the conversation to the baseball game on the lounge TV. Jeremy ordered a double Jack Daniels, and, as the bartender went off to fill his order, Rice returned to the original subject.

"I was hoping you would get back here earlier," Rice continued, though his speech had slowed, and he seemed to be staring at Jeremy's face. "I had Tad follow Fadil just in case you decided we ought to pay him a visit."

They went back to the baseball conversation as the bartender placed the drink in front of Jeremy and said, "You want to run a tab?'

'No, I'll take care of it now. Just bring me the check," Jeremy said, and downed the drink in one swig. He added hoarsely through the searing sensation of the liquor, "Oh, but before you do, bring my friend and me another round."

The lights in the bar suddenly got brighter as the manager gave his customers a subtle hint the bar was about to close.

"Is there something wrong?" He squirmed under Rice's intense look.

"Yeah!' Rice said. "Now that I can see better, you look like hell! What happened?"

"Thanks for the compliment. You wouldn't believe me if I told you." Jeremy downed the second drink, paid the bill and rose to leave. "Signal

Tad and find out where Fadil is holed up. I think we need to have a look at what he's got."

"I'll get right on it and let you know," Rice said and added as he walked with Jeremy towards the elevators, "By the way, give your room a good sweeping. You had a visit from one of the maids. I have a feeling she wasn't there just to turn down your bed, and leave you a chocolate."

"I will," Jeremy said as he pressed the button to call the elevator. "See if you can come up with an anonymous set of wheels, and pick me up in 20 minutes by the pro shop just below The Mansion restaurant. I need to change into something a little better suited to the job."

"Sure you don't want to tell me about your evening?" Rice pursued the line of questioning, a devilish grin spread across his face. "Whoever she was, I'd say her tastes run beyond just plain kinky."

"Some other time. Hey, maybe I could even introduce you to her!" Jeremy smirked back at him and the effort brought a shooting pain to where Alanna's nails had raked his face. "She might put a little excitement in your life."

"Thanks, but noooo thanks. I think this job's excitement enough for this old man." Rice laughed, and dropped the subject as they boarded the elevator.

* * *

Checking, then double-checking that he was not being followed, Rice exited the hotel through a side door, a gym bag in hand. The area around the hotel was filled with cars and vans.

In the back of the lot, and off to one side, was a black panel van with no markings, just what Rice had been looking for. He approached the door of the van, pulled out a small control box, pressed the button and, electronically, destroyed any burglar alarm mechanism the van might have been equipped with. Then, using a small set of tools he carried in his pocket, he set about requisitioning the vehicle for government duty.

* * *

The black van slowed, and its lights went out as it approached the pro shop. It halted as Jeremy stepped out from behind some bushes, opened the passenger door and got in.

"You do nice work, Rice," Jeremy said, honestly. 'What part of your flight manual covers auto theft?"

93

"The part where you've had to ditch in enemy territory, and are in need of transportation home," Rice replied.

"Where's Fadil?" Jeremy asked, as he checked to make sure there was a round in the chamber of his pistol.

"He's at the White Oak Motel on New Circle Road. It's not too far from here," Rice said, as he put the truck in gear and headed out the curved drive. "Tad said that Fadil went right to his room, and hasn't left or had any visitors.

"The motel is only a two-story job," Rice added. "Fadil is on the second floor, third door from the end in the east wing. The windows are all solid plate glass so you'll need a diversion to go in his front door. Not the best situation, but, hey man, a super snoop like you shouldn't have a bit of trouble. Right!"

"Confidence is everything, Rice. I wish I had yours," Jeremy retorted, as he adjusted his bulletproof vest.

They pulled in the motel drive and headed towards the back entrance. Tad was waiting to let them in, since all the perimeter doors could only be opened from the inside after 11 p.m.

"What have we got to work with?" Jeremy asked Tad as they came through the door.

"Not much," Tad replied. "This place is too small for any elaborate ventilation system we might use."

"Is there a supply closet on this floor," Jeremy inquired, as he made his way up the stairwell to the second floor. "How many of the rooms on this floor are occupied?"

"Three, his at this end and two at the other end," Tad said. He pointed to a metal door halfway down the hall. "The supply closet's the metal door on the right. I've already taken care of the lock."

"Great!" Jeremy said. "Here's what we're going to do."

He ran through the plan quickly, and back over it once more to make sure there was no confusion. There wouldn't be much time, and no margin for error if they were to pull this job off without Fadil knowing he'd been had.

Jeremy turned too quickly, and his bruised and battered ribs howled in protest. A grimace covered his face, and his breath caught in his throat. He paused for a moment, his body doubled over, his hand rubbing his sore rib cage.

"Hey! Are you all right?" Bill seeing the pain in Jeremy's face moved towards him.

Jeremy nodded in reply, and then said, "Yeah. I just need a minute."

Tad looked at Rice questioningly, and Rice just shrugged his shoulders and said, "He's into kinky ladies now. What can I tell ya!"

They smiled at each other, as Jeremy, painfully, straightened up and said. "If you two giggly girls have your orders straight, I suggest we get on with this job."

The two men nodded, and Tad headed for the rooms at the end of the second floor corridor, while Rice moved back down the stairs. Jeremy took up his position in the supply closet where he donned an oxygen mask, and readied his equipment.

At the bottom of the stairwell was a large coin operated soft drink machine. Taking out his tool kit, Rice worked the lock on the machine. The front of it opened revealing storage racks filled with soda cans and the change box, pulling that section forward, exposed the machinery. An expert at this kind of maneuver, Rice knew that his sabotage would not be detected, even on close inspection by the arson investigators. He had rigged it so that the eventual blame for the smoky diversion he was about to unleash would be placed on faulty wiring. Finished, he took up his position in one of the unoccupied first floor rooms.

A couple of minutes passed. In the stairwell, there was a barely audible whooshing sound, and smoke began to pour out of the crevices of the machine. It swirled around the machine for a minute then, started up the stairwell. Drawn by the draft the stairwell created, it began to fill the hallway of the second floor.

Seeing the smoke moving down the hall in his direction, Tad proceeded to knock on the doors of the two occupied rooms. Waking the occupants, he steered them in the direction of the fire exit, assuring them that the fire had been reported.

As soon as the hall was clear, Jeremy slipped the oxygen mask over his face. He moved quickly to Fadil's door, banging on it loudly, at the same time yelling, "Fire!"

Fadil, disoriented by the sudden rousing from a sound sleep, frightened by the sounds of impending disaster, and the acrid smell of smoke, panicked and opened the door without checking through the peephole. The last thing he was to remember was a puff of smoke hitting him full in the face. He coughed, gasped, and with a light shove from Jeremy, fell backwards onto the bedroom floor.

Switching on his flashlight, Jeremy systematically searched the room. The book he was looking for was hidden in the false lining of one of Fadil's suitcases. Being sure to notice its position, and any other detail that might reveal it had been disturbed, Jeremy set about photographing its contents,

Meanwhile, downstairs, Rice ran interference by assuring the management the upstairs guests had all been evacuated, and were waiting at the other end of the building. Once he felt certain no one would head up to the second floor, he blended back through the crowd of curious onlookers to the van.

Tad was already there, and they gave each other a thumb's up. Rice began wishing Jeremy would hurry up, as the sound of the approaching fire trucks was getting closer by the second.

"Damn, Jeremiah, hurry up!' He said out loud, as the fire trucks wheeled into the parking lot, and firemen began making their way into the smoke-filled entrance of the motel.

Rice's head spun sideways and he whipped his gun out of his holster as the side door, away from the view of the crowd, opened and a rather pungent-smelling Jeremy eased himself down onto the van floor.

"Move out of here," he said. "We're in business!"

Chapter 11

It was almost 7 a.m., and Alanna was in a hurry to reach Keeneland before the morning sales session began. As she passed her office on the way to her car, she heard a noise. Stepping inside, she saw Angela on her hands and knees amongst the rubble, busily gathering up the scattered papers. Angela rose from her task as Alanna entered.

"You had a burglar last night, Miss Reynolds?" She said, indicating the disarray.

"Yes, I did, Angela," Alanna replied. "It's okay, they didn't get anything."

"Did you call police?" The housekeeper expressed her concerned.

"No, Hannibal and I took care of them. Since they didn't get anything, I'd rather not bother with the police," Alanna said, as, for the first time, she realized the tremendous destruction she and Jeremy had caused to the room.

"I have to get to the sales grounds, so just stack the papers, and, when I have time, I'll sort them out. Sorry for the mess," Alanna said, apologetically. "Bye, I've got to run."

Not waiting for a response, she exited the room and the house.

* * *

"Good evening, sir," the sales company valet said as he hurried to open the door of the BMW that had pulled up to the front of the sales pavilion. As Jeremy took the valet stub, he made mention that he needed the car parked close at hand, then he thanked the valet, and headed in the front entrance. The sale was already in progress. The lighted board showing that catalogue No. 85 was now in the auction ring. He noted that Alanna's Sun Star colt was catalogue No.115, so there would be at least an hour before the colt would be in the ring.

Jeremy was on his own this evening. He'd sent Rice to Langley with the film he'd taken last night in Fadil's room, and had Tad busy keeping an eye on Fadil. He hoped the boys back in ciphers got the information decoded quickly. Time was of the essence.

Jeremy was relieved to read in the morning's Lexington Herald-Leader that a fire, which had occurred late last night at the White Oak Motel, had resulted in only minor damage to the motel and only one injury. An Arab businessman, the article had stated, had suffered a minor case of smoke inhalation. The gentleman, whose name had been

97

withheld at his request, had been treated at St. Joseph's Hospital and released. Fire inspectors had determined that faulty wiring in a vending machine had started the fire.

Rice was good at what he did, Jeremy thought, really good!

Jeremy followed the hallway that lined the seating area of the pavilion, He went down the steps beyond the bar area, and through the door that led to the indoor walking ring. Once there, he strolled leisurely around the ring, admiring the three beautifully turned-out, young horses that paraded within it. Each horse behaved differently. The bay colt was cool and collected, walking sedately next to his handler. The gray filly, following the colt, pranced nervously, occasionally kicking out with a hind leg at nothing in particular. The chestnut colt behind her was on the verge of launching himself. Between airy, sprightful steps, he would rear up on his hind legs and paw the air. Each displayed, in its own way, the fine breeding, beauty, grace and fire that is the Thoroughbred racehorse.

As the horses moved by him, Jeremy's mind wandered. This mission was like a time bomb waiting to go off. He wondered if Alanna and he would survive the explosion.

Jeremy smelled the perfume first. It was the same one Alanna had worn last night. She came and stood alongside him. As the people either side of them left to tend to their business, leaving them alone, she turned to him. Their eyes met, and before he asked the question, he knew the answer.

"I'm sorry about last night," she said, apologetically. "I had no right to take my anger out on you."

"Apology accepted," he replied. Then he asked the obvious. "What have you decided to do?"

"You can tell Granton I'm in," she said, without hesitation. "A good place for him to brief me would be at my bay house in Miami. I'll be there on Thursday. I'll be waiting for him on my dock at 10 p.m. He asked in his letter if I would like to make arrangements for Jake's burial. I made them this morning, so please tell him I'd like Jake's body sent here to St. John's Catholic Church on Thursday morning."

Then, in a barely-audible voice, she added coldly, "I want that Arab bastard!"

"We both want him, Alanna, and we'll have him, I promise you that," Jeremy said, relieved that at sometime during the night she was able to make peace with his part in the Balkan incident. Still, he had mixed emotions at her decision to rejoin the Agency. "As for you coming back in to the Agency, I wish you'd reconsider your decision."

"You saw the contents of that envelope. There never was a choice for me to make." Her voice had a distinct sadness to it. "Granton knew that from the beginning."

And, with that, she turned and walked away.

* * *

"What did you find out from Fadil?" Francois inquired of his secretary as his limo made its way to the sales grounds. The morning had been off to a bad start with the news of the fire at Fadil's motel. Even though he had no proof, his gut feeling was that the fire was a set up, and Fadil's security had been breached. He wasn't sure by whom, since there now were many interested players in this game, but his instincts seldom proved wrong.

"Did he find anything missing or disturbed?"

"Non, monsieur," Phillip replied. "He found everything as he had left it. Nothing had been removed from the room, and the strand of hair he had put between the pages of the book was as he had placed it.

"He believes," Phillip continued, "that he was overcome by smoke when he tried to return for the briefcase."

"And what of Mr. Jergens?" Francois inquired.

"He returned to his room an hour before the fire and did not leave the hotel until a half hour ago," Phillip said. "He made only one stop before coming to the sale, and that was for dinner in the hotel dining room."

"And the men with him?" Francois continued the questioning.

"The red-haired fellow was in the bar until Jergens returned," Phillip informed him, "then they both retired to their rooms. As far as we know, the co-pilot went to his room directly after dinner and did not leave.

"The pilot and co-pilot left the hotel early this morning and flew out of town." Phillip added. "The flight plan the pilot filed indicated that he was headed for his home field in Arizona. It will be a couple of hours before we can check to see if he arrived at his destination."

"I have a bad feeling about Jergens, Phillip," Francois confided. "So far I have nothing concrete to substantiate those feelings. Keep a good eye on him, if he's for real, we'll know soon enough. I don't think he's smart or clever enough to keep up this facade forever. If he is, then Phillip, he'll prove a formidable adversary."

The limo pulled up in front of the pavilion. Francois picked up his leather-bound sales catalogue, and he and Phillip exited the car and headed into the pavilion.

"Have you checked Jergens' line of credit with the sales company?" Francois inquired as he went in the door.

"Oui, monsieur," Phillip replied, following close behind. "My sources tell me that he has credit in excess of 10 million dollars."

"Mr. Jergens may not be a problem, as yet." Francois considered the information he'd just received. "But, he certainly has the potential to be."

As Francois entered the hall surrounding the main sale area, he checked the lighted board, and found the colt into the ring to be No. 90. It would be a half hour before Alanna's colt came in the ring. But, since he had also planned to bid on No. 96, he entered the main area of the pavilion, and proceeded to the seats reserved in his stud farm's name.

"May I join you," Alanna said.

Francois turned and smiled at the sight of her. She was dressed in a cream silk camp shirt and khaki gabardine trousers; the gold locket once more graced her neck. Her attire made her look business-like and elegant at the same time.

"Of course, of course," Francois said delighted. He rose and stepped into the aisle so that she could take the seat next to his, which Phillip had discreetly vacated.

"Merci, Phillip, vous etes gracieux," she said, by way of greeting to the man, who returned her greeting with a slight bow and a smile, and remained standing until she'd taken her seat. Then she turned back to Francois, gave him a warm smile and added, "Thank you for a wonderful evening, Francois."

"Ah, Alanna, you are such a treasure. Only you could brighten what has been a dismal day," he said, his eyes drawn to the locket.

Francois took the locket in his hand, snapped it open and said, "Such a beautiful locket. And the picture?"

"My mother and father," she replied, with a note of sadness in her voice, of the photo that had replaced Dar's. "They're both dead."

"Ah, that is so sad. You must miss them," he said, adding. "Have you anyone? Brothers? Sisters?"

"My parents have been dead for some time," she replied, her smile remaining, but the sadness plainly visible in her eyes. "My maternal grandparents raised me, but they're dead as well. Since, I have no other family, I miss them all a great deal."

"It's hard to believe a beautiful, young woman like yourself is so alone," he remarked, somewhat skeptically, "I am amazed that you are not overwhelmed by men vying for your affections?"

"My horses are my life, for now, Francois," Alanna said.

"I see,' he said. Then taking the hint, he changed the subject, "Well, if that is the case, you must be getting nervous, as I see your colt is due to sell soon. I, too, am beginning to feel the anticipation. Has Mr. Jergens been by to see him again?'

"No, he hasn't," she responded, letting a trace of disappointment lace her reply.

"I spoke with him for a moment at the walking ring, but he didn't mention the colt," she added, establishing her motives for talking to Jeremy should Francois' men, the ones she'd detected following Jeremy, report her contact with him. "I thought I was going to see a real bidding duel between the two of you. Now, it looks like he might have lost interest in the colt."

Alanna, playing to Francois' ego, said, "Or, perhaps the fact he knows you will be bidding on the colt scared him off."

"Jergens hardly struck me as a man who scares off easily," Francois grudgingly reassured her, and then added, "I suspect that maybe all he needed was one look at the colt, and the colt's owner, to make his decision. I think you'll have your duel. Better with dollars than with swords, wouldn't you agree, my Cherie?

"Definitely!" She said, moving forward in her seat in preparation to leave. "You must excuse me. They'll be calling the colt down to the walking ring shortly, and I want to be at the barn in time for a final inspection."

"Well, I will be right here to make sure no one steals him," Francois said, standing to allow her back into the aisle. "Good luck, though it is I who will need luck to buy him."

"Then, good luck to you," Alanna said. "May the most generous bidder win!" Giving him one of her most enchanting smiles, she left.

Francois thought about how Alanna was able to affect him like no other woman ever had, her presence causing him to forget everything else, certainly not a desirable reaction at a time when he needed his wits about him. He longed to possess her. That in itself, he realized, was an awesome undertaking. But he'd made up his mind. If he succeeded in nothing else on this trip to America, it would be that.

The filly he'd been waiting for entered the ring, and he put his thoughts of Alanna temporarily aside, and began to bid on the horse.

* * *

Jeremy moved toward the chute where the horses waited to make their entry into the ring. He positioned himself along the wall in full view of the bid spotters, who were seated on a raised platform just to the back of the auctioneers' stand.

He saw Alanna come through the pavilion door, and start to head toward the stable area. She stopped and turned in his direction and their eyes met. He knew it wasn't enough for her to just "be back in". For this mission to succeed, nothing could stand between them.

It was just a look she gave him, and yet, it said everything. It said everything was all right.

Alanna and Jeremy's nonverbal communication was interrupted by her fellow horsemen, who suspecting that her colt might be a big seller, perhaps even the sales topper, began gathering around her to offer encouragement and wishes of good luck.

Held up by the well-wishers, Alanna had been unable to give the colt a last inspection before he made his appearance in the walking ring. The inspection proved unnecessary. As the colt entered the walking ring, the local TV station's cameramen began filming what could be their lead story. The horse that topped the Keeneland Summer Sale was always big news, even to those not interested in the horse business.

The colt responded to the attention like a true media star, turning his head from side to side, as if in acknowledgment of the adulation being accorded him. His blood bay coat glistened. His sleek muscles rippled with each powerful step he took. His large, intelligent brown eyes, set in his beautifully sculptured head, emphasized his class.

He took his turn in the holding area, and waited with calm dignity for the door to the sales ring to open.

Alanna was about to make her way to her seat in the sales pavilion, when she saw Francois, obviously alerted by his men to the fact that Jeremy intended to bid from out back, and his entourage come through the pavilion door and take up a position opposite Jeremy. Though she had wanted to see the colt in the ring, she decided the real show was going to be back here. Choosing a place to stand where she could observe both Jeremy and Francois, Alanna anxiously awaited the bidding to begin. She looked up at the television monitor above the bid spotters stand, saw the door to the ring slide open and the colt enter.

The announcer's voice cut through the murmuring of the crowd, the rapping of his gavel bringing them to attention.

"Entering the ring now," he began, "we have hip No. 115, property of Wicklow Stud. This is a bay colt foaled February. 6, by SUN STAR, two-time Horse of the Year. Leading sire five times. Sire of more than 100 stakes winners and 20 champions, including STAR STRUCK, champion 3-year-old colt and NORTHERN LIGHTS, champion older mare in France.

"Out of OCEAN BREEZE, champion 3-year-old filly, winner of the Filly Triple Crown. Ten wins in 15 starts, earnings of $1,004,534. Half-sister to TIDAL WAVE, champion 2-year-old colt, 8 wins at 2 and 3, $1,450,375, and from the family of CLEAR SAILING, TREASURE ISLE and many more.

"Ladies and gentlemen, this is the last colt to be sold at public auction by the now deceased, renowned sire SUN STAR. This is the colt you've all been waiting for!"

The auctioneer took over. "Thank you. All right, who'll give me $250,000 to start him? Thank you, I have $200,000 to start."

Francois had opened the bidding with what he hoped was a sufficient amount to warn off Jeremy.

The auctioneer continued, "Two hundred, do I hear three? I have three hundred thousand from Rob. Thank you, sir!"

Jeremy had been equally quick to counter Francois' bid, serving notice that he intended to hang tough.

The auctioning of the colt continued with sporadic bids from other individuals, but the bulk of the bidding was between Jeremy and Francois. The bidding was quickly nearing the previous year's record of three million dollars, and showed no sign of slowing.

Eye to eye, Jeremy and Francois faced off, each countering the other's bid with unwavering determination. The surrounding area buzzed with conversation from an audience, who had not seen prices to match these since the mid 1980s when the Arabs went on a binge, and spent this kind of money on a regular basis.

The last bid had been Francois', but he had just exhausted his budget, and, as yet, his adversary had not capitulated. Surely, Francois thought, Jergens would not continue beyond this. To his surprise, Jeremy's next bid came without hesitation.

"I have three million, two hundred and fifty thousand, do I hear three million, five?"

For the first time, there was a lull in the bidding, tipping off Jeremy that Francois may be close to backing off. Francois had to make a decision that would result in the balance of the cost of the colt coming out of his pocket. Francois nodded in the affirmative, and Jeremy breathed a sigh of relief as owning the colt never was his intention.

"I have three million, five, do I hear four million?" the auctioneer continued. "I have three million, five! Do I hear four million?"

This was it. Francois had to hope it would do.

"I have three million, five, do I hear four million?" the auctioneer's chant reverberated throughout the pavilion.

Jeremy dropped his eyes, indicating that he had reached his limit and would not bid further.

"I have three million, five, do I hear four million?" The auctioneer repeated. "I have three million, five, do I hear four million?"

There was not a sound in the place.

"Three million, five once, three million, five twice, sold out back for three million, five hundred thousand dollars!" The auctioneer concluded, as the gavel fell, knocking the colt down to Francois.

The crowd broke out in applause.

"Ladies and gentlemen!" The auctioneer cautioned. "Please hold your applause until the colt has left the ring. Thank you."

Jeremy had planned to make a quick exit after bidding on the colt. Just before the colt had come into the ring, he had gone out front, and requested the valet bring his car around to the front door and park it. He'd made the excuse that he had a plane to catch directly after bidding on a horse, and the valet said that he would see that Jeremy's car was there waiting for him. Jeremy knew that even as the under bidder on the colt, the press and probably Francois would be looking for him after the sale, each for their own reasons, neither one of which would be of benefit to Jeremy.

The milling of the crowd, excited by the sale, gave Jeremy a chance to head for the front entrance. However, as he started up the steps, he saw the press coming toward him, accompanied by their photographers. He turned to go the other way and saw Francois trying to force his way through the crowd, heading right at him.

Suddenly, he felt a hand take him by the elbow.

"Thank you for bidding on the colt, Mr. Jergens!' Alanna said, as she steered him through the crowd, along the walking ring and toward the back door. "We appreciate your support."

Alanna understood the financial workings of the Agency. She knew they had the wherewithal to spring for this kind of operational expenditure, but she knew Jeremy could not risk ending up with the colt, and the publicity the purchase would draw. Jeremy had timed his exit perfectly, and, in bidding, had provided her with a nice windfall.

Under her breathe, she said, "My sales manager, Julie, is waiting to get you out of here." Alanna motioned in the direction of the dark-haired girl waiting just outside the back door.

Jeremy shook her hand, appeared to say something in response to her congratulations, and then hurried out the back entrance. Julie followed him at a discreet distance through the curious crowd, and into the darkness beyond the ring, where her car was waiting.

The press and Francois hurried around to where Alanna and Jeremy had been standing. By the time they reached Alanna, Jeremy was gone.

Chapter 12

"This way, Mr. Jergens." Julie called to Jeremy, when they were a safe distance away from the pavilion. They slipped into the shadows, and she led him to a beat up old Ford Pinto parked in the darkness along the stable area road.

"Sorry, about the car. It belongs to one of the grooms. Miss Reynolds said to find something that wouldn't call attention to us," Julie said, as she opened the squeaky driver-side door.

"Good choice!" Jeremy concurred, somewhat tongue-in-cheek.

She got in, reached across the seat, and opened Jeremy's door.

"Sorry you didn't get the colt, Mr. Jergens. He's a good one," Julie said.

"Well, first off, Julie, thanks for rescuing me from the gentlemen of the press. As for the colt, I'm sorry I missed him, too," Jeremy said, feigning regret. "But, I'm a gambler by profession, and one thing a smart gambler understands is that you have to set a limit and stick to it. I'm just a novice at this horse racing stuff. I'd hate to get started off on the wrong hoof."

They both broke into laughter at Jeremy's pun, and then she cranked up the old car, and headed in the direction of Wicklow Stud.

* * *

Alanna heard voices and laughter coming from the sun porch as she let herself in the kitchen door. She followed the sounds, and, as she entered the porch, she found Julie busily entertaining Jeremy with some of her and Alanna's old horse "war" stories.

Seated comfortably in a high-backed, white, wicker chair, drink in hand, Hannibal ensconced happily at his feet, Redford curled up in his lap, Jeremy was obviously enjoying the entertainment.

Both turned their attention to Alanna as she entered the room.

"Mind if I join the party?" she said, as she made her way to the bar and poured herself a tall glass of sugar-free tonic water, and squeezed a lime into it.

"This is the most exciting sale I've ever been at!" Julie said, still unable to get over the last hour's excitement. "I can't believe the Sun Star colt brought three and a half million. Wow!"

"Yes, it's pretty hard to believe," Alanna replied, eyeing Jeremy with some skepticism. "Thanks to you, Mr. Jergens, Wicklow Stud is the center of world attention."

"Isn't that great!" Julie interjected.

"Yes, I guess it is," Alanna replied, trying to show some enthusiasm.

"I'm sorry I missed your colt. As I explained to Julie, I had to set a limit. It's the way I do business. Maybe I could convince you to take me on as a client, and find me a nice colt I can afford," Jeremy added. "With a little luck and your help, I still might be able to get a nice horse."

"It's a possibility," Alanna replied.

Julie, taking her cues from the conversation, said, "I know you two have business to discuss, so I best be on my way. It was nice meeting you, Mr. Jergens."

"You were a real help this evening, I won't forget it," Jeremy said, setting the cat gently on the floor and rising to say his farewell.

"Yes, thanks, Julie. You handled everything just right." Alanna added her gratitude. From her pants' pocket, she removed two slips of paper and handed them to Julie. "Oh, by the way, Julie, Francois gave me the release forms for the horses he bought. Please make arrangements for them to ship here tomorrow. They'll be staying with us until he can arrange for them to ship to France."

As Julie took the forms, and made ready to leave, Jeremy pulled out his wallet and removed two $100 bills. Handing them to her, he said, "Julie, here's a little something for your effort tonight."

"This isn't necessary, Mr. Jergens," Julie said, trying to resist the offering.

"It's more than necessary, Julie. Thanks again," Jeremy insisted.

"Thank you!" She said, squeezing the money in her fist in a gesture of delight. "See you in the morning, Miss Reynolds. Good night."

She took her leave, and Alanna took a deep breath.

"How's your drink?" she asked Jeremy, as she moved behind the bar and he handed his glass to her for a refill. As she reached for the bottle of Jack Daniels, which she knew to be his brand of choice, he took a seat on one of the cane-backed mahogany bar stools across from her.

She mixed his drink, handed him back his glass, refilled hers, and then came around, and sat on the bar stool next to him.

"What a difference a day makes," Jeremy sang the first verse to the song, "twenty-four little hours.."

"God, how can you be so corny at a moment like this," Alanna said, leaning back in the chair and shaking her head.

"Hey! I read somewhere that a wise man once said, 'It's a good thing we can laugh. Otherwise we'd all go crazy'. You need to laugh more, Alanna. Yesterday, I almost bit the big one just down the hall, remember?" Jeremy pointed out. "Today, I'm here sipping drinks with my almost executioner like it never happened. Like I said..." and again he sang, "What a difference a day makes."

"You know, Jeremy, you have a nice voice," Alanna said. Getting up from the stool, she added, "Let's go outside, it's getting stuffy in here."

There was a nice breeze, and it carried with it the floral scents of a southern summer night. Alanna made herself comfortable on one of the lounge chairs, kicking off her shoes, removing her earrings, and closing her eyes.

Jeremy sat on a stonewall that formed the patio's outer boundary, trying to make out, in the semi-darkness, the figures in the field. For a minute neither of them said anything.

"Broodmares and foals," Alanna said.

"What?" Jeremy stirred by Alanna's comment, returned to the present from his mental distraction.

"That field is one of the fields where we keep the broodmares and foals," Alanna reiterated.

"Mmmm." Was Jeremy's only reply, and he seemed to lapse back into his thoughts.

"Are you thinking something I should know?" Alanna asked, unable to figure out why Jeremy, atypically, was so withdrawn.

"Well, for starters, I'm a little confused. You used to be a nice girl," Jeremy began. "Oh, sure, you ran around with the likes of Dar and Granton and Jake and me, but that didn't make you a bad person. But, this Francois thing..."

When he turned and looked at her, Alanna couldn't tell if Jeremy was serious or kidding, as he was inclined to be kidding where she was concerned.

"Is it that you don't know that the sleazy bastard would sell anything, including his mother, for a price," Jeremy said, in all seriousness. "Or, that you've changed so much that you don't care?"

She didn't reply, just looked at Jeremy with an even look.

"Well?" Jeremy pushed for the answer he was so curious to know.

"If my fraternizing with 'sleazy' elements of society bothers you so much, Jeremy, just consider that Francois is no different than that murderous Russian we had to cozy up to get those missile plans, or that Lao opium dealer we used to get to that POW, or that Asian skunk we had to deal with to get arms to those Afghani freedom fighters," Alanna remarked.

"The horse business, wonderful as it is, and as much as I love it, is really not much different than the intelligence game. The stakes are different, horses not state secrets, but the modus operandi is somewhat the same. There are nice people in this business, and there are the sleazy ones. The Agency was a great training ground for this business. I learned how to deal with the dirt without letting it rub off on me. But, if you must know the real reason for my association with Francois --- it was Jake. I thought he might need an in to the man some day. I never dreamed I would be the one needing it."

"Francois is a dangerous man, Alanna."

"I can handle Francois," Alanna said, confidently. "And if I find out that he's the one responsible for Jake's death, he'll see just how dangerous I can be."

"What took you so long getting back here?" Jeremy asked, shifting gears. "Julie was about to run out of war stories. I really liked the one about how that Barerra filly made you miss out on the Irish Breeders' dinner by whopping you on the nose, and making both your eyes match the color of your burgundy gown. And I thought intelligence work was dangerous!"

"You made Francois very happy by bowing out, though I suspect he'd wished you'd done it earlier," Alanna replied. "He insisted we celebrate his purchase with dinner, but I said I was too tired and that he'd have to settle for a drink there at Keeneland."

"So, what's the deal?" Jeremy inquired.

"Well," she said, with a Machiavellian smile, "the sale of that colt to Francois will more than keep the banker wolf away from my door, and, with a little careful planning, it should put the intelligence wolves in bed with Francois. Not literally, of course."

Both their hearts skipped a beat simultaneously as the door chimes rang.

"Can't be anyone I know," Jeremy said, as they exchanged bewildered looks.

Starting for the front door, Alanna said, "If it's Francois, the French doors at the end of the patio lead into the breakfast room. The pantry door is the first one on the left as you come into the kitchen. The far wall of the pantry is a false door that leads to the bedrooms upstairs. I guess you can figure out what to do from there."

"Which one's yours?" Jeremy said, jokingly.

"Drop dead!" She replied, and headed for the door.

Relieved, but surprised, she saw the figure of Bill Rice in the security monitor hidden behind a decorative molding above the door.

"Well, hello, Mr. Riker," Alanna greeted Rice, using his alias. "This is a surprise. Is there something I can do for you?"

"I certainly hope so, ma'am," Rice replied, somewhat shyly. "I went to the sales grounds to get Mr. Jergens and, wouldn't ya know, everyone was already gone. I remembered him sayin' he planned to bid on your horse, so I found your barn. I was lucky that girl Julie had come back to check the horses for the night. She said she thought he might be here. You haven't seen him, have you?"

"Well, Mr. Riker..."

"Bob's fine, ma'am," Rice said, respectfully.

"Bob, why don't you come out to the porch and have something cool to drink," Alanna said, as she stepped from the door, and gestured for him to enter. "I think your search is over."

"Jesus, Rice," Jeremy said, in surprise as he entered the porch. "How'd you know I was here?"

"I came to pick you up, Mr. Jergens," he replied, somewhat confused that Jeremy would use his real name in front of the woman.

"I forgot Julie would go back to the sale grounds to check the horses for the night," Alanna said, to Jeremy, in explanation. "I neglected to tell her not to let anyone know where you were."

"A... Ma'am, I'd say she figured that out for herself," Rice said, confusion still in his voice as he rose to Julie's defense. "Because she did a whale of a job of interrogating me before she did tell me."

"Alanna," Jeremy said, to end Rice's dilemma. "I'd like you to meet our right-hand man, Bill Rice."

"Bill," Jeremy continued the introductions. "This is Alanna Reynolds, our new associate."

There was neither an immediate response from Rice at the announcement, nor a look of surprise on his face. When he did respond, it was only to confirm his earlier suspicions.

"Unforgettable blue eyes," Rice said, "The same unforgettable blue eyes I caught a glimpse of on a package I picked up on a lonely stretch of beach in a far off, unfriendly land."

Rice looked Alanna in the eye and awaited a denial. There was none.

Without further comment, Rice extended his hand and said, "Good to be working with you, ma'am."

"Thank you, Bill, I'm just as pleased to be working with you, but I'd really be pleased if, when we're not professionally involved, you'd call me Alanna, she said, accepting his hand and shaking it firmly.

"It'd be my pleasure, Alanna," Rice said, a smile spreading across his face.

"Why don't you get yourself something to drink, Bill," Alanna said, indicating the bar. "You'll have to excuse me, gentlemen, I have to give my farm manager a call and see how things went here today."

As she left the room, Rice, not knowing the extent of Jeremy and Alanna's previous relationship, commented, "She's an absolute knockout, and she's damn good at what she does. That was a hell of an operation I picked her up from. It'd put gray hairs on the best of 'em. And, she was solo!"

"You don't say!" was Jeremy's only reply.

Changing the subject to the more important business at hand, Jeremy asked. "How did it go at the head shed?"

"It went okay. I saw the old man," Rice said, "he said for you to call him."

"Instead of calling him, I think we'll just head back there tonight. Where did you leave the plane?" Jeremy asked.

"In Louisville. It's parked at Triangle Flying Service over at Bowman Field," Rice replied. "I figured Francois' men might look for it at Bluegrass Field, and they might even try Standiford Field in Louisville, but I doubted that they'd think to look at Bowman. It'll take us an hour and 20 minutes to get there. I had Tad drive your rental car back to the hotel from Keeneland. I figured you'd want to turn it in."

"Call him, tell him to check us out and dump the car without drawing a crowd, and that you'll pick him up in half an hour," Jeremy instructed. "I'll meet you at the plane. I'm sure I can get Alanna to drive me there."

"What's the hurry? Couldn't hurt you to stick around for the night? You can't see Taylor until in the morning anyway," Rice suggested. "We could leave at first light, and be there before he has his first cup of coffee.

"You could buy the lady dinner," he added. "If I were you, I'd find some nice romantic place to wine and dine this beauty. Maybe, she'd even put you up for the night." He punctuated his last comment with a wink.

"Well, you're not me, Rice," Jeremy replied, seemingly annoyed at the suggestion.

"Yes, sir!" Rice responded formally to Jeremy's terse reply.

"I'm sorry, Bill, my comment was uncalled for," Jeremy said apologetically, realizing Rice's suggestion was not meant disrespectfully. Had the woman not been Alanna, Jeremy might have come to that conclusion on his own. "Miss Reynolds has other interests. Some other time, maybe."

"It's okay. I was out of line," Rice said, now sensing it was more than 'other interests' that stood between these two. "I'd better get going. I'll catch a pay phone on the way in, just in case Francois' goons are tracing numbers. Say good night to Alanna for me."

"I'll do that," Jeremy said. "I'll call the plane when I'm on my way."

Alanna returned just as Rice was about to leave.

"Off already?" she said.

"Yes, ma'am," Rice replied, taking the outstretched hand that she offered him.

"Well, it was nice to meet you, Bill," Alanna said, and as she put her other hand on top of his in a warm gesture of friendship, she added, "I never got to thank you for the ride home, I just wanted you to know I appreciated it."

"Alanna, you're always welcome in my taxi," Rice replied, his neck and face reddening in embarrassment at the touch of her hand on his, and her expression of gratitude.

Regaining his composure, he said, "Well, I've got to run."

She started to show him out, but he stopped her saying, "It's all right, I can find my way out. See ya soon."

"Good night, Bill," Alanna said, as she watched him depart.

"Nice guy," she commented, as she turned her attention back to Jeremy, who had once again focused his attention on some point in the darkness beyond the patio.

She didn't intrude further on his solitude, but instead sat back down on the lounge chair and waited for him to speak.

The horses, which Jeremy had been unable to see earlier, had gathered as a group on the top of a rise in the field. They were now silhouetted against a star-filled background, and illuminated by an ever-brightening moon. A cricket's song filled the fragrant air that was borne on a light, warm breeze. It was as serene a moment as Jeremy had ever known.

"I never thought I'd see you again," he said, without turning to face her, melancholy edging his voice. "Do you have any idea how many times I woke up in a cold sweat, hearing Dar's screams, seeing the anguish in your eyes. I would have given anything for the ending to be the other way around."

When he turned, his face appeared drawn; his voice was heavy with sadness. "It won't work, Alanna."

She remained unresponsive.

Thinking she wasn't listening, he shouted, "Damn it! It won't work, there's just too much between us. It's suicide!"

When she still remained silent, he headed for the door.

"Jeremy! Stop!" Alanna ordered his retreating form, as she rose from the chair.

He stopped, but did not turn around.

"Look at me, Jeremy," she said, quietly.

He turned and slowly raised his eyes to meet hers.

"Jeremy, how many missions have you and I worked on?"

Jeremy did not reply. He had made up his mind and he wouldn't be coerced.

"How many? Answer me!" she demanded.

"Twenty, thirty, who keeps count?" He replied, reluctantly, shifting his weight from foot to foot, anxious to be away from this place.

"Enough," She concluded for him. "Enough to know that emotions never stopped us from doing a job before. It's hardly a reason to think they'd get in the way now."

"Things are different now," Jeremy said, "Obviously, not for you, but they are for me."

Tired of trying to reason with Jeremy, Alanna's temper began to flare, "I can't for the life of me understand why, all of a sudden, emotions are a factor in our working relationship.

"Of course," she said, deliberately drawing what she knew was an erroneous, but stinging, conclusion. "All this emotions stuff could just be a bluff. Maybe Dar wasn't the only thing we left behind that chain link. Maybe, we left your guts there as well. Word has it, that the only real action you've had since then wear skirts."

"You've got a lot of nerve questioning my courage, lady!" He denounced her accusation vehemently, adding caustically, "Who was it that turned in her Jane Bond kit just because her boyfriend bought it?"

"Touché. One good low blow deserves another," Alanna said, calming herself. "I am sorry, Jeremy. I didn't mean to call you a coward. No one knows better than I that you're not.

"Now that we've cleared the air," she said, calmly. "Let's get on with this discussion."

"The air is not cleared," Jeremy responded defiantly.

"Suit yourself," Alanna said, somewhat exasperated with Jeremy's stubbornness.

Then, she mellowed her voice and appealed to Jeremy's loyalty. "I'm taking this job with or without you, Jeremy, but this is serious business, and I really need your help. Together, we can pull this off. We have the skill, the experience, but most of all, we have the incentive. You know its true, Granton knows it, and God bless his duplicitous soul, Jake knew it. Let's do it, Jeremy! Together. Let's get those bastards, then maybe we can both have lives free of shadows and ghosts!"

Jeremy, trying to return to the subject matter he was really pursuing, said. "What about us?"

Alanna did not reply, and as the silence dragged on, he waited impatiently, hoping to hear the answer he wanted break the silence.

"There is no us, Jeremy," Alanna said, without malice in her voice. "When you let me go back to Dar without trying to dissuade me out of some kind of loyalty to him, you ended what might have ever been an us. Let's just leave the us out of this and do what needs to be done."

The resulting silence that fell between them was leaden.

"If that's the way you want it, lady, you've got it," Jeremy said, finally, as he slumped down into a seat at the wrought iron table.

"Maybe it isn't the way I want it, Jeremy," Alanna said, trying to ease the pain she knew they both felt. "Maybe, that's just the way it has to be."

Jeremy, frustrated, tired and feeling more than a little empty inside, changed the subject. "I need a ride to the plane."

"Where's it parked?"

"In Louisville, at a place called Triangle Flying Service over at Bowman Field. Do you know where that is?"

"Sure do. I just need to see to a few things here, and then we can leave. I'll be back in a minute," Alanna said, as she left the porch.

Jeremy felt a real tug-of-war developing inside him. Alanna had been only half right about emotions not affecting their previous missions. From an operational point of view the missions had never been compromised, but every time he was within touching distance of her, his heart bled.

Seeing Alanna again had stirred all the old feelings and regrets. Wow, he thought, it must be time to start thinking of hanging up your cloak and dagger when you seriously start dreaming about hearth and home, and that's exactly what being in this house had made him do.

"Okay. Let's go," Alanna called, from out in the hall.

Jeremy felt like he'd grown roots, and it was only with a terrible effort that he managed to get up from his chair and follow the sound of her voice.

"I think we'll go out the back way," she said, to him as he appeared in the hall. "This way."

She led him to the basement, and through a door that opened to an underground passage.

"This portion of the house was built on an old foundation," Alanna explained the unusual exit. "The former residence was an old southern mansion. It was part of the Underground Railroad that smuggled slaves to the north. When the man who built this house discovered it, he chose to let it be."

She hit a switch and the tunnel lit up. "He did modernize it a bit."

They followed the tunnel to its end, which was a root cellar surrounded by high bushes, and trees, and whose door exited facing away from the house. Alanna doused the lights and opened the door, letting in the fresh night air to replace the tunnel's mustiness.

"Come on," she said, and led him out of the sheltered area, and through the ankle deep, dew laden field grass.

"Where are we headed?"

"The barn over there," Alanna indicated a large black tobacco barn on the far side of a black, four-planked fence. "We park one of the farm trucks on the other side of it."

Alanna reached the four-foot fence, and, taking hold of the top rail, vaulted over it, landing without a sound on the other side.

"Showoff," Jeremy said, as he followed suit, not to be outdone.

"Bravo!" Alanna said, and added under her breath. "You always were good at jumping things."

"Very funny!" He growled. "I'd almost forgotten what a wise ass you can be."

"It's been so long since I've had you to abuse, I have to make up for lost time," Alanna said, as they reached the front of the barn. Just to the side of it was a dark green Dodge pickup. She took the keys out of her pocket, and unlocked the doors.

Jeremy climbed into the passenger side, and Alanna started up the truck. Without turning on its headlights, she headed it down one of the tree-lined lanes toward a thickly wooded area, where even what little moonlight there was could not penetrate. Jeremy looked uneasily in the direction they were heading.

"If you're worried that I can't see where I'm going, you're right. I thought I'd use the Braille method," she teased. "Actually, I know this path like the back of my hand. Just relax."

The vehicle edged its way slowly along the path, the occasional limb brushing its side, finally, when Jeremy thought his eyeballs would pop from trying to see in the dark, she came to a stop and said, "Here's the key. Open the gate."

"What gate?"

"The one three feet in front of this truck," she said, confidently.

Jeremy got out, felt his way along the truck until it ended, then struck out into the darkness. Several paces from the truck, he ran into the metal gate. He undid the lock, swung it open and after Alanna drove through it, relocked it. Stumbling back through the small fallen limbs, he got back in the truck.

"Do that often?" Jeremy asked, brushing only God knew what off his head and arms.

"No. First time for this route," Alanna replied, without bravado. "Jeremy, when are you going to learn to trust your instincts?"

"When I develop radar like a bat," he replied, sarcastically. "Which, obviously, you've already done."

The truck's wheels gripped asphalt as they reached a deserted county road. Alanna waited until she'd rounded a corner and then turned on its headlights. The road wound around for a couple of miles before joining the main road. It was only a short distance from there to I-64, the route to Louisville.

As the truck cruised along, Alanna said, "You know, this ride is going to cost you."

"Hey!" Jeremy reminded her. "I already added seven figures to your bankroll. The least you can do is give me a lift."

"Wasn't your money."

"So what's this luxury cruise going to set me back?"

"Dinner."

"Dinner?"

"Heck, yes! Dinner," Alanna said, as she reached behind the rear view mirror and pressed a button that activated an automatic debugging device. Feeling their conversation now secure, she added, "You know, that meal you were always trying to get me to join you for. The one, for which, when I relented, you always proved to be good company."

"Flattery will get you anything from me, dear lady, even dinner," Jeremy replied, buoyed for the first time that evening by their conversation. "Pick the spot!"

"If you're not in a big hurry to get back to Washington," she said, while turning on the radio and tuning it in to a soft rock station, "Le Relais would be my choice."

The thought struck Jeremy, as he was about to answer her, that from now on he'd make the time to be with her, but he replied, "How far out of the way is it?"

"It isn't out of the way. It's right at Bowman Field."

"Then I guess I have the time."

"Good, I'm sure you'll like it."

Changing the subject, he remarked, "You know for a civilian, you're very security conscious," alluding to the debugging device.

Looking over at Jeremy, she replied, "Jake used to love to come and stay at the farm with me when he wasn't off on assignment. It was just a precaution..." She left her comment hanging in mid-sentence and once again fixed her gaze on the road ahead. Her hands gripped the steering wheel tighter as she fought back the tears that threatened to dissolve her composure.

The gesture was not lost on Jeremy, who had been wondering, now that they were on friendly terms again, how long it would be before Alanna opened up to him on the subject of Jake's passing. He wanted to reach out to her, but afraid that she might reject any physical contact initiated by him, he resisted the impulse. Talk to me, Alanna, he begged her silently; as he caught sight of an errant tear, exposed by the headlights from an oncoming car, slide down her cheek. Now's the time, talk to me. I know you need to get this out of your system.

The silence was nerve racking. In an effort to ease the emotional tension, Jeremy undid his tie, unbuttoned the collar of his shirt, and, after assuming a more relaxed position in his seat, began humming to the music playing on the radio.

When nothing more than a stifled sniffle was forthcoming from her, he finally said, initiating his comment with a hearty laugh, "Hey, did I ever tell you about the time I took Jake hunting in the Rockies, and a bear chased us up a tree?"

When there was still no response save for another stifled sniffle, he added, "I guess I must have."

"You didn't, but Jake did," she replied, regaining her composure somewhat. "Since your association with him was no secret after our little

117

fiasco in Newmarket, he used that story to help break the ice between us when we were first getting to know one another. But, I heard it many times after that. It was one of his favorites."

"Yeah, but in his version he gets all the credit for saving our skin," Jeremy added, encouraging the conversation by elaborating on the tale. "The way he tells it, he just jumped down from that limb above me he was perched on, and scared the bear off."

"And, that wasn't how it happened?" Alanna inquired, the sadness beginning to fade from her voice.

"Hell, no!" Jeremy chuckled, as he pictured the predicament in his mind. "The truth of the matter was that we both thought that bear was either going to eat us for dinner, or keep us pinned there for a week. All of a sudden the limb Jake was on let go, and he went crashing through the branches to the ground, all the while hollering like the devil, himself, was waiting for him at the bottom. That damn bear got so confused and scared by all the racket, he just took off."

"That is definitely not the version I heard," she said, laughing and remembering how Jake was inclined to make a good story better. "But nothing you can tell me about him could make him less of a hero in my eyes."

"I wasn't trying to take anything away from him, Alanna," Jeremy replied, with sincerity. "There never was a more honorable man, or a truer friend than Jake."

"You know, Jeremy, there were many times when I thought about how different my life would be if the Agency had assigned someone other than Jake to get me back home after Newmarket. Especially since I elected to not to follow his initial advice and took off on my own instead."

"I never understood why you didn't just go home."

"Sheer stubbornness, I guess. When I woke up that morning in the Bedford Lodge, I was faced with a terrible dilemma. Until then, what had happened to us the previous night just seemed like a bad dream that would disappear with the dawn, but the only thing that was gone with the sunrise was my old life and you. All my dreams, my hopes for the future were shattered with the realization of the seriousness of what I had done in that pub. I'd killed five men. I knew it was self-defense, but justifying the act didn't ease my conscience any. I wanted to run, to hide --- honestly, for a few minutes --- to die. It was the first truly terrifying moment of my life…"

"Damn!" Jeremy said, interrupting her unintentionally, when he noticed the time on the truck's clock. "Sorry, to interrupt you, Alanna, but I forgot to call Rice, and tell him we're on our way. Does this thing have a phone? Can you believe, I left mine in my briefcase."

The truck was equipped with a farm radio, but no cellular phone. So, Alanna pulled off the highway at the next exit, and into the first gas station that had a pay phone. Jeremy got out and went to make his call.

Alanna was relieved to have Jeremy gone for a few minutes. Saying Jake's first words of comfort to her had caused a lump to form in her throat, and pent up tears to break free and begin their journey down her cheeks, putting her on the verge of totally breaking down. That was something she did not want to do in front of him.

As Jeremy carried on his conversation with Rice, Alanna pictured in her mind what transpired after her and Jake's initial meeting. How Jake had warned her of the danger she was in, and how it was imperative that she return home immediately. She, of course, had not paid one wit of attention to Jake's warning. With her friend Mark Quinn's help, she was able to sneak off to Ireland and hide out in a cottage in Arklow that Mark was house sitting for a friend. She'd given Dar, Jake and the Agency quite a scare, not knowing if she was safe or in enemy hands, but she had made her point, especially to Dar. She'd come home when and if she was ready and on her terms.

Alanna's thoughts returned to the present as Jeremy made his way from the phone back to the truck.

"Okay, we're all set," he said, as he opened the door and climbed back into the truck. "Rice and Clark have already had dinner, so it's just the two of us."

As they pulled back onto I-64, he tried to revive their conversation. "So, carry on. What happened next?"

"If you don't mind, Jeremy, I'd rather not talk about Jake any more tonight," she said, the sadness back in her voice. "It's going to take me a long time to get used to the fact that he's gone. We had such great times together, and I owe him so much, that the memories of him, even the good ones, are just too painful for me to talk about now."

"It's okay. I understand."

And their conversation faded as they each drifted off into their own private thoughts.

Alanna exited off I-64 onto the Watterson Expressway. From there, it was just a short drive to the Taylorsville exit and Bowman Field. The entrance to Le Relais was to the right of the historic terminal's main

119

entrance. Alanna parked the truck in the lot in front, and they went inside. Anthony, Le Relais' manager and host, welcomed them as they came through the door.

"How are you this evening, Miss Reynolds?"

"I'm fine, Anthony, I hope we're not too late for dinner?"

"No, not at all," he replied, as he motioned for them to follow. "Let me get you seated, and I'll send a waitress right over with the menus."

He started for a section of the dining room that was fairly well filled.

"If you don't mind, Anthony," Alanna said, stopping their forward motion. "Could we have something a little more private, like the table against the wall there?" She indicated one on the other side of the room.

"But, of course. Won't you come this way," he replied, turning his attention to Jeremy and giving him a knowing smile, then leading the way.

As they made their way to their table, Alanna noticed Nick, the restaurant's cashier, who was a dead ringer for TV's Lovejoy, wave to her. She excused herself for a minute and went to say hello.

Anthony waited for her to rejoin them, and then seated them.

"Your waitress will be here directly," he said. "Can I get you something to drink while you're waiting? We have an excellent selection of wines." And with that, he handed Jeremy a wine list.

"Miss Reynolds loves champagne," Jeremy said, not even bothering to look at the list or consult with Alanna. "So why don't you bring us a bottle."

"Any particular brand?" Anthony inquired as he started to point out those available.

"Just bring us the best one you have, and make sure it's nice and cold," Jeremy replied, thanking the man with a smile and a look that said 'that'll be all for now.' Then turning his attention to Alanna, added, "I hope that meets with your approval."

"It meets with my approval, but it might not meet with your expense account," she said, as she placed her napkin on her lap, and accepted a menu from the waitress.

Jeremy picked up his napkin and accepted his menu. After the waitress ran through the specials, and announced that she would be back to take their orders, he replied, "This dinner is not on Uncle Sam, Alanna. It's my treat to celebrate our reunion."

"Nice thought, thank you."

The champagne being served interrupted their conversation. When the server had left, Jeremy raised his glass in a toast. "It's too bad it took a tragedy to bring us back together, Alanna, but however it happened, I'm glad it did. Here's to the future and to us."

"To the future," Alanna said, raising her glass and touching it to Jeremy's, ignoring the second part of his toast.

Much to his dismay, Alanna kept their dinner conversation to either light talk, or, when no one was within earshot, their assignment, strictly keeping away from anything of a personal nature. In the end, Jeremy gave up trying. Just before the waitress brought their after dinner coffees, he excused himself and went to the men's room.

As Alanna watched him walk away, she thought, how that was just like Jeremy, optimist that he always was, to think that now, with all the human and logistic obstacles removed, they could just pick up where they'd left off that night in Newmarket. But, there was at least one little piece of baggage he'd forgotten about.

Though, their one-night-stand in the Bedford Lodge had been initiated by her, Jeremy's subsequent abrupt departure had wounded her pride, and deeply disappointed her. For a long time after the incident, Alanna had been angry with herself for having succumbed to the passion of the moment, and for becoming physically and emotionally involved with a perfect stranger.

Six months after the Newmarket incident, she and Jeremy were reunited professionally by the Agency. Not having any knowledge of what went on in that room in the Bedford Lodge, and encouraged by Jake to do so, the Agency had no reason not to team them up. In deference to the success of her and Jeremy's future professional relationship, and because, she, at Jake's urging and intercession, had renewed her personal relationship with Dar, she'd never brought up the subject of their brief encounter. She'd simply tried to put the experience behind her, as she assumed he had.

But now, she and Jeremy were the only ones left, and the questions of why he'd left, why after professing his love for her, he had never tried to find her, or explain his actions, once again nagged at her.

The waitress set the coffees down just as Jeremy returned. He thanked her and sat down.

"I have to compliment you on your choice of restaurants," he said, as he tore open a pack of sugar, and poured it into his coffee. "The food here is great."

"I'm glad you liked it." Alanna said, after which, she took a sip of her coffee, a silent, deep breath, and asked, "Jeremy, I was just curious."

"About what?"

"Did you ever know or care what happened to me after you left me that morning in Newmarket?"

Since, in all of the years they'd been together, the matter of their Newmarket affair had not surfaced before, Jeremy was caught off guard by her question. He took a sip of his coffee to give himself time to organize his thoughts, and then he raised his eyes to meet hers and said, "When I left that morning, my main concern was my assignment, which as assignments go, was off to a fairly bad start. I knew you were in good hands, that Jake would take good care of you, though I never imagined 'how' good that would be.

"What could go wrong went wrong on that assignment. Some mole in MI-6, who was working in the British embassy in Washington at the time, gave the operation away. That's why the KGB was on to our meeting. I got the job done, but when I got back, the Agency had me lay low for a while to see if my cover had been blown. It wasn't until I got back to headquarters that I had an opportunity to try and find out anything about what had happened to you. Much to my amazement, what I found out was that you had been recruited and we were to be working together. How's that for a shocker?"

"A shocker! Why so? Was it because you thought you'd never see me again, that you could write that night off as just another one night stand."

Jeremy looked away for a minute, as the underlying reason for the discreet distance that Alanna had maintained between them throughout their working relationship suddenly became clear.

When once again their eyes met, he said, "If that's what you've believed all these years, why ask me about it now?"

"It's not what I wanted to believe, it's what I thought," Alanna replied, her look never wavering from his, "and since, there's no one to hurt anymore if I bring up the subject, I want to know the truth, whatever it is."

"The truth!" Jeremy said, a hint of sarcasm in his voice. "I don't think you really want to know the truth."

"And, why is that?"

"Because, it's going to force you to rethink our relationship," he replied, "and after our conversation earlier this evening, I'd say you're not prepared to do that."

"My question still stands."

"Very well," Jeremy said. "Before we met, Alanna, I'd done a lot of things in my life I wasn't entirely proud of, but sleeping with a close friend's lady wasn't one of them. Even given our unusual circumstance, and the fact that I was completely captivated by you, what I did bothered the hell out of me. There I was trying to outwit every KGB sharpshooter from St. Petersburg to West Germany, and every time there was a break in the action, my mind would turn back to those moments we'd spent in each other's arms. I was so distracted that I'm sure that poor bastard I was sent to get out of Mother Russia never thought he'd make it."

He paused for a moment, sipped at his coffee, trying to calm his nervousness, and then went on with his explanation.

"God, this is hard. I have an aversion to confessing, as you know, so you can take some pride in knowing that you're the first person to ever get one out of me." He looked up at the ceiling and then, shaking his head in dismay, said, "The truth! The truth is I was sick inside over what had happened between us. But it wasn't caused by any remorse I'd felt over betraying a friendship, as it should have been, that was making me regret my making love to you. Oh no, that wasn't it at all. I was sick because I realized my love for you, Alanna, was as real as love gets, and I was afraid that in taking advantage of you in a moment of weakness, I'd lost all chance to have you, maybe forever.

"And, I was right. By the time I got back to headquarters, Jake had managed to patch things up between you and Dar. You seemed really happy. What could I do, I didn't fit into the picture anymore --- except professionally. Yes, I'd wondered how you'd fared after I left, and of course, I cared, but wondering and caring weren't enough by then, they weren't enough to do me, or us, any good. Earlier, you said there was no 'us', that that one night in Newmarket was it."

He laughed sadly, and added, "Well, there's your truth. Still think bringing up the subject didn't hurt anyone?"

Chapter 13

It was a good thing that the ride from Le Relais to the Triangle Flying Service was a short one, because from the time Jeremy had finished answering Alanna's question and paid the check, until she'd parked the truck in the lot behind the Triangle's hanger, they had not spoken, the mood of the evening becoming suddenly awkward.

As Alanna and Jeremy walked toward the waiting plane, Rice, who was waiting in its doorway, could see that things had deteriorated between them. Afraid that she would leave before he had a chance to give her the message and some equipment he'd received for her from Granton, he shouted above the sound of the plane's engines for her to wait.

"Alanna, hang on a minute. I have some things to give you," he said as he hurried down the steps.

He handed her the message, and, as she read it, Rice gave Jeremy a "What happened?" look.

Jeremy's answer was a just slight shrug of his shoulders, but his eyes said it was personal.

The note was from Granton, expressing his sympathy, welcoming her back to the fold, agreeing to meet her Thursday night for a briefing, and finally, assuring her Jake's body would arrive ready for burial on Thursday morning as requested. After reading it, she handed it to Jeremy for disposal.

Rice then handed her a leather case. She opened it, and took out what looked like a very small cellular phone.

"Let me have it for a minute, Alanna," Rice said, extending his hand to accept the instrument, "and I'll explain how it works."

She handed it to him. With a flip of his hand, he opened it. Pointing to the keypad, he explained, "Granton wanted you to have this so we could reach you at a moment's notice, anywhere. It works by satellite connection, but has a special scrambling device, so the signal is impossible to intercept. Don't worry if someone should happen to pick it up by accident or otherwise, because it also works as a regular cellular phone. If you want to contact us, all you have to do is press the star key twice, followed by the number key, and you'll be patched through immediately.

Handing it back to her, he asked, "Have any questions?"

"No, I understand, and thanks," she replied, putting it back in its case and then sliding it into her purse.

"Well," Rice said, to Jeremy. "If you're ready, we'd better get going."

"I'll be with you in a minute," Jeremy replied.

"Have a safe trip back," Alanna said, to Rice.

"You take care, ma'am," Rice said, and retreated to the interior of the plane to allow Alanna and Jeremy a moment of privacy.

"Sorry, I won't be able to make the funeral," Jeremy said, as Alanna turned her attention away from Rice and back to him. "I'll be in touch with you as soon as I know anything. Remember, if you need Granton, or me, use the telephone numbers I gave you, or your new toy."

She did not respond, so he said, "Well, I better go." And started to turn to leave.

"Jeremy," she called to him and he turned back to her. "I don't know if what you said tonight will make anything change between us, but I want you to know I appreciate your telling me it all the same. Let's just do this job, and then we can see where we're headed personally."

He held out his hand, and she put hers in his and smiled.

He squeezed it reassuringly, and returning the smile, said, "Hasta luego, querida."

* * *

Alanna watched the plane lift skyward from behind the wheel of the truck, then she drove out the gate to the main road and home. It was late and except for the occasional vehicle, I-64 was a very dark, lonely place.

The darkness melted into a vision of Hunter's, an old coaching inn on the river Vastry in Rathnew, the place Alanna and Jake went on their final evening together in Ireland. They sat at a table overlooking the river nursing their drinks. They had spent the last four days getting to know one another. Jake had watched her train, and been impressed by the level of her physical fighting skills. He has also been impressed by her seeming natural ability to outwit him initially, and stay hidden until she decided it was time to reveal her whereabouts. He had taught her how to shoot, something Dar had neglected to add to her arsenal of weapons, and to trust someone again. They had learned enough about each other in that time to know they would be lifelong friends --- family, but for the first time in days, they were having a hard time making conversation.

"Alanna, things are in order now with your case and I don't mean to offend you, but right now you are not a high priority to anyone except

Dar. I am about to be reassigned. That's why I wanted to spend this time with you.

"If you ever need anything," he said, his voice husky with emotion at their parting. "You'll always have a way to reach me, I'll see to that. In the past few days, you've become the closest thing to a daughter, to a family, I'll probably ever have.

"Christ," he paused, taking a deep breath. "I sound like a melancholy old fool. Forgive me."

"No you don't, Jake." She reached across the table and took his hand in hers. "And thanks to you, I have what I need now to face my life again, a friend."

"I have a feeling that this little episode has made a girl into a women -- a woman who knows what's best for her," he said, and she caught the glint of a tear in his eye. "Whatever you decide to do with your life, Alanna, I'm behind you a hundred percent."

"Tell me something, Jake. Why did you choose the intelligence business?"

"I'm afraid there's no simple answer to that question," Jake replied, reflecting on a lifetime of experiences. "I chose it for lots of reasons, some idealistic, some not. Basically, it's my way of helping to keep the stars and stripes aloft and you, my dear friend, out of harm's way. Good enough?"

"Good enough."

They ate dinner, then moved on to the pub where a band was playing a variety of Irish melodies. Over after-dinner drinks, Alanna finally brought up a matter that had been bothering her for some time.

"Jake, what ever happened to the agent I met that night?"

"What agent?"

"Don't be coy, Jake. He said his name was Jeremy Slade."

"Oh! Slade! Why are you so concerned about him?" Jake saw a hint of blush cross her cheeks.

"Oh, well, you know, you told me about all those dire things that could happen to him, and I, well, it bothered me."

"Never lose sleep over Slade, my girl, he has more lives than a back-alley tomcat," Jake said. Suddenly, remembering that Jeremy and Alanna had shared a room that night, he added. "Yes, ma'am, if there's a way out of a situation, you can count on him to find it.

"Word of advice, Alanna. I mean... You know... should Slade ever cross your path again. He's a rogue and a ladies' man. He only commits himself to one thing and that's his job."

"Are you sure about that?"

Catching the tone of her voice, he replied, "Maybe not where you're concerned."

"You're too honest, you know that, Jake."

"Keep that a secret, it would be bad for my image."

The waiter refilled their coffee cups. Jake checked his watch as he tried to stifle a yawn.

"It's not the company, it's the age." He reached for the check, and signaled for the waiter. "I've got to head back to Dublin bright and early tomorrow morning to meet that rookie they're sending in to replace me. The 'expert tracker' that's supposed to hunt you down and bring you home." And he laughed at the thought.

"Suppose he doesn't have anyone to hunt down?" Alanna asked.

"Does he?" Jake questioned, his attention back on her.

"No. I'm going back," Alanna said, determination clear in her voice.

Jake waited for the waiter to take the bill and money, and depart, before saying, "Are you now?"

"I have a little money put away, and I know of a small farm for rent in Middleburg, Va. It's been advertised in '*The Chronicle of the Horse*'. But, I'll need a place to stay until I can make arrangements to rent it. Got any suggestions?"

"My having to work with Dar makes it impossible for you to stay with me," Jake said, thinking how mad Dar was going to be when he found out Jake had spent this time with her and not told him. "But, there are a lot of Agency people away on temporary duty, so there's bound to be a place available where you can stay until you can make other arrangements. Tomorrow, I'll call Langley and tell Dar you're coming home."

"No. I don't want him to know."

"Trust me, Alanna, it's the best way to handle this," Jake advised her. "I'll tell him that you're planning to stay with a friend and when and if you want to see him, you'll call him."

"You won't tell him where I am?"

"No. The Agency has no interest in detaining you, and his interest in you is strictly personal. I'm not obligated to divulge your location to him for strictly personal reasons," Jake said. Despite whatever he might have said earlier in Dar's defense, he felt it would serve Dar right if she never came back. "In fact, I haven't the faintest idea which friend it is you're staying with, do I?"

"Thanks, Jake."

127

"Alanna, I know that you love the horse business, and wouldn't be interested in giving it up, but I'd like to propose something to you."

"What?"

"I think that you have the skills and the intelligence to be a real asset to the organization I work for. Maybe, I shouldn't even be bringing this up to you without first consulting the powers that be, but if you think you'd be interested in coming into the Agency, I'll go to bat for you."

"I don't know, Jake. You're right about the horse business, it's what I want to do for the rest of my life?"

"What if that were part of the deal, Alanna?"

"What about Dar? Do you think he'd go for the idea?"

"I don't know? He couldn't argue that you can't handle the work. If he objected at all, it would be for strictly personal reasons, and unfortunately, his objection would carry a lot of weight, because he's got a lot of seniority. But, my opinion carries a lot of weight too. I have considerably more seniority and am the senior member of this special group. However, may I suggest that before we even approach the Agency on your coming in, that you two settle your differences. This group I'd like you to join is too tight knit for lover's quarrels."

She didn't respond.

"Give it some thought, Alanna, I don't need an answer now."

"The answer's yes, Jake."

It was amazing how much her life had changed since she'd made that fateful decision, she thought as she exited I-64 at the Versailles exit and headed up route 60 toward her farm. Nowhere in her life's plan had she included the possibility of being employed in the field of international espionage, yet, she had become a willing and skilled player in the game. But, when she'd stopped to weigh the emotional cost to her of her participation in the intelligence business against the benefits to her country's security, she had come out a poor second.

"Duty and honor, before all else," Jake used to say. Could it be any other way now that she had been brought into this new intrigue? Not hardly, and she knew it.

It was only a short drive from I-64 to the back road that led to her farm. She pulled in the back gate, and once again made the trip up the pitch-black lane to the side of the barn without lights. She was about to retrace her steps back to the house when she heard a buzzing sound. Reaching into her purse, she pulled out the small communicator Rice had given her. When she flipped it open and hit the talk button, she heard

Jeremy's voice say, "Bad news, Querida, they've got a delivery date on the nuke. We're in business for sure."

* * *

Alanna entered the house and started up the stairs to her bedroom, but changed her mind, and instead went to the office to check her messages. There was one from her farm manager, Rick, saying Francois' horses would arrive by ten in the morning; one from her housekeeper, saying her car wouldn't start, and that she'd be a little late in the morning — and one from Francois.

The one from Francois said, "I am sorry to call you so late, Alanna, I know you said you were very tired, but I wanted to get word to you before you left in the morning. Please call me when you get up. I know that is quite early, but I am also an early riser and you won't awaken me. I need to see you about something of great importance tomorrow morning, so please call. The number is 272-4381, ext. 801. Bonne nuit, mon Cherie."

Turning off the recorder and the light, she said, "Bonne nuit yourself, you bastard, soon it will be bonne nuit forever!"

* * *

The flight from Lexington to Washington had been uneventful. Rice had been ordered to land the plane at a private airstrip, where a car from Security met them and took them back to Rice's condo.

At 6 a.m., the phone in the condo rang. It was Catherine calling for Jeremy. She told him that Granton had asked her to contact him, and to let him know that a meeting had been set up for ten that morning in Rosslyn. It was to that meeting that Jeremy now was headed.

With some difficulty, he'd found the Arlington Towers Apartments. He parked Rice's Jeep Cherokee in the underground parking garage, and took the elevator up to an Agency "safe" apartment on the fourth floor. A CIA security man was waiting for him.

"Mr. Taylor will be along directly," said the burly, dark haired man as he ushered Jeremy in. "Like something to drink while you're waiting?"

"Got any Diet Coke?"

"Sure do. Have a seat."

Jeremy checked out the rather sterile looking decor of the apartment, and then took a seat on the couch.

"Here ya go," the security man said, as he handed Jeremy the iced beverage.

"Thanks."

The man returned to his vigil at the window. Five minutes later, the door opened, and Granton came in.

"Everything in order, Judd?" Granton asked, as he greeted his man.

"Yes, sir, Mr. Taylor. I'll be just outside the door, if you need me," the security man replied, and immediately left the apartment, leaving Granton and Jeremy alone.

."Did you get bunked in with Rice okay?" Granton said to open the conversation.

"Yeah. He's got a nice place," replied Jeremy.

"I'll see about getting you a place tomorrow."

"I'd appreciate that."

"How did it go with, Alanna? I assume she was upset by the pictures?"

"Upset?" Jeremy shook his head and snickered under his breath. "Yeah, I guess you'd say she was upset. She thought I had a hand in putting that little package together. I learned the hard way that her combat skills are as sharp as ever. I spent an hour in an emergency room getting X-rayed and narrowly missed you claiming this body from the morgue. Shit! I forgot how good she was at that stuff."

"Have you patched things up?" Granton asked, worried by Alanna's loss of control. "Can you work together?"

"After she cooled down, we worked things out," Jeremy replied. "Those pictures were a hell of a thing to drop on her. You've got the conscience and the heart of a rock."

"I needed her in," Granton said, not apologetically. "She had a choice, you or the pictures."

"I doubt she realized there was a choice," Jeremy remarked. "And counting me as one of them, didn't really leave her with any choice, now did it?"

"Water over the dam, Jeremy. It worked, that's all that matters," Granton brushed Jeremy's criticism aside. Changing the subject, he asked, "How'd she take the news about Jake?"

"Jake was all she had left. It broke her up pretty good," Jeremy said, the sadness in his voice reflecting his feelings of loss as well. "How did they get on to him, Granton? I'd sure like to know who the hell's been looking in your 'Eyes Only' files?"

"I wish I knew," Granton said, sitting down in a chair. He looked pensively at the opposite wall for a moment, then said, "What really worries me, Jeremy, is that if he knew about Jake, it's a good bet he can finger you, and maybe Alanna."

"That little thought has been gnawing away at the back of my mind for the last couple of days, too," Jeremy said, in agreement, while parking himself on the corner of the bed. "If he can finger us, the operation's a bust right from the start."

"Well, we can't let Francois out of our sight, and we have to be there when they deliver the merchandise. The only one capable of getting that close to him is Alanna. I have to go with the two of you, and hope he just got lucky with Jake.

"In the meantime, I've had Security and CI working on this mole problem around the clock, but until he makes a mistake or a move, they've got nothing to go on. If only we had some kind of lead, something to start with!"

There was silence for a moment. Jeremy rose from the bed and walked to the window. He separated the closed drapes just enough to take a quick peak out without exposing himself. Then, turning back to Granton, said, "It could mean nothing, Granton, but while we were still on the ground at the Farm, the shuttle landed and parked alongside us. One of its passengers took a great deal of interest in our plane. He was too far away for me to identify, because he had a hat and glasses on, but he saw, and I think, recognized me. It looked like he even asked one of the ground crew about the plane. Like I said, it might not mean a thing."

"The Farm shuttle, huh?"

"If whoever made Jake can make me," Jeremy added, "it's more important than ever that you get our man in Ireland to come in on this. Whether our mole fingers me or the opposition just gets lucky again, if I'm taken out, then Alanna's got no backup. What's the holdup with him, anyway?"

"He just hasn't responded to our calls. He always was a moody bastard, but I'll get him for you, because we do need a backup."

Granton made a note in his pocket secretary, then said, "Any idea where Francois will be off to next?"

"Alanna says he always goes to the yearling sales at Saratoga in upstate New York."

"Well, you've still got your cover, looks like Saratoga's your next stop. I'm going to brief Alanna tomorrow night. Did she say if there was anyway she could be in Saratoga too?" Granton inquired.

"Yes. She's got six yearlings selling there. It couldn't be a better set up if we'd arranged it that way."

"That's an understatement," Granton replied. "Let's hope this lucky string of coincidences holds."

Changing the subject, Jeremy said, "What have we heard from the Moscow station on this nuke thing?"

"The station says that the Russians deny having any nukes missing. They claim their inventory is complete, and that they're cooperating 100 per cent with the Moscow station."

"Well, somebody's blowing smoke here." Jeremy said. "Either Francois' Russians don't really have a nuke, and we're chasing our tails, or the Russian government is lying through their teeth. Why don't we ask the Russians to let the Moscow station confirm their inventory?"

"That's a good idea. However, we'd have to get it approved by the State Department first, and you know how touchy they are on that stuff. It may require that the Director go back to the President, but our people must confirm that inventory.

"I'm going to have CI check the manifest on that Farm shuttle and see if it'll give us a lead. Who have we got baby-sitting Francois?"

"Only Alanna, for now."

"I think I better get a team down there to cover this bastard until he gets to Saratoga. You and Alanna can take it from there. When do you have to be there?"

"Not for a week, at least," Jeremy replied. The sale doesn't start until the second week of August, but the races start the last week of July."

"Good. In the meantime," Granton said, "I have a difficult assignment for you. While I was briefing the Director on SABRE's progress, I mentioned that it probably would be a good idea for you to spend time living your cover. You cost Francois a bundle, so he's really going to make an effort to check you out thoroughly.

"The Director contacted Walter Morris, the resort's owner, and Morris is more than happy to have you come out to the resort for a week or so. He's putting you down on the company roster as a partner, and is going to set you up with a suite and an office. The staff will be told you are coming into the firm, so you'll have legitimate cover. Hopefully, this will satisfy Francois' curiosity, and, Jeremy, for God's sake, quit mooning over Alanna, otherwise you might make that asshole so jealous that he bumps you off for that."

"Damn, I always get the tough assignments!"

"Okay, Mr. Jergens, I've got to be running. Stay in touch and don't enjoy yourself too much." Granton said, rising from his seat. As he headed to the door, he added, "Oh, by the way, I had to approve your expense voucher this morning. Couldn't you have rented something cheaper than that BMW convertible?"

"Hey, just living my cover, boss!"

* * *

Jake's body had arrived in Lexington at 6 a.m. aboard a Delta flight. A hearse, which Alanna had arranged for, met the plane and took his body to the church. When it arrived, Father Frank Dombrowski, the pastor, gave Alanna a call.

"It's Father Frank, Alanna, I hope I didn't wake you?" The priest said, when she'd answered the phone.

"You didn't, Father, I've been up waiting for your call. I take it my friend has arrived."

"He has. It's a beautiful coffin. The papers that accompanied it said the casket could be opened for viewing, if you were interested."

"Yes. I would like to see him one last time."

"I've arranged for the mass to be at ten. If you come by after nine, I'll have the coffin set up in the chapel so you can say your farewell in private."

"Thank you, Father, I'll see you a little after nine."

Alanna pressed the disconnect button, and when she heard the dial tone, dialed the number Francois had left on her message machine.

It rang twice and Francois answered, "Alanna?"

"Good morning, Francois," she replied, forcing herself to sound cheerful.

"Yes, it is a good morning!" His cheerful response was obviously not forced.

"My farm manager informed me that your horses would arrive here by ten this morning. He'll call you as soon as they have been settled in." Alanna kept her voice friendly, but just a tad businesslike, "Was there something else you needed?"

"Yes, there is. I must see you as soon as possible," Francois said, with great excitement in his voice. "My clients are very pleased to have purchased your colt, in spite of the cost. As you know, I am also a partner in him, and I think I have a proposition that might interest you. How soon can you meet me here?"

133

"I'm very happy your people are pleased with the colt, and I know that you'll do right by him, Francois, but I can't meet you this morning."

"Surely, you can spare an hour or two." Francois' elation began to ebb.

"I'm sorry, I just can't."

"What about lunch?" His enthusiasm returned.

"Today is just impossible, Francois. I have a funeral to attend, and then I am going out of town. Perhaps we can get together at Saratoga? I'll be there Monday, so that I can watch my horses train before the yearlings get there for the sale."

"No. I must see you today. What time is your flight?"

"Noon," she replied, somewhat frustrated "As much as I'd like to see you, today, Francois, it's just impossible."

"What time is the funeral?"

"At ten. Why?"

"Would you object to my invading your privacy?"

There was a distinct silence at Alanna's end of the phone.

"Alanna?"

"You can meet me at the entrance to the Lexington Cemetery at 10:45. We can talk for a few minutes after the burial service."

"Fine. I will see you at 10:45. And Alanna," Francois added, "Do not think I am making light of the circumstances. You have my deepest sympathy."

"Thank you, Francois."

* * *

Francois' limousine was already at the entrance to the Lexington Cemetery, when the hearse, followed by the priest's car, and Alanna's Volvo, pulled in. It followed behind the short procession as it wound its way through the tree-lined lanes until it came to a secluded area, where it stopped and everyone got out. The pallbearers attended to the casket.

Alanna wore a black linen suit. Her only accessories were a simple strand of pearls around her throat and a wide-brimmed black straw hat. She carried the only flowers, a bouquet of red roses.

The men sat the casket down, and Alanna placed the roses on top of it. Then she took her place to one side of the coffin with Francois at her side. Father Frank stepped to the head of the coffin, and began the burial prayers. At the end of the prayers for the dead, he raised his head and said, "Miss Reynolds has asked me to read this eulogy she has written on behalf of her friend.

"Jay was more than my best friend. He was my inspiration, my solace and my strength." he began. "He was a man who subscribed to the highest of standards and possessed boundless enthusiasm for whatever task he chose to tackle. No one, whose privilege it was to know him, is likely to forget the candor of his speech, the courage of his beliefs, or the warmth and genuiness of his friendship. Jay never dodged a responsibility, never refused to take on a difficult or unpleasant job, if it needed to be done. What he preached, he practiced. What he believed, he believed with heart and soul. He fought hard for every cause in which he enlisted, especially, for our rights and freedoms.

"Jay was and always will be an ideal. The example he set will continue to influence and inspire those who knew him. Though his passing leaves an enormous void in my life, his spirit will remain forever alive in my heart."

The tombstone set to one side of the grave read:

> J. DAVID CLARK
> You have filled my life with riches
> for there can be no greater
> treasure on earth, than
> true friendship and love.
> Love,
> Alanna.

The service over, Francois turned to her and said, "I am truly sorry, Alanna. I had no idea how much Mr. Clark meant to you. I should not have imposed myself on your last moments with him."

"He was like a father to me, Francois," Alanna said, as she wiped a tear that had freed itself from the reserve she was trying to maintain. "We adopted each other many years ago. We were both orphans in our own way."

"Had he been ill long?"

"No. He died quite suddenly," she replied, as she turned in the direction of the priest, who was making his way back to his car. He waved farewell, and she signaled with her hand for him to wait.

"Francois, please excuse me for a moment. I must speak with Father Frank before he leaves."

"Certainly. I'll wait by my car."

As Alanna passed the casket on her way to the priest's car, she stopped momentarily. Resting her hand gently on it, she said a farewell prayer, kissed the coffin, and from the bouquet, she took a single red rose.

She then proceeded to where the priest stood waiting and said, "Thank you for everything, Father. It was such short notice I can't believe you were even able to get the tombstone. I know this would have meant a lot to my friend, and it means a lot to me."

"I only met the gentleman a couple of times when you brought him to mass with you, Alanna, but it was obvious that he was very fond of you. To look in his eyes, was to know a good man."

"He was a very good man, Father," Alanna said, as she offered her hand to the priest. "Again, I want to thank you and I apologize for running, but I have a plane to catch."

"Have a safe trip, and good luck at Saratoga."

"Good-bye, Father."

Alanna walked back toward the cemetery road and Francois' limousine. He was leaning against its side in conversation with his secretary, Phillip. The conversation stopped when Alanna came within hearing distance.

As she approached the men, she said, "Bonjour, Phillip."

"Bonjour, Mademoiselle Reynolds," Phillip replied. Then, in retiring to the car to give Alanna and Francois privacy, he said, "Pardon, s'il vous plait."

"I have heard you converse with my countrymen on many occasions, Alanna," Francois said. "And I have been meaning to tell you how very good your French is. Did you learn to speak it in your travels?"

"I majored in it in college, Francois, but I really learned it in my travels."

"Yes, a language must be used to be learned well, I sometimes have trouble with my English for that reason. I'm sure it comes in handy in this business with so many Frenchmen to deal with."

"Yes, it is an asset. I'm sorry to rush you, Francois, but my plane leaves at noon. What is it you were so excited to tell me?" She said, with genuine interest.

"Ah, yes. Alanna, I have a great idea," Francois said, full of enthusiasm. "I think it would be wonderful if you would retain an interest in this colt. Then, when he has completed his career on the track, we could stand him at stud on your farm. It is time Wicklow Stud had a stallion facility, do you not agree?"

"Stallion facilities are an expensive proposition, Francois," Alanna said, skeptically. "And, traditionally, one-stallion studs do not fare very well."

"You would not have to stand just one stallion, Alanna. With my connections in Europe, you could offer the finest roster of European stars at your stud."

"That's a very nice thought, but the facilities for and the operating cost of such an operation are just out of my league."

"Ah, my dear Alanna, money is the least of your worries."

"I wish I could agree with you, Francois. What I made on that colt will pay my stud fees, mortgage and operating expenses for the year, but what I have left has to go for future operating expenses, and not some fancy dream."

"I'm not talking about your money, Alanna. I'm talking about investors' money."

"What kind of investors, Francois?"

"French, European, Arab, a conglomerate."

Arabs, naturally, she thought. Then, she said, "I'll think about it, Francois."

"Good. We'll discuss it further at Saratoga. Did you say you would be there on Monday?"

"Yes, but right now I have to run or I'll miss my plane."

"My plane could take you."

"You're kind to offer, Francois, but it isn't necessary. I do need to go." She offered her cheek and they exchanged the traditional air kisses.

"Consider this offer well, Alanna, it is a great opportunity for you to become part of a powerful international group."

"Heady stuff for a country girl, isn't it, Francois?"

"You are hardly a country girl, Alanna." Francois replied, with a smile. "See you in Saratoga."

Chapter 14

Passenger traffic was light at Bluegrass field. The Delta flight to Miami was three-quarters empty. Alanna gave the flight attendant her boarding pass as she entered the aircraft.

"Seat 4-B." The young woman indicated the aisle seat in the last row in the first class cabin. "Can I help you with your bag?"

"No, thanks, I can manage." Alanna smiled, and moved down the aisle to her seat. She put the garment bag in the overhead compartment, her briefcase and purse under the seat.

As with checking the rear view mirror of her car, when traveling by air, she still maintained the old safety precautions of making reservations at the last minute and always taking carry-on luggage.

The flight made a quick stop in Cincinnati, then head to Miami.

On arrival at Miami International Airport, Alanna gathered her things and left the aircraft. She walked briskly down the long hallway that joined the concourse to the terminal. At a toy store in the terminal, she stopped and purchased a large stuffed tiger. It gave her an opportunity to make sure she hadn't been followed. Out of the air-conditioned terminal, the humid Miami heat made her catch her breath.

A voice with a heavy Cuban accent beckoned her from the curb, "Looking for a cab, senorita?"

"Yes, I am," she said, as she made her way to the taxi parked along the curb.

The driver hurried to open the curbside back door, and helped her with her bag. "I will put your bag in the trunk."

"Thank you," she said, as she settled into the back seat.

The cab driver slid behind the wheel, and edged the cab into traffic.

"Buenos tardes, Miguelito." Alanna let herself relax as she greeted the driver. "Como esta usted y tu familia?"

"They are very good, Senorita Reynolds," he replied in English, and added with pride, "My English, it is much better since your last visit, no?"

"Yes, it is much better," she smiled at the young man, who looked back at her in his rear view mirror.

The cab got off I-95 at exit 2 and proceeded into the heart of Little Havana. Miguelito radioed his headquarters, notifying them that he was minutes away. He reached his headquarters by way of several back alleys, where the garage door waited open for the anticipated arrival.

As the cab pulled to a stop, its rear door was opened by a short, stout man in mechanics' overalls. "It is good to see you again, Senorita Reynolds."

"It's good to see you, Carlos," Alanna said, as she hugged him affectionately. "You're looking well. I've been told you've had heart surgery?"

"Si, si, but, I am as good as new, now."

"What's the word on our friend in Havana?"

"Ah, el barbudo? He never changes. Cuba will only be rid of him when the devil takes him," Carlos said with a shrug of his shoulder. "Well, let me get your car so that you can be on your way."

He motioned to one of his men. "Get the senorita's car, Hugo."

The man returned with the white Mercedes 450SL, its navy convertible top up and the air conditioning running. Miguelito loaded her bag in the trunk.

"Thanks again, Carlos. You take good care of my car while I'm away. I appreciate it very much."

"As we did for Dar," he said. "He is still missed greatly here in Miami."

"Yes, I miss him, too," she said, as she sat down behind the wheel. She took her sunglasses from her purse and added, "Take care, Carlos, I'll let you know when I'll be bringing the car back. Hasta la vista."

"Adios," he said, as he signaled one of his men to open the garage door.

* * *

It was a beautiful day for a drive along the beach. Alanna put the top down on the Mercedes and headed east across the McArthur Causeway to Collins Avenue. She drove north on Collins until she reached a place where the road split to one way. She turned west on a side street and doubled back to 63rd St. Once across the bridge, she turned right at the first street which led to an island gatehouse.

Alanna waved to the guard, who, recognizing her, raised the gate allowing her to enter. The drive, lined with palm trees, wound along the edge of the island, ending at a high wrought iron gate. Alanna used her card to open the gate, and proceeded down the drive into the courtyard of a sprawling Spanish-style ranch house.

As the car pulled to a stop, 14-year-old Lorenzo Valdes hurried to open the door.

139

"Bienvenida, Senorita Reynolds!" he said, excitedly, a broad grin on his handsome face.

"Gracias, Lorenzo," she said, as she got out, put her arms around him and hugged him to her. "Every time I see you, Lorenzo, you get more good looking. You're going to break a lot of ladies' hearts."

His olive complexion betrayed a hint of blush at her compliment and, obviously embarrassed, he quickly changed the subject.

"I have been practicing the wounded black tiger kata you showed me when you were here last month. Will you watch me later, so that I can show you what I have learned?" He asked, shyly.

"Lorenzo," his mother, and Alanna's housekeeper, called to him from the front door, "do not bother Senorita Reynolds. Forgive him, senorita. He could hardly wait for you to arrive. He has been practicing what you taught him every day since you left."

"It's all right, Carlotta," Alanna shouted back from behind the car, where she was unloading her bag and the stuffed tiger. She handed the tiger to Lorenzo. "Here is a little souvenir for you Lorenzo. I hope you learned your lessons well, I intend to put you to the test."

"Thank you, senorita, I will not disappoint you," Lorenzo said with pride as he carried Alanna's bag and the tiger into the house.

"Take Senorita Reynolds' things to her room, Lorenzo," the woman said as she greeted Alanna with a warm hug. "Angela told us a friend of yours passed away. We are all very sorry to hear that."

Angela and Carlotta were cousins. The De Santes family had employed them and their family as housekeepers and caretakers for many years. Their loyalty to Alanna was assured.

"Thank you, Carlotta," Alanna replied as she returned the hug, and entered the plant-filled vestibule of the house. It was cool and fragrant. The sounds of tropical birds, permitted to fly free, gave it the feeling of a rain forest.

The house had been left to Alanna in Dar's estate. It had belonged to his parents, who had left it to him. The furnishings were antiques, treasures that had been in the De Santes family for generations. Before Dar's death, it had been their favorite retreat.

Keeping the house now that the Thoroughbred market was bad was a definite luxury. Alanna kept it more out of sentiment than necessity, and also because it had been the Valdes home for many years.

"Will you be having dinner at home this evening? I have a very nice steak I can grill for you."

"I'll be staying in, but don't fuss. A salad is really all I want, it's too hot for anything heavier." She started in the direction of her room, then added. "Oh! Carlotta. I'd like to eat early, say about six o'clock, then you can have the rest of the evening off."

"Can I get you anything now? A glass of lemonade, perhaps?"

"No, thanks, maybe later, I think I'll change into my swimsuit, work out a little with Lorenzo, and then take a swim."

"That is good. It will relax you. You work too hard."

"You and Angela worry too much about me, Carlotta," Alanna said, gently admonishing her.

"You need someone to worry about you, but it should be a rich husband, not two old Cuban women."

"Someday, maybe, Carlotta," she said, as she disappeared into her room.

Alanna placed the purse and briefcase on a bedroom chair. She slipped out of her traveling clothes and into a sleek black maillot swimsuit, over which she donned a black Gi, securing it around her waist with a black belt.

Barefoot, she walked across the cool Spanish tile floor to the gym. It was a large square room with a well-padded floor, high ceilings and mirrored walls. Between the top of the ceiling and overhanging roof was a screened area that let in light and air. Huge fans hung from the ceiling, silently circulating the air and cooling the room.

She did a quick warm up, and soon Lorenzo appeared at the door. He hesitated in the doorway.

"Come in Lorenzo, let's see what you have learned from our last lesson," she said.

He came to the middle of the room and assumed the stance for the start of the wounded black tiger kata. Alanna came to where he stood to adjust his position. When she laid her hand on his shoulder, it was hot, very hot, but it did not burn, instead, it felt soothing. It was the same sensation Angela's son, Michael, had experienced at her farm, but she did not get the same reaction.

"There is nothing to be afraid of," she reassured him, as he jumped away. "What you feel is the power of the Chi. With practice and concentration, you, too, will be able to feel and project its warmth."

"Now, the last time I was here, we worked on the final moves of the tiger kata. The strongest of the animal forms. Let me see what you have learned. Do the entire kata, Lorenzo. Remember, the success of the tiger

141

kata lies in its big, powerful, and explosive moves. I want to see those qualities in your kata."

Lorenzo bowed to her. Then began the tiger kata. He worked his way timidly through the opening moves, growing bolder as he gained confidence. When he finished, she praised his efforts and made suggestions as to how he might improve certain moves.

"I think we should have a short sparring session. What do you think, Lorenzo?"

"Oh, yes, Senorita Reynolds! Sparring is the best part of the lesson."

"Well then let's get started," Alanna said. "You use the tiger form. In contrast to the strong moves of the tiger, I will use the White Crane form, the bird style."

"How is the bird style different from the tiger?" Lorenzo asked, never having seen the White Crane form performed.

"The Crane or bird method relies on speed and agility. The force in this style is created by whip like movements of the arms and high swift kicks. You know I discourage high kicks, because they leave you off balance and vulnerable. I will illustrate the kicks anyway for reference, and, because on rare occasions, they may be useful. The style also makes use of a unique hand strike. Instead of a blade hand or fist, the fingers of the hand form a beak. This hand position can be very deadly. A hard strike to the temple with this hand position will kill your opponent.

"You must always be careful, Lorenzo, to only use as much force as is necessary to end a confrontation without ending someone's life. The exception to this rule is, if it is a matter of your opponent or your life, then you must use all the force at your disposal. Is that clear, Lorenzo?"

"Yes, senorita, it is clear."

"Okay, let's go," she said, as she took a position opposite him.

They bowed to each other and assumed a sparring stance. Lorenzo's hands became like the paws of the tiger -- his fingers, the claws. He sank his weight low, as he assumed a horse-stance position. The expression on his face acquired the look of a snarling cat.

She allowed him the first strike. When Lorenzo could no longer contain his impatience, he leaped forward, propelled by powerful, young leg muscles. At the same time, he struck out forcefully with a claw-like hand. Alanna countered by simply sidestepping the attack. Lashing out with her hand, as a bird would with its wing, she slapped him gently across the side of his face. Had Alanna used the beak hand, or any force at all, she could have hurt him severely.

"Where is your defense, Lorenzo?" she asked, as he stumbled backward from the surprise sensation of the slap. "When you attack someone, you must also be prepared to defend yourself, especially, if your attack is unsuccessful. Concentrate!"

Alanna understood how frustrating it was for Lorenzo to spar with someone of her caliber. She recalled her own novice attempts at sparring with Dar. She once compared it to sparring with a shadow. No matter how hard she tried, he always seemed to be just out of reach.

Before Lorenzo could get too discouraged, she called a halt to the sparring.

"That's enough for today, Lorenzo."

He immediately came to attention facing her. They bowed in respectful courtesy to one another.

"Lorenzo, when you practice, do each move in front of the mirror, slowly. Feel every move. Close your eyes. Sense each muscle movement. Visualize the move in your mind. Remember, each movement must flow into the next. The power must develop like water that is flowing through a pipe. A pipe that is wide at the beginning, and then becomes narrower and narrower until finally the water bursts from the opening with a tremendous surge. So, do you understand what I mean?"

"Yes," Lorenzo smiled wearily. "I am sorry I am so slow to learn."

"Patience, Lorenzo," she said, encouragingly. "Don't be so hard on yourself. It takes a long time to do this well. You're doing just fine."

"Sometimes, it is hard to be patient."

"Ah, yes, I know. In the martial arts, Lorenzo, being patient is a very important asset, because in the martial arts, timing is everything. Now go, the lesson is ended."

They bowed to each other, again. Then Lorenzo left the room, bowing as he exited the door.

Alanna thought, as she watched him leave, how little contact she'd had in her life with children Lorenzo's age. Dar had wanted to get married and have a family, but, orphaned early in life, she was unreceptive to the idea. The fear that, because of their occupation, they might leave their children orphans only solidified that opinion. She left the room, and, with it, the memories.

The patio covered the entire distance between the house and the waters of Biscayne Bay. The tri-layered decks, made of cedar and stone, were lushly landscaped with trees, shrubs and a rainbow of tropical flowers. It ended at a boat dock on the bay. On the second level of the deck, set in a basin, with a waterfall spilling into one end, was a large pool.

Alanna removed her sweat-soaked Gi. She stepping under the outside shower for a moment to cleanse her body then dove into the clear, azure water of the pool. As her body broke the surface, and slipped into its depths, she was enveloped in silence, her problems forgotten.

* * *

The twin 440-hp MerCruiser engines, powering the Tempest 44 Riviera through the calm waters of the Intercoastal waterway, purred softly. Though the boat could travel at speeds in excess of 60 mph, the speed it was presently proceeding at was barely above idle.

Granton was in no hurry to reach his destination. When he had devised his plan to bring Alanna back into the Agency, he had hoped that the Director's assumptions were correct; that time and distance from the Agency would have eased her animosity toward it, as well as toward him and Jeremy; and that having time to look back on the Balkan incident, with less emotion, would make her more forgiving. With this hope, he had chosen Jeremy to give Alanna the news of Jake's death, and to try and recruit her back in. But, apparently time had not healed the old wound completely, and she had rejected Jeremy.

Contrary to what Jeremy thought about his lack of heart, and even as hard-nosed as he was, Granton had found resorting to sending her the pictures distasteful. Dar had been Alanna's life. All she had left of him were memories. Now, thanks to Granton, her last memory of Dar would be of seeing his final agonizing moments.

If her initial reaction to Jeremy was as bitter as Jeremy had said, then there was no telling what her reaction would be to him.

Granton could never make himself understand how a women as angelic looking as Alanna could be so lethal. He knew she did not relish taking a life, and avoided it at all costs, but the instinct to kill was there. When she made up her mind there was no alternative, the end came swiftly for her victim. In hand-to-hand combat, within the Agency, she had no equal.

But, Alanna had other qualities that had made her a valuable asset to the Agency, as well. She was self-motivated, ingenious, had excellent command of at least five languages, and was a brilliant strategist. She was cool, fearless and determined, completing missions that, had they been assigned to a lesser qualified operative, would have been given only a marginal chance for success.

It had been an incalculable loss, the day she resigned from the Agency. Now, he had a chance to rectify that loss -- to have her back.

It was pitch dark when the Riviera entered Biscayne Bay.

"Where to from here, sir?" Paul Talbot, Granton's driver and bodyguard, asked. The other two bodyguards who occupied the boat were women. A ploy to make the craft appear to be two couples pleasure boating on the bay. Granton gave him the final coordinates, and cautioned him to make his final approach slowly.

Granton had been to this house many times and remembered how, in the daylight, the house looked vulnerable, innocent. But, anyone trying to invade that peaceful, serene setting was in for a huge surprise. So well protected was its perimeter, that small fish and birds had trouble penetrating it undetected. Dar was very security conscious, and so, he imagined, must Alanna still be.

Paul allowed the boat to speed up as it entered the open waters of the bay. It took only a few minutes to cross the distance to what appeared in the dark to be a large house set on a rise. He powered down a respectful distance from the house, but could barely make out the dock, until a line of lights flashed on illuminating the docking area.

As Paul edged the boat alongside the dock, one of the female security people jumped onto the dock to secure it. The woman caught the bow spring line that Granton threw her, then took up the bowline and secured it.

Granton stepped out of the boat, and turned to take his briefcase from the other woman. As he turned back toward the house, some very discreet indirect perimeter lighting came on. It made the deck, one level up from where he was standing, visible.

He heard Alanna's voice call to him from the darkness of the upper deck. "I'm up here."

"Sir, would you like us to check out the area first?" Joan, a tall, brunette, asked, somewhat unnerved by the dimly lit area and the fact no one was on the dock to meet Granton.

"No, it's okay," Granton said, knowing this was not normal operating procedure for them.

"Darlene," he said, to the woman still in the boat. "You stay with the boat. Paul, when I get inside the house, you see to the front of the house, and, Joan, you stay out here on the upper deck."

They acknowledged his orders, and Granton proceeded up the steps to the house. He could barely see Alanna waiting for him in the semi-darkness, clad, as she was, in black silk camp shirt and matching slacks.

145

As he came to her, she extended her hand in greeting and said, "It's been a long time, Granton."

"Much too long, Alanna." He took her outstretched hand in his, and gripped it firmly.

"Come in," she said, as she removed her hand from his grip and stepped through a sliding door into a large glassed-in porch. He followed her lead. She closed the door behind him, and drew the curtain.

The house was very still, and, as with the exterior, dimly lit.

"We can go into the den."

"That will be fine," Granton replied, remembering from past meetings here with Dar and Alanna, that the room was soundproof.

As they passed through the living room, with its massive floor-to-ceiling fireplace, and beyond the formal dining room, with it heavy Spanish furnishings, Granton marveled at how big the house was. The den sat in the center of the house. None of its walls touched the outside perimeter of the house and it had no windows or skylights. It had been designed for the kind of meeting they were about to have.

"Still sweep this thing?" Granton asked Alanna as she led him through the door.

"Only for special occasions like this."

Indicating the round conference table in one corner, she said. "Why don't we sit there? Can I get you something to drink?"

"Sure, thanks," he replied, amazed and relieved that things were going so well. "What have you got?"

"How about a Chevas on the rocks with a splash of soda and a twist of lime?" Alanna said, as she slid the louvered doors open to reveal a well-stocked wet bar.

"My wife always forgets the twist of lime. Even after 25 years of marriage, she still forgets the lime."

Alanna brought his drink, and set it on the coaster in front of him, then sat down in the chair to his right.

"Thanks," he said, as he took a sip of the drink, and held it up as a toast to his satisfaction with it.

"You're looking very well, Alanna. The horse business agrees with you." Granton risked a negative response, but needed to hear her say the words of acceptance himself. "Are you sure you want back into the Agency?"

"Yes." Simple, straightforward, no hesitation, it was typical Alanna.

"Well, the Agency is pleased to have you back. Shall we get on with this briefing?"

146

"Definitely."

"Alanna, I know that Jeremy has brought you up to date on the basis for operation SABRE, and where it stood when he was with you," Granton said. "What I'd like to do is apprise you of the latest developments, and answer any questions you might have about the operation, and your part in it. Do you have any questions so far?"

"No."

"Good. Then you know that Francois has arranged the sale of a back-pack nuke to a Hizballah cell headed by a man named Kamal Shabban." As Granton spoke, he removed a file folder from his briefcase, and slid it to her. Alanna turned it to face her, but did not open it.

He continued. "You also know that we have broken a code that indicates that Francois expects to have the package in his hands by the third week of August. The deal is drugs and cash for the nuke. We have no idea what Hizballah has planned for the nuke.

"At our last meeting, Jeremy suggested that we have the Moscow station ask the Russians for permission to inventory their nuclear arsenal. Normally, the Russians would be pretty touchy about such a request, but the last thing they'd want, now that they're trying to get into our coffers, is to have us suspect they're selling a nuke to Arab terrorists. We ran the inventory, and found their stores intact. It was perplexing because Jake's contacts are usually very reliable."

"Do we have any idea which contact Jake used?"

"We still don't know for sure." Granton stopped for a minute to sip on his drink. Continuing, he said, "Whoever it is, he must have know Jake was dead, because he put Jake's plan B into operation, which was to call the Paris station and ask for a Mr. Wilson. That's the code name Jake gave his contact for his courier at the station. The contact spoke with Mr. Wilson, and told him he had a package for Jake. The courier told him where to drop it, and I got it in the cable traffic this morning. The reason we couldn't find a Russian nuke missing is because it isn't a Russian nuke, it's from the Ukraine!"

"You know Granton, it sure was wonderful when all the Agency had to occupy itself with were simple things, like, who was trying to make off with a stinger missile, or the latest war strategy plan, or the plans for Star Wars. Oh, but with the recent change of heart about missile defense in Washington, they still must be after that one. Yes, it almost makes you wish for the 'bad old Soviet Union days' to be back, doesn't it?" Alanna drolly asked the rhetorical question.

147

Contemplating verbally the consequences of the fall of the Soviet Union, she added, "Instead, now we have to worry about every two-bit dictator getting his hands on a nuclear toy or two, courtesy of the collapsing ex-Soviet economies. A truly scary thought!"

"I agree, Alanna, but what's puzzling about this scenario is that the Ukrainians are as anxious to have our dollars and our sympathies as are the Russians. It doesn't make sense for them to throw the good will theyve built up with us out the window over one nuke."

"The hard-liners in the Ukraine might not agree with you." Alanna alluded to the inner struggles for power going on in all the CIS states.

"You have a point and they may be involved in this," Granton concurred. "Since, the Ukrainian government also claims its arsenal is intact, we've asked our Kiev station to make the same request for an inventory of them, as we did of the Russians. If they allow us to inventory their stockpile, we should know by Monday if one of their nukes is missing.

"Wherever this nuke is coming from, Alanna," he continued. "Our first hope is that we can stop it at its source. If that isn't possible, then it will be up to you to be where it's delivered and get the damn thing before they can use it. Couldn't be simpler, could it?"

"If you say so."

"Any questions?"

"Not so far."

"As Jeremy probably also told you, there is the possibility a mole has surfaced." Granton advised Alanna. "I suspect that Jake was sold by someone within the Agency. I believe, but have no proof, that it is the same individual who blew the job in the Balkans. Since Jake's death was reported, I've had Security and CI working around the clock on this.

"God forbid the mole would blow your or Jeremy's cover, this operation would be finished and we'd probably have a world crisis on our hands. Hizballah will use that nuke if they get it, there's no question of that."

"How come you never shook this maniac loose after the Baltic disaster?" She asked, remembering the painful consequences of that breech of security. "It was so obvious that it was an inside job."

"The same problem we're faced with now, no leads," Granton said, sitting back in his chair and folding his hands across his lap. "This person, obviously, has access to information that can keep him one step ahead of us. How he gets that information is something else no one seems to know. We haven't heard from him since the Balkan incident that we know off. Whoever employed him for that operation paid him well, because he's been able to lie low and survive all the internal investigations our other mole hunts produced. That is, until now."

For a moment, they each contemplated the seriousness of having this person, who seemed to have such easy access to the most classified of information, running loose. Granton knew Alanna must be weighing the risks against the benefits of this mission.

To put her at ease, Granton said, "I'm hoping Jeremy has provided me with a lead that will unearth him. He thinks a guy getting off the Farm shuttle may have recognized him. The guy took an inordinate amount of interest in Jeremy's plane at the airfield. Could just be innocent interest, but we're trying to identify the guy now, and find out the connection.

"It seems another problem has arisen concerning Jeremy, a problem that could jeopardize this mission almost as much as a mole." Granton waited to see if Alanna would volunteer anything. When she didn't, he said, "I got the impression from Rice that Francois thinks Jeremy has a romantic interest in you. Of course, we both know he doesn't. Right!"

"Are you asking me or telling me?"

"Maybe a little of both."

"Then I guess you'd have to say, the answer is a little of both."

"God, some things never change," And he shook his head in dismay, his suspicions confirmed. "Well, if it's true, we can't have Jeremy continually exposed to Francois. I guess Jeremy's request to bring in another agent to assist in backing you up makes sense."

There was no response from Alanna, but he could almost sense her non-verbal objection. After a moment, she said, "Do I know this person?"

"No you don't." Then, Granton answered the question that he knew she was thinking, but too professional to ask. "Alanna, I know that you prefer working with people you're familiar with, especially, on tough stuff like this. But, if for some reason Jeremy can't function effectively, we need a backup for you."

"What's wrong with Rice as backup?"

"Rice will be there to back you up, but he's only a pilot. This guy is better. Much better."

She didn't seem convinced.

"What's the story on wonder agent, and when do I get to meet him?"

"He's ex-MI-6."

"British Intelligence!" And she rolled her eyes in disgust.

149

"I said ex-MI-6. He's been working on a contract basis for us for a long time. In fact it was Dar who introduced us to him."

"And I don't know him?"

"You never had a need to know him."

"Well, it looks like I do now, so what else can you tell me."

"He spends a lot of time in the Orient, and, like you, is well versed in the martial arts. But, more importantly, he's a natural for this job. He grew up on a horse farm in Ireland, and he knows the horse business -- maybe as well as you do."

"Sounds like he's the man for the job. Why not get him to do it instead of me?" She said, her voice edged with sarcasm.

"Somehow, I can't see Francois relating to him in quite the same way as to you, but, then, you know that."

"So, what's his name, and when can I expect to meet him?"

"His name is Aiden Doyle and you can expect to meet him as soon as I can get him to answer his phone, and get his butt over here," Granton replied, with an uncharacteristic air of humor.

She smiled at his remark, and that broke the coolness that had predominated throughout the briefing.

"Speaking of Francois, just before I flew down here, he made me an interesting offer." Alanna said, referring to her and Francois' conversation in the cemetery. "He offered to make me a part of his European conglomerate."

"You're joking?"

"No. I'm not. He wants me to retain an interest in the colt I just sold him, so that after the colt's syndicated and finished with his racing career, he can return to Lexington and stand at stud on my farm. Funds for this little venture are to be provided courtesy of his European and Arab business partners, of which I would become one."

"The gods have smiled on us for once, Alanna." Granton was overjoyed at the news. "Of course you will take him up on his offer."

"If I accept his offer, is the Agency willing to cover the cost of my share?"

"God, you've gotten to be a hard-nosed business woman."

"Well?"

"If we have to."

"You do."

"In that case, we will."

Granton finished off his drink. Then he leaned forward, rested his forearms on the edge of the table, and folded his hands together. In a more personal tone of voice, he said, "Alanna, there was a time when you and I had a very good working relationship, a friendship. Despite what has transpired in the interim, I hope that will be the case again."

"I don't have a problem with that," Alanna assured him.

"Good, I'm really glad to hear that," he said, reaching for his briefcase. Then he said, "I came here tonight for two reasons, Alanna, the first we have already accomplished. The second reason is bittersweet." While he spoke, he withdrew a large manila envelope from the briefcase. "As you know, Jake had no close blood relations living. You were his family, as far as he was concerned."

At the mention of Jake's name, Alanna rose and turned away from Granton.

Granton rose too, but did not go to her, instead he said, "In his will, of which he made me executor, he named you, Alanna, beneficiary of all he had. In this envelope I have a copy of the will, his financial papers, the keys to his cottage in North Carolina, his apartment, and his car. The Finance Department will see that you receive the proceeds from his insurance."

Granton could see the news was upsetting her. In the past, she had rarely displayed any signs of emotion in front of him, but now, he saw her shoulders shudder.

"There is something else that Jake wanted you to have. It is usually only passed on to blood relatives, but the Agency has made an exception in this case. Please face me, Alanna."

She turned. "I'm sorry, Granton, I didn't mean to be rude."

"I know. Jake's death is difficult for me to accept, too." Granton assured her. "But, I am pleased to be able to give you this."

From within the envelope, Granton removed two official looking papers and a box. He opened the box, and, extending it to her, said, "Alanna, in 1978, Jake risked his life by going into Czechoslovakia to save two of his agents, whose cover had been blown. One of the agents was severely wounded and had to be physically carried out. For his heroism, Jake was awarded the Intelligence Star, which I now give to you in his memory."

Alanna came forward, and took the box containing the three-inch, circular bronze medal, which bore the seal of the Central Intelligence Agency, and the words "For Valor" on the front. On the reverse, were the words United States of America, and, in small scroll-like plaque the name J. David Clark.

"Thank you, Granton." She clutched the medal close to her.

He also handed her the two certificates. One was a citation stating the reason for the awarding of the medal, which Granton had already explained. The second was an official certificate, signed by CIA Director, and dated 1st day of May 1978.

"You know that you cannot display any of this," Granton cautioned her.

"I do."

"I have also requested the Awards Department issue a second medal, the Intelligence Cross, in his honor for his valor in his final mission," Granton said, as a final tribute to his long-time friend. "When it is awarded, you will receive it as well."

"This is a great honor, Granton," Alanna said, as she set the certificates and medal on the large oak desk. "Jake was all I had left. I wish you were bringing him to me in place of this medal. But, he died an honorable death, doing what he loved --- no one can hope for more than that."

Then they were both silent, each absorbed momentarily with their own memories of a man they called friend.

Checking his watch, it revealed the time to be 11:45 p.m.

"I have to go, Alanna." Granton said, this time putting his arm around her shoulder in a gesture of support. "If I've caused you pain, I am truly sorry. I admire your ability to put aside your feelings to serve your country in this task you've been given. I promise that I will support you in every way possible to see that you succeed and return safely."

Alanna touched the hand on her shoulder in response.

She walked Granton to the door.

He turned to her before leaving, and, extending his hand in farewell, said, "Good night, Alanna. Take care of yourself, and if you need anything, just call me."

"Good night, Granton."

Without looking back, he headed down the terraced patio to the dock and into the MerCruiser, where his bodyguards joined him.

Alanna watched from the doorway as Granton's boat headed out into the bay. She remained there until its running lights disappeared beyond the horizon.

* * *

After reading the updates on Operation SABRE that Granton had left with her, Alanna spent most of the remainder of the night lying on a lounge chair beside the pool, enjoying the breeze, the solitude, the sound of the bay waters lapping up against the boat dock, and doing some serious thinking.

It was the first opportunity she had had to consider all the angles of this mission, and the part she was to play in it. So far, everything had simply fallen into place, as Jake knew it would, because she was perfectly positioned by way of her occupation and contacts to make her initial entry into the operation without suspicion. But, from here on in, access to the areas she needed to penetrate would not be so easily achieved. Like Jake, one wrong move and her cover would be blown as well. There were too many sophisticated players in this game for her to hope that playing upon Francois' obvious fascination with her would be enough to see her through.

Jeremy posed still another problem. Normally, he would have been her first choice as her backup, but after seeing him almost blow his own cover, acting as he had in front of Francois, she wasn't sure he could handle the job. No matter how they had felt about one another in the past, professionalism had prevailed. The necessity to maintain that level of professionalism on this assignment seemed to have escaped him. Whatever had caused him to lose focus on the importance of this key operational ingredient concerned and perplexed her.

The addition of Aiden Doyle to the team also concerned her. It was not unusual for one intelligence officer not to have knowledge of the identity of a fellow officer. This was simply good operational procedure and helped keep identities of intelligence officers from being blown, either purposefully or unintentionally, during the course of carrying on the business of gathering intelligence and doing espionage work. But, if Dar had recruited Doyle, and, if he had considered him such a hot shot, why hadn't he requested him for one of their missions. Even Granton seemed to exude a certain reticence where Doyle was concerned. It left her with an uncomfortable feeling about the man.

As for the unearthing the mole, dangerous as that situation was it would have to be Granton's and the Agency's concern, for to even make the slightest attempt to expose him from her end would surely alert the opposition and give her identity away.

What she knew for certain was that, from here on in, things would happen fast, that nothing could be taken for granted, and that working this far out in the open meant their lives were, without question, on the line.

* * *

"Good morning, senorita. I hope you slept well. It was a pleasant night to be out under the stars," Carlotta said, as she placed the glass of orange juice on the table next to the lounge chair, and stood looking down on Alanna's prone figure.

Alanna rubbed both eyes with her hands to get the sleep out of them. She had no idea when she had dropped off to sleep, but the sun was already well up in the sky so she knew she had be asleep for quite some time.

"Yes, it was very peaceful," she said as she reached for the glass and took a sip. "Thanks for the juice, Carlotta."

"Will you be having breakfast?" Carlotta asked.

Alanna thought for a moment before saying, "I should go for a run, but to be really honest, Carlotta, I think I'll just loaf away the day. I may not get another chance to do it for quite some time. So the answer is, yes, I'll have breakfast. Make it a big one; bacon, eggs, the works. I'll just shower and dress, and I'll see you in the kitchen in 20 minutes."

As Alanna was pulling on a pair of jeans, the phone rang. Hopping on one foot, she made it to the bedside table, and picked up the receiver.

"Ola," she said.

"Ola, yourself," replied the slightly annoyed voice she recognized to be Jeremy's.

Alanna sat down on the bed, and hit a switch under the table that made the phone she was talking on a secure line.

"Where the hell have you been?" Jeremy asked, concern evident in his voice. "I called and called last night, but there was no answer. I was worried sick."

Alanna had taken the phone off the hook before she had gone out to the pool last night, so as not to be disturbed. Obviously, Carlotta had made sure it was working again. In reply to Jeremy's question, she said, "I was out on the high seas, if it's any of your business, which it isn't."

"With who?"

With who, she thought, why does there always have to be a "who" in men's minds. But, if he wanted to think that way, she'd accommodate him. "That is none of your business," she said. "Where are you, and what is it you're so desperate to talk to me about?"

"Well at least we've established there was a who," Jeremy said, less than enthusiastic at the supposed revelation. "Let's just say that I'm immersing myself in my work."

"How many woman does it take for you to do that successfully?" She could play his game.

"Would you believe me if I said none?"

"Not for a minute!"

"Alanna, you have no faith in me. I told you I'm a changed man."

"It's not a matter of faith, Jeremy, it's a matter of, of... For the life of me I can't think what it might be a matter of. Now, what did you really call for?"

Glad to hear that they were back on their old bantering terms, Jeremy changed the subject to more serious matters. "Does this line have ears?"

"No."

"Good. I just talked to Granton. I'm glad to hear that things went well last evening."

"He gave me Jake's Intelligence Star."

"I know. That was a hell of a thing Jake did."

They were silent for a moment. Then Jeremy said, "Granton told me that he discussed this mole business with you. He wanted me to let you know that they have narrowed the suspects on the Farm shuttle to three men --- Andrew Schulhoffer from Commo, Todd Keswick from Finance and Chet Rakeland from Technical Services. Any of them ever come in contact with you?"

There was more silence on the line as Alanna mentally ran through the names.

"No, I don't believe I've ever had anything to do with any of them. Have you?"

"Unfortunately, yes. Rakeland."

"How'd that come about?"

"He set up some bugging devices for me in a safe house in Turkey where I was meeting an agent I was hoping to turn."

"That's not enough to hang the man."

"I realize that. They're still keeping an eye on the others as well. But, I saw someone talking to one of the ground crew. Security is trying to locate the crewman, and see if he can pick the guy out of a group of photos."

"What do you think about that nuke coming out of the Ukraine?"

"Possible," Jeremy said, thinking, happily, how like old times this conversation sounded. "But, if it's coming from them, I'd wager it's a black market item."

"Any chance they'll put us out of a job, and nail it in country?"

"I doubt it, but we'll know better Monday when we establish whether they've got one missing or not."

"Tell me about Aiden Doyle, Jeremy."

"What's to tell, Alanna? He's got the cover to do backup and he's good," Jeremy replied, without fanfare.

"Oooo, that's an impressive sales pitch. I thought he was your idea?"

"He is."

"Really! Well, I would have never guessed it by your enthusiastic appraisal of his capabilities," she said, intrigued by Jeremy's reticence to elaborate on the new man. "I hear he spent a lot of time in the Orient, and that he can out Kung Fu and out horse me. I'd say that those are pretty impressive credentials. He must have stolen your favorite geisha girl that you have such a modest opinion of him."

"It's a long story, Alanna. The Agency would refuse my expense voucher if I took the time to tell it to you over the phone. But I could arrange a private briefing, if you're that interested in the subject," Jeremy replied, getting a dig of his own in. "Suffice to say, he's the right man for the job."

"Don't trouble yourself, I'll get the story from him, personally. He's probably a more reliable source on the subject than you are anyway," she teased. This kind of harmless exchange had been part of their repertoire for a long time. It was one thing that made the sometimes unbearable strain of their job bearable.

"Is he a viable commodity as yet?"

"He'll show."

"What makes you so sure?"

"You're the bait."

* * *

Chet Rakeland threaded his way through the desks in the CIA's Technical Service Division until he reached his. He set his briefcase down, and thumbed through his mail. As he was about to pick up his phone to report in to his supervisor, one of the secretaries from personnel stopped by his desk.

"Hi, Chet," she said, as she sat a hip sexily on the front corner of the desk.

"Lila." he said, giving her his best foxy smile. "How's it going?"

"I thought maybe you'd give me a call this weekend," she said, with a sexy pout.

"I couldn't, sweetheart. Duty calls," he replied, indicating the briefcase.

"Uh, Chet," she said, hesitantly and looked around to see if anyone was listening.

"What, sweetheart," he said, only half paying attention to her as he opened his briefcase, and searched through it for the file containing his report on the assignment he'd just completed.

"Chet, are you in some kind of trouble?" She said, again looking to see if she had been overheard.

"What makes you think that, sweetheart?" He said, while keeping his attention on the paperwork in his briefcase. But now, he was all ears to what she had to say.

"Chet," she said, nervously, "Security has pulled your file."

"Hey, not to worry, dear. When you have my kind of job," he said, blowing off the announcement, "they run checks on you all the time."

Which was true, but he had an unsettling feeling that this security check was not routine.

"Well, I just thought you should know, Chet," she said, getting up and preparing to leave as she noticed his supervisor approaching. "I gotta run. Call me?"

"Yah, I will," he said, without feeling.

Chapter 15

"I think Saratoga is my favorite sale," Julie said as she sat scrunched down, resting in the front seat of Alanna's Volvo, her bare feet propped up on the dash. She had just picked Alanna up at the airport in Albany, and had turned the driving chores over to her.

"Keeneland is still my favorite sale," Alanna reflected on her own preference, as she headed the car north from Albany airport on I-87 towards Saratoga Springs. "But I love everything about Saratoga — the racing, polo, champagne picnics on the lake, creme brulee at Mrs. Londons — mmmm . . .

"I second the mmmm — heavenly creme brulee. God, just the thought of it makes my mouth water," Julie said, sitting up in the seat as they approached their exit.

As the Volvo made the wide arching turn off I-87 onto 9-N, Alanna thought about how lucky she was to be a part of the wonderful world of the horse -- lucky to be able to experience the beauty and romance of the places associated with it.

Saratoga was a town created by history and legend, filled with a mystic, old-fashioned charm and elegance. It was a place, where thousands of people came each August to escape the mid-summer heat of mid-town Manhattan, to enjoy the cool air of the Adirondack Mountains of upstate New York. Joining them for the first two weeks of this ritualistic exodus were the international buyers and sellers of the Thoroughbred horse.

Whatever consequences her decision to rejoin the Agency might bring were forgotten as she turned onto Union Avenue and drove past historic Saratoga Race Track

"Listen to that, Julie," she said, as she ran her window down, and the joyous sound of race fans cheering their favorite horse home filled their ears. It was opening day, and the place was packed.

Alanna turned onto East Avenue, and then left at George Street, where she managed to find a parking spot. Julie took her suitcase from the car and went to check on their stall location, while Alanna stopped at the sales office to see whether the paperwork on her yearlings was in order, and to secure seating in the pavilion for herself and her new client, Mark Jergens. Then, they met in front of the snack bar and got a cold drink.

"What time are the horses due in?" Alanna asked, as she made a note on her reminder pad to get some potted mums for decoration around their stable area.

"Five in the morning," Julie replied, finishing her drink and tossing the cup in the trashcan.

"Do you want a ride to your rooming house?" Alanna offered.

"No, thanks." Julie said, "I told our stable crew I'd meet them here and we'd go to dinner."

Alanna finished her drink, and disposed of her cup, then asked, "You have my phone number in case you need me, and enough money for expenses?"

"Sure do." Julie replied, picking her suitcase up off the ground.

"Fine, then I'll see you at 4:30. Have a nice evening," Alanna said.

She left the sales grounds through the chain link gate, then drove to the house on Salem Ave, which she rented each year for the month of August. She let herself in with the key that Mrs. O'Boyle, the owner, had left for her at the sales office. After unpacking, she changed into a sundress, low-heeled pumps and a broad brimmed, straw hat and drove to the track.

Alanna parked in the horseman's lot, and, showing her owner's license, was admitted through the gate and into the paddock area. The horses for the next race were being led around the walking paths under the trees. She went from tree to tree examining each entry, comparing the physical horse to the pedigree listed under the name in the program.

"Pick me a winner," a voice from behind her requested.

"You should be the one giving me the advice, Mr. Brown," she replied, without turning around, having recognized the voice of her friend, John Brown, the handicapper for the New York Post.

"I've been watching for you all afternoon. Did you just get in?" he asked, as he came and stood alongside her, and pointed with his program to a horse circling the tree to their right. "The bay over there, number six, Alliance, has been training gangbusters. He's coming off a layoff, but he loves this track and his trainer's a genius at getting a horse right just off works."

"I got in about an hour ago," she said, as she checked the horse out in her program. "Is he worth a bet?"

"He'll probably go off at 8 to 1. I'd say he's worth a small wager," he said, as he acknowledged, with a wave, a greeting from one of the owners watching his horse being led around under an adjacent tree.

159

"Would you be interested in having dinner with me and the Silvermans at The Wishing Well tonight?"

"Yes, I would, John. How are the Silvermans?"

"They're great, and they're looking forward to seeing you." He looked anxiously in the direction of the main paddock, and said, "I've got to run. I see the owner of the favorite for the stakes race today. I need to ask him a few questions for an article I'm working on. Are you still on Salem Ave.?"

"I am."

"Great. Then, I'll pick you up about eight. Okay?"

"That will be fine. See you then," she said, as he started in the direction of his quarry.

"Oh," he stopped and turned to her, adding, "If you feel like coming up to the press box, and watching the steeplechase race from the roof, I'll be back up there in about 20 minutes."

"Thanks, but I'll just watch it from my box. See you at eight," she said, to his now departing figure.

"You have so many admirers, Alanna, a man is hard-pressed to keep track of them all." Francois voice came out of the throng of voices surrounding her.

He had come up behind her without her noticing him.

"I hear he has already managed to gain the pleasure of your company for the evening," he added, with a look that conveyed disappointment.

"Francois," she said, extending her hand and offering her cheek for a kiss.

He took her hand, and they exchanged kisses on both cheeks, after which he did not relinquish her hand.

"I had no idea you'd be in Saratoga so soon," she said, although she had full knowledge of Francois' whereabouts via the men surveiling him. "Julie told me that your yearlings are doing beautifully at the farm. Did you have a chance to see them before you left Lexington?"

Still holding her hand, he said. "Yes, I did see them, and they looked very well. Your manager gave me a tour of the farm. You have done wonders with that farm since you've been there, Alanna. I had been a guest of the previous owner, and know he had let it fall into disrepair. It will make a very elegant stallion facility, if you are prepared to accept my deal.

"Why don't you come to my box?" Francois said, more as an order than a request. "You can meet one of my associates. A gentlemen, who may become a part of the syndicate I am putting together to race this colt. You can help me sell him on the virtues of coming into our little group."

"You forget, Francois," Alanna said, taking her hand from his, and in a tone that indicated ordering her to do anything would not get the desired response, "that I'm not sure, as yet, that I want to be a part of this enterprise. However, if you like, I will come to your box and meet the gentleman."

Francois took the hint, writing her independent attitude off to her Americanism. He said, apologetically, "Forgive me, Alanna, if I was overbearing, sometimes I forget that I do not command all that I see. Please, do come and meet him."

They walked to the grandstand, and took the elevator up to the level on which Francois' box was located. As they approached the box, Alanna could make out the figure of a tall, broad-shouldered man in a dark business suit, looking through binoculars at the horses charging down the home stretch.

They entered the box just as the horses crossed the finish line. The man lowered his glasses and turned to the face them, his hard, coal black eyes immediately settling on Alanna. Being no stranger to the Arabs' custom of women not looking men in the eye did not prevent Alanna from doing just that -- cold stare for cold stare.

"Hakeem, may I present Alanna Reynolds, the breeder of the colt we have been discussing." Francois carried out the introductions, noting the look Hakeem gave the woman and the manner in which it was returned. "Alanna, this is Hakeem Saleh of Dubai."

"Miss Reynolds." Was all Hakeem said in reply.

Matched with no less coolness by Alanna's greeting.

"Mr. Saleh."

"Alanna, why don't you sit here," Francois said, holding the back of a chair, the seating arrangement placing Francois between the two of them.

"Thank you, Francois," she said, accepting the seat, while never taking her eyes from those of Hakeem's.

Suddenly, the cold, black eyes that were set in a face carved of granite and framed with thick, wiry black hair and full beard relinquished their hard stare, and Hakeem said, "I have heard a great deal about you from Francois, Miss Reynolds. He holds you in very high regard."

"This must be your first venture into the horse business, Mr. Saleh," she replied, ignoring the compliment. He did not fit the mold of the typical royalty of Dubai. "I don't recall seeing you with the regular contingent from Dubai."

"We travel in different circles. You seem to be very observant of our customs," he said, and it was obvious he was trying to evaluate her as well.

"Your culture is of great interest to me, and your people do me the honor of buying my yearlings. Their patronage is greatly appreciated."

"From what Francois tells me about the quality of your horses, they are very wise to do so," he replied, with a smile that did not diminish his cold stare.

From behind Alanna and several boxes to her right, a man aimed his binoculars, that were a cover for a camera equipped with a telephoto lens, at the horses that were entering the track for the feature race. Nonchalantly, he swept the area of the grandstand that contained Francois' box. Holding his finger on the shutter release, he let the automatic film advance do its work, as he captured the area on film.

Francois had remained silent during the exchange between Hakeem and Alanna. He observed how, though Hakeem's appearance and manner intimidated most people, as was Hakeem's intent, his demeanor did not seem to affect Alanna in the least. An interesting reaction on her part, he thought.

Alanna stayed in Francois' box until the feature race was run. Then she left, but not before agreeing to meet with Francois for lunch the next day to discuss further the deal on the colt.

"I think you are interested in more than the lady's horses, Francois," Hakeem said, once Alanna had retreated out of hearing distance.

"I find Alanna very refreshing, Hakeem. She reminds me of a filly I had when I was young. She was a beautiful filly, elegant and full of fight -- full of life. I loved her more than any other horse I ever had, because she was always a challenge to me. A man must have a challenge to stay young, stay sharp, do you not agree Hakeem?"

"If you say so, Francois, however, you may want to reconsider bringing her into the group?"

"And why would I want to do that?"

"A feisty horse is a challenge, Francois. A feisty woman is trouble."

* * *

The Falcon 900-B pulled into the parking area reserved for it at Albany airport. Jeremy was in the passenger compartment, gathering his papers together, when Rice came back with word that Granton was on the phone.

"Granton, is there something wrong?" Jeremy said, as he picked up the receiver.

"I hope not. Yesterday, one of the men I sent to do surveillance on Francois while you were in Arizona got a picture of Alanna with Francois and another man. Counter Intelligence identified the man as Hakeem Saleh."

"Christ," Jeremy replied. "Isn't he on the State Department's Watch List? How'd he get into the country?"

"I don't know, another foul-up at State, I guess. We're checking it out now. We have to warn off INS and the FBI. If, they pick him up they'll blow this operation. The Presidential Finding we have for this operation will insure that they cooperate. Have you ever had any contact with him?"

"No, I just know of his handy work, like blowing up airliners and Marine barracks," Jeremy replied. "I'll be seeing Alanna shortly, and I'll pass the word about Hakeem on to her."

"Fine. Did Security get you Jake's briefcase?"

"Yes, they did."

"Then, that's all for now," Granton said, pausing for a moment to make sure he hadn't forgotten anything. "Oh, by the way, I got Doyle. He'll meet you up there."

"Have any trouble hiring him on?"

"Initially, but when he found out who he'd be working with, he signed right up for the job."

"He's a bastard," Jeremy said, with a laugh.

"You won't get any argument on that appraisal from me, but remember, he's our bastard."

"Right. Thanks for getting him for me. I'll get back to you later," Jeremy said.

* * *

The Saratoga Yearling Sale is a small, very select sale, similar to the Keeneland Summer Sale. The stable area, unlike Keeneland's, is small, as well as unique, blending well with the rest of the town's Victorian architecture. The sales pavilion is the only concession to modern design.

The pavilion, like Keeneland's, is round, but its exterior walls are of plate glass. Traditionally, the townspeople gather outside on the evenings of the sale, and watch the proceedings from behind these glass walls. The blue bloods of society, business, entertainment and politics, as well as horseflesh, are on display for all to see.

Alanna thought about the physical toll this sale took on its participants. It was the only sale that required the sellers to have the stable area mucked out by 5:30 a.m. This meant it was sometimes necessary to rise as early as 4 a.m., as Alanna had this morning, or even earlier in the case of very large consignments, and often continue late into the night entertaining clients. She was convinced that it was a good thing it wasn't necessary to carry on this routine for any length of time because a steady diet of it would make a person old in a hurry.

Alanna had made arrangements to meet Jeremy at her trainer's barn on the Oklahoma side of Saratoga Race Track.

At 7 a.m., she left instruction with Julie, stopped by the snack bar for an orange juice, and crossed East Avenue to the stable gate entrance. The guard at the gate checked her owner's badge, which allowed her access to the track. He wished her a good morning and she headed on down to barn 58.

"Good morning there, lady." Her trainer, Allen Miles, greeted her from aboard his horse. "Your yearlings get in all right?"

"They did. Thank God," Alanna replied, as she came up to the horse and patted him on the neck. "I'm supposed to meet my new client, Mark Jergens, here this morning. Have you seen him?"

"Yeah, he got here a few minutes ago. Right now, he's over there by the training track." Miles pointed in the direction of a figure that was barely visible in the early morning fog that shrouded the area.

"How long will it be before my colt goes, Allen?"

"I want to work him this morning, so I'd like to wait until this fog lifts some. It'll probably be another hour," he replied. "If you and your client would like to get some breakfast, I'll hold him until you get back."

"Sounds good." She appreciated his thoughtfulness. "We'll be back in an hour."

"Take your time," he said, as he headed to the track with two of his charges following behind him.

Alanna had four horses in training with Allen, but only one was entirely hers, and she stopped by his stall on the way to the track. The mahogany bay colt was tied to the back of his stall, his groom rubbing him vigorously.

"Hello, handsome," she said sticking her head in the door. Recognizing her voice, the colt cocked his head sideways and gave her welcoming whinny.

"Ah, you are too kind, senorita. It has been a long time since anyone has called me handsome," Pablo, the colt's groom, said as he peered from under the colt's neck, a mischievous grin on his face.

"You two suit each other well, Pablo." She laughed at the old man's comment. "I'm not sure which of you is the orneriest. How's he doing? Alan tells me he's going to work this morning."

"He will blow them all off the track, senorita," Pablo reassured her. Coming around to the back of the colt, he patted him firmly on his muscular rump. "With all this power, all they're going to see is his tail."

"You've taken good care of him, Paublo, he looks great. I'm going to breakfast with a client, but I'll be back in time to see him work."

"Si, senorita, he'll be ready when you get here."

* * *

The fog still lay heavy over the training track. The horses appeared out of the mist like ghostly visions, their arrival foretold by the sound of pounding hooves and heavy breathing.

"Good morning," Alanna said, brightly, as she approached Jeremy across the dew-laden grass.

Jeremy turned and rested his back against the track railing. He looked very preppy, dressed in khaki trousers, blue and white striped, button down shirt, and a navy, cotton, crew neck sweater.

"You're awfully cheerful for this early in the morning," he said, glad to be back in her company and have her reaction be the same. "It's too damn early for anyone in his right mind to be up. We really could have met later."

"Complaints, complaints! Just remember, Mr. Jergens, some of us really live our cover, while others just play at it," she teased, as she moved next to him and set her elbows on the rail.

"This is like a moment out of time," Jeremy said, turning and leaning his elbows on the rail alongside her. "This is a beautiful place."

"Yes, it is." And she took in a deep breath of the clear morning air. "My trainer tells me that my colt will not be going to the track for another hour. There's a little restaurant across the street. Let's walk over and get some breakfast."

"Better yet, let's take my car. I have something for you." He pointed in the direction of the black BMW convertible.

"If you insist." She moved toward the passenger side of the car parked on the grass behind them. "Didn't you rent one of these in Lexington?"

"As a matter of fact I did, I kind of fell in love with the thing. Besides, it bugs the hell out of Granton to see it on my expense report. Actually, this one came from Technical Services."

Jeremy followed behind her, opening the door and helping her in. "Thank you, Mr. Jergens you are so gallant. Is this a part of the cover or has your alter ego transformed you into a gentleman."

"Hey, I told you, I'm a changed man," he said, feigning hurt feelings, then he added, "Actually, Francois' secretary has been watching us from that shedrow, otherwise I'd have let you get the door yourself."

Jeremy was a happy man this morning, and the smile his little joke brought to Alanna's face made him even happier. Here he was, in this beautiful place, doing the work he loved, with the woman he loved.

He slapped the trunk of the car as he went behind it, and said in a resounding, joyous voice, to no one in particular, "Yes!"

"What was that all about?" She asked, as he got behind the wheel.

"Youthful exuberance!"

"At your age?"

"I have a young heart," he said, and reaching over the backseat, he picked up a tattered old briefcase and handed it to her. "I also have a present for you."

She recognized Jake's briefcase immediately. In the meantime, Jeremy headed out of the stable area, and did a quick jog around the corner to the parking area of the restaurant.

"Where did it come from?" She asked, as her fingers lightly traced its edges.

"The Paris station shipped it back along with Jake's other belongings."

Alanna opened the case with a key she had on her key chain. Initially, there appeared to be only a letter in it. She placed the letter on the dash. Then, taking a small penknife from the hip pocket of her jeans, she gently slid the knife down one side of the briefcase and lifted up its false bottom. Set in the foam padding, where the indention made by a second gun was very evident, was one of the two guns Jake carried.

"Annabelle, my you've aged well, lady. Where are you Gloria?" she said, as she searched under the foam for the 9mm Beretta, his other weapon of choice. Not finding it there, she freed Jake's Walther PPKS from its snug compartment in the case's bottom. As she checked to make sure it wasn't loaded, she added. "You know, Jeremy, this is the first gun I ever fired. I wonder where the other one is. Do you know if it was on him when he died?"

"I couldn't tell you. I didn't know what was in the case and the guy who gave it to me didn't offer any explanation. A little eccentric of Jake to name his guns, don't you think?" Jeremy said, shaking his head at a peculiarity he did not know his friend and mentor had.

The case also contained extra magazines and two custom-made silencers, one for each of the guns.

"Jake must have been carrying the Beretta the day he was killed. Yet, it seems odd that he would have been, because, when he was undercover, he almost always carried the Walther. And why would he not have taken the silencer and the extra magazine for the Beretta with him?" she wondered out loud, as she put the Walther back in the case and then set the case on the floor between her feet. "Since he took time to include a letter in the case, he must have packed it ahead of time."

She retrieved the letter from the dash, opened it and read:

Dear Alanna,

A week ago, I discovered that my cover might have been blown. I immediately advised headquarters of my suspicions, and they gave me permission to return to Washington, but my intentions are to stay on this job as long as possible.

The fact that you are reading this letter means that I misjudged how close to uncovering me they were, and have gone on to my just reward, whatever that may be.

It is also a pretty good bet that the Agency has asked you back on my recommendation. I did so in a letter I sent to Granton yesterday. It is with great disappointment that I find it necessary to do so. Should you accept their invitation, I am enclosing some information that I think is vital to your succeeding. This mission is doubly dangerous, because somebody knows who we are, all of us, I think.

I truly wish I was not convinced that you are the only one that can pull this off, and I hope that by putting you in harm's way I haven't condemned you to the hereafter.

Be careful my dearest one, and please <u>remember,</u> "take care of the girls and they'll take care of you." In my heart, you are the daughter I never had. I have never loved anyone more. I am with you forever in spirit.

God's speed,
Jake

Alanna scanned the enclosed information. Jeremy started to say something, but she hushed him with a gesture of her hand, and quickly finished reading. He had been reading over her shoulder and noticed that the print was getting fainter. Before he could finish, the print had completely disappeared leaving three unmarred, blank white pages in Alanna's hands.

"What the hell!" He said.

"It's magician's paper made in Austria," Alanna explained. "You write your message, after the ink is dry, you seal the letter in this special envelope. When the pages are exposed to the air again, the ink breaks down and the print disappears.

"The words are gone," She said, wadding up the now blank sheets, "gone forever, like their author."

Then in silence she thought about what she had just read. While all of what Jake said in the letter was important, his words "remember, take care of the girls and they will take care of you", became indelibly etched in her memory. Because they begged the question, if the impeccably thorough Jake had packed this case, why would he use the plural "girls", if he knowingly only meant for her to have the one gun?

Without verbalizing her thoughts, she put the briefcase back on the rear seat, and said, "I'll fill you in later, if you missed anything. Now, let's eat."

* * *

They sat across from one another, waiting for breakfast to be served. Alanna sipped her coffee and watched Jeremy play with his spoon. Turning it end to end, tapping the table with each turn.

Alanna found Jeremy handsome in a clean cut, outdoorsy way. The kind of man the ads portrayed dressed in corduroy trousers and fisherman's knit sweater, sitting in front of a roaring fireplace in some log cabin in the Rockies, his faithful golden retriever lying at his feet. He had a whale of a personality, a real charmer. The ladies loved him. Men liked and respected him. He was honest, dependable, loyal to a fault, and when you got beyond his chauvinistic facade, warm and caring.

Alanna had a great deal of admiration for Jeremy. Before they had started working as a team, he'd had one of the most difficult jobs in the Agency. Clever and resourceful, he was one of the best at working behind enemy lines. His specialty was bringing out those people the opposition would have rather kept: defectors, sleepers, and other agents whose cover had been blown. Dangerous work. He'd had a knack for it.

It was rumored, and believed, among the Crown Jewels, that Jeremy knew the Russian border better than the Russians and that the same was true for the rest of the former communist bloc nations.

"Solved any great world crisis yet?" Alanna said, deciding to interrupt his daydreaming.

He put down the spoon, but let his fingers play over it. Raising his eyes to meet hers, he said, "Alanna, the man I'm bringing in, well..."

"Has fangs and sleeps in a coffin! For Pete's sake, spit it out!" She urged him.

"He and I don't get along very well."

"Now, there's a first! Someone you don't get along with. See, I knew he'd stolen your favorite geisha!"

"Believe me, it's not an operational problem," Jeremy reassured her. "And, he's good, Alanna. He's what you'll need, if I lose my effectiveness, or worse."

"You're not going to lose your effectiveness, or worse..."

Alanna cut her statement short as the waitress appeared with their breakfast.

"Sorry it took so long, folks," she said, apologetically, with a big bright smile. "The chickens must have slept in this morning."

"I don't blame them," Jeremy said, returning her smile with one of his own. "I wish I could have too."

The waitress nodded in agreement, and then headed over to the table by the window to take an order.

"From the remarks Granton made, it sounds like he has an attitude problem," Alanna said, resuming the conversation between bites of breakfast.

"If Dar were alive, he could maybe explain him to both of us. He knew him well. They pulled off some real hair-raisers together. Dar certainly didn't have a problem getting along with him."

"When do I get to meet him?"

"He'll be here sometime later today. I'll arrange for the two of you to meet."

"Does he know about me?"

"Yes. It's safe to say that's the only reason he's in on this deal."

"Why should I be a factor in his decision?"

"A promise he made to Dar, that if you ever needed his help, he couldn't refuse to help you."

"And you knew about this promise?"

"Dar made it a point to tell me. Even from the grave he looks after you." Jeremy picked up the check, and said, "Come on. Let's go."

"I'm not sure I'm comfortable with this," she said, as she went out the door.

"I was sure you wouldn't be, but give him a try. If you don't like him, you can always do to him what you tried to do to me in your office, but stay on your feet and away from coffee tables."

They looked at each other and laughed.

* * *

The stable guard waved the BMW on through the gate.

"Looks like your ardent admirer has returned with a backup," Jeremy said, the sarcasm in his voice evident.

"Jealous?" Alanna teased.

"Should I be?" He asked.

"Don't waste your energy."

"Good, I won't."

Parked in front of Alanna's trainer's barn was Francois' limousine. He was leaning against its fender, discussing data from The Daily Racing Form with Hakeem. He looked up as he heard the car approach.

"I'll just drop you off," Jeremy said, as he stopped at the far end of the barn. "There's no sense raising his blood pressure."

Alanna started to get out of the car, but he took hold of her arm. "Alanna, I almost forgot. One of our people got a picture of that Arab with Francois. Watch your step around him. His name is Hakeem Saleh and he's on State's Watch List. Unfortunately, somebody at State was asleep on watch. He's here illegally."

"I figured as much. He's passing himself off as a wealthy Arab from Dubai, but I doubt he's even seen the country," she said, as she slid her arm through his hand, letting her hand stop for just a moment in his before completely liberating it. He squeezed it gently, and she said, "I'll get the briefcase from you later. Bye, I've got to go."

Jeremy didn't wait for her to reach the other men. Instead, he turned the car around and headed out the gate. As he did, he kept watch in his rear view mirror.

As he watched her walk over to Francois and Hakeem, he thought how different this assignment must feel to Alanna. In the past, she had no exposure whatsoever to the opposition in the formative stages of an operation. Jake, Dar or he did any setting up. It was her job, once the objective was established, to go in, execute the operation, and get out without the opposition knowing it had been had.

It took guts, courage and real talent to get in and out of the target area without a trace. Alanna was so good at it that Jeremy often thought she had the power to make herself invisible. Some of the target areas she'd infiltrated had demanded almost that level of stealth. On the rare occasion that things didn't go as planned, and she had to meet the opposition on their field of play, she was usually able to extricate herself from the situation with a minimum of fuss.

Being a seductress had never been in her job description, he and Dar and Jake had seen to that. Jeremy thought that if one could see into the hereafter, Dar was probably giving Jake a good pounding for putting their girl in that position.

The fact that playing the seductress was a necessary part of this assignment, and a strictly new element in her repertoire, worried Jeremy. As a rule, the seductress role was best played by a less independent minded woman -- a woman who didn't mind kissing up to the opposition, Alanna's tolerance for the condescending male bordered on nonexistent. So far, she was carrying off the duplicity well. Maybe, maturing a little had elevated her forbearance to an acceptable level, at least enough to allow her to maintain this pretext to the end. He hoped so.

* * *

"Good morning, Alanna," Francois said, as she came up to them. "I see Mr. Jergens is still attempting to gain entrance to the equine industry?"

"He's still in the market for a classically bred colt," Alanna replied, in a friendly tone that completely ignored the sarcasm in his voice.

"Good morning, Mr. Saleh." She diverted the conversation to the other man.

"Good morning to you, Miss Reynolds," Hakeem said. The ignoring of Francois' innuendo by Alanna did not escape his observation.

Out of the corner of her eye, she saw her colt emerge from beneath the shedrow.

"Would you gentlemen like to see my 2-year-old colt work?" She said to further distract Francois thoughts from Jeremy.

"Which colt is this, Alanna?" Francois' interest was now piqued.

"He's a Sun Star colt out of my good mare, Carina." She said, pleased to see her ploy had worked, and that Francois had returned to a

171

more congenial mood. "I had to hold him out of last year's summer yearling sale because he ran a high fever right before the sale. He didn't recover from the aftereffects of the fever until December, so I decided to keep him.

"This will be his first official work, and I'm as nervous as a three-legged cat in a kennel full of Dobermans."

"An interesting, but unenviable position for either you, or the cat to be in, is it not, Miss Reynolds?" Hakeem said, seeming to be taking an ever-increasing interest in the woman.

"Come. Let us see what he can do." Francois ignored Hakeem's remark and drew Alanna away before she had a chance to respond.

They stood along the rail as the colt and his stablemate took to the track. The two young horses jogged along the outer rail, past the three observers and Alanna's trainer, who had joined them, and around to the back of the track.

Because it was their first work, both colts had jockeys mounted on them, in place of their regular exercise rider. When the jockeys reached the appropriate spot on the far side of the track, they turned their mounts in the opposite direction, and allowed them to gallop off with the flow of traffic. They maintained a steady gallop, dropping lower and lower onto the track until they were right along the inner rail. As they reached the spot they were to work from, the jockeys dropped low onto their mounts' necks, and the colts began to accelerate.

New to this move, they were a little slow off the mark, but there was no question which one had the talent. At first Alanna's colt stayed alongside his buddy, then his rider chirped to him. Daylight appeared quickly between the two colts, as Alanna's colt kicked in the afterburners, and drew away effortlessly from his stablemate. With each powerful stride, he increased his lead, crossing the finish line ten lengths in front of the other colt.

"You've got yourself a good one, lady," her trainer said, as he held out the stop- watch with its impressive evidence for Alanna to see.

Her face lit up. "Fantastic!" she said, with delight.

Francois, who had also noted the exceptional time of the work, said, "That was very impressive, Alanna. Do you have any partners in this colt?"

"I'm not sure anyone has the kind of money it would take to own a piece of him, Francois."

Not easily dissuaded, Francois said, "Well, we'll see. We can discuss it at lunch this afternoon, if we still have a date?"

"I'm flattered that you're so interested in the colt, Francois. Lunch is still on, but only if we can make it a short one. We'll be busy showing the yearlings today, and I need to be at the sales grounds as much as possible. Care to give me a lift there?"

"You're always in such a hurry, Alanna, but we can make it a short lunch," Francois admonished her gently, "and, yes, I would be happy to give you a lift."

Francois' limousine stopped at the gate nearest her stabling area. As Alanna was about to leave, he said. "I will see you at noon. Tonight, I must dine with Hakeem, as we have business to discuss, but I hope you will do me the honor of having dinner with me tomorrow night?"

"Yes, tomorrow would be fine," she said, and turning to Hakeem added. "I hope you are enjoying your stay in Saratoga, Hakeem. Will you be staying for the sale?"

"No, I will be departing soon." His flat, cold eyes again betrayed the smile on his lips.

"Then, it has been a pleasure meeting you," Her comment and her smile reflecting a warmth she didn't feel.

"Have a good sale, Miss Reynolds, and if Allah sees fit to let it be, we shall meet again," he said, without a change in his demeanor.

"Have a pleasant trip." To hell, she thought.

As she started to exit the back of the limo, Francois caught her elbow and drew her back into the car.

"Before you go, Alanna," Francois said, "have you considered my invitation to the charity ball on Friday?"

"I have, Francois," she replied, applying a little charm to her acceptance. "I would love to attend the ball with you. Thank you for inviting me. Now, I really do have to run. You gentlemen have a nice day."

* * *

If Alanna thought her diversion had taken Francois' mind off of Mark Jergens, his first action, as he entered the large country house he'd rented on Saratoga Lake, proved her wrong.

"Have you come up with anything new on Mark Jergens, Phillip," Francois asked his secretary as he came through the front door and headed for his temporary headquarters set up in its library."Sir, the men I sent to Phoenix have verified that Mr. Jergens does indeed own a resort hotel. In fact he returned there after the Keeneland sale." Phillip relayed the information his further investigation had netted.

It worried Phillip, who had been employed by Francois for the better part of 25 years, and was privy to even the most sensitive information, that Francois' energies, which should have been focused on the deal with Hizballah, were instead focused on a woman. Even worse was Francois' obsession with the man whom he perceived as a rival for her favors. It was extremely out of character.

"Everything about him checks out positively. The only change in his status at this sale is that he has appointed Miss Reynolds as his agent."

"Are you sure of that, Phillip?" Francois said, and mumbled something else indiscernible on his way into the library. Not waiting for a reply he ordered, "Tell Roberto I want to see him."

"Oui, monsieur." Phillip, who had followed Francois as far as the entrance to the room, turned to carry out the order, but was stopped by Francois.

"Oh, and Phillip, arrange to have two dozen yellow roses sent to Miss Reynolds." He went to his desk and took a small white note card from his briefcase, wrote on it, sealed it and handed it to Phillip. "The sales company will have the address where she is staying. Send one of the men with this note, which I would like sent with the flowers. Do it, immediately."

"Oui, monsieur," Phillip said, and went off to carry out both orders, closing the library door quietly behind him.

The door had barely shut, when there was a knock at it.

"Come in,"

"What can I do for you, monsieur?" Roberto said, as he entered the room, and came before the desk at which Francois had taken a seat.

"Roberto, I would like you to take care of something for me this evening."

"Of course, monsieur?"

* * *

Francois got up and walked to the window, which had a splendid view across an expansive lawn to the mountains.

Francois remembered his father saying that the Italians were probably the only people more irrational then the French when it came to being in love. The operative word here was love. He had lusted after many a beautiful woman, but had never loved one. Alanna was the kind of woman you loved and respected, not lusted after

This situation that had developed with Alanna and Mark Jergens disturbed him. He realized how quickly he, Francois, had become

174

obsessed with her. Even to the point of making uncharacteristic decisions based on jealousy, an emotion he had never previously permitted to rule his life. He knew what he was doing, but he couldn't seem to control himself. Since ambition had, up until his falling for Alanna, been his only love, it was easy for Francois to rationalize his actions. He never let anything stand in the way of getting what he wanted, and he had no qualms about using whatever means or methods it took to accomplish that end.

Mark Jergens bothered him in many ways, not the least was what appeared to be a romantic interest in Alanna. But, more importantly, something just did not ring true about the man. Francois' instincts told him so, in spite of what the reports on the man confirmed or denied.

Francois knew that it was not unusual for some newly wealthy American to appear out of nowhere and sink a fortune into the Thoroughbred business. And, it was also not unusual for someone like Jergens to seek out Alanna's help in selecting the right horse. Selling horses to people was what Alanna did for a living, and as highly regarded as she was in the business, a new person would be smart to enlist her aid. Yet, his uneasy feelings about the man persisted. After tonight, Francois thought, I might just be able to concentrate on more pleasurable things.

Chapter 16

Alanna had driven back to her house on Salem Avenue to change clothes. She had just gotten out of the shower when the doorbell rang. Slipping into her robe, she hurried to the door. Through the front window, she could see a black and white truck with the name of a florist emblazoned on its side. At the door was a young man holding a basket of bright yellow roses.

"Good morning," he said as she opened the door. "These are for Miss Alanna Reynolds."

"Thank you," she said, accepting them.

Alanna closed the door and carried the flowers into the living room where she placed them on the table next to the sofa. She removed the card and read its message.

Dearest Alanna,
   The sun's brilliance is but that of a distant star in your presence.
Love,
Francois

   Too bad you're not a nice man, Francois, she thought.

* * *

The sales grounds were a hive of activity when Alanna finally returned. She saw a car pulling out of a space near her stalls, and hurried to pull into it. She picked her straw hat and purse off the seat next to her and pressed a button on the underside of the steering column, activating the car's sophisticated alarm system.

Skip Morrison, an old Agency friend whose specialty was beefing up Technical Services' motor pool, had added a few optional extras to Alanna's car not found on Volvo dealers' lists -- things like improved handling, bullet proof windows and body, undercoating protection for land mines, grenades and the like. He had also replaced the original tires with steel reinforced ones, and added little goodies like the ability to produce an oil slick or smoke screen, fire tear gas, and should anyone decide to break into her Volvo, a burglar system that would deliver 6000 volts of discouragement. She thought, with amusement, that maybe it was a little overkill for a horse breeder, but Skip did not believe in half measures where security was concerned.

176

Alanna stopped to speak to one of the sale's directors before passing through the pedestrian turnstile that led into the stable area, which was bustled with people showing and inspecting yearlings. She noticed that the gentleman inspecting one of her yearlings was her old friend from Ireland, Paddy Ryan.

He saw her approaching, and turned his attention away from the yearling to her. "And here I thought you were going to sleep in all day. How's my best girl?" He said, greeting her with a warm embrace that knocked the straw hat from her head.

"I had to make a quick trip back to the house," she said, as she returned his embrace with equal enthusiasm, ignoring the fallen hat. "It's so good to see you, Paddy! Where's Michael?"

"He's around the place somewhere. I'm sure he'll turn up shortly," Paddy replied, and then stood off a bit to take a good look at her. "You're lookin' well, lass."

"Being in Saratoga in August always lifts my spirits, Paddy," Alanna remarked, as she turned to retrieve her hat. She found it in the outstretched hand of a stranger. He had an Irish look about him, but more continental, as indicated by his slicked back, black hair and designer clothes, which were of the latest European fashion. He was tall and slender, but strong. His interesting face -- lean and angular, had a nose that was a trifle long and off center; full, sensuous lips and deep, dark, haunted eyes.

She could hear Paddy introducing him in the background.

"Alanna, I'd like you to meet an old friend of mine, Aiden Doyle."

Alanna controlled her surprise on learning the man's identity, having expected their introduction to come by way of Jeremy.

"His father, Regan, owns Ballydale Stud," Paddy advised. "You remember it. It's the one up the road from me with the big manor house.

"Aiden," Paddy continued the introductions, "this is Alanna Reynolds."

"Yes, as a matter of fact I do remember the place, Paddy. Ballydale is very impressive, Mr. Doyle, and your father is quite the horseman. Welcome to Saratoga, and thank you for retrieving my hat," Alanna replied, while extending her hand to accept the hat.

"It's a pleasure to meet you, Miss Reynolds," Aiden returned the greeting in an accent smoothed to where only the gentle Irish lyricism remained, and with a look on his face that said I know you're surprised to see me, I meant for you to be. "My father would be warmed by your kind words of praise both for himself and Ballydale.

177

"Please," Alanna said, trying to ignore his intense visual appraisal of her, "call me Alanna."

Aiden's concession to a smile was the turning up of the corners of his mouth and the slight rise of his left eyebrow. It was enough to soften his features. "I will, if you drop the Mr. Doyle."

Paddy, satisfied he'd done his civil duty in introducing them, had returned to inspecting her yearling, while Aiden continued the conversation, "I've been looking forward to meeting you, Alanna."

"Is that so, Aiden?" Alanna remarked, as she led the way to her tack room where she deposited the errant hat, her purse and her catalogue on a table.

"Absolutely. Why, ever since Paddy convinced me to come along on this trip, he's done nothing but talk about you," Aiden said, not following her into the room, but remaining at the door, where he leaned his shoulder against the frame. "Unlike most of his ravings, he didn't do you justice."

"Mmm, so it was Paddy that convinced you to come, was it?"

"I guess I can't give him all the credit," he said, the corner of his mouth giving up another sly smile. "A certain promise I made a while back, and my curiosity, finally decided the matter. Like it or not, it would have been impossible for me not to come."

Turning, she responded in a voice that elicited mild skepticism and seriousness, "Curiosity can be a dangerous motive for embarking on an enterprise such as this."

"Life would be very boring without an element of danger in it, don't you agree?" Aiden countered, his smile replaced by the haunted look. "Anyway, how dangerous can meeting you be?"

"You're absolutely right, Aiden. How dangerous can meeting me be?"

The discussion seemed to hang on that remark, but only for a moment as Paddy, putting his arm around Aiden's shoulder and peering into the tackroom, said, "I don't mean to interrupt you two, but the powers to be are pagin' ya over the loudspeaker, lass."

"Are they, Paddy? Thank you for letting me know," Alanna replied, as she exited the tackroom, Aiden abandoning the doorway to let her pass. "I guess I need to see what they want. If you gentlemen will excuse me?"

"Not to worry, lass, you carry on with your work. We've got to be runnin' along anyway, but we'll get together later," he said, pleased to see that Aiden seemed taken with the young woman. "You must have dinner with us soon. Aiden, here's, got some cash burning a big hole in his pocket, and I told him you'd be the one to handle his dealings."

"I appreciate your confidence in me, Paddy. We could have dinner tonight, if that suits you and Aiden."

"It does, indeed," Aiden replied.

"Good, then I'll call you when I'm finished here. Where are you staying?" she asked.

"One of those big old Victorian houses on Union Ave. Here's the number." Paddy wrote it on a piece of paper that he tore out from the back of his sales catalogue and handed to her.

She placed the piece of paper in her pocket and said, "I'll look forward to seeing you all later." Then, giving the men one last parting smile, she hurried away.

Even as she blended into the crowd, Alanna could feel Aiden's penetrating look following her. As she crossed the road and passed through the turnstile that led to the main sales ground and out of Aiden's scrutiny, she was struck by the audacity Aiden had displayed at making contact with her initially instead of Jeremy. But, she thought, the Irishman with "an attitude" was definitely an interesting character.

"So, what do ya think o' the lass?" Paddy asked, as soon as she was out of earshot. He fancied himself a matchmaker of sorts, and felt that both these people, who he cared so much for, had been single far too long.

"I don't know her well enough to say, Paddy." Aiden replied.

"Well, a blind man could see she's quite a looker!"

"Ah, it's whether she appeals to my masculine nature that your wanting to know, is that it?" Aiden said, and consented to relinquish another one of his meager smiles. "Well, I have to say, I prefer tall, long legged lasses."

"You're kidding with me, of course, now aren't you, lad?"

"Now, Paddy, just because I don't fancy the type, doesn't mean I don't like the lady." And he let it rest at that.

* * *

Having taken care of business in the sales' office, Alanna headed back across the street. Paddy and Aiden had already gone, but in their place was a welcome sight.

"Oh, Michael, I'm so glad you're here!"

"You certainly have a way of makin' a man feel special, my girl. How've ya been keepin' yourself?" Michael Quinn rose from the braiding box he had been sitting on and kissed her.

"Just fine, thanks. Let's go to the Spuyten Duyvil and have a drink. I need some information," she said, as she took his hand and led him in the direction of the little tavern that occupied a portion of the sales grounds.

"If information is what ya be lookin' for, woman, a pub's the place to get it out of an Irishman, for sure," he laughed, as he followed after her.

They chose a table set outside on the patio. Since most of the buyers were busy looking at yearlings, the place was empty save for a couple at the far end of the patio.

The waitress brought Michael a Guinness Stout, and Alanna a glass of white wine.

"Tell me about Aiden Doyle."

"Ah, you've met my friend, have ya?" Mark replied. "And he's piqued your interest, has he?"

"Yes, you might say he has "piqued" my interest. Tell me about him, Michael."

"Where would you like me to begin?"

"The beginning."

"Well, he's a tragic story he is, Alanna." Michael began, the joy in his voice gone. "He's the only living child o' Susan and Regan Doyle. His four brothers and two sisters were killed when their home caught fire one Christmas Eve. Aiden was just a babe then. He was the only one of the children saved, because he'd been sick and was sleepin' in his parents' bedroom."

"Hmm, how awful," Alanna remarked sympathetically.

"T'was for sure," Michael agreed, "But that wasn't the worst of it. Aiden's oldest brother, Kevin, was Regan's favorite, when he died the old man just lost it. He ignored Aiden the whole time he was growing up. No matter what Aiden did to please him, it wasn't enough.

"It was a shame," he said, shaking his head, "because Aiden was good at most everything he did, yet he never got a nickel's worth o' credit for it. His mother, God rest her soul, tried to make up for the father's abuse, but the lad's been scarred, nonetheless. And Paddy's, why he's been like an uncle, no, I guess it'd be closer to the truth to say, a father to him. Took him in hand, Paddy did, kept him from goin' bad."

"How'd you get to know him?"

"Aiden and I were schoolmates and best friends at Clongows Wood College, that's the equivalent of your junior and senior high school. We played on the same football team, ah, I mean soccer to you Yanks. Then we both worked at the National Stud in Newmarket for a while. I went on to work for the people I work for now, and he went on to the university.

"He's got degrees in Eastern and Middle Eastern Philosophy from Cambridge, and an MBA in business from Oxford. How's that for fancy degrees?"

"Pretty impressive. What does he do for a living?"

"Consulting or some such thing. He helps you Yanks talk turkey to that Asian and Arab lot. One thing's for sure, the man ain't on the dole. He has enough money to travel the world, but mostly, he stays in that cottage I let you use."

"The one in Arklow?" Alanna interrupted, somewhat surprised by the discovery.

"The very same one."

"How interesting!" Alanna said, mulling over all the coincidences involved in this potential new partnership between Aiden and her. "Any military service?"

"Yeah. I seem to remember him tellin' me," Michael replied, "that he spent a couple years or so in the Royal Marine Commandos.

"Ah, but, here's the best part about him, lass," Michael said, looking both ways, then leaning towards her like he was about to reveal a national secret, "Besides the obvious, that he's good lookin', well educated and comfortably off --- true to the male Irish tradition of marrying late, he's still single."

Michael took another drink of his Guinness, and added. "Now, that's all I know for sure, but, if you'll stick around for awhile, and buy me a couple more o' these brews, there's a whole lot more I can make up."

When she didn't respond, he asked, "So, what do ya think o' the lad?"

"Impressive, but not my type," Alanna answered, and seeing Michael about to protest, added, "but, that doesn't mean he and I can't be friends."

"Friends!" Michael responded, incredulously. "Is that the best ya can do? Lordy, lass, what more could ya be lookin' for in a man."

"I'm not looking for a man, Michael."

"Well, lass, if I can do no better than that at convincing ya to give the bloke a shot, it's just as well I get back to work," he said, cuffing her playfully on the shoulder from across the table, a move, which only served to bring on a big smile, a shaking of the head, and a gentle warning from Alanna.

"Off with ya', ya' woman beater, before I have your hide."

Feigning fear, Michael rose from his chair, his arms raised in a gesture of surrender, "My dear mother didn't raise any foolish lads, I know when to leave."

With that he finished off his drink, toasted her with the empty glass, and left, turning back a few seconds later to give her a quick salute before disappearing around the corner of Barn 3.

She smiled at his departing figure, then took a sip of her wine and let her mind lapse into deep thought, allowing the information Michael had revealed to her to fill in some of the missing gaps in the puzzle that was Aiden Doyle.

"Well did you learn anything that interested you, or that you didn't already know?" Aiden's voice coming from the bar entrance of the Spuyten Duyvil startled her out of her thoughts.

"There are volumes I don't know about you, Aiden, so anything and everything I can learn about you interests me." Alanna, having quickly regained her composure, remarked to the man who had taken the seat across from her. She was hardly surprised that he was able to eavesdrop on them so successfully, since Michael's and her conversation had been anything but clandestine. But, she hoped he'd somehow missed the last, more personal part. "I thought you left with Paddy."

"I begged off viewing any more yearlings." His eyes met and held hers. "I thought maybe, you and I had more important things to see to."

"How right you are," she replied, not letting their eye-to-eye contact diminish any. "But, this is hardly the place, or the time, to discuss such delicate matters."

She concluded her comment with a beautiful smile, a diversion of her line of sight to directly behind him, followed immediately by her saying, "Well, Francois, is it time for lunch already?"

"You were so concerned that we keep it short," Francois said, as he made his way to the table, "that I arrived a bit early."

When he came alongside their table and looked into the face of Alanna's companion, his face registered a look of surprise and delight.

"Aiden Doyle," he said, greeting the other man who had risen to meet him with a warm embrace. "Where have you been keeping yourself?"

"China, mostly," Aiden replied, and indicated the seat next to Alanna, who was surprised at the fact Aiden and Francois were so well acquainted. "Join us and let me buy you a drink."

Francois looked to Alanna, and said, "A quick one maybe, if Alanna can spare the time."

Putting her arm on the back of the neighboring chair, indicating that he should take a seat beside her, she said, "Certainly, Francois, a quick drink won't disrupt my schedule."

"This is quite a surprise seeing you here, Aiden." Francois said, as he moved behind Alanna and settled into his seat. "China, you say! What takes you there?"

"Consulting, Francois," Aiden replied, as he signaled for the waitress. "I assist some major U.S. and European companies in their dealings with mostly Asian governments."

"Very good!" Francois remarked, genuinely impressed. "And, you are here because....?"

"I miss the horse business," Aiden explained. "So, I thought I'd get myself a horse or two to race. Paddy... You know, Paddy Ryan?"

"Very well." Francois replied. "Your father introduced me to him years ago, when we first started doing business on a regular basis."

"Well, Paddy put me on to Alanna." Aiden continued, with only a brief look over at Alanna to see her reaction, which appeared to be one of mild interest. And he gave her a nod and a smile. "Since I plan to race on the continent, and since she's bred so many horses to win there, Paddy felt that she was the one to see that I got the right horse."

The waitress took their orders, Alanna refraining from a refill of her wine, and they resumed their conversation.

"That's very interesting, and Paddy is certainly right about Alanna," Francois said, patting her hand that was resting on the table. Then, returning to Aiden's business, he said, "Asia is an area into which I have been thinking of expanding my interests. I may have use of your services, Aiden."

"Well, then, let me give you my card," Aiden said, reaching into the breast pocket of his linen sport coat and removing a leather business card holder. Selecting one of the cards, he passed it over the table to Francois. Selecting a second one and handing it to Alanna, he added, "Perhaps, I should give you one too, Alanna, after all, if we're going to do business, you'll need to know where to reach me."

While the waitress served the drinks, and Aiden and Francois discussed business, Alanna read the front of Aiden's business card.

Classically elegant in form, it identified his business as Jade Enterprises, Ltd., with its headquarters in Hong Kong, and branch offices in London, Singapore and Riyadh, Saudi Arabia.

When Alanna returned her attention to the two men's conversation, Francois was doing his best to sell Aiden a piece of the Sun Star colt he had purchased from Alanna.

"I could possibly be interested," Aiden was saying. "I'll have a look at his pedigree."

"Excellent." Francois replied, enthusiastically.

Out of the corner of her eye, Alanna caught sight of Julie rounding the corner of Barn 3 in a hurry.

"Uh, oh! Looks like trouble," Alanna said.

"Alanna," she said, almost out of breath, "The Raise A Star filly got cast in her stall. Her legs are wedged up against the door and she's having a fit. We can't find a way in. You better hurry."

Without a word to either man, Alanna got up and hurried to her barn, Julie right behind her, both of them careful to slow down when passing the other young horses being shown, so as not to frighten them. Aiden and Francois followed quickly behind them.

When they arrived at the barn, a crowd had gathered at the filly's stall. Two of Alanna's grooms were standing in front of the stall door trying to calm the cast filly, who was neighing and squealing shrilly in fright and pain, lying on her side, with all four of her legs jammed tightly against the door of the stall.

Alanna calmly made her way through the crowd and gently asked them if they would mind moving away from the area, as their presence and the noise they were creating were adding to the filly's fears. They dispersed willingly.

"Should we remove the kick board?" The one groom asked, anxiously, reaching for the wooded board that covered the distance between the bottom of the stall screen and the ground.

"No." Alanna said, quietly so as not to startle the filly. "If you do, her legs will be free, but then they'll be hung up under that metal screen door and she'll really do some damage to herself." Then she asked the grooms to stand back, and she assessed the situation.

Francois and Aiden watched, as, without moving the metal screen door, Alanna eased herself up and over the top of it. Once inside, she took hold of the top board of the doorframe, which allowed only enough room for her fingertips, and lifted her body off the door screen. Hanging by her fingertips, she moved along the width of the door and stall

184

framing until she was in a position away from the filly. Silently, gently, she let herself down onto the straw bedding. Then while talking quietly and calmly to the filly, she moved her away from the door by pulling her hindquarters into the center of the stall with her tail.

There was a collective sigh of relief from the observers outside, as the filly rose to her feet, shaken, but otherwise not seriously injured. Alanna took hold of the filly's halter and talked to her until she stopped shaking and allowed the vet, whom Julie had called as a precaution, to inspect her.

"Is she all right?" Francois said, with concern, as he peered into the stall.

"She's lost some hair on her legs," Alanna said, as she emerged from the stall and brushed the dust off of her clothes. "Hopefully there won't be any swelling, otherwise, she just scared herself almost to death."

"You did that very well." Francois congratulated her on her effort. "Don't you agree, Aiden?"

"I guess when you learn this business from the pitchfork up, as I've been told Alanna has," Aiden observed, complimenting her on the depth of her horsemanship, "you get handy at accomplishing feats like that. Am I right, Alanna?"

"A crisis a minute, that's the horse business," she replied, with a laugh that broke the tension of the moment.

Seeing the dirt-smeared state of her clothing, she turned to Francois, and said, "I think I should pass on lunch, Francois. I'm entirely too grungy to grace your table."

"Alanna, You could never be too "grungy" to grace my table," Francois assured her, "and you must be starved by now. It's almost two o'clock. Come with me and have the wonderful lunch Gilbert has prepared for you. You can freshen up before we eat."

Turning to Aiden, Francois said, "Join us, Aiden."

"Thanks, Francois, it's very kind of you to invite me, but I have to beg off." Aiden replied. "There's an old friend I've been meaning to see while I'm here, and I've a mind to do it this afternoon. That is if I can find him."

"Before you go, Aiden," Alanna interjected, "let me give you the address of that gallery where you can get that Sun Star print."

Playing along, Aiden said, "I'd appreciate that. I can pick that up this afternoon as well."

"I have some paper in the tackroom, if you come with me, I'll write it down for you." Alanna said, hoping Francois would take the hint and leave them for a minute.

"While you're taking care of Aiden, Alanna," Francois said, reaching into his pocket and pulling out a palm-sized walkie-talkie, "I'll have the car come around and pick us up at the gate here." And indicating the exit closest to them, he added, "I'll meet you there."

"Fine, Francois," Alanna said, from the tackroom door. "I won't be but a minute."

As Francois headed for the gate, Alanna went into the tackroom and on a piece of paper wrote her address and drew a map directing Aiden to the empty lot behind her house, where she indicated on the paper he should park his car.

Aiden remained on watch at the door in case Francois, having forgotten something, returned before she finished.

"Here," she said, handing him the now folded piece of paper, "this should help you find what you're looking for."

"I can't thank you enough." Aiden said, taking the paper and putting it in his jacket pocket. "I'll see you later."

He turned to leave, then stopped and turned back to her. "Oh, by the way, Alanna, just so we start this association off right, let me just say that my curiosity about you, though it did exist, was a very small factor in my coming here. And as for adventurism, it's for the bored and immature, two things I've never been accused of. I'm here because the promise I made was a debt of honor between honorable men. That debt of honor demanded that I be here for you, and that's really why I came."

Then relinquishing another of his meager smiles, he added in parting, "Be careful that gourmet lunch doesn't have some erotic ingredient in it. That man's desperate to have you, 'grunge' and all!"

"Thanks, for the advice," she remarked, smiling while doing so, "but handling lecherous men was covered quite adequately in my training. I think I can handle lunch with Francois. I'll see you at dinner."

When Alanna arrived at the gate, Francois' limo was parked at the curb with its rear door open and its engine running. The driver held the door as she and Francois entered the car, then he settled behind the steering wheel and drove off.

Ten minutes later they were pulling under the sheltered portico of the his rented country house, a grand old Victorian, set on a large, tree covered lot at the edge of town. It had a huge screened porch overlooking the gardens, on which Guilbert, Francois' chef, had set a beautiful luncheon table. Guilbert was awaiting them as they made their way from the vestibule.

"Bonjour, mademoiselle. I hope you will enjoy the luncheon I have prepared for you." Guilbert said, with an elaborate bow, graciously ignoring the rather disheveled state of his boss's guest's appearance.

"Bonjour, Guilbert. I've heard so much about your culinary talents that I'm sure I will. My, the table is lovely!" Turning to Francois, she said, "If you don't mind, Francois, could someone show me where I might clean up a bit."

"But, of course." He summoned his housekeeper, and within moments, a stout women in her sixties with a pleasant smile appeared. "Natalie, please show Miss Reynolds to the guest room."

Natalie smiled broadly and indicated for Alanna to follow her. As they mounted the long staircase to the second floor, they chatted amiably in French, the woman commenting on her lovely accent. Halfway down the upstairs hall, she showed Alanna into a lovely, sun-filled bedroom done in pink and white Victorian decor. The housekeeper opened the door to the attached bathroom and set a fresh towel on its sink.

"If mademoiselle needs anything, just ring this bell," she said, indicating a button on the wall next to the shower.

"Thank you, Natalie, this will be fine."

"Very well," Natalie replied and left the room, closing the door behind her.

Alanna freshened up, then headed back downstairs.

"Feel better?" Francois said, rising from his seat and pulling the chair next to him out for her.

"Yes, thank you," she replied as she took the seat he held for her.

She noticed that he had been studying the racing form in her absence and offered, "I have a very good tip on tomorrow's fourth race, if you're interested."

"Always," he said, looking up from his paper, "unfortunately, gambling is one of my obsessions."

"Really! Well then, I've been told that Gratify will be hard to beat."

Guilbert brought in lunch and they began to eat.

"Tell me, Francois," she asked, giving him a particularly lovely smile, "what other obsessions do you have? I know so little about you, except what I've read and we know how inaccurate that information can be."

"What would you like to know, Cherie?" Francois replied, setting down his fork and turning his attention to her.

"Everything!" She said, letting her warm smile permeate her voice. "Tell me about your childhood, your parents. What you do with your time when you're not searching the world for the perfect racehorse."

"Ah, yes, my parents," he began, somewhat reluctantly, for discussing his childhood was not without pain. "I was not close to my parents, or shall I say they were not close to me. They traveled a great deal so most of my childhood was spent at boarding schools, or in the company of governesses.

"My mother never wanted children, but she adored my father and agreed to start a family. When she produced the son my father longed to have, me, on the first try, she terminated her childbearing career. She also, immediately, divested herself of the mothering role.

"Father was a hard, but fair man. I think he did not know how to be a father, but he was a good money manager and teacher. Since my family has been wealthy for generations, my father's only task in life was not to lose the family fortune. He was successful at enhancing it, as I have been. As for my interests outside of horse breeding and racing -- they are few."

"You never married?" Alanna continued the questioning. "Didn't you want a wife and family?"

"Yes. Many times I have stopped to consider this void in my life," he said, with a trace of melancholy in his voice. "But until recently, I'd never found a woman who could compete with my first love -- money."

"Well, I'm very happy to hear that you've found someone, Francois," Alanna remarked, genuinely. "Does she share your feelings?"

"I'm afraid you'll have to answer that question, Alanna, since you are that woman!"

Chapter 17

Jeremy had decided, after seeing the look on Francois' face when he dropped Alanna off at the stable that it was in both his and Alanna's best interest to make himself scarce for a while, so he spent the morning driving around Saratoga Lake. After about an hour, he pulled off the road at a small fishing camp and picnic area. He parked the car under the shade of a grove of trees, went in the camp store, bought a sandwich and soda, and sat down at one of the picnic tables overlooking the lake.

He thought about how nobody connected with this operation could have foreseen that Francois would envision his relationship with Alanna as more than platonic, or could have conceived of how quickly he would become possessive of her.

Have I really been so unprofessional, he thought, that my feelings for Alanna were so evident to a stranger? One thing he knew for sure was when a man is interested in a woman, detecting a challenge from another man is instinctive, and that was where in his problem with Francois lay. How, he wondered, could one night with a woman screw a man up so badly for the rest of his life?

Where Alanna's access to Francois was concerned, Francois' desire for her was an asset, but where Jeremy's backing her up was concerned, Francois' jealousy was a nightmare. They'd just have to see that this snag in the plan didn't interfere with the operation's success.

The obvious solution, Jeremy reasoned, was for him to find a romance of his own, one that he could flaunt, one that would ease Francois' mind. Yes, what he needed was a little distraction, preferably a beautiful one.

* * *

Jeremy returned to his room in the Adelphi Hotel late afternoon. He took a shower and had a short nap. He was awakened at about 7 p.m. by the phone ringing. When he picked it up, there was static on the line, then there was a noise like his party had been disconnected. He immediately hung up the phone, and took his cellular phone, equipped with a scrambler, out of his briefcase, and dialed Alanna's number.

Her answering machine answered his call, when it finished cranking out its message, he said in a sing-song Chinese voice, "Ho Ho's Chinese restaurant calling, your order is ready, missy."

189

He heard a scrambler click in followed by Alanna's laughing voice, "Ah so, Ho Ho, so where's my dinner? I'm starved. What have you been up to this afternoon?"

"I took a nice drive around Saratoga Lake. Great country. If I live long enough, maybe I'll retire here," Jeremy replied. "You say you have a taste for Chinese. I think we're crafty enough to duck Francois' troupies, so why don't I get Bill and Tad, and we'll be right over to get you?"

"Thanks, but I'll have to pass. I'm having a problem with one of my yearlings," Alanna said, the long day showing in her tired voice. "She got down in the stall and jammed her legs up against the wall twice today. The second time she banged herself up pretty good. So, I've made arrangements to ship her to one of the farms here until she settles down, and then I'll ship her home."

"Sorry to hear that. Other than that, how was your day?"

"I met Aiden."

"I don't believe it." Jeremy said, the annoyance clear in his voice. "No, on second thought, I do believe it. Damn, he always has to do things his way. Asshole."

"Don't make such a big deal out of it, Jeremy. Maybe it was easier and less conspicuous to get in touch with me first," she said, knowing that wasn't the case. "He must have tried to reach you and missed you, he was on his way to do just that when he left me."

"He could have tried, I guess," Jeremy said, backing off on the hostilities. "I've been out most of the day. How did your lunch go with his highness, Francois."

"Good. That international conglomerate he wants me to join sounds pretty legit," she replied. "Unless, of course, some of them are fronting for the evil empires out there. There's no way to know that until I have Granton run this list of members he gave me through the Agency's, the FBI's and Interpol's computers.

"We had a surprise guest for lunch," she continued. "Hakeem showed up. Even Francois seemed surprised at his appearance."

"That's interesting," Jeremy remarked. "You'd have thought he wouldn't be pushing his luck, staying in the country knowing he's on the State Department's undesirable visitors' list."

"Well, if he's concerned, you'd never know it. Luckily he didn't show up until I'd had a chance to pick Francois' brain a bit."

"Learn anything interesting?"

"Nothing new about Hakeem, and mostly background stuff on Francois," Alanna said, through a stifled yawn. "Excuse me, these four o'clock mornings get to you in a hurry."

"Well, then it's a good thing you're passing on dinner out. You'd be lousy company, probably fall asleep in your chow mien," Jeremy kidded. "Besides, I'm sure that you consumed your entire daily quota of calories eating that fancy French lunch."

"You got that right. I can feel my hips expanding as we speak," she joked back. "Look, I have to get back to my barn. I was supposed to join Aiden and the rest of the Irish mob at the Firehouse Restaurant, so my guess is you can catch up with him there. If you miss him, at least you'll have had a good dinner."

"Good idea," Jeremy said. "By the way, why do you think Hakeem showed up at lunch?"

"I'm not sure. Maybe to make sure I didn't charm anything of value out of Francois. He plays back and forth between being suspicious and then interested in me."

Alanna hesitated for a moment, then added. "I've seen a lot of cold characters in my time, Jeremy, but believe me, this man's eyes make a snake's look positively warm and caring."

"Well, you can't always judge a person by the look in his eye," Jeremy said semi-seriously. "After all, those baby blues of yours have iced a man or two in their day, and look what a sweet thing you are!"

"Since I am too tired to come up with a put-down to equal yours," Alanna said, feigning mock indignation, "I shall simple terminate this conversation. Good-bye and get to work!"

"I'm going! I'm going! You are such a poor sport," Jeremy said, laughing softly. "I'll talk to you later."

Jeremy pressed the disconnect button, then got a dial tone again, and rang Bill Rice's cellular phone.

"Parker's Auto Works," Rice answered using his telephone identifying code.

"My BMW's got a knock in it, can I schedule a service?" Jeremy said, in his coded reply.

"Hey, it's about time you called, Jeremiah, we're starved," Rice muttered. "Is this anyway to treat your loyal crew?"

"Hardly, I agree, but you know what an ogre I am," replied Jeremy. "There's a place up the street called The Firehouse, that I understand is pretty good. Let's give it a try. I'll meet you in the lobby in ten minutes."

"We'll be there," Rice said, and hung up.

The men were waiting near the front entrance when Jeremy came downstairs. He drove to the restaurant, which was only a few blocks from the hotel. A quick look around the restaurant did not reveal Aiden, or his friends anywhere among the crowd, so they took a table and ordered dinner.

After dinner, Jeremy dropped Rice and Clark off at the hotel and told them to stick close to the phone in case Doyle tried to contact him. In the meantime, he would make a tour of the town to see if he couldn't run across him. Jeremy tried Lillian's and the Ramada Renaissance without success. He'd heard that a place called Siro's was a good spot. Located on Lincoln Street, behind the thoroughbred track, it was a favorite hangout of the racetrack and sales crowd. He made it his last stop.

Just as he pulled up, a parking space opened at the end of a line of cars parked facing the racetrack fence. He parked the BMW, activated the special security device, and, out of habit, checked gun in his holster, making sure it had a full magazine and a round in the chamber.

There was a lot of noise and music coming from the tented area Siro's had erected to accommodate the additional crowd. It had tables and a bar, and a band that was playing music suitable to the older crowd the restaurant generally attracted. The place was packed.

Jeremy made his way through the mob, a waitress took his order, and as he waited for the drink to appear, he scanned the revelers. When his drink arrived, Jeremy moved on through the tent. Aiden was nowhere to be seen, but he ran into some people he'd met at the sale in Kentucky, and in order not to seem suspicious, stopped to chat. He continued his search entering the main building by way of a back entrance. Passing through the dining room, he once again stopped to talk to some familiar faces. There was still no sign of Doyle. He made his way to the bar area, where a group of American and British horse people were lending their voices to oldies being played on the bar's piano, but turned up a blank there as well.

Jeremy finished his drink, and decided to call it a night. He set his empty glass on a table, and headed for the front door. The valet, standing at the end of the canopied walkway, came forward to meet him.

"Can I get your car for you, sir?" he inquired.

"No, thanks," Jeremy smiled and replied. "I parked up the street."

"Well, then have a good evening, sir." the boy said, and returned to his post.

The driver's side of Jeremy's car was bathed in the light from the street lamp. He approached it from the opposite side of the street, avoiding a line of cars cloaked in blackness by overhanging tree limbs.

He had an uneasy feeling about the man he noticed sitting on the trunk of the car next to his. Their eyes made contact as Jeremy crossed the street to his car and started to insert his key in its lock. The man made no move to leave his position, but the uneasiness persisted.

Before Jeremy could unlock the car door, he heard the engine of a car parked on the opposite side of the street start. There was a screeching of tires and even with his back to the car, he knew it was headed in his direction. It was on him in a second, its headlights glaring off of the BMW's side window. As he turned to face it, the driver hit his brights, blinding Jeremy.

If they'd wanted him dead, he knew they had him. He started to reach for his gun. As his body angle turned slightly to his left, he caught sight of an object, a bat, coming swiftly in his direction. Instinctively, he raised his arm to deflect the blow.

It missed his head, but came down heavy across his shoulders and upper back. His arms were numbed by the impact, making it impossible to get to his weapon. He turned his back to the man with the bat, and tried to steady himself against the car with his right side.

By this time, the two men in the car were out and on him. Pinning him against the side of the car, they delivered a couple of solid punches to his mid-section, knocking the wind out of him.

"Go easy." He heard the taller of the men, who obviously thought they'd knocked him unconscious, say. "We're just supposed to rough him up a bit."

"I say we get rid of the bastard," the one who resembled a Sumo wrestler growled. "He's fuckin' trouble."

"Argh!" Jeremy cried out, as he tried to break free and the Sumo wrestler struck him across the back, driving him to the ground.

"You're probably right. Who's gonna miss him?" The tall one agreed, realizing now that Jeremy had heard everything they'd said. Cautioning the other men, he added, "There's too much light here, let's get him in the car and finish him off up the road. We can dump the body in the lake. Be sure to get his wallet and jewelry so it looks like a robbery."

The one who had wielded the baseball bat, said, "He's got a gun."

"Get it," said the tall one, whom Jeremy decided was the leader.

As the Sumo wrestler went to roll Jeremy over to get at the gun, he felt Jeremy's hand grab hold of his arm, followed by Jeremy's foot slamming against his chest. Straightening his leg and using the man's own momentum, Jeremy pitched him over his head and into his buddies.

In the confusion that ensued, Jeremy had just enough time to hit the button on his watch, which triggered the self-starting mechanism in the BMW and unlocked its door. The car's engine roared to life, further adding to the chaos.

Leaping painfully to his feet, he managed to reach the car door before the leader drew his gun and fired.

The bulletproof door shielded Jeremy from the shot. He slid behind the wheel, threw the car into reverse, then dropped it into first and peeled out, barely missing the gunman and the rear end of their car, which he now could see was a big Mercedes sedan.

A right turn onto Nelson, and another right on Union put him on 9P, heading past the front of the track, and in the direction of the lake.

Jeremy's breath came in small gasps, as his ribs, which were still sore from the encounter with Alanna, protested the additional abuse they'd taken. As for his arms, his left one was completely numb, and for all practical purposes, useless. It made driving the stick shift BMW extremely difficult.

He looked in the rear view mirror, and saw that the Mercedes was right behind him. Outnumbered and incapacitated, he knew that he needed a way to get rid of these guys, and quickly.

The cars flew over the Northway bridge. From there, the road bent slightly to the right, and went from four lanes to two, then it straightened and the pursuing car was able to get off a couple of shots.

The road bore to the left, then the right and rose as it reached a small hill. At the top he passed the Canterbury Restaurant, and the road to Kaydeross Park. It curved to the right and down towards the narrow, green metal-covered bridge that crossed Saratoga Lake.

As he headed towards the lake, an idea began to form in Jeremy's battered head.

He was grateful for the late hour, because the bridge they were approaching was narrow and during the day, a steady stream of cars made their way across it. Hitting the bridge in daylight at the speed the two cars were traveling at would have been suicide. Now, it was empty, the area on either end of it lit only by the security lights from gas stations and bait shops.

The cars flashed across the bridge and on down the road. Jeremy poured on the speed. He needed to put some distance between the Mercedes and him if the plan he had in mind was to work.

Barely holding the wheel steady with his injured arm, he reached with his good one under his seat, and pulled out a pair of night vision glasses, and put them on.

He had arrived at a place in the road where 9P curved gently to the left, and another road bore off to what was a group of cottages set on the lake. As he set his car into the curve, he deliberately hit his brakes, which illuminated his brake lights and gave away his location, insuring that the car behind would follow.

The main road had a metal guardrail running the distance of the cottages. Where 9P came closest to the lake, the rail ended and the side road once again merged.

"Hurry up," the Sumo wrestler type sitting in the front passenger seat shouted. "If we don't finish him off, we're dead men."

"He'll have to slow down here, this road gets pretty curvy." The driver, who had driven Francois to dinner down this road the previous evening, assured his accomplices.

"Well, just don't lose him."

Suddenly, Jeremy's car disappeared.

"Holy shit, where'd he go?" The driver slowed the Mercedes, and the men vainly searched the dark areas and driveways for signs of Jeremy's car. "He's got to still be around here somewhere."

"I told you to stay up with him," the Sumo wrestler type retorted.

"Shut up and look for him," the driver snarled. He was fed up with his partner's whining. "If you had listened to me in the first place, we wouldn't be here. The orders were to rough him up, not kill him. The boss is going to have our heads."

"He'll have yours for sure if this bastard gets away. He can identify all of us."

The driver glowered back at his partner, then turned his attention back to the road.

They were creeping along at 30 miles per hour. Where had he gone?

* * *

At the place where the roads met, Jeremy, sure they had followed, turned off his lights and sped on.

The road was pitch dark. Some of the cabins that sat along the left side of the road still had their lights on, but the light was too far back to have any effect on road visibility.

The dark road did not hinder Jeremy's progress, as the night vision glasses provided more than enough light. Another switch on his dash had allowed him to turn off all of the car's lights, even interrupting the signal to his brake lights, which now permitted him to use his brakes without giving away his position.

Unseen, he had quickly covered the distance to the spot he had chosen. The lake along this stretch of road was not more than 20 feet from the water's edge. The shoreline was lined, sporadically, with narrow floating docks that jutted out into the lake.

He drove a tenth of a mile beyond this point, slowed, and pulled off the road into the parking lot of the Saratoga Boat and Tackle Supply store. Removing the night vision glasses, so that the lights from the Mercedes would not blind him, Jeremy pulled back onto the road heading toward the pursuing car.

As Jeremy's car straightened out on the road, he punched down on the accelerator and the BMW leaped forward in response. It rounded the turn and was now headed directly for the Mercedes, unseen by that car's occupants.

Keeping his car a little to the left of the centerline would, he hoped, give the driver of the Mercedes no option but to swerve to his right. Jeremy waited until the last possible moment, then he hit his brights.

The men in the Mercedes were gripped with fear, as virtually out of nowhere, the oncoming car hurtled toward them in the middle of the road. Panic stricken, the driver's first reaction, was as Jeremy had hoped, to get out of the oncoming car's way. Without thinking, the driver of the Mercedes hit the accelerator and swerved the car to the right. Too late, he remembered the only thing to his right was the lake.

The Mercedes shot off the road, and landed with a belly flop into the dark water. It sank slowly, its passengers trying vainly to open its doors.

* * *

Jeremy headed back to Saratoga. He had to get some help and quick because the burning pain in his shoulder and back was becoming unbearable. The strain of maneuvering his car at high speed had aggravated whatever injury he had sustained. His body was functioning on auto-pilot. Sweat was pouring down his face, and he was nauseated.

Earlier that day, Jeremy had stopped by Alanna's house to deliver some instructions from headquarters. He had parked his car, as she had instructed, in an empty lot behind her house. Now, barely able to stay conscious, he searched for the street the empty lot was on. Going back to the hotel in his condition, he knew, was out of the question. He hoped Alanna hadn't changed her mind about going out for the evening.

The street sign said Fox Hall Drive. I'm almost there, he thought, as he fought the black unconsciousness that threatened to engulf him, I've got to make it. Then he was at the lot, pulling the car onto the grass and to the trees that bordered the back of Alanna's yard. He opened the car door, and fell out of the car, and onto the ground.

When he hit the ground, it felt like he'd fallen on a grenade. Fiery shafts of pain penetrated every inch of him.

Alanna, returning from a late-night run, ran to the man she had just seen crumple to the ground, and who now lay in a huddled, moaning mass.

Jeremy was about to lose consciousness, when he heard the sound of Alanna's voice and felt her touch. It seemed to give him new energy.

"Oh Lord, Jeremy," Alanna said, bending down, and gently touching him on the shoulder. "What happened?"

He could barely see her, dizziness hampering his vision. How had she known he was there? Hell, he didn't care how she knew, he'd never been so happy to see anyone in his life. But, the only response that he could give to her question was a groan.

Not knowing the extent of Jeremy's injuries, but seeing that he was in excruciating pain, Alanna said, "Jeremy, I'm going to call an ambulance."

"God, no, you can't. It'll spoil everything." He gasped out the words. "You can fix me up."

Alanna shook her head at his stubbornness. Her hand gently stroked his sweat-drenched face and in a steady, soothing voice, she said, "Then we have to try and get you into the house. If, I help you, can you make it?"

"Yes." His voice was hoarse with pain.

She knelt down beside him. "I'm not going to touch you. You just lean on me whatever way is comfortable for you. Take your time."

Slowly, agonizingly, he got to his feet. They moved across the back yard, using every available solid object en route for support. She took him into a back bedroom and sat him down on the bed.

197

Gently, she helped him out of his jacket. She could see by the position of his shoulder that it was out of joint. He groaned and grimaced as she removed his empty holster from the injured shoulder. Hopefully, the gun is somewhere in the car, she thought. Then, she removed his shirt, and eased him into a prone position.

He was breathing rapidly, and she was afraid he'd go into shock.

"Listen to me, Jeremy. Slow your breathing down, take deep breaths, come on you can do it." She encouraged him.

When he seemed to have that under control, he tried to speak. "What were you doing out there?"

As she laid a light blanket over him, she said, softly, "I was out for a run. I can see that your shoulder is out, but can you tell me where else you hurt. I'd rather not move you if I don't have to."

"Back, shoulders, ribs - - left arm numb," he barely mumbled. "Baseball bat."

"Keep breathing deeply. I'll be right back," Alanna said. Getting up and going around the bed, she pulled down the window shades, and turned the bedside lamp down low. She went to her room. There from a small bookcase, she took out a book. Instead of pages, it contained vials of liquids and powdered herbs. She selected four vials. From another book-like box, she took jars of salves and healing oils. She replaced the faux books, and went into the kitchen.

While the water heated, Alanna removed a homemade chamomile tea bag from an airtight can. She placed one in a mug, and filled it with boiling water, and let it steep. While the tea brewed, she took a large bowl and poured the powdered herbs into it, adding enough witch hazel into them to bind them into a poultice. Cutting a length of cheesecloth into several pieces, she submerged them in the wet pasty poultice mixture. When the tea had reached its proper strength, she removed the bag, stirred in a measure of a powdered herb called valerian, a teaspoon of honey, and a few drops of a secret ancient Chinese sedative.

When she returned to his room with the poultice bowl and tea on a tray, Jeremy was so still, she was afraid he had lost consciousness.

"Jeremy," she said, tentatively.

He groaned a response.

"Here, drink this. I'll help you," she said, as she set the tray on the nightstand, took the teacup in her hand, and slipped her arm carefully under his head, raising it so he could drink. "I think I know what's wrong with you. If, I'm right, I'll have you good as new."

"And if you're wrong," Jeremy tried to joke.

"Sue me." She laughed at his attempt at humor despite his pain. "Remember, this was your idea."

The tea had a sweet, spicy aroma. Initially, it had a sweet taste, but its aftertaste was bitter, which made it almost undrinkable.

"Auck!" he said, and gagged at the first taste of the tea. "What is this stuff?"

"Don't ask," she replied, and had Jeremy been able to see anything, he would have seen a sly grin break the corners of her mouth. "Just drink it, all of it. Then, we'll give it a minute or two to work."

"This stuff is terrible," he complained. "One of these days I'm going to have your witch doctor's license revoked."

"I wouldn't do it tonight, if I were you. Now, quiet. Just relax and finish the tea."

Soon, Jeremy found that he craved the tea, and when it was gone, so was the searing pain.

She could see the drug was beginning to work. Jeremy's breathing was more normal, and a relaxed expression had replaced the painful grimace on his face.

Alanna removed the blanket, and climbed on the bed. She straddled Jeremy's body and removed his trousers.

"Hey! What are you doing?" Jeremy protested with weak, but uncharacteristic modesty.

"Quiet, quit making such a fuss! You'd think this was the first time I'd seen you in your Jockey shorts," she said, gently. "If this potion and the treatment I'm about to give you doesn't kill you, well it probably won't be the last time I see you in them."

"With my luck -- you better take a good look now," Jeremy said, sleepily. "I wouldn't count on any 'next times'."

His attackers had managed to avoid bruising Jeremy's face and that was to the good, but the bruises on his body were quickly becoming visible.

"Relax now," she said, letting her hands stroke his face gently and soothingly. Before he drifted completely off, she whispered in his ear, "Come on, Adonis, ease yourself over on your stomach, so I can work my black arts on you."

He turned over and mumbled, "Oh, how I wish you would! This must be a dreammm..." And then there were no more sounds from Jeremy as he slipped into a deep, painless sleep.

Now that the drug had a good hold, Alanna began to probe his body gently. Dar had not only taught her the fighting arts of Shaolin, but the healing arts, as well. He even arranged for her to spend time in China with the old Grand Master who had been his teacher, perfecting this part of her training.

Here we are, she thought, in the middle of one of the most important operations of our careers, and Jeremy's in pieces. And what do I have for backup -- an Irishman with an attitude.

It wasn't hard to figure out where the orders for this little escapade had come from. How could any man be so stupid and consumed with jealousy that he would resort to this to eliminate the competition? The realization that Jeremy might have died in that empty lot, if she hadn't been on her way back from her nightly run, made her furious with Francois.

Her body shook reflexively, and she thought how she cringed inwardly every time Francois touched her. It was necessary for her to propel herself into another dimension, another personality, to maintain the facade she projected to him.

She encouraged Jeremy to turn back over, where a tour of his left arm and shoulder confirmed her earlier suspicions. Placing herself in a position of leverage, she first worked on his neck, then his shoulder and arm, resetting the shoulder, a move that would have been excruciatingly painful had Jeremy not been sedated.

On his shoulder and the areas that showed the worst bruising, she placed the pieces of poultice soaked cheesecloth, which she covered with moist hot towels. The areas less bruised were treated with a mixture of the salves and oils. She filled the dispenser of a vaporizer with a few drop of orange blossom oil and let the soothing scent permeate the room. Throughout the night, she remoistened the cheesecloth and replaced the hot towels. About 4 a.m., she removed the poultices, washed and dried his back, shoulders and chest, covered him with a blanket, turned out the light and left him to sleep off the drug.

* * *

Granton laid the Wall Street Journal on the end table next to his leather recliner. He looked at his watch and yawned. It was almost 4. He thought he'd head off to bed, and get an hour or two of sleep before he had to head in to work. A decision that he knew would inevitably leave him groggy for the rest of the day. He hadn't had many sleepless nights in the past, but operation SABRE was fast increasing their numbers.

He tucked the chair's footrest back into its closed position, turned out the lamp, and got up and headed for the door. Just as he closed the door to the room he used as his home office, he heard one of the phones on his desk ring. He went back into the room, and when he realized that the ringing was coming from the phone with the secured line, he hurried to answer it.

"Granton here," he said, in greeting, and was surprised to hear Alanna's voice on the other end. In order to limit her exposure, it had been decided to let Jeremy make all contact with Granton.

"Granton, Jeremy got beat up. Someone worked him over with a baseball bat." Alanna advised their boss of the incident.

"God, almighty. Do you know who did it? How serious is he hurt? Do we need to get him to a hospital?" Granton distressed by the news, fired off questions.

"He showed up at my place, just barely conscious, and in serious pain. He had a dislocated shoulder, and some pretty severe bruising over most of his upper and middle torso area. I didn't push him for details, since I was more concerned with taking care of his pain. He's asleep now and resting comfortably. I think he'll be all right in the morning, but we'll have to wait and see."

There was silence on Granton's end of the line as he pondered the situation.

"Do you need any help?" he asked.

"No. I can take care of him myself."

"Did he have a run-in with Francois?"

"Not that I know of. Jeremy was gone all day. He took a ride around the lake to stay out of Francois' way."

"I think you should have him stay put there, at least until we can determine what the situation is."

"That's fine with me."

"Have you met the Irishman yet?"

"Doyle stopped by my barn this morning with an old friend of mine, Paddy Ryan. We were supposed to have dinner this evening, but one of my yearlings got sick, and I had to cancel. He must have talked to Jeremy by now, because when he left me, he was on his way to do just that."

"How are things going with Francois?"

"Fine."

"Good." Feeling satisfied that Alanna had everything under control, he said, "Have Jeremy give me a call in the morning, if he's up to it. If not, you get back to me. Well, I'll let you get back to your patient."

"Thanks, I will. Good night." she said.

"Good night." he replied, and hung up the phone.

* * *

Jeremy's mind had played crazy tricks on him all night, flashing back to various events in his life, some happy, some frightening, like his first firefight. He was cruising through another episode. It was where he and Alanna were running from the Serbs. It seemed to be a required part of any nightmare he had, but this time it was taking a different twist.

In the original version, Dar's last cries had eliminated any reason for her to go back, so Jeremy had let go of Alanna's hand in order to speed their progress. The going had been slippery and tiring, and she had begun to drop back. When Jeremy had turned to try and encourage her to catch up, she had disappeared.

This is where his new nightmare took a turn for the worst. In the original dream sequence, he'd safely carried her back to the pick up point after discovering she had passed out due to blood loss from wounds that weren't visible.

In the new version, he arrived at the top of a knoll only to discover the Serbs had beaten him to her body. There were eight of them, but he opened fire anyway, hoping to drive them off. Instead one of them picked Alanna up and headed back towards the munitions plant, while the others returned his fire. Somewhere in the distance he could hear himself shouting after her. "Alanna! Alanna...."

"Open your eyes, Jeremy." He heard Alanna say gently. Her voiced sounded like it was right next to him. Still, in his mind he could see the man making off with her. He tossed fighting the imagined enemy.

"Jeremy, wake up," Alanna said, more firmly this time. "Come on, open your eyes."

Jeremy stopped tossing, and opened his eyes to a room filled with the soft light of morning, the odd lingering aroma of a mixture of camphor, vinegar and orange blossoms, and his partner's reassuring smile.

"You had a pretty busy night, my friend," she said. "But, I think you're going to survive nicely."

"What did I say in my ravings?" He was almost embarrassed to ask.

"Nothing anyone else will ever know," was her reply. "You have my word."

She could sense his embarrassment, so she changed the subject.

"After I was sure you would make it," she said, while straightening up the room, and opening the shades, "I went to your hotel, and got you a fresh change of clothes and your toilet kit. And, I slipped a note under Rice's door, letting him know where you were."

He didn't have to ask if anyone had seen her. He knew they hadn't.

"I called Granton," she said, now standing at the foot of the bed.

He was not surprised that she had called in. It was correct operational procedure. However, he knew if Granton believed his cover had been compromised, Granton could remove him from the operation. It was the last thing Jeremy wanted to happen.

"What did he say?"

"He wanted to know how you were, and who did it." She related last night's conversation with Granton in brief. "He said for you to stay here until we figure out what happened, and determine how much damage has been done to the operation. And," she added, "you're supposed to call him."

Jeremy didn't say anything. He just lay there, looking up at the ceiling.

"Come on, get yourself out of bed," she said, as she started out of the room. "I have to get back to the sales grounds, but I'll make you some breakfast before I go.

"The bathroom is through that door." She pointed to a door to his right. "Why don't you clean up. But, before you do, drink that," and she indicated, with a nod of her head, a steaming cup of liquid sitting in a saucer on the night stand.

"Oh, God, do I have to?" Jeremy grimaced at the thought of the taste of the previous night's beverage.

"Yes, you do, and every last drop. And," she warned, punctuating the words with a finger pointed in his direction, "don't even think of spilling it down the drain."

"Now, what makes you think I would do that!" he grumbled, disgusted that she had read his thoughts. "What's in it?"

"Nothing much."

"What is nothing much?" he insisted.

"Just some Paconia, red dates, ginger and some licorice," she finally conceded the formula. "Now is that so bad?"

Afraid to move his injured shoulder, he rubbed his good hand over his face to wake himself, then replied, "I suppose I'm about to find out."

"Okay, quit stalling," Alanna said. "Down the hatch with that stuff, and then make yourself presentable. Breakfast will be ready by the time you've finished dressing."

Other than touching his hand to his face, Jeremy had not yet made an effort to move. "Are you crazy? Are you telling me I can just get up and carry on like nothing happened last night?"

"If I worked my magic well enough, you can. But, if you don't give it a try, I'm going to get a bucket of ice water and move you myself." As she left the room and headed down the hall to the kitchen, she said, tauntingly, "Lying around, sleeping in until all hours, why you'd think we were on vacation, or something!"

He shouted after her, "Hey, is this stuff any good for my sex life?"

There was no reply, so he gave in and tried sitting up, tentatively at first, then completely -- nothing, no pain, anywhere.

* * *

Jeremy found his way to the dining room. The kitchen opened on to it, separated only by a breakfast bar, atop which Alanna was making a cup of tea. He was adjusting his shoulder holster and his gun as he approached.

"I see you found my gun."

"Luckily, it had fallen on the floor of your car. Have a seat," she said, indicating the place already set at the dining room table. She brought him a glass of fresh-squeezed orange juice, and two poached eggs on buttered toast rounds. From under her arm, she removed a folded newspaper, and set it, opened to the front page, on the table next to the plate of eggs. "You're headline news today."

"Have you read it yet?" he said, pointing to the article with his fork.

"Yes, I have," she replied. "You 'deep sixed' three of Francois' men. Of course, the cops think they had a DWI accident. The driver tested positive for alcohol."

"Oh, shit. They were Francois' men," Jeremy said.

"That surprises you?" Alanna asked.

"No, but I'd hoped..." And his voice trailed off.

"So, other than the fact that you're depressed because Granton's going to have a fit when he hears this, how do you feel?" She asked, as she set his steaming cup of black coffee and her tea down on the table, and took the seat across from him.

"The ribs are still sore," he replied, rubbing his hand gingerly over his rib cage. "But, the pain and numbness are gone from my arm, and so are most of the bruises from my body. How do you account for that?"

"It's all in the hands," she said, raising both of them in front of her, and wiggling her fingers. "Still want to close down my little shop of horrors."

"Hell, no!" Jeremy said, through a mouthful of egg and toast, adding when he swallowed the food. "You just keep practicing that black magic. It's not every intelligence agency that has a resident sorceress. You never know when I might need your services again."

Alanna took a sip of her tea. Then, as her fingers played along the rim of the cup, she asked, "Did you ever make contact with Aiden?"

"No," Jeremy took a sip of his coffee, and added, "I was out looking for him when Francois' men jumped me. He could have called the hotel while I was gone. Rice will know. He was monitoring all my calls yesterday evening."

"It turns out he's life-long friends with Paddy Ryan and Michael Quinn." Alanna inquired. "Were you aware of this?"

Jeremy stopped eating, and said, "No, but I'm not surprised. He grew up in that area."

"Then can I assume you're aware of the fact that he's on a first name basis with Francois?"

"No, as a matter of fact I didn't know that either," Jeremy said, somewhat annoyed. "If that jerk would get in touch with me first, like he was supposed to, I might have been able to find out what gives with him. Did he say whether he'd tried to contact me when he got to town?"

"He never said. We never really had a chance to discuss the matter. We were never alone long enough. However, I did give him your phone and room number at the hotel, and my phone number, address and directions on how to get here, so you'll probably hear from him soon."

Jeremy dropped the subject, and finished his breakfast. He set his fork on his now empty plate, and looked up into Alanna's sky blue eyes that were looking beyond him as though someone were there.

He turned and looked; there was no one. "What's bothering you, Alanna?"

"Nothing." Her eyes refocused on him.

"Let me rephrase that. Tell me what's bothering you, Alanna. Is it Doyle?"

"Should he bother me?"

"I suppose not. Maybe it's just me. Maybe I just can't get used to his ways. Just mismatched chemistry, I guess."

"Is it important for him to have some effect on me?"

"Only if it's good," Jeremy said.

"Well, then so far, so good," she replied, getting up and starting to clean off the table.

As she reached for his plate, he caught hold of her hand.

"Thanks, for taking care of me last night."

Her smile returned and she said, "Sure, anytime. I'm glad you're okay, Jeremy." Gently freeing her hand, she collected the dishes and went into the kitchen. From in front of the sink, she reminded him, "I have to go. Call Granton."

* * *

"Well, what's the next order of business on Rakeland?" Granton was asking Chief of Security Karl Heinz, as their meeting was about to conclude.

As Heinz was about to reply, one of the secure lines on Granton's desk rang.

"Yes?" He said in greeting and immediately recognized Jeremy's voice.

"It's Jeremy."

"What happened to you last night?"

"I got worked over by three guys," Jeremy said, knowing this conversation was necessary, but dreading the consequences. "Now, it turns out, they were Francois' people."

"Are you sure of that!" Granton asked.

"Yeah, I'm sure," Jeremy replied, hesitantly. "It's in the morning paper."

"What! You made the paper!"

"No, I didn't, but they did." Jeremy qualified his answer. "The paper said that the driver was intoxicated, and ran off the road. All of the men in the car drowned. They traced the car to Francois."

"You didn't have anything to do with this mishap did you?"

"No, not according to the paper."

"That's not what I asked you."

"Just protecting my ass, boss."

There was silence for a moment. Then Granton said, "I think it's time you ended your stay up there. Turn the backup duty over to Doyle and get to safer territory."

"That might take a bit of doing," Jeremy said, stalling for time. "The jerk hasn't gotten in touch with me yet."

"Well, get it done and get out," Granton said, and switched the conversation to the matter of Rakeland. "Karl Heinz is in my office.

We've been discussing the matter of the mole. We think we have his identity pinned down to Rakeland.

"Ed Simecek, the ground crewman out at the Farm, ID'd Rakeland as the one who asked about your plane. Simecek said Rakeland even called you by name. Karl checked the file on the Baltic operation, and it showed he was on TSD support for the operation. The other two guys never have had any dealings with the CROWN JEWELS, or had access to any information on CROWN JEWEL activities. So, I think we can eliminate them.

"We've got Rakeland under 24 hour surveillance, phone taps, mail coverage -- the works. CI is going into his background and his contacts to see if they can work a connection from that end. Nothing has turned up yet. Rakeland's been watching his step, which leads Karl to believe that somehow he knows that he's under the gun. Karl's looking for who warned him. We have also advised Jerry Myer, head of TSD, not to assign him to anything sensitive.

"And, we've run into another complication on the nuke." Granton relayed the information he'd just received from the Kiev station. "We pulled an inventory of the Ukrainian nuclear arsenal, and, according to their records, nothing is missing."

"Well, somebody's blowing smoke somewhere," Jeremy said. "The deal is going forward like they've got full confidence they're getting the thing. Francois and his organization are not people to be messed with. So, somebody's lying."

"Well, we're going to proceed like we're sure they have access to one," Granton advised. "In the meantime, get a hold of Doyle, and get out of there."

Chapter 18

"Roberto, you are an idiot!" Francois' anger was at fever pitch.

Roberto shifted from one foot to the other. "But, monsieur, I never thought..."

"It is very obvious that you didn't think, Roberto, otherwise you would have seen to this job yourself instead of sending those drunken fools." Francois paced the floor in front of the library's picture window, the glorious view now ignored in his rage. "A simple job, it was a simple job and you bungled it. Amazing! Amazing!

"What is worse, we have no knowledge of whether or not the men ever got to our Mr. Jergens. I can not believe the incompetence..."

Francois slammed his fist down on the desk, making the normally unflappable Roberto flinch. Phillip, who had been observing the proceedings from the back of the room, flinched as well. Hakeem, who was settled comfortably in a leather arm- chair, looked on, less than amused with the fiasco unfolding before him.

"What can I do to rectify the situation, monsieur?" Roberto asked, his apprehension growing.

"What can you do? What can you do?" Francois yelled. "You can go to hell, that's what you can do, and the quicker the better. Get out of here before I shoot you myself!"

Without further comment, Roberto hurried out of the room. Phillip attempted to follow, but Francois stopped him.

"Phillip, get Rene on the phone," Francois said, as he continued to pace the room, trying to control his mounting anger.

"Oui, monsieur," Phillip said, as he exited the library and headed to his office up the hall.

"There is just no getting rid of Jergens, Hakeem. It is almost as though he leads a charmed life," Francois said, anxiously waiting the ringing of the phone.

On the first ring, he picked up the receiver. The heavily accented voice of his pilot responded to his greeting.

"Rene," Francois ordered, "Roberto will be needing a ride. His fare is good to about the middle of the Atlantic. See that his baggage goes with him."

"Oui, monsieur," was Rene's unemotional reply.

"And, Rene."

"Monsieur."

"I want you to continue on to Paris. You will pick up two passengers, and bring them here as quickly as possible. Phillip will provide their description. Are you clear on what you are to do?"

"Oui, monsieur. I understand perfectly."

"Very good, then get on with it," Francois said.

"Isn't this rivalry getting out of hand, Francois?" Hakeem asked in a voice that matched his cold expression. "Jergens bids, unsuccessfully I might add, on a horse you covet for purely personal reasons, shows only a business interest in a woman who has shown only mild interest in you, and you resort to violent methods to eliminate him.

"Overreacting, my friend, is very dangerous," he warned. "It is unwise to pursue this issue, and I think, this woman. She has poisoned your judgment, perhaps to the point where our deal is in jeopardy. Perhaps, Francois, we have chosen the wrong man for the job."

"You have not chosen the wrong man, Hakeem, and you know it," Francois replied, keeping his voice even. "There is more to this Jergens fellow than meets the eye. I am sorry to say that I think he plans to use Alanna as a pawn."

Francois turned from the Arab, and looking out the window, he said, "She is very special to me, Hakeem."

"I can see that, Francois, but how do you think she will feel about you when she discovers what you really are?"

"After this deal is complete," Francois said, turning back to face Hakeem, "I will have no more need for this line of work. I intend to retire, then I can be what she believes I am."

"You fool yourself, my friend." Hakeem's remark was accompanied by a cynical laugh. "You are a greedy bastard, as am I. No amount of money will ever be enough, especially, when we know there is so much more to be made. No, she will grow to hate you, and then you may find it necessary one day to make her fare good for only half the trip. Spare yourself and her the pain."

"It is not your concern," Francois, not appreciating the Arab's intrusion into his private life, replied.

"Ah, but it is, Francois. Anything that affects this deal is my concern," Hakeem countered. "I will leave now. When you have this dilemma resolved, let me know and I will return."

The Arab rose and left the room.

Francois sat down at his desk, and pressed the call button. A few minutes later, Phillip was at the door.

"Oui, monsieur?" Phillip said, upon entering the room.

"Phillip, have you been able to reach our contact in Washington?"

"Non, monsieur. We have had no word from him." Phillip replied. "When I call, all I get is a recording saying the number has been disconnected. It is possible the Americans are on to him."

"Let's hope not. I need to get in touch with him, Phillip." Francois said, drumming him fingers on the desk pad. "It is a certainty that the CIA has replaced their agent. I must know who it is."

"I agree, Monsieur. May I suggest sending a message via the 'live' drop?"

"Yes, yes, do that, Phillip." Francois wrote a message on a piece of notepaper and handed it to Phillip, who started towards the door.

"Oh, Phillip!"

"Oui, Monsieur?"

"You did a good job of handling the police and the press on the matter of the accidental death of our men," Francois remarked. "Thank you."

Phillip just nodded his head in recognition of one of Francois' rare expressions of gratitude, and proceeded to carry out his new assignment.

"Damn!" Francois said out loud, as he sat down in the amply upholstered, leather chair situated behind the large, cherry desk. Then, he thought to himself, if my men did not make contact with Jergens, then I have nothing to worry about. However, if they did, Jergens would know by the article in the paper that the people who had tried to assault him were my men. If indeed Jergens knows, and has chosen not report the incident to the police, then it can only mean one thing: that it is as important to Jergens as it is to me to keep this matter under wraps. What reason could Jergens have for wanting to keep such an incident under wraps? Could it possibly be that, by exposing me, he would be exposing himself?

Francois reached for the phone. He placed a call on a secure line, and waited as the phone in a luxury apartment in Neuilly-Sur-Seine summoned its occupant.

It seemed to ring forever before it was answered by a seductive female voice.

"Oui?"

"Nenet, it is Francois."

"Ah, Francois," the voice oozed its deadly sweetness, "it has been too long. To what do I owe the pleasure of this call?"

"I have taken the liberty of sending my plane for you and your friend. I hope you are free to enjoy a few days in Saratoga."

"Well, as a matter of fact, Francois, my friend and I had plans to take care of some old business in Madrid," the sultry voice of the women, whose code name was taken from the Egyptian Book of the Dead, replied.

"I will make it worth your while to change those plans, my sweet." Francois responded to the woman's need to bargain.

"Oh, but certainly, my dear Francois, if your little outing promises to be profitable as well as enjoyable, I am sure we can change our plans."

"How very generous of you, Nenet," Francois replied. "We will discuss the details of your visit when you arrive. Phillip will be in touch with you directly. Au revoir, my angel." And he hung up the phone.

* * *

Chet Rakeland made his way to his desk, as he had every morning since Lila had dropped the news of Security pulling his file. Outwardly, nothing appeared to have changed with his routine, but he had become very cautious, even to the point of having the second phone line in his apartment, the one he used for his extracurricular activities, disconnected. Now, if the Agency had a tap on his line, all they'd get would be a bunch of giggly female callers and his old maid aunt.

He was busy working on a report, when he heard his supervisor's voice behind him say, "Chet, would you step into my office for a moment."

"Sure, Bob, I'll be right in," he replied, and a chill ran down his spine, as it did these days whenever anyone in authority said anything to him.

He closed the folder of the report he was working on, and put it in the safe in his desk. When he arrived at the supervisor's office, he found the door opened. He knocked anyway, and his supervisor, who was in the midst of a telephone conversation, waved him in.

"That's perfect, Dave," the supervisor said, to the caller. "As soon as I have the results of that report, I'll get back with ya, buddy. Take care." He laughed at something the caller said, and hung up the phone.

Turning his attention to Rakeland, he said, "Chet, it's your turn to go on the lecture circuit. Starting Monday, you'll be doing your thing over at the school in Alexandria. Can you finish that Cortland report, and have it to me before you go over there?"

"I'm finishing it up now," Rakeland replied, relieved that this encounter was simply business as usual. "I should have it ready to be typed tomorrow afternoon."

"Fine. Well, that's all I needed you for, you can get back to work." And with that, Bob picked up the phone and started to place a call.

Rakeland went back to his desk, and pulled the Cortland file back out of his safe. He opened the folder, but he couldn't get his mind to focus on the job. Instead, it insisted on dwelling on the possibility that he had been discovered.

He tried to dismiss the thought by telling himself that he was overreacting. What he'd told Lila that day, about it being normal procedure for someone in his position to have his file pulled every once in a while, was true. So, maybe they weren't on to him. Maybe, it was only his guilty conscience creating this paranoia. Still, he couldn't shake the feeling that "big brother" was watching him.

The worse thing about having to lay low was that the Agency probably already had a replacement for Jake Carter in the field. He needed to find out who that person was, but not being able to operate freely, meant getting the information would have to wait. There was one thing Rakeland was sure of, the man he'd seen boarding the Falcon 900-B at the Farm was Jeremy Slade. The ground crew employee he'd questioned about the plane had said that it had been leased by the Agency for an operation. A costly piece of equipment like the Falcon 900-B usually meant it was a big operation.

Five years ago, Jeremy would have been the undisputed choice as a replacement for Jake. However, today that might not hold true, for Rakeland knew another little secret. He knew Jeremy was considered a burnout. He also knew that there was one thing the Agency would never do, and that was to assign an operation of this magnitude to a burnout.

Somebody had gotten Jake's job, and it was costing him big bucks not knowing who that somebody was.

There was another thing laying low had hampered him from doing. He had to get a message to his clients. He knew they'd probably been trying to get in touch with him, and that they would be alarmed when they discovered the number they were cleared to call him on had been disconnected. They'd break contact immediately if they conclude that he was under suspicion. It would cost him the job.

Rakeland's growling stomach reminded him it was lunchtime. He put the file back in his safe, and locked it. Two other people from his department were on their way to the Agency cafeteria, so he joined them.

As he came away from the cafeteria food line and made his way to a table, he noticed Ray Stasio from the Operations Division sitting at a table by himself. Stasio was a case officer assigned to the station in Ankara, Turkey.

He diverted his course so that he passed by Stasio's table.

As he came up to the man, Rakeland said, "Hey, Stasio, how ya doing?"

When Stasio seemed not to recognize him, he added, "Chet, Chet Rakeland, from TSD, I gave you a hand on a job a couple of years back."

His memory jarred, Stasio replied, "Hey, Rakeland, how the hell are you?"

"Good. Good." Rakeland shifted his tray as if about to drop it.

Stasio started to rise in an attempt to catch the falling tray, but Rakeland righted it before he succeeded.

"If you're not sitting with anyone, why don't you join me?" Stasio invited.

"Thanks, I will." And Rakeland sat down across from the thin, dour looking man.

A camera, hidden in a briefcase at the foot of one of the security men observing Rakeland from the upper tier of the cafeteria, quickly recorded Rakeland and Stasio in conversation.

Before Stasio had a chance to leave the cafeteria, the security man operating the camera, ordered his partner, "Evan, make a pass by their table and eyeball that guy with Rakeland, then wait out in the hall. I'll let you know when he's on his way out, so you can get an ID on him."

Without comment, Evan headed to the lower level and made a pass by the table, but one aisle over from it, calling no attention to himself. He waited out in the hall until word came from his partner over his hidden communicator alerting him that Stasio was on his way out.

As Stasio headed up the corridor to the elevator, the security man headed back toward the cafeteria. At the point that their paths intercepted, the security man quickly noted the number on Stasio's badge.

"Q1127A, repeat, Q1127A." The security man passed the information to his partner via his communicator.

"Got it." Came the reply.

An hour later, the Chief of the Middle East Division, Arthur Limbach's phone rang.

"Limbach, here," he responded.

"It's Granton Taylor, Art, how've you been?"

"Worked to death, as usual, Granton. What can I do for you?"

"You have a man in your division by the name of Ray Stasio. I'd like to borrow him. He has some input into an operation I'm running."

"That's fine with me, chief, should I send him right up."

"Thanks, Art, I'd appreciate it if you would." And Granton added in conclusion, "Oh, and, Art, this is a tight one, strictly need to know."

"You got it. He'll be right up."

Fifteen minutes later, a curious Ray Stasio found himself in Granton Taylor's office. Taylor was in the company of two men whom Stasio failed to recognize.

"Thank you for coming by, Ray," Granton said, putting down the file he'd been reading and rising from the chair behind his desk. "This is Tom Paine and Joe Poole from the Chief of Security's office.

Stasio wasn't sure why, but suddenly, as he acknowledged the two men and they returned his greeting, he felt his pucker string close in on his Adam's apple.

Sensing Stasio's nervousness, Granton said, "You're not in any kind of trouble, Ray, we need your help. Have a seat." Granton indicated the chair across from him. Stasio took a seat, his shoulders relaxing as Granton's announcement relieved his anxiety. The security men also resumed their seated positions.

"Ray you were observed having lunch in the cafeteria with a guy from TSD named Chet Rakeland. How well to you know this man, and where did you meet him? Tell us about it."

"I knew him in Ankara. He was on temporary duty supporting some of our operations. I had to get the guy set up with a room and stuff, and handle him while he was there. He serviced some taps and bugs we had going, and did some new stuff. I wasn't really close to him; he was never really friendly, kind of a loner. Except, that is until today, when I ran into him in the cafeteria, he was as friendly as could be."

"What was your conversation about? Anything in particular?"

"No, just talk, but he was very friendly."

"Ray, we have reason to believe that this guy is going try to meet with you again." Granton further explained the situation. "If he does, we want you to go along with him. You don't have to do anything, just be friendly, and report the conversation to us.

"Just so that you'll understand the seriousness of this matter, I am making you privy to some top secret information that indicates that this man probably caused the death of one of our top intelligence officers."

Oh, shit! Stasio thought.

"We also believe, that at some point, he will attempt to get operational information from you. We intend to use you to see that the information he gets is false. Do you have a problem cooperating with us on this?"

"None at all, sir!"

"That's good." Granton indicated the man sitting closest to the door, and said, "Poole will be your handler. He'll brief you. Just do what he tells you."

As Stasio headed back to his office, he smiled to no one in particular and thought, if I pull this off Granton will have to reward me. I think the job of Chief of Station in Acapulco ought to do it. Good-bye Ankara!

* * *

Jeremy tried the telephone number Alanna had provided for the house on Union Street where Doyle was supposed to be staying. Twice, there was no answer. On the third try, the owner of the house answered, and he was told that Mr. Doyle had gone to the sale and the races, and she had no idea when he'd be back.

Would he like to leave a message?

Would he ever, but the one he gave her was not the one he would have liked to have left.

The phone rang. Jeremy waited until the answering machine took the call, and he heard Alanna's voice before picking up the receiver.

"How are you?" she said. "What did Granton have to say?"

"I'd feel a lot better," he replied, and Alanna could sense the unhappiness in his voice, "if Granton hadn't told me to turn the backup over to Doyle and get out of town. Shit!"

"You can't blame him, Jeremy. You're putting your life and the mission at risk, if you stay."

"I know," he said, wearily. "So, now I get to play case officer from some boring office in nowheresville."

"Feel sorry for yourself, if you must, but at least you'll be alive and useful. Doyle's got all those great qualifications, so let him do what you hired him for."

"Are you going to be all right with him?"

There was no answer.

"Alanna!"

"Doyle and I will be fine. You just listen to Granton, Jeremy."

"I'm scared for you, Alanna."

215

"I'm scared for me too, Jeremy, but you're getting killed because that jerk, Francois, is jealous of you won't help me. Knowing you're there behind me, that'll help me."

"I won't be close enough behind you!"

"I've got to go, Jeremy. We'll talk when I get home. Bye!"

* * *

Alanna was just crossing the road, when she saw Paddy, Michael and Aiden looking at yearlings from a consignment stabled next to hers. She ignored the look Aiden gave her, and headed over to her barn, where an agent from the British Bloodstock Agency was looking at a yearling.

Activity at the sales grounds had slowed considerably as the races were now underway, and many of the buyers had gone to spend the afternoon at the track. As the BBA agent left, and Alanna's yearling was returning to its stall, the Irish trio made their way over to her barn.

Alanna went into her tack room to check on some equipment. When she came out, they were waiting for her.

"Good afternoon, gentlemen." She greeted them warmly. "Would you care to see a yearling or two?"

"You're lookin' lovelier than ever this afternoon, Alanna," Paddy said. "You bet we'd like to see some yearlings. Michael and I would like to see 68, 73 and 105. Anything special you'd like to see, Aiden?"

"Yes, I like to see 89," he replied, looking directly at Alanna.

"Is that the only yearling you'd like to see, Aiden?" Alanna asked. "May I suggest 93 as well?"

"If you think 93's worth a look, let's have it."

"Julie we need 68, 73, 89, 93 and 105. We'll have 68 and 89 first, please."

The grooms hurriedly polished off their yearlings and led them out for inspection. Alanna had them spaced far enough apart that her conversation with Aiden could not be overheard.

"We missed you at dinner last night." Aiden said, under his breath, as he pretended to go over the confirmation of the yearling poised before him. "I was looking forward to having a drink, and a little in-depth conversation with you afterwards, just the two of us, of course. By the way, where, the hell is Slade? I called his room twice, and never got an answer. I even went by his room before we headed off to dinner."

"Sorry about dinner, the filly I rescued yesterday got into trouble again. I had to ship her home," she replied, also under her breath.

"Anyway, it's not me you should be concerned about discussing things with."

"Let him have a walk, will you." Aiden said to the yearling's groom, and the boy led the horse off away from them.

"I've been trying all morning to call him." He wrote a comment in his catalogue, and as the boy returned with the colt, he said, "Once more, would you, please."

And the boy and the horse moved off again.

"Francois tried to have him killed last night," Alanna said.

Aiden never took his eyes off the colt or changed his tone of voice. "Where is he?"

"He's at my place. You need to get over there. Now!"

Paddy and Michael, having finished inspecting their yearlings, rejoined them.

"That's a real nice filly, Alanna," Paddy said, of the last yearling he'd looked at.

"Yes, she is Paddy. Her half-brother looks like he might be stakes material. At least that's what the trainer told me."

Aiden, having finished looking over the second yearling, turned his attention back to the group, and said, "Ninety-three's a right nice colt, Alanna."

"Well, I've had enough of looking at horses' behinds in this heat," Paddy said, while wiping his brow with his handkerchief. "What da ya say we go over to that Spittin Devil, or whatever you call it, and get ourselves some liquid refreshment, lads. You, too, Alanna, take a break, lass."

"I think I will join you, Paddy, I could use something cold to drink," Alanna replied. "I'll just be a minute. I need to let Julie know where I'm going."

"I'm going to pass, Paddy," Aiden said, as Alanna headed to where Julie was standing, holding one of their yearlings for a client's inspection. "Alanna gave me the address of a gallery where I can get that Sun Star print I've been wanting. So I think, if we're finished looking at yearlings for a while, I'll take a run over there and get it."

"Well then," Paddy said, "we'll meet you for lunch at Mrs. London's. It's on Caroline St. You can park in that lot off Union Ave. It's easier than fighten' those blessed one-way streets."

"Right," Aiden said, and without waiting for Alanna to return, left.

When Alanna returned, Aiden was gone.

"Aiden chose not to join us," Paddy said."

217

"That's fine with me, Paddy," she said, starting in the direction of the bar. "Shall we go?"

* * *

Rice had left Tad Clark to monitor the bug TSD had installed in Francois' limousine, while he went in search of Jeremy. He'd been surprised to find the note under his door that morning. It didn't give any details other than, if he were looking for his boss, he could find him at the enclosed address, and to park in the vacant lot behind the house.

He cruised past the house on Salem Avenue. Seeing that there were no cars parked in the drive or anywhere in the vicinity, he proceeded to the street that backed up to the house, where he found the lot.

There was no sign of Jeremy's car. He parked his rental car, and walked through the trees to the back of the house. There were two doors, one to the garage and the other to a sun porch. He peered through the garage door, and saw Jeremy's car parked inside. When he tried the door, he found that it was locked, so he went to the sun porch and knocked on the door.

Jeremy caught a glimpse of Rice making his way from the garage door to the sun porch. Before Rice could knock twice, he was at the door.

"I'd like to think you're here because you and Alanna decided to make this more than a working relationship, but I have a feeling that's not the case," Rice said, in the way of a greeting.

"I wish I could tell you your first inclination was correct, but I'm afraid it's your second one that's accurate," Jeremy replied, closing and locking the door behind Rice.

"The morning paper said Francois lost three of his men in an accident." Rice pointed out the article in the newspaper. "When I put that piece of news together with the note I found shoved under my door, it wasn't hard to figure who'd encouraged Francois' men to see if that Mercedes was amphibious. Was I right?"

"Well, they had orders from Francois to make my evening unpleasant. In fact, they'd taken it upon themselves to make the unpleasantness permanent. I didn't have a choice, but I as you can see I survived."

"Not without help, I take it?"

"Right again," Jeremy replied, acknowledging, but not elaborating on Alanna's assistance. "I'm glad you're here. We need to find Doyle." Dejectedly adding. "I've been ordered to turn the backup duties over to him."

"What?" Rice was stunned. "Taylor's replacing you, and Tad and me too? Why?"

"Granton's afraid if Francois keeps this up, it'll blow the mission."

"So we get dumped in favor of the Irishman?" Rice said, knowing full well that Jeremy was even more disappointed at the news than he was. "Hell, I was just gettin' into this game."

"Doyle can handle it," Jeremy replied, "and we have to think of Alanna. If Francois begins to feel too threatened, he could put a lot of pressure on her to do things that none of us want her to do."

"I got that loud and clear. So what do we do now?"

"Find Doyle, and keep a eye on Francois and the Arab until Granton can send Doyle some help.

"Grab a seat. There are some things we need to go over." Jeremy said, indicating to Rice the dining room table on which he'd set the telephone, and a pad he was making some notations on. "Want a cup of coffee?"

"Sure, just black," Rice said, as he took a seat.

"Where's Tad?" Jeremy went to the counter, and filled a cup.

"Minding the bugmobile."

"Get anything?"

"Yeah, last night Francois and that Arab went to dinner in Albany. Tad kept them company while I sat around waiting for Doyle to show, which of course, he didn't. What is with that guy?"

"It's hard to say, Rice. He made contact with Alanna, so we know he's here," Jeremy said, as he handed the cup to Rice, and sat down across from him.

"Well, anyway," Rice continued. "I brought along the tape so you could hear for yourself what they had to say. One thing they found immensely funny was how it was going to be real hard for anyone to figure out where they were getting their little goody. Something about how it wouldn't show on any inventory list because it was made out of spare parts. Got any idea what he meant by that?"

"Are you sure he said that?" Jeremy said, suddenly excited.

"Yeah, I'm sure! Here! Listen!" And he pulled a cigarette pack sized tape player from his pocket, stuck the tiny earpiece in his ear and turned it on. He ran it, stopping occasionally to pinpoint conversations, when he reached the desired spot, he handed Jeremy the earpiece.

"Good, God. That's it. Damn it, that's why we couldn't find the bugger," Jeremy said, grabbing the phone and starting to dial. Before he could complete the call there was a knock at the sunporch door.

219

Jeremy set the receiver back on the phone, and pulled out his gun. He took up a position against the wall next to the telephone stand, and motioned to Rice to see who was at the door.

"I can see him from here and I don't recognize him." Rice said. "He's about 6 foot, black hair, dark eyes, slender-- kind of."

Jeremy put his gun up, and went to the door.

"About time you showed, Aiden," he said, caustically, as he opened the door for the Irishman.

"Should have known I'd find you lollygaggin' at the lady's place," Doyle replied, with equal rancor, as he stepped into the sun porch. "It's the first place I should've looked."

"You boys on the same team by any chance?" Rice interrupted Jeremy and Aiden's verbal exchange.

Neither man said anything in response.

Then Doyle put out his hand to Jeremy, and said, "Can't accomplish anything with this attitude, now can we?"

"You're right, Aiden." Jeremy shook the Irishman's hand and motioned for him to join them at the table. En route, he introduced Rice. "Aiden, this is Bill Rice. He's my pilot and backup man. We have one other man, Tad Clark. Right now, he's manning the bugs."

Aiden nodded to Rice, and offered his hand, which Rice shook.

"Coffee?" Rice offered.

"No thanks," Aiden declined the offer.

"You look pretty good for an assassin's target," Aiden remarked, alluding to the previous night's incident. "They couldn't have been too competent?"

"I owe my present good health to my sorceress friend," Jeremy replied. "You ought to have Alanna give your attitude an adjustment sometime. She's a real miracle worker."

Jesus, let's not start again, Rice thought. Don't these two ever back off.

"I see nothing's changed between us, Jeremy," Aiden said, a crooked smile replacing the serious expression on his face. "She may have worked miracles on your body, but you're not a good sell for an attitude adjustment. However, I might just have her give mine a fine tuning after I've helped you out of this mess. Might be, she'd be more successful with better material to work with."

After hesitating for a moment to let the full impact of the verbal swipe sink in, he added, "Now, shall we cut out the dickering and get on with it."

"In a minute," Jeremy said, as he reached for the telephone, less than happy that he'd brought up the subject of Alanna. "I was just about to call Granton with some information Tad picked up with the bug we have planted in Francois' limousine."

Before he could dial Granton's number, Rice's beeper went off.

"Hold up a minute, Jeremy," Rice said, as he read the message coming over the beeper's display. "Tad wants me to call him right away."

Jeremy slid the phone over to him, and Rice made the call. When Tad answered, Rice turned the phone over to Jeremy.

"What have you got, Tad?"

"Francois' pilot, and some guy named Roberto, are on their way to the Albany Airport," Tad replied. "I can't make out exactly what this Roberto's connection is with Francois, but, from the tone in his voice, I'd say he's in deep shit.

"He's been trying for a half hour to tell the pilot how it wasn't his fault his men got drunk, and bungled some kind of job they were sent on last night. He's really pissed with them, says he doesn't even know if they even made an attempt to pull it off. And, he's worried that he may be out of a job. I thought you'd want to know about this immediately."

"Thanks, Tad. Keep on them. We'll be at the hotel when you get back." There was a pause as Tad signed off, and Jeremy hung up the phone. He leaned back in the chair, sighed a huge sigh of relief, and without commenting on Tad and his conversation, lifted the receiver back up, and dialed Granton's number.

"Yes," Granton's greeting ended the ringing of the phone.

"It's Jeremy. You're not going to believe what I just found out."

"Try me?"

"The reason that nuke isn't showing up missing from anyone's arsenal," Jeremy began, "is because it's not listed on anybody's inventory list. And the reason it's not on anyone's inventory list is because it's made from spare parts."

"Did I just hear you right? It's made of spare parts?" Granton said, the surprise evident in his voice. "How do you know that?"

"You heard me right. Francois told Hakeem that on their way to dinner last night." Jeremy replied. "Tad picked it up while he was monitoring the bug we planted in Francois' limo."

"Christ, that's just great," Granton exclaimed. "Now they've got their hands on a nuke nobody even knows exists. I wonder how many other little packages like this are running around Russia and the Ukraine untagged. I need to get in touch with our Moscow and Kiev stations right away."

"Hang on a minute, Granton. I've got more news. First of all, Doyle is sitting here with me, and I am about to brief him. But, more importantly, Tad overheard one of Francois' boys saying that they have no idea whether or not those men he sent to get me ever even made an attempt to do the job."

There was silence on the other end, and then Granton said, "That may be, Jeremy, but your hanging on there is still a risk."

"Give me a break, Granton," Jeremy pleaded his case. "If I really felt I was a liability to this operation, you wouldn't have to yank me, I'd quit. Francois isn't dumb enough to pull this twice."

Another silence filled the airwaves, as Jeremy held up crossed fingers.

"I'm going to trust your judgment on this, Jeremy." Granton said, while trying to ignore the sigh of relief that came across his line, "but, just in case you're wrong, I'm going to set up a contingency support group for you. I'm going to arrange for a small group of FBI agents to be set up in Saratoga in case you run into any more trouble. We know that the Bureau doesn't really like us running operations inside the U.S., but in this case, this operation has such high priority, I can get the Admiral to get with their Director and order them to support us. I'd like to talk to Alanna about this, so have her give me a call. By the time she gets back to me, I should have things in place."

"I appreciate you doing this, Granton." Jeremy replied, grateful for his superior's support. "I have a plan of my own to take the heat off of this situation."

"Just be careful what you do, Jeremy."

"I will," he said, as he gave the thumbs up to Rice. Then changing the subject, he added, "Any news on Rakeland?"

"It looks like he's beginning to feel the squeeze. If he's going to come up with any more information on this deal for his patrons, he's going to have to make a move and soon.

"Yesterday, he approached Ray Stasio, a case officer from our Ankara station, who's back here for debriefing. We think he plans to use Stasio at some point. We've already enlisted Stasio's aid so that we can feed him some bogus information.

"According to Security, Rakeland's day to day routine hasn't changed much. He made three stops on his way to work this morning -- a bakery, a supermarket and a laundry. All we can do now is wait for him to make a move."

"If he's our man, I sure wish we could take him out," Jeremy said. "He makes me very nervous."

"I understand," Granton concurred, then in closing added, "Oh, and until the heat is off you, Jeremy, you let Doyle make the bulk of the contact with Alanna."

"I will."

"I'll expect to hear from Alanna." Granton reiterated, and with that, the communication was ended.

"Got a reprieve?" Rice asked.

"For now."

* * *

The late afternoon sun temporarily blinded Alanna as she turned off of Lake Avenue onto Salem. She pulled into her driveway, and parked the Volvo, but she did not immediately kill the engine. Instead, she sat in its air-conditioned comfort, trying to find a moment's peace from what had been a very hectic 24 hours.

Not wanting to think of anything personal, especially not about Jeremy, who waited inside, she focused her attention on the house. It was a pretty house, she thought, this red brick, ranch house. Simple and homey, it sat on a fair-sized, shaded lot in a neighborhood of similarly typed homes. Located only a couple of blocks from the racetrack and the sales grounds, you could hear the sounds of the cheering crowds through its opened windows. For four years, it had provided a comforting retreat, a welcome respite from the sweltering heat of August in Kentucky and the rigors of farm life.

Unable to keep her personal thoughts at bay, Alanna considered how much her life changed every time Jeremy made an appearance in it. He had a way of turning her somewhat secure world upside-down. Fate had not been kind to their personal relationship, and it had, on several occasions, tested their professional relationship pretty thoroughly. But it had, over the years, created a unique bond between them, a bond that made them a potent force in the intelligence game.

Jeremy had done a masterful job of masking his feelings for her over the course of their relationship. But, last night's drug induced sleep had roused the demons that lurked within him, and his feelings were exposed, the thread that had wound its way through each troubled dream that night was his love for her.

223

Even she could not deny, that being as close, physically, to Jeremy as she had been last night, stirred some old embers.

She thought about Jeremy waiting inside the red brick house, and wondered how his conversation with Granton had gone? Was their partnership history? Could she carry out this mission as well with Aiden? How would she handle this evolving personal issue?

Alanna sighed a heavy sigh, shut down the engine, then after gathering up some papers from off the back seat, got out of the car, and headed to the front door. As she unlocked the door and entered the vestibule, she called out, "If you're hiding under the bed, it's safe to come out now."

"Very funny," Jeremy remarked, from his reclined position on the couch, in the shade darkened living room.

"Before you get busy doing something," he said, as he got up and followed her into the dining area, where she was in the process of setting her papers on the table. "Give Granton a call."

"I will, in a minute," she said. Then turning to him, added, "But first take off your shirt and let me have a look at your shoulder."

"Hmmm," Jeremy replied, a sly grin spreading across his face. "Why that's the best offer I've had all day."

"I'm not impressed," she remarked, sarcastically, recognizing one of his famous 'harmless' teases coming on. "Let's face it, it's the only 'offer' you've had all day."

"Are you implying that I'm hard up?" He said with mock indignation, as he took off his shirt, which revealed a tastefully muscled chest, tinged a slight yellow-green from last night's bruising.

"Of late, yes, I'd say your hard up," she said as she checked his shoulder and examined her handiwork on the bruises.

"You could change that."

"I could," she replied, teasing him with a sexy smile. "But, I won't."

"Damn, just my luck," he responded with an accompanied shrug of his shoulders, which elicited a loud, "Ouch!"

"Go easy on that shoulder." The tempting tone in her voice replaced by one bearing a stern warning. "It may feel better, but it's far from healed."

"So I noticed."

"I'll call Granton then I'll make you some tea to ease the pain."

"Oh, God, not more tea!" Jeremy protested. "You know a little Jack Daniels would work just as well, and taste a hell of a lot better."

"Suit yourself," she said, as she picked up the phone with the secured line, and dialed Granton's number. There was a brief pause, and then she merely said, "It's Alanna."

After that, her end of their short conversation was limited to acquiescing comments, and a brief parting salutation. "Mmmhmm." Pause. "Mmmm." Pause. "That could work." Pause. "I understand." A pause followed by a light laugh, "Thanks, Granton. Good-bye."

"Well?" Jeremy asked, as she replaced the receiver on its base and headed into the kitchen.

"I'll tell you in a minute," she said, as she went to the refrigerator. She removed a bottle of spring water from the refrigerator; filled a six-ounce glass with ice, then took a bottle of Jack Daniels from a cabinet under the kitchen counter. She poured liquor over the ice, then opened the bottle of water and took a drink. Handing him the glass, she remarked, "Sorry, I was dying of thirst. It must have been 95 degrees in the shade out there this afternoon."

"Salud!" He said, raising his glass in a toast, a gesture she returned. "So, what's the deal?"

"The FBI has assigned three agents to us. They will be set up in an apartment here in town," Alanna said, as she wrote a telephone number on a piece of paper and handed it to Jeremy, "and will keep this phone number manned 24 hours a day. We are to make sure everyone has the number. The FBI does not know who we are, but if there's trouble, we are to call this number and say, that this is Operation QUILL, and that we need immediate assistance."

"Does Granton really think we're going to need these guys?"

"He must. We have 'em."

"I think his going to all this trouble because of the incident with Francois is overkill," Jeremy said, following a sip of his drink. "Francois is not crazy enough to try something like that twice, even to insure himself of your undivided attention."

"Francois certainly is risking a lot in order to have me to himself," Alanna remarked, as she screwed the cap back on the water bottle and replaced it in the refrigerator. "I'd be really flattered if he were the genuine article."

"Heck, I've risked everything for you, and I consider myself the genuine article," Jeremy said, the twinkle returning to his eyes, "how come you never seem flattered by my efforts?"

"God! You're incorrigible, Jeremy, and what's worse, you have a one track mind."

"Of course, I'm incorrigible." He laughed as he added, "And, you love it."

Chapter 19

Rakeland unloaded his car, trying unsuccessfully to juggle the things he'd picked up at the supermarket, the cleaners and the bakery without squashing his loaf of bread.

"Damn," he said, as he caught the loaf from slipping out of his hand with his elbow mashing it flat against his side. He maneuvered the key in his apartment door, and kicked the door open with his foot.

"Shit," he said, as he set the distorted loaf on the hall table. He deposited the other grocery bags on the kitchen floor, and took his laundry into the bedroom. There, he hung most of the cleaned items in the closet. The one suit in the load, he hung on a hook on the back of the closet door. Reaching under the plastic cover and the jacket, he removed the laundry tag that was pinned to the trouser.

From an overhead shelf, he removed a large battery operated flashlight/emergency radio unit. He opened the back of the unit, removed the batteries, and reaching into it, removed a small, flat, black box. He set the main unit down, and taking the black box and laundry ticket went into the bedroom, and set them on the nightstand next to his bed.

He took off his jacket and hung it over the oak valet, kicked his shoes off, loosened his shirt collar and tie, and sat down on the edge of the bed. Taking the black box in his hand, he ran his finger over a small switch imbedded in the side of the box, and watched as a green light next to it began to glow. Then, he picked up the laundry ticket, and inserted it in a slot in one end. A moment passed before the green light went off, and the box expelled the ticket from the open end.

The ticket now bore a line of letters on its reverse side. Using a codebook he had hidden behind the mirror in the bathroom medicine chest, he deciphered the message. The message was short. "Communicate. Now."

Great, he said to himself, knowing his place was bugged and unable to do anything about it without giving himself away. Okay, if communication is what you want, communication is what you'll get.

The CIA security man watching the front door signaled to his partner that Rakeland was leaving his house on foot. When it was determined in what direction he was headed, security people stationed along that route stood ready to cover Rakeland's every move. Their tag led them to an Italian restaurant. Rakeland was seated and ordering a drink, when the security team, made up of a man and woman, walked into the restaurant, and was seated two tables from him. Nothing out of the ordinary took place except that in the process of eating his meal, Rakeland managed to drop some tomato sauce on his jacket. He was observed making an attempt to remove the spot with water and a napkin, and then he finished his dinner, and returned home.

Rakeland made a great show in front of his window of watching TV, then preparing for bed. He turned out the apartment lights, and went to bed. When he felt he'd lulled his surveillors into a stupor, he used the soft glow from the room's nightlight to make his way to the far wall and his desk. Taking an ordinary looking 3x5 piece of paper from the desk drawer, he made a list of supermarket items on it, then slid it behind the calendar located in the front of his pocket secretary. He removed a headless straightpin from the back seam of the pocket secretary, and proceeded to insert the pinhead into almost imperceptible holes in the calendar's days, dates and numbers sections, affecting an encoded message. He, then, took the paper, and inserted it into the inside pocket of the sport coat with the spot on it that he had rehung over the oak valet.

The next morning, as two men from security watched from their car, Rakeland carried the soiled sport coat into the laundry and deposited it on the counter.

"Take care of that jacket," Rakeland said to the clerk, "It's made out of China silk."

"Not to worry," the man behind the counter said. Recognizing the words China silk as an identifying code, he immediately did a check of all the pockets, stopping long enough to finger the message in the interior pocket. "We handle all delicate items with extreme care."

Handing Rakeland a claim check, he said, "Your jacket should be ready tomorrow afternoon, if you care to pick it up then."

"Sounds good to me," Rakeland replied, and turning to leave, said, "Have a good one!"

* * *

The black Mercedes limousine flashed its headlights as it splashed to a stop in front of the Au Pere Tranquille. Hakeem, the collar of his jacket pulled up around his neck as a buffer to the Parisian downpour, stepped out from the shelter of the bistro's doorway, and hurried to the waiting vehicle.

He did not wait for the driver to open the door. Slipping quickly into the automobile's dark interior, he took a seat facing backwards. As he settled into the rich leather upholstery, and readjusted his collar, his associate, Kamal Shabban, greeted him from the facing seat.

"So, Hakeem, how was your vacation in Saratoga?" Kamal inquired.

"Very interesting," Hakeem replied.

"And our friend, Francois," Kamal continued the inquiry, "is he having an interesting time, as well?"

Hakeem did not respond, at first, and then he said, "We have a serious problem, Kamal."

"The package," Kamal inquired, concern evident in his voice. "There is another complication with the package's delivery? Francois knows that time is of the essence now. With this one blow, we will totally change the balance of power in the Middle East. Israel will have met its match in Kamal Shabban. And once we have dealt with Israel, the Americans will be the next to feel the pain."

"No," Hakeem replied. "Francois assured me that the package is on schedule. But, I feel a risk still remains."

There was silence again, and when Hakeem did not seem willing to come forward with further details, Kamal asked, "What causes you such anxiety, my brother?"

"If I did not know Francois half so well," Hakeem replied, disgust hung heavy on his voice, "I would think the man has turned senile overnight."

Again there was silence from the younger man.

"And, why is that, Hakeem" Kamal inquired further, his voice tinged with irritation. "Tell me. Must I pull this from you word by word?"

"Francois has become infatuated with a young woman."

"Hah!" Laughed the old Arab. "This is what you interpret as senility. Hah, Hah!" His laughter rang out in the cavernous back seat.

"I am really surprised at you, Hakeem. What is so unusual about that? Francois is getting to the age when you younger men usually interpret we older men's fascination with younger women as an expression of senility. Hah, Hah, that is very humorous, Hakeem."

Not wishing to seem disrespectful to his superior, Hakeem let Kamal enjoy what humor he saw in the event, then he added, "His infatuation with this woman would not have caused me such concern had he not almost created an international incident to insure that another man would be unable to compete for the lady's attention."

The laughter faded from Kamal's voice and eyes, turning them brutally cold.

"Are you serious, Hakeem?"

The look on the younger man's face was answer enough.

"I apologize for my lack of trust in your judgment, Hakeem." After pausing briefly to gather his thoughts, he continued. "Tell me about the matter."

Hakeem filled in the old Arab on the details as the car headed out of Paris, and on to Montmartre, where their safe house was located.

"He has hired Nenet to do in this Jergens fellow." Hakeem concluded his explanation just as the limousine pulled through the heavily guarded entranceway, and started up the drive of the chateau.

"That is troublesome indeed," Kamal remarked, as he waited for his driver to come around and open the door. "Let us go inside and see what we can do to salvage this situation."

Once inside the chateau, they went directly to Kamal's office, where he placed a call to a Hizballah contact in New York City. He gave the contact the information on Jergens, which Hakeem had secured from Francois' secretary, Phillip, and instructed him to do a thorough background check on the American.

While they awaited word, Kamal changed the subject.

"Hakeem, I must ask you to divert your attention from our dealings with Francois for a while in order to assist Hamas in a project of great importance."

Hakeem did not respond, knowing he had no real choice in the matter. What Kamal ordered, Hakeem was expected to do

"The PLO police have again joined forces with the Israelis in a raid on a Hamas safe house in Gaza," Kamal said, as he removed a cigar from an elaborately carved teak humidor. He paused in his conversation to offer one to Hakeem, who declined the offer. After snipping the end, lighting it and taking a satisfying drag on the cigar, he continued, "PLO police, assisted by Israeli soldiers, killed two Hamas leaders and arrested five others. Hamas feels it is time to strike back decisively at the heart of these PLO traitors. They must feel the sting of retribution for this continued harassment, so they will understand what price is to be paid for turning on their Arab brothers. Hamas has asked specifically for your help in engineering a response that will make clear to them the folly of their decision to join with Israel."

"Do they have anything specific in mind, Kamal?"

"They have some preferences, Hakeem, but the eventual target and the method that will be employed against this target will be entirely of your choosing," Kamal replied. "Hamas respects your past successes in matters of this nature and they are willing to abide by whatever you recommend."

"I can leave for Damascus in the morning," Hakeem replied.

"Very good. I will tell them to expect you."

* * *

The Saratoga Sales pavilion and grounds had been transformed into a gossamer wonderland for the annual ball.

From the valet parking lot in front of the pavilion, green and white canvas strips formed a walled walkway that led behind the pavilion to the "ballroom." The walking ring, where the yearlings were paraded before entering the ring had been made to look like an old fashioned carousel. A circular green and white canvas roof was supported by brass poles, positioned on the poles were carousel horses, each depicting a different famous mythical equine figure.

A hardwood dance floor covered the surface of the walking area, and the aisles, down which the horses were led into and out of the pavilion, held the orchestra.

In the center of the dance floor was a working carousel with three white horses, each adorned with saddles and bridles of gold and simulated precious gems. Wide pastel streamers of grosgrain ribbon extended from the center pole to each outer pole, where they were tied in large bows. From under the floor came a dry ice mist. Stirred by the spinning carousel, it moved along, and over the floor, giving the illusion that the dancers were dancing on a cloud.

Most of the ball's guests were socializing at their tables, or around the bars that had been set up in the grassy area bordering the dance floor, when Alanna and Francois arrived. So beautiful was she, in her ivory, cloud satin and lace, sheathed ball gown that all eyes turned towards the couple as they entered.

Francois, sensing the attention they were receiving, said proudly, "Look at them, Alanna, they are in awe of your beauty. I am lucky to be the man whose arm you are on. Come. Our table is this way."

They stopped to greet friends and associates along the way. As they approached a large round table, at which several couples were already seated, he said, "I see some of my guests have already arrived."

The guests included some of Francois' business associates, and a few French dignitaries and their wives. Their initial reaction to Alanna was typically cool until she responded to their greeting in her perfectly accented French. From that point on, she was warmly received.

Francois, noting their acceptance of her, was especially pleased.

231

"I see Hakeem chose not to join us this evening," Alanna said, trying to see whether Francois would be willing to discuss the man.

"He sent his regrets, but he had to return home," was all the response she could get. She dropped the subject.

As the evening wore on, she could see that all the attention the men at the table were paying her was causing the women to become a bit hostile. In order to placate the situation, she called Francois' attention to Paddy Ryan, who had finally made eye contact with her, and was waving his arms to attract her attention, "There's Paddy Ryan. Would you mind if we went by his table and said hello?"

"No, of course not," he said, "I, too, would like a word with him."

They excused themselves, and he led the way to Paddy's table.

"Holy Mother of God, have you ever seen anything more lovely?" Paddy exclaimed, as he stood with his arms outspread waiting to greet her. He gave her a hug and a kiss on the cheek.

"Good evening, Paddy." Alanna returned the kiss and the compliment. "You're looking pretty dapper yourself."

"Paddy. It is a pleasure to see you again, my friend," Francois said, shaking the other man's hand. "And, how is Mary?"

"Fit as the day she was born, that woman is, Francois. But, it's kind of ya ta ask," Paddy remarked, before indicating the men seated across from and next to him, who had risen to greet the couple. "You remember Aiden Doyle and Michael Quinn, Francois?"

"But, of course. Aiden. Michael." He acknowledged the men with a handshake.

"You're a lucky man, Francois, to have such a beautiful woman for your companion this evening," Aiden said, to Francois, but with his attention focused on Alanna, who met his admiring gaze with an uncharacteristically demure smile. "I would guess that you are the envy of every man here."

"I would have ta be concurring with Aiden's observation, Francois," Michael agreed, giving Alanna a conspiratorial wink, and a corresponding nod of his head in Aiden's direction, which elicited a roll of her eyes, and a sly grin in response. Then he added, "And how are you tonight, my dear?"

"Very well, thank you Michael," she said. "You gentleman all clean up so well I hardly recognized you in those tuxedos."

"You'll be joining us for a drink, now won't ya?" Paddy said indicating two empty seats across from him and next to Aiden.

"Would you care to join your friends for a minute, Alanna?" Francois left the choice to her.

"Yes, thank you, I would," she replied and moved to take the seat on Aiden's right that Francois held for her.

"If you don't think it rude of me to discuss business for a moment, Alanna," Francois inquired, "this is an excellent opportunity for me to further persuade Paddy to consider standing his stallion, Sanctity, at my stud next season."

"Of course not, Francois," she assured him, a smile confirming her approval.

Francois immediately launched a conversation with Paddy that excluded the others.

Aware of this, and seeing his chance, Paddy interrupted Francois' sales pitch, "We've already been discussin' this business off and on for six months now, Francois. I think we might just be needin' more than a few minutes. In the interest of not boring the others at this table with our negotiations, may I suggest, that is if you have no objections, that Aiden or Michael ask Alanna to dance."

Knowing he could not refuse Paddy's suggestion gracefully, Francois said, "Forgive me, Alanna, if you care to, have this dance with Aiden or Michael."

Michael gave Aiden the nod.

Rising from his chair, then turning to Alanna and offering his arm, Aiden said, "Would you do me the honor of this dance, fair lady?"

"How could I refuse such a charming invitation?" Alanna replied, rising and taking his arm.

As the couple made their way to the dance floor, Alanna noticed Jeremy seated, with his back to her, at a table to her left.

"I think it might be wise," Alanna said, giving a gentle tug on Aiden's arm in the direction of Jeremy's table, "if I make a point of introducing you to my client, Mr. Jergens."

"A necessary evil, I suppose," Aiden responded unenthusiastically, and allowed himself to be led in Jeremy's direction.

"Don't look behind you, Jeremiah," Rice, who was seated facing the approaching couple, said quietly to Jeremy, "because what's coming is about to break your heart, buddy."

"Let me guess," he said, noting the almost sadistic delight in Rice's expression. "Alanna and Francois have come to pay their respects."

"Worse!" Rice said, just before the couple arrived within earshot. He rose to greet them. "Miss Reynolds, you look absolutely... well, there's just no word in the spoken language to describe how lovely you look."

With that, Jeremy turned to see Alanna on Aiden's arm.

"Thank you, Mr. Riker," Alanna said, smiling and winking at Rice, whose face bore a smile worthy of the Cheshire Cat's. Then turning her attention to the two other men at the table, she asked, "Mr. Jergens, Mr. Cominski, I hope you all are having a pleasant evening."

Jeremy joined the conversation by rising from his seat, facing the couple and commenting sullenly, "I can't remember when I've had such a fine time." Then he said, seemingly forgetting where he was and as though there was no one else around to hear, "Trust me Alanna, you have never looked more beautiful than you do tonight."

Alanna, surprised that Jeremy would be so blunt, played down the compliment, "Well, thank you for saying so, Mr. Jergens."

Then returning the subject of their conversation back to the men, she said, "I'm delighted to hear that you all are having such a wonderful time." Indicating Aiden, who stood to her left, she added. "Gentlemen, I would like you all to meet Aiden Doyle. Mr. Doyle is here from Ireland to buy yearlings. Aiden, this is my client, Mr. Mark Jergens. Mr. Jergens is in the resort business in Phoenix, and is also in the market for yearlings. The tall, handsome, red-haired gentleman is his pilot, Bob Riker, and this handsome gentleman is Ted Cominski, Mr. Jergens' co-pilot."

Aiden shook hands and exchanged greetings with each of the men, an event that did not escape Francois' ever-watchful eyes.

"Would you care to join us?" Jeremy said, pulling the chair next to him away from the table, and inviting Alanna to sit beside him.

"It's kind of you to offer, but I've accepted this dance with Aiden," Alanna said rather enjoying this tantalizing game. "I just didn't want to miss this opportunity to say hello."

"That was thoughtful of you," Jeremy said, glumly. "Don't let us keep you from your dance."

Aiden had kept quiet, but Alanna's arm, linked through his, said volumes.

"Well, have a good evening," Alanna wished them well as she and Aiden turned and headed toward the dance floor.

"Nowheresville is looking more attractive every minute," Jeremy said out loud, but to no one in particular as he watched Aiden assist Alanna up a step and onto the dance floor.

"Hey, man," Rice said consolingly, sensing now how much more there was to this relationship then met the eye, "take it easy, this is a tough game, and a deadly serious one and she's playing it by the rules. I'm not entirely sure why, but you're taking this too personal. Anyway, if it's the lady you're worried about, I'd say it's even money that you're the favorite on her program, even if she won't admit it."

"I'd bet the farm that Rice here's right about those odds," Tad concurred with his partner.

Jeremy gave a heavy sigh, and then turned his attention to the milling crowd of partygoers. "Well, I promised to find myself an attractive diversion. Seen anything interesting with those eagle eyes of yours, Rice?"

"I've seen lots of possibilities, but they all seem to have the escort problem solved," Rice replied as he perused the crowd.

Suddenly, leaning forward, he said, "Hey, Jeremiah, There you go!" and he nodded in the direction of a tall redhead leaning up against one of the bars, looking kind of lost.

"Not bad, not bad, at all, Rice," Jeremy said, rising from his seat. "Don't wait up for me, gentlemen."

* * *

Except that dancing with Aiden had presented an opportunity to introduce him to Jeremy where Francois could witness the introduction, making any further meeting of the men less suspicious, Alanna was not happy with Paddy's suggestion.

"Here, let me help you," Aiden said, as he assisted her up the step to the dance floor.

"Thank, you," she said, lifting her skirt with her free hand, so as not to step on the hem.

It's all so unreal, she thought, as Aiden took her in his arms and they blended into the swirl of dancing couples, the mist rising and whirling around them. And, I don't mean just this place. Help me Jake, she implored her dead mentor and friend. I am truly scared, the unthinkable sensation permeating her soul. Make them all go away --- Jeremy, Aiden, everyone. Just leave me to do this on my own. There are too many distractions, and I am at the center of most of them. Too many ways we can be exposed and this operation fail ---and it must not fail.

"You are the epitome of a silent partner, Alanna," Aiden said, breaking her concentration. "Is it the company?"

"No," she said, and let a warm smile replace the former serious expression, but she did not elaborate on her thoughts or attitude.

"Then, what?" Aiden asked forthright.

"You scare me, Aiden."

Her forthrightness took him back a bit. "Scare you! Did I miss something in my briefing? Was I, or was I not, brought here to help you? How can that scare you?"

"I didn't bring you here, Aiden," Alanna replied, trying not to sound unkind in saying the words. "Jeremy and a promise brought you here. A promise made to a man, who, if he were here today, would be as concerned as I am about the way this operation is shaping up."

Seeing that her seeming lack of appreciation for his presence was causing Aiden some discomfort, she added, "Please, Aiden, don't take my criticism personally. I appreciate your concern, and your desire to honor your commitment. It's just that you know so little about me, that's why you can't possible understand why I am so disturbed at how this operation is unfolding."

She continued her conversation as he whirled her gracefully around the floor, the other dancers blurred images. "I'm not sure how it happened, but there are too many people involved, and too much time for things to go wrong before we can make our move. There's just too much chance for error. It's not my style, Aiden. I am the shadow, the night. I work alone. Stealth and darkness are my allies."

"In the past, maybe," he said, and, seeming to forgive any slight her remarks may have caused him, he tightened his hold on her and pulled her closer to him. "But, like it or not, my dear lady, this is a light-of-day operation. Just keep me close and believe in me, and I'll see to it that you don't get hurt."

"Surviving is not what's important here, Aiden," Alanna replied, her body stiffening slightly. "Succeeding is."

"In that case, I apologize for being so presumptuous," Aiden replied gently, letting a smile soften his expression. "You have an angel's body and a warrior's heart, and I failed to acknowledge and respect the difference. I hope you will forgive me."

When they arrived back at the entrance to the dance floor, Francois was waiting for them. They whirled to a stop in front of him, and he said, "You two dance with a grace that would put Fred Astaire and Ginger Rogers to shame."

"That's kind of you to say, Francois," Aiden replied, as he relinquished Alanna's hand to the Frenchman. "Thank you for the opportunity to dance with your lovely friend."

Turning back to Alanna, he said, "Thank you, Alanna, for the pleasure of this dance."

Alanna smiled, and nodded her head in response. Then, as she and Francois took the floor, Aiden returned to his table.

* * *

As it turned out, the lost-soul look on the redhead's face was the result of a drug induced high, which was quickly apparent to Jeremy the minute she opened her mouth and responded to his overture. He had finally managed to disengage himself from her company, and was headed back to his table when, in swerving to miss a waiter, he collided with a woman making her way through the crowd.

"Excuse me!" he said, apologetically, as he grasped her arm in order to keep her from being bowled over.

"Oh, mon dieu!" she said, in a husky sensuous voice, as she struggled to keep herself upright. Once steadied, she accepted his apology with a smile and a look that matched her voice, "It is quite all right, monsieur, no damage has been done."

God, she's gorgeous, Jeremy thought as he gave the tall, sultry looking woman the once over, while she straightened her black satin dress, that clung like Saran Wrap to her well-endowed figure, and smoothed her coal-black hair, that was drawn back away from her face, and into a braid secured at the back of her head. Her full, ruby-red lips and smoldering dark eyes, shielded by long dark lashes, stood in stark contrast to her ivory skin.

"How clumsy of me!" Jeremy fumbled for words to keep the conversation going.

"Au contrare, monsieur," she replied, giving him a thorough going over, "I should consider myself fortunate to have run into such a handsome gentleman. Only one thing could be more fortuitous, eeef you are unattached."

"I am indeed unattached, mademoiselle," Jeremy said, loving the lusty quality of her voice, and encouraged by a dismal evening seeming to have taken a turn for the better. "May I assume that you are unattached as well?"

"You may, monsieur,"

Then sighing slightly, she said, "I am the guest of some friends who have horses racing here. But..." she added, as she let a sexy pout form on her lips, gave him a look that would melt steel and slipped her arm through his, "I am afraid I am not, how do you say...oh, yes, horsy, so I have found the evening dreadfully dull so far."

"My, that's too bad," Jeremy remarked, with feigned sympathy. "As a matter of fact, I was a little bored myself, and was about to find more stimulating surroundings. You wouldn't care to join me, would you?"

"Oh, monsieur..."

"Mark," Jeremy interrupted. "My name is Mark Jergens."

Through another barn burner look, she continued, "As I was saying, Mark, I am not sure it would be polite to leave...but, oh yes, I would love to go with you."

"That settles it..." he hesitated, waiting for her to respond.

"Au, pardone, Monsieur Mark, my name is Claudette Dupré."

"Well, Mademoiselle Dupré," he said, leading her in the direction of the dance floor, hoping Francois would get a good look as they passed on their way out, "my car is this way. Shall we go?"

As Claudette moved in front of him in order to negotiate the crowded aisle more easily, he noticed, to his delight, that the black satin dress she wore was cut to a deep "V" in back, revealing an ample amount of smooth, silky skin.

* * *

Despite the dubious company she was being forced to keep, and the whole nasty business she was involved in, Alanna found that she was enjoying the evening. The place was gorgeous, the music beautiful, and so far, her dance partners were more than equal to the task. She had just resigned herself to making the best of it, when Francois' voice intruded on her thoughts.

"It looks like your client, Mr. Jergens, has found himself a charming companion, Alanna," he remarked pointedly, almost gloating at the fact, as he turned her so that she had a clear view of Jeremy and the woman as they passed the entrance to the dance floor.

It took a moment for Alanna to recognize the woman's face, but when she did, there was no doubt in her mind, who she was, or what her purpose in being here was. She had wondered why Francois' attitude toward Jeremy had changed so radically since this morning. Francois had even gone so far as to invite Jeremy to stay at his chateau, when, as they had stopped to greet Jeremy as they passed his table on the way to theirs,

Alanna had informed him that Jeremy planned to attend the yearling sale at Deauville.

Now, she knew why. At no time in her life had Alanna's emotions and instincts been as thoroughly tested as they were at that moment. In a split second, she experienced surprise, fear, pain, a moment's panic, hatred, and the urge to kill the man who held her so tenderly in his arms, and had professed such great love for her.

In spite of this emotional rush, she maintained a cool calmness, and responded in a voice that projected only mild interest, "Yes, I see. Well, Mr. Jergens is an attractive man with an outgoing personality. I'm delighted that he's found someone attractive to spend his time with."

Jeremy knows I'm up here, Alanna, thought. Look this way you jerk, her mind shouted silently to him, as he nonchalantly followed the woman past the dance floor, never giving Alanna or Francois so much as a glance. Honestly, Jeremy, any other time you'd be giving me one of you're gloating smirks. This is no time to abandon tradition. Look this way, dope! But, he didn't and now the dilemma began.

God you are a rotten, persistent bastard, Francois, she thought, as her mind sought a logical excuse to end their evening together. In desperation, she let her eyes roam the crowd in hopes of seeing Aiden, Paddy, Mark, Bill or Tad, and getting someone's attention. Aiden was nowhere to be seen, Paddy and Mark had left their table, and were in deep conversation with a group of people from the British Bloodstock Agency, and Bill and Tad were amusing themselves by carrying on a conversation with the couple at the table behind theirs, putting their backs to her.

All during these moments that seemed like hours, Francois continued to babble away about things that made only a passing impression on her conscious mind. Even if she managed to think of some way to leave Francois without raising his suspicions, she had no means of transportation to pursue the departing couple, nor was she dressed for the task this situation would entail.

She heard Francois say something that demanded an answer, which she provided, quickly turning her concentration back to solving the problem at hand. Well, she thought, I've got no choice. It's time for you and me to part company, Francois.

She pulled Francois closer to her and closed her eyes, a gesture Francois found totally to his liking. Eyes closed, she summoned her internal powers. All the energy contained in her Chi was aimed in the direction of her foot. Suddenly, there was a sharp cracking sound, and were it not for the hold Francois had on her, Alanna would have fallen to the floor, as the high heel of her shoe gave way under the extreme pressure.

"What the...!" Francois said in surprise, as he quickly responded to her loss of balance enabling her to remain up right. "Are you all right, Alanna? What in the world happened?"

"My, goodness," she exclaimed, hopping a step to get her balance. Then, resting one hand on his shoulder, she reached for her right shoe.

"I don't believe it! The heel broke," she remarked with false astonishment as she offered the shoe up for his inspection.

The heel was not broken off in the normal weak spot where it joined the shoe, but in the middle of the steel shaft, a feat that is normally impossible.

"Come let us sit down," he said, and he made a move to assist her to their table.

"Oh!" Alanna cried out, faking the distressing sound as well as the pain in her ankle, as she gingerly lifted up her bare foot

Francois put his arm around her waist, and, lifting her off the ground, carried her back to their table, a move that caused the other partygoers to flock around the couple to see what had happened.

"I'm fine," she said, reassuring them. "I just took a little misstep."

Realizing it was nothing serious, they all resumed their previous activities, some of her closer friends making kidding remarks as they departed.

"Are you sure you're okay, Alanna," Francois was very concerned. "Perhaps we should go to the hospital, and have your ankle x-rayed."

"I don't think that's necessary, Francois," Alanna said, then not wanting him to think there was nothing wrong, she added, "I'm sure it's just a mild sprain. A good soaking in Epsom salts and hot water, and it'll be as good as new."

"Well then," he said, "let me take you home, and I'll help you soak it."

Great, just what I don't need is you playing doctor, she thought. How am I going to get out of this one?

"Is something the matter, Francois?" she heard Aiden say as he made his way through the departing crowd.

"Ah, yes, Aiden," Francois said, with genuine concern in his voice. "The heel on Alanna's shoe broke, and I am afraid she may have sprained her ankle. She is making light of the situation, but I think it would be best if it were attended to."

"Honestly, gentlemen," Alanna said, finally catching Aiden's eye and giving him a look that said I need to get out of here. "I just need to get home and soak it and get to bed. I do have a four o' clock morning to look forward to, you know."

"Well, then let us go," Francois said, starting to make a move to lift her again.

"Look, Francois," Aiden said, interrupting his forward motion with a touch of his hand on the Frenchman's arm, "I think Alanna's probably got the right idea. A good soaking, and resting that foot elevated, is all they'd recommend she do even if you took her to a hospital.

"You have all these guests here to entertain," Aiden said about the other people at the table, who seemed more interested in the inconvenience Francois absence would cause them, than in Alanna's plight. "I was just on my way out, so why don't I take her back to her place. She can rest and you can see to your guests."

"Thank you for offering, Aiden, but I wouldn't think of it," Francois said, once again bending to pick her up. "Alanna is my responsibility."

"Please, Francois, I think Aiden's right," Alanna said, not wanting to create a confrontational situation, but hoping she could sway his decision, "You must attend to your guests. I won't have any trouble taking care of this myself, and I just as soon be alone so I can get some rest."

He was silent for a moment. Neither Alanna, nor Aiden dared say anything lest they sway him in the wrong direction.

"I don't know," Francois said, hesitatingly.

"Please, Francois, I'll be fine. Really," she assured him.

"Are you sure it isn't a bother, Aiden."

"Not at all."

"Well, then, alright," Francois said, reluctantly, not really convinced it was the best alternative, but he did have an obligation to his guests.

* * *

Every time Jeremy stepped through the front doors of the Adelphi Hotel he felt like he was stepping back in time. One of the last of the grand old hotels that had graced Saratoga during its heyday as a gambler's paradise, she had been lovingly restored to her earlier Victorian splendor. The lobby had a certain mystique, a romantic ambiance created by the rich dark wood paneling, soft lighting, ornate Victorian furniture, ceiling fans, and a subtle tropic touch of strategically placed potted palm trees.

Jeremy let the woman precede him through the lobby, then guided her by the elbow to a table in an alcove off of the main barroom. A waitress came and they ordered.

Jeremy glanced at his companion, who returned his look with an exotic smile.

"What are you thinking about, Mark?" she asked.

"I was thinking how well you speak French, but I'd be willing to bet France is not your home," he replied.

"A very astute observation, my friend. And where would you say I am from?" she inquired, surprised by his perceptiveness.

He studied her intensely for a moment before saying, "Morocco. Southern part. Possibly, Marrakech."

"Very impressive and correct," she said, trying to keep a growing concern that he might know who she was out of her voice. "May I ask how you arrived at that conclusion?"

"But, of course," he replied, as he uncharacteristically shoved to the back of his subconscious the little alarm bell that had just gone off in his head. "I have a friend who has a casino in Agadir. Your accent is a familiar one there. I've visited my friend and his casino in Marrakech many times, although not recently. The twilights there are magnificent."

"I cannot disagree with that observation, either," she said, his explanation alleviating some of her anxiety. As she accepted her drink from the waitress, she inquired, "What do you do for a living, Mark? You do not appear to be one of the horsy set, either."

"I have a resort hotel in Phoenix, Arizona. And you?"

"I am an artist of sorts," she said, with an undercurrent of laughter. Then turning the conversation away from the personal, she commented, "This place has an artist's touch. Is the entire hotel done in this style?"

"I guess. Every place in it that I've been, it seems to be."

"The rooms as well?" she continued her inquiry, leaning a little closer to him and using her sensuous dark eyes to flirt with him.

"Yes, the rooms definitely are in this style? Care to see one?"

"If that could be arranged, I'd love to. I'm very interested in this period of Americana."

"Well, there'll never be a better time than right now," he said, while signaling for the waitress to pick up the signed check.

"I couldn't agree with you more," she said, placing her hand in his proffered one, and following him in the direction of the stairs.

* * *

Alanna rose from her seat with Aiden's assistance. Putting her one hand through his bent arm for support and using the other to hold her purse, shoes and lift her now too long dress, she began limping toward the exit. When she was well into the canvas-lined walkway, and sure she was out of the line of sight of Francois, his men and his guests, she quit limping and began dragging a surprised Aiden by the arm as she ran in the direction of the valet parking area.

"Hey, I thought you were hurt?" he said, amazed at her change of demeanor.

"I faked it," Alanna said. "I don't have time to explain now. Quick! Where's your car?"

"I parked it up the street a piece in case I needed it in a hurry," he replied, pointing in the direction of a line of cars parked along the curb

"Well, I need it in a hurry, so lead the way and step on it," Alanna pushed him out in front of her and they both took off. Neither her slim cut dress, which flared slightly at the bottom, nor running over the pebbled surface of the parking area in her stocking feet slowed her down any.

"Where are we going?" he asked, as the reached the silver, Lexus opened the driver side door and flipped the switch that unlocked the door on the passenger side. "And, would you care to tell my why you dumped Francois."

"The Adelphi Hotel, and I hope that's the right decision," Alanna replied as she slid into the seat and closed the door. "As for my dumping Francois, I had no choice. Jeremy's been set up, and if my choice of destinations is wrong, he's about to enjoy his last roll in the hay."

"Come on, Alanna, you wouldn't begrudge the old boy a little female companionship," Aiden joked, not yet understanding the seriousness of the situation. "I didn't think you were the jealous type."

Alanna shot him a caustic look that caused his laughter to die instantly.

"Jeremy's been looking for a way to make his and my relationship look like it's strictly horse business," Alanna explained, her look and voice now taking on a distinctly worried tone. "So, he told me he was going to try and meet a woman at the ball that would help convey that message to Francois. I don't know how she finagled it, or why, in all his travels, Jeremy hadn't become aware of Andrea Mersant, but our friend left the ball with the world's most formidable female assassin. Her code name is Nenet, but a better one would be Black Widow, because by an account from the lone man to survive one of her attacks, she waits until she reaches orgasm before she kills her victim."

"I don't understand why you're so worried about Jeremy. He's a big boy. He's been around. You don't think he would just pick up this woman and then jump in the sack with her, do you? Aiden said, an anxious note beginning to creep into his voice.

One look at Alanna's facial expression, and he had his answer.

"Jeremy's not one to waste time on the preliminaries if he has a willing partner," Alanna said, that night with Jeremy in the Bedford Lodge all too clear in her memory. "And, he has a willing partner!"

Alanna picked up the car's cellular phone. She dialed a number, and said to the receiving party, "This is Operation Quill. I am in need of your immediate assistance. You are to go to the Adelphi Hotel on Broadway. If I'm right, you will find Andrea Mersant in room 204. She is an assassin wanted by both the Brits and the Germans. She always has a bodyguard posted wherever she is, so be careful when you approach the room. Her target is the gentleman in the room. His name is Mark Jergens. Jergens is clean, so you are not to detain him. You are also not to detain the bodyguard. Do you understand?"

The reply was obviously in the affirmative as she concluded by saying, "Time is of the essence, so I'd get going immediately if I were you."

Alanna would not have recognized the woman, Andrea Mersant, except that Dar had pointed her out when she'd made an appearance at a restaurant they were dining at while on a vacation in Marrakech. Andrea had not seen them at the time, because she had been busy plying her seductive charms on a wealthy-looking Arab businessman. Dar had also pointed out the bodyguard, whom he said always accompanied her.

With Jeremy and Andrea having such a big head start, it was strictly a guess, albeit a pretty safe one, as to which way they had gone. If annihilating Jeremy were on Andrea's agenda, they'd be headed to someone's bedroom, and since a dead corpse in her room would be hard to explain to the hotel management, Jeremy's room seemed the logical choice. But, if Alanna were wrong, then neither she, nor the FBI would be able to get to him in time and to save him.

"Aiden, do you know where the Adelphi is?" she asked, sitting forward slightly in the seat, as if her position would help them arrive at their destination faster.

"I know where it is, but since you've already called in the cavalry, what's the hurry?"

"They may not get there in time, or if they do, they might tip their hand when they take the guard at the door and cause Nenet to forego her pleasure in order to collect her pay."

"In that case, do you know any short cuts?" he asked, as he started the engine and pulled out onto East Ave.

"Take a right here at Madison," she said, pointing to the street immediately to their right. "Then take a left on Caroline. Phila St. goes directly to the hotel, but it's one way, and unfortunately not our way."

Aiden did a double take, as Alanna ran her hands up her dress revealing a lot of leg, and removed what was left of her tattered stockings.

"They may not be long, but they're beautiful," he said and followed his comment with a low wolf whistle.

"What did you say?" she asked, her mind having been elsewhere.

"Nothing. Not a thing!" Aiden replied, and then thinking what Paddy would have said in response to his comment, he laughed to himself.

They were fast approaching Caroline St.

"That's Caroline St., and that street is Phila," she said pointing to a street that jogged off to the left. "I'm not sure which of these other streets will be the fastest ..."

Before she could finish the sentence, Aiden turned the car right onto Caroline. Fishtailing, he made the hard left onto the one-way Phila, and took off, tires screeching, swerving back and forth to miss the oncoming traffic that blew their horns at the oncoming speeding silver intruder.

"Whew! That was beautiful!" Alanna exclaimed, as she steadied herself by gripping the dashboard.

"Where to now?" Aiden said, as he dodged the oncoming traffic.

She could see the four-story, brown and cream facade of the Adelphi looming straight ahead of them. Its lobby doors were in a direct line with Phila St., where it dead-ended into Broadway. Traffic on the main street was bumper to bumper, and had the intersection of Phila St. and Broadway completely blocked.

"This will have to do," she said, as they reached the end of Phila St., and a stream of blaring horns and protesting drivers. As she prepared to bail out of the car, she said, "I think you're a terrific driver, in spite of what everyone else on this road thinks."

"Wait! Where are you going?" Aiden yelled after her.

"Damn!" was all the comment he could muster as he waited a break in the traffic, and an opportunity to park the car and follow.

245

* * *

Jeremy's room was on the second floor. Not liking unexpected guests, he'd chosen one with no balcony or fire escape, yet not an impossible distance to drop to the ground should he be faced with an intruder through his hall door.

He opened the door and they entered. His suite was not large, but it was done tastefully. It had a fair-sized bedroom, an adequate sitting room off to the left, and a large bathroom through a door to the right of the bed.

"Very nice," she said, as she walked to the window and pulled down the shade. Jeremy lowered the light to a soft glow. She walked towards him, and they met in the middle of the room.

As she stood in front of him, she reached up and slid her hand behind his head. He let his arm slip around her waist and gently pulled her to him. Their lips met, first tentatively, then with increasing fervor. She moaned and her lips parted, permitting his tongue to enter. His hand caressed the silken skin along her spine, moving upwards until it reached the nape of her neck.

He started to let her hair down. She moved away from him.

"I prefer it up," she said, and in order not to break the mood, her hand moved to her left shoulder and slowly removed the strap of her dress from it. Then she removed the strap from the other shoulder and let the dress fall to the floor. Standing naked in front of Jeremy, she proceeded to stroke her breasts with her hand until her nipples became erect.

She closed the short distance between them. Once again, she placed her hand behind his head. Throwing her head back, she arched her back and gently pulled his head down to her breast.

Jeremy kissed her breasts, then lifting her in his arms, carried her to the bed.

* * *

Alanna barely missed catching her dress in the car door as she slammed it shut behind her, leaving a frustrated Aiden to figure out how to get out of the traffic jam and park the car.

This damn tight skirt, she thought, as she lifted it high to give her legs more mobility. Her bare feet slapped the pavement, as she ran across Broadway, weaving her way through the stalled traffic. Reaching the other side of the street, she slowed to a walk and composed herself. She checked to see if there was anyone about, that looked like the FBI, but the place seemed quiet. As she entered the Adelphi lobby, she let her skirt down to a length that covered her bare feet, and headed in the direction of the cocktail lounge.

As elegantly as she was dressed, Alanna knew the desk clerk would not question her. He only glanced up momentarily, smiled, bid her a good evening, then turned his attention back to his newspaper.

Finding the bar empty, she headed around the corner, down the hall and out the back porch to the garden area behind the hotel. Normally, the area would have been well lit. The spot under the awning served as a dining area, the brick patio behind that, set with Adirondak lawn chairs, and matching tables, was a favorite gathering place for guests to sit and have a drink. But, due to the lateness of the hour, the entire area was empty, and in deference to people sleeping in the rooms adjacent to the courtyard, the lights had been turned very low.

Alanna moved along the patio walk towards the end of the back wing of the hotel. Looking up, she saw the light go out in what she knew was Jeremy's room. She listened to see if there was any activity other than what must surely be taking place between Nenet and Jeremy. There didn't seem to be.

I can't wait any longer, she thought, as she looked down at her dress, up in the direction of the window, then considered her options. The door would have been easier, but knowing Nenet's method of operation, it would not be the route of choice.

Please, God, she prayed silently, don't let me be too late.

Reaching behind her, she slid the zipper down and let the dress fall among the flowers, which grew at the base of the wall, then stood contemplating her next move, clad only in her ivory lace and satin teddy.

Thankfully, the Adelphi was an old building. The bricks, ravaged by time, were rough, the mortar between them chipped away. She looked up again at the window, positioned herself under it, closed her eyes for a second, then placing her fingers in the grooves between the bricks, she began to climb the wall.

Scaling a wall in this manner was an old Ninja trick and a very useful one, but it required nerves of steel, great concentration and strength. Once committed, the only way down was hard and fast.

She kept herself tight against the building, alternating her hands and her feet "crab claw" style. Slowly, painfully, she inched her way to the windowsill. Quickly, she made a grab for it, first with her left hand, then with her right. Luckily, although the shade was drawn, the window was open.

Alanna hung for a moment, suspended from the thin window frame. She took several slow, deep breaths, then began to pull herself up. As her head and shoulders reached the window bottom, she slid over the sill and without a sound, slithered snake-like to the floor.

Having come to the room the other day for Jeremy's clothes now proved a blessing. Seeing it in the daylight, Alanna could visualize it perfectly in the dark. As she lay facedown on the floor, she closed her eyes, and concentrated on the layout of the room, and let her other senses, heightened to a fine degree, fill in the blanks.

Her sense of smell detected a heavy musky scent, the kind emitted when two bodies are heavily engaged in sexual activity. Her hearing determined their location, and the sound of their breathing told her that the woman was positioned on top of the man.

She could hear Jeremy, sense his motion, could almost feel him thrusting into the woman. The soft moans of pleasure coming from him reminded her of a moment such as this that they had shared. Quickly, she shook the thought.

As her mind developed the scene unfolding before her, Alanna's hands were preparing the method of attack. Quietly, she rolled onto her back. Raising her left arm slightly, her right hand reached for the stay that formed the side support of her bra. She lifted the small flap that covered it and drew from what was actually a hollowed out tube, a four-inch long piece of icepick.

She extracted it carefully. The hollow tip contained Cylon A, a deadly derivative of Cyanide and Curare. The tip, in order to protect Alanna, was sealed with a non-toxic crystal plug. The pick was cushioned and insulated in the tube by a Styrofoam cork. Her objective would be to aim and throw the projectile so that when it reached its target, Nenet, it would lodged itself in the base of the skull, between two vertebrae, known as C-2 and C-3.

At the instant of penetration, the crystal plug, warmed by the body temperature, would vaporize instantaneously, releasing the poison. The poison, which would effectively cause dissolution of the spinal cord, would immediately cut off all nerve control to the respiratory system and the heart. Nenet's death would be instantaneous and silent.

There was still no sign of assistance from the FBI. She knew that, in a matter of minutes, and despite the danger she ran of spoiling the mission, exposing her identity and for certain, because of Agency regulations against what she was about to do, getting fired from the job, she would be forced to act. Nenet was a master of the Black Widow art of seduction and execution. To achieve orgasm, she killed her lover. Alanna could tell by the sounds coming from the bed that that moment was imminent.

The sounds of lovemaking would cover her approach, but the icepick, she knew, would have to be thrown in pitch darkness, and at the exact moment the woman would raise her body to an upright position.

Turning back onto her hands and knees, Alanna started across the floor in the direction of the bed, using the same floor hugging, crab style she had used to scale the wall.

She reached the foot of the bed, in a direct line with, and behind the two lovers. She rose silently, in full control of her body. She had reduced her breathing to a minimal level, removing any unnecessary noise that might distract her.

Alanna raised her arm and set the hand, holding the pick, in a throwing position. Then, focusing all her attention on the sounds directly in front of her, she waited.

Suddenly, it was there, the sound and the motion that she had been waiting for. Until that moment, Nenet's body had been bent over Jeremy's, moving her hips in rhythmic motion that coincided with his thrusts. About to reach the moment of release, she came erect, at the same time her right hand started up towards the back of her head. The reed-thin dagger, her trademark, was hidden in the braid on the back of her head.

Just as suddenly, there was shouting in the hall. A man's voice could be heard identifying himself as the FBI, and ordering someone to raise his hands and face the wall. Instinctively, Alanna rolled back into the shadows and behind the love seat that was set to the right of the window she'd entered through.

She saw Andrea's hand hang in the air behind her head for a moment as she tried to decide the merit of following through on her assignment, or making a break for freedom. The possibility of life in prison or worse won out, and Andrea quickly disengaged herself from her and Jeremy's flesh entwined position, and made for the open window.

"Jesus, what's going on?" Jeremy said. He had been completely immersed in his euphoric state, and was just beginning to become aware of the sudden activity, as Andrea headed for the window.

Knowing she could not let Andrea get out of the room, Alanna sprung at her from the shadows and before the woman knew what hit her, delivered a karate chop to the back of her neck that sent her, unconscious, to the floor. In the same motion, Alanna took the opportunity to make a silent exit through the window.

Jeremy, not sure whether to focus his attention on Andrea, or the banging at the door, only caught a brief glimpse of first one, then two people at the window. One figure fell to the floor, while the other silently disappeared out the window.

"I'm coming. I'm coming. Quit your banging," he yelled to the impatient FBI agent, who had identified himself and demanded to be let in.

Alanna climbed out the window, hung momentarily from its windowsill, then dropped to the ground, letting her body roll on landing to lesson the impact. She quickly grabbed her dress and hurried into the shadows of the hotel's porch. She noticed Jeremy take a quick peek out the window, but she resisted the urge to make her presence known. Instead, she slipped on her dress, tidied her hair and went to make her exit the way she'd come in, through the main lobby.

As she passed through the bar area, she heard Aiden's voice call softly to her from a dark corner. "Well, did the cavalry arrive in the nick of time?"

She did not want to discuss what she had just witnessed.

"Well, did it?" Aiden persisted.

"Just barely!"

When she was not forthcoming with any further details, he said, "Well. If we're not going to discuss the gory details over a glass of brandy, I guess I'd better get you home. That is before Francois finds out you're not tending to your injury."

He slid from the booth he was seated in and joined her, but before they could leave, there was a great commotion coming from the direction of the stairs. Nenet, handcuffed and wrapped only in a sheet, was putting up a great fuss as she was being led away by the agents to FBI headquarters.

Aiden quickly grabbed Alanna by the arm, and shoved her unceremoniously into the darkness of the booth. He slid in beside her, and before she had time to object, took her in his arms, shielding her from view with his body, and kissed her. He could feel her start to resist. As the melee made its way into the lounge area, he looked her in the eye and said, "This is no time to be coy, Alanna. Kiss me like you mean it."

"Why not!" she said, and as his lips met hers, she kissed him like she meant it.

Chapter 20

Francois' secretary had a distinct feeling of déja vu as he watched Francois lose his temper with Nenet's bodyguard. The poor man was trying to explain how the FBI had shown up and arrested Nenet for being an illegal alien, and for being wanted by the British MI5.

Phillip was sure that the man would have been happier locked in jail then facing the tirade the Frenchman was unleashing on him.

"How could they have known? How in the hell could they have known?" Francois repeated to himself, trying to understand how his plans had once again been foiled and Jergens had survived the unsurvivable.

"They said MI5 has had a tail on Nenet since we left London, monsieur. She is wanted there." The bodyguard fed Francois the disinformation he had been told. "They planned to have the gendarmes stop us when we left Paris on a commercial flight, but when we left on your plane, they had to turn the arrest request over to the Americans."

"And why are you not locked up with Nenet?"

"Neither the Americans nor the British have a quarrel with me. I am simply a bodyguard doing his job."

"This whole thing is impossible. How could one man be so lucky?" Francois said exasperated, and he was not referring to the bodyguard. One thing Francois knew for sure was that he could not wait to be back home where events were more predictable.

* * *

"Jesus! What the hell's going on?" Rice said to Clark. As on their return from the ball, they were bumped and jostled by the FBI agents, and their prisoner, as the entourage made its way out the front doors of the Adelphi and to their waiting cars.

He recognized the woman wrapped in the sheet as the one Jeremy had left the ball with earlier that evening. Though Rice had not seen an ambulance out front, a sudden panic seized him. He rushed into the hotel and sprinted up the steps to Jeremy's room. Clark followed, close on his heels.

"Mr. Jergens! Mr. Jergens! It's Riker, are you all right?" Rice shouted as he pounded on Jeremy's door.

There was a heart-stopping few seconds of silence before Rice heard the door being unlocked.

"Come on in," said an obviously dejected Jeremy, who was now fully clothed, and standing just slightly behind the open door. The room was a shambles. Though Jeremy had had time to dress, bedding and clothing were still strewn everywhere.

"God almighty, are you all right? What's been going on here? Who was that woman?" The questions tumbled out of Rice's mouth.

Jeremy didn't answer Rice. He didn't close the door, leaving that for Clark to do. He just went over to a love seat, sat down and covered his face with his hands.

Rice looked over at Clark and shrugged his shoulders. Jeremy didn't appear to be hurt physically, but something serious had happened to him.

"Who was that woman, Jeremiah?" Rice asked, free now that they were behind closed doors to use Jeremy's real name.

Still nothing.

Rice turned to Clark, shrugged his shoulders again, and, while motioning him to leave, said, "Tad, why don't you check and see if we have any messages. I'll stick around here for a minute, and see if I can't straighten this mess up a bit."

"Sure," Tad said, and quickly exited the room.

Rice did not pose any more questions. He just sat down in one of the chairs and waited.

Jeremy finally removed his hands from his face, and said, "The woman was an assassin, Rice," he said, in a tone that told Rice the woman had physically missed her mark, but that Jeremy had been mortally wounded nonetheless.

"I take it those guys hauling her off were our friends from the FBI," Rice remarked. Then asked, "Any idea who tipped them off?"

"Alanna."

"Are you sure?"

"She was here."

"In this room? With you and that woman?" And then lightening struck home and Rice knew from where Jeremy was bleeding. "Oh, God, she didn't see you screwing that bitch?"

"I don't know how long she was here, but she was here long enough to see Nenet, that's what the FBI guys said was her code name, didn't make it out the window before she was apprehended. I have to assume she was here for part of the time."

"What are you going to do? How are you going to explain this to Granton? You think she'll still want to work with you?" Rice couldn't get the questions out fast enough.

Jeremy let his head fall back against the back of the loveseat, and closed his eyes.

"What *am* I going to do, Rice? That's a very good question!"

* * *

All the way back to her house, Alanna remained silent. She and Aiden had waited until the Adelphi lobby was clear, and then they had exited the hotel, his arm around her, holding her close to him, as real lovers would do.

Aiden had no idea what had transpired in that hotel room, and Alanna refused to say, but whatever it was, it had left her in a deep funk.

He drove around to the empty lot behind her house, pulled the car up behind some trees, and shut off the engine. Then he simply waited for her to make the first move.

Finally, while still staring straight ahead, she said, "Thanks for lending a hand this evening."

"It was in my job description. What else could I do?" he replied, turning to face her.

"Right. I forgot," she said, and reached for the door handle to let herself out.

Aiden reached out and, grasping her arm, stopped her.

"If we're going to be partners," he said, "don't you think you ought to level with me?"

She ceased moving forward, but her head remained turned towards the door. "I'm tired, Aiden. Jeremy can fill you in."

"I'm sure he will, but I'm not worried about him. I'm worried about you. And, I want to know what happened."

Alanna slumped back in the seat. "Nenet, that's the woman's code name, is an assassin. Her modus operandi is to seduce her victim, and deliver the coup de grace just as she is about to reach orgasm."

"Oh, hell!" Was all Aiden could think to say, as the full picture of what had gone on in Jeremy's room hit him.

"An appropriate response," she agreed.

This time, when she opened the door, he didn't stop her.

"Good night, Aiden," she said, without looking back at him, and then she disappeared through the trees in the direction of the house.

Aiden did not know what to say. He knew Alanna and Jeremy had worked together for years. He assumed that because of it they had become very close. He thought about how he might react if it had been him in that room and the person making love was a female partner of his.

253

It was no use trying to rationalize the situation. Until now, he had never had a female partner, so the point was moot.

He drove back to his boarding house. As he was undressing for bed, the phone rang.

"Yes," he said.

"I need to talk to you." He recognized Jeremy's voice.

"I bet you do!" Aiden replied, somewhat sarcastically.

"Save the sarcasm, this is serious." Jeremy said, and he gave Aiden directions to a bait shop on Saratoga Lake. "I'll meet you there in half an hour."

"Right," Aiden replied, and hung up the phone.

* * *

At first Aiden did not see the black BMW, which Jeremy had parked in the shadow of the trees near the lake. Aiden killed the lights on his car, and parked alongside the other car.

Jeremy was sitting on a picnic table facing the lake. He did not turn, even to check if the approaching figure was Aiden.

"You must have a death wish, leaving your back exposed like that." Aiden said, as he came alongside the table.

"Couldn't happen at a better time." Jeremy replied, sullenly.

"Do I detect a note of self pity in that remark?" Aiden said, as he stepped around to face the other man.

"Detect whatever the hell you want," Jeremy retorted, "I asked you to meet me out here so I could brief you as to where we're at with this God damn mission, and turn the backup over to you."

"Is that what you and Granton want?"

"It's what he'll want when Alanna fills him in on what happened tonight."

"Care to fill me in on what happened?" Aiden said, taking a seat on a picnic table facing Jeremy's. "I missed all the action. My only part in this was to play chauffeur." He deliberately left out the after-action action in the hotel bar.

"Hell, I don't know half of what went on myself," Jeremy said, angrily. "I had this plan to find a woman I could use to get Francois to stop thinking I was trying to compete with him for Alanna and ..."

Jeremy went on with his explanation, but Aiden was no longer listening, for Jeremy had summed up the situation brilliantly with his last remark.

Aiden's eyebrows rose at this revelation. When he'd come aboard, no one had briefed him that a problem like this existed. In her explanation of the night's events, Alanna had completely omitted this factor. Since, as yet, he had not had an opportunity to be with Alanna and Jeremy when they had been together, or Alanna with Francois, he had assumed all was well. Now that he thought about it, it had never been quite clear to him why Francois' goons had made the first attempt on Jeremy's life. So that was it.

Aiden had gotten to know a few things about Francois over the years that his father had dealt with him. Sure Francois was obsessed with money, power and racehorses. However, it was common knowledge that Francois considered women to be nothing more than a diversion, fancy trinkets on his arm. No woman had every gained the kind of power over him, that would make her an obsession.

Aiden had not been surprised to see Alanna on Francois' arm at the ball. After all, she was certainly the most attractive, desirable, not to mention available, woman around. Who else would Francois have chosen? And, of course, it was her job to get close to him. But Francois, obsessed to the point that he would kill to have her, that was a new side to him. And surely, he would not have considered Jeremy competition unless Jeremy had given him good reason to assume he was.

"I still don't understand the problem," he lied, now understanding perfectly well what the problem was. "You were screwing the woman, and Alanna saved your neck before your friend, and I say that reservedly, could end the relationship — permanently.

I'd say the deal played out perfectly. So, why do you want to quit?"

Aiden's remarks reflected such indifference to the feelings of the personalities involved that Jeremy almost wanted to punch him. Instead, he asked, "What did Alanna say?"

"Not much."

"That's what I was afraid of."

"Look Jeremy, Alanna, from what I know, is a professional," Aiden said, while toying with the keychain in his hand. "She's not going to let a little incident like this, however embarrassing it might be for both of you, affect this mission. I'd wager that she doesn't tell Granton any more than is necessary to get you off the hook.

"And, as far as Francois goes," Aiden continued, reassuringly, "you let me handle him. He's no fool, but by tomorrow night he won't believe you have any more interest in Alanna romantically than I do."

"How do you propose to do that?"

255

"Simple. I'll just tell him that the word is you really like boys."

Jeremy was sure now that he was going to kill Aiden. He looked across at the man to see if he were smirking, anything that would let Jeremy know Aiden wasn't really serious about what he'd just proposed to do. But, Aiden's face was deadly serious.

"Your choice!" Aiden said. "It's for sure you can't be interested in her and your pilot too. Well, I guess you could, but... "

"No, not in this lifetime. Anyway, how would you explain Nenet to him?"

"Easy, you've been known to go both ways at times, but only with prostitutes."

Aiden got up to leave, but, in parting, said, "Think it over. It makes sense if you still want in on this. It's my guess Alanna still wants you in on this. It might be the price you have to pay for failing to remember who and what you are."

Being diplomatic was not one of Aiden's strong suits.

* * *

Alanna lifted the skirt of her gown high as she made her way barefoot through the dew-laden back yard of her house. She let herself in through the garage door, and turned on the kitchen light. Her wet feet left small imprints on the vinyl floor as she made her way to the dining room, where she opened the case that contained her secured satellite linked phone. She lifted the receiver to call Granton, hesitated, then set it back down again.

Pulling out one of the dining room chairs, she sat down, closed her eyes and considered her dilemma.

If she picked up that phone and reported in to Granton right now, Jeremy was history. Considering what had transpired that night, he should be. It was probably a safe assumption that Francois had no idea that Jeremy and she were Jake's replacements. It was his obsession with having her that was the driving force behind these attempts on Jeremy's life. But, whatever was motivating Francois to act so irrationally, the bottom line was that he wanted Jeremy out of the picture, and her desire to keep him in it jeopardized the mission.

The only good thing about this evening was that it had given her a chance to see Aiden in action, and he had proved to be very effective. The fact that he had let the situation play itself out as he had, not rushing in and complicating matters, but still being there to mop up afterwards, said volumes for his professionalism and his skill, and boded well for their working together successfully.

She knew that the final decision as to whether Jeremy stayed or went was not hers, but Granton's. But, she also knew she could have a huge effect on that decision. Granton would not have any knowledge of what had transpired until well into tomorrow afternoon. The report of the arrest of Nenet would have to filter through the various channels — FBI headquarters, the Attorney General's office, Admiral Porter's office and finally to Granton. How she handled things between now, and when she reported in to him, would be the decisive factor.

The single most important consideration was could they pull this mission off if Jeremy stayed on as part of the team. The only way to insure they could was to face the immediate problem, Francois' determination to get rid of Jeremy, head-on, without exposing her true identity, and take the pressure off Jeremy.

Doing so could prove very risky concept, because, if the ploy failed to achieve the desired results, the mission could collapse on itself, and she would be to blame for its demise.

The thought struck her that the mission being blown could already be a possibility, after all Francois had assumed she was injured and would be going home. He may have tried to call to check up on her. There was no telling what he might have thought if he had been unable to reach her. An even worse scenario was if he had gotten pangs of conscience, and tried to visit her at the house and found out she was not there.

Quickly, she rose from the table and went to check her answering machine. The message light was not blinking, so no one had called. She went from there out to the garage, where she rewound and played the tapes from the video cameras that had been set up to do surveillance on the house. The tapes did not show anyone approaching the house or stopped at the curb. She breathed easier, knowing she was safe where this potential complication was concerned.

There was little Alanna could do to rectify the situation now, so she returned to the house, turned out the lights, and retired to her room. As she passed the room Jeremy had spent the other night in, the scent of camphor and orange blossoms that lingered there, caught her attention. She stopped for a moment in the doorway, and looked at the bed he'd slept. She imagined him lying there helpless, and in pain, as he had been the other night, professing, in his drug induced slumber, how much he loved her. One of him having sex with Nenet quickly replaced the image. The hurt she felt at the contradiction in Jeremy's words and his actions went very deep. The best solution to this crisis, she knew, was to remove the problem — him.

* * *

Alanna woke to a brilliant flash of lightning, followed quickly by an earth shaking roll of thunder, and the sound of raindrops with the density of nails hitting the panes of her bedroom windows.

By the time she had dressed and was backing her car out of the garage, the early morning storm had dissipated, with only a steady, light drizzle remaining. As she cut through the back streets on her way to the stable area, the lightning and rain again intensified.

"Hope this rain doesn't continue all day," said Frank Sights, her neighbor in the shedrow, who was standing in the doorway of his tack stall, drinking a cup of coffee.

"How are you this morning, Frank?" Alanna asked, stopping to chat for a moment, on the way to her barn. "Don't worry, it won't keep the die-hards from looking, and they're the ones with the bucks."

"I'd feel loads better if this dang lightning would go away. Makes me and the horses nervous as hell," he said, visibly ducking as a flash illuminated the stable yard followed quickly by a clap of thunder indicating the lightning strike had been very near.

"Whew, that was close."

"Well, keep a low profile, Frank, and you'll be okay," she smiled in understanding at his fear, and continued on to her tackroom.

Julie and two of the grooms were huddled by the coffee pot, their wet rain slickers hung to dry on the tack cleaning hook, which was suspended from a rope tied to the center beam of the barn. Alanna hung hers alongside theirs, and accepted coffee from Julie.

"Lousy morning!" Julie remarked.

You'll never know how right you are about that, Alanna thought, but instead she replied, "Actually, it's kind of energizing."

"Yeah, you'd get good and energized if you stood out under one of those trees for very long," David, one of the grooms, quipped. "Real energized!"

"How was the ball?" Julie asked. "I stopped to look at the decorations before we headed out for dinner last night. It must have been really beautiful under the lights."

"It was," Alanna replied. "I was having a great time until I broke the heel on my shoe and twisted my ankle."

"Is it all right?" Julie asked, though she assumed it was, as Alanna seemed to be walking perfectly sound.

"It's fine. It was just one of those things that hurts like crazy for a minute, then feels fine just as quickly. But, I had to leave Francois to fend for himself for the rest of the evening," Alanna said, in way of preparing her crew for any inquiries by Francois as to her condition, should she not be around to tell him herself.

She had had a restless night, the "Jeremy" dilemma allowing her little sleep. In spite of deliberating the matter into the wee hours, she still had no real answer to the problem.

"Hop to, you guys!" Aiden's voice startled the bunch of them as his form filled the doorway of the tackroom.

"Ah, a great Irish morning if ever there was one," he said, indicating the mist that was now falling outside the shedrow, which had replaced the torrent of water that had preceded it. "You'd better get a move on or that last horse on the right is going to need pontoons to stay afloat."

With that said, he had to sidestep quickly to avoid the rush of bodies that shot out the door and in the direction of the endangered animal.

Alanna did not join them. Instead, she filled a cup with coffee, and offered it to him. He removed his raincoat, hung it next to hers and took the cup, helping himself to sugar and powdered creamer.

"Did you talk to Granton?" he asked, as he turned to face her. She had moved into the doorway, her back now to him and was watching the rainfall.

"No?" She replied.

Fairly certain everyone was out of hearing distance, he said, "I met with our friend last night, and he filled me in on what happened. Well, as much of what happened as he could remember."

"Humph!" Was the only response he got from Alanna, her back remained to him.

So he continued. "I'll admit, it' a damn awkward situation, but I'm sure there's a way to handle it."

"Oh, really! How?" she said, finally turning to face him, nothing of value readable in her expression.

"I'll be damned if I know!" He tried to get her to smile, by relinquishing one of his own, but he failed, so he added,. "That would be up to the brains of this operation. Since I'm only the muscle, it doesn't fall on me to solve the mess."

"If any of us had any brains, we'd be doing something else for a living," she retorted.

"I thought I was," he said. "I just dabble in this sort of thing when I'm called on to slay dragons and rescue fair damsels in distress."

At that remark, Alanna did crack a smile.

"Ah, that's better," he said, his lyrical Irish brogue making his words almost musical. "There's a way out of this. I promise ya."

"And, what way is that?"

"I suggested to our friend that I let slip the word to Francois that he prefers boys, but he didn't take kindly to it."

The suggestion brought a wide-eyed, silent gasp from Alanna, who said, "I would give anything to see him have to pull that off."

Thinking how she must be feeling about Jeremy just now, he replied, "I'll bet you would."

Then changing the subject, he said. "Well, I don't know about our friend or Francois, but I had a great time at the ball."

"Really!"

"Without a doubt," he replied. "While everyone else was plotting mayhem and stewing over the results, I got to dance with the belle of the ball and even kiss her. The best part was I got her to kiss me."

That kiss was something Alanna had purposefully allowed to fade from her memory.

When she did not comment, he said, "Well, it might not have been an earth shattering event for you, but I rather enjoyed it and after thinking about it later, I'd half hoped you'd enjoyed it too."

"Guess I was too busy worrying about real time stuff, like this mess our 'friend' has gotten us into, to be emotional about an operational diversion."

"Oh! Right!" he said, with merriment in his voice, and that devilish gleam still in his eyes. "I forgot. That's all it was, a textbook operational diversionary kiss. How stupid of me to be so naive."

"I'll admit," she said, smiling. "It was a very effective diversion."

"Well, good. At least it served some purpose." Then his voice took on a more serious tone. "As for reality, have you got any thoughts?"

"I think, for now, it would be best if our friend left the area," Alanna said, not knowing at this stage what that would accomplish other than taking the heat off Jeremy, and allowing her the luxury of not having to face him after last night's experience.

"Is that for his benefit or yours?" Aiden asked, as if reading her mind.

"For the benefit of the operation, hopefully," she replied, not letting his intuitiveness shake her composure. "I don't really have a plan. I have to be straight with Granton when I talk to him, but I think he will agree that getting our friend out of the area quickly is the best immediate solution. I'll depend on you to let our friend know of this decision. They tell me that Arizona is very pleasant this time of the year. So, it shouldn't work too much of a hardship on him to wait this out there."

"You're all heart, Alanna, banishing the man to paradise."

"Would it suit you better," she said, looking him straight in the eye, "if, I said that the two of you can stay and straighten out this mess and I'll go to Arizona. I know it would suit me just fine."

"No, it's for sure you're the brains, so we can't have you going off, and frying them in the desert sun. I'll give him the word to pack up and ship out," he said, finishing his coffee and heading toward the doorway.

As he passed her, she said, "You have my undying gratitude for handling this most unpleasant task."

He stopped, faced her and smiling, said, "I always collect on undying gratitude IOUs, so be prepared to pay."

"Just hope you survive this fiasco, so you'll to be in a position to collect."

"Amen," he replied, with a note of skepticism in his voice. As he headed off he added, "I'll catch you later."

"Later," she repeated his farewell as she watched him walk off. Men! She thought, one-track minds, and the sex train was always on it. Yet, she did smile to herself when she thought of the kiss they had exchanged in the Adelphi bar, and the interesting response it had aroused in her.

* * *

Phillip followed the housekeeper into Francois' bedroom, and remained to one side as she rearranged his pillows and served him breakfast in bed. The rain was pouring down and Francois had decided the weather, like life, was treating him badly at the moment, so the best remedy was to remain in bed until a more civilized hour. He had tried to contact Alanna upon rising, but when he only succeeded in reaching her answering machine, he concluded that she was better, and had gone on to see to her horses. He would see her later.

The housekeeper finished seeing to Francois, then exited the room.

"Yes, what is it Phillip?" Francois asked, although not caring particularly to hear about any more plans gone awry.

"We have had word from our friend in Washington," Phillip announced.

Francois was not certain by Phillip's tone of voice whether this was a good or bad development, but he resigned himself to pursuing the inevitable, and asked "And what does he have to say?"

"The message was short," Phillip replied, "but it said that he is working to find out if the gentlemen Monsieur Shabban removed, has been replaced, and if so, who has replaced him. There did not appear to be any indication at his headquarters that the agent had been replaced. Something he found to be a bit strange. However, he said that he would make certain of the fact. He also said he would be in contact with us again soon, and suggested we use the live drop method to communicate with him, but to vary the drop point."

"And what does that last request suggest to you, Phillip?" Francois asked, now certain that the rest of the day would be equally as dismal as its beginning.

"That he is being watched," Phillip replied.

Francois did not say anything, so Phillip asked. "In that case, Monsieur, should we break off contact with the man?"

Francois thought for a moment and then said, "No, but be cautious. His information has been excellent in the past, and it is obvious he is aware that he is being scrutinized, and is taking steps to avoid detection. He is not going to risk his neck unnecessarily. We will wait and see what he delivers. It is hard for me to believe the CIA would let the matter of the intelligence officer's demise go unresolved. But, who knows? The American Congress is unpredictable. They may not have realized the importance of the man's mission, and are willing to write the loss off. If so, it is to our advantage.

"And what of our incompetent friend Nenet and her bodyguard?" he inquired further.

"The man is to be deported today. As for Nenet," Phillip replied, "the FBI has her in custody. Since, the Americans have no particular quarrel with her, I assume they will simply detain her until the British arrange for her to be extradited."

"Phillip, contact of our Arab friends in New York, and see that they get her a good attorney — a very good attorney. Make sure that he advises her, confidentially of course, that it is I who is seeing to her welfare, so that she is not tempted to tell the true purpose of her visit state side."

"I will, monsieur," Phillip said, making a quick note in his pocket secretary. As he started to leave, he said, "If you will excuse me, monsieur, I will get on with my work."

He was halfway to the door, when Francois called to him.

"Phillip."

"Oui, monsieur?"

"In light of what our Washington friend has said, do you think I have been overreacting over this man Jergens?"

Phillip weighed his reply, then said, "I do, monsieur."

"Perhaps you have better instincts than I, Phillip."

"Will monsieur be needing anything else?"

"No, Phillip. You may go about your work."

* * *

Rakeland's attempts over the last two days to come up with more information on the French matter had met with mixed results. It hadn't helped that he had been relegated to a training mission at one of the Agency's outposts, and did not have access to the array of personnel from whom he might normally be able to extract this kind of information.

Still, some good had come of his situation. Last night, he had told his boss that he needed to stay late to complete his reports on his students' progress. By doing so, he had been able to gain access to one of the few computers that was tied in to the main computer at headquarters. Using his technical expertise and his hacker's skills, he was able to break into the section housing information on Operation SABRE. To his amazement, the operation appeared to be dormant. With the only current activity being DeGare, the Agency's inside man, mopping up after Carter and ending with a reference to Carter's body being returned for burial. There was no mention of the body's final destination, an omission that did not concern him, since he cared little where they had put Carter's remains to rest.

He knew there had to be more. It was simply too implausible that the Agency would simply drop the matter, but if there was more, why wasn't that information available? What he needed was a reliable human source. He wondered how much Stasio was privy too now that his residency at headquarters seemed to be permanent. Maybe it was time to invite his new friend to lunch.

* * *

Alanna had accepted an invitation to have breakfast with Paddy and Michael at Mother Goldsmith's. She had just secured her seat belt, and was about to start her car, when the small cellular phone Rice had given her buzzed. She picked it up, pressed the talk button, and held the device to her ear.

"I'm sorry, Alanna." She heard Jeremy's down cast voice say. She did not answer. In all honesty, she had dreaded this moment and could not summon up an answer.

"Are you there?" he asked, tentatively.

"Yes." was all she could say. The pounding in her chest was so loud she thought he must have been able to hear it at the other end of the line.

"Say something. Anything." He pleaded.

Silence.

"Alanna!"

"Are you leaving?" she said, to change the subject.

"Yes."

Silence.

"It's what you want, isn't it?" he asked. Then without letting her reply, because he knew it was, he added, "I don't blame you. I guess you were right, some things never change."

Silence.

"Do you want me to call Granton? I should be the one he hammers on about this, not you."

"No," she finally found her voice, and replied. "It's best I do it. He's more likely to see it in its proper perspective if I'm the one to break the news. I plan to do it early this afternoon."

"I feel like shit."

Silence.

"Will you call me?"

"Yes."

"I understand," Jeremy lamented. "If I were in your shoes, I wouldn't have much to say to me either. We'll be leaving in half an hour. Do you have my number in Arizona?"

"Yes."

"Well... okay. I guess I'll hear from you when I hear from you. Take care of yourself, Alanna and I ..."

He was about to say something else, but sensing that it was another of his professions of love, she stopped him. "Don't say anything more, Jeremy. Have a safe trip." And she disconnected the call.

Chapter 21

It was nearly 2 p.m. before Francois finally made an appearance at the rain-drenched sales grounds. He found Alanna sitting alone at a picnic table under the canopied area of the concession stand. She did not look at all cheerful.

"Your face reflects the day," he said, as he took a seat across from her.

She had seen him coming, but had made no attempt to change her outward demeanor, which reflected her reluctance to face the inevitable reporting in to Granton.

"I expect that it more clearly reflects the kind of day I've had," she replied, not even attempting a smile.

"Yes, I'm sure an injured foot is a disadvantage in your circumstance." He offered sympathy, thinking that her injury was the basis for her depressed mood. "I tried to call your home earlier today, but you had already left. I hope your foot is better."

"My foot is better. Thank you."

Francois was silent for a moment, waiting for further comment from her, but when none was forthcoming, he said, "I too feel a bit down, and will be very happy when this sale is over, and I can return to France. Except for our time together and my purchase of your beautiful colt, my stay in America has not been joyous."

I can't imagine why not, Alanna thought. You've certainly created enough havoc to make any self-respecting scoundrel deliriously happy. But instead, she replied, "I thought you were having a wonderful time. What could possibly have happened to make you feel otherwise?"

Unable to be truthful about the reason, he countered with a somber laugh and a lie, "Nothing, really. I guess the rain has made me feel a bit melancholy, that is all. Certainly, nothing to trouble you about."

Then, seeming to brighten up, he said, "Anyway, there are only two more days of the sale to go, and then I can look forward to your visiting me at my chateau."

When Alanna's demeanor did not brighten along with his, at the suggested visit, he said, "Nothing has changed, has it Alanna? You are still coming to Deauville?"

Alanna allowed a brief moment of silence before she looked him square in the eye, and said, "For some reason, which I have not been made privy to, my new client, Mark Jergens, suddenly decided to go home this morning."

265

She did not continue, but instead kept eye contact with Francois with such an intense, angry look that it made him squirm, a first for Francois. He was sure that she couldn't possibly know that he had been attempting to achieve just such an end, yet her eyes were almost accusing him of it.

Careful, Alanna, she thought to herself, don't play your hand too strong.

Then she gambled, and let the bomb drop, "That being the case," she said, being careful to allow her disappointment to show in her voice, "I have canceled my plans to attend the Deauville sale, and of course, I will have to decline your kind invitation to stay at your chateau."

Alanna knew that if Granton were listening under the table, he would have had five heart attacks by now. Life is risky, so be it.

Francois was so taken aback by this announcement, that even being as well practiced as he was at maintaining a poker face, he was unable to conceal his disappointment.

"You can't be serious, Alanna," he said, in a voice that bordered between disappointment and panic. "How can Jergens leaving possibly have such a huge effect on your plans?"

"Well, it could and it did," she said, adding matter of factly. "In fact, I've already gone ahead and canceled my flight arrangements."

"This is unbelievable, Alanna!" Francois said, incredulously. "You have been coming to Deauville for years without the benefit of a Mr. Jergens. Why is his presence so important?"

"Look, Francois, Jergens' business meant a lot to me. He had plans to get deeply involved in horse breeding and racing. I could have counted on representing him for a long time to come. That's the kind of client every bloodstock agent covets." Alanna said, maintaining eye contact with the Frenchman, but now without accusation in it.

"I realize that your involvement in horse racing and breeding, though certainly run like a business, is merely a diversion for a man of great wealth. For me, it is a business and my only means of livelihood, and I must run it accordingly. Because of the volatility in the economy right now, I need big money, a steady client like Jergens. In fact, I could use two or three like him. Losing him means that right now I cannot justify an expensive trip to France without the potential monetary benefits representing a client like Mr. Jergens could provide. So, no Jergens, no Deauville, it's as simple as that."

Alanna disengaged her eye contact with Francois. Instead, she let her eyes rest on the cup of tea on the table in front of her that she had been clasping with both her hands, and silently allowed Francois a moment to mull over the predicament.

Undaunted, he said, "Alanna, I really can't believe you would even consider missing Deauville. My offer of hospitality aside, an international agent needs to be seen internationally. Anyway, money alone cannot be the reason you are refusing to come. The funds you will receive from your summer sale yearlings will more than tide you over for a while. And, in coming to the sale, there is always the chance that you could pick up a client even more valuable then Jergens.

"What about Aiden Doyle?" Francois argued on. "You've been acting as his agent here, and so far, he hasn't been able to get anything that suits him. You could convince him to wait until Deauville. There will be plenty of yearlings there that would make excellent racing prospects for him, and you could always emphasize the point, that unlike purchasing a yearling here, he would not have the unnecessary expense or the risk of shipping them overseas. And, do not forget that once you have joined my consortium, the potential business you could pick up from its members is limitless."

He took a breath and then concluded his argument. "This headstrong position you've taken simply makes no sense to me."

Alanna had spent the morning in anticipation of this encounter. Though face-to-face psychological warfare had, in the past, not been a necessary part of her job, the lessons Jake had taught her on the subject had been learned well. She knew that in the person of Francois, she was up against one of the preeminent psychological warriors, so a slip, any slip, in her plan would mean her undoing.

There could be no smoke and mirrors attempt at inducement here. Francois was a logical man; consequently only logic could win this battle. To lead Francois to the edge of the psychological minefield she had laid for him was one thing. To get him deep within its perimeters was another, and she needed him so deep that the only way out was to surrender.

Surrender, to Alanna, meant that Francois would willingly, albeit unknowingly, assume responsibility for bringing Jeremy safely and effectively back into the operation. It was a task, she realized, that might prove almost as difficult as the U.S., during the Cold War, getting the Soviets to surrender after we had fired the first nuclear missile at them.

"I realize, Francois, that on the surface, my situation appears very simple," Alanna said, launching her attempt to get him to make that first fatal step toward complete surrender, "however, the reality is much

267

different. Due to the depressed market for Thoroughbred horses, many of my, my clients', and my partners', horses entered in last year's sales, went unsold. This includes the colt you saw work the other morning, which I had hoped would bring a big price at last year's summer sale and bale me out, and who, because of unforeseen circumstances, did not. It caused me to have to borrow a great deal of money from the bank to stay afloat. My farm and my best broodmares secured that money.

"I met with my tax attorney and my banker before I came here. None of us believes there will be that big or sustained turn around in the horse market very soon. It is our collective consensus that I take a very conservative approach to running my business for at least the foreseeable future. That means liquidating my lesser stock and using the money I got for the colt you bought to pay off the loans on my farm and my good mares. Had Mark Jergens stayed on, I could have used my sales proceeds to stabilize my base of operation, and used any monies I earned through agenting for him to expand. Meaning, to take part in your consortium — with him out, I'm out."

Hook extended. Will he bite?

Francois folded his hands in front of him and looked down at them. At one point, he looked her in the eye, almost as if in doing so he expected she would smile, say she was just kidding and that things would remain as they had planned, She did not oblige him, and once again his eyes reverted to his hands. Francois took a long time to respond, during which time Alanna made no further comments.

"I apologize to you, Alanna," he said, finally, and with great sincerity. "You are right. We enjoy the same passion, horses, but we operate our business in different levels. I have never had to consider options where my passions were concerned. I have always had enough money to indulge myself as I pleased. I know you do not operate under the same circumstances. You have had to struggle to maintain what you have, and it is obvious that you take great pride in successfully doing so."

Here is where this kind of ploy gets sticky, Alanna thought. He's bought my story, but which direction will he go? She had tried in advance to anticipate the possibilities in order to have a ready response, but the enemy was clever enough to mount a challenge of his own.

"It truly disappoints me," Francois said, solemnly, as he took both her hands in his and looked into her eyes. For a moment, Alanna could not read in them what line he was about to take, and she began to fear the worst. Unaware of her apprehension, Francois continued on, "to think that a poor prognosis for the future of the horse industry would succeed in denying me the great moment for which I have waited a lifetime.

"After all of my planning, my looking forward to doing what I am about to do in front of my many friends at my chateau, and with the benefit of my Grandmother's heirloom ring to offer you, I am forced to propose marriage to you in this less than romantic place. Be that as it may, I am asking you to marry me, Alanna. I am asking you to let me allow you to enjoy what you love without ever experiencing another worry about how you will pay for that pleasure. In saying yes, and by becoming my wife, you will have given me the greatest treasure I could hope to have — your love."

This had been one of the scenarios that Alanna had considered earlier, but when she had, she had not given enough consideration to the impact it would have on either of them. Francois had often hinted at marriage, but she had assumed he did this on a regular basis to entice a woman into giving him what they perceived was all he wanted — sex.

But, it was obvious from the gentle way in which he held her hand, the warmth in his voice, and the love that was very evident in his eyes, that he was serious. Suddenly, she was caught in the minefield with him. If she said yes, she would have access to everything that was his. She would need no pretext to infiltrate even the most secret enclaves of his chateau, for she would be its new mistress. It would be her home. It would also mean that she would not have to risk anyone else's life to complete this mission. A quick tying of the knot before they left the states, and everything would be at her disposal.

The flip side to this windfall was that for her to marry Francois was the equivalent of selling her soul. Even if that marriage was a marriage of convenience with the duration good for less than the length of the honeymoon. If, he laid one hand on her, she knew she would kill him. No way to start a marriage.

She had deliberately tried to look surprised at Francois' proposal. This did not necessitate an Academy Award winning performance since the depth of the emotion surrounding the pronouncement did indeed surprise her. And since he feared rejection, Francois chose to let her get used to the idea, rather than pressing her for an answer.

But, how should she answer? Yes was out of the question, but so was a resounding no.

"Got yourself in a good one, girl." Jake would have said, and she could almost hear him laugh.

Finally, she turned her hands up so that she now held his hands and, allowing her voice to reveal a kind of stammer, she said, "I...I don't know what to say, Francois."

"Say yes," he replied. "It's very simple and I promise you will never regret saying it."

"I...I....," she began, as if she were going to answer in the affirmative, which caused Francois to hold tighter onto her hands as if in doing so it would assist in her decision. "I'm afraid for now the answer has to be no."

Was that a maybe she had just given him? Luckily, Francois was so fearful of rejection by her that he chose to focus on the modifier "for now."

Still, he asked, "If you are seriously considering my proposal, which I assume you are by your choice of words, what does timing have to do with you accepting or not?"

Suddenly the path out of the minefield for her was plainly visible, and she explained her hesitancy in accepting his proposal by saying, "Francois, everyone in Lexington, maybe in all of the horse business, knows that my farm is going through hard times. If I marry you now, without getting Wicklow Stud back on a firm footing on my own, people will say that I married you for your money, and not because I loved you. I wouldn't want anyone to think that of me, and I surely wouldn't want anyone to make light of our relationship and laugh at you behind your back. I am truly honored that you feel the way you do about me, and that you want to save me the burden of contending with this problem, but I really want and need to work this out for myself. When I do, and I will do it, then we can have another go at this, if you are still interested." And as she concluded her statement, she stood and leaned across the table and kissed him.

By the look on Francois' face, she knew she had caused him to step on and detonate the first mine.

"I cannot say I am happy to hear your reply," he said, trying to ease his somewhat bruised ego, "but I understand you are a proud woman, and insisting you change your mind would not succeed in accomplishing anything. I feel my best alternative is to do what I can to see that you succeed without embarrassing you in the process. So what can I do?"

When you're like this, Francois, Alanna thought, you make it very hard to hate you. However, I know that just a millimeter below that seemingly gallant, warm exterior lays the cold, merciless heart of a snake. So it does me good to know that twisting this emotional knife into your gut is causing you some real pain.

"I'm sorry, Francois, I'm not sure how you can help."

He thought for a minute, then said, "Let me think about it for awhile, Cherie, maybe I can think of something."

* * *

It was more than an hour since Francois had left to go back to his house. Alanna debated what to do. She knew that if she wanted to be the one to break the news about Jeremy to Granton, she needed to contact him soon. She could not depend on anything of value resulting from this past encounter with Francois, and waiting any longer to see if something might develop, might mean the difference between lessening the impact of the news of the debacle, or having Granton go ballistic when he read the FBI's version of it when it reached his desk by way of the Admiral's office.

Reasoning that to wait much longer invited disaster, she started to head for a private place where she could contact him. She hadn't gone more than half way across the walking area, when she heard her name paged. She changed direction and stopped at the telephone room to see who had paged her. The woman at the desk handed her a pink slip with a name and phone number on it. It was Francois'.

She stepped into one of the phone booths reserved for local calls, and dialed the number. Phillip answered and said he would get Monsieur La Croix.

"Alanna," he said, joyously. "I have thought of a way to help you."

* * *

"Are you serious, Alanna?" Granton said, after she had finally contacted him on her secure phone, and as though she had just proposed the most ludicrous of ideas to him, which she had. "You can't be serious. After what happened to Jeremy last night, you actually believe Francois is going to call him in Arizona and convince him that he should attend this sale, and then not try anymore of his nonsense when Jeremy gets there?"

"Nothing is for sure, Granton," she replied, having neglected in her debriefing to say anything about Francois' proposal, "but, I have good reason to believe that Francois thinks smoothing things over between himself and Jeremy, and convincing Jeremy to reconsider coming to

271

Deauville, is in his very best interest, so it behooves him to honor his commitment."

"Well, of all the..... This is the craziest thing I've ever heard of," Granton railed. "And, the downright scariest. If Jeremy has any sense, which I know he doesn't, he'll turn this dumb idea down cold."

"Deauville is four days off," Alanna reminded him. "The plans are set and Jeremy is a big part of them. I am well aware how dangerous this idea is, but I don't think we have a choice other than to go with it. Four days, Granton. It's your decision."

"I'll reserve my decision until I've talked with Jeremy."

"Whatever you decide is fine with me." Alanna said.

There were lots of things Granton liked about Alanna, but two of the things he liked best were her ability to think on her feet and act accordingly, and to accept orders with a strictly professional detachment. And never was it more obvious how valuable having the intelligence officer in place able to operate under a natural cover than in this case. Not even the most sophisticated legend builder in Cover Division could have hoped to educate his charge in all of the intricacies of Alanna's business so that she could have operated in the fashion she had.

Not that the Cover Division didn't do good work. The way Jeremy's cover had withstood Francois' close scrutiny attested to that fact, but operating under deep cover as opposed to an official cover, such as the one created for Jeremy, or as an employee of a branch of the U.S. government like the State Department, always worked best. In Alanna's case, her cover was so deep it was almost impenetrable.

"How soon will you be free so that we can get together for a planning session?" Granton asked, and he felt a sudden surge of adrenaline as he anticipated the mission heading into high gear.

"The sales are not over for a couple of days," Alanna said, "but, all of my yearlings will be sold by tonight, so I could be available by tomorrow afternoon."

"I would like to hold this meeting at your place in Miami, if that's all right with you? It's as safe as anyplace, and we already have access to a large warehouse in the area where we can set up a mockup of the room in Francois' chateau that you'll probably have to infiltrate."

Had it not been for Rakeland, whom Security and CI now was convinced was their mole, and, on whom they were beginning to close the trap, Granton could have held the meeting in Washington and used the Farm, or their satellite facility in Alexandria to recreate the room.

But, getting Alanna that close to Rakeland was cutting the risk factor too close.

Granton had to admire Rakeland's panache. Save for his making the mistake of being too obvious while observing Jeremy's plane leaving the Farm, they probably still wouldn't have a clue who he was. Granton knew that Rakeland, having gone undetected this long, would surely have gained access to the information he needed, and blown this mission wide open.

"My bay house is fine. Francois has no idea that it even exists," Alanna replied in agreement. "How did you find out which room Francois plans to store the nuke in, and then manage to get plans to it?"

"Jake pinpointed it in his last report," Granton replied. "He didn't have any idea what the room looked like, but he got a key clue to finding that out. One day, while he was doing surveillance on the place, he managed to get the license number of a truck that came to service the chateau's security system.

"It was a British plate, so I got in touch with a friend of mine, Robert Elders, who is with MI5, and had him trace it. It turned out that the truck belongs to a firm called Finley's International, Ltd. They specialize in very sophisticated security systems, and do business world wide," Granton explained. "In fact, they do work for Scotland Yard, MI5, MI6 and some of the other branches of the British government.

"I'm sure Francois was not aware at the time he hired this company to install his system, that they have a practice of reporting to MI5 or MI6 any security systems they install outside the country that they deem might be of an interest to Britain's national security. The owner was about to file just such a report on Francois' installation to MI6, because, over lunch at the local cafe, his men had heard rumors that Francois was French Mafia connected.

"My friend at MI5 took the report and forwarded a copy of it to us. But what we really needed were copies of the plans for the security system, and any photos of the room that were available. Elders didn't want to take a chance on sending one of his men over to photograph the plans with a mini-cam, because he thought the resolution would be better if he had the originals at headquarters, where the pros could make certain the prints were clear enough that, if you need to, you could tell what size screws they used in the hinges. So, since he knew the head of the company, he laid the Official Secrets Act on him and got him to personally deliver a complete set of the plans and pictures."

273

"How complicated a setup is it to penetrate?" Alanna asked, her adrenaline beginning to get pumped as well. This was her bailiwick, and she was confident that whatever security was in place, she could subvert it one way or another. Anything that was made by humans to keep other humans out, she reasoned and felt confident, she could, with Agency technicians, help defeat.

"Let's just say, it will take everything you've learned so far and then some, for you to get in and out of there without getting caught. Security systems don't come anymore sophisticated than this setup. Francois paid a lot for it, but he got his money's worth. Of course, you will have an edge. You'll at least know what you're up against, and hopefully, we can provide you with a little technical assistance to undermine some of it. The rest, Alanna, will be up to you."

"Well then, when shall we meet?" she asked.

"Can you arrange to have the house vacant day-after-tomorrow?"

"I can."

"Then let's plan to get together about 10 in the morning," Granton instructed. "It'll be just you, me, Aiden and Jeremy. After lunch, Rice and Clark can join us at the warehouse. I want everyone to know the layout of that place well enough to see it in his or her dreams. Rice and Clark will get briefed there. Then you can stay on with the crews from Technical Services, and they'll familiarize you with your equipment, and run you through a virtual reality mock up of the situation."

"Virtual Reality mock up!"

"Absolutely, it's TS's latest toy," he replied, with some amusement at her surprise. "See what you've been missing."

"I'd be more impressed," she said, quite seriously, "if you told me they had a transporter room like the one they have on Star Trek."

Granton laughed and agreed wholeheartedly. Then he concluded their conversation by saying, "I know, Alanna, that I don't have to tell you that things are going to get real serious from here on in. So, think about what you have to do very carefully, because if you have any doubts about any arrangements, or any person involved in this business, now is the time to say so. That includes Jeremy. You may want to reconsider your insistence at having him along. If you do reconsider, call me before we meet, and I'll take care of the matter.

This, in the end, will be your show. A wrong choice now could mean you and maybe everyone else involved could be lost. You are going to be at the mercy of two very hostile and lethal entities in the form of

Hizballah and Francois' group. There will be times, while you're in that chateau, that you'll be your only ally. So, consider everything well."

"I'll do that, Granton."

"Good. Then until the briefing, take care."

And the line went dead.

Alanna quickly placed another call.

"Carlotta," she said, when she heard her housekeeper in Miami's voice answer. "I called to say that since things have gone very well at the sale here in Saratoga, and I have a few days before I leave for France, I thought I'd come back down there, and take care of a few things, and maybe take a couple days and go to Disney World. I would like you and your family to join me."

Carlotta had not heard her employer make such a suggestion since Dar passed away.

"Thank you, Senorita Reynolds, Lorenzo will be very happy to hear that we are going to Disney World," Carlotta replied, accepting the offer of the vacation gratefully, but knowing full well that Alanna, in the end, would not be coming with them. It was her subtle way of saying that she wanted the house to herself.

"I may be having overnight guests while I'm there, Carlotta, so please make sure the guest rooms are made ready."

"We will expect you and everything will be as you wish, senorita."

"Thank you, Carlotta. Oh, and tell Lorenzo we will have time for a lesson while I'm there."

"I will. He will be happy to know that as well," she said. "Have a safe journey."

Her conversation concluded, Alanna returned to her stable area. There were several people inspecting her remaining yearlings, among them Enrique D'Agustino of British Bloodstock Agency's Italian office, and Francois. They were exchanging comments about one of her colts, who was posed in front of them for their inspection.

Seeing Alanna approaching, Francois called her over.

"I was just telling Enrique how good I think this colt would do in Italy," Francois said, as she joined the men.

"Really, Francois!" She said, cheerfully, and then greeted the Italian warmly. "Hello, Enrique. How are you today?"

"I am very well, indeed, Alanna. But, I must say you have some very expensive help."

"I have?"

"Indeed, you have," Enrique replied, a glint of humor in his eyes. "I haven't seen Francois work this hard to sell a horse, since — well, since I don't know when, but, it's been a long time."

"Well," she replied. "I hope he's doing a good job."

"He is," Enrique assured her.

"Excuse us, Enrique," Francois said, in way of parting and shook the man's hand, "I need to speak with my boss for a moment."

"Of course, of course, Francois," the Italian replied, and returned his attention to the colt.

Francois steered Alanna in the direction of the chain link fence that bordered the stable yard. Once out of hearing of the crowd, he said, "Well, everything is taken care of."

"What do you mean, Francois?" Alanna asked.

"I have contacted Mr. Jergens, and convinced him to reconsider coming to France for Deauville," Francois announced proudly. "It was not an easy task, but I assured him Deauville was a sale not to be missed."

"I can't believe it. You're sure he's coming?" Alanna tried to sound overwhelmed by Francois' news.

"Yes, Cherie, he is coming." Francois said. "And to make sure he would have a good time, I have invited him to stay with us at the chateau."

Oh great, Alanna thought, that's a good maneuver Francois. Have him where you can watch him.

"And he agreed to stay at your chateau?" She said, hoping Jeremy had declined the invitation.

"He did."

"Well, Francois, you've been so efficient that I guess I'd better rebook my flight."

"That won't be necessary, Alanna. When I told Mr. Jergens that you'd canceled your reservations, he offered to fly you over on his plane. I thought it was most generous of him, don't you agree."

"Yes, very generous. I guess I'd better get in touch with him, and make arrangements for the flight."

"Yes, I would," he said, then putting his arm around her shoulder, he added, "I hope you are pleased. If there is anything else I can do to further solidify your empire, let me know."

"I don't know how to thank you, Francois."

"Marry me."

Chapter 22

Alanna was glad to finally be rid of Francois. It was going to get harder and harder to keep him in hand, and having to be under the same roof with him for the duration of this mission was going to prove a dicey situation indeed.

She had gone home to dress for the evening sale. Just as she was about to head out the door and back to the sale pavilion, the phone rang.

"Alanna.' She heard Jeremy's voice say and she quickly turned on the scrambling device.

"How are you, Jeremy?" she asked, with no particular inflection in her voice that might have told him how she was feeling towards him.

"I'm okay." he replied, evenly. "Did Francois tell you he called?"

"Yes."

"Was that your idea?"

"Indirectly.

He didn't say anything for a moment, and she remained silent on her end.

"I spoke with Granton," Jeremy finally went on with the conversation. "He's concerned about this situation between me and Francois, and he thinks I should reconsider accepting his invitation. He thinks it's too risky."

"He may be right."

"So what do you want me to do?"

"Follow your best instincts and do what you feel is right," she said. "If you pull out, I'll understand."

"I can't pull out, Alanna."

"Then, I'll see you in Miami."

With that, they concluded their conversation, but Jeremy did not hang up his phone. Instead he held on to the receiver as though, in doing so, he could hold on to Alanna.

Finally, he replaced it on its base. Turning to Rice, who had been sitting on a couch in Jeremy's make believe office at the Arizona resort, he said, "File a flight plan for Miami. We'll leave tomorrow night."

* * *

Rakeland had been careful to make his call to Ray Stasio from a public telephone in the Tysons Corner Mall. He did this, after having first rid himself of his Agency tail. Stasio's unlisted home phone number was one of the better bits of information he had been able to glean from his excursion into the Agency's computer system.

Rakeland had tried to find a number for Jeremy Slade, but either Slade had no permanent state side number, which could be the case if he were still tracking dopers in the Southern Hemisphere, or if he did, only someone like Granton Taylor had access to it.

He was about to hang up after the sixth ring, when a woman answered.

"Hello," she said, in a voice that announced her birthplace as Boston.

"Hi, Mrs. Stasio?" He replied, hoping he had the number right.

"Yes, this is the Stasio residence."

"Mrs. Stasio, my name is Chet Rakeland," he began. "I'm a friend of your husband's. We work together, and I would like to speak with him if he's in."

"Yes, he is, Mr. Rakeland," she answered. "If you'll hold for a moment, I'll get him for you."

"I will. Thank you." Rakeland said, pleased with his good fortune.

Soon, he heard the receiver lifted, and Stasio say, "Chet, how are you? How'd the hell did you get my number?"

"I'm fine. Thanks, Ray. The number was in our Turkey file," he lied.

"Well, what can I do for you?" Stasio also lied, because he had been expecting this call, and knew exactly what Rakeland wanted.

"Nothing in particular," Rakeland kept up the pretext. "I was just thinking about you and Turkey the other day, and thought I'd invite you out for a beer, or whatever, and we'd reminisce about old times."

Not wanting to appear too anxious to oblige, Stasio hedged, "Well, I don't know when I'd have time to do that Chet. The boys at the office have me working all kinds of hours."

The comment led Rakeland to believe something was going on somewhere.

Not easily discouraged, Rakeland persisted. "Hey guy, you've got to break for lunch some time. What say we hit that new place in Rosslyn, the one with the microbrewery? Do you know the one I talking about. It's just a block or so up from the Key Bridge Marriott. I hear they brew a pretty good lager."

Stasio refrained from answering immediately, then said, "Yeah, sure. I know where it is, why not. When do you want to get together?"

"How does tomorrow suit you?" Rakeland didn't want Stasio to get suspicious, but there wasn't a lot of time to get this thing done, so he'd have to risk rushing the meeting.

"Tomorrow? I don't know, Chet," Stasio stalled some more and dropped a little bait. "We've got a heavy duty meeting until two in the afternoon, I couldn't get there until 2:30 at the earliest. Isn't that a little late for lunch?"

"Nah, it's a great time." Rakeland came right back at him. He was even more convinced that they needed to talk if Stasio was now privileged to be in on "heavy duty" meetings. "The main lunch crowd will be gone, and they'll serve us quicker. I'm game, if you are?"

Again there was a pause, and then Stasio said quite enthusiastically, "Sure, let's do it. I could use a break."

"Great," Rakeland said, completely pleased with himself. "I'll see you there at 2:30."

* * *

Rakeland had asked the hostess to seat him at a table that allowed him to see most of both sides of the street. But that was far enough back away from the windows, that if anyone were to try and look in on him or eavesdrop, they could not do it easily, nor could they do it without looking obvious.

Losing the Agency guy tailing him to the restaurant proved even easier than losing the two guys tailing him last night. Either he was getting better at losing them, or they were getting worse at maintaining a tag. What he didn't know, or obviously suspect, was no one at the Agency was particularly interested in keeping a close eye on him at the moment, because he was about to meet with an Agency man.

He was beginning to get a little edgy, because it was now almost 2:45 and still there was no sign of Stasio. Just as he was about to give the meeting up, he saw a cab pull up across the street, and Stasio get out.

"Sorry, I'm late," Stasio said, apologetically. "That meeting took forever. Some of those old windbags are in love with the sound of their voices."

Rakeland got up, shook Stasio's hand and concurred, "Hey, don't give it another thought. I know exactly what you mean about windbags. God, have we ever got a bunch of those over at TS!"

They ordered lunch. Rakeland waited until they had a couple beers, and Stasio appeared to be relaxed before he started to tap him for information. Until then, he had kept the conversation to topics concerning Stasio's family; his home state of New Mexico, and his favorite football team, the Denver Broncos, all background information Rakeland had gathered via the computer. When Rakeland felt the most opportune time had arrived, he began his "getting the information" game by first giving some valuable information of his own.

"Boy, I'll tell you those mothers at TS have got me running all over the place," he said, in a conspiratorial tone. "The boys in Ops must have some big boom and bang job in the planning, cause I've been working overtime teaching a bunch of commando yahoos how to work all kinds of sophisticated commo and eavesdropping gear."

"It must be exciting," Stasio said, between bites of salad. "I mean, you know, what you do. Messing with all that neat technical stuff must be real exciting."

"Yeah, I guess it's all right work," Rakeland replied, his voice hinting at boredom. "I'd have rather been in Ops, though. You know, where the real action is. TS is fun and interesting work, but there's not much action."

"Hell," Stasio replied, after taking a big swallow of his beer. "I've been in Ops almost my entire career, and I can count all the exciting moments I've had on one finger, and that one happened by accident."

Rakeland laughed off-handedly, and said, "Yeah, I guess you've got to be someone like Jeremy Slade in order to get any real action out of your job."

He hesitated for a moment to see what kind of reaction he'd get. When none of value was forthcoming, he added, "I worked with Slade on a job over in the Balkans a few years back. The guy got himself in a bad way after that mission got blown. Lost his cool, washed out. I hear he's chasing dopers in South American for the DEA now. You know the guy I mean, Ray?"

Stasio assumed a thoughtful expression, while he took a moment to gather his thoughts before answering. After doing a routine, but thorough background and security check on him to determine his trustworthiness, Granton had made it a point to brief him on certain aspects of Rakeland's prior career involvement with the Special Ops Division, which included his short, but deadly, association with Jeremy Slade. Granton had suspected that since it was Jeremy whom Rakeland had seen boarding the plane, it might be the logical starting point in his shakedown.

"Jeremy Slade?" Stasio answered, questioningly.

"I guess you could know him by another name. Hard to know if people's names in that section are what they are. You know what I mean?" And he winked, reinforcing the conspiratorial nature of their conversation. When he still didn't get an affirmative response, he continued, "He's a big guy, about six foot two, well-built, athletic. Got kinda sandy-brown colored hair and green eyes. A real Agency cowboy, and boy does he like the ladies — I mean like big time!"

Stasio wanted to laugh at Rakeland's last bit of description, but he refrained and instead said, "I didn't know who you meant in the beginning, but now that you describe him, I think I do know who you mean. Although you're right, that's not the name he was using when I knew him in Ankara."

Well, that's not much help, Rakeland thought disappointedly. If Jeremy were involved in the operation in France, and Stasio had any knowledge of it, he'd have known whom he'd meant right off the bat. He had to take a shot, and find out exactly what area Stasio was working in. If he wasn't working in the European Section, he might not know anything at all about Operation SABRE. It was really risky to be so specific, but he had no choice. First, he better get off the Slade track, that approach was looking totally unproductive.

"Yeah, it would be a great deal to be someone like Slade, but hey, we can't all be James Bond, now can we?" And he laughed heartily at his own joke.

"You're right about that," Stasio remarked with a slight slur to his voice, "and as far as I'm concerned Slade, or whatever his name is, can have that kind of life." He took another deep swig of his beer to give Rakeland the impression he was heavily under its alcoholic influence, and then led with bait of his own. "I, myself, am happy with what I'm doing."

Hoping he could illicit an answer before Stasio had time to think what he was saying, Rakeland asked, "Where do you work?"

"The European Division," Stasio replied quickly, as though Rakeland had succeeded in catching him off guard.

"Boring place, Europe." Stasio volunteered. "Now the Middle East or the Russian desk, they are the busy ones."

"I thought you were stationed in the Middle East?" Rakeland backtracked, a little confused by Stasio's answers. "If you liked it so well, why'd you switch?"

"I didn't have a choice." Stasio fed Rakeland the disinformation he'd been told to lay on him. "They lost some guy in France, and they needed a replacement."

"Really!" Rakeland replied, honestly amazed at this piece of news. But, in reality, he thought, Stasio, Jake Carter's replacement — never. Carter, he knew was the consummate professional. It had taken him months of work, and all kinds of finagling to uncover his identity. This guy was a total dupe. No way could he be Carter's replacement.

"Actually, what I mean is," Stasio, seeming somewhat embarrassed, clarified his earlier statement, "I replaced the guy at headquarters who they sent to France to replace the guy they lost."

Ah, now you're making more sense, Rakeland thought with relief.

"They lost an Ops guy in France, and replaced him with a 'feather merchant'?" Rakeland replied, somewhat astounded. In his description of the individual sent to replace Carter, he had used the common slang term Ops people used in referring to staff from the Intelligence side of the Agency.

"Nah, they replaced him with another Ops guy." Stasio again volunteered.

Emboldened by Stasio's obviously intoxicated state, and his seeming willingness to discuss what would have been otherwise classified information, Rakeland continued his line of questioning, stating innocently, "I'd like to be working on that Operation. I'll bet it's a good one."

"I don't think so," Stasio said, matter-of-factly.

"And what makes you think that?"

"The guy's just there to mop things up," Stasio said, authoritatively. "Apparently, nothing of value had developed during the course of that operation, and then somehow this intelligence officer bites the dust, so the stiffs from the National Security Council pulled the plug on it."

"I'll tell ya," Rakeland said. "That's the trouble with the intelligence business in this country. We got all those old geezers lookin' over our shoulders, who don't know shit about what's going on in the world, and telling us how to run our business. Doesn't happen that way in Russia. You can bet your ass that those KGB guys, or whatever they're calling themselves this week, don't have to put up with that kind of crap. They want to waste a guy they waste him. They do what they want, when they want to do it. That's the way intelligence should work."

"Ever thought of going to work for them?" Stasio asked, and then thinking better of his statement, laughed and said, "Just kidding, Chet. I sure the hell wouldn't want to work for them. With all its faults, the Agency's my home."

"Amen!" Rakeland said, raising his glass in a toast.

It was almost five when he and Stasio parted company. Since it was too late to go back to the office, he headed home. All during the drive back, he mulled over the things Stasio had told him looking for anything that might knock a hole in the story he'd been told. But, either Stasio was the best actor in America, which Rakeland sincerely doubted, or what he'd said happened to Operation SABRE was the truth. Still, a nagging doubt persisted.

He turned up a back street that led to a shoe repair store, one of four drop sites he had set up with Francois, but quickly changed his mind about dropping Francois a note. Hell, what would he say, if, he said the operation was dead, and for some reason it turned out not to be, he'd be in a world of hurt. Francois did not take kindly to being misled. No, it was better to give this thing a little more time, and in the meantime, he'd explore another way to corroborate Stasio's tale.

* * *

Kamal Shabban welcomed the two Arabs into his study of his Montmarte home, and invited them to sit down. While they were getting settled, Kamal's houseman brought in a pot of coffee, and poured small cups of the strong, sweet liquid for the men. Then he retired from the room.

The older of the two men, Hassan bin Laden, was short and stout, and was dressed in a fine custom-made Italian silk suit, and hand-crafted Italian shoes. His hair was neatly cut, and he was clean-shaven, save for a small, well-trimmed mustache. He wore an expensive Piagett watch, and a large, ornate white gold ring on his right hand.

Hassan was an importer by trade, but dabbled in the construction business as well. He was wealthy, well educated, well connected politically, and had, for a long time, been a major financial supporter of the Palestinian cause. He was also Kamal's oldest and most trusted friend.

Kamal and Hassan were among the few dissident Palestinian leaders to be spared death at the hands of the Israelis. Hassan's survival was due largely to the fact that his part in the Palestinian campaign was a behind the scenes one.

In contrast, the other man, Mohammed al Khatib's, clothes were more workmanlike, consisting of khaki slacks, a plaid shirt and a leather jacket. His jewelry was limited to an off brand, much worn, military style watch. He was of medium height and build, with thick and somewhat unkempt black hair. His face was covered by a full beard, that concealed a heavily pock-marked complexion, and bushy eyebrows that made his narrow, close set eyes seem that much narrower and closer together. A physical trait that had always made Kamal feel slightly uneasy around him despite the fact that his deeds were such that his loyalty could never be questioned.

Mohammed's main purpose in life was to kill as many Israelis as possible before he, himself, was killed. Kamal never really knew whether the delight Mohammed took in the bloodshed he created was due to his love of or his dedication to the Palestinian cause, or whether he simply delighted in carnage for carnage sake. Whatever the reason, Mohammed had, over the years, inflicted heavy casualties on both the military and the civilian population of Israel. His survival was always in doubt, but his luck, like Kamal's, had held.

"Hakeem has not yet arrived?" Hassan asked, as he set his coffee on the table beside the over-stuffed leather chair in which he was seated.

"He will not be joining us tonight," Kamal replied. "He is away on business."

"I see." Hassan acknowledged the intent of Kamal's evasive reply by not pursuing the subject. Instead, he remarked, "Khalil will be arriving late. He too had business to take care of before coming here."

The third man expected at this meeting, Khalil al Otaibi, in appearance, fell somewhere in between the two men already assembled. Despite the fact that Khalil had come from a poor family, he had managed to get a university education. Smart, clever and a skilled negotiator, his job was to act as the main conduit between Kamal's group and the other Palestinian organizations. But Khalil had the jackal's scent for blood, and often took it upon himself to orchestrate and lead raids on Israeli targets.

"We can start without him," Kamal replied. Then, turning to Mohammed, he said, "In four days, Mohammed, I will require a least 25 or 30 of your best men to act as guards for a special shipment I am to receive in France."

"That will not be a problem," Mohammed replied. "Where shall I send the men? And do you wish me to accompany them?"

"Yes, you are to accompany them. They are to come to Francois De La Croix's chateau. The town the chateau is located in is quite small, and since I do not want your presence to draw attention, make sure they arrive at night and in small groups. Also, see that they are well armed and have sufficient ammunition. I do not want to have to rely on the kindness of others for supplies, especially since they may be more concerned with their own welfare than ours. You will also need a vehicle to transport the merchandise in. It should not call attention to itself, but it should have armored protection."

"I understand," Mohammed assured him, a nefarious smile appearing on his face. "That too can be arranged."

Kamal picked up a large manila envelope from the coffee table, and motioned for Mohammed to take it.

"This envelope has the information you will need to take charge of the shipment." Kamal said, as Mohammed took the envelope from him. "It will be kept in Francois' safe until we are sure it can be removed to our chosen location safely. The security set up for the room the safe is located in is excellent. Francois has agreed to let us take over security for the area after we have paid for the merchandise. It will be up to you and your men to see that no one gains access to the room, or tampers with the merchandise."

Mohammed nodded his head in the affirmative.

It is necessary that we receive the parcel at Francois' chateau," Kamal explained, "because it is the most secure place to do so, but the timing of the arrival of our parcel couldn't be worse. There will be a sale of Thoroughbred horses going on in Deauville at the same time, and since Francois is the head of the French Thoroughbred Breeders Society, he must entertain the people who attend the sales. Despite my recommendation for him to change his plans, he is still planning to entertain guests at his chateau while we are there. He believes it will actually draw less attention to him and us. Perhaps he is right, but the prospect worries me."

"I can see why it would, Kamal," Hassan said, in agreement. "Is there no way to change his mind?"

"I'm afraid not, Hassan," Kamal replied. "Francois is a man used to getting his own way, and one who thinks he always knows best."

Hassan shook his head in understanding, and frowned in dismay.

"So," Kamal continued his instructions to Mohammed, "it will fall to you, Mohammed, to see that the parcel remains secure without calling undue attention to yourself or your men. Do I make myself clear? Do you have any questions?"

This was an unusual assignment for a man given first to shooting, and later to asking questions.

Mohammed was silent for a moment, and then he said, "If we are to be so exposed to the general public, what you are asking me to do will not be easy?"

285

"I didn't say it would be easy, my brother," Kamal said, "I simply said for you to do it."

"Does that mean I must treat errant guests like curious pussy cats instead of spies?" Mohammed asked caustically, his tone bordering on the insubordinate.

"If need be." Kamal replied, ignoring the sarcasm in his lieutenant's voice. "But, with discretion, of course."

"As you wish." Mohammed responded, his demeanor signaling his resignation to carrying out the task, but his voice revealing his true feelings, which were, that the task would be impossible to accomplish as his boss had ordered it done.

"I think that is everything you need to know for now, Mohammed." Kamal said, in way of dismissing the man. "If I think of anything else, I will be in touch with you."

At those words, Mohammed extinguished a cigarette, finished his cup of coffee and rose to leave. Neither of the other two men rose with him. He started for the door, then turned back and said, "Kamal, what have you heard concerning the American that I took care of that night in Trouville?"

"The gendarmes found him dead in his car by the side of the road just outside of town." Kamal related the tale he'd been told. "We do not know for sure, but we are fairly certain that he did not make contact with anyone before he died."

"Has he been replaced?"

"That is something that we do not know. Our source has been unable to determine if, in fact, he was replaced."

"Then I shall assume the worst."

"I think it would be in our best interest that you assume so," Kamal said, in agreement. "Unlike Francois, I have every confidence in my belief that the Americans will not give up their quest to stop us."

Mohammed nodded his assent, bid them Allah's blessing and departed the room.

"We shall give Khalil a few more minutes to join us, Hassan," Kamal said, as the door closed behind the departing Arab. "If, he does not arrive soon, we will assume he was unable to make the meeting, and carry on, as I have a great deal to discuss with you."

Reaching into a drawer on his desk, Kamal produced a box of cigars and offered one to Hassan.

"Cigar, Hassan?"

"Thank you." Hassan said, helping himself to one, and preparing it properly with the small tool Kamal provided, he accepted a light from the cigarette lighter Kamal extended to him.

"So, tell me Hassan, is your family well?"

"They are indeed, Kamal, thank you for asking," Hassan replied. He did not inquire regarding Kamal's family, for Hassan knew better than Kamal how they were doing. As Kamal's friend, it had been up to Hassan to see that money was funneled secretly to Kamal's family, who were still living under cover in the United States.

The wait to conduct further business served a second purpose for it was not Kamal's intention that Mohammed hear any more of the plan. It would allow sufficient time for Mohammed to leave the house and be on his way.

Kamal and Hassan passed the time smoking cigars, sipping coffee and discussing generalities. When they'd heard the front door close and the sound of Mohammed's car's driving off, they resumed discussing their plans.

"Do you still think you can pull this off, Kamal?"

"More so now then ever, my friend," Kamal replied, his excitement very evident. "For what I didn't tell you was that we have been very fortunate in securing from one of the Russian Mafia organizations more than we bargained for. The deal we originally made was for nuclear material, but what we will actually be receiving is an operative bomb."

"Are you serious, Kamal?" Hassan said with great surprise, as he moved to the edge of his chair. "How did this happen to be?"

"Francois can sometimes be very stupid and stubborn," Kamal said, "but mostly he is a very shrewd businessman with many contacts. He got wind of a member of a Russian Mafia organization, who had access to Ukrainian nuclear scientists with a need for some quick cash. They just happen to have access to an area where the Ukrainian military stored spare parts for various weapons, among them tactical nuclear devices. They were able to pilfer enough of the spare parts to assemble a working bomb. Of course, the new deal he put together for us cost us considerably more than we originally agreed to, but with a device that is ready to use immediately, we will be ready to act on our plan much sooner than even I ever dreamed possible."

"How effective is this weapon and do we need any special training to detonate it?"

"It is extremely effective, and will serve our purpose perfectly," Kamal remarked. "A nuclear device of this size will obliterate an area

287

approximately a quarter of a mile in diameter along with considerable peripheral damage.

"The man delivering the parcel," Kamal assured his associate, "will be sufficiently adept at deploying it to show whomever we choose to position the weapon how it is done."

"Then the destruction would be considerable?" Hassan remarked, with amazement.

"It would."

"What effect will the radiation have on the target area?" Hassan pursued his inquiry into the bomb's capabilities.

"Marginal, thankfully." Kamal replied. "It is not our objective to poison the environment forever."

"And the target, Kamal, have you selected one?" Hassan asked.

"Yes, Hassan. There is only one target whose destruction would serve our ends and that is the Pan-Arab Israeli Peace Conference," Kamal said, again without hesitation. "which I have learned will be held in the Saudi city of Ta'If."

"How can you even consider an attack in Ta'If, Kamal?" Hassan said, alarmed at even the suggestion of destroying an Arab city very evident in his voice. Then by way of suggesting that caution in executing this decision be exercised, he added, "To kill a few of our brothers on foreign soil is bad enough, and risks our incurring the wrath of our brethren, rather than insuring their support, but to risk the population of an entire Arab city, well, I don't know Kamal if that is wise at all."

"Do not worry yourself Hassan, we will see that the blame for the bombing falls not on our shoulders, but on the shoulders of the Zionist radicals. We will not suffer any loss of face over the incident," Kamal said, keeping an even tone, though he was somewhat upset at his colleague's lack of understanding at the necessity of following through on this decision. "It is unfortunate to be forced to sacrifice so many Arab lives, but their souls will surely rest with Allah, martyred in the battle for a truly free Palestine."

Hassan puffed nervously on his cigar and drank the last of his coffee before asking, "Who will see that the bomb gets to its destination?"

"Who else, but Hakeem!" Kamal replied, without hesitation. "But, he will need your assistance."

"And what am I to do?" Hassan inquired, not convinced of the merit of Kamal's decision, but committed to seeing their cause through to the end.

"You must gain access to the construction company that will provide the concrete barriers that they will use to secure the area around whichever building is chosen to house the conference. Whichever facility they choose will probably already have some of these barriers in place, but they will add additional ones to heighten their security."

"I am sure I can arrange this, but what possible interest could Hakeem have in these barriers, Kamal?" Hassan asked.

"Security will be extremely tight in the area, even days before the conference, and once the conferees arrive, they will sweep the area for bombs constantly. There will not be an opportunity to bring the bomb into the area then, so it must already be in place and undetectable, before security measures reach that level."

"What has getting to the concrete barriers prior to the construction have to do with getting the bomb in place?"

"Everything, my friend," Kamal said, a sly smile spreading across his face. "For one of those concrete barriers will contain the bomb, set and ready to go off, and completely undetectable."

"But they deliver those barriers weeks in advance? How can you be assured the timing device will work for that length of time?"

"Never fear, Hassan," Kamal assured, his friend and patron, "we will make sure that the load containing the barrier, with the bomb encased in it, will not be delivered earlier than two weeks before the conference. We have been assured that the timer on this nuclear device is accurate up to a month prior to detonation. When the bomb goes off there will not be an Arab terrorist, save, of course, for the unlucky souls involved in the conference, eligible for them to blame within a thousand miles of that place. And, they will not be under suspicion, because they will have already have passed through security legitimately.

"Since, it will be obvious to all that it was a nuclear explosion, and since no one will have any idea that we were in possession of a bomb with such capabilities, the only other logical suspect will be the Zionist extremists. It is no secret that they harbor a similar desire as we do to derailing the peace effort, and they have the wherewithal, the nuclear capability to carry out such an attack. Does that set your mind at ease, Hassan?"

"It is a very clever plan, Kamal, and I will do what I can to assist you in carrying it out."

They stopped their conversation as they heard a car hurriedly come to a stop in the driveway in front of the house. They heard a car door slam, followed soon after by the ringing of the doorbell. Seconds later, an out-of- breath Khalil al Otaibi was shown into the room.

"Kamal!" He said, excitedly. "Turn the TV on to the CNN International channel. Quickly!"

Kamal obliged his request, and as the picture appeared, they could see a chaotic scene which the commentator was describing as the bombing of an Israeli cafe that had been hosting a party for Israeli soldiers and their families. The commentator said that Hamas had claimed responsibility for the bombing. The pictures continued on the screen, but the sound disappeared as Kamal pressed the remote's mute button, and said, "I expect Hakeem will be returning soon."

Chapter 23

As Alanna pulled her car into the drive of her Miami bay house, she saw Leonardo, Carlotta's husband, loading luggage into their faded, old Chevy station wagon. She pulled her car alongside the vehicle, and shut off the engine.

"You've got enough bags there, Leonardo, to be away for a month," Alanna said, as she gathered up her purse, a manila envelope and some groceries from off the front passenger seat, and got out of the car.

"Ah, well, senorita, you know Carlotta," Leonardo replied, laughing softly, as she stopped next to him, and watched him load up the family's gear, "she has to be prepared for any eventuality."

"Oh, yes, how well I know." She laughed with him, remembering how often she had had to repack her bags before a trip after Carlotta had attempted to pack every decent outfit in her closet in them.

"Can I help you get your bags into the house," he offered.

"No, thanks, Leonardo, I didn't bring a bag. Everything I need is already here," she said as she set the articles on the hood of her car, and opened her purse, and removed an envelope from it.

"Leonardo, take this," she said, handing it to him. "It's a little something extra for your trip."

He took the envelope, and took a quick look inside. There was a small stack of $100 bills in it.

"Oh, senorita, this is too much. You have already paid for the hotel and the admission to the park." Leonardo said, while trying to hand the envelope back to Alanna.

She refused to take it, saying, "Please keep it, Leonardo, I want you and Carlotta and Lorenzo to have a good time."

"You spoil us, senorita," he replied.

"It gives me great pleasure to do this for you." Alanna said, with great sincerity. "You and Carlotta take good care of me, Leonardo. You treat me as though I'm a member of your family. I really appreciate that and all of you. So let me do this small thing for you."

Leonardo reached out and hugged her warmly, at the same time assuring her, "You are a part of our family. A very special part."

She returned the hug, then turned and retrieved the articles from off the car's hood, and headed to the front door.

She had only gone a few feet when she heard Leonardo say, "Oh, by the way, senorita, your house guest arrived while you were gone. Lorenzo has been entertaining him."

She turned to acknowledge his statement, and noticed that he wore a strange expression on his face. A least a strange expression for Leonardo, who usually maintained a certain dignified demeanor. It was one of those smirky expressions that implied a shared secret.

He paused for a moment as if deciding how best to put his next statement, then said, "He is mucho hombre, no, senorita?"

Thinking he was referring to Jeremy, who she had not been expecting to arrive until the next morning, she replied, "If you say so, Leonardo."

"I say so!" he said, smiling and winking conspiratorially to add emphasis to his appraisal.

Alanna just laughed, shook her head and headed for the house. Once inside, Carlotta, who was wearing a similar expression as her husband, met her. In a whispered tone she said, "Ah, senorita, your friend has arrived. He is...how do you say — very, ah, interesting. Ah, no, that is not the word I am looking for. Very..."

"Macho?" Alanna said, thinking how Jeremy always did have a way of impressing people.

"Ah," she said, laughing heartily. "Ah, maybe, macho, but I think much more."

Carlotta waved in the direction of the gym and said, "When he arrived, I told him that you would not be here for a few hours, so he and Lorenzo have been working out in the gym to pass the time until you returned."

"That's interesting!" She replied, in surprise. Jeremy. Working out in the gym. That was a new one. She started for the gym anxious to see what was going on, completely forgetting the parcel in her arms.

"I'll take the groceries into the kitchen, if you like, senorita," Carlotta offered.

"Yes, please do, Carlotta. Thank you," she said, handing the bag over to the woman.

As Alanna approached the room, she could hear the thud of a solid blows and kicks being landed to the punching bag that was suspended from the ceiling in one corner of the room. Entering, she notice Lorenzo standing with his back to her observing a man, who, in the space of the few seconds it took her to recognize him, landed several punches, strikes and kicks to the bag that would have made him the envy of any martial arts expert.

"Well, hello!" She said, stepping into the room.

The pair turned towards her, Lorenzo coming over quickly to greet her. His voice full of excitement and admiration, he said, "Señor Doyle is good, no, Senorita Reynolds?"

"He's fast and powerful, Lorenzo, but it remains to be seen if he's good," Alanna replied, with a smile that suggested she thought he might be.

"That's not what he told me," Aiden said, wiping his face on a towel. As he turned his back to her to reach for his shirt, Alanna saw that his lean, well muscled body was marred by several old, but still angry looking red scars across his back. These were evident for only a split second as he hastily put on the shirt.

While his back was still turned to her, he added, "Lorenzo said that in an even match, he thought you'd knock the livin' daylights out of me."

"Thank you for your loyalty, Lorenzo," Alanna said, as she put her arm around his shoulder and gave him a friendly hug.

"I could not lie, senorita," he said, shrugging off the hug as an embarrassed teenager might do. "He only has to see you perform to know I have spoken the truth."

"Ah, an honest lad, a rare commodity today," Aiden remarked, as he joined them, again wiping his face with the towel.

Turning to Lorenzo Alanna said, "Lorenzo, you'd better hurry and get cleaned up. I think your parents are about ready to leave."

"Oh, yes," he said excitely. "I almost forgot."

Offering his hand to Aiden, he said in parting, "It was a pleasure meeting you, Señor Doyle."

"My pleasure entirely, Lorenzo." Aiden said, returning the handshake.

As Lorenzo started up the hall, he said, over his shoulder, "If you get brave enough to spar with Senorita Reynolds, be careful she doesn't take advantage of you." And, he laughed.

"I'll heed your warning, lad. Have a good time on your trip," Aiden replied good- humouredly.

Aiden waited until Lorenzo was well out of hearing, then he said, "I hope you don't mind me arriving early, Alanna. You did mention I'd be welcome and I saw no point in going back to Ireland for a day, then flying back here, or hanging out in some boring Miami hotel."

"No, I don't mind at all." she said, warmly. "In fact, it's better that you came today. The traffic in here tomorrow won't look so heavy, and it'll give us a chance to get acquainted. It's something I think we should do, since I'm not sure how much use Jeremy is going to be to me since he agreed to stay at Francois' chateau."

"I guess he didn't want to leave you that exposed and on your own, but he played right into Francois' hands," Aiden replied.

"Well, " Alanna said, seeing that Aiden had become quite perspired while exercising. "It's out of our hands for the moment, so why don't you take a quick shower, and dig out your bathing trunks and we can take a swim. Here, if you like, or if you prefer, we can drive to the beach."

"I do need to get a shower and change, but if you don't mind I'll pass on the swim," Aiden replied.

Remembering the scars on his back, Alanna said, "That's fine with me. I assume Carlotta has you settled in a room, so why don't you have a shower, and meet me on the patio, and I'll make us a drink and we can talk."

"I'll just be a minute," Aiden said, heading off in the direction of the guest room.

While he showered, Alanna touched base with Granton by phone, though for her own reasons, she did not inform him that Aiden was staying there. Then she filled an ice bucket with ice, and headed out to the patio. She was sitting at a table on the upper deck reading the Miami Herald, when Aiden appeared wearing tan linen slacks, a cream cotton cashmere blend polo shirt, and saddle-tan basket weave leather loafers, without socks. His coal black hair, still wet, was slicked back against his head.

"Do you always dress like an ad for Gentleman's Quarterly?" Alanna asked, smiling while she inquired, so he would not take offense.

"You don't approve of my dress?"

"On the contrary, it's in very good taste."

"Well, in that case, I will take your inquiry as a compliment."

"Let me get you a drink," she offered, as she rose from her chair and went over to a rolling cart that sat to the left of the table. "What would you like?"

"Jaimesons, neat, if you have any, no, on second thought, considering the heat, a gin and tonic on ice might be a better choice."

"I agree," she replied, and then asked. "Care for a slice of lime with it?"

"I would, thank you," he said, as he took a seat at the table and picked up the paper, which he began to read,

She fixed the drink, and not wishing to interrupt what he was reading simply set it before him, and returned to her seat.

"Thanks," he said. Then picking up the glass, he raised it in a toast, "May we be in heaven before the devil knows we're dead."

"That's a cheerful thought," Alanna remarked, as she picked up her glass of orange juice, and clinked his glass with hers.

"I see Hamas has been playing in the streets with their toys that go boom again," He said, referring to the frontpage article that told of the bombing of an Israeli cafe.

"Yes, I saw that," Alanna replied, as she shuttered to think how many people would die if she was not successful in keeping Hizballah from getting its hands on the nuclear device Francois was planning to deliver to them.

She dismissed the thought, although not easily, then after letting Aiden take a few more sips of his drink, she said, "Tell me about you and Dar."

He had resumed reading something in the paper. Without bothering to put it down, he answered her from behind it, "We were friends."

Both of them were silent for a moment, Aiden seemingly engrossed in his reading, Alanna simply sat observing him. Then she picked up her glass and rose from her seat.

"I'll leave you to your reading," she said, with no discernible sign of irritation at his refusal to talk in her voice. "I have some things to do."

She had moved off a few feet in the direction of the house, when she heard him say, "Refill your glass Alanna and sit down, it's a long story."

When she turned back to him, he had put down the paper, and was sitting with his elbows on the table, and his hands folded in front of him. He motioned for her to take a seat, and she did.

"I am telling you this, Alanna," Aiden advised, his eyes holding hers, "not because you believe you're entitled to know because of our mutual relationship with Dar, but because I've gained a great deal of respect for you since we've met, and I want you to know. However, what I am going to say is for you alone, and not to be repeated to anyone. Is that clear?"

She nodded and after hesitating momentarily, he continued.

"I was working for MI6," he began. "We had been heavily infiltrated by KGB moles, something that had been going on since MI6's inception. The men in charge deliberately overlooked the matter, and swept any proof of such allegations under the rug, because nobody wanted to admit their old-boy system of vetting out intelligence people was unreliable. My employers preferred to cover it up rather than acknowledge it. As a result of this overt ignorance, many of our operations were being exposed and compromised, and far too many of our people were losing their lives."

He paused for a moment, leaned back in his chair, took another sip of his drink, and let his gaze settle somewhere out over Biscayne Bay. Then, while still looking out over the water, he went on. "I was on one of those ill-fated missions. I was sent into eastern Thailand, to a Cambodian refugee camp just inside the Thai border, where I was to pick up one of our people and get him home. It was supposed to be a quick in and out kind of affair. What I didn't know was that the Khmer Rouge were hot after this guy, and had been tipped that he was on his way out. They made a raid on that camp just as we were about to leave, and got the both of us. They took us back to their camp. He didn't last long, and though his agony was short lived, they made damn sure that his exit from this planet was a painful one."

Again, he paused and took a long sip of his drink, as though he needed the liquor to bolster his courage to continue. "I wasn't as lucky. I'm not sure whether that was because the other guy gave it up so quickly, or just because they had another victim to work their tortuous art on, but they did a number on me."

He didn't elaborate, but she had seen the scars on his back, a lasting and all too visible reminder of that experience.

"I quickly lost track of time," he said, the anguish at relating this tale evident in his voice, "even though I tried hard not to, because I thought it would save my sanity. After a while, I wondered if having all that will to survive was really doing me any good. I had tried to escape once and had succeeded, but I was so weak, they didn't have any trouble tracking me down. That only made them madder and the torture worse.

"My rescuers were a cadre of Thai Border Police alerted to my predicament by one of the doctors at the refugee camp, and accompanied by an American intelligence officer," he said, now settling his gaze back on her, "That American was Dar. I was told that when they rescued me after eight days in that tiger pit the Khmer Rouge kept me in, I was filthy from my own excrement and blood, starved, dehydrated, semi-conscious and one step from the grave."

"Dar was in Thailand?" She said, in surprise. Knowing this incident had to have taken place while they were together, yet she had known nothing about it.

"He was conducting some kind of intelligence training at the Thai Border Police Training Center at Phitsanulok when the message from the refugee camp came in. They asked him to come along because the doctor at the camp had mistakenly reported me as being an American. The cadre was made up of the best of their Thai ninjas. They slipped into the camp after dark. But, because the Khmer Rouge had moved their camp twice since I'd been captured, they had no prior knowledge of where I was being kept, so they had to search the camp for me. A couple of Khmer Rouge guards spotted them, and tried to make sure they didn't find me alive. One of the Thais said that Dar found me first and took both the Khmer Rouge guards out, then defended the area until the other Thais arrived to help him get me out of the pit.

"Dar knew by the first words that came out of my mouth, that I was Irish, but he told them I was American, so that they'd make a special effort to get me to a hospital as quickly as possible. He also had them take me to the best hospital in the area, the Seventh Day Adventist Hospital near Bangkok. When he knew I was going to make it, he left.

"That probably would have been the last of our relationship, but about a year later, I accidentally ran into him in a hotel lobby in Hong Kong. He didn't recognize me because my appearance had improved considerably from the last time he'd seen me. But I recognized him, even though I was only half lucid the whole time he was around me in Thailand.

"We each were in a business that allowed us to make contact with one another without raising anyone's suspicion. Once we got to know one another better, he asked me what I'd been doing in that Cambodian refugee camp. My instincts told me that he already knew, so I told him the truth. He told me to be more careful next time, that there might not be a friendly force handy to save my neck. I told him there wouldn't be a next time, because, about a month after I got back to England, another friend of mine was killed in a similarly botched operation as the one I'd been on. I'd decided then that was all I wanted of an organization that didn't look after its own people, and handed in my resignation. He told me to keep in touch. When he got back to the States, he handed in a background report on me, and after I had passed their security check, he requested permission to recruit me as a contract agent.

When he made the pitch, I wasn't too excited about signing on, but he convinced me to do it. Once in, he made me promise that if I was ever asked to assist on an operation that involved another intelligence officer, code-named CHAMELEON, I would not, under any circumstance, turn the assignment down."

Again there was silence. Throughout the final stages of his story, Aiden had not taken his eyes off Alanna, nor she him.

"And that's why you're here," she said, finally, "to repay him for saving your life?"

"No," he replied. "I'm here to help you. That's what he asked me to do."

"What's caused the animosity between you and Jeremy?" she said, changing the subject.

"Jeremy!" Aiden replied, smiling and shaking his head. "I honestly don't know, Alanna. Bad chemistry, I guess. It's nothing personal. We met on an operation Dar was running out of Singapore."

"Was that the only time you worked together?"

"No, we've crossed paths on several occasions," he replied. "Don't let it worry you. He and I work together just fine."

Then turning the tables, he said, "What about you and Jeremy? Francois didn't just dream that he was interested in you. Jeremy must have given him good reason to be suspicious."

Alanna suddenly diverted her eyes from Aiden's, looking instead out across the water as he had done before. She realized that she should have anticipated that he would be curious about their relationship, but his question, nevertheless, caught her off guard.

"Why the stall?" he said, sensing her reluctance to answer. "Just spit it out."

"Jeremy and I have been partners for a long time," she replied, once again making eye contact with him. "During the operation that we lost Dar on, he saved my life. Other than that, there is not much to tell."

"If that's true, why did seeing him make love to that female assassin put you in such a funk?" Aiden questioned her response. "You said yourself he was looking for someone he could appear to be involved with to try and convince Francois he wasn't interested in you. It seems to me he was just carrying through with his plan. If you hadn't recognized her as an assassin, and had to save his neck, would you have given his going off with her a second thought?"

"No, I wouldn't have," she replied, truthfully.

It wasn't the answer Aiden had expected, so he pursued the matter.

"That's a very interesting answer, and I believe you," he said, suddenly entranced by the complicated emotions working here. "The old out of sight, out of mind philosophy?"

"Hardly, Aiden." Alanna, now having had time to get her thoughts together, replied. "Jeremy has always found it necessary to bed anything in skirts that is half-way attractive and offers no resistance to him. He makes no secret of it."

"But, what he does obviously bothers you, right? More specifically it hurts you, yet, you still care for him?"

"Yes," she said, and there was a trace of sadness in her voice.

"Why?"

Alanna was silent again, searching her soul for a way to say what she had never said to anyone else.

"Do you love him?" Aiden asked.

"One time, long ago, I thought I did."

"And you don't now?"

She was silent for a minute. Then, he could see her eyes becoming moist. Realizing he had noticed this, she lowered her head and turned in her chair so that she was facing to the side.

"I'm sorry, Alanna," Aiden said, apologetically, and got up from his chair. He came over to her, and stooped down next to her. He took her hands in his. "I had no right to get so personal. What's between you two is your business."

She raised her head and looked at him. He smiled at her and touched her cheek gently with his hand. "I'm sorry I made you sad. I didn't mean to."

It was the sincerity of his words and his gesture that made her decide to do something totally out of character. "Come with me," she said, as she rose from her chair and started into the house.

He followed her to a room whose door she unlocked with a key. It was the room she and Granton had had their meeting in. She turned on a wall switch as she entered, illuminating the room, which, since it had no windows or skylights, was pitch black inside.

"Close the door behind you and come in here," she said, indicating the door they'd entered the room through.

He did, and then he came over to where she was standing. She went to a wall of bookshelves, removed a book, pressed something and part of the wall moved away revealing another room. It, too, was pitch black except for the light that filtered in through the open door. Alanna disappeared into the blackness, which vanished as she turned on a lamp that sat on an end table situated between two leather chairs.

"Come in here," she said. "I want to show you something."

He came into the center of the room, whose walls, he could now see were filled with pictures and other memorabilia. There were lots of pictures. The kind you take of family and friends. One he noted especially, because it seemed to be the only one of its kind. It was of a young man and woman all dressed up in their Sunday best, each holding the hand of a pretty little blonde girl of about three.

There were many others, some he noted particularly such as the one of an elderly couple standing beside a beautiful young blonde woman, whom he had no trouble recognizing as a college-age Alanna, dressed in a cap and gown, proudly displaying a diploma. There was one of them smiling proudly as they stood next to her mounted on a beautiful gray horse, a championship ribbon hanging from the browband of his bridle. There were pictures of her and Dar taken in different settings, their facial expressions indicative of the love they'd shared for one another. And, there were pictures of her and an older, gray-haired man, whom he deduced was Jake Carter from the description of the man Granton had given him. One of them was of Jake and Alanna fly- fishing in a stream; one was of them trap shooting. Next to Jake's pictures, framed in a small shadow box was an Intelligence Star, and next to it, the Citation awarded with it, which he read. There were no pictures of Jeremy.

"No one," she said, while concentrating her gaze on the pictures on the wall, "has ever been in this room but me, and now you. This is all of my family, and, unfortunately, they are all dead."

Aiden did not know what to say. The loss of his father's love now seemed almost inconsequential in comparison to the losses suffered by the woman standing next to him.

"Everyone I ever cared deeply about is dead except for Jeremy," she confided, "and though I do care a great deal for him, I think that there just might be too much excess baggage between us for me to love him anymore."

"You didn't have to show me this room, Alanna, or tell me that." Aiden said, suddenly feeling like he had invaded and desecrated some sacred place.

"Yes, I did!" she said, as she walked to and touched, lovingly, one of the pictures of Jake. "Jake would have wanted me to, because he would have felt what I feel, that you would understand."

* * *

Aiden woke to the sound of water lapping up against rocks, and the cry of sea gulls, that came into his room through opened French doors. He checked the clock on the nightstand, and noted that it was only a little after seven. Knowing he had plenty of time before their meeting with

Granton, he laid his head back on the pillow and while gazing up at the ceiling, tried to piece together the enigma that was Alanna Reynolds.

Just before he had been contacted about signing on to this operation, he had given serious consideration to getting out of the intelligence business. Since Dar's passing, his Agency assignments had been mostly relegated to intelligence gathering on the drug trade, and political climate in the areas in which he operated his business. He had produced a lot of good intelligence for them, but he missed being assigned the covert, para-military type operations he and Dar had done.

The chance to once again participate in a covert para-military operation was as much a deciding factor in his taking this assignment, as was his promise to Dar. Until he'd actually signed on, he'd had no prior knowledge of the fact that CHAMELEON was Alanna, or that she had been the woman in his Dar's life, because despite their close friendship, Dar seldom talked about his personal life. And, in still another ironic twist of fate, she was a much admired and loved friend of the man he considered his real father, Paddy Ryan and his best friend Michael Quinn.

The more he learned about Alanna, the more fascinated he became with her. She was so very complex, one minute she was the perfect spy: tough, efficient, capable, confident, level-headed, in control, and the next minute the she was the perfect woman: gentle, feminine, devoted, sympathetic, caring. He could see why it was so easy for men to fall in love with her. Especially men like Dar and Jeremy, and even, he now sensed, a man like himself -- men who could appreciate both sides of her persona.

It was this realization that had made his inquiry into her feelings for Jeremy two fold. He needed to know how to handle their relationship from an operational standpoint, and he wanted to know where he stood in the scheme of things. What she had shared with him in that room last night had been a glimpse inside her soul. In doing so, she had, without words and without him asking, expressed a profound statement of her trust in him.

All through the rest of last evening, through dinner, during the quiet moments they'd shared having a brandy and watching the sunset, they had deepened the understanding and the bond that had begun to develop between them. He knew that if it were necessary, he would die rather than break that bond, and that he would let lie dormant any urge to express the deeper feelings he now harbored until a more suitable time.

301

His thoughts were interrupted by the sound of something splashing into the water of the pool, which was located just below his bedroom's balcony. He got out of bed and as he made his way outside, slipped on his robe. Looking down from the balcony into the pool, he could see Alanna's slender figure swimming laps while submerged underwater. Pretty good, he thought, as he counted the laps she was able to complete before surfacing.

When she did surface, he called down to her, "Is there room enough in that bath tub for two?"

"Absolutely," she said, as she floated over onto her back and looked up at him.

"Then, I'll be down in a minute," he replied, and disappeared back into the room.

Alanna smiled to herself. Having bared his soul to her, it now seemed that Aiden was able to bare his scared back to her as well, comfortable in the knowledge that the sight of those scars would not be a turn off to her. She liked that development in their relationship, and after sleeping on what had transpired between them last evening, she'd decided that she also liked him.

* * *

As Alanna, carrying an ice bucket, was about to enter the conference room, she noticed Aiden heading towards the front door with his suitcases.

"Leaving without saying good-bye?" she asked, a trifle confused, since he was to have stayed another night before heading off to France to do the advance work for the operation.

Aiden set the bags down against the wall just inside the door, and as he was walking over to her, replied, "After giving our discussion about your relationship with Jeremy some thought, I decided it would be wiser if he didn't know I'd spent last night here. This operation is complicated enough. We don't need him reading things into my stay here that don't exist. Wouldn't you agree?"

Though nothing of a romantic nature had transpired between them since he'd arrived, Aiden's bluntness in indicating that there was nothing between them took her by surprise.

"Personally," she said, the tone of her voice cool. "I don't really care what he thinks happened between us. But, if it makes you feel more comfortable working with him, I don't have a problem pretending yesterday never happened." And without further comment, she entered the conference room.

Bad choice of words, Aiden, he thought to himself as he reconsidered his statement while following her into the conference room, but now is not the time to apologize for using them. Let her be a little cool towards you, it'll carry this strictly business, client/bloodstock agent relationship off better.

"Is there anything I can do to help?" he asked, as he looked around the room and noted that sometime earlier she had set out pads of paper and pens on the conference table, and pulled down a large movie screen which now covered one of the room's walls.

"No, thanks," she said, with a smile, the coolness completely gone from her voice, which surprised him at the quickness of her change in attitude. "I think I've seen to everything."

Alanna set the ice bucket on the sink behind the bar, and from behind it, gave the room a quick once over to see if she'd forgotten anything. Turning her attention back to him, she asked, "Would you like something to drink?"

"Thanks, but I think I'll wait until the others arrive." He had barely finished his statement when the doorbell rang.

"That's probably Jeremy," Alanna said, as she started out from behind the bar to answer the door. "Granton won't be here for at least another half hour, and he'll come by boat."

Aiden motioned for her to stop, saying, "Make yourself busy doing something, and let me get the door."

She just smiled, nodded in reply, and returned to fussing with things behind the bar.

Aiden proceeded to the front door.

Jeremy, not expecting his greeter to be Aiden, inquired suspiciously, "Been here long?"

Ooooow! Bad attitude, Aiden thought, and considered how he would have like to readjust it by knocking Jeremy on his ass. Instead, he stepped back inside opening the door wide enough for Jeremy to see his bags set against the wall, and said, "Actually, I just got here, myself. Alanna was busy setting up the conference room, so she asked me to get the door."

That seemed to satisfy Jeremy. Aiden understood how Jeremy might be a little off- tempered and nervous considering that he wouldn't have the slightest idea how Alanna would accept him since the fiasco in Saratoga. Jeremy had probably been hoping to get her alone for a few minutes before he and Granton arrived to see if he could set things right again. It would have been what he would have hoped for had he been in a similar circumstance.

"She's in the conference room," he said, pointing the way, which was probably unnecessary, since Alanna had already told him that they held meetings there on a regular basis when Dar was alive.

"Thanks," Jeremy said, his voice taking on a more friendly tone as he headed off in the direction of the room, Aiden behind him.

As the two men entered the room, Aiden called to Alanna, who had disappeared somewhere behind the bar.

"Alanna?"

"I'm right here, Aiden, thanks for getting the door," she said, as she stood up from behind the bar, bringing with her a couple of bottles of liquor.

As Alanna's eyes settled on Jeremy, Aiden sensed the tension building in the room.

"I think if you don't mind," he said, "I'll go sit out on the deck, and wait for Granton to get here. I could use some air. That plane was awfully stuffy,"

He noted that Jeremy's stance became more relaxed at his suggestion.

"Sure," she replied, thinking it a thoughtful gesture on Aiden's part, and one Jeremy did not deserve. She had been able to hear Jeremy's greeting to Aiden and the tone of voice he'd used. "Care to take a drink out with you?"

"No thanks," he said. "I'll wait." And turning, he left the room, and headed up the hall.

"Pretty familiar with the terrain around here, isn't he?" Jeremy said, when Aiden was out of hearing distance. He regretted, almost immediately, the brusqueness of his words, but he was nervous as hell.

The warmth in her reply to Aiden was replaced in her reply to him with a distant coolness, "I showed him around the place before you got here." Then very formally, as though she were addressing a stranger, she added, "Care for a drink?"

"It's that bad, huh?" Jeremy said, grateful Aiden had allowed him this privacy, but unhappy at the way this was going. "You're really pissed off at me?"

Alanna just stared across the room at him for a minute, then she said, "I don't really know how I feel about you any more, Jeremy. Frankly,

I'm beginning to feel a little numb towards you, and maybe that's for the best."

For a moment, they just stood silently facing one another across the room.

"I guess I can't blame you," he said, finally, a great deal of remorse in his voice. "I could offer a lot of insincere, stupid excuses for what I did, but the fact is I am how I am. I'm not always proud of it, especially when you're the one I hurt when I do something like this, but much as I'd like to change, I don't seem to know how to do it.

"So what can I do," he asked, and not in jest, his voice still heavy with sadness as this time he saw no forgiveness in her eyes, "to make you at least be comfortable being in the same room with me without killing me over and over again with those daggers coming out of your eyes? I'll do anything you want except sign off of this operation."

If Jeremy had dreaded this moment, his apprehension didn't even come close to that which Alanna had felt, for she knew there were no easy answers to their problem and yet the onus would be on her to straighten this mess out.

Alanna had once asked Jake why she was always so attracted to the wrong kind of man. Why she couldn't just say yes to one of the nice, rich Lexington horsemen who seemed so anxious to wed her.

Jake had replied, that if she found being attracted to men like Dar and Jeremy a problem, she only had to look inside herself and see what motivated her to know the answer. If she found it necessary to live on the edge, he'd said, she would never be happy with a man whose idea of excitement in life was riding The Beast at King's Island. Men in the intelligence business, he'd advised, were natural liars and finaglers. It was their stock in trade, and I think, aggravating as that trait was in these men, it was part and parcel of the individual.

Since, he'd decided, she didn't have sense enough to marry someone who could pass a flutter test without first having to rehearse his answers, he'd told her she should stick to having great love affairs, and being on her own. He said he was giving her that piece of advice on good authority, since that was the way it was necessary for him to maintain his relationship with his friend Catherine. They'd both gotten a good laugh out of that appraisal of her situation, but over the years she'd begun to believe that what Jake had said was all too true.

"I apologize if I seem to be staring daggers through you," she said, and her apology caught him off guard. "I admitted, that had I not recognized Nenet, and gone off after you to save your neck, I wouldn't have given your going off with another woman a second thought."

"You wouldn't have?" he asked, surprised and disappointed.

"No! Especially considering the circumstance," she replied. "Why you even told me that's what you were going to do. Knowing you, I didn't expect that you would kiss her good night at the door and leave it at that. We even discussed how hard up for the company of a lady that you've been lately, so it was a natural."

"I hate this!" Jeremy said, as he walked up to the bar and sat down, angry and dejected, on one of the bar stools across from her.

"You hate what?" she asked, innocently.

"Don't do the innocent routine with me, Alanna," he said, raising his voice a notch and looking her straight in the eye. "You know damn well what! Rant and rave at me. Take another shot at kicking the living shit out of me. Tell me to take a long walk off a short pier like you used to, but, for God's sake, don't expect me to believe it doesn't matter. Because, I can see it in your eyes — it matters!"

The innocent look vanished, and, not taking her eyes from his, she said, "You're right, Jeremy, it matters and it hurts, but I have to make myself not care, because in the scheme of things our relationship is of no importance except where it is dependent on us making this operation work."

Jeremy sank back against the back of the barstool. For a moment he looked away, then he looked back. Her demeanor remained emotionless. Her answer, brutally truthful as it was, Jeremy knew, had summed up the situation perfectly and so he had no response.

"Incoming!" They heard Aiden yell from the porch and they assumed Granton's boat was approaching.

With time running out on their discussion, Alanna said, "Let go of me, Jeremy. Newmarket was a long time ago. Do us both a favor and let go, because you don't even know that if you had me, you would really want me, and I don't want another broken heart."

Then, not giving him time to argue with her over her decision, she left the room.

As she came onto the patio, she could see Granton's boat about to dock. Hurrying over to Aiden, she said, "Would you go inside and make sure Jeremy's all right? I'll stall Granton for a few minutes."

"Sure," he replied, and set off in the direction of the conference room.

When Granton, Alanna and the two men from the Special Operations, who would be assisting Granton in the briefing, entered the room, they found Jeremy and Aiden seated at the conference table in conversation, each with a cup of coffee before him.

"Good morning, gentleman," Granton said in greeting, and walked over to shake hands with the two men, who had risen from their seats. He set his briefcase down on the table, and introduced the two Special Ops experts to Jeremy and Aiden, referring to the two intelligence officers by their temporary aliases. "Patrick, Jim this is Dan Fryman and Russ Romano from Special Ops."

The men shook hands, and, after helping themselves to coffee, took their seats at the table either side of Granton. Alanna took a seat between Fryman, the Ops' man Granton had indicated on the way in would be briefing her, and Aiden. She did not make eye contact with Jeremy, who had taken a seat on the other side of Aiden.

If Granton noticed a certain coolness that pervaded the room, he did not indicate so, and went on with the briefing. He began with a rundown of the current information he had on the operation, and an overview of how it would run.

"Our mission is definitely a 'go', people," he said, to those assembled at the table, while passing out briefing folders to Alanna, Jeremy and Aiden. Granton's two assistants had already removed theirs from their briefcases, and set them on the table.

"Yesterday," he continued, "we got word from our Kiev station, that last week Ukrainian security forces took two of their nuclear scientists into custody on charges that they have been attempting to sell nuclear material. After questioning the men in typical non-humanitarian Ukrainian style, one of the men confessed to putting together a tactical nuclear device, which, he said, was sold to a Russian Mafia contact. He told them the man's name, but naturally it was not his real name, so they lost the trail. We are assuming that this is the device that Francois is making available to Kamal's group.

"We have no way of knowing, at this point, the exact timing for the bomb's delivery. Bits and pieces of information have been floating back to us from JESTER'S old contact, but so far he has not advised us of a delivery date. We know the place of delivery to be Francois De La Croix's chateau in Normandy, and we assume that, because the procurers of this device are going to want to unload it quickly, that they plan to deliver it soon.

"Surveillance conducted by the Paris station has revealed that a meeting was held the day before yesterday at Kamal Shabban's house in Montmarte. Those attending the meeting included Hassan bin Laden, who is involved in the construction and importing business, and who sources say, is one of the main fund raisers for Hizballah; Mohammed al Khatib, one of Kamal's lieutenants and trigger man, and Khalil al Otaibi, who likes to pass himself off as a rug merchant, but who has spent more time making bombs than rugs.

"Hakeem Saleh, Kamal's right hand man was not in attendance. He was seen leaving France by air two days before the meeting, and was later spotted by one of our people in Damascus. We have no proof, but we suspect that he may have had something to do with the bombing of that Israeli cafe by Hamas the other night.

"Francois left New York yesterday, and since his return home, he has been under surveillance by the Paris station. We have learned that he has acquired a very prestigious art collection, which will be on display at his chateau during the Deauville horse sales and race meet. We think he is using the exhibit as a cover in order to beef up security around the chateau.

"Yesterday, a panel truck arrived at the chateau. The driver and passenger were identified as Arabs connected with the French Hizballah cell. The Paris station traced the license plate, and found that the truck belongs to one of Hassan's construction companies. It was followed later that day by a large delivery truck, likewise driven and occupied by Arabs. So, it would appear that Francois and Kamal are laying the groundwork for receiving the bomb. Hopefully, JESTER's source will provide us with an exact date of delivery before you leave.

"We have drawings, maps and pictures done in great detail of the chateau, its layout, its grounds and the surrounding countryside that you can familiarize yourselves with. A mockup of the secured tower, in which the bomb will be held for safe keeping, has been set up in one of our warehouses, and will be available tomorrow for a hands-on training session.

"So here is what we're going to do." Turning to Alanna and using her alias, he says, "Diane, because of her experience in surreptitious entry, will gain entry to the pavilion room housing the device through a window. Our people have made a feasibility study of this entry, and believe that it is possible to accomplish. Thanks to our MI5 friends, we have the full layout of the room and the entire security device installed by Finley's. These warning and detection devices are highly sophisticated, but again our feasibility study shows that they can be bypassed. Alanna will enter the room wearing special clothing. She will be carrying an inert timer detonator for the nuclear device that we have obtained from the Ukrainians. Alanna will open the safe. The Ukrainians have informed us that these devices are generally shipped in crates. The detonator device should be packed in a similar but smaller crate, with a top that is usually secured by two wing nuts. Alanna will open the safe, then the detonator box, and remove the live timer detonator device and replace it with the inert one. The live detonator, which Alanna will carry from the room, will then be passed to Aiden at an appropriate time.

"So that you understand what this will accomplish, I want to review with you the operating principles of this particular nuke. The device is a sphere roughly the size of a soccer ball and weighs in at about 37 pounds. The entire outer surface of this sphere is composed of small squares of explosives. Each square has its own electrical squib to detonate it. The device has a timer and a detonator that is screwed onto the outer surface.

The timer can be set for any time up to 30 days. This type of timer is very accurate. When the timer goes off, it activates the detonator, which sends an electrical jolt simultaneously to all the squares on the outer surface of the sphere. All of the squares detonating at once will implode toward the center, which contains an amount of fissionable nuclear material.

The implosion squeezes the nuclear material into a tight ball, which starts a chain reaction that will level everything in its path for a quarter mile. There are other highly technical aspects to this device, which, for the purpose of this operation, need not be explained. The reason for switching the timer detonator, with an inert one is, obviously, that it leaves this bomb totally useless. Without the live timer detonator there is no way to detonate the bomb."

Speaking to Alanna, Jeremy and Aiden, Granton said, "Fryman and Romano have all the details of the operation outlined in those folders I've given you. I want you to get together with them now, and go over the information with them. "Are there any questions?"

Since there were none, Jeremy and Aiden picked up their folders, and headed off to another room with Romano, while Alanna, who, along with Fryman, had remained seated at the table, prepared to go over her folder's contents.

Before she and Fryman could get started, Granton touched her lightly on her shoulder and said, "Mind if I borrow your car. I'll be flying back to Washington later this afternoon, so while you're going over this information, I think I'll go out and check on the setup in the warehouse."

"Sure," she said, getting up from the table and heading out of the room, "If you come with me, I'll give you the keys, and show you where it's parked."

* * *

It was late afternoon before Granton returned. When Alanna appeared at the door to let him in, he asked her to step outside for a moment.

"Is everything all right between you and Jeremy, Alanna?" He said, looking her straight in the eye. "I couldn't help noticing how quiet the three of you were all during and after my briefing."

"Everything is okay, Granton," she lied, and suspected he knew it. "Everyone's just feeling a little tense right now."

"I'm not buying it, Alanna." Granton advised her rather bluntly. "I've never, in all the years I've had occasion to deal with him, seen Jeremy act like this.

"I know that you think things will go better with this deal if you have someone you feel comfortable with on your team," he said, in a more moderated tone of voice, so as to let her know he understood her feelings. "But, just remember, Aiden is very capable and reliable. Don't let old loyalties cause you to make a decision you'll regret later."

"I know you're concerned, Granton." Alanna replied. "But, please believe that I would never risk this operation or our lives for the security of his company. Jeremy and I have always been able to work past our personal problems. It will not be any different this time."

"Very well," he said, but she could sense the misgivings in his voice.

They concluded the briefings late in the afternoon, after which Fryman and Romano left with Granton.

Alanna was cleaning up in the conference room. She sensed there was someone in the room, and turned to find Jeremy standing in the doorway.

"Are you still speaking to me?" he asked.

"Of course," she said, with no sign of the animosity in her voice that had appeared in their earlier conversation.

"As usual, you're right about us, Alanna," Jeremy said, as he moved slowly across the room in her direction until he stood looking down at her. "The night we were together in that hotel room in Newmarket was the first time my life felt complete, really happy. Then, I let it all slip away. Deliberately and stupidly, I let the source of that happiness slip away. So, I have no one to blame for how our relationship has gone but myself. I don't even know if things would have turned out differently if I had made the effort to pursue your love. In the end, you may still have chosen Dar over me. But, I know I'll regret not finding out for sure for the rest of my life. There is one thing I do know and that's nothing will change my feelings for you — ever."

Alanna, not knowing what to say, lowered her head.

Jeremy, very gently, took hold of her chin and raised it up until they were once again eye-to-eye, then he smiled and said, "You don't have to say anything, Querida, I just wanted you to know."

He kissed her gently on the forehead, then turned and walked back to the doorway. He picked up his briefcase, and then turned back to her, "Aiden says he's not scheduled to be in France for another day. I thought maybe if you could tolerate his company for a night that you could put him up here. It would give you two time to get acquainted and go over the plans."

She didn't immediately answer, so he asked, "Do I hear an objection?"

"No," she replied. "He's welcome to stay."

"Good," he said. Then as he turned and started down the hall to the door, he added, "You don't have to show me out, Querida, I know the way. See you at Homestead."

* * *

As Alanna made the half-hour journey across Miami to the CIA-leased warehouse along the perimeter of Miami International Airport, she thought about yesterday. Sad as it was, she felt a certain relief at having things out in the open with Jeremy about their relationship. She knew it would make working with him easier, at least for her. It also would make working with Aiden easier, as he would not have to deal with the tensions that their never knowing where they stood caused.

She had really enjoyed last evening with Aiden. They had cooked steaks on the grill, and then sat out on the deck and went over the operation in detail. The atmosphere between them had been relaxed and friendly.

Aiden had even brought up an interesting angle that either the Agency had forgotten, or that they had dismissed as unimportant, and that was her conduct when dealing with the Arab men. On this assignment, she would be pretending to be associating with them in a

311

social setting. Thus, he had suggested gently, if she wanted to avoid attracting undo attention to herself, she might consider conforming, albeit not too obviously, to some Arab customs.

Aiden had given Alanna examples of how to respond to introductions, how to act in their company and what to wear. He'd said he didn't expect her to don a veil, but modest garments would win her their respect, and make dealing with them easier. He said that he understood that her ultimate goal might be to kill them, but first she had to foil their plans, and that meant not giving herself away.

Aiden's professional approach to preparing for an operation impressed her. Alanna knew that his knowledge of the Arab world and its people would be a real asset to them.

"Good luck and be careful," he'd said, before he'd gotten into the cab that had taken him to the airport this morning. "Remember, I'll be there if you need me."

Alanna realized that even in the short a time she had spent with Aiden, what she had learned about him made his becoming part of this operation a very reassuring factor.

Alanna stopped reminiscing long enough to find the warehouse, which was located halfway down a street lined with several unoccupied warehouses. Using a remote switch that Granton had given her before he'd left yesterday, she opened the perimeter gate, and drove through into the large vacant parking lot. The gate closed automatically behind her.

Following Granton's direction, Alanna drove around the building until she came to a loading dock. She drove down into it. On the far right was a large overhead door. She pulled in front of it and sounded her horn. A couple minutes later, the door opened and a man she recognized as Dan Fryman waved her through.

She pulled up to him, and ran down her window.

"How are you this morning, Dan," she said.

"I'm doing great, Diane," he replied. Then referring to the mousy brown wig and nondescript brown contact lenses she was wearing, added, "I almost didn't recognize you."

"That's the idea," she replied, with a smile.

"Well, if you're ready to get started," he said, while pointing to a parking place next to a Ford pickup, "just park your car over there, and follow me."

Alanna parked, and they headed in the direction of a metal staircase. At the top, they passed through a door that he opened by placing his hand on a glass plate, which, after it read his prints, allowed the door to open. They went along a long deserted hall until they came to a heavy steel door. Here, he pressed a button and then spoke his name into a device, which having identified the voice as his, allowed him to open it.

The room was centered within the building. Its thick walls were sound and bulletproof. On entering, a tall, slender black woman greeted them.

"Dr. Mavis Clark," she said, offering her hand to Alanna, and smiling warmly. She accepted the hand Alanna offered her in return, but did not wait for Alanna to say her name as she had already been supplied with her alias. "I hope you're ready to get to work. We have a lot to cover in a short time."

"I am," Alanna assured her.

"Good, then follow me and I'll introduce you to my staff, and we'll get started.

Her staff consisted of Dr. Craig Wayland, who was the Agency's preeminent expert in Visual Reality training, and Dr. David Wu, the computer expert who designed and ran the training program.

"Do you understand how Visual Reality works, Diane?" Dr. Clark asked Alanna.

"My briefing gave me the basics on it, but no, I don't know how it works," Alanna replied.

"In that case," Dr. Clark advised, "may I suggest that we begin by having Dr. Wu familiarize you with the Visual Reality training concept and the equipment we use. Then he can give you a short demonstration of how it actually works. Your first encounter with Visual Reality can prove to be a little daunting and disorienting, understanding how it works should make you feel more comfortable experiencing it.

Alanna nodded her agreement. Then, for the next two hours, he proceeded to explain to her the concept, the equipment, and the program, and ended the briefing by demonstrating it capabilities.

When they were finished, Dr. Clark had them take a short break. Then, they began the real training.

"Please follow me, Diane," Dr. Clark said, and led the way to a small room.

Once inside, she opened a large metal suitcase, which contained various articles of clothing and equipment.

"Diane, my specialty within Technical Services is the development of special clothing and equipment, which allow our intelligence officers

313

to achieve operational capabilities that normal clothing and equipment would not allow.

She removed a matte-black hooded suit, which resembled those worn by scuba divers. It appeared made of a very thin fabric.

"The room you will be asked to penetrate has a very sophisticated security system," she began, as she removed the suit from the case and handed it to Alanna for her inspection. "The system is multi-layered, so that each individual system will act as a fail safe measure to the other. Consequently, your equipment must be multi-dimensional, non-restrictive and minimal, so that you will be able to operate within this environment in complete safety and with complete freedom of motion. That is critical because time is of the essence in your transversing the area protected by the system.

"One level of security involves a timing device. Another involves a motion detector. What this amounts to is that if you go too fast you will trip one alarm, on the other hand, if you go too slow you will trip another. Your body temperature and breath can also trigger other sensor alarms, so while you cannot be encumbered by bulk of any kind, you must be encased in clothing that will not give away your presence by either means. Do you have any questions, so far?"

"No," Alanna replied. "My briefing yesterday covered the security system in great detail. I was amazed at its intricacies, and will forever be in your debt if you have something in that case that can help get me through it."

"I was amazed at the intricacy of its design as well," Dr. Clark said, smiling. "But, then, problem-solving is what makes this job interesting. I can't guarantee, Diane, that you won't get caught, because I have no way of controlling your actions inside that room. The equipment I have designed for you will do its job, that is all things being equal. First, that you use the equipment correctly; second, that your own skills are up to the task; and third, that lady luck is with you, and someone doesn't just stumble onto you innocently."

Alanna nodded in agreement, and the doctor went on.

"Defeating the first stages of entry into the room are mainly mechanical and will be up to you. Though they are by no means unsophisticated, they are not at the same level as those inside the room. You must get into the room quickly, because although the security setup that is governed by temperature changes does allow for a certain small variance, like the air conditioning going on, a sustained change will trigger an alarm. It's the same principle that would detect you in the room, as even the smallest amount of body heat exposed to the heat sensors in the room, for any length of time, will trigger an alarm."

Indicating the suit Alanna held in her hands, she advised, "That is the purpose of the suit you are holding. It is made of a fabric called Tempra-Seal that will let your body breathe. That is very necessary, because the stress you will be under will cause your body to heat up. If the suit did not allow for your body to breathe eventually you would pass out. But, by the same token, there are minuscule sensors within the fabric of the suit which can determine the temperature of the air around you, and cool the body heat escaping the suit to that temperature."

"Amazing!", Alanna replied, while feeling the fabric and noting no visible sign of its wondrous capability.

"Their room also has a system of laser beams that are invisible to the naked eye," she said while reaching into her case and removing a facemask. "Needless, to say if you break a beam, an alarm sounds. Since your breath would also give you away because it, too, exudes heat and motion waves, I have devised this mask, which will solve all the remaining problems. It is made of a very flexible compound, which will feel almost like a second skin. The eyepieces will give you superior vision in low light situations and will allow you to see the laser beams. That includes excellent peripheral vision, which will be a very important feature for you. Meanwhile, the breathing piece, which is equipped with the latest version of the rebreather device covert scuba teams use, will allow you to breath normally without your breath entering the room.

"Rebreathers require some sort of oxygen supply, don't they?" Alanna asked.

"Normally they require only a small supply since the air you are breathing is recirculated air. This one's supply is carried in a flexible collar that you will wear around your neck. The thin boots you will wear are made of the same fabric as the suit. The soles, though designed to grip surfaces well, will not attract or hold dirt, so that they will not leave tracks on the floor. The gloves, likewise, are made of the same fabric."

Dr. Clark reached into her case and pulled out another mask and suit, both similar to the first ones she had shown Alanna.

"You will wear this mask and suit for our training session today," she said, exchanging the first mask and suit she had given Alanna for the second ones. "The glasses in this mask, which are connected to the computer by wireless infra-red sensors, will allow you to experience the same sensations and sights through our Visual Reality set up as you will experience in that room. The suit, also equipped with infra-red sensors, will duplicate the same sensations as the original, but will also allow you to manipulate the computer-generated images that comprise the Visual Reality training program we have designed to simulate your entry and egress from that safe and that room.

She concluded by asking Alanna, "Do you have any questions, before we get on with the real, or should I say 'virtually real', business we're here for?"

"None that I can think of?" Alanna replied.

"Good," Dr. Clark replied. "Then I will leave you to get into your gear, and when you are ready I will turn you over to Drs. Wayland and Wu."

Chapter 24

Francois leaned against the fender of his car, the double-edged sword of delight and dread playing havoc with his nervous system. The last few days had passed in a blur of unsettling events, most of which had caused a steady rise in his blood pressure.

Before leaving for the airport, Francois had asked Phillip to see if any messages had been received from Rakeland. None had been, and that made him more nervous. What if they'd arrested Rakeland, and gotten him to talk?

Phillip had sensed his anxiety and assured him that had Rakeland been arrested they would know. He'd said that Rakeland had agreed, that should he be caught, he would pass a message to them through his lawyer.

That knowledge put Francois a little more at ease. But, he was still a bundle of nerves as his eyes followed Jeremy's sleek sliver and blue aircraft as it made a gentle arcing turn over the English Channel before beginning its final approach to Deauville's Saint-Gaitien airport.

"You seem extremely nervous today, Francois," Kamal said, from his seat inside the limousine. "I am wondering if it is caused by your excitement over seeing your young lady friend, or your feelings of apprehension over having insisted on drawing such a crowd at such an inauspicious time?"

Kamal had insisted on coming to the airport on the pretext that he wanted a first hand look at the American, Mark Jergens. Francois knew that, as with his background check on Jergens, Kamal had produced nothing to suggest the man was anything other than what he presumed to be. So, since Kamal considered himself something of a ladies man, Francois suspected it was Alanna, and not Jergens, who was the object of his curiosity. Francois had made it plain that Kamal's company was not appreciated, but Kamal had not been dissuaded by his objection.

"If I am nervous, Kamal, for once it is a good nervousness," Francois replied caustically. He came to a standing position next to the car as the plane settled lightly to the earth and began to taxi in their direction. Then, in a gentler tone, he added, "I have waited 50 long years for this moment, my friend. The anticipation has made me feel young again, very young, indeed!"

"Then I shall not cast dark clouds on your moment, Francois." Kamal said.

"I would greatly appreciate it if you did not, Kamal."

Karen A. Lynch

The plane pulled up, and stopped before them, its engines still screaming, while the ground crew hurriedly rolled the stairway into place.

The aircraft's door was opened from within by one of its crew, but a couple of minutes passed before its first passenger appeared in the doorway. It was Alanna, elegantly dressed in a periwinkle blue silk suit. On seeing Francois, she smiled warmly, waved and made her way down the stairs, and into his waiting arms.

"My darling, I am so happy that you are here," he said, with great emotion, but keeping his public display of affection to gentle kisses on both her checks, which she returned. "I hope you had a good flight."

"I did, Francois," she replied, her voice and smile so full of warmth and happiness it lifted Francois' spirits to new heights.

"And, where is your Mr. Jergens?" He asked, looking up toward the entrance to the plane. "Can I possibly be so lucky as to have you all to myself?"

"Unfortunately not, Francois." Came the reply from just inside the plane and a second later Jeremy emerged onto the top of the stairway. He paused briefly to speak to his pilot, who, immediately following their conversation, returned to the interior of the plane. Jeremy then proceeded down the stairway, a friendly smile on his face.

"I'm really not here to buy horses, Francois," he said in jest, as he stepped onto the tarmac and offered his hand to Francois. "I just felt this lovely young woman needed a chaperone. How are you?"

"Well, and you?" Francois said, ignoring what once would have been a confrontation remark, and shook his hand.

"Just great," Jeremy replied, "It's kind of you to offer me your hospitality."

"It is my pleasure to do so," Francois said, in a tone that sounded convincingly genuine.

"Come," he said, indicating the waiting car. "You must be exhausted after your long trip. May I suggest we get underway, so that you will have time to relax and freshen up before the evening's festivities begin. If you are hungry, we can stop for lunch in Honfluer, where there is a very good seafood restaurant on the harbor."

"Thank you Francois, but we had lunch on the plane," she replied, as she took the arm Francois offered, and allowed him to lead the way. "Actually, what I would like to do when we get to the chateau is to go for a run. Being cooped up in even that lovely a plane for so long has gotten my muscles tied up in knots."

318

Francois seemed to ignore her first remark, and instead steered the conversation to her comment on the plane.

"Yes, the Falcon 900 is a lovely plane," Francois agreed, turning to take one last look at the aircraft. "She is the finest aircraft our French manufacturer, Dassault, makes. I envy you Mark, you are fortunate to have her."

"She's corporate property, but I am lucky to have the use of her," Jeremy said to Francois, as he walked beside Alanna. "She is definitely a beauty, and I have been very pleased with her performance."

There were two cars parked 50 feet in front of them. One was a Mercedes limo the other a Mercedes sedan. "I have arranged for a car to transport your crew to the chateau," Francois said to Jeremy, as he indicated the waiting sedan with a wave of his hand.

"That very kind of you, Francois, but that won't be necessary, they're not staying," Jeremy replied, as a cart arrived loaded with his and Alanna's luggage. "I bought some paintings and antiques for the resort last time I was in France, so I'm having my crew fly on to Paris, and pick them up.

"Since, I won't be needing the plane until I'm ready to head back," he added, "I gave my crew some time off to enjoy the city."

"You are a very generous employer," Francois remarked, as he motioned for his driver to load the luggage. "In that case we are ready to leave."

While Jeremy and Francois carried on their conversation, Alanna glanced in the direction of the rear of the car. She could just barely make out through the darkened windows of the limousine the figure of a man sitting in the back seat. For a moment their eyes met, and, without even having a clear view of him, she knew it was Kamal Shabban, the man the file on Operation SABRE had indicated was responsible for Dar's death and most likely Jake's as well. It was Kamal Shabban whom she had come to kill.

From within the car, Kamal's hawk-like gray eyes met hers, and for one inexplicable moment, Kamal sensed he'd seen the eyes of death. Never had such a cold chill filled his soul. "You will meet your death at the hand of Azreal, the angel of death," an old Arab wise man had once told him.

The moment passed, and the look was gone. Surely you are imagining things he thought. The woman is such a gentle, almost angelic looking beauty; no wonder Francois covets her so. But, the key descriptive word that stuck in his mind was angelic.

Francois opened the door and Alanna and Kamal came face to face. This time Kamal sensed no threat for she smiled demurely in his direction.

"Alanna, Mark, I would like you to meet one of my other guests, Kamal Shabban," Francois said, indicating the Arab attired in conservative European fashion seated in the rear of the car. "Kamal, may I introduce Monsieur Mark Jergens, and my very special friend Mademoiselle Alanna Reynolds."

They shook hands all around as they took their seats in the car, Alanna remembering to make her hand contact brief as Aiden had instructed.

Kamal's handshake with Jeremy had been strong, but brief, as was their eye contact. While in contrast, his hand contact with Alanna was minimal, but his eye contact was steady and long. He noticed that this prolonged eye contact, which required the person in question to dwell on his scar ravaged face and hard eyes, did not seem to cause her undo discomfort, something it frequently did to others.

"Forgive me for imposing myself on your reunion," he said to her graciously, briefly looking over at Francois to see his reaction, "but I was very curious to see what manner of woman could cause my normally level-headed friend to suddenly become so addled.

"I can see now that his condition is well justified. However, his description of your beauty did not do you justice, for the most delicate and beautiful flower created by Allah pales in comparison of it."

She acknowledged his compliment with a demure half-smile, a slight nod of her head and a simple "Thank You."

Yet, he sensed she was not as delicate a flower as her outward appearances would lead one to believe. No, indeed, the steady way she matched his eye contact told him that she possessed great inner strength and determination, for he had yet to meet the women, and seldom the man, who having looked him in the eye, was not intimidated by him. She was not, and that was very evident. Nor, was her head turned by his compliments. A very strong woman, indeed, Kamal thought. Only the shell resembles a flower, while the core is rock. He looked forward to knowing her better.

Francois, not wanting to create a scene in front of the Americans, pretended to ignore Kamal's having been so obviously forward with Alanna. Instead, he instructed his driver to take them to the chateau.

"We will go straight home, Jacques," he said, from his seat next to Alanna. Then turning to her and smiling, he advised her, "We will be there in 40 minutes. I am anxious, Alanna, for you to see my home. I hope you will find it comfortable and to your liking."

"I'm sure I will, Francois," Alanna said, turning her attention from Kamal to Francois, and allowing her demeanor to warm considerably. "I have heard that it is a wondrous place and very beautiful. I am anxious to see it."

She addressed her next comments first to Francois, then to Jeremy, who had been keeping a low profile since entering the car. "I understand, Francois, that your chateau was the first to be built in the new Renaissance style. On the flight over, Mark was telling me that one of the his resort restaurant's themes is the Renaissance period."

Then turning to Jeremy, she said, "Maybe, you'll be able to go back to Arizona with a few new ideas for your restaurant's decor, Mark."

Alanna's comment allowed the subject of discussion for the duration of the drive to the chateau to center on the chateau's history and architecture, rather than on her or Jeremy. A move, she sensed, that did not coincide with the Arab's desire to scrutinize them further.

Though it was not obvious to the rest of the car's passengers, Francois took great delight in Alanna's ability to so gracefully take control of the conversation, which left Kamal with no option but to abandon his.

The chateau, built on a rise, could be seen above the roofs of the houses and shops, as they entered the small village of La Croix. One could see its pavilions as they rose majestically towards the clear blue August sky.

The main road through town wound upwards past the old Gothic church of St. Acceul, which Francois informed them was famous for its choir windows of fine contemporary stained glass. Once out of town, they turned off of the main road, and onto a private drive that led past Francois' stud farm's stallion and broodmare complex, which was set among brilliant flowering gardens and lush green pastures. The drive ended at the well-guarded entrance to the chateau.

As the limousine approached the heavy iron gates, four heavily armed guards emerged from the stone guardhouse. Two to each side, they approached the vehicle weapons at the ready. Even though they knew the car, Francois' orders were to always approach any vehicle, even his, with extreme caution — to assume nothing. Upon clearance from the head guard, the limousine continued on in.

The chauffeur headed up the main drive, which was surrounded by vast, beautifully manicured lawns and gardens. He turned left over a bridge that had once crossed over a water-filled moat, and through another well-guarded gate into the cour d'honneur (the court of honor.) The car pulled up to the north entrance, where Phillip and two male servants met it.

The servants rushed to open the car doors for Francois and his guests. The one on Alanna's side offered his hand in way of assistance, which she accepted.

As she and Jeremy stood in the courtyard taking in the magnificent structure surrounding them, Alanna said, "Oh, Francois, your place is unbelievably beautiful."

However, Jeremy, who was just as awed as Alanna at Francois' home, was thinking how in Francois' case, crime really did pay and big!

He did not voice his thoughts, instead, he said, "It's pretty spectacular, Francois. It puts my little resort homestead to shame."

"I'm glad you both like it," Francois replied, with pride. "Now, come inside and we will get you settled, and then I will give you a tour of my home and we will visit."

* * *

"I really don't understand why my going jogging is such a problem, Francois." Alanna was saying to Francois as she stood before his big oak desk.

"I am sorry, Cherie," he said as he finished putting his signature on a letter, then rose to come and stand before her. "I know you feel the need to get some fresh air and exercise, but as I have explained," he voice became gentle, almost condescending, such as one might use with belligerent, but loved teenager, "since I have this art exhibition here I have had to employ many security people to insure its safety. You may have noticed some of them as we drove in. It would be quite dangerous for you to go jogging around the area unescorted, because these people are unfamiliar with you, and serious about their responsibility and they might unintentionally do you harm."

"What are they going to do — shoot me?" She asked, feigning ignorance of the situation, but desperately wanting an opportunity to get a look at the exterior of the building as well as a lay of the land surrounding the chateau.

"Unfortunately," Francois replied, concern for her safety in his voice, "that is a real possibility."

Taking her gently by the shoulders and escorting her to the window, Francois indicated the many people wandering around the area armed.

Then he said, "If you were to go jogging right now, Alanna, you would need an escort known to these people to insure your safety. Since, as you can see my dear, I am in no shape to go jogging with you, your going on your own is simply too dangerous for me to permit. I hope you will understand that my concern is purely for your safety, and that until I can find one of my people, who is up to the task, I must beg you to be patient concerning this matter."

Alanna was about to answer, when she heard a familiar voice behind her, say, "I believe I am up to the task, Francois."

When she turned in the direction of the entrance to the room, she found Hakeem standing in it.

"Hakeem," Francois said, and went to welcome the Arab. "Come in, come in. I had no idea you had arrived."

"I just got in a few minutes ago," he said, after exchanging greetings with Francois.

Hakeem, approached Alanna, and offered his hand, which she shook briefly, "I see, Miss Reynolds, that Allah has seen fit to once again grant me the pleasure of your company."

There was a glint of something Alanna neither liked, nor could fathom in Hakeem's cold, dark eyes, but she replied graciously, "Thank you, Hakeem. I'm pleased to see you again too."

Turning to Francois, he said, "I couldn't help overhearing your conversation as I passed the library door on my way to my room, Francois. I, too, feel a bit sluggish from my journey, and would enjoy a short run. If you would trust me with this lovely lady, I would be happy to see that no harm comes to her."

Hakeem waited patiently, as he could see both Alanna and Francois had doubts about accepting his offer.

Finally, Alanna said, "It's very kind of you to offer to escort me, Hakeem, but I think my jogging today presents more of a problem than it's worth. I can wait until tomorrow and just have..."

Francois, not wanting to deny her anything, and having the seeming solution to the problem at hand, interrupted her, saying, "I think you should take Hakeem up on his offer, Alanna. Considering the amount of cigarettes he smokes, you should be able to keep up with him quite easily."

Knowing that arguing the issue would only cause suspicions to arise, Alanna relented. "I guess that settles the matter, Hakeem." Alanna replied, as she turned to leave the room. "I'll be ready to go in a minute, I just need to get a sweatband from my room."

"I will change and meet you in the courtyard," he said, but he did not follow her out of the room. Instead, he remained to discuss some business with Francois.

As she started up the stairway to her room, Alanna looked up and saw Jeremy leaning against the marble railing about half way up. As she came up to him, he indicated the room she'd just come out of with a toss of his head and said, "I couldn't help overhearing. Some escort. You'd be safer with Jack the Ripper."

"Well, there's nothing I can do about it," Alanna replied, unhappily, and under her breath so that no one could over hear her. "If he gets out of hand, he'll just have to run into a tree accidentally, and kill himself."

"Hmmm, now I don't know who's in more danger, you or him?" And he laughed.

"Well, excuse me," she said, as she continued on up the stairs. "I mustn't keep my escort waiting."

As Alanna disappeared beyond the top of the stairs, Jeremy heard voices in the main hall below him. Hakeem and Francois had come out of the library, and were standing in the hall talking. He coughed to warn them of his presence, knowing that since Francois only marginally trusted him, he wouldn't want it to appear as though he was eavesdropping on them.

"Mark," Francois said, startled at the thought someone was in earshot of his conversation with Hakeem, but thinking it was courteous of Jergens to have given him warning. "Come. Meet my friend and partner, Hakeem Saleh. Hakeem, this is Mark Jergens of Phoenix, Arizona. He is my guest and Alanna's client."

Jeremy approached the men, and he and Hakeem exchanged handshakes, the strength of which would have made a hand wrestler proud.

"Mr. Jergens, it is a pleasure to make your acquaintance," Hakeem said, as they eyed each other up. It was then that Jeremy realized Alanna had not exaggerated when she'd commented on the coldness in Hakeem's eyes.

I can't say the same, Jeremy thought, but he smiled and said, "Good to meet you."

"Well," Francois said, to Jeremy. "Alanna has insisted on having a run, and Hakeem has been foolish enough to volunteer to go with her, So, why don't we, more sensible men, go into the library and have a drink?"

"An excellent suggestion, Francois," Jeremy said, in agreement. "I'd much rather be raising a glass, than jarring my knees any day."

Jeremy noticed that even when Hakeem smiled, which he did at this remark, his eyes remained cold. Pick a big tree, Alanna, he thought, it's going to take a whale of a trunk to do this sucker in.

"Well, enjoy your drinks," Hakeem said, and after nodding to Francois, he headed down the hall to his room.

* * *

Alanna had been waiting in the courtyard for 15 minutes before Hakeem finally appeared. She was not upset by the delay as it gave her ample opportunity, without drawing undo suspicion to herself, to explore the exterior of the building that faced on the courtyard. It would be one of these walls that she would have to scale in order to get to the pavilion that housed the safe.

From the information contained in her briefing file, she knew that this chateau had been built in the second half of the Renaissance period. It differed from those built early during that period in that it was a quadrilateral. Also, unlike it predecessors, it did not have round corner towers like those on fairy tale castles, but square pavilions.

Though different in many ways, the chateau still maintained some of the military features of the fortified castles, one of which was that each pavilion still had turrets angled in the recesses formed between the projecting pavilions and the adjoining buildings. She noted that each of these was heavily armed.

When Hakeem did finally appear, he was dressed in khaki camouflage fatigues, and a pair of desert style combat boots. A khaki camouflage bandanna was wrapped around his forehead.

He noticed her appraising his outfit, and couldn't help doing a little appraising of his own. He had half expected her to be wearing very short shorts and a skin-tight top that was the attire of choice for the women he saw jogging on television, and on the European roadways. Instead, she had on a simple royal blue jogging suit.

"Disappointed?" she said,

He laughed, and surprising her, he replied truthfully, "Possibly, but not any more than you, I suspect."

"Do you always jog in battle gear?" She asked.

"I had not anticipated jogging on this trip, so I left my jogging suit in my camel pack," he said, trying, with humor, to release some of the tension he felt between them, which again surprised her.

When she smiled obligingly at his joke, he continued with his pre-conceived fabricated explanation.

"Actually, I am in my country's reserve army," he half-lied. "Even those of us of royal lineage must serve. In fact, I just returned from a training mission. But, don't worry, I am quite comfortable jogging under these conditions." He indicated his clothing, and then added confidently. "They won't slow me down."

"Well, then shall we go," she said, in a tone that indicated she'd swallowed his story. "I trust you know the way?"

"I know the way," he replied, and started off in the direction of the main gate.

"How far would you like to go?" he asked, over his shoulder as they passed through the iron main gates, and without incident, the armed guards. There was no sign of a double meaning to his statement in his voice, but she could not resist a dig of her own.

"Until you're ready to quit," she said, challenging him.

He turned back towards her while still jogging; a sly grin now featured fully on his face, and replied. "Then Francois may be forced to file a missing persons report, as we will not be back for a long time."

They took a path to their right that appeared before they reached the stable yard, which led them in the direction of woods that bordered three sides of the chateau.

Playing with fire can be dangerous, Alanna, she chided herself. Just look at where he's headed with you — into the deep, dark woods!

Soon, the only sounds around them were those of singing birds, their feet hitting the ground and their breathing — mainly his. Occasionally, he would look over his shoulder to see if she was keeping up, an act he found necessary because her footfalls were so soft and her breathing so quiet, he could not tell if she was behind him without looking. This was true even after they had covered a distance, which even he found stressed one's lung capacity.

All of his life Hakeem had trained in the heat and the sand of the desert, a combination that was guaranteed to make your body fit and your breath strong. But, now they had traveled for many miles, up and down hill, across some pretty rough terrain by normal jogging standards, and still the she showed no signs of tiring.

Just when Alanna sensed Hakeem's pride was about to kill him, and he thought his lungs would burst, he heard her call to him. Alanna had to shout, because the blood pounding in Hakeem's ears made hearing difficult.

"I think this is far enough," she shouted. When he'd acknowledged by slowing his pace that he had heard her, she added, in a more moderate tone, "I'd like to turn back, if you don't mind. It's getting late."

The last few miles they'd jogged, he had not chanced looking back for fear she would see the fatigue he was feeling in his face. When he finally did turn to face her, she was still jogging in place to cool down. She bore not the slightest sign of shortness of breath or fatigue. He was amazed and frustrated, but showed neither.

"Would you care to rest before we go back," he asked, trying not to gulp in air too obviously.

"Yes, if you don't mind," she replied, walking to a low rock wall set back off the path, and taking a seat on it. He knew her reply was a face-saving gesture to him, since she was obviously not in need of such relief herself.

Hakeem sank to the grass. He unbuttoned the left breast pocket of his now thoroughly soaked shirt, and pulled out a pack of Marlboros and a silver lighter.

How ironic, Alanna thought, noting the cigarette's brand, the Marlboro man replaced by the Marlboro terrorist. That image would certainly make an eye-catching roadside billboard. She also noted that he wore a Rolex watch and a large, but simple ring, consisting of an onyx set in a silver band

Hakeem lit the cigarette he'd taken from the pack, and lay back down on the ground face up, his eyes looking up to the sky. When he'd had a chance to recover his breath, and take a few drags on the cigarette, he said, "You are in excellent shape, Miss Reynolds, both physically, and I think, mentally. You must train seriously when you are at home."

She was in the process of taking a drink of water, so she had to pause before replying untruthfully, "Not really."

Then, noting that he'd neglected to bring something to drink, she attempted to change the subject by offering him some of her water. "Care for a drink?"

He rose up, supported by both his elbows. "I would, thank you."

Hakeem easily caught the bottle she'd tossed in his direction, and holding the bottle above him, allowed the cool water to pour from it and into his mouth, not touching his lips to the bottle's rim.

"Foolish of me not to have thought to bring my own," he said, as he raised the bottle in a gesture of thanks. Then, he said, "I do not mean to seem impolite but your performance on the road belies your answer, although why you would choose to lie about such a mundane matter intrigues me."

When she did not seem phased by his accusation, he asked, "Who are you, Alanna Reynolds? What mystery hides beneath that golden exterior?"

"Mystery? I'm not any more of a mystery than you are, Hakeem," she replied, her gaze intent on him. "Why, I'm just a simple girl from Kentucky, who is much too busy running a horse farm to train for marathon races and who is here, as are you I've been told, to buy a horse. If you find that that makes me mysterious, then so be it. You are here to by a horse, aren't you?"

Hakeem laughed at her ability to so smoothly turn the focus of their conversation from herself to him. But, after rising to a sitting position, and taking a long drag on the cigarette, he replied in a tone that said he was unconvinced by her answer, "If you are a simple country girl, Miss Reynolds, than I am Little Bo Peep.

"Everything about you is mysterious," he insisted. "On each occasion that I have observed you, I have been amazed at what you can achieve with just a simple smile.

"For example," he said, between drags on his cigarette, "take my friend Francois, who, at a word from him, has the mightiest of men quaking in their shoes. Upon seeing your smile he becomes like a whimpering puppy. That, my lady, is a very powerful smile."

He put his cigarette out by rubbing it on a rock that lay near him, then rose from the ground, and came to stand before her, his proximity close, but his demeanor unthreatening. While handing her back the water bottle, he said, "I have observed and decided, that you have the same effect on a man as does polished gold, or very fine diamonds. Your brilliance dazzles him until he can no longer think, or see, or want anything but you. Yet, unlike the gold or the diamonds, I believe you cannot be bought. Not by anyone, least of all Francois, despite his great wealth. He who desires to posses you may find that desire difficult, perhaps even impossible to fulfill unless he has a very special key."

"What are you saying, Hakeem, that you believe you have the key?"

"Hardly," he said, with a hard laugh and a shake of his head. "No, I do not have the key, Miss Reynolds."

He paused for a moment, then looking her straight in the eye, added, matter-of-factly, "At least, not yet!"

* * *

Phillip had reported to Francois that Henri, who had been scouring the surrounding area in the chateau's Land Rover, had found Hakeem and Alanna returning along one of the forest paths. Rene had indicated that Alanna had looked no the worse for wear, but that he could not say the same for Hakeem, a bit of information Francois took secret delight in.

Francois had liked Hakeem from the moment he'd met him. He liked him because, while he was brutally proficient at his job, he had a way of making you feel comfortable in his presence. You always knew where you stood with him. He thought that Kamal was lucky to have him as his right hand man, because there was no question where Hakeem's loyalty lay. It was that confidence in his loyalty to friendship that had convinced Francois to trust him with Alanna, from Rene's report that trust seemed not to have been misplaced.

* * *

Alanna let the hot water pour over her body. Hakeem, she thought, was a complete contradiction. On one hand, he had exhibited no qualms about jogging for miles with her behind him, trusting his completely exposed and unprotected back to her, the perfect target. On the other hand, he was quick to reject her replies to his questions, even to blatantly say she'd lied. She doubted that he suspected her true identity, but she knew he was very smart and observant. With his constant scrutinizing of her every move, he could easily become suspicious if she were not careful.

Suddenly, her attention was drawn to the shower curtain, which had billowed slightly inward warning her that someone had opened the bathroom door. She moved against the back of the shower stall wall to give herself the maximum room to maneuver.

A towel appeared at the corner of the curtain and she heard Jeremy, in almost a whisper, say, "You can slip this on and come out of there, or if you'd like company, I'd be happy to join you. Whatever your choice, turn up the water, this place has ears everywhere.

Alanna snapped the towel out of his hand, and wrapped it around her, then she turned the shower up to high, and stepped out into the bathroom. Grabbing a second towel from the towel bar, she wrapped it around her wet hair.

"I see you survived the forced march. Did he?" Jeremy asked.

"Just barely," she replied, as she secured the towel on her head.

"Sorry to interrupt your shower, but this place is so full of bugs," he explained, holding out a sample of one in his hand for her inspection, "that I thought this would be the best place to have a chat."

"I'm happy to hear your motives for invading my privacy were purely business related," she replied, as she gave the bugging device a cursory inspection.

Deliberately ignoring her remark, he said, "They've been through our luggage on the pretext of unpacking it. Have you found anything missing?"

"I noticed that when I got back from my run. Everything is fine," she replied, drying her hair with the towel as she spoke. "Weren't you taking kind of a big risk just to tell me something you were sure I already knew?"

"Not really." he said, "Francois asked me to knock on your door on my way up to my room, and relay the message that we're to meet in the Guard Room in 20 minutes, so you better hurry and dress. Although, were we in different circumstances, I'd say what you're wearing was perfect."

"God!" She said, with mock disgust as she shoved him in the direction of the bathroom door. "Give it a rest."

"See you down stairs and be careful," he said, as he started out the door.

She smiled in way of assuring him that she would be, then closed and locked the bedroom door behind his retreating figure.

* * *

As Alanna entered the room, she found Francois explaining to Jeremy the history of one of the fine tapestries that graced the wall next to the Guard Room's huge fireplace.

From there, they set off on a tour of the chateau, in which three areas were notably off limits. One, the stairway that led to one of the pavilions had two guards posted at the bottom of it. Francois did not offer any explanation for the guards, or the omission of the other rooms on the tour. Neither Alanna nor Jeremy asked for one, though both noted their locations and made mental notes to check with headquarters the next time they made contact for clues as to what the rooms might contain.

Cocktails were served at seven in the grand, formal hall. A favorite of Francois', it had heavy ceiling beams supported by stone corbels, frescoed murals of the histories of nine "valiant" knights — Hector, Alexander the Great, Julius Caesar, Joshua, Judas Maccabas, David,

King Arthur, Charlemagne, and Godefroi de Bouillon — covered the walls. The furniture dated from the 17th century. It was an exquisite room.

The men, in formal dress, were on their second drink when Alanna made her entrance. She wore a bright red China silk, full-length, oriental-style sheath with high Mandarin collar, gold frog closures and long sleeves. The cuffs of the sleeves and the hem of the dress, which was spilt to the knee on both sides, were edged in thin gold braid. Her only jewelry was a pair of long dangling gold earrings and a beautiful black lacquered comb painted with red and gold dragons that she wore in her upswept hair.

The look, though modest in terms of the amount of skin it exposed and elegant of form, was none the less exotic, sensual and by the looks on the men's faces as she entered — totally devastating.

The men dominated the conversation at dinner, which Alanna did nothing to change, and after coffee and brandies in the library, they drove to the casino in Deauville.

Upon arriving, Hakeem and Kamal quickly excused themselves, and headed for the private rooms. Jeremy found a high stakes poker game, and Francois and Alanna cruised the floor until they found a blackjack table to their liking.

Alanna took a seat on the side of the table that allowed her to see the casino entrance. When she saw Aiden come through the door, and enter the main salon, she placed her hand over Francois' to get his attention, and said, "Would you excuse me for a moment?"

"Certainly. Hurry back." He kissed her hand and watched her head off in the direction of the powder room, then turned his attention back to the table and the game.

After a few minutes in the powder room, she headed back to the table. Aiden, who was now playing roulette, turned just as she reached him, and bumped squarely into her knocking her red silk purse out of her hand and to the floor.

"Lord, Alanna, sorry, I didn't see you coming," he said, apologizing profusely as he knelt to retrieve her fallen purse, making sure to turn his back so that no one could see him quickly switch it with the matching one containing the inert detonator he had concealed under his dinner jacket.

"It's quite all right, Aiden," she replied, and accepted the switched bag from him. "I didn't realized you'd arrived in town already."

"I got in an hour ago," he said, while giving her the once over. "Beautiful dress."

"Thank you."

"Looks just like the one a friend of mine asked me to pick up for him in Hong Kong," he remarked.

"It was a gift from a friend," Alanna replied.

Changing the subject, he smiled and asked, "Will you be ready to have a look at some yearlings with me in the morning?"

"That I will," she said, smiling in return. "I'll meet you at the entrance to the cafe under the sales pavilion at 8, if that's not too early?"

"Give a lad a break, lass. I intend to be here when this place closes. Eleven would be more to my liking."

"As you wish." she said, turning to leave. "We meet at the same place at 11."

"Who are we meeting at 11?" Francois, who had appeared out of the crowd, asked.

"Aiden." Alanna replied. "I've arranged to look at some yearlings with him. You will join us, of course."

"Aiden, how are you?" Francois offered his hand in greeting to the Irishman. "When did you get in? You must come and stay at the chateau."

"About an hour ago," Aiden said. "Thank you for the invitation Francois, but I'll be staying with old friends of father's while I'm here."

"That is disappointing," Francois replied, "because I was hoping to be able to do a little business with you while you were here."

"And what kind of business would that be?" Aiden asked.

"Word from my friend at the British Bloodstock Agency is that you purchased Sanctity from Paddy Ryan. Is this true?"

"It is indeed. He needed the cash."

"Then, if I can tear you away from your game, we must talk now," Francois said, then turning to Alanna, he added "Would you care to join us, or would you prefer to try your luck at the tables. I do not want to spoil your evening with business, but I would consider any advice you would choose to give invaluable."

"You two go ahead and play horse traders," she replied. "I think I'll just mingle. I see a few old friends I'd like to say hello to."

"In that case," Francois said, signaling to one of the pit bosses, who came straight over to them. "Jean-Pierre will see that you are supplied with chips or whatever else you need.

"Take good care of Miss Reynolds, Jean-Pierre," Francois said to the man, indicating Alanna to him.

"Most certainly, Monsieur La Croix."

Jeremy had watched the purse exchange between Alanna and Aiden from the poker table. He'd noted that it had gone smoothly but with little time to spare, as Francois had quickly made his appearance at Alanna's side. God, he thought, if he continues to keep close tabs on her, things could get very sticky.

The other players called his attention back to the poker game, anxious for him to make a move. When he looked back in the direction where Alanna, Aiden and Francois had been, they were gone. A quick look around the room found Aiden and Francois heading into the lounge, but Alanna was nowhere to be seen.

"I say mate, if you can't keep your mind on your cards, maybe you should fold, and let the rest of us get on with it," the man sitting next to him said in an irate Australian accent.

"You're right friend. Sorry." Jeremy said, apologetically, as he laid down his cards and raked up his chips, pocketing them. He got up and started circling the room looking for Alanna He made his way from table to table and room to room searching the casino, which as the evening had worn on, had become quite crowded.

Alanna had left the main salon, and, after stopping to chat with a few fellow Kentuckians, who were trying their luck at a roulette table, she moved over to the blackjack table she and Francois had been playing at earlier and placed a bet. She won, let the money ride and won again. The room was fairly crowded, with a number of people standing behind her watching to see if her luck would hold.

She was about to up her wager, when she became conscious of an aroma coming from directly behind her, laced with the scent of cloves, the same scent of cologne she had noticed Hakeem wearing. When she looked behind her, she found him standing there.

"Please, don't let me intrude on your game." he said, through his stark white teeth and dark smile, indicating with a look at her stack of chips. "I would not like to ruin your run of luck."

Alanna gave him a half smile and turned her attention back to her hand. The dealer dealt, and again she won. Not caring to have Hakeem continue to breathe down her neck, she collected her winnings in the drawstring chip bag Francois had given her, picked up her purse and rose from her seat. Hakeem allowed her to rise, but before she could head to the lounge, and the safe company of Francois and Aiden, he took her by the arm.

"My friend Kamal noticed that Francois had abandoned you, and sent me to invite you to join us." Hakeem said, indicating one of the doors of the private rooms.

"Tell Kamal I appreciate his offer," Alanna said, as she unsuccessfully attempted to free her arm from Hakeem's grasp without creating a scene, "but I was just about to rejoin Francois."

"Francois is busy trying to buy a horse, he is poor company at the moment," Hakeem replied, as he tightened his grip on her and aimed her in the direction of the room. "Kamal and I have nothing more to occupy our time than each other's company. Surely, you can spare us a few moments of your time."

If Alanna considered refusing him an option, Hakeem's hand, firmly placed on her elbow, dismissed that idea promptly. No vast arsenal of martial arts skills capable of freeing her from his grasp was worth anything at this moment. To free herself by force would unmask her completely.

"You are perfectly right, Hakeem," Alanna said, changing her tactics, and no longer fighting his grip. "This is my night off from the horse business. I'm sure I'll find visiting with you and Kamal much more interesting."

Then, without turning to face him, she moved off in the direction of the room, saying as she went, "Shall we go."

Even though Alanna had capitulated, Hakeem did not relax his grip. His hand remained on her elbow until they were well into the private room, a gesture that did not escape Kamal's attention.

Once inside the room, Hakeem escorted her to a chair across from where Kamal was seated, took the silk purse and chip bag from her, and suggested that she be seated.

Could it be possible that Hakeem had seen Aiden switch the purses, she wondered. She did not want to look back and see what he was doing with it for fear that showing concern for it would raise suspicion and cause him to search it. The purse was hard-sided, and though the inert detonator was concealed in a false side, if one opened the purse and looked carefully, he would notice that there was a discrepancy in the size of the purse's interior as compared to its exterior.

"Thank you for joining us, Miss Reynolds," Kamal said, moving forward in his seat, and assuming a more relaxed position. It was obvious the woman had not come without some encouragement from Hakeem, yet she seemed relaxed enough, and not unduly upset over Hakeem's somewhat roughshod treatment of her. "May I offer you a drink?"

"Yes, thank you," she replied, casually. "I wouldn't mind having a tonic water on ice with a slice of lime, if that is possible."

"It most assuredly is," Kamal said, as he motioned to one of the other two men in the room, obviously his bodyguards, to see to her drink.

The man made the drink quickly, and, as she turned to accept it from him, she could see her purse sitting on top of the bar where Hakeem had taken a seat. His hand was playing over the top of it.

"Francois is like a man born again, since you have shown a...how do you say... ah, yes, a personal interest in him," Kamal began the interrogation. "He has told me that he has serious intentions where you are concerned."

When Alanna did not comment on his statements, he went on, "I understand that you have been in the horse business for most of your life, is that true?"

"It is," she replied politely, but she did not volunteer anything or elaborate on his statement.

"Please do not take this as an insult, Miss Reynolds," he said, stopping for a moment to take a sip of his coffee, then continuing, "but in our culture a woman of your beauty, intelligence and age would have been married and with family many years ago. Yet, you are still single, and there does not appear to have ever been a significant love interest that we can find in your life."

"You have checked on my life," she asked, feigning surprise. "What right have you to do that?"

"Please, once again, do not take offense," Kamal said, his velvety tone of voice trying to cover for what his hard, intimidating eyes were actually saying. "Francois and I have a significant business relationship, and who he associates with, especially on such a personal level, is of utmost interest to me. I did not mean to imply anything, by your lack of attachment to a particular male, other than curiosity. As I said, in our culture a woman like yourself would be a great prize, I assure you that you would not have found Arab men as easy to dissuade as you obviously have your other suitors."

"If Hakeem is any example of an Arab's persistence," she replied, and turned and gave Hakeem a look that said such persistence was not appreciated, "I'd say you might be right."

"Tell me about yourself, Miss Reynolds," Kamal said, in an authoritative manner.

335

"If you know about my love life, you must know all that there is to know about me," she replied, sounding annoyed, as any woman might be, at this intrusion into her privacy, but not giving an inch.

"There must be things we don't know," Kamal persisted. "In everyone's life there are always things that are not available on the record, or obvious to an observer. So, Miss Reynolds, tell me about those things. Why don't you start by explaining why you haven't put your degrees in French and Russian to better use. They would be of great value to you had you chosen, for example, to go into foreign service work."

"I use my French quite frequently in the horse business, and I majored in Russian because my grandfather was Polish-Russian, and I'd been taught to speak it when I was a child. It was an easy degree to achieve, so why not add it to my resume," she replied, quite truthfully, but neglecting to add that she also spoke fluent Spanish and acceptable Mandarin Chinese, which she had learned from Dar. "I speak Polish fluently as well, but my university did not offer a degree in it, or I would have a degree in Polish as well."

"And, seeing what degrees you were pursuing, no foreign service ever came to your college in an attempt to recruit you," he asked, probing closer to the truth.

"My school did not encourage recruiting by foreign service agencies," Alanna again replied truthfully to a fact they would already be aware of if they had checked her out as thoroughly as it appeared they had.

"My intentions, since I was a child, have been to be in the horse business. There was never any doubt in my mind, no matter what degree I pursued in college, in which direction my life would go after graduation. Horses are my life. Whether you are convinced of that or not is not my concern, but my life is as simple as that."

Where are they going with this, she worried? Is this really just a simple going over they give everyone that associates with Francois, or has Rakeland succeeded in unearthing the truth? Why had no one missed her? Where were Jeremy and Aiden? God, even Francois' loathsome presence would be a welcome sight now.

"You have been very truthful and cooperative, Miss Reynolds," Kamal said, but something in his voice told her he wasn't finished probing. His next question confirmed that suspicion, "Tell me about the man whose funeral you attended before you left Lexington. The man, J. David Clark, who was he to you and ....

Before Kamal could finish his question, the door burst open, and Francois stormed into the room. He observed the group and without saying anything to Kamal and Hakeem, walked over to Alanna and took her by the hand, "Come Alanna," he said, gently. Then giving the two Arabs a look that conveyed his displeasure with the situation, he added, "I'm sorry to intrude on your visit with my friends, but I think it's time we went back to the chateau."

"I'm ready, if you are," Alanna replied, as she rose from her seat and allowed him to escort her to the door. She purposely refrained from making eye contact with Kamal. He had not found out more than he already knew during the course of his interrogation. There was no need to aggravate him with a sarcastic look into further pursuing his investigation of her.

However, Hakeem was another matter. "Just a moment, Francois, I almost forgot something," she said, just as they were about to leave the room. Turning back, she walked over to the bar. With her back turned to Kamal and Francois, she picked her purse and chip bag up off of the bar, and then, after quickly giving Hakeem a look that was the equivalent of the proverbial "finger", she rejoined Francois who was waiting for her at the door.

"I'm sorry to have left you alone for so long, Alanna," Francois said, in a concerned, apologetic tone, as they headed through the crowd of people and to the main entrance of the casino. She, however, sensed an underlying anger towards the Arabs that was seething just below this calm demeanor.

"It was inconsiderate of me," he went on. "I hope Kamal and Hakeem treated you with respect, and did nothing to frighten you. Arab men have a very different opinion of women, especially western women."

"I'm fine, Francois, but I was growing weary of their conversation." Alanna said, squeezing his arm affectionately, which brought a smile to his face. "Thank you for rescuing me."

"Rescuing beautiful damsels in distress is the time-honored task of the French nobility," he replied, smiling down lovingly at her as he escorted her out of the casino. "I am proud to have lived up to my heritage. May I suggest, Alanna, that someone accompanies you, while Kamal and Hakeem are here. My Arab associates would not hurt you, but they can be overbearing, and I imagine, frightening to a woman such as yourself."

337

"Yes, I believe you're right, Francois. I'll remember to do that in the future," she replied, thinking that his suggestion was a point well taken.

When Francois' car arrived and there was still no sign of Jeremy, she asked, "Isn't Mark coming back with us?"

"He said that he wanted to gamble for a while longer," Francois replied, as the doorman opened the door, and Francois allowed Alanna to precede him into the backseat. "So, Aiden said he would drive him back to the chateau later. Actually, it was Mark who called my attention to the fact that you were missing. He'd been looking for you, and got worried when he couldn't find you."

So that's how my French knight in shining armor managed to turn up in the nick of time, she thought.

"Actually, I am happy that he decided to stay," Francois said, as he moved closer to her and slipped his arm around her shoulders, briefly turning his attention from her to signal the driver to be off. "Since you have arrived, we have not had a minute to ourselves, and I have very much wanted to be alone with you."

While the driver was waiting for a break in the traffic before pulling out, Francois put his hand to her cheek and turned her face to his.

Oh, God, I don't think I can do this, Alanna thought.

Just as he was about to kiss her, there was a knock on the car's window. Francois hesitated, then turned and seeing that it was Jergens, lowered it.

"I'm glad I caught you before you left," Jeremy said, as he bent over and spoke to Francois through the open window, while not missing the look of relief at his appearance that was visible on Alanna's face. "I remembered that we had a early morning, so I changed my mind about closing down the place. I hope you don't mind if I ride back with you after all."

"Not at all," Francois replied, with little enthusiasm, as he slid back to his side of the seat while opening the door for Jeremy to enter.

"Ah, I see you found Alanna."

"Yes," Francois replied. "She was visiting with Hakeem and Kamal in one of the private rooms. That is why you did not see her."

"That must have been interesting. Did you learn anything new about Arabic customs during your visit?" Jeremy asked her.

"Not really," she replied. "They were more interested in learning about our ways than educating me to theirs."

"I see," he said, understanding her previous dilemma perfectly now.

338

* * *

On their return to the chateau, Jeremy gave Alanna the opportunity to gracefully extricate herself from his and Francois' company by suggesting they have a nightcap.

"If you gentlemen don't mind, I'd like to pass on the nightcap," she said. "The day has finally caught up with me, and I'm beginning to feel very tired. I think I'll just go on to my room."

Obviously disappointed, but in no position to argue the matter, Francois took her hands, kissed them gently, and said, "Yes, you must be exhausted. The trip over, jogging all over the countryside, and partying all evening must surely have taken their toll. Good night and rest well. We will see you in the morning."

"Good night, Francois," she said, as she gently slid her hands from his grasp. Then turning to Jeremy, she added, "Good night, Mark. Remember, we have an early morning."

"How could I forget?" Jeremy replied. "Count on me to be there. Good night."

As Alanna climbed the stairs to her room, she felt as though the thick stone walls of the chateau were pressing in on her. Even though she and Jeremy had the means to communicate with headquarters and Granton, she knew that this could only be done under the gravest of circumstance. The communicators worked by secured satellite transmission and their signals were, for the most part, undetectable to groups as technologically unsophisticated as the Arabs and Francois. Still, they might be observed doing so, and blow the operation. Which meant, for the moment, they were on their own. The only safe means of communicating with headquarters was through Aiden, who was, unfortunately, not always handy.

Something else had begun to worry her. While it appeared Francois had accepted them at face value, the Arabs appeared not to have. So, maybe Rakeland was the Arabs' man and not Francois'. Not that it really mattered when you considered that the Arabs and Francois were in this together.

And, how had they known about Jake's funeral? Hopefully, the answer was as simple as Francois had told them, since he had been there for it as well. But, why would they be so interested in who the man she buried was, especially since she had provided Francois with an explanation already. Maybe, she told herself, what they had said was true. Maybe, anyone that had as close a relationship with Francois as he hoped to have with her was fair game for their in-depth scrutiny. And, maybe, if she really believed that, she could expect to see Santa Claus come down her chimney next Christmas.

Come on. Now is not the time to get paranoid, she reminded herself. They had you where they wanted you. If they'd had anything to prove that you were other than what you claimed to be, they would not have waited so long to spring it on you. It's for sure, that you would not have walked out of that room on Francois' arm; in fact, you probably would not have walked out of that room at all.

Alanna entered her spacious bedroom, which was furnished in a distinctively feminine renaissance style. The room's lights had already been turned on ,and there was a fire in the fireplace and a tray, with a brasier of hot tea and a plate of light biscuits, on the night table next to her bed. Although in a room of this size the fireplace offered little in the way of warmth, it had obviously been lit to lend atmosphere to what would have been a rather dreary, damp room. This was Alanna's first stay in a castle, but she had spent many nights in rather large, old country houses in both England and Ireland, and all seemed to share this damp dreariness no matter the season of the year.

She noticed that her bed had been turned down, and one of her sexier nightgowns laid out on it by the maid assigned to her. Perhaps the choice of gown was a little hint from the maid, more likely, it was an order from Francois. It bothered her that there was so little privacy here, but unless you actually called for someone, things seemed to get done with ghostly efficiency.

As she closed and locked the heavy door behind her, she took in the tranquil pastoral scenes portrayed in the tapestries draped on the walls. She thought about the ancient intrigues that must have transpired here within the confines of the chateau, maybe within this very room. None, she was sure, could have compared in worldly significance or in far-reaching consequences to the one that was about to take place.

Alanna went to the large ornate walnut armoire. From within it, she took a white silk robe. While her back and the two doors of the armoire shielded her movements from the view of any hidden cameras in the room, she used the robe to cover both the purse she had been carrying and her jewelry box, which she picked up from off one of the armoire's shelves.

Alanna carried them into the bathroom and turned off the bathroom lights. There, protected by the darkness, she transferred the inert bomb detonator from the hidden panel in her purse to the false bottom of the jewelry box. She took the velvet bag of BB sized lead weights that had occupied the space in the false bottom, and which had been placed there to simulate the weight of the detonator, and poured its contents down the shower drain.

Then, in the privacy of the darkness, Alanna undressed, and slipped on the white silk robe. When she was finished, she carefully covered the purse and jewelry box with her red silk dress and took it back to the armoire, where once again shielded from view by her back and the doors, she replaced the purse and jewelry box and hung up her dress.

Finally, Alanna turned out the lights in the bedroom, then took one of the candles from the fireplace mantle, and set it on a wooden footstool in the middle of the room. She sat down on the floor 12 feet from the candle, assumed the lotus position, began to concentrate on her breath, and for the first time that day, let her mind relax.

* * *

The black Peugeot sedan sped down the dark narrow Normandy road banked high on both sides with hedgerows, their towering blackness broken only occasionally by a pasture gate, driveway or deserted crossroad.

The illuminated clock on the car's dash read 2 a.m., but Aiden seemed not to notice or be affected by the lateness of the hour. He slowed briefly as he passed through the empty streets of a small village, accelerating quickly once he reached its outskirts. Five miles on, he took a turn to his right, down a narrow lane, and followed it for a mile until he came to an iron gate. There he stopped and waited.

A few minutes passed before he saw the signal. Three flashes of light, then three more, followed by a single flash. He answered with his own signal, and soon saw a figure clad in dark clothes approaching the gate. The figure had a rifle in his hand, pointed in his direction.

"I'm afraid I'm lost," Aiden said, to the man, who now stood just the other side of the gate. "Can you tell me the way to Calle?"

Recognizing the code, the man responded, "For the right price, I can."

"Name your price." Aiden replied, completing the code.

The man unlocked and opened the gate. Once Aiden had driven through it, he relocked it. Then he walked back into the woods, returning astride a motorcycle fitted with a silenced muffler and shielded headlight. He signaled for Aiden to follow with his lights off, and took off down the lane.

The path led to an old farmhouse, surrounded by three rather ramshackle outbuildings. The motorcycle rider pulled into the largest of the three buildings, which upon closer inspection turned out to be an old dairy barn. Aiden pulled in behind the parked motorcycle, and turned off his engine.

"I'm Russo," the motorcyclist said, in heavily accented English, as he offered his hand to Aiden, who had just gotten out of his car.

"Aiden Doyle."

They shook hands, and Russo said, "Follow me."

The old door creaked on its rusted hinges as they entered the house. Russo led the way with his shielded flashlight as they crossed the worn plank floor of the hallway. It led to a trap door under the main staircase. He lifted the door and motioned to Aiden to watch his head and mind the steps. Then, bending low, he disappeared through the door. Aiden followed, closing the trap door behind him, and likewise ducking to miss the low beams of the cellar ceiling, while being careful to place his feet squarely on the narrow stairs.

Once in the cellar, Russo led Aiden to another door. He stopped and rapped out a signal. A man Aiden quickly recognized as Bill Rice opened the door.

"Good to see you, Doyle." Rice said, moving away from the door to give the two arriving men room to enter.

The room was far more modern than the house above it. Brightly lit, it contained a work area that centered on a large, light table for enhanced map work. Along one wall were computers, weather equipment, sophisticated communications equipment, and a large screen with a satellite hookup.

As Aiden was observing the operations setup, the door at the far end opened.

"Doyle! Good ta see ya man," Tad Clark said, as he entered the room carrying a tray bearing a freshly brewed pot of coffee, cups, spoons and all the fixings.

"This is sure some setup, ain't it?" he said, referring to the room they were in. "And the one back there's not bad either." Meaning the room he'd just come from that contained a fully equipped, modern kitchen, bath and dormitory style sleeping accommodations.

"Wouldn't suspect it from looking at what's at ground level, now would you," he asked as he set the coffee down on a buffet located against the wall opposite the electronics.

"That's for sure." Aiden replied. "When did you guys get here?"

"We had to fly that bird all the way to Paris and drive up here, just in case Francois was still doggin' our trail. We got here at dinner time." Rice said, as he walked over to the buffet, and helped himself to a cup of coffee, then offered one to Aiden, "Care for a cup."

"Who does this place belong to?" Aiden asked Russo, as he joined Rice at the coffee bar.

"The farm belonged to my family. They were killed in the war fighting with the resistance." Russo replied. "This room was constructed especially for this type of work. I was only a child when they were killed. I still own the property, but I can no longer live on it. The memories are too...

He did not finish. No one bothered to pursue the answer further.

"Well, let's get to work, gentlemen," Aiden said, as he moved over to the light table, set down his cup of coffee, and proceeded to spread the plans for the operation, which he'd taken from his briefcase, on the table."

"Russo, are you sure the train will be on time?" Aiden asked, as he pointed to an area on the map he'd just unfold, which pinpointed a rail yard just north of the village of La Croix.

"Yes," Russo replied. "We have information from a reliable source that the train carrying the chemicals is on schedule. No one wants that load sitting around in their yard any longer than necessary.

"I have some satellite shots of the train taken this morning," Russo said, collecting a bunch of pictures from the top of a Hewlett Packard laser printer that sat to the right of one of the computers, and laying them before Aiden. On one picture, he circled two of the cars, which were located midway down the train, with a marking pen, adding, "These are the ones we're to hit."

"When are the helicopters due in?" Aiden asked Rice, while he gave the satellite pictures a thorough going over.

"Any time now."

"What are we getting?"

"Two UH-1Hs. Hueys." Rice added the latter just as a dig, knowing full well Aiden would know what the helicopter's initials stood for. "Their dressing 'em up to look like the ones some Hollywood film crew has here to film a balloon race scene for a movie they're making."

"Either of them armed?" Aiden asked, this time while his attention was focused on an enlarged section of the map of the area.

"Not that I know of." Rice replied, as he too looked over the terrain they'd be operating in. "Think we'll need 'em armed."

"Not if things go according to plan."

"And, if they don't?" Rice asked.

"Then we'll wish they were, won't we?" Aiden said, looking up at Rice, his eyes saying what he had not.

"Then maybe we should lay in that option?"

"It may be too late for that, Bill." Aiden said. "The U.S. has no airbases here in France. That makes it damn hard to just order up an armed chopper at a moment's notice. If we tried to fly one in from England or Germany, the French would have our heads."

I guess you're right. We'll just have to hope all goes off as planned."

"Amen, to that!" Clark said.

Aiden unsuccessfully stifled a yawn, and Rice said, "Hey, man, why don't you sack out for a couple hours. Tad and I have already caught a few winks. I'll wake you when the choppers arrive."

"Sounds like a good idea," Aiden replied, as he considered the wisdom of Rice's suggestion. "I'm having a hell of a time keeping my head upright."

* * *

Francois had obligingly had a nightcap with the American, though he would have rather pursued his original objective, which was to finally get Alanna to himself. Once Jergens had retired to his room, it was too late for him to impose his company on her without looking out of line. So, now feeling wide-awake, he decided to wait for his partners to make their appearance. They had a little explaining to do concerning their actions this evening. Though Alanna had covered for them, he'd sensed when he'd entered that private room that all was not well. He meant to make clear to them, that where Alanna was concerned, they were to mind their manners. Otherwise, deal or no deal, he'd make life very unpleasant for them.

Just as Jeremy began to think seriously about turning in, he heard voices in the west hall. As the Arabs came abreast of the library's doors, Francois opened them.

"Gentlemen, would you care to join me for a moment." Francois said, in a tone of voice that said this was not an invitation but an order that broached no argument, not even from the likes of Hakeem and Kamal.

"But, of course, Francois," Kamal replied, and indicated to Hakeem, who had begun to walk off, that he should join them.

"I trust you found Miss Reynolds' company pleasant this evening, and I hope she found yours pleasant as well," Francois began his inquiry into the purpose of their visit with Alanna.

"Of course, I cannot speak for the lady, Francois, but I found Miss Reynolds quite charming," Kamal replied. "From my observation of her, I would say that, should she agree to be your bride, my heartiest congratulations would be in order."

"And you Hakeem, what do you think? You have spent more time with her than even I have?" Francois asked of the man, whose concession to obliging Francois' order to join them, was to remain standing in the doorway.

"If I thought you could really have her, Francois, I would count you a lucky man," Hakeem replied, with a look on his face whose meaning Francois could not decipher.

It was a response so out of character for Hakeem that it took Francois, and even Kamal, aback. There was a deafening silence before Francois dared ask, " What do you mean, Hakeem? What has she said to make you suspect that to be the case?"

For a moment it seemed Hakeem was bent on keeping whatever he knew to himself. Finally, he said. "She said nothing, Francois. But, I have had ample time to observe both you and her. I told you that you were making a mistake in pursuing her when we were in Saratoga, and my opinion is still the same. She is too smart for you, Francois. You will never be able to keep your dirty little secrets from her. Should you manage to find a way to convince her to become your bride, you, and I fear, she, will regret the decision for the rest of your lives."

"If she loves me, what I do will not matter to her. She will go along with whatever I say," Francois insisted angrily.

"Never, Francois!" Hakeem said, and turned and disappeared into the darkness of the hall.

"What do you make of that?" Francois asked Kamal, somewhat shaken by the finality of Hakeem's pronouncement.

"It is one man's opinion, Francois," Kamal replied. "You know her better than any of us. No one is better qualified to judge her suitability than you. She is strong-willed, but she is still a woman, and I dare say, one who likes the luxuries of life. You have an abundance of those to offer, in addition to the fine man you are."

The flattering, consoling remarks from Kamal were all that Francois needed to soothe over his earlier anger at the two men — exactly the reaction Kamal had sought.

"Well, you must excuse me, Francois," Kamal said, "I have reached the end of my endurance for the night. I must retire."

"Certainly, Kamal," Francois replied. "We will be leaving for the sales grounds quite early, so I probably will not see you until lunch. You will be pleased to know that what I have promised you will be delivered this afternoon. I have arranged for it to be delivered while I, and my guests, are away at the sale. This will allow you and your men to see to its safe placement in the tower. Yesterday, I gave Hakeem the combination to the safe, and advised him how the tower's security system works, so he and his men can handle the details."

"Excellent, Francois!" Kamal said, with obvious pleasure in his voice. "Our task is almost at an end. You have my undying gratitude."

"I have your money, Kamal. That is gratitude enough," Francois replied.

Kamal bid Francois good night, and started to his room, midway down the hall, he reversed his course. Stopping in front of one of the other guestroom doors, he knocked and said, "Hakeem, it is Kamal. Are you still awake?"

The light coming from under Hakeem's door told Kamal that he was. A couple of moments later, Hakeem opened the door.

"May I come in?" Kamal asked.

Hakeem nodded in the affirmative, and stepped back to allow Kamal to enter. He was still dressed in the tuxedo he had worn to the casino. Spread out on a desk next to the window was a pistol, broken down, and a cleaning kit. Hakeem still held a cleaning rag in his hand.

"Francois has told me that we shall have our package tomorrow, and that he has made arrangements for you to handle it," Kamal said, surprised that Hakeem had known earlier about the arrangements, but had said nothing to him. "Why did you not tell me this?"

"Francois wanted the honor of informing you himself."

"I see," Kamal said, and was about to turn and leave, when he hesitated, turned back and looked into Hakeem's expressionless face. "What troubles you, Hakeem? The woman?"

"No. The woman is Francois' concern."

"Then, all is well with you?"

"It is." Hakeem replied

"Very well." Kamal said, resignedly. "Let me know when the delivery has been made."

"I'll do that," Hakeem said, as he closed the door behind Kamal.

* * *

"Sort trente deux, s'il vous plait," Alanna said, to the head groom, and he went off down the shedrow to bring the yearling who bore the number she had requested.

"I wish I knew if and when that damn thing was going to show up," Jeremy said, as he fingered his sales catalogue idly. "We can't hang around here forever."

Alanna did not respond, as the groom arrived with the yearling, and stood him before her for her inspection. She went through the motions of physically appraising it, then asked the groom to walk it away from her and back. She made careful notes on the catalogue page and even called Jeremy's attention to the flaws she found. He feigned interest, but deep down he was beginning to feel the pressure building.

When she thanked the groom, and sent him and the yearling back to its stall, she said to Jeremy, "You may not be able to, but I can, and if I have to I will."

"You're serious! You'd stay."

"Until I knew one way or the other what was happening with that thing."

"What about Francois?" Jeremy asked, though, in his heart, he knew and dreaded the answer. "I managed to keep his grubby hands off you last night, but you're not going to keep him at bay forever, especially if you stay on alone."

"I'll handle what comes," she said, with no emotion in her voice.

"Christ!" Jeremy said, in disgust and helplessness.

Alanna was feeling much the same as Jeremy, but realizing the futility in expressing her feelings, she chose to change the subject.

"Try and look a little interested in the next yearling I pull out, will you," she scolded, "You're supposed to be interested in buying one. At least that's what the script says."

"You're right. I'm sorry," Jeremy said, apologetically. "Where are we headed to next?"

"Yard A on the far side of the walking ring," she replied, and headed off in that direction.

They stopped when Jeremy's pager went off. It was the signal for them to part company. Alanna went about the business of looking at yearlings, while Jeremy went on to the sales office to make a call.

Alanna had just pulled out another yearling, when Francois appeared at the main entrance to the sales grounds. It was nearly lunchtime so

347

much of the area had cleared of people. He had no trouble locating Alanna, but Jergens was nowhere to be seen.

"Where is your friend," he asked, as he came along side her. He noted the catalogue number of the yearling she was looking at and referred to the catalogue page.

"He got beeped by his office on one of those satellite pager things, and went off to call in," she said, as she made some marks in her catalogue.

"How are things going?" He asked. "Have you found anything of interest?"

"Yes. Two nice colts for Mark, and I found a filly I wouldn't mind having if the price were right."

"It's almost noon," Francois said, referring to his Rolex watch. "You've been at this since 8. Why don't you break for lunch?"

"That's a good suggestion," she replied, closing her catalogue. "Let me just find Mark, and ask him if he'd like to join us, and then we can go."

"If you must," Francois said, but he had a just-kidding smile on his face.

Francois watched Alanna walk off and considered what Hakeem had said about her last night. There was no doubt that she was smart, and as far as he knew from her business dealings, honest. It was something on which he knew she prided herself. So, was Hakeem right, was he deluding himself? Did he honestly believe she'd close her eyes to what really went on at La Croix?

Francois chose not to answer his own questions, first because he was afraid the answer would not be to his liking, and second, because Alanna had just emerged from the sales office, and was headed towards him, wearing the most beautiful of smiles.

Mark has some business to take care of for the resort," she said. "His office is faxing him some papers to review and sign, so he sends his apologies, but he will not be able to join us for lunch."

"How disappointing," Francois said, and they both laughed, knowing he was not disappointed at all. "Shall we go?"

Jeremy watched Alanna and Francois leave the sales grounds from the sales office. When he was sure they were well on their way, he headed out of the building, and to the Rue Jules Saucisse, the street bordering one side of the sales grounds. As he reached the curb, a taxi pulled up in front of him.

"Taxi, monsieur?" the driver asked.

"Can you take me to Calle?" Jeremy inquired.

"For a price I can." The driver responded with the second part of the identifying code.

"Name your price," Jeremy said, concluding the code.

Reaching back, the driver opened the rear door and said, "Entre, monsieur. I am sure we can arrive at a mutually agreeable price."

Jeremy got in the cab, and it drove off.

* * *

Rice had awakened Aiden just as the sound of an approaching helicopter was heard in the distance. They remained below, while Russo went to signal in the aircraft. When he confirmed on transmitter device that it was safe to come out, Aiden, Rice and Clark joined him.

"What the hell!" Rice said, as he approached the lone helicopter, which he recognized as an Aerospatiale.

"Where's the other chopper?" He yelled to the pilot, over the noise of the rotor blades.

The pilot signaled that he was unable to hear. The four men waited until he'd shut down the craft, and was standing before them to question him further.

Rice, whose responsibility it was to evacuating Jeremy and Alanna from the area when the operation was complete, assumed command of the situation.

"Bill Rice," he said, approaching the pilot and co-pilot and offering his hand.

"Good to know ya, Bill," said the pilot. I'm Andrew Gunter and this is my co-pilot Chris Wright."

"What happened to the Hueys?" Rice said, pointing to the Aerospatiale. "Where's the second helicopter?"

"We had a screw up," Gunter, said. "The transport bringing them from Germany had problems, so we were forced to get what we could."

All night Rice had mulled over Aiden's lamenting the lack of weaponry on at least one of the Agency's helicopters. He'd though that given his and Clark's experience with Huey helicopters, they might be able to solve that problem. Since the aircraft would be U.S. government property, he was sure that bastardizing them would not cause a national crisis. By the same token, he was also sure that whoever owned the Aerospatiale would not take kindly to the type of alterations he'd had in mind for the Huey being made on their aircraft no matter the reason.

"Damn," was all he said, but his mind was already searching for a way to handle the problem.

"Better get this thing under cover," Rice said to Russo and Clark.

To Aiden and the Aerospatiale crew, he said, "Let's go back inside. We need to revise our Hotel Alfa plan."

"What plan?" asked the co-pilot, who had never served with the military.

"That's military talk for haul ass, man," Gunter replied, and looked at Rice, and rolled his eyes.

By the time Russo and Clark joined them in the operations room, Rice was going over the original extraction plan with the chopper's crew.

"Damn! Situation normal, all fucked up! He said in frustration to Clark, and walked away from the table.

Aiden wasn't quite sure why Rice seemed so upset. True, two helicopters would have been better than one, especially if Rice and Clark had to accompany him on the extraction. It was obvious that that would not be a possibility given the limited passenger capacity of the model Aerospatiale they had, but one was better than none, in his estimation.

"Look we'll make do, Bill," Aiden said, "I can get out on the ground, if space becomes a problem."

Rice returned to the map spread on the table. He made a circle with his finger the diameter of the chateau's entire area.

"The problem is not just a matter of passenger capacity," Rice explained. "What if hostilities break out and you need help? What if you, Jeremy and Alanna get split up and time's a factor? What if someone's wounded, or trapped? What if this Goddamn bird decides to get temperamental and won't fly? Where's our backup?"

It was in the middle of this tirade, when they heard the front door of the house open, and the sound of footsteps on the floor in the hall above them.

Russo killed the lights, and the men assumed cover positions. Russo, Aiden and Rice drew their pistols.

There was a rap on the trap door, then three raps, and then another single rap.

"It's okay." Russo said, switching on the lights, and running up the stairs to unlock the door. When he came back down, he was followed by a young blond haired man, who he introduced as his cousin Patrice; and Jeremy, who introduced himself to the helicopter pilots.

"Well, this is a happy group," Jeremy said, noticing the scowls on most of the men's faces.

350

"It's a sentiment I'm sure you're going to share, Jeremiah," Rice said, as the men reassembled around the table. "Come over here and get a load of what's happened."

"How are things going over at the chateau?'" Aiden asked, not meaning to change the subject, but having interests of his own. "What happened in that room last night with Alanna and those Arabs?"

"She said they gave her the fifth degree," Jeremy replied.

"You think they suspect her?"

"No. I think that's just their style. Hakeem's spent enough time with her for their relationship to qualify as a common law marriage," Jeremy said, in jest. Then added, seriously, "If they suspected anything, we'd surely know it by now. Things are quiet, too quiet. If our target doesn't arrive on schedule, we won't have a legitimate reason to stick around. That is except for Alanna, and she's prepared to stay 'till the end."

"Not alone." Aiden argued.

"She won't have much choice," Jeremy said, and the implications of that possibility were clearly etched in his voice. "We can hang around as backup out here, but for all practical purposes, she'll be on her own in that chateau with that horny Frenchman, his mob and the Arab hordes."

"Now that's a combo that'll give you something to think about," Clark said, and while his voice had a humorous overtone to it, the message behind his words was clear.

Rice was about to launch into another tirade, when Jeremy caught his eye and gave him one of those "empty this place" looks. So, instead he said, "Look guys, why don't we go out and have a look at that bird and see if there isn't anything we can come up with to improve this situation.

"You go ahead, Rice." Jeremy said, "Aiden and I have a few things to discuss."

The other men filed out, Rice being the last one to mount the steps. Before he did, he looked over at Jeremy, who signaled him not to return for at least 15 minutes.

"Have you heard anything from headquarters?" Jeremy asked Aiden.

"No," Aiden replied, "I was about to check in with them when you arrived."

"Well, let's see what the head shed has to say," Jeremy said as he entered his code into the computer, and then accessed the communications program. It was 5:30 a.m. Washington time, but the picture and the voice that answered Jeremy's call was Granton's.

"Sleeping on the job, boss?" Jeremy kidded his superior, whom he knew probably would not leave his office area until this operation was over.

"How'd you guess?" Granton replied.

"The bathrobe gave you away." Jeremy said.

"A man can't hide a damn thing with this new visual conferencing. How are things going at your end?"

"They're going, but I sure wish we knew if that thing was going to get here on schedule. Any word from our contact?" Jeremy asked.

"Nothing." Granton replied. "How's Alanna doing?"

"Okay, but we had a shaky moment last night. The Arabs tried a little light-handed interrogation. They didn't find out anything they didn't already know, but they'd really done their homework on her. It made us really nervous. You don't think Rakeland put them up to it, do you?"

"I don't think so," Granton replied, but his voice had a touch of uncertainty in it. "We've kept him pretty much under wraps, and had Stasio feed him some disinformation that we allowed him to confirm by letting him hack into a phony SABRE file. The Rakeland matter, however, has now been more or less taken out of our hands."

"Why's that?"

"Ever since the fiasco with the Anderson case, we've been required to turn cases like Rakeland's over to the FBI. Especially, once we've confirmed our suspicions that we have a potential mole," Granton said. "When Rakeland coerced Stasio into giving him classified information and then hacked his way into the computer to confirm it, his case became FBI property."

"That's shit!" Jeremy said, "What if he finds something out while they're trying to prove their case? Will they let us know in time, or are we going to have to find out the hard way?"

"I've assigned one of our best people to act as liaison with them. The FBI understands that Rakeland poses a significant threat to an active operation, and that extreme caution is to be used. They also have been told that I am to be informed personally of his every move. That was the best I could do, Jeremy, the law's the law."

"Shit!" Jeremy reiterated his frustration.

"I take it from the point of origin of this message that you successfully rendezvoused with our French agents." Granton asked.

"We have, but we ran into our first snag when only one helicopter showed this morning," Jeremy replied. "And, the wrong kind, to boot."

"Let me see what I can do about it," Granton said.

"We'd appreciate it. Rice is working on the problem too, but if things go wrong, we'll have a real problem getting everyone out safely."

"I understand. Tell Rice to check in with me. Anything else?" Granton asked.

"No," Jeremy said, "This will probably be the last chance we have to talk. From here on in, I'll have a hard time slipping away. Aiden will keep you informed."

"Right." Granton replied. "Good luck. I'll see you when it's over."

"God I hope so." Jeremy said. Then turning to Aiden, he asked, "Do you need to talk to Granton?"

"Not at the moment." Aiden replied. And Jeremy signed off the communication.

"I've got to get back to the sales grounds before Alanna gets back from lunch with his majesty," Jeremy said, the sarcasm thick in his voice.

"Shit!" He said, again, clearly exasperated by the state of uneasiness that existed with each aspect of this operation.

Aiden understood full well that the underlying reason for Jeremy's anxiety was Alanna. "Relax, Jeremy. Everything will work out fine. We've got a good, knowledgeable, experienced crew working on this. Hell, it's not the first time things have gone buggers with an operation we've worked on, and this helicopter thing's only a small nuisance. We've always managed to pull'em off in spite of it."

"Sure!" Jeremy replied, obviously unconvinced. "Well, I'm out of here. I'll see you tonight at the chateau."

Aiden watched as Jeremy climbed the stairs, and disappeared out the door. What Jeremy didn't know was that, if there was a delay and Jeremy had to pull out, he would never allow Alanna to remain in the chateau alone. His purchase of Paddy Ryan's stallion Sanctity, the horse Francois wanted so desperately, was his personal backup plan. He had laid the bait and the groundwork with Francois last night at the casino. The horse was his ticket in. He meant to keep his promise to Dar, but he now had his own reasons for seeing to Alanna's safety.

The rest of the men returned from their jaunt to the makeshift hanger just as Jeremy left. They were busy sounding out ideas with one another as they came down the steps.

Rice went immediately to the secure phone. He took out a small black leather phone book, and paged through it, stopping when he'd found the number he'd been looking for. He dialed, and a phone on the other end of the line began to ring. On the eighth ring, he decided to hang up. Suddenly, a gruff voice, he recognized from out of his past, answered.

"Yeah, wha'dya want?" It said.

"Doc? God damn, Doc, is that really you, man?" Rice responded warmly. "I was afraid by now they'd retired you and your tool box to some old VA mechanic's home."

"What the fuck? That you, Rice? I hear you're still livin' a charmed life." The old helicopter maintenance officer huffed, but the delight at hearing his friend's familiar voice was obvious.

"I can't believe with that candy-assed job I hear ya got, you'd be needin' my help, but I gotta feeling that's why you called. Tell me I'm wrong?"

"You always were a perceptive bastard, Doc."

"Cut the fuckin' flattery, Rice and give it to me straight.

"It's a tough one, Doc. I need a Huey, Charlie-type, like yesterday. Armed to the teeth and fit to do battle. How are you fixed for miracles?" Rice said, looking back at the men around him, and crossing his fingers for luck.

"You should have stayed a memory, Rice." He could hear the disbelief in his old friend's voice. "Just like that, you want a fully-armed, combat-ready Huey! How about I throw in an assault team, a couple of Cobras, a few B-52s and some heavy artillery/"

"Nah," Rice said, laughing. That'd be overkill, Doc. I just need a Huey gunship."

"You must be callin' from a fuckin' VA loony bin, Rice"

"I guess that's what it would sound like to me too if I were in you shoes, Doc, but listen..."

Rice proceeded to fill in his friend on a need to know basis. Eliminating anything from the briefing that was top secret, but underscoring the seriousness of the operation.

"You've got to help me, Doc, you're my only hope." Rice concluded, and held his breath during the silence that followed.

Finally, the gruff voice said, "I'm not promisin' anythin', mind ya. You gotta number I can reach ya at?"

"No, I'll just have to call you," Rice said, almost afraid to hope his friend could come through. "I really appreciate this, but make it quick — real quick."

"Gim' me a couple hours, Rice. Remember, I'm not promisin' nothin'."

"Right two hours. Thanks, Doc."

When he turned back to the group, he noticed that Aiden and Russo were busy plotting out an area on the map.

"Have you got everything we need?" Aiden asked

"As far as I know, we have everything," Russo replied.

"Then, we just wait, and hope we've got their delivery schedule figured right." Aiden said, "Waiting's the hard part."

He didn't get any argument from the other men.

It was lunch time, so Russo threw together a peasant lunch of cheese, sausages and crisp French bread for the men, which they ate while going over the plans for the dozenth time. Exploring all the possible what ifs they could think of. When a couple of hours had passed, Rice replaced his call to his friend.

"Doc?" Rice said, when the man answered.

"The luck's still with you captain!" Doc replied. "There's just what you need sittin' large as life at a joint military air show at Orly. It's got the pods and the guns, but no ammo on board, o'course that's the least of our worries. You'll need to make a pit stop for fuel along the way. Can you arrange that?

"Just a minute," Rice said. He put his hand over the receiver and turned to Russo and asked, "Can we arrange for a fuel stop midway between here and Orly?"

Russo nodded in the affirmative, and Rice took his hand off of the receiver and said, "We've got that covered on this end, Doc."

"Then you're set," Doc replied. "I've arranged for the chopper to develop a mechanical problem that will require my personal attention. My man there will tell them that I've authorized you to pick it up ASAP. And for, God's sake Rice, bring it back in one piece! There'll be hell to pay if you don't."

"I hear ya, Doc," Rice replied, this time crossing his fingers behind his back. "You always were a genius at appropriations. Tell your man that I'm on my way, and thanks, I owe you one."

"You bet your sweet ass you do, Rice. Be careful."

Rice hung up the phone, and turning to Clark and Russo, said, "Come on, guys, let's go get that baby.'

Tad finished his coffee, and joined Rice. As they headed for the stairs, Rice said to Aiden, "We'll try and make it back tonight, but more likely we won't get in until early morning."

Aiden nodded his head in reply, and the three men left.

"Why don't you men get some sleep, everything's on hold for now," Aiden said, to the crew of the Aerospatiale. Pointing to the door at the other end of the room, he added, "There are bunks and showers through that door, and a kitchen that Russo said is well-stocked, so make yourselves at home."

"Good idea, I could use a nap," Gunter said, picking up his canvas duffel bag and heading toward the door.

"I could use a sandwich and a nap," Wright said, as he picked up his bag, and headed off after Gunter.

"I'll be leaving shortly," Aiden advised them, before they left the room, "but Patrice should be back before I leave. I don't anticipate needing you guys anytime soon, but if we have an emergency, he'll let you know."

When they were gone, Aiden leaned back in his chair, and propped his feet on the table. He thought about how agitated Jeremy had been. Since, he'd worked with him on several occasions, he knew that this was not normally how he acted. It was Jeremy's concern for Alanna that was causing the problem. Aiden knew that if Jeremy didn't get control of his emotions, and soon, he ran the risk of being the one to expose her. He'd meant to say something to Jeremy, even though he knew his advice would not be appreciated, but, with all the activity and people in the room, he'd never gotten the chance.

Aiden heard the door upstairs open, footsteps on the hall and then the familiar signal on the trap door.

"It's me. Patrice." He heard the visitor say, and he went to let him in.

* * *

Francois was not the only one worried about Rakeland's status; Rakeland was beginning to worry about it too. It was only a subtle change in the way the people tailing him were now going about their business, but to an expert like Rakeland, it said a serious change had taken place in the Agency's perception of him. It said, they suspected him big time, and had turned the matter over to the FBI for closure. He was in deep shit!

It was time for Rakeland to make a big decision about his future, a decision that did not require a lot of mulling over. It was time to leave. But, before he did, he needed to make one more score, one that would ensure him a secure retirement, one that would keep his Swiss bank account in the six figures, at the very least. It looked like Francois and Operation SABRE were a dead deal, but there was a lot of other information that he had access to that would take care of his problem.

Tonight, he would get that information, and tomorrow, he'd be out of here. That Russian dacha was looking better all the time.

* * *

"Did you know, Alanna, that many of the great artists came to Honfluer to paint, because they considered the light here to be perfect?" Francois asked, between mouthfuls of his seafood salad.

They were having lunch at an outdoor cafe on the harbor, and taking in a spectacular view of the village of Honfluer.

"I think the beauty of the village was as much an incentive for them to come here and paint as was the light, Francois." Alanna replied, thinking what a charming, romantic place this was, and how wasted its enchantment was on them.

Francois put down his fork, looked out over the harbor, and, for a moment, said nothing. Then, turning his attention back to her, he said, "Alanna, I want to again apologize for the rudeness of my Arab friends."

"I've already forgotten it, Francois," Alanna lied, but sweetly. "So please don't give the matter another thought."

Alanna kept on with her lunch, but Francois obviously had no more appetite for his. Instead, he again lapsed into a momentary, thoughtful silence. When he emerged from it this time, his tone was serious.

"Alanna, I know that in being in the horse business you are used to dealing with a lot of different personalities," he began, and she responded with a nod of her head, and an agreeing smile.

"I am not sure how well you are apprised of my business dealings," he continued, somewhat nervously, "but they are vast and varied, as are the people I deal with.

Here, he again paused, reluctant to go on, contemplating her reaction to what he was about to say. But feeling, out of love for her, the necessity to clarify his situation, he proceeded.

"Alanna, if you agree to be my wife, as I hope you will, then I want you to know all there is to know about me," Francois said, his voice almost hoarse from the nervousness he was feeling.

Oh, no, Alanna thought, as she put down her fork and looked him straight in the eye, hoping he was not about to bare his soul and force her to make a choice that would, to save her good girl image, include leaving the chateau.

He could see he had her full attention, and refused to allow the voice inside him that shouted caution to be heard. Instead, he pressed on.

"Alanna, my Arab friends might not be the only ones concerned about your loyalty to me if we are married," he said, trying to make his point without elaborating too much, but he was finding the words to do that difficult. "There will be others I deal with who will expect the woman I marry to be one 100 per cent behind me, no matter what I do."

Careful, Alanna, she cautioned herself, he's on a slippery slope to a full blown confession, and once you know the truth, you're hooked or dead. End this now!

"Dear Francois," she said, interrupting him with a gentle smile, and understanding tone to her voice. "I appreciate your wanting to be honest in our relationship, that is so rare these days that it makes me admire you all the more, but whatever, it is that you want me to know about you, I think it should wait. I would feel most uncomfortable knowing very personal things about you. I'm not saying our relationship won't work out, but if for some unforeseen reason it doesn't... Well, I hope you can understand, until our relationship is further along, baring your soul to me is more responsibility than I want."

The relief on Francois' face was plainly visible, which was supported by the tone of his reply. "I am sorry, Alanna. I am under such pressure lately, and I am so afraid that I will lose you, that I have lost my better judgment. Thank you for restoring me to my senses."

"I understand, Francois," she said, taking his hand in hers and squeezing it in a comforting manner. Then changing the subject, to relieve the tension, she suggested, "Why don't we finish our lunch. I could spent the rest of my life here, this place is so lovely, but I do need to get back to the sales grounds, and you have a ball to get ready for."

"I love you, Alanna," he said, almost with tears in his eyes. "You're the best thing that has ever happened to me. I am truly blessed.'

I think not, she thought.

The drive back to the sales pavilion was a quiet one. Francois sat in sullen silence, obviously regretting his decision to confide in her, especially since she had rejected his attempt to do so. It had been a bizarre turn of events that no one had anticipated. Alanna hoped it would not create a wedge between her and Francois that would undermine the mission.

Hoping to shake Francois out of his doldrums, Alanna changed the subject to something she thought might be of interest to him.

She opened her catalogue, and indicating a particular pedigree to him, said, "Francois, I was hoping you would have time to look at this filly that comes up for sale this afternoon. She has a pedigree that I think would eventually cross beautifully with the Sun Star colt's."

"Let me see," he said, reaching for her catalogue. She handed it to him, and after a moment's consideration, his enthusiasm was renewed, and he asked, "Have you had a chance to look at her? What do you think she can be bought for?"

"Yes, I have. She's put together beautifully, with a really attractive head, and a good athletic way of moving. Her only drawback is she is on the small side, but that's because her family tends to be small," Alanna replied. "Her being small will discourage some buyers, so I'd say about 300,000 euros should buy her."

"Well, then," Francois said, "since I cannot be there to bid on her, would you do so for me. I will call the sales office, and advise them that you will be bidding on my behalf."

"Of course, Francois, I'd be happy to," Alanna said, as the limousine pulled in front of the entrance to the sales grounds, and the driver came around to open the door for her.

"Good. Then, until this evening, au revoir," Francois said, giving her a gentle farewell kiss on the cheek.

Turning to face him after she had stepped out of the car, she said, "I'll call you, and let you know if I succeed in getting the filly."

"Bonne chance, cherie!" Francois said, smiling, and then he signaled the driver to be off.

Alanna found Jeremy in the cafe below the sales pavilion, slouched in his seat, sipping on a glass of wine, and making incomprehensible doodles on a blank page of his catalogue.

"Interesting!" she said, as she sat down across from him, and turned his catalogue so that she could see his handiwork up close. "I'd be interested to know how a psychiatrist would interpret this artwork. It might give me some insight into how that muddled brain of yours works."

"You don't need a shrink to tell you what's on my mind," he replied, looking her in the eye, while leaning forward, and reaching across the table to retrieve his catalogue. "At least not where you're concerned."

"How true," she said. "That is one aspect of your psyche that is an open book. In fact, it's been read by so many people that it's almost a best seller."

"How discouraging," Jeremy replied, somewhat sarcastically, "and here I thought I'd been doing a pretty good job the last two days of playing the eunuch in your company."

"Oh, you have done a good job," she said, teasingly. "Why, you've even got me convinced that you're not interested in me anymore."

Jeremy did not respond to her reply. Instead, he took his wallet out of the inside pocket of his sport coat, removed several euros from it, and set them on the check the waiter had left on the table. Then, he picked up his catalogue, and while rising from his seat, said, "Come on, let's make like tourists. I've got things to tell you."

Alanna followed him out, and when they reached the front of the sales grounds, Jeremy had her pose in front of the entrance while he took her picture with a camera loaded with a special film created by the Agency's Technical Services. Film, whose individual frames the photographer could code with a click of a button to either be developed or not. In turn, she took one of him.

After pulling a tourist map of the city from his pocket, and their mulling over its contents, they headed up the narrow brick sidewalk lined with cars and horse vans towards the center of town. To any observer, their actions reflected those of the average tourist. They stopped to admire the gardens of the well-kept houses along their way, taking a picture in front of one of them. If, by chance, they were overheard, their conversation was as banal as were their actions.

Two blocks from the sales grounds, they came upon an old Catholic church.

"I'd like to stop in here for a moment," Alanna said, as she headed for the church's massive dark wooden doors. Before she entered the church, she removed a decorative lace handkerchief from the breast pocket of her pale blue, linen shirt and placed it on her head.

She held the door open as she waited for Jeremy, who had lagged behind her, to join her. He had been raised as an Episcopalian, but it had been many years since he'd seen the inside of a church for any reason other than to use it as a rendezvous point. He stepped inside. The door shut behind him with a resounding thud that echoed throughout the church's tomb-like interior. The only light came from the sunlight streaming in through its large stained glass windows.

This time Alanna did not wait for Jeremy. She walked slowly up the aisle. Midway up it, she genuflected before the altar, and slid into one of the pews. She knelt and bent her head in prayer.

It was an ancient church, and when a shaft of shifting sunlight suddenly penetrated its dark, musty solitude, Jeremy experienced a moment of deja vu. As the sun broke through one of the side stained glass windows, its beam of light fell hauntingly on the figure of Alanna kneeling in prayer. She turned at that moment to motion him to her side, and, for a split second, she looked like the angelic vision he'd seen just before he'd passed out after being wounded in combat. He shivered, but not because he was cold.

A second later, the shaft of light was gone, and only Alanna, again urging Jeremy with a gesture of her hand to join him, was left.

Jeremy walked up the aisle, slid into the pew and sat down beside her.

"You look terrible," she said, to him in a whisper.

"Churches and I don't mix," he said.

Taking the hint, Alanna changed the subject. "This is as good as any place for us to talk. I doubt that they have this place bugged. What did Granton have to say? Has Aiden got everything under control? What about Rakeland?"

"Things are proceeding as is usually the case in this business — a big SNAFU. You know, situation normal all fucked up." Realizing what he'd said in this holy place of worship, he looked quickly to the altar as though he expected a bolt of lightning to strike him dead, and he added, "Sorry, Lord, for the heathen slip of the tongue."

Alanna smiled wryly at his apology, and then commented on his earlier statement. "Well, that's not encouraging. What's happened?"

"I was just fooling," Jeremy said, recanting his original appraisal of the situation. "We've had a few things get muddled, but Aiden and Bill have them under control, and are ready to carry out their end of this. If you need to get any messages out, you need to use Aiden. He's the only one free to come and go from this place now with no questions asked."

Jeremy had changed his mind about telling her about the helicopters, because the problem really was of no concern to her. She had enough things of her own to worry about.

He reached into his pocket and held out a vitamin-sized capsule to her.

"Aiden said to swallow this tonight after the ball." Jeremy instructed her. "It's a transmitter. He's afraid that, when they're ready to come in to get us if we get separated, and there's trouble, he won't be able to find us fast enough. He wants some way to pinpoint us in a hurry, and he says this will do the trick. It's not an Agency issue, but something he and Dar came up with, and used on occasion when they worked together.

"As for the objective, Granton said that if our source's information is correct, the bomb should be delivered some time this afternoon. We'll

361

know for sure it's there if Kamal's men instead of Francois' are manning the guard stations when we return to the chateau."

"So that's why Francois wanted us out of the way this afternoon," Alanna said. "Taking care of the preparations for tonight's ball is just a cover, so that he can be there when it arrives.

"And Rakeland?" She asked "What's the word on him?"

"They baited him and he bit, so they know he's the man," Jeremy replied, hesitating a moment before telling her the rest. "And in digging deeper, they are fairly certain he's the one who blew the Balkans mission as well. That means he knows who I am."

"Oh, Lord!" she said, dejectedly. "So... Have they grabbed him yet?"

"No. They've had to turn the matter over to the FBI for closure," he said, and she sensed the feeling he was not at all pleased at this development. "It's been the law ever since that fiasco the Agency had with Anderson. I'm sure you heard about that mess even out in the boon docks of Kentucky."

"I did," Alanna replied. Then with a genuine sense of foreboding in her voice, she added. "But, what if they slip up. With him on the loose, there are no assurances that he can't still compromise this mission and us."

"True, but it's too late to worry about it now. We can't dwell on it. We just have to do what we came here to do, and then haul ass out of here," Jeremy said. Adding in a very serious tone, "And I do mean haul ass, Alanna. If Francois ever finds out the truth about you... God! I don't even want to think about what he'd do to you. So, don't take any chances, and don't wait for me, or anyone else that's left in there. Get yourself out and way clear of that place. Do you understand me?"

"Yes."

"Promise me you'll do as I've asked," he said, emphasizing his fear of the possibility by taking hold of both her shoulders, turning her to face him fully, and then gently lifting her chin with one hand so that she was forced to look him in the eye. "No heroics just get out of here. Promise me you'll do it, Alanna. Promise me! I want to hear you say it."

For what seemed like a long time, she didn't reply. Her thoughts went back to her conversation with Francois that afternoon and its implications. Francois had lost control of his emotions because of her, and to a man to whom control meant everything, his losing it added a whole new element of danger to this mission and to her.

As her eyes searched Jeremy's, she was struck by the love and concern so evident in them. She reached up tenderly to touch his face, and said, "I can't promise you that, Jeremy. No matter what the consequences, I could no more leave you than you could leave me."

And then, she kissed him. It was a tender kiss, but lacked the passion Jeremy would have hoped for. He tried to hold her in his arms, but she pulled away.

"That was a kiss for luck, Jeremy, please don't read more into it then that," she said, gently stroking his cheek once more before rising from her seat and leaving.

* * *

The chateau was lit in a festive glow, its reflection danced off the highly polished surfaces of the stream of cars and limousines that carried Francois' guests through his security gate, and to the main entrance.

A recently installed x-ray monitor, hidden in the decorative overhead wrought iron gateway, and the metal grating the vehicles passed over, allowed the guards to check for weapons and explosives without the vehicles' occupants' knowledge. It had not been activated in time to detect the weapons Jeremy had smuggled in on his person during his and Alanna's arrival the previous day. This was due to an electrical blackout that had been conveniently arranged by Agency personnel, and which had disrupted the chateau's electrical system for an hour before and an hour after they had passed through the gate.

As Jeremy entered the ballroom, he surveyed it quickly for signs of anyone he recognized or who might recognize him. It was early and the room was fairly empty, making his job easier. He spotted no one and approached Francois.

"Well, there you are, Mark, finally," Francois said, offering his hand, and, at the same time summoning a waiter with a tray full of champagne to offer Jeremy refreshment. "I was pleased to hear that Alanna succeeded in buying that filly for me, but I am disappointed she is not as yet by my side to help me greet my guests."

"I apologize for being so late, Francois," Jeremy replied, accepting Francois' hand, and after shaking it, helping himself to champagne. "Alanna wanted to have your vet take a second look at the filly before she signed for her. She'd thought she'd seen a bit of swelling on one of her hind legs when she was in the sales ring, but it turned out to be nothing more than ruffled hairs on her leg. After giving 275,000 euros for her, she though she ought to make sure."

"I appreciate that. Alanna is the consummate professional."

How right you are about that, Jeremy thought.

"I understand you were not so lucky," Francois said, referring to Jeremy once again being the under bidder on the high-priced colt of the afternoon."

"I guess I'm just destined to be the bridesmaid in this game," Jeremy replied, as to his and Alanna's well-timed exit from the bidding on the colt. "Alanna says when the one I'm meant to have comes along, I'll get him."

"She is very wise, and a very good judge of value," Francois advised. "I would heed her advice."

"I intend to do just that," Jeremy said. Then making a move to leave and make himself scarce, he added, "Well, Francois, I'll leave you to greet your other guests, and catch up with you later when you're not so busy."

"Enjoy yourself," Francois urged, "There will be many eligible ladies for you to meet here this evening. Wealthy and beautiful ones, I might add. I will see that Phillip introduces you to the more interesting of them."

"That's very considerate of you, Francois." Jeremy said, accompanying his reply with a suitable lecherous grin. "I appreciate your thoughtfulness."

As a couple approached Francois to greet their host, Jeremy slipped away.

* * *

Alanna floated towards Hakeem like a heavenly apparition approaching on silent footsteps. Her white satin and organza gown was exquisite. Its bodice and ballgown sleeves, which she wore off her delicate, fair-skinned shoulders, were frosted with re-embroidered Alencon lace and seeded pearls. The basque bodice was cut low in front and back. Small, pink, silk roses accented the sleeves and the back bow. Her golden hair was piled high with soft curls, which were intertwined with delicate baby's breath and tea roses of a matching pink. She was all a man could imagine elegance, grace and beauty to be.

She glided on feet hidden from view by the length of her gown along the length of the balcony, stopping to inspect each of the famous paintings in turn that hung upon its wall.

He stood in the dark alcove, knowing she could not see him, but sensing that she knew he was there. He was sure of it when she chose to stop, directly across from where he stood, silent, motionless, to admire the Monet hanging there at length, the scent of her perfume, flowery yet intoxicatingly erotic, drifted back to him.

She turned to face him and he emerged from the shadows.

"Allah has blessed you with keen senses, to go along with your fleet feet and strong lungs, Miss Reynolds," Hakeem said, as he stepped into the dimly lit hall. He was an imposing figure dressed in formal attire, a thought that had also struck her that night at the casino. It changed his image completely. "I have been told that you are leaving the day after tomorrow. If that is true, it leaves me little time to change your opinion of me."

"Of what importance could changing my opinion of you be?" she replied.

"It is of considerable importance to me," Hakeem said, as his eyes devoured her. "After all, if you and Francois are to be married, as is his intention I believe, we will be in contact with one another quite frequently. I would prefer you did not view me as an adversary. So, to help improve your opinion of me, I would like to start by apologizing profusely for my actions last night."

She turned away from him without answering, and proceeded on to the next painting. Hakeem followed behind her, keeping a discreet distance, impressed that his presence did not seem to frighten or intimidate her.

Alanna had had to turn away rather than answer him, because the only answers that came to mind, especially after the once over he had given her, would not have improved their relationship. She had come this way to check and see who was manning the guard posts at the bottom of the stairwell leading to the pavilion housing the bomb before she made her appearance in the ballroom, and had not anticipated running into Hakeem. But, if she thought ignoring him would cause him to leave so that she could accomplish this task, she was wrong. He followed behind her like a puppy on its master's heels.

Alanna stopped before a painting by Berthe Maria Pauline Morisot from where she could see that the guards at the bottom of the staircase were indeed now Arabs.

"It is interesting how much she looks like you," Hakeem remarked from behind her of Morisot's painting entitled *Young Woman in a Party Dress*, and which portrayed a beautiful young woman, her blonde hair done in the fashion Alanna's was and wearing an off the shoulder dress much like her own. "You lack only the fine jewel she is wearing around her neck to complete the similarity. I am sure that is an oversight Francois will correct upon your marriage to him."

She had not really looked at the painting, her interest being elsewhere, but when she did turn her attention to it, she saw that he was right. The resemblance to her was uncanny right down to the young woman's startling blue eyes.

"Correct me if I am wrong, and it may only be, in truth, an old wife's tale" Hakeem said, moving to a spot just behind her where she could feel his hot breath on her bare shoulders, "but I believe the young woman in the portrait is Morisot's youngest daughter, who died very young and under quite mysterious circumstances."

"I have no idea if you are correct or not, Hakeem." Alanna replied in a tone that showed she was unflustered by his remark, though the idea and the way he'd presented it were both chilling.

Again she moved on, trying to ignore him as best she could, but by the time she had arrived at the next painting, she found it was hung just beyond where the guards were posted, at the foot of the dark stairway that led to the pavilion.

"Now this is an interesting painting. Don't you agree?" Hakeem said, referring to a Cezanne portrait entitled *Three Skulls*. As he spoke, he put his arm around her waist, and forcefully guided her to a position directly behind the guards, and right in front of the picture. The men stood up in alarm at his action, but a look from him caused them to return without question to their original postings.

"There are many other valuable paintings further up this stairway," he said, drawing her by his hold on her waist farther up into the darkness. "Let me show them to you."

"I think I've seen enough for tonight, thank you." Alanna said, as she attempted, again without the luxury of using her fighting skills, to free herself from his grip. "Francois was expecting me to join him in the receiving line, and I'm quite late already."

Ignoring her, he asked her, in a tone of voice both cold and menacing, "Do you know what is at the top of the stairway, Alanna?"

"One of the pavilions," she replied, while keeping any evidence of her growing apprehension out of her voice.

"Has Francois shown you the interior of any of the pavilions?" He inquired, all the while advancing her toward the door of this one.

"No, we've been too busy," she replied, now completely fascinated by the irony of the situation. The Agency had planned and schemed to get a look at the interior of this room, and here she was approaching its door. The very room she had to infiltrate the following night. The only bad part about this deal was that she was accompanied by a man, whose sole purpose, she suspected, in letting her see inside the room, was wholly dishonorable and undoubtedly dangerous to her health.

"I'm not interested in seeing what's in that room. So, if you don't mind I'd like to leave now," she said, in no uncertain terms. Knowing that relying on her training to infiltrate the room, rather than encouraging this situation any further was the right course of action.

Hakeem removed his hold from around her waist, but when she tried to move around him, and head back down the stairs, he blocked her path with his huge frame.

"I won't hurt you, Alanna, if that's what you're thinking," Hakeem said, in a voice only slightly less cold that the one he'd used previously. "Let me show you the room. The view from it is the most spectacular of all the pavilions, and since you're leaving so soon, I'm sure you won't have another opportunity to see it."

She looked into his hard dark eyes, which she could only now see thanks to the light of the flashlight he had conveniently produced.

"Do I have a choice?" She asked.

"Not really," he replied, as he used the flashlight's beam to enter in a code, find the slot to put his hand in for identification, and the handle to the door of the room.

He pushed the door open, snapped on a light and gestured, with a nod of his head, for her to enter. Once inside, he closed the door and, she saw, reactivated the alarm.

The room was exactly as the artist's renderings had depicted it. Since he had suggested she see the view, she walked across the room's parquet floors to the window. The somewhat primitive, but effective, security system guarding the window was plainly visible from where she stood.

"Did I not tell you that the view was beautiful from here?" Hakeem asked, as he came and stood behind her, and took in the view from over her shoulder.

"I must admit it is," she replied. And, it was. The view of the chateau, its courtyards and the surrounding lawn area, with its reflecting pools and fountains, was magnificent under lights.

Now that Alanna had seen the view, she wondered what other plans Hakeem had for her. She began to wish someone would miss her as they had at the casino, and mount a rescue, but as the minutes passed, the possibility seemed unlikely.

Slipping by him, she moved to the center of the room, and let her eyes wander around it. Why not, he'd provided the opportunity. She made it a point, however, not to let her gaze fall for too long on any one place or thing.

"An odd mix of decors," she said, gesturing around the room with her hand, and calling attention to the fact that half the room was done as a den and trophy room. Its walls, paneled in mahogany, and hung with various wild animal heads and hides, while the other side housed a bank of computers and a safe. The safe.

"This is Francois official office, he runs his empire from here," Hakeem replied, while holding his position at the window.

"And, you are privileged to have the keys to the empire?" She asked, in reference to his knowing the combination of the security system.

"He trusts me to look after his empire."

"I see. Well, now that I've seen the view and where the empire is run from," she replied, "I'd like to leave."

"Don't be in such a rush, Alanna," he said, for the first time using her given name. "It is early. Most of the guests have not yet arrived. Once you get amongst the crowd, I will have little time to visit with you. You excite my curiosity. A strong, intelligent, and I must say opinionated woman like yourself is a rarity among my people, I find that very stimulating"

I hope your curiosity is all I excite and stimulate, she thought, because everything else is off limits.

Hakeem moved from the window to a large, elaborately carved walnut armoire. When he opened its door, she could see that it held a bar.

"Could I offer you something to drink?"

Oh Lord, what an opportunity, she thought. She had already spotted the location in the portrait hanging behind Francois desk from where she had been told the infrared motion detector beam originated, and gotten a sense of the actual distance from the window to the door of the safe. Fifteen or twenty more minutes, and she'd have everything pegged. But, to stay, she knew, was to invite disaster, either from Hakeem or Francois. And what about Kamal? What would he think of this arrangement?

"You're very kind to offer, but no thank you," she replied, declining the drink gracefully. "If talking is what your interested in, I'll see that we have time to do that tomorrow. In the mean time, I would like to leave.

To emphasize her point, Alanna started for the door. Hakeem intercepted her just as she arrived at it. He reached out for her arm to stop her, and that is when she decided enough was enough. She blocked his grasping hand by reaching out and taking hold of his arm at a point where exerting pressure brought about a searing, mind-numbing pain. She did it so quickly that he had no time to react. He cried out and crumbled to his knees from the pain. She had held her grip on his arm for only a second, but the move was so effective that even that brief time was enough for her to make her point. In addition, it was such an innocuous move that one could have thought it an accident, rather than an exhibition of her skills.

"Sorry!" she said, pretending to be surprised at his reaction, but remaining alert and prepared for any further action she might need to take if he turned hostile. "I must have grabbed you the wrong way."

His immediate reaction had been to rub the area of his arm she had grabbed. When he finally made eye contact with her, the deadly cold look he normally wore was twice as icy. Then, he kind of blew himself up to his full height in front of her, and she thought she was going to have to resort to stronger measures. Instead, after a few seconds had passed, he simply said, "I think you should be getting back to your friends."

With that, he turned his back to her to shield the security systems combination pad while he entered in the code, and after having his hand print identified, opened the door, and let her walk to freedom.

* * *

Jeremy anxiously watched the balcony for any sign of Alanna. When he'd left her at the door to her room, she had said she would be down in about an hour. It was well beyond that now, and still she was nowhere to be seen. He was not alone in his concern, for he'd noticed Francois glancing at the balcony staircase frequently as well. Aiden had arrived about 15 minutes ago, and now both men stood in conversation where Jeremy could scan the balcony without being obvious.

"I'm going to go see what's keeping her," Jeremy said.

"Give her a little more time," Aiden advised. "Women always take longer to dress than they say they will."

Jeremy was about to argue the point when Phillip showed up with a beautiful auburn haired woman on his arm.

"Monsieurs," Phillip said, as he and the woman joined them. "May I have the honor of presenting Mademoiselle Isabella Cassini. Mademoiselle Cassini, this is Monsieurs Mark Jergens, who is from America, and Aiden Doyle from Ireland."

The men graciously turned their attention to the woman and greeted her, Aiden going so far as to kiss her hand. Despite this gesture, she immediately made it known it was Jeremy she was interested in.

"I have only had the good fortune to visit America on one occasion, Señor Jergens," she said, in a very sultry Italian accent that labeled her a Neapolitan. "but I was most entranced with the beauty of your country."

The music had begun, and taking a cue from a look Aiden shot him, he asked, "Well, if you allow me the pleasure of your company for this dance, maybe you can tell me about your visit."

"It would be my pleasure, senor," she said, removing her hand from Phillip's arm and taking Jeremy's arm.

As they headed off to the dance floor, Aiden said, "Good work, Phillip. Got any more like her handy?"

"If Monsieur Doyle likes, I think I can arrange a similar match," Phillip replied, with a subtle smile.

"No thanks, Phillip. The hunt is the most intriguing part of the game," Aiden said, indicating with a look the possibilities available to him. "If you don't mind, I'd just as soon find my own quarry."

"I tend to agree with monsieur," Phillip replied. "Good hunting."

Aiden waited for Phillip to disappear into the crowd before he nonchalantly headed for the balcony staircase. As he arrived at the top of the stairs, he heard angry voices coming from down the hall. He recognized them as Hakeem's and Kamal's. Because of his knowledge of Arabic, he was able to decipher what they were saying. It made him quicken his efforts to reach the spot for it was Alanna whom they were arguing over.

Alanna had no sooner escaped Hakeem's grasp, then she'd run into Kamal and his henchmen, Khalil and Mohammed, who gave new meaning to the word cold-blooded. They were as surprised to see her coming out of the pavilion as she was to see them. But the shock was only momentary as Kamal, angry that she had been allowed into the room, ordered her to return to it.

Her refusal to return was supported by Hakeem, who blew off Kamal's outrage and, in Arabic, subtly warned him that by making so much of the event, he was calling undue attention to the importance of the room. In fact, Hakeem informed Kamal that he had taken her there on purpose in order to dispel any curiosity she might have as to the room's contents. He did nothing wrong, he claimed, and she saw nothing out of the ordinary, so Kamal's outrageous behavior was unwarranted.

Before the action could get any hotter, Aiden showed up at the bottom of the pavilion's stairwell.

"Alanna," he said, and the commotion at the top of the stairs ceased immediately. Though he'd understood every word, he continued as though he had heard nothing out of the ordinary, "Francois is looking for you. If you can tear yourself away from the company of those gentlemen, I'm sure he would appreciate your presence in the receiving line."

Before Alanna could respond, Hakeem took her by the arm, and pushing his way through Kamal and his men, cleared a path for her to leave. Once through, she did not stop to thank him, but hurried to join Aiden at the foot of the stairs.

"What was that all about?" Aiden asked, as they headed down the hall and to the main staircase.

"I honestly don't know, Aiden," Alanna replied, unflustered but obviously confused. "Hakeem all but dragged me into that room, made a half-hearted pass at me, then got me out of what could have been a real hairy situation with Kamal and his merry men. I'm sure he did it to save his own skin more than to save mine, because Kamal was furious with him. But, whatever his reason, it got me out of there. Your showing up when you did didn't hurt things either."

"Well," Aiden said, as they descended the stairs. "I wasn't kidding about Francois being annoyed about you not being in that receiving line, so may I suggest you get your beautiful self over there in a hurry."

His remark stopped Alanna dead in her tracks. It wasn't so much what he'd said as how he'd said it. He stopped and turned to her. She seemed surprised. He smiled and said, "I know your going to be tied up for a while with his majesty, but when you get free, save a dance for me. I seem to remember the last one as being a very pleasant experience."

* * *

The retreating pair had barely rounded the corner when Mohammed, furious at the shoving he had received from Hakeem, rushed at him. Before he could strike a blow, Hakeem had pinned him to the stairwell's stone wall, the razor sharp blade of his lightning-fast drawn knife poking into the tender part of Mohammed's neck.

"Never... lay a hand on me!" Hakeem hissed, into Mohammed's startled face.

"That's enough, Hakeem," Kamal said, from behind him, while barring Khalil with an outstretched arm from aiding his comrade. "I will not have dissension in the ranks."

The knife remained at Mohammed's throat, while Hakeem turned to Kamal and said, "Do not question my motives, Kamal. My reasoning, as always, is sound."

With the conclusion of that statement, Hakeem removed the blade from Mohammed's throat, shoved him in the direction of the other two men, and, without looking back, disappeared down the stairs.

"Should I go after him, Kamal?" Khalil asked, drawing his gun and starting after Hakeem.

"No, Khalil," Kamal said, the anger no longer in his voice. "Let the randy goat go."

And, he laughed out loud at the thought.

* * *

Even though Francois had been busy playing host, he had not failed to notice Alanna's continued absence.

Earlier, he'd had Phillip check her room. She had gone, and no trace of her could be found. The result was that a small fear began to nag him.

Francois was about to have Philip take over his duties, and go look for her himself, when he saw her standing at the far end of the room.

"Will you excuse me," he said, to the couple with whom he had been engaged in conversation, and after motioning to Phillip to take over greeting the new arrivals, he made his way to her.

"How truly beautiful you are!" He said, as she stopped, wearing one of her most alluring smiles as a greeting, in front of him.

"Thank, you, Francois," she replied, graciously. "You look very... How do you French say, soigné?... yourself."

Quickly, she added, "I do apologize for being so late. There has been so little time to view the paintings since my arrival that I thought I would view a few of them on my way down. It is such an extraordinary collection that time slipped away without me noticing. I hope you'll forgive me?"

"Of course," he said, offering her arm, which she accepted. "Come spend a few minutes with me in welcoming my guests, and then we will dance. I cannot wait for my guest to see how lovely you are, and what a lucky man I am."

* * *

Jeremy escorted Isabella back to the group of people she had indicated she'd come with, leaving her with the promise of another dance later. He helped himself to a glass of champagne from off a tray a waiter carried passed him, then found himself a break in the crowd of onlookers along the dance floor from where he could watch Francois and Alanna as they circled the floor.

Her face was alive with color, full of life as she whirled, skimming across the floor as if on air. A far cry from the deadly pale look she'd worn in the flashback of the Balkans incident that he'd had during his ride back to the sales grounds with Patrice this afternoon.

It had come on again, as they were driving along through the peaceful countryside, suddenly, like so many of the flashbacks he had of Vietnam.

First had come the terror that he'd felt when he'd first discovered she was no longer following him as they tried to make their escape back to the extraction point. Then, the helplessness he'd felt when searching through the darkness, calling to her, only as loud as he dared, and hearing no reply. The anguish he'd felt when he, finally, out of sheer luck, had stumbled over her unconscious, bleeding body. How, for days, as she'd lay in that hospital bed, unconscious, fighting for her life, Jake and he agonizing over whether she would survive or not.

But, most vivid was the feeling of overwhelming loss when he'd realized he could not have lost her anymore surely if she had died than he had when she came to and he'd seen the loathing in her eyes.

The pain resulting from that knowledge was so wrenching that he had almost taken his own life. It was Jake who had made him see the futility of taking that course of action, as he had so many times in the past, when he was about to make a rash decision.

Jake had said "give her time, she'll come around."

Returning to the present, he thought, well, Jake, you were almost right, she almost came around, I had my chance to make it work and I blew it. Maybe she's right; maybe I should just let go. Nah! No way. Not possible. The word quit was not in his vocabulary, and most especially where she was concerned.

Jeremy took another sip of his champagne, and was entertaining the possibility of cutting in on Francois, when he noticed Aiden headed his way.

Aiden swiped a glass of champagne off a passing tray, and joined Jeremy.

"She finally turned up," Jeremy said, indicating Alanna coming into the room with a nod of his head.

"I know," Aiden replied, "but under unusual circumstances."

Jeremy turned his attention back to his associate, and shot him a look of surprise.

"How so?" He asked.

"What do you know about Hakeem?" Aiden asked.

"He's the badest of the bad asses in that bunch. He'd take his own mother out, if she got in his way. Why do you ask?"

"He bears serious watching," Aiden replied. "Alanna said that he waylaid her while she was checking on whether there had been a change of guards at the bottom of the pavilion staircase. Which, by the way, there was, so it's here. Then, she said, he all but dragged her into the pavilion. She managed to have a quick look around, but she decided to get out of there before Hakeem proceeded to carry out whatever his real intentions were, and she'd have to blow her cover to save her hide."

"Are you serious?"

"Damn right, I'm serious!" Aiden replied, under his breath, but emphatically. When I finally located her, she had just managed to get away. As we were leaving, we could hear Hakeem having a hell of a row with Kamal over the matter.

"What was interesting, was that he wasn't taking any guff over his actions from Kamal. Alanna said that Hakeem had the combination and clearance to enter that room. That he bragged that Francois trusted him to watch over his empire. We could be seeing a switch of loyalties in the progress here. Whatever this new relationship with Francois entails, the bottom line is that for some reason Hakeem is fixated on Alanna. Whether that's because he's got the hots for her, or because he's baiting her, remains to be seen. "Whatever his interest, his constantly watching her leaves her very vulnerable. Unfortunately, we've only got a few hours until this operation is a go, so I don't see that there is anything we can do about it."

"Hell," was all Jeremy could say in response.

Aiden had just turned his attention back to Alanna, when he noticed Phillip approach Francois on the dance floor.

"Well, that's enough business for the moment," he said. "Alanna's promised me a dance and this looks like the perfect time to claim it."

Before Jeremy could respond, Aiden was headed in her direction.

As he made his way through the crowd, Aiden thought that the trouble with being in the business of espionage, spying in general, was that you were never sure if you were the hunter or the hunted. Ironically, as in this instance, often you were both. You doubled the intrigue, when one of your own, such as Rakeland, is out to get you. It was a classic case of paranoia personified.

Aiden reached the couple just as Francois was about to escort Alanna off the dance floor. The band had begun playing another waltz, and as he came up to them, he said, "Mind if I have this dance with Alanna, Francois?"

Francois responded to Aiden's request by smiling and relinquishing Alanna's hand to him. "Please do, Aiden, I have to take an important call."

As Francois and Phillip left Alanna and Aiden, and made their way to the library, Francois asked, "Who is the call from, Phillip, that you found it so important to interrupt me?

"Rakeland, monsieur."

Chapter 25

Rakeland looked nervously first to his left, and then to his right. As he did so, he passed the phone receiver from one ear to the other.

"Hurry up, damn it! He said, under his breath, to the emptiness at the other end of his connection.

Again, he looked around. In the midst of his turn to the right, he suddenly heard a click, and realized he had been disconnected. Quickly, he replaced the call — line busy. He tried the alternate number he'd been given with the same results. He alternated between the two, hoping that it was just a normal busy problem and not a sign that Francois' secure lines had been breached by the Agency. But that was the inevitable conclusion Rakeland came to when all his efforts to re-establish his connection failed. It was an irony not lost on him, since tapping phones had been his specialty, and it was his comrades, or should he say his former comrades, who, presumably, were now intercepting his call.

He stood a moment longer in front of the pay phone, as if trying to decide whether to make another call. It was obvious to him now that he had little choice other than to run, but the watchers were watching him, and he had to use great care. Whoever they were, FBI, Agency Security, they must not have gotten the official word to pick him up.

Though he knew that after what had transpired less than an hour ago, they soon would. They would not be suspicious about him leaving his office so late. He had made a habit of working overtime, so as to establish that as a normal pattern of behavior. The most important thing now was not to move fast, not to do anything stupid, and panic them into thinking that he was running and arresting him, which he knew they had the authority to do.

Slowly, he walked away from the phone, even stopping nonchalantly to buy a paper at the all-night newsstand. He knew trying to duck out on the watchers here was impossible. The time he'd spent at the pay phone had given them more than enough opportunity to cover every avenue of escape. He needed to keep his cool a while longer. At least, until he could maneuver them into following him somewhere where even with the manpower they had relegated to his tail, they would find themselves spread thin, and give him the out he was looking for.

Ever since he'd known for sure that the Agency was onto him, Rakeland had been smuggling out extra clothing in his laundry. The laundry man, his contact with Francois, had them packed and ready to go in a locker at the bus terminal. He'd also begun wearing a money belt containing $10,000 in large bills. He had tickets to Paris on three different airlines, and a set of fake travel papers he'd had made in Hong Kong, which included passports, visas to three different countries, credit cards and drivers licenses, all in fake names.

Just last week, he had mailed the keys from his Swiss bank's safe deposit box that he'd had duplicated to different postal boxes in Paris, which he'd had the presence of mind to open last year in the phony names on his passports.

What Rakeland didn't have was a briefcase full of secrets to sell. That plan had gone awry when he had been discovered while hacking his way through the Agency's top secret computer files. When he'd realized he'd been discovered, he'd quickly signed off the computer using the code that had allowed him to breach its security. A code that belonged to a staffer authorized to access that area, and whose use, he hoped, would confuse Security. Then, he quietly left the building.

He had, however, come away with one gem, or should he say "Jewel." On a hunch, he had been cruising through the files that contained reports on just completed training exercises of covert agents. Low and behold, what had he found? Operation SABRE. Not dead at all, but very much alive and running. And there **she** was, the mysterious one, the one that there were only rumors in the halls about, the one he'd heard about for years, but never seen, the most precious JEWEL in the Agency's CROWN — code name CHAMELEON.

She was Carter's replacement.

Five years ago, there had been a rumor that she had left the Agency, but obviously that was untrue, and now she was somewhere in France about to make her move, a move that, if it proved successful, would cost Francois, and him, a bundle.

The big question was, how could he turn this fortuitous discovery into big bucks if he didn't know where she was, what she looked like, or when, and how she would strike? There had been no answers to these questions anywhere in the file, and he had no time to search further.

His only hope was to bluff Francois into thinking he knew, then get to the chateau where it might be possible for him to flush her out. That was just one more reason he needed to rid himself of his tails, and leave this place. It excited him to think that his final act of treason, the final blow he would inflict on the Agency would be to take out, preferably with his own hands, their most valuable asset — CHAMELEON.

* * *

Jeremy was about to find a dance partner when he saw Aiden signal with his head for him to follow Francois and Phillip.

He did so careful to keep his distance, and an eye out for anyone who might suspect his intensions. He arrived at the door to the library just as Francois picked up the receiver, and felt his heart sink when he caught an earful of Francois and Phillip's conversation.

"You are sure it was Rakeland?" Francois asked his assistant as he kept trying to re-establish contact with his caller.

"Oui, monsieur," Phillip replied. "He identified himself clearly, and was still on the line when I went to get you."

"Well, something must have caused the phone to disconnect. I will wait for a few minutes, and see if he calls back."

It was at that moment, that the pager attached to Jeremy's belt began to pulse. He quickly reached for it. A message was scrolling repeatedly across its liquid crystal screen.

It said, "Fire in kitchen. Call immediately."

To Jeremy the "ops immediate" message meant one thing — their cover had been blown.

* * *

With the "ops immediate" message having been sent, Granton could do little more than sit back and wait for his now vulnerable operatives to make contact and assure him that they were all right.

Things had happened fast since the chief of security, Karl, had awakened him. The young man, John Tracher, whose code Rakeland had used to access the Agency's top-secret computer files, had accompanied Karl.

The only break that they had had so far in this mess was that Rakeland had assumed that the person assigned that code would be home in bed at this hour. Fortunately for the Agency, Tracher, who was returning from a visit with his family, and had arrived at Reagan International Airport just a couple hours before, had decided to head straight to the office, and catch up on some work instead of heading home. A workaholic, he'd felt guilty about having taken the extra time off, and, since he was wide awake, he'd decided to make up for lost time.

When Tracher went to log on, he saw that his code had already been entered. Using an alternate code that he'd been issued as a security precaution to log on, he was able to identify which file had been accessed using his original code. He could also tell that whoever was perusing the file knew he'd been discovered, for the intruder had quickly gone off line. Realizing the seriousness of the situation, Tracher immediately notified security.

About a half hour after Tracher's discovery, Granton had received an "ops immediate" message from Paris saying that their man, Patrice, while running a tap on the chateau's phone system, had intercepted and interrupted a call from Rakeland to Francois. They said that Patrice did not want to run the risk of Francois discovering the tap, so he was not able to disrupt service on the line for any length of time. The best he could do was to monitor each call, and terminate any conversations that endangered the mission.

Granton realized that this was no guarantee that Rakeland could still not make contact. Although if he had other means, it was unlikely Rakeland would have risked using the public phone system. Still, Granton could assume nothing.

"Did you get word to the F.B.I. to haul Rakeland's ass in?" Granton asked Karl from behind the door of his private bathroom, where he was changing into his work clothes.

"The minute Tracher let me know what was going on," Karl replied. "They said they'd pass the word on to the people tailing him, and get back to us when they had him in custody."

"Use my phone to give them a call and light a fire under them. If he gets away, our people are dead."

* * *

With no one to leave in his place, Jeremy had to decide whether to continue monitoring Francois and Phillip's activities, or break the news to Alanna and Aiden. He opted in favor of the later, figuring that if anything further developed with Rakeland, headquarters would keep him abreast of the situation via his pager. It was more important he get back to his partners, and decide with them how the situation should be handled.

Aiden was waiting for him along the far wall of the ballroom next to one of the large glass doors that opened out onto a flagstone patio. Meanwhile, Alanna was now dancing in the arms of a distinguished looking gentleman in a military dress uniform, one Jeremy recognized, that was from Spain.

When Aiden saw Jeremy reenter the room, he walked out onto the patio. Jeremy made his way around the edge of the dance floor to the patio side of the room, and, after making sure no one was paying any attention to him, exited through one of the opened doors. He walked over to a far corner of the patio, and motioned for Aiden to follow him.

"We're exposed," he said, quietly, when Aiden reached him.

"How badly?" Aiden replied.

"I'm not sure." Jeremy said, while keeping an eye out over Aiden's shoulder for Francois or Kamal's men. "You need to get back to the farmhouse, and contact headquarters and assess the damage. We know the package is here, what we don't know is if it's still a viable option to finish this job, and get out with our scalps in place."

"Where's Francois?"

"When I left, he was still in his office. It sounded as though Patrice was able to interrupt the call, but that doesn't mean Rakeland can't get the word through some other way."

"I think we should do this thing tonight," Aiden said. "Do it and get out of here."

"Can we still pull it off as planned?"

"When did anything ever go down as planned in this business?" he replied, sarcastically. "The last I heard, Rice and Clark had not made it back with the chopper, but that's the least of our worries. If we go tonight, you and Alanna will just have to get out of here the best way you can. Russo, Patrice and I can handle the outside diversion, and we'll do our best to help get you out. What are you going to do in here to keep them busy while she goes in?"

"I'll think of something," Jeremy replied. "This is all moot talk since whether or not we go ahead with this is her decision."

Aiden nodded in agreement, then said. "Well, I'm out of here. I'll get word to you as quickly as I can on the damage. Signal me if it's a go."

With that, he turned and headed back into the chateau.

Jeremy was about to do the same, when he saw the glow from a cigarette deep in the shadows at the far end of the patio. As he started for the door he'd come out of, Hakeem came out of the darkness.

"Are you having a pleasant evening, Mr. Jergens?"

Jeremy knew that Hakeem had been too far away to have heard anything, and his talking to Aiden should not have caused suspicion, but one never knew what conclusions an adversary might draw under these circumstance.

"I am, indeed. And you?" He replied.

"I am not the social type," Hakeem said, as he reached Jeremy's position just outside the glass door. "But, I have found certain people of particular interest this evening."

For a moment they stood facing one another, neither saying a word.

Then, Hakeem said, "Well, I'll leave you to enjoy the rest of the party."

They nodded to one another, and Hakeem disappeared into the crowd inside.

Jeremy shook off the bad feelings left by the cold look Hakeem had given him, and headed into the ballroom. There, he saw that Alanna was dancing with an Asian man, who was not much taller than she was. He made his way though the dancers to a place where he could intercept them.

"Would you mind if I cut in?" Jeremy said politely to her partner. The Asian bowed and smiled, and relinquished Alanna's hand to him.

"Before I give you the bad news," Jeremy said, taking her in his arms and waltzing off with her, "I'd like to say you look wonderful."

"Thank you. Are we blown?" was her reply.

"I believe so," Jeremy said, unhappily, as he looked into her eyes. "Aiden's gone to do a damage assessment, but we know that Rakeland made an attempt to contact Francois, and headquarters just ran up the red flag on my pager."

She did not respond for a moment. Then she said, "Can Aiden be ready to go with this job tonight?"

"Yes."

"Then, if they don't come and get us, and throw us in those dungeons below anytime soon, we go in."

"Are you sure?"

"I'm sure," she said. Then, breaking the tension with a smile, she added. "In the meantime, hold me close. My knees are shaking."

"With pleasure," he replied, returning her smile and drawing her closer to him, "but only if you return the gesture — mine are shaking too!"

* * *

"Whatever he wanted, it couldn't have been very important," Francois said, rising from the seat he had taken at his desk, while waiting for Rakeland to call. "Otherwise, he would have called back."

"That is probably true," Philip replied, in agreement. "Monsieur Rakeland has been very useful in the past, but since that man Anderson was caught spying for the Soviets, he has become very erratic. He would be wise to get out before he is discovered."

381

"I would not be surprised if he is not already under suspicion," said Kamal, from his position at the entrance of the library.

"Sorry, for the intrusion," he said, as he came further into the room, closing the door behind him, "But, I could not help overhearing your conversation. Do you always make a practice out of leaving your door ajar when you discuss such matters?"

"Did you notice anyone other than yourself eavesdropping on our conversation, Kamal?" Francois replied, the irritation at the implication Kamal was making clearly present in his voice.

"No, I did not, but then I just happened by this way," Kamal said, in response. "It is hard to say who might have been privileged to your conversation before I arrived."

"Your are right, Kamal." Francois conceded the wisdom in the other man's observation. "Rakeland called, but before I could get back to the phone to speak with him, he either hung up, or was disconnected. We have no idea why he called, and he has not attempted, as far as we know, to repeat his call. So, I have decided to return to my guests. If what he has to say is important, I am sure he will call back."

"Before you go, Francois, did Miss Reynolds say anything to you about being in the pavilion this evening?"

Francois appeared stunned by the revelation.

"The one..."

Before Francois could finish, Kamal nodded in the affirmative.

"No she didn't. But, how could that be?"

"Humph!" Kamal replied, while shaking his head. "Hakeem let her in."

"What?" Francois' initial shock was eclipsed by this pronouncement. Totally confused by the motivation for this out-of-character move on Hakeem's part, he inquired further. "What could have possessed him to do such a thing?'

"I have no idea, Francois. The matter baffles me as it baffles you." Kamal replied. "When I questioned his motivation, he became irate, and claimed I was making too much of the issue, which... maybe I was. After all, if we have no reason to believe your friend is anything other than what she says she is, what harm could it have done?"

Francois did not respond. He could only envision in this mind the many times Hakeem happened to be around where Alanna was. All the instances could, of course, have been coincidental, but then, maybe they were not. He was sure it was not Alanna's fault, for, if anything were true, it was that she seemed to dislike Hakeem.

"It is a curious occurrence," Francois finally remarked. "However, they are both above suspicion, so may I suggest we write what happened off as some eccentricity on Hakeem's part, and forget the matter."

But, from the look in Francois' eyes, Kamal knew Francois would not forget the matter. It had been the perfect opportunity to drive a wedge between this newly formed alliance he feared was developing between Hakeem and Francois, an alliance that strengthened Hakeem's base of support and weakened his. Kamal knew Hakeem had the respect of most, if not all, of the Fundamentalist leaders, but whether he aspired to more than his present status within the organization had never become a topic of discussion between them. Hakeem was an ambitious man, thusly, Kamal concluded, one could assume he did. One thing he could not, nor would not, tolerate in his organization was disloyalty.

If the nuance of this verbal exchange was lost on Francois, it was not lost on Phillip. So, when Kamal suggested he and Francois get back to the ball, Phillip said, "Monsieur, before you leave, may I see you about a matter concerning the brunch tomorrow. I have to place an order early in the morning, and I know you would not want to be disturbed about the matter at such an early hour."

"Certainly, Phillip," Francois replied. Then turning to Kamal, he said, "You go on Kamal. This is nothing but a boring household matter, but I must see to it."

Kamal bowed slightly, and, as he turned to leave, caught Phillip's eye. He held eye contact with the other man long enough to imply he knew the real reason for his delaying François's departure.

If, there was an implied threat in the gesture, Phillip ignored it. Kamal might doubt Hakeem's loyalty, he thought, but Francois need never have any doubts about mine.

By the time Francois got back to the ballroom, Jeremy had relinquished Alanna to the arms of a portly German businessman. He had positioned himself where he would be the first person François encountered on his return.

"Francois!" Jeremy called to him as he came through the archway, and began a search of the area, obviously, looking for Alanna. His face wore a worried expression and when he spoke, he spoke in an anxious tone.

"Mark. Have you seen Alanna?" He asked, walking up to Jeremy, but still allowing his eyes to search the dance floor.

"Yes. She's dancing with the one of your German colleagues... Is something wrong?"

383

"No. No. I am just upset that I have allowed things to interfere with my being with her this evening," he replied, but his tone was not convincing.

"I'm sure she understands that you have other guests to see to. Speaking of which, Aiden said to tell you that he was sorry to have to leave without saying good-by..."

Francois stopped. Turning to Jeremy, he asked, "Did he say why?"

"He received word that his father was not well, and he went to call home."

"Oh. I see. I am sorry to hear that. I hope whatever is troubling his father is not serious," Francois replied, this time the tone of his voice was genuine.

"You must excuse me," he said, as he began walking in the direction of the dance floor. "I must find Alanna."

Alanna saw Francois at the edge of the dance floor. When he spotted her, he made his way through the dancers, while smiling and exchanging congenial words with them in passing.

The man she had been dancing with saw Francois approaching. Bowing in mock deference to him, he allowed Francois to cut in.

As they waltzed off, Alanna could sense a change in him, which she surmised had been brought on by more than the alcohol she smelled on his breath.

"Is something wrong, Francois?" She asked, waiting for him to drop the Rakeland bomb.

Instead, he looked at her, and said, "Tell me about your little excursion into the pavilion with Hakeem."

So, that's what's up your craw, she thought, with relief. She never thought she'd see the day that she'd be covering for Hakeem, but if Hakeem wasn't telling what happened behind closed doors, then neither was she.

"Hakeem was just being sociable," she lied, but in a nonchalant tone, that was meant to convey the triviality of the incident. "I was admiring the paintings on my way down here when we met in the hall not far from one of the pavilions. He asked if you'd had an opportunity to show me the view from them. I told him no. That with both of us being so involved with the horse sale, and my visit this trip being so short, it was a good possibility that I wouldn't have a chance to see it before I left.

"He told me that the view from the pavilion we were standing at the bottom of was particularly nice, especially at night, and he offered to show it to me. I didn't see the harm in going along with him, as he hasn't

384

been anything but a gentleman in the past. He was on this occasion as well," albeit, with a little help from me, she thought.

"The only strange thing about the incident was, that we ran into your partner Kamal and some of his friends as we were leaving. With all the fuss Kamal made over his seeing us leaving the place, you would have thought we'd just stolen all the gold out of Fort Knox."

Then, smiling sweetly, she added, "It did, however, keep me from coming down here and joining you sooner, and I do apologize for that."

The relief at knowing that Kamal's insinuations were unfounded was evident on Francois' face, and in his voice.

"No apology is necessary, Cherie," he said, his improved attitude reflected is his more animated dance steps. "You are in my arms, and that is all that matters."

When the dance ended, they went back to mingling with his guests. As they moved from one group to the other, Alanna waited to put plan "B" into action. On Jake's advice, she always included several well thought out options for each mission. Which one she would chose to use would depend on how the evening's events proceeded.

It was Francois, who eventually made the decision for her. At one point in their circuit of the ballroom, they arrived at the entrance to a small, secluded alcove. He led her into it, and then taking her into his arms, he said, "Alanna, I was hoping that this evening would not end with us parting company as we have in the past."

Alanna was not surprised by what Francois had suggested, in fact, if anything, she'd wondered why she hadn't faced this dilemma of their making love sooner. Yet, she had always harbored the hope that the mission would be finished, and she would be far away from him before his hormones got the better of his chivalry.

Unfortunately, it appeared, that his inebriated state was about to get the better of both his hormones and his chivalry for without waiting for her to reply, he began kissing her. For one tension-filled minute, his kisses became so passionate that she thought he was going to take her right on the spot.

It was then, as she fought to maintain a balance between keeping Francois convinced she was interested in him, and maintaining her dignity, that the awareness sunk in of how easily a mission might be scuttled when you play at seducing the enemy without any intentions of following through with the seduction.

"My goodness, Francois," she said, breathlessly, while managing to loosen his grasp on her, "what if someone walked in on us?"

Karen A. Lynch

"That would be their problem," he said, laughing drunkenly, amused by her concern.

His hand continued to caress her face, it moved downward from there until the back of it slid across the cleavage of her bosom.

"If you find getting caught making love in public objectionable," he said, the liquor making what was supposed to be a romantic overture sound anything but romantic, "then say I may come to your room tonight and make love to you. I promise, that if you agree to do so, you will not be disappointed."

She pulled away from him, eyes lowered, her insides boiling. This was more than she could endure — even for God and country. Every fiber within her urged her to kill the bastard, instead, she turned away from him so he would not see the loathing in her eyes and said, "Please, Francois, I'm just not ready to get involved with you on that level!"

"I am sorry, Alanna, but I am overwhelmed with desire for you," he replied, though his apology had a hollow sound to it. "I have been very patient, because I have a great deal of respect for you, but you must understand, I am a man and I cannot be patient forever. If you are sincerely interested in pursuing this relationship with me, I see no reason why I must…"

He broke off his statement as the meaning of hers became clear.

" Ah," he said, sadly, "I see now how it is, Cherie. He paused, then added wearily, "Some dreams can never be, no matter how we wish them to be real."

"I'm sorry, Francois," she lied.

"Not as sorry as I," he replied, unhappily. Then he offered her his arm, and said, "Well, then, come, let us return to the party. At least we can enjoy the moment."

Before she could make a move to accept his arm, there was a noise in a hallway behind them.

"I'll be right back," he said, as he hurried off to investigate the source of the noise. When he turned his back to her, she reached behind her neck and undid the clasp that secured the chain from which her locket hung. She leaned slightly forward, and the locket fell to the floor. Then she gave it just enough of a kick with her foot to send it sliding off into the shadows.

"I could find nothing," he said, when he returned. "I must be hearing things."

But Alanna knew there had been someone there, but now only the sent of cloves remained.

386

"Come," he said, again offering his arm, which she took and the started toward the ballroom floor. Just as they were about to emerge from the alcove, she pulled up sharply, removing her arm from his.

Francois turned to see that she was standing with her hand at her throat at a point where, just minutes before, she had been wearing the locket.

"I've lost my locket," she said, in a voice that sounded on the verge of tears. "Oh please, Francois, help me find it. It was my mother's. It's all I have to remember her by."

"Of course," he said, and headed back in direction from which they had come. Alanna lagged behind, appearing to search for the locket.

"Here it is," he announced, stooping down and picking it up off the floor, glad for the small face-saving victory.

Smiling, he walked over to her, and handed it to her.

"Thank you, Francois," she said with relief, as she took it from him by the chain, and pretended to examine the clasp for the flaw that had allowed it to slip from her neck.

"The clasp must be broken."

Then, she opened her evening bag, and dropped the locket into the small interior pocket.

"Come, let us get back to my guests," Francois said, and without any argument, she followed him.

Once in the main ballroom, he left her and went to mingle with his friends. Alanna also mingled, dancing with several of the guests. At one point, Jeremy made like he was going to approach her, but a look from her warned him off. Instead, he asked one of the other woman he had been introduced to by Phillip to dance, all the while keeping Alanna in sight. He had not missed the gesture she had made as he'd approached her; the one where she had touched her hand to her now naked neck. He had not missed the wordless message that her gesture, and the missing locket, conveyed. The mission was well and truly on, and the first blow had been struck.

* * *

Rakeland knew he couldn't go home, but he headed in that direction, initially to lull the watchers into believing there was no cause for alarm. He laughed to himself, as he thought about how stupid Anderson was not to have suspected that he and his wife were being watched, and for not knowing when to call it quits and get out.

Rakeland had most of his escape plan laid out for months, now he had the edge. They'd never get him.

He knew that his tails employed multiple cars positioned to intercept him at various points, supposedly not to alert him that he was being followed. Using one of the Agency's more sophisticated eavesdropping tools, he was able to listen in on a conversation between two of the trailers while they were waiting for him to leave the Agency parking lot, and to get the radio frequency they were using to communicate with one another. Now as he tuned in to their conversation, he knew where the next car would intercept him. He had purposely driven this same route so that he could determine how long it took the next car to pick him up.

At one point in the trip, there was a 30 second delay before the next car came on line. It was a short gap, but one he had planned to take advantage of. As he approached that point, he prepared to make his move, sure enough, as he turned the corner, the car that had been behind him continued on straight. The way the surveillance worked, the other car would pick him up at the next corner. But, the next car's view of his oncoming car was blocked by a line of delivery trucks parked on their side of the street. They couldn't see him until he actually passed them.

He watched in his rear view mirror as the car that had been tailing him crossed the intersection, and disappeared from view. At that point, he was halfway down the block and in the waiting surveillance car's blind spot. He was also at the entrance to a long alley that ran alongside a multi-level parking garage.

He quickly turned the car into the alley, slowed it to a crawl and bailed out. As the car, which he had rigged to continue at that slow speed to the far end of the alley went on, he jumped the wall of the parking garage, and ran up a flight to where the car he had stored was parked.

The squeal of tires from down the street told him that the waiting surveillance car had realized he was not about to pass them and had come looking for him. By the time he had the back door to his waiting car opened, other cars had arrived on the scene as well.

He removed his shirt and threw it on the floor of the backseat. From under a blanket on the back seat, he took out a woman dress, a mask of a woman's face and a longhaired wig. He slipped the mask over his head, followed by the dress, and then put on the wig. As quietly as possible, he shut the back door and got into the front seat. There, under another blanket on the passenger seat was an inflatable male dummy. He hit a switch on the dash and a small compressor attached to the dummy inflated it. Then, he started the car, and, without turning on the lights, he and his companion drove out of the garage on the side of the street away from the alley, and headed for Dulles International Airport and his flight.

* * *

Granton was aimlessly paging through some reports, killing time until he heard from his operatives in the field, when the Chief of Security burst into his office.

"Rakeland's loose!" Karl said, breathlessly, having run the distance from his office to Granton's.

Granton rose from his desk. The implications of what he'd been told etched in his expression.

"Mother of god. How the hell..."

"He bailed out of his car in an alley en route to his apartment," Karl explained. "He had the car rigged to coast to the end of the alley, and stop before it hit the wall. The car's windows were tinted, so the agents following him had to approach it cautiously on the chance he was still in it. They figured he had another car in the parking garage that abutted the alley, and was long gone from the area by the time they finally got to his car."

Anticipating Granton's next question, Karl added, "They've sealed off the area tighter than a drum, including access to all airports within driving distance of D.C. With luck, they'll have him in custody soon."

"Christ! He's the one with all the damn luck," Granton replied, dropping his head into his left hand, and shaking it in exasperation. Then, rubbing his chin in his hand, he contemplated his next move.

"Abort the mission, Granton. We still have time to get word to our people." Karl advised.

"It's too late for that, Karl." Granton said. "The last word I had from Aiden was that the mission was already running. All we can do now is let them know what's happened here and be ready to assist them, if necessary."

* * *

Aiden got the word that Rakeland was on the loose via a communication over his satellite-fed field radio.

Jeremy got the word over his pager, which kept scrolling the message. "Fire in kitchen out of control. Return, if possible."

Alanna got the word from the look on Jeremy's face.

Of course, having as limited contact with headquarters as they did, and Aiden already in the field carrying out his part of the plan, neither Alanna nor Jeremy could possibly know all the details involved in what was happening with Rakeland. However, just the fact that he had tried to call Francois, and had made a run for it, combined with the encoded message from headquarters, which meant he could identify them and was making every effort to do so, made Rakeland's intentions implicitly clear.

What all this meant for Alanna and Jeremy was that now they were probably on a suicide mission. Knowing how much time it would take them to complete the mission, it was hard for her to imagine how Rakeland, having slipped surveillance, would not be able to make contact with either Francois, or the Arabs, and blow their cover before they could get out.

Whatever the reality of the situation was, she intended to fulfill her two goals. Which were, first, to disarm the nuclear device, and then, to eliminate Kamal Shabban and as many of his "friends" as was humanly possible.

She checked her watch. It read 10:27. From where she was standing, she could see Francois standing near one of the room's many fireplaces amongst a group, which included some military men from Eastern European countries, and Kamal and two of his men. He was in the midst of an animated conversation when suddenly he reached out and grabbed onto the fireplace mantle as if he were in need of support. The man to the right of him took his elbow, and another man rushed off towards Francois' library.

Seconds later, Phillip appeared with the man and they hurried toward Francois. As they crossed the dance floor, Phillip grabbed the arm of a distinguished looking man, said a few words to him, and quickly moved on, the other man hurrying off in the other direction.

By this time, one of the guests had brought Francois a chair and Alanna had made her way over to him.

"Francois, are you okay?" She said, seemingly real concern in her voice.

"I will be all right, Cherie," he said, breathlessly. "I just felt a little dizzy. Too much champagne I suspect."

But, judging by the color of his complexion, she doubted he'd be all right, at least not for a while.

Francois suffered from a heart condition known as arrhythmia. Only those closest to him and the CIA, and, maybe, Russian Intelligence, knew of his illness.

That is why, as one of her operative options, Alanna had provided herself with the locket dusted with an herbal compound. When the compound penetrated Francois' skin and entered his bloodstream, it had interacted with his heart medication, causing his heart to go out of rhythm. This medical condition, attended to immediately, would leave Francois physically uncomfortable, and mildly incapacitated. But it would be temporary.

The dusted locket was a method of delivery that was foolproof and undetectable. The small quantity of the herbal extract needed to affect an imbalance in Francois' medication made it impossible to trace even by blood testing. And who would suspect anything in the first place? After all, she had been wearing the locket against her bare skin. Skin, of course, protected by a coating of specially formulated flesh colored makeup, which followed by a dusting of a similarly formulated powder, would not allow the invasive compound on the locket to penetrate her skin.

It was obvious by the expression on Francois' face that he was happy to see Phillip.

"Monsieur, are you all right?" Phillip asked, knowing full well that Francois was not.

Offering his arm for support, he added, "Here, let me help you into the library. Dr. De Vries has gone for his medical bag. He will meet us there."

By this time, the other guests had noticed the commotion, and gathered around. Francois stood, brushing off assistance from those who offered, and said to the crowd, "Please go on with your partying. I am fine."

Then laughing, he added reassuringly, "Too much of the fruit of the vine."

They laughed with him, and slowly dispersed. The band resumed playing and Francois, no longer resisting the assistance of his secretary and his butler, made his way to the library.

Alanna followed. She was allowed into the library, and took a seat in a chair a respectful distance from where Francois' doctor was examining him. They spoke in low voices so she was unable to hear what they said. But, it was not necessary for her to hear for she knew what the prognosis and the prescribed treatment would be.

The doctor finished examining Francois. He took some medication out of his bag, and handed it to Phillip, while instructing him on its use. Then he gathered up his gear, gave Francois some final instructions, and encouraging words, and turned to leave. As he did so, he caught sight of her sitting off to the side. He smiled and gave her a reassuring wink of the eye, and left.

In the meantime, Phillip had gotten Francois a glass of water with which to take the medication. After swallowing the pills, Francois said to her.

"Please come here, Alanna."

As she came over to him, he said to his secretary, "Would you leave us for a minute, Phillip."

"Certainly, monsieur," Phillip replied.

Phillip gave Alanna a sympathetic smile as he passed her on his way out of the room. Then, before closing the door behind him, said, "If you need anything, monsieur, I'll be right outside."

"Thank you, Phillip," Francois said, in a tired, depressed voice.

Alanna took a seat in the chair next to his. Francois leaned back in his chair and closed his eyes. He took a deep breath of the oxygen that flowed through the tubes now attached to his nose, which ran from an oxygen tank Phillip had set up next to his chair. His condition had caused even the simple act of speaking to make him short of breath.

When Phillip left the room, Francois said, "I am truly sorry, Alanna, for how I acted earlier this evening. It was the drink speaking. Excuses aside, I had no right to demand anything from you..."

His voice trailed off, and he took a short rest and another deep breath of oxygen before continuing.

"I ask your forgiveness."

"Everything is all right," she said, reassuringly, while touching the top of his cold hand.

He smiled weakly, and said, "The doctor says I must get some rest, so I will be retiring directly. Phillip will explain what has happened to me. I want you to know everything. It is only fair."

Alanna rose and stood before him.

"Sleep well, Francois, and I will see you in the morning."

When she looked back over her shoulder on her way to the door, she could see that he was already half asleep in his chair.

Phillip was waiting outside the door.

"Will he be all right?" Alanna asked him.

"Oui, mademoiselle,' Phillip replied. "Monsieur has a heart condition called arrhythmia. In most instances, it does not preclude him from living a normal life, but, occasionally, even though he is on medication, something will set off an imbalance, and what you have seen happen this evening is the result. He will be fine again in the morning."

"I'm glad to hear that," she said. "Well, I guess I'll retire too."

"Bon nuit, mademoiselle."

"Bon nuit, Phillip."

Phillip re-entered the library as Alanna made her way to her room. As she mounted the stairs, she could feel the adrenaline begin to flow. It had been five years since she had undertaken anything similar to what she was about to do, but she could feel that her system was prepped and ready for to the effort to come.

As Alanna approached her room, she saw a man standing to one side of the door. He turned in her direction and she could see he was the taller, better built of the two Arab guards posted at the bottom of the pavilion staircase earlier that evening.

In answer to her inquisitive look, he said, "Hakeem has asked me to stand guard at your door."

"For what reason?" she asked.

"He has heard rumors that there are thieves among the guests," he replied, "who plan to remain in the chateau after the other guests have left and rob those remaining here overnight. He thought it wise that someone watch over you while you sleep."

He apparently had been told to expect an argument from her, thus she saw a hint of surprise in his expression when she said, "Please tell Hakeem he has my thanks for his concern."

As she entered the room, she added, "Though your presence is reassuring, I still plan to bolt my door as an added precaution. Oh, and please tell anyone who wishes to disturb me that I have had a hard day, and plan to take a sedative to insure I have a good night's sleep, and that they are not to wake me before morning unless it is an extremely urgent matter."

He nodded his assent, and turned his attention back to his duty.

Alanna leaned her back up against the door she had just shut and bolted behind her. If Hakeem suspected her of intending to interfere with their plans, and had sent someone to make sure she didn't leave her room via the bedroom door, it was a sure bet he would not forget the windows, and that there were people watching them as well.

The surveillance would complicate matters. She would now, more than ever, have to rely on the diversion Aiden was about to unleash to attract attention away from her.

She looked down at the face of her watch, which, despite the darkness in the room, was visible. In exactly four minutes, an Agency satellite would pass overhead. She removed her evening clothes and slipped on her robe. At the two-minute mark, she went to the first window and casually drew the drapes. By the time the satellite was in position to receive her signal, she was positioned in front of the second window. She held up her wrist as if to check the time, at the same time pushing in on the stem of the watch, causing it to send out a single burst, high-energy signal which the passing satellite would receive, and forward in various forms to Aiden, Jeremy and Granton, telling them her end of the mission was set to go.

Then, she casually closed the drapes, and prepared to dress for the job to come.

Chapter 26

Aiden sat at the rough-hewn table in the basement of their farmhouse headquarters, now dressed in his black commando outfit, instead of the tux he had worn earlier that evening. He ran a soft rag over the surface of his Beretta pistol, which he had just finished cleaning, and thought how, in a few more hours, this operation would be finished — for better or worse.

Two days ago, Aiden had arrived in Pont l'Eveque, where he had met a Frenchman, Peter DeLoux, a CIA contract operator assigned to the Paris station, and who Aiden had worked with previously.

DeLoux had provided him with the necessary clothing for him to pass himself off as one of the local farm hands. Using this disguise, they were able to gain access to the grounds of Francois' chateau under the pretext of delivering feed for the livestock. Though under close scrutiny of the chateau's many guards, they were still able to get a good idea of the lay of the land.

Aiden had been furnished satellite shots of the area, but he liked to physically have a dry run of the area he would be operating in, if at all possible. Now the successful dry run they'd had, and some aerial shots he had taken of the chateau, and the small town bordering it, from a small plane he had rented, had given him a good feel for the place. That, along with the information the Agency and Russo had provided him with at the farmhouse last night, had led him to believe they could pull this mission off with ease, provided nothing went afoul. He felt even more reassured this morning, when Rice had sent word that he was in possession of the helicopter, and was on his way.

That was then. But now, knowing that Rakeland was on the loose, and could blow the operation at will, he wasn't so sure. It meant everyone's life was on the line, most assuredly Alanna and Jeremy's, stuck, as they were, in the midst of people who had no qualms about dealing out death.

He finished cleaning the weapon, and it inserted into its holster, which nestled under his left arm. The room was still except for the occasional garbled voices that floated over the radio that Russo, who'd arranged for the helicopter's refueling stop and returned to the farmhouse late that afternoon, was now manning. He was waiting impatiently, as were they all, for the word to go.

Patrice, Peter and the two Aerospatiale pilots played cards at a corner table. Every once in a while, they looked in Russo's direction, revealing their anxiousness to be on with the job.

Aiden rose, and picked up his coffee mug. He refilled it, and headed for the door.

"I'm going outside," he said, to Russo as he exited the room, his remark acknowledged only by the wave of the hand from Russo.

As Aiden came out onto the porch, he observed that it was a good night for an operation. The sky was clear and full of stars, but there was no moon to expose their movements. He sat down on the top porch step, took a sip of his coffee, and thought about this evening, and worried. How could he keep his promise to Dar if he was so out of touch with Alanna during the course of the operation? He wished that Granton had taken his suggestion of letting him be the one to remain inside the chateau with her.

Granton had nixed the idea, saying that since the operation was already set up with Jeremy to be the inside man, he felt making such a change now was not in their best interest. Of course, Granton had no knowledge that Aiden's agreeing to come aboard had been influenced by a promise.

Aiden's present thoughts were replaced with a mental picture of he and Alanna as they danced earlier that evening. She had seemed extremely calm despite the doubts about the viability of this mission that he knew she must have been having, smiling all the while, and exchanging small talk in passing with couples she knew.

"When I leave this evening, Alanna," he'd said to her. "leave with me."

She gave him an understanding smile, and replied, "I can't leave, Aiden. I'm too close to getting this done, and I'm committed."

"If it's your promise you're concerned about keeping," she'd said, as her smile became more intimate, and her hand moved from its place on his shoulder to gently caress the nape of his neck. "I release you from your obligation, as Dar would have under the circumstances. Please understand that I also have a promise to keep — both to myself, and Jake. Jake gave his life for this mission. It can't and it won't fail. I intend to see to that."

He had been silent after that, and simply took pleasure in the sensation of her in his arms, for he knew nothing he could say would change anything. Should he have told her how much he'd come to care for her? How he had bought Paddy's stallion, Sanctity, with a dual purpose in mind. Initially, he'd made the purchase because he knew that Francois' desire to own the horse would serve as a tool that would allow him to keep a closer eye on her at the chateau should he find that necessary. Should that not prove necessary, it was his hope that his father would share Francois' enthusiasm for standing the stallion, and thus pave the way for his return to the family's farm. There, he hoped to begin a new life, even entertaining a small hope, as had probably many men before him, that she might be a part of it. But, no, none of that could be said now.

Instead, he'd said, "If its no good trying to talk you out of this madness, then know this Alanna, I will do my best to see that you succeed."

"I never had any doubt that you would," she'd said, her expression warm, but serious. "Dar would only have entrusted the best of men with the kind of responsibility with which he entrusted you. It says a lot for how he must have felt about you, and for your friendship with him."

And, how do *you* feel about me, he wanted to know, but he knew better than to ask. Another time. Another place. Maybe...

Instead, he asked, "Did anyone ever tell you that you have a beautiful smile?"

Her smile intensified at his compliment. A slight blush, that ever so lightly colored her cheeks, and a soft, gentle laugh, accompanied the smile. Then, she'd said, "Some have, but I believe it's more of a compliment coming from you."

* * *

Wumph, wumph, wumph, wumph.

Aiden's thoughts, and the chirping, croaking symphony provided by the creatures of the night, which had been his musing's background music, were interrupted by the distant, but familiar sound of a Huey helicopter making its approach. He heard Peter come through the door behind him at a run, and watched as he quickly headed to the clearing behind the barn to activate the infrared landing lights.

Aiden set down his cup, and slowly followed after him.

A couple of minutes later, the helicopter appeared as a black mass against an even blacker sky. For security purposes, it landed without its running lights on. Now, it was visible to the naked eye only because there was no starlight.

Aiden had remained near the barn, away from the landing zone. Yet he could feel the force of the prop wash as the aircraft settled to the earth. Even from this barn-side vantage point, and in the darkness, he could see that the Huey was well outfitted. Beside the two rocket pods, it had a door-mounted 50 cal. machine-gun, and a 40 mm grenade launcher on the front.

It was apparent, that if Rice had also come up with the necessary ammo for the weaponry available, the Huey would provide excellent backup firepower should the need arise.

Aiden joined Rice as he made his way from beneath the Huey's rotor blades, which were slowly winding to a halt, and to the house. Tad Clark and Peter remained behind to refuel the craft, secure it, and erect the camouflage netting over it.

"Good job, Rice," Aiden said, as the men joined up. "It's vintage Vietnam."

"Felt like old times flying that bird," Rice replied, as he gave the Huey a quick, melancholy, backward glance before moving on. "Times best forgotten."

Neither man said anything more en route to the house, though Rice displayed an uncharacteristic nervousness by slapping his leather flight gloves against the palm of his free hand as they walked.

Aiden had been told that when Rice was 24-years-old, he had been an aircraft commander during the last months of the Vietnam War, and that Clark had been his peter pilot, helicopter jargon for co-pilot. They had flown some harrowing missions, as had many of their cohorts. But, Rice and Clark's record of kills and rescues during that abysmal conflict was a standout even among the best of them, and both men had been highly decorated for their efforts and their bravery. Aiden was sure that flying the Huey from Paris had brought back a lot of memories, good and bad. Memories that could give a man, even a man of Rice's caliber and mental stability, a case of nerves.

Halfway to the farmhouse, they saw Russo and Patrice come out onto the porch. Russo raised his arm and pointed to his wrist watch, and then gave them an emphatic thumbs up signal — a signal that meant their end of the operation was officially up and running.

Then, Russo and Aiden hurried to where their car was parked, and headed off to carry out their assignment.

* * *

A quarter mile up from where they'd left their car under the cover of a thick grove of trees, Aiden and Russo hid in the high grass bordering the railroad tracks. The night was ink-black, save for the starlight, and silent, all night creatures in their vicinity having stopped giving voice in their presence. In the distance, they could hear the sounds of the approaching train, and feel its thunderous vibrations transmitted through the ground they lay on.

One hundred feet from where they lay, the track made a turn. It was the first of three in this S-shaped curve in the track. The light stream from the train's headlight was now visible, and they could hear and feel the train slow as it neared the entrance to the curve.

They steeled their nerves, as the train slowly rounded the bend. Even with its speed reduced to a crawl, the iron monster shook the ground as it passed before them.

"Now!" Aiden shouted.

Leaping to their feet, the dark clad figures ran toward the last of several tanker cars that were strung between a multitude of box and flat cars. They boarded it unobserved and separated, Aiden making his way to the tanker car in front.

Working swiftly, they planted their explosive charges under the metal catwalk that ran the length of each tanker car. Then they removed the identifying plaques off the sides of the cars, replacing them with ones that indicated both cars' contents to be highly toxic, the manifest in the La Croix train station office already having been altered to correspond with the changed rail car signs.

Before the train had worked its way out of the S-shaped curve and had built up speed, they had completed their work, jumped to the ground, and disappeared into the bordering woodlands.

* * *

Granton was in the midst of trying to make up his mind how to handle the latest developments concerning Rakeland, when the telephone rang. It was the secure line on which he made outside calls, calls that went neither through his assistant's desk, nor the Agency's switchboard. Its ringing caught him by surprise, because he rarely received incoming calls on it. Few people knew the number, and they were mostly family.

Thoroughly occupied with the operation in progress, he debated momentarily whether to take the call, then fearing it might be a family emergency, he picked up the receiver, and said, "Yes?"

"Granton?" asked an unfamiliar voice at the other end of the line.

"It is," he replied. "Who are you?"

Well, Granton, we've never met, but you know me.... shall we say almost intimately," replied the voice with insolent overtones.

399

Rakeland? Granton's mind could hardly grasp the possibility that Rakeland, the focus of the area-wide FBI manhunt now in progress, had had the audacity to phone him directly. And on a phone line that was so secure, the only way he could have gotten it was to have hacked into the most secret of the Agency's computer files.

"Could you be more specific," he asked, while signaling for Catherine to come into his office. As she came through the door, he pointed to the phone and cautioned her, with a finger over his lips, not to speak.

"Come on, Granton," Rakeland sneered, "neither of us has time for games. You know damn well who I am."

While Rakeland responded, Granton motioned for Catherine to take the piece of paper on which he had hastily written, "Rakeland on line. Call Security. Trace call."

Upon reading the note, her eyes grew wide in amazement. She did not speak, but rather she hurried out the door to do as she was told.

"So, what is it you want, Rakeland?" he asked, nonchalantly.

"Well, I guess you know I'm in a world of trouble. Seems there are a lot of folks out here looking for me, probably on your orders," Rakeland replied. "I don't really want very much. I just want out of here with no complications, and with sufficient funds to see me through until I find new employment."

"Sounds like you've gotten in touch with the wrong man, if that's what you want," Granton, stalling for time, said. "It seems the head of your department is the man to talk to. It's not my job to help you with change of employment plans, or to discuss any severance pay you may feel you have coming."

"Ha! Severance pay!" Rakeland hooted in reply. "Hell, Granton, if you want to call the tidy sum I'm going to hit you up for severance pay, be my guest, but believe me this is going to be the biggest severance payoff in the history of this Agency."

He laughed again, and then added, "Good joke, man, and people around headquarters said you didn't have a sense of humor. Shows you what they know."

As Rakeland was finishing, Karl Heinz, Chief of Security, came through the door. He was accompanied by one of his people, and a man from Technical Services.

Granton cautioned them not to speak, so Heinz took a pad from Granton's desk and wrote, "Secure line. Can't trace."

Granton rolled his eyes in exasperation, and motioned for Heinz to stay and the rest of the people to leave. When the others were out of the office, he switched to speaker phone mode so that Heinz could listen in on his and Rakeland's conversation.

Impatient that Granton had made no reply, Rakeland said, "You there, Granton?"

"I am."

"Well, then, I suggest we cut to the chase, because unless we strike a deal before we end this conversation, I am going to blow your fuckin' SABRE operation sky high, and, along with it, the last real jewel in your crown. Just so there is no confusion on who that might be; it's the one who bears the code name CHAMELEON. I am correct in saying, **she's** the one that took Carter's place, aren't I, Granton?"

Granton had to stifle a gasp at the revelation that Rakeland was onto CHAMELEON, and that he knew it was a woman. Whether he could identify her physically was something Rakeland had not alluded to as yet, and Granton hoped he could not. It would be some small measure of security left for Alanna.

Again, the impatient and increasingly nervous Rakeland did not wait for Granton to reply.

"You're fooling yourself, Granton," he said, to strengthen his bargaining position, "if you think you have all my avenues of communications with my clients in France cut off. You don't."

Then, he softened the tone of his voice and added, "Look, I realize how important this operation is to Middle East security. I haven't exactly been a patriot in the past, but this is different. And the woman, you don't want her dead, do you, Granton?"

"I'm sorry, Rakeland," Granton replied. "But you've gotten some bad information. The SABRE operation was killed by the National Security Council weeks ago."

"Try handing that malarkey to a real fool, Granton. My info's solid. Quit stalling. A secure Middle East, and saving that woman's life is worth a lot more than I'm asking."

"Which is?" Granton finally, but reluctantly asked.

"I know you can get your hands on a million dollars without much hassle, and can pull those FBI dogs off my tail."

"The money part I can do, Rakeland," Granton said, hoping this deal was for real, and that he could avert the disaster that Rakeland's blowing this operation would cause. "But, the Feds are not mine to control, so I'll have to work on that part of the deal. How do you plan to collect your "severance pay?"

"That information will come later," Rakeland replied. "You just get the money, make sure the Feds are off my ass, then take yourself for a drive around town in those fancy wheels you drive. I'll be in touch with you. Oh, and don't worry, I have your car phone number too."

"Thought of everything, haven't you, Rakeland?" Granton said, feeling suddenly helpless.

"I certainly hope so," he replied. "Oh, and, Granton, just so you don't think you have all day to take care of this, if you're not in your car when I call, say in about an hour and a half, I'm going revert to my unpatriotic old self and make that call to France. Are we clear on all of this, Granton?"

"Very clear, Rakeland."

"Good! Good!" Rakeland replied, smirking laughter in his voice. "Well, until later, au revoir, or whatever the hell those Frenchies say."

Then, before Granton could reply, the line went dead.

"Well, what are you going to do, Granton?" Karl asked.

"Hell, he knows that I can't pull the FBI off him," Granton replied. "So, I figure this is just a brazen bluff on his part, an ego thing, to show us how deeply he's penetrated our system. But, on the chance its not, and he is really fool enough to think he can pull the scam off, I have to come up with the money, and arrange for it to at least look like the Feds have backed off."

Motioning for Karl to follow him, Granton said, "Come with me. I'm going to need your help."

* * *

Rakeland entered the ladies room of the Dulles Airport British Airways travel lounge, checked to see if there was anyone around, and then tossed the cellular phone on which he had made the call to Granton into the trash bin. He shook the bin a bit to ensure the phone fell to its bottom.

A woman came through the door. She gave him a brief impersonal smile before positioning herself alongside him at the vanity mirror. While she rearranged her hairdo to her satisfaction, he fussed with his own, and even applied another coat of lipstick from a tube he took from the cosmetic bag in the purse he was carrying. He kept up the primping until she was finished and left.

His female disguise, which he had embellished at an unoccupied Agency safehouse he'd broken into after he'd eluded his tails, had fooled even the most seasoned of the personnel manning the roadblocks out of the city and into the airport grounds. In less than half an hour, he would be aboard his flight, and on his way to France. He knew this ladies' room offered the kind of innocent looking haven he needed until it was time to board the shuttle to the plane.

He laughed to himself when he envisioned Granton running about, trying to accomplish the tasks he'd given him. Especially, since Granton's efforts were for nothing, as he had no intentions of ever meeting him. Why should he? The million dollars Granton had to offer was a piddley sum in comparison to the money he would be paid when he exposed CHAMELEON.

And even though he hadn't said so, and there had been no indication of it in his voice, Rakeland knew Granton must have been amazed and greatly disturbed at the knowledge that he had penetrated the Agency's security so thoroughly. Maybe it was a fool's venture, but he had gotten a great deal of satisfaction out of personally rubbing that knowledge into the Agency's collective noses.

Yes, indeed, he thought with great delight, this was a red-letter day for him and his brethren, the intelligence moles of this world. In about eight hours or less, he would be a very wealthy man. Then, after undergoing a little plastic surgery and assuming the new identity he had already created for himself, he would have most of the world's exotic destinations available to him. There, he could spend his wealth and live the rest of his life undisturbed.

But, the most seductive pleasure that lay ahead was the possibility that he would get to take out CHAMELEON.

* * *

Jeremy mingled with the ball guests until almost all of them were gone. He noticed that the Arabs did the same, though Hakeem's presence was notably lacking. He was aware of the veiled surveillance he was under by Kamal's men, but did not let on to the knowledge since he was equally interested in Kamal and his men's activities.

He nonchalantly glanced at his watch, yawning while doing so to cover his real intentions for looking at it, which were to calculate approximately how much longer it would be before Aiden's diversionary tactics were to begin.

403

Karen A. Lynch

Moments ago, he'd felt the back of his watch grow cold, then return to normal, a signal indicating Alanna would soon begin her end of the operation. While she carried it out, it would be up to him to see that those inside the chateau kept their minds and their attentions on Aiden's diversion, a task that would have been somewhat easier if Francois had not suddenly taken ill.

Alanna must have had a good reason for resorting to the tactic she'd used to disable Francois, because Aiden's diversion was planned with the thinking Francois would be available to manage the various armed groups within the chateau. Losing Francois made his job just that much tougher.

By his calculations, the boom and bang stage of this operation would be underway in 30 minutes. Until then, he would return to his room.

As Jeremy headed down the hall to his room, the beeper in his trouser pocket began to vibrate. He removed it, and read the message from Granton, which said. "Fire out of control. The main roof has collapsed."

It meant Rakeland was headed their way.

Checking on Alanna before retiring was not in the plan. He knew to do so might be risky, but this news from headquarters warranted the risk, and he turned and headed for her room. As he rounded the corner, he saw a man standing just to the side of her door. As he came closer, he could see that it was one of Kamal's men, the tough, ugly looking one.

Shit, now what the hell is this all about, he thought.

The man turned to him as he approached.

"Is there something you want?" he said to Jeremy.

"I'd like to say good night to Miss Reynolds." Jeremy replied in a level tone, so as not to give away his surprise and concern.

"She has already retired, and asked not to be disturbed," the Arab said, while moving his body into a position that put him between Jeremy and the bedroom door.

"Well, ordinarily I wouldn't impose myself on her," Jeremy replied again in a firm but non-confrontational tone, "but I've had bad news from back home concerning my business, and she needs to know that, if she intends to fly back with me in the morning, she'll need to be ready early."

The Arab was about to offer further resistance, when Hakeem stepped around the far corner and said, "I am sorry to hear you have had bad news, Mr. Jergens, I hope it is not too serious."

404

"It's serious enough that I need to get back as soon as possible," Jeremy replied, again surprised, and now even more concerned for Alanna at Hakeem's presence. "I'd leave tonight, but my plane is in Paris and I've given my pilots the night off. I'd be hard pressed to find them, and get them here any earlier than they were already scheduled to arrive.

"By the way," Jeremy said to Hakeem, with a nod of the head in the direction of the other Arab, and in a tone that allowed for the annoyance he was feeling to show a bit. "Why the guard dog?"

"As I explained to Miss Reynolds," Hakeem replied, "we have reason to believe that thieves may be hiding in the chateau, waiting to rob unsuspecting guests after they retire.

"So, that Francois needn't be concerned for Miss Reynolds' safety," he added, indicating the man with a slight nod of the head. "I have asked my friend, Mohammed, to remain at Miss Reynolds' door to insure that she is not harmed.

Pretty lame excuse, Jeremy thought, but now concerned that Alanna might have been taken from the room, he demanded, "Nice of you to be so considerate, but I still need to talk with her."

"Of course you must," Hakeem said, with a cool smile and a sideways nod of his head, which told Mohammed he should stand aside. Then, he came forward and knocked on Alanna's door. "Miss Reynolds, could you please come to the door."

Just as Alanna was about to suit up for the operation, she heard the commotion outside her door. Checking her watch, she silently cursed the un-timeliness of the interruption, and then quickly hid the clothing and equipment in the armoire.

She had already turned down her bed, and mussed up the bedding to give the appearance it had been slept in, so all she needed to do now to look convincing was to slip on her robe and ruffle her hair a bit. This she did as she approached the door.

She refrained from opening it until Hakeem called to her a second time. They would expect a delay after all she was supposed to be asleep.

When he did, she waited another moment before opening it slowly, and only wide enough for her to look out.

Jeremy felt a sense of relief at her appearance. Especially, since she did not indicate that there was anything to be concerned about.

"Is something wrong?" she said, stifling a yawn. Then with concern in her voice, she quickly added, "It's Francois, he's all right, I hope?"

"Do not concern yourself about Francois, Miss Reynolds. He is resting comfortably," Hakeem replied. Then indicating Jeremy standing behind, he said, "We are sorry to disturb you, but Mr. Jergens has a problem."

Alanna looked to Jeremy, who said, "I'm real sorry to disturb you Alanna, but I got a message on my pager saying I have a problem back home."

"Oh," she said, opening the door a bit wider and stepping out into the hall. "I hope it isn't serious."

"I'm afraid it's as serious as it gets," Jeremy said, knowing that she would understand the meaning behind this message. "So, I plan to be out of here as early in the morning as is possible. If you're planning to fly back with me you need to be ready."

"Yes, I do intend to leave with you, and I'll be ready," she said.

Hakeem moved between Jeremy and Alanna, and said to Jeremy, "Well, Mr. Jergens, since you have an early morning, and you have seen to it that Miss Reynolds has her traveling instructions, may I suggest you return to your room. The less people we have wandering the halls, the easier it will be for my men to see to everyone's safety."

"Yes, of course," Jeremy replied, without argument. "Good night, Alanna."

"Good night, Mark," she said. "I'll be ready to go whenever you are."

Jeremy gave her a half smile, nodded and headed to his room.

Alanna turned her attention to Hakeem. He watched Jeremy head up the hall, then turned to her, and said, "Please accept my apology for disturbing your rest. I will see that it doesn't happen again."

That would be very helpful, she thought, but she said, "I'm just glad it wasn't bad news about Francois."

"Francois will be disappointed to find that you are leaving," Hakeem said, with no hint of surprise in his voice.

"We've already discussed the matter, and he understands."

"Then, I hope your decision to return home is a temporary one," he said, a rare, almost warm smile softening his normally cold appearance. "I will miss our spirited discussions."

I can't say the same, she thought, but instead said, "We have had some interesting moments."

"To be sure," he said. "Well, good night, and if I don't see you before you leave, may Allah go with you on your journey."

Having said that, he turned and left.

Alanna looked briefly after him, then at Mohammed, who had resumed his post beside the door. Finally, she re-entered her room, and closed, and locked the door behind her.

* * *

On his return from setting up the diversion, Aiden got the same message about Rakeland heading their way, but in greater detail, by way of a televised computer hookup with headquarters.

"Abort the mission, Granton!" Aiden demanded, after Granton briefed him on the situation. "Alanna and Jeremy can still get out of there, if you do it now. We'll get that damn bomb another way."

"It may be too late to call it off, Aiden," Granton replied. "The FBI lost Rakeland's tracks hours ago. In his conversation with me, he made it clear that he had a way to communicate with that bunch that we can't block, so he may have already blown their cover. If he hasn't, we have to take the opportunity to take care of the problem now."

Aiden knew Granton was right. At the moment, it looked as though luck was holding on their side. Anyway, the initial phase of the operation was already up and running. He and Russo had planted the explosives, the bill of lading in the train station's office had been changed, and Alanna had signaled she was set to proceed. He knew she would never abort the mission, and that she would go ahead with her end of it with or without the diversion he was about to create.

So, he simply said, "Wish us luck, Granton, we're going to need a hell of a lot of it."

"Do you have everything you need?" Granton asked.

"We do." Aiden replied.

"Then good luck and go to it," he said.

Aiden broke off the communication, signaled to Peter that it was time for him to leave, and headed for the door. He got in his car, and, with the headlights off, drove out to a seldom-traveled country lane that would take him to the place he was to meet Russo and Patrice.

As he drove, he thought how if only this fiasco would hold together until rendezvous time, they'd succeed. A possibility that now depended heavily on how sharp their people were on this end. Rakeland was headed their way, most certainly by air. They had to determine what flight he'd managed to get on, and either intercept him in the air, or before he had a chance to clear the air terminal grounds.

Alanna had two signals she could have sent, a "good to go", or one that indicated she was under some sort of duress. She'd sent the first, so unless she'd been compromised after that, she was prepared to carry out her mission. He had to make this diversion convincing, otherwise, she would have a little chance of completing it undetected and getting away safely.

Aiden parked the car off the road, and behind a high stonewall that surrounded a deserted farm a quarter mile from the rail yard. He got out and removed his black nylon equipment bag out of the trunk. He ran silently along the inside of the wall until he came to the edge of the rail yard. There, in a clump of trees, he met Russo and Patrice.

"How did it go?" Aiden asked Russo.

"Everything is set." Russo replied.

Aiden opened the cover that concealed the luminous dial on his watch. He checked the time, and said, "Come on. Let's get into position."

The three men slipped along the wall, and headed to a secure position parallel to the tracks. They crouched low behind the wall, and waited and listened a moment to make sure they had not been detected by the railway guards.

Aiden kept checking his watch. The train was already 15 minutes behind schedule. What could be holding it up?

Just as he was about to call his headquarters, he heard the train approaching. It lumbered into the rail yard, and came to a screeching, metal banging stop 400 yards in front of them. It was scheduled to remain there until mid-morning to allow for the daylight loading of a shipment of cattle, which were milling about a holding pen on the opposite side of the track, their loud, panicked mooing, adding to the din.

Through his night vision binoculars, Aiden watched the guards make a cursory inspection of the train. Another 15 minutes went by while this was accomplished, taking Aiden further off his schedule. Despite the delay, they were still within the operation's time frame.

The wait was necessary as it was not in the script to annihilate innocent bystanders. Finally, the activity and sounds died down. Slowly, they rose up to a squat, and checked to see if the area was clear. Then with Russo, wearing a pair of night vision goggles, in the lead, and using the wall as cover, they moved quickly down the line of railway cars. Russo signaled to Aiden when he saw that they were within radio signal range of the two tanker cars that had been rigged with the explosives.

Russo returned his night vision equipment to his pack. Aiden and Patrice had already put on their protective goggles, and were in the process of adjusting their gas masks. Russo did the same.

Aiden consulted his watch for the last time, and signaled Russo that it was time. He armed the two detonators, and pressed one of the detonators, which blew up the first car.

Even though they were a safe distance away, the concussion from the blast was tremendous. The white-hot flames shot skyward. Soon the chemicals in the tanker began escaping, even in the dark of a moonless night the cloud of green smoke was visible to the naked eye.

Aiden pressed the remaining detonator button, and the second car was ripped apart by the explosion. It, too, caused shock waves to reverberate across the ground they lay on.

The two cars quickly became engulfed in flames, spewing forth, billowing clouds of green smoke. Once the area was free of falling debris, the men quickly disappeared into the shelter of the bordering woodlands. As they cleared the area, they could hear the panicked, disorganized shouts coming from the train crews and the railway guards. In the distance, emergency vehicles could be heard hurrying to the scene, the sound of their sirens wailing eerily through the late night air.

While the emergency equipment was en route, railroad personnel quickly checked the bill of lading for the two cars that had exploded. They noted that the chemical, supposedly contained in them, was listed as Perchloride of Mercury. The appropriate gear was donned and evacuation orders given. It would be a long, dangerous night for those summoned to the scene.

* * *

Jeremy lay in his bed. Hakeem's scrutiny of Alanna had always bothered him, but now, his posting of a guard at her door, whatever his flimsy excuse might be — well, that was a real concern.

He had been surprised that Alanna had shown so little concern with the matter. If her reaction was as disarming to Hakeem as it was surprising to him, and as long as the Arabs kept their surveillance to the exterior of her door, then some good might actually come of this unexpected maneuver.

He tossed and turned, unsuccessfully trying to rest, as the moments slowly passed until it would be his time to act. He envied Aiden, out there, doing something. He hated the waiting. It gave him too much time to think, to reflect on the what ifs, and the might have beens. It was especially torturous when the opening of a bedroom door might mean the end of your life, or, more importantly, the life of the woman you loved.

Jeremy tried to put the thought out of his mind by reflect the good times with Alanna. Both knew what deadly danger they were in, more so now, than at any time in their careers. They knew they could count on each other, and their wealth of experience. In the past, that had always been enough. Would it be now? He prayed that it would.

But, if worse came to worse, he could go to his grave knowing Alanna had forgiven him for his all his failings, real and imagined. Yet, her forgiveness was little consolation to him, when what he really wanted was her love.

Alanna being in the room in Saratoga while he was having sex with Nenet may have sealed the ending of their personal relationship. And after seeing how happy she'd been dancing in Aiden's arms tonight, and remembering her same reaction when they'd danced together at Saratoga, he'd realized, sadly, that her loving him might never be a possibility. Whatever happened tonight, they had to get out alive. Survival had always been important, but now surviving meant another chance, it meant pursuing that possibility, however slim.

Now Jeremy laid in the dark, stillness of his room, trying to stoke the fire, the adrenaline he would need to carry him through the coming turmoil. He began to think it was a lost cause. The searing emptiness caused by the thought of losing Alanna overwhelmed his senses. Then he felt it, the small metal disk on the back of his watch go cold, giving the go-ahead signal, followed by a rush of the formerly elusive adrenaline.

Seconds later, there was a brilliant green flash of light. It illuminated the room, giving it an otherworldly glow. It was followed by an explosive sound that roared and rumbled within the walls of the chateau.

At this instant, Jeremy knew Alanna was making her move. He grabbed his robe. Wrapping himself in it, he let himself out into the hall. People were beginning to stagger from their rooms and mill in the hallways, half asleep, confused, disoriented.

Francois, having been only mildly sedated, came out of his room, and though groggy, began giving orders. Then, he headed to Alanna's room.

"What are you doing here?" he said to the Arab.

Quickly the man explained Hakeem's intentions at posting him there. Francois ordered him to step aside and the Arab did so immediately. Francois knocked on the door, but there was no answer. When there was no answer the second time Francois knocked, the Arab took it upon himself to intercede.

"Mssr. La Croix, Miss Reynolds said that she planned to take a sleeping pill before retiring. Perhaps she is well under its influence by now, and doesn't hear you knocking."

Francois tried the door, but it was locked. For a moment, he thought about having the Arab break it down. But then, not exactly sure what the emergency was, and not wanting to panic Alanna needlessly, he backed off.

"If the situation warrants it," he said. "I'll send for her. If she still doesn't reply when you knock, break it in."

The Arab nodded, and Francois moved unsteadily down the hall to the stairs. En route, Jeremy intercepted him.

"What the hell was that? Is Alanna okay?" Jeremy asked, feigning ignorance and concern. Then noticing how unsteady Francois was, he added, "Should you be up, Francois? Here let me help you."

"Thank you." Francois replied, accepting Jeremy's assistance. "I have no idea what it was.

"Phillip! Phillip!" He shouted for his secretary, who he now saw headed up the stairs in their direction at a run.

"Monsieur, the north-west pavilion reports a tremendous explosion at the rail yard," he announced, upon reaching them. "Our security people have contacted the police, and we were told we would be informed of the situation as soon possible."

They heard the sound of running feet on the marble floor and turned to see Kamal and Hakeem hurrying toward them from the other direction. They signaled to Francois.

"Excuse me, Mark, if you will. I must see to my associates." He turned toward the two Arabs, then turned back to Jeremy and said, "Sorry. About Alanna, apparently she has taken something to help her sleep. Until we see what this emergency amounts to, I suggest we let her do just that. No sense in worrying her needlessly. Do you not agree?"

"Most definitely," Jeremy replied.

"Then," he said, again turning to leave, "why don't you go on to my study and fix yourself a drink. We will join you there shortly, and we can await further reports on this event together."

* * * * *

Outside, the guards, seasoned from a variety of similar missions, stood stunned by the intensity of the explosion. Normally, an explosion of this magnitude would not have distracted them, but rather heightened their alertness, except, that to a man, they recognized the signs as those

411

of a Perchloride explosion. The point was not lost on them that if the winds were right, and they held their ground; soon they would be inhaling a lethal substance. With that thought in mind, they abandoned their posts to better equip themselves.

With no other choice but to trust that Aiden's diversion had worked, Alanna disengaged the simple alarm on her window and opened it. Her matte-black Tempra-Seal jumpsuit was now covered by an off-white one, which would blend with the stone façade of the chateau wall that was illuminated by the courtyard lights.

She stepped out onto the ledge, and turned her back to the courtyard, blending perfectly into the coloration of the wall. Though the walls appeared smooth from afar, in actuality they were 12 inch blocks with deep grooves, offering sufficient hand and foot holds for her to ascend unaided. Even so, as with the wall of the hotel in Saratoga, climbing it required the same unwavering concentration, incredible strength, and nerves of steel, only on a significantly larger scale.

She knew instinctively that there was no sense worrying whether someone had spotted her. She'd know all too soon if they had.

With her eyes level in front of her, she climbed. From memory, she gauged the distance to the top, proceeding cautiously, but quickly upwards. She reached the third level ledge, grasped it with one hand, then the other, then hung suspended for a moment before summoning her internal power, Chi. Closing her eyes and forcing the power into her upper body, she slowly pulled herself up. As her hands came level with the ledge, she spread them flat across its narrow surface, widening her base of support, and allowing her the use of her arms and shoulders to finish the task of raising her body onto the ledge.

Alanna rested only a moment before walking the narrow ledge like a tightrope walker to the south pavilion roof. Once in the shadow of the roof, she removed the white coverall, wedging it securely behind one of the ornamental window frames.

The steep slope of the roof rose before her like a mountain peak. A quick look over her shoulder revealed a ghostly green cloud headed slowly, but surely, in her direction. If the Agency's weather information were correct, a front due to move in within the hour would change the direction of the wind away from the chateau, removing any danger. She needed to get the job done before that happened and the enemy below realized that fact.

Alanna tackled the roof. Time was of the essence, and it was passing swiftly. Reaching the peak, she straddled it, then made her way down the other side. As she worked her way behind the blind side of the turret, she overheard men, their conversations punctuated with anxiety over the approaching mist.

She continued over the pavilion's roof and to the large double windows. They presented the first obstacle. Guarded by a combination of alarms, her method of entry required her to bypass only one. Clean and simple, it would allow her to cover her tracks completely on exiting.

This particular alarm consisted of a magnetic switch set in the window jam. If you attempted to open the window without first shorting out the switch, the connection would be broken and the alarm would sound.

Alanna undid the buckle closure on the holster attached to her belt. From it, she removed a silenced, battery-powered drill the size of a 380 Automatic. Into it, she secured a bit fitted with a collar, which would allow the bit to penetrate the wood just to the point of contact and no farther, preventing her from overdrilling into the alarm mechanism. Then, she took a small strap with snaps at either end from the holster, and clipped one end to the drill, the other to her belt.

She inserted the drill in its holster long enough to take a pair of highly refined infra-red eyeglasses from a pouch attached to the other side of her belt. She put them on, and the once dark window frame was brilliantly illuminated.

She started to drill. The slight noise the bit made entering the wood seemed deafening to Alanna in the surrounding silence. The bit quickly reached its preset limits and she removed it. Then using the bit, she filled the hole with window foil, leaving a length of it dangling to retract later.

Looking through the window, Alanna determined at what angle she needed to drill the middle of the frame to release the latch. She removed the collar, and began to drill at an upward angle. When the bit bored through the other end, she inserted a six-inch long rod through the hole.

She was about to test the accuracy of the insertion, when out of the corner of her eye she saw the alarm panel light on the door go from red to green. Quickly, she pulled the rod so it did not protrude from the hole, and then backed out of sight into the shadows.

A guard entered and made a cursory inspection of the room. He stopped momentarily at the window, but it was more to check on the progress of the advancing green cloud than the window itself. He left the room, reactivating the alarm on his way out, leaving the light on the panel once again glowing a bright red.

Alanna moved back to the window and slid the rod through. Short. Damn!

Once again she drilled and inserted the rod. This time it was perfect.

The rod contained a core, which was manipulated from her end. It released a hook and line, which she maneuvered from under the latch, raising and releasing it. She withdrew the line and hook back into the rod. Carefully, she pushed on the window, hoping the foil she'd inserted had done its job of short-circuiting the alarm. It swung in, the only sound, a low-pitched squeak from an ancient hinge.

Quickly, so has not to disturb the temperature in the room, she removed the night vision goggles and replaced them with another pair. Then she reached to the back of her head, and pulled down the full facemask, which was also made of Tempra-Seal, and equipped with the Tempra-Flow breath filtration system – a rebreather.

Alanna entered the room, closed the window behind her, making sure to secure the latch, and pushing the protruding end of the rod back into its hole. With a piece of adhesive paper, she picked up the shavings made by the drill, which thankfully, the guard had not seen, and disposed of them in the pouch on her belt.

The safe was behind the false panel to her left. Directly across from it was the large fox hunting print she had seen earlier that evening. Then, she was just able, with her naked eye, to detect the small red light in one of the huntsman's coat buttons, which was the heart of the security system. Now, with the aid of the second pair of glasses, she could easily see the infrared beam, which covered more than half the room, including the area containing the safe.

The room's security system was simple in principle, but difficult to defeat. The beam was set at a sensitivity determined by the owner. It measured movement in its field of vision and the temperature within the room. As long as the red light remained on, it meant the system had not been breached. If set too sensitive, a fly crawling across the floor could set it off.

Usually one would set it slightly slower than a human would normally move. Unless an intruder were aware of its presence, once they'd gotten through the perimeter defenses, they would tend to move around the room at a normal pace, thus setting off the silent alarm.

If by chance they moved at the correct pace, their body temperature, which would be higher than the contents of the room, would give them away and activate the secondary alarm. Once activated by either, the room would fill silently with a non-odorous, short-lived paralytic gas,

414

which attacked through the pores in the body, so not even a gas mask prevented the individual from its affects. The gas could be quickly removed from the room through an exhaust system in the ceiling so the guards could apprehend the intruder before they had a chance to recover the gas's affects and escape.

Earlier, Hakeem had turned off the alarm's ability to activate, but that did not affect the beam's sensitivity level readings, which remained on, as they were controlled by an independent system and were only turned off for maintenance or adjustments. Even though Alanna had not anticipated having the opportunity, a small computer that she'd carried in her evening bag, made to look and operate as a hand held organizer, but which had a feature that enabled it to detect and measure the level of gasses, or infra-red beams of any kind in her vicinity, had recorded the beam's setting.

What its reading told her was that someone wanted to make sure nothing or no one reached the safe undetected. A turtle at normal speed might not set it off, but anything moving any faster probably would.

Alanna's jumpsuit and mask would take care of the temperature and gas problems, but the defeating the motion detection device was her problem to solve. Alanna had done seemingly impossible things on previous missions, and this red eye demanded the impossible be done and now. What she had to do was move across the width of the room so slowly as not to be moving at all. One inconsistent, erratic move, an over-fatigued muscle twitching, a sneeze, something as simple as taking too deep a breath, anything, and the light would disappear,

Alanna closed her eyes and concentrated on her breathing, adjusting it to a slow, even flow. Then trusting to her skills, she opened her eyes, and began her arduous journey by slowly moving backwards into the beam's path, facing the light, so as to keep a constant vigil on the unwavering sentry's response to her intrusion.

Her martial arts training had taught her that the real, truly devastating, power that results from any martial arts move, is the direct result of how much control the practitioner has over his or her muscles, breathing and mind. The great masters were able to slow down the process until they literally could feel every tiny movement that built toward the final explosive conclusion. The training to achieve this control is excruciatingly painful, both mentally and physically. It was one aspect of Alanna's training Dar had concentrated on, bequeathing her this master's skill early in her martial arts career. At the time, what she had viewed as torture had later proven to be the definitive edge

415

between success and failure on many a mission. That ability would now be put to the ultimate test.

Each second was an eternity. Each step, an agonized release of energy, each beat of her heart, like the pounding of a drum in her ears.

Slowly, she closed the distance, the light daring her to lose patience, enticing her to make that fatal move, and then, when she felt the distance had become endless, she sensed the wall behind her.

She froze, as suddenly she heard the sound of boots scuffing against the stone stairs as they approached the door, and then voices outside the door.

"Hakeem wishes the room to be inspected," she heard the new arrival announce to the guard outside the door.

"I was just in there a few minutes ago, and it is secure," the guard said, in defense of his ability to do his job.

"No matter," she heard the second man say. "Hakeem feels this explosion might be a diversion. Open the door," he commanded.

She heard a chair scrape against the floor as the guard rose to do his superior's bidding.

Alanna's eyes darted from the red eye to the corner of the room, six feet away. A shadowy ledge several feet up offered the only visible cover. Unless she could reach it, remain undetected, and return to this exact spot before the system was reactivated, all advantage would be lost.

She heard the men joking nervously about the cloud of gas, and then the sound of the guard inserting the key in the lock. At the instant the red light went green, Alanna leaped sideways, sunk to a squat position and then sprung up towards the ledge. She grabbed hold of its edge with both hands, swung sideways, catching the flat part with her foot, and pulling herself up onto it. Flattening her body against the wall, she disappeared into its shadowy depths.

"I can't believe Hakeem has grown so paranoid," the one guard said in his native tongue, as he and the other man entered the room. "Everything is secure. See for yourself. Even the spirit of Allah could not go undetected in this room."

The other Arab, an older, more seasoned looking man, grunted his agreement as he moved around the room, scrutinizing all the nooks and crannies. He, too, stopped when he'd reached the window Alanna had entered through, but as with the guard, his attention was focused on the cloud rather than the latch, which in any event appeared normal.

"The cloud," he said, "it appears to have stopped moving this way."

The guard joined him at the window, and after checking the mist's progress for himself, said, "If it is what they say it is, we should be gone from this place. Whatever we are guarding here must be very valuable. Even Kamal and Hakeem are not willing to leave it. Pray to Allah that you are right about it not moving this way, or soon we all will be dead."

"Come, there is nothing here," the older man said, and turned and started for the door.

"Ah!" he said in exasperation, and turned his attention to the panel that concealed the safe. "I almost forgot that Hakeem wanted the safe checked as well."

He pressed one of the blocks of walnut that lined the doorframe. It slid down to reveal a digital panel into which he entered the combination. The panel moved towards him and he stepped behind it. He checked the contents of the safe, closed it back up and then joined the guard at the entrance.

"There is not so much as a mouse here. Let us go," he said, as he gave the room a quick visual going over. Then they exited and he closed the door behind them, all the while carrying on a conversation with the guard about the veritable merits of staying or leaving the area given the threat outside.

As the door closed, Alanna dropped silently to the floor. Knowing she ran the risk of the door reopening, or the alarm being activated before she could get to the safe, she, nevertheless, hurried to the safe's door. She hit the panel that housed the combination pad, and when it opened, entered the combination. Though she could not see it, just as she stepped into the safe, and closed the door behind her the red light blinked on.

Alanna looked around the interior of the safe, there were drawers in one wall of different sizes, framed paintings leaned one against the other on another wall Against the third wall stood a couple of statues, the old piece of furniture, and a table with an odd assortment of boxes on it.

Oxygen was at a premium in the safe once the door closed, but her rebreather took care of that problem. Still, she knew the diversion would not last forever and that didn't leave much time to find the bomb and disarm it.

It was obvious that the drawers were too small to hold what she was looking for, so she turned her attention to the table. She scrutinized the boxes carefully, some were labeled, and some were not. Almost all of them were large enough to hold the bomb. It would take too long to search through each of them, so she hoped something would give the correct one away.

In the front bottom row, there was a box from a museum in China, another from an antique shop in London, and a third from an auction house in New York. All seemed to legitimately occupy space in the safe. Set atop them, were two boxes from a museum in Madrid and next to them, a box clearly labeled Waterford Crystal.

It was not until she moved the middle pair of boxes that she saw the misfit. It sat underneath a box that bore the markings of Sotheby's, the famous auction house. It was a white box, featuring a large picture of a soccer ball and labeled Kiev/Dinamo, 101 Krschatic Boulevard, Kiev, Ukraine.

Now this is a strange place to keep your soccer equipment, she thought. But, of course, this is not just any old soccer ball, is it? It's a Ukrainian soccer ball. Let's have a look. She removed a small geiger counter from her kit, and when she activated it, she knew her search was over.

Carefully, Alanna lifted off the Sotheby's box, and slid the soccer ball box to her. The weight of the box surprised her. She lifted it. How heavy do you think a soccer ball is, a pound or two? The tactical nuclear device she was looking for weighed 37 pounds. She guessed that this soccer ball weighed in somewhere in that neighborhood. She checked around its perimeter to see if it were sealed in any special way. It wasn't. So, she lifted the top. Under it, there was a thin Styrofoam layer, the same kind you would find in such containers to stabilize and protect the contents. Very carefully, she lifted it and beneath it encased in a thin bubble wrap bag was the ball.

The bag was sealed with clear tape. She lifted a corner of the tape, and it peeled away from the bubble wrap without tearing either the wrap or itself. Almost a bigger trick than disarming this device was rewrapping it so it didn't look disturbed in any way.

Since the tape was obviously designed not to stick permanently to the wrap, she simply removed it and stuck it to another area, where it would be safe to use when she resealed the bag.

That was the easy part. Now came the hard part. She removed the sphere from the wrapping. It looked, for all practical purposes, like any other professional soccer ball, its stitched leather cover not giving any hint of the dangerous weapon hidden inside. Neither, at first glance, did there seem an easy way to access the ball's interior without noticeably damaging the outer covering.

Alanna ran her fingers along the seams. At first they had looked normal, but on closer visual inspection, and now under her touch, she realized that one seam that encircled the ball was thicker than the others.

She removed a screwdriver from her tool pouch and carefully slipped it along the edge of the seam. It slid easily between what she now realized were two very thin strips of Velcro. She separated the strips with the screwdriver until she could fit her finger between them. Then using her finger, she separated the entire length of the seam, and pealed away the cover.

There inside was the bomb.

But, what on first inspection had seemed an easy victory, on further inspection revealed a serious setback, for the bomb was without its detonator.

Alanna checked her watch. Time and her diversion were both running out.

One of the scenarios presented her in training by the Agency's Technical Services people was the possibility that, for security reasons, the detonator might be in another location. But, they had felt, that the chance of this in this was slim. The reasoning being, that, since the people at the receiving end of this transaction probably were not well versed in handling the device, if it were completely assembled and ready for use on arrival, it would be far safer, and the device's performance could be guaranteed to be more reliable.

Guessed wrong.

There was nothing more to be done with the bomb. Without the detonator it was just nuclear trash. So, she carefully replaced the outer cover, rewrapped it in the bubble wrap, and returned it to the box. Before replacing the box among the others, she made one last, quick search of the area to ensure she hadn't missed anything that might connect this box to the one holding the detonator. There was nothing.

She turned to the wall that housed the many lockboxes. It could be in any one of them, and no way could she search them all.

Very slick. Someone was prepared for this invasion.

The clock was ticking, which left little time for appreciating her adversary's foresight.

Alanna set herself in the lotus position on the floor, closed her eyes and imagined all the things that had happened since her arrival at the chateau. Somewhere in that space of time lay the clue.

As she quickly called to mind bits of events and conversations, a picture formed. On the tour of this pavilion, conveniently provided by

Hakeem, she remembered seeing a trophy case, and a comment Hakeem had made when she'd paid passing interest in it.

"Soccer, as you Americans refer to our football," he'd said, "is a passion of Francois' almost the equal of his love of horses and beautiful women. And, supporting under-financed foreign teams is one of his many benevolences."

Following a wild guess, a hunch, such as this with so little time left was at best risky, at worst, madness, not just because she could be completely wrong, but also because it required her to extend her time and the distance she must travel in the glare of the ever-watchful red eye.

But the feeling was strong, and she knew to trust her instincts

Slowly she slid from behind the door and once again faced the glaring red eye. Carefully, still facing the beam, she closed the door of the safe and the code panel. Then, with the same painstaking slow pace, she traversed the distance away from the window and toward the trophy case.

The good news was that the case was outside the range of the red eye, but that led her to believe it was protected by a security system of its own. Before risking opening the case, she looked through the glass doors at the trophies and plaques it held. They were all from small, third world countries, except for one. A rather large, ornate trophy, that was inscribed with the same team name as the box in the safe. Was it coincidence, or a trophy of another sort?

From her tool pouch, she removed a palm-sized scanner, and ran it the height and width of the case. The response printed on its screen told her there was an electronic security monitor present.

She replaced the scanner and removed a similar device to the one Rice had used to disable the security system on the van he'd requisitioned for the motel job. As she held it up to the case, it flashed a red warning light. She pressed a button on the device's side and immediately the light went green. What the device had done was to temporarily break the electronic circuitry in the security system, allowing her five minutes to do what she had to do before the system would reactivate.

Alanna didn't waste time. She opened the case and removed the trophy. Judging by its construction, there was only one place the detonator could be hidden – the base.

Alanna checked the base carefully. Then with the help of a small screwdriver from her pouch, she unscrewed the brass plaque on the base and removed it. There in a small compartment was the detonator. She removed it and replaced it with the inert copy. Then, she replaced the plaque and set the trophy back in the case, being careful to set it in the dust-free space it had rested in before. Seconds after she closed the case, the red warning light on the security detector flashed on.

Again there were boot steps on the stairs and the sound of multiple voices approaching. She held her position. The voices joined with the guard outsides voice in what seemed a celebration. She looked out the window and saw the green cloud receding.

Alanna had to hope the celebrants stayed put, because she had no choice now but to make a move. She had to recross the entire width of the red eye's range. Halfway through there was a thump on the door. Lesser-trained souls would have jumped out of their skin, setting off the alarm, Alanna never changed pace until she reached the other side and the window.

Only when she was outside on the ledge and had removed her headgear did she allow herself the luxury of a deep breath. The cool fresh night air filled her burning lungs.

She shut the window, and with the help of the rod, relatched it. Then she removed the rod, and filled the hole with window putty. Next she removed the window foil, and also filled that hole.

After double-checking that she had left no trace of her presence, she retraced her steps. When she reached the roof's peak, she checked on the progress of the green cloud, and saw that it was gone.

When she reached the crevice where she had concealed her white camouflage suit in, she stopped and put it on. She did not return directly to her room. Instead, she climbed down the south side of the inner wall to the windows of Francois' office, where she found, thanks to Jeremy, a window that had been left open.

She entered and located the video unit that contained the VCR where Francois had left the tape Aiden had given him of the stallion Sanctity's races. She replaced it with a replica that contained the live detonator. Back out the window, she resumed her journey to her room.

Chapter 27

It had been a wild ride for Rakeland, but he had learned his Agency lessons well, and had made it to France undetected.

He hailed a cab outside the terminal, and was soon headed for Paris. The driver turned onto the Rue Lamarck, and stopped before the entrance to the Hotel Ermitage. The 1870, villa-like, Napoleon III style hotel was located just a short uphill walk from the Basilica of Sacre-Coeur, and around the block from Kamal Shabban's headquarters in Montmarte -- another bit of intelligence he'd learned from his latest computer hacking job. He was sure he would not have any trouble getting through to Francois now.

* * *

The intercom buzzed on Francois' desk. Tired, still a little weak from his heart problem, and more than a little short tempered from a sleepless, nerve racking, night, his response was brusque.

"What is it?"

"This is the main guard post," came the reply. "There is a Mr. Doyle here. He says he has an appointment with you."

Aiden. The tapes, of course, he'd forgotten.

"That is correct. Send him in."

Francois stood, pausing for a moment to steady himself. He crossed the room to the video unit, and started to remove the cassette from the VCR. He hesitated for a moment, half thinking of replaying it. Instead, feeling he was too tired to enjoy it, he ejected it, slipped it into its jacket, picked up its mate, and set them both on his desk. Then he sank wearily in to the chair behind it, and summoned Phillip on the intercom.

As he waited, he thought of the panic the events at the railyard had caused in the town and at the chateau last night. Thankfully, there had never been any real danger to anyone. But whoever had been so negligent, or stupid, as to have misread the manifest, confused the contents of the cars, and caused such a panic should be fired, or better still, jailed.

Before he had time to raise his anxiety level further, he heard Phillip's knock on the door.

"Entre, Phillip," he said.

"What can I do for you, Monsieur?" Phillip replied upon entering.

"Mr. Doyle is on his way here." Francois said, as he sat back down behind his desk. "When he arrives, please bring him here and have the maid bring us some coffee."

"Will there be anything else?"

"No, that is all," Francois said

"Oui, Monsieur."

It bothered Francois a great deal that Rakeland had not tried to make contact again since his interrupted call last evening. He must have had something important to say to risk a direct call. It would have been very dangerous for them to try and reach him, as it was now obvious he had been uncovered. So, they just had to sit tight, hope he called again, and pray that he had not been arrested.

No matter how hard Francois tried, he simply could not shake his suspicions of Jergens. Though he had no proof the events of last night were any kind of a diversion, or that Jergens had anything to do with it, especially since a check of his safe and trophy case had revealed all to be in order, and he was aware of Jergens' whereabouts the entire time, still, he did not trust the man. He would be glad when this deal was finished and the Arabs gone. Never had he had such bad feelings about anything as he did now about this deal.

It was already nearly 10:15 a.m. Alanna and Jergens were scheduled to leave at noon. Rakeland had precious little time to get a message to him, if indeed what he had to say had anything to do with Jergens.

Francois could not detain Jergens on a hunch. Already too much had happened between he and Alanna that could turn her against him forever. She would never stand for it.

There was a knock.

"Come in," Francois said, as he rose from his seat and adjusted his robe.

Phillip opened the door, and showed Aiden in.

"Aiden, good morning," Francois said, moving forward to greet his visitor. "Please forgive my appearance, I'd forgotten our appointment in the aftermath of yesterday's excitement. How is your father feeling?"

"He is better, thanks," Aiden replied, "but how are you? I heard you fell ill last night as well."

"I am much better this morning." Francois said.

"I didn't hear until this morning's news reports about the train explosion," Aiden said, hoping to get a read on Alanna and Jeremy's present situation. "I hope everyone here was all right."

423

"Everyone was quite concerned, but as it turned out, the matter was not as serious as it seemed." Francois said. "In fact, Alanna slept so soundly, I doubt she knew anything was amiss until she was served breakfast this morning and told the news."

That bit of information was good news to Aiden, as it meant Alanna was not a suspect in the incident.

Indicating the room's sitting area, Francois said, " Please, have a seat and join me for coffee. I invited Alanna and Mark to join us, but I'm sorry to say they had to decline as their plane will be arriving shortly, and they will be departing for home."

Aiden would have rather collected the tapes and left, but to do so would have been rude, so he took a seat, and said, "That's quite all right, Francois. I can't stay long either. I need to get back to Ireland, and see to my father. I hope you understand."

"Of course," Francois replied, en route to his desk, where he retrieved the videotapes, and handed them to Aiden.

"Thanks," Aiden said, accepting them. Then in way of small talk, he inquired," Have you heard what caused the explosion?"

"The authorities suspect a bomb of some kind, I've been told," Francois replied. "Sadly, of late, my country has become a playground for every terrorist group with capital enough to buy a stick of dynamite. Normally, they just use us for a base of operation. I hope this is not a sign of things to come."

Then to change the subject, Aiden asked, "How did you like the tapes of Sanctity?"

"Excellent, excellent," Francois replied, enthusiastically, as he sat in a chair opposite Aiden's. "I thought about viewing them again just before you came, but I didn't want to hold you up."

The thought of Francois trying to run the tape that now, Aiden hoped, contained the real detonator, caused Aiden a momentary panic, but it was not evident to Francois.

Quickly, should Francois now change his mind and decide to review the tapes, he said, "It was my idea to have a dozen copies of the tapes made to send to potential share holders. I will have a set sent to you first for your comments."

"That is a very good....." Francois reply was interrupted by a knock on the door. "I believe our coffee has arrived.

"Come in," he said.

But instead, it was Phillip.

"Mssr," Phillip said, "I am terribly sorry to bother you, but a matter of some urgency has come up."

Both Aiden and Francois took this pronouncement with foreboding, though each for a different reason.

Seeing his opportunity to leave, Aiden said, "Let's have coffee another time Francois. Both of us have a busy day ahead of us."

Francois, knowing Phillip would not have interrupted without a good reason, rose from his seat and replied, "Yes, perhaps you are right Aiden."

Aiden gathered up the tapes and walked to the door, Francois close behind him.

At the door, he bid Francois goodbye, and said, "I'll be in touch, and I'll have the copy of the tapes to you directly."

"Very good," Francois replied, "Again, I apologize for the intrusion."

"No apology necessary," Aiden replied, shaking Francois hand, and then allowing one of the maids who had accompanied Phillip, to show him out.

* * *

"Well, Kamal, how are things going at the chateau?" Rakeland said, in opening his conversation on a cell phone one of Kamal's associates at his headquarters had provided for him.

"Things are going very well here, should they not be?" Kamal asked, surprised that it were he and not Francois that Rakeland was speaking to.

"Actually, Kamal, despite what you think, things there are probably not going well at all. Especially, if who I think is there is," Rakeland replied, with an underlying snicker in his voice. "In fact, I practically guarantee you things are not well there."

"You are playing games with me, Rakeland, and I am not fond of games. What is it you are trying to say?" Kamal asked, anger rising in his voice.

"Just that," Rakeland said, his voice serious this time, "if, the list of guests at that chateau includes an American, oh, say about 6'2'', brown hair, hazel eyes, accompanied by a women, whose description I unfortunately do not have, but who is rumored to be very beautiful, I would say things there are about as bad as they can be. Are they, and are they still there?"

"Yes, there are two Americans here that fit that description, a Mark Jergens and an Alanna Reynolds," Kamal replied, apprehension now evident in his voice. "They are scheduled to leave within the hour. Please, Rakeland, no more games, what is it you are trying to say?"

"Well, the Mark Jergens is an alias, his name is Jeremy Slade, but Alanna Reynolds," he said, thinking back to an old file he'd come across once long ago, that contained the name of a new intelligence officer recruited by none other than the late Jake Carter, "now, she's for real."

"You know them, Rakeland?" Kamal asked, tension now building in his voice.

"Slade, yes, Miss Reynolds, no. No one really knows the elusive Miss Reynolds. But, my friend, the bad news is, if those two are there whatever you and Francois had cooked up, it's a dead deal," Rakeland said, the sarcasm back in his voice. "Because, those two Americans are, I am proud in a strange way to say, the best the CIA have in way of clandestine operatives. And if they are leaving, they have accomplished their mission – big time."

Kamal stood in stunned silence as he weighed the enormity of that possibility. He and Hakeem had inspected the weapon no more than a half hour ago. The room's security had given no evidence of being breached in any way, and everything that was connected to the weapon, including the detonator, was as they had left it. Hakeem had assured him of this, even pointing out the subtle booby traps he had laid to indicate if it were otherwise.

Rakeland was mistaken, or crazy.

"You are mistaken, Rakeland," Kamal replied, his thoughts momentarily distracted by Hakeem entering the room. He waved Hakeem over to him, and said to Rakeland, "Hold on, I'll be with you in a minute."

"Hey, take all the time you want, Kamal," Rakeland replied, "I'm in no hurry. But, in the meantime, if I were you, I sure wouldn't let 'em leave. At least, not 'til I had a little talk with 'em. On second thought, I am in a hurry, 'cause I'm on my way up there. Make sure nothing happens to them before I get there. I want the pleasure of taking them out myself."

Kamal did not have time to reply before Rakeland hung up. He put down the now silent phone, and said to Hakeem, "It was Rakeland. He says that the Americans have compromised our weapon. They are from the CIA.

Hakeem said nothing.

"Have they left?" Kamal asked.

"No." Hakeem replied.

"Then see that they don't," Kamal said, as he headed for the door "I must speak to Francois immediately."

* * *

Aiden's car had barely cleared the gates of the chateau before he sent a message to Jeremy's pager. It said, "Get out now!"

Jeremy got the message almost immediately. His first thought was to warn Alanna, but when he opened the door to his room, he found two Arabs outside it, their guns aimed in his direction. He had just enough time to hit the face of his watch, before slamming the door on the Arabs, who proceeded to empty their weapons into it.

* * *

Alanna felt the back of her signal watch go cold at the same moment she heard the first shots.

She knew Jeremy was in trouble, but her first thought now had to be to stay free. Her bedroom door was locked, but that would not hold them for long, and the sound of footsteps running down the hall headed in her direction indicated the need for her to disappear, and immediately.

* * *

The four Arabs sent to get Alanna stopped in front of her door.

One of them, Mohammed, the Arab who had been stationed outside her door and whose voice she was familiar with, was there to encourage her to open the door willingly.

"Miss Reynolds are you in there," he asked, his tone friendly, "are you okay? There has been some trouble, and Francois asked us to bring you to him for your safety."

There was no reply from within.

"Miss Reynolds, can you hear me?" he asked, once more pleasantly.

When there was still no reply, he tried the door. When it would not open, he said, "Break it in."

* * *

"This is madness," Francois said to Kamal, who had found Francois in his office preparing to make a call. "Your men shot Jergens? Is he dead?"

"No," Kamal replied, "but his leg wound is serious enough that I have instructed my men to get him to talk before he dies.

427

"How much do you value Rakeland's information, Francois?" Kamal asked, as he made his way to one of the windows and looked out.

Francois noted that Hakeem remained standing silently at the door to the room. His presence now seemed threatening rather than reassuring as it had in the past, though Francois could not understand why it should be so.

"It has always been reliable in the past," he replied, his attention back to Kamal. "I can understand suspecting Jergens, Slade, whoever Rakeland claims him to be. I have always suspected there was something about him that meant trouble, but Alanna, never. I have known her personally for years. She is not a spy.

Their conversation ceased, as Mohammed and his men rushed into the room.

"She is gone, Kamal," Mohammed said, "nowhere to be found."

Kamal looked to Francois, who was quick to offer, "Just because she was not in her room means nothing, she...."

"What did you find in her room?" Kamal's question ended Francois efforts at a defense.

"Her bags, which we searched and found nothing out of the ordinary," Mohammed replied.

That's because I destroyed everything after the operation was completed, Alanna thought silently from her hiding place in the room. Or almost everything, and she patted the pockets on the belt she now wore. It was ingenious of Technical Services to come up with a zippered bag she could deposit everything in, and a liquid that would liquefy its contents, so that all incriminating evidence could simply be poured down a drain.

But she was saddened and angry to hear Jeremy had been shot.

She owed her present great vantage point to the plans within the plans of the chateau that Jake had provided her. They had clearly laid out a series of secret passageways to safety the first owner of the chateau had ordered built as a precaution against an attack the walls of the chateau could not repel. She had committed the layout to memory and had disappeared from her room with the help of one such escape hatch, whose trapdoor was cleverly concealed in plain view in the plank floor. She had followed the passageways until they had brought her to a place behind a large panel in Francois' office, where she was able to view the goings on in the room through what appeared from the outside to be the center of an ornate carved flower set among many similar flowers.

"I don't understand why you had to shoot Jergens, Slade, whoever he is," Francois said. "He could not have suspected you were on to him. What if he dies? How will we know what he may have done to the device?"

"He closed the door on my men and tried to escape." Hakeem replied for Kamal. "Though I instructed them not to injure him, they shot through the door and caught him in the leg and head. His leg wound is serious, but he was just grazed by the bullet to his head, which knocked him unconscious long enough for my men to grab him. We put him in one of the dungeons. If Miss Reynolds is who Rakeland says she is, we doubt she will leave without him."

"So you see, Francois, we always have Miss Reynolds to answer our questions should we lose him." Kamal said. "She will be found, I assure you."

The dark sadistic look present in Kamal's eyes did not escape Francois' notice.

Alanna stifled the emotional outcry that begged for release. She leaned against the passageway wall, took a deep breath, and said a quick prayer.

"That is very clever of you, Kamal," Francois said, turning slowly until he was facing in the direction of the panel behind which Alanna was hiding. "But how is she to know he is there? Unless, of course, you think these walls have ears."

Alanna, who was still leaning back against the wall, came forward and peered through the hole, and then jumped back when she noticed Francois looking directly at the spot on the panel. He couldn't possibly see her, but did he suspect she was there?

"Are you insinuating that they do, Francois?" Kamal said, also focusing his eyes on the spot Francois seemed preoccupied by.

"If they did, Kamal, I would certainly advise you of the fact. No," he said, turning his attentions back to the Arab leader. "These walls have no ears, or eyes for that matter."

Had Francois just covered for her or was he just lulling her into believing that, Alanna wasn't sure, but she wasn't about to stay there any longer and find out if it was another trap. Instead, she moved away quietly toward the dungeons, where she knew for certain there lay a trap.

"We were just planning to visit Mr. Slade, if that is his name," Kamal said, "and see what he might be willing to tell us in return for some pain relief and tender care for his wounds. Care to join us?"

"In a moment," Francois replied. "I had a call from the main gate before you arrived, and I must return it."

"Very well," Kamal said, and started for the door. He turned back, a cruel, evil smile on his face, and said, "Oh, you can tell them that Rakeland is on his way here and to let him in. He made me promise not to kill either Slade or your Miss Reynolds. He feels that is his right to do."

With that, Kamal and Hakeem and their men left, leaving Francois to mull over the possibility that the women he loved not only did not love him, but had actually used him, and was in reality not the beautiful, gentle, horsewoman he knew, but a first class spy. He stood for a moment looking out over the large expanse of his estate. Normally, this knowledge would have hurt and angered him beyond belief. But, of late, he had grown to despise Kamal so thoroughly that the fact they were so certain she had pulled off her mission almost delighted him. Suddenly, a feeling of despair overwhelmed him.

Phillip, in the room the entire time, stood silently, watching with sadness this strong, willful man whom he had worked for so long, whom he admired, even loved as one does family, break into silent tears. He rushed to close the doors so others would not see this uncharacteristic show of weakness.

"Is there something I can do Mssr.?" He asked.

"I am destroyed, Phillip," Francois said sorrowfully. "The heart has gone out of me."

"Perhaps they are wrong. Miss Reynolds could be at the stables looking at the horses," Phillip offered in her defense, as he knew this was the real cause of Francois' despair.

"On the chance that they are right Phillip," Francois said, his tone becoming very determined. "We can't let them find her."

"What are you suggesting Mssr?"

"The passageways, Phillip. I believe she is in them."

"What makes you think that, Mssr. How could she possibly know about them?"

"I don't know Phillip, I just know a moment ago I felt her presence in this room, felt her eyes on me, but when I looked at the panel, I sensed she had gone."

"What can we do Mssr?"

"I can't do anything Phillip," Francois said, taking his longtime assistant by the shoulders. "I must keep them thinking I am on their side. Anyway, she does not trust me. She would never let me approach her."

"Then she is lost."

"No, Phillip, she trusts you. You must find her, and get her out of here," Francois said. "You must be very careful, as they will kill you if they find you are trying to help her. I am almost embarrassed to ask such a sacrifice of you, but there is no one else I trust."

"I will do it Mssr.," Phillip said, and headed in the direction of the panel.

"Thank you, Phillip, I am forever indebted to you," Francois said, "but do not use that panel. They must see you leave, otherwise they will suspect something is not right."

"Very well, I will use the entrance in the wine cellar," Phillip replied.

"Bonne chance, good luck, Phillip."

"Ah, yes, and to you, Mssr."

Phillip exited the office and headed down the hall toward the kitchen. From around a corner further down the hall Kamal, smiling self-assuredly, said, "Take your men, Mohammed, and follow him. I think the mouse will lead you to the cheese."

* * *

Francois composed himself, and returned to his desk. From a drawer, he removed a secure communication device equipped with earphones. Donning the earphones, he pressed the send button, Henri, his head security man, responded.

"Yes."

"We have a situation, Henri," Francois said, in just above a whisper. Knowing his man would know what to do based on previous conversations on the possibility of dealings with the Arabs going wrong and the contingencies that were put in place to contend with such a scenario.

"I understand, Monsieur." Henri replied.

"A change, Henri," Francois said. "We will need every man in the chateau, but leave your best shot on the Paris gate. Rakeland is due to make an appearance soon. Kill him.

"It will be done."

"Fine. Meet me where they are holding the American, whose name it now seems is Slade, Jeremy Slade.

* * *

431

Aiden drove his car into la Croix. He turned up a side street, and drove until he came to a deserted garage. Stopping in front of it, he got out, opened the door, and drove inside.

He put on a pair of gloves, and carefully wiped the car clean of prints. Then he covered it with an old paint-splattered tarp, and leaving it, made his way to the rendezvous point, the small Catholic Church on the hill.

As he walked, he felt the inside of his pocket. A quick check of the videotape case had revealed that Alanna's efforts had been successful. Now all that remained of Operation SABRE rested safely against his chest. He hoped Jeremy had gotten his message, and that he and Alanna were on their way.

He entered the church. As he sat in the dark stillness of the ancient structure, his every self-preserving instinct told him to go back to the car and drive off. But, he could not.

He pictured himself with Alanna in the lobby of the Adelphi Hotel. He closed his eyes, and once more felt the touch of her lips on his. He would not leave this place without her. Her surviving this with his help was now more than just a promise to a friend. It had become the reason for all the years of training he'd endured, for all the skills he had acquired and perfected, but more importantly, it had become the real meaning of his life.

He waited. Time passed. No one came.

* * *

Jeremy was vaguely aware of the sound of people approaching. He didn't have any idea where he was, though wherever it was it was dark and damp. There was a dull pain in his head, but the pain in his leg was considerable. Though he couldn't see it, he'd felt his leg wound and what he'd felt was not good. The bone in his leg was broken, that was for sure. The weakness he felt was from the blood he had lost, and was still losing. In the dark, he had ripped his shirt, and made a tourniquet out of it. He knew he needed medical treatment, but that possibility looked remote if not impossible given the circumstances.

It had been a stupid decision to run, but he had hoped a ruckus would alert Alanna and give her time to escape. He'd never dreamt he would be shot. He knew that it would have been better had he been captured physically fit, because he would have still been an asset to the operation, as there is always the chance to escape. But, wounded as he was, he had become an enormous liability, and a trap for Alanna. Though he had told her to save herself at all cost, he knew she would not leave without him, and in his condition, that meant she might not leave at all.

"Well, Mr. Slade," Kamal's voice could be heard from behind the bright light that now blinded Jeremy, and which had come on suddenly after the opening of the door to his cell. "That is your correct name, is it not?"

Jeremy did not reply.

"It is not in your best interest to be uncooperative, Mr. Slade," Kamal said. "I am sure that you are aware that your wound is in need of attention, which we would be happy to provide in return for your help with a small matter.

Again, Jeremy remained silent. It was then that Kamal kicked Jeremy in his wounded leg, causing a cry of pain that echoed throughout the bowels of the chateau.

* * *

Alanna stopped in her tracks as Jeremy's cry reached her. She only had a moment to absorb it implications, when a sound from behind her drew her attention. Someone was coming, and they knew their way around because they were coming quickly.

She considered what to do, and decided that despite Jeremy's predicament, whoever it was needed eliminating now. Running along the length of the center of the passageway's ceiling was a deep indentation a third the width of the tunnel. She knew narrow ledges and a handrail ran the length of these indentations, another safety featured the farsighted builder had included.

The passageway was unlit, but Alanna could see clearly with the aid of her night vision goggles. A tiny flashlight she wore around her neck emitted just enough light for the goggles to work, but not enough to be seen by the human eye. As she was about to disappear into the depths of the ceiling, the sounds of more people coming could be heard behind the first.

The beam from a flashlight preceded the first person around the corner and into the tunnel Alanna was in. She recognized immediately that is was Phillip. He, too, had heard the sounds of other footsteps, and had turned off his flashlight, and was backed up against the wall, probably hoping his followers would head off down another passageway.

But they did not, and in a moment the bright light of the lead man's flashlight came around the corner and fixed its beam on him. Alanna had removed and stowed her goggles so as not to be blinded by the

433

flashlights. She recognized the first voice as that of the Arab, Mohammed.

"Well, Phillip," he said, "what brings you to these dark haunts?"

"I am checking them for security purposes." Phillip answered calmly. "May I ask why you are following me?"

"Kamal thought maybe you might be looking for Miss Reynolds, and he sent us to help you," Mohammed replied.

By his sarcastic tone, Alanna knew that if indeed Phillip were looking for her, it was not to help the Arabs find her. Phillip's tone of voice had been brave and calm, but his body language gave away his fear.

When Phillip did not respond, Mohammed said, "Well, I do not have time to waste on you, Phillip, my men will see to you. I have more important things to do.

"Ahmed," he said, turning to the man directly behind him. "Phillip seems to know where he is going, so maybe he already knows where Miss Reynolds is. Perhaps you and Salem can convince him to take you to her."

Turning his attention back to Phillip, he said, "I suggest you cooperate with my men, Phillip. You do not appear to be a man who could endure much pain."

"Find her," he said, to his men, and headed back the way he had come.

For a moment there was silence, then the man nearest to Phillip, Ahmed, landed a heavy blow to his midsection. Phillip cried out and dropped to his knees doubled over in pain.

"Time is short," Ahmed said to Phillip. "Tell us where she is."

He picked Phillip up by his hair, and was about to strike another blow, when suddenly his motion was halted in midair. His partner, Salem, watched Ahmed's eyes glaze over, followed by a gurgling sound. Ahmed lost his grip on Phillip as he fell to the ground dead.

Both Phillip, who now stood shaking against the wall, and Salem, stood their ground. Salem suddenly pulled a pistol from his belt and aimed it at Phillip. Before he could fire, he, too, fell dead, his gun falling harmlessly alongside his crumpled body. Eliminated, as was his cohort, Ahmed, by the same type poison dart intended to save Jeremy from Nenet's assassination attempt.

Phillip, thoroughly shaken, started to move backward in the direction he had come. He had heard no one, seen no one, but mysteriously both of his assailants had died swift, sure deaths. Even though the area was illuminated by the light from the Arab's flashlights, which lay on the ground beside them, he could see no one.

"Why are you here, Phillip?" He heard Alanna's voice say from somewhere in the depths of the passageway.

"Alanna, I hope you believe me when I say Francois sent me to help you," Phillip replied, his backward motion now ceased.

"Why would he do that?"

"Francois, as I think you must know, has not always chosen to do the right thing," Phillip said, his voice strong and containing no hint of duplicity. "But in your case, Alanna, there is no question his feelings for you are real and honest. He sensed you were here in the passageways, and asked me to come and help you. I am afraid I was not very clever, and Kamal's men were able to follow me. The passageways are safe no longer. You must let me help you to get free of this place."

"I appreciate your efforts, Phillip, and Francois' concern," The voice from the depths replied. "You can help me best by getting yourself and all the innocent help out of here before all hell breaks loose. I am best left on my own. Take the flashlights with you. Goodbye, Phillip. Good luck."

"Good bye, Alanna. God be with you."

He waited for a moment, but if she was still there, she said nothing. So he picked up the flashlights, and took the passageway that let to the help's quarters, his mission clear.

* * *

Aiden raised his head. He heard the sound of an approaching helicopter. Rising, he looked at the alter once more, crossed himself, and turned and walked from the darkness of the church, and out into the bright afternoon sun.

The blue and white Aerospatiale helicopter, now bearing the logo of the Marlin Production Company, came to rest in a small clearing behind the church. As he approached the helicopter, he checked his watch. If all had gone well, they should have been there by now.

Suddenly, he quickened his steps. Then he broke into a run.

The co-pilot waved in recognition. "Good to see you, sir," he said. "Are the others on the way?"

"You must get aboard, sir," the pilot said. "According to our orders, we can't wait much longer."

The aircraft door had been opened for him to enter. There on the floor, he recognized the long black satchel containing the emergency cache he and Russo had assembled.

Good man, Russo, he thought.

"Are you sure they're coming, sir? Please get aboard." The pilot asked again.

"No, I'm not sure." Aiden shouted over the sound of the rotors.

"I must call the base," the pilot said as he radioed the staging area.

* * *

Curtis, Rice, Russo and Clark sat glued to the radio in the staging area. Since, their return with the Huey, no one had heard anything. The last communiqué with the operatives had been at the onset of the explosions.

The time set for the rendezvous had past. They had just gotten off a communiqué to headquarters alerting Taylor of the missed rendezvous.

Rice and Clark, and Russo, who had volunteered for the gunner position on the Huey, had gone over their plan a dozen times. It never got any easier, or less dangerous.

Upon their return from Paris, they'd run their own check of the aircraft, including a trial run over a remote mountain lake to check the electrical system. That night, stowed safely in the barn, the Huey's identifying marks were painted out, and the fuel tank topped.

It was armed with two rocket pods, each equipped with seven rockets. Four M-60 machine guns were mounted on each side, and one, to be operated by Russo, hung by a bungee cord from the ceiling.

It would be critical that they expend all their ammo before making a pickup. Otherwise, the additional weight of the passengers would make liftoff impossible.

Rice had practiced the run many times in his mind, yet he knew that when the time came, he'd be flying by the seat of his pants. No matter how well you planned these things, the enemy always had other ideas.

The radio interrupted his thoughts. It was the pilot of the Aerospatiale. Rice hoped it was a confirmation that they had lifted off with all aboard.

Instead the voice said, "Base this is Hawk One, we have one, we repeat one for liftoff. Liftoff imminent unless advised otherwise."

Rice came on the line. "Hawk One, this is base. Hold your position. I repeat, hold your position. Do you roger that?"

"CPT Rice. CPT Rice, do you read me?"

The voice was Taylor's coming over secured satellite communication system from CIA Headquarters.

"This is Rice. I copy you."

"CPT Rice this is Taylor, I have been monitoring the situation via satellite, does Hawk One have the package?

There was a moment's silence, then Rice said, "Hawk One, is your passenger in possession of the package?"

There was a momentary silence from the other end, then "My passenger is in possession of the package. But I'm short two passengers, did you copy that?"

"That's a Roger, Hawk One," Rice replied. "Mr. Taylor, we have the package."

"Then, he is to depart immediately. Do you copy that, CPT Rice?"

"I copy, but we still have people unaccounted for, Mr. Taylor."

"I understand, but I am ordering you to instruct Hawk One to depart immediately. Do you understand CPT Rice?"

"I hear you, sir, and will convey your order," Rice said, anger in his voice, "but, no, I do not understand. We have two people in the hot zone, with no backup, and you want me to order Hawk One out?"

"Those are my orders CPT Rice. You are now their back up."

"Hawk One, you are ordered to lift off immediately. Do you copy, Hawk One?"

"I copy that Base. Am preparing to depart," were the final words from the pilot.

Suddenly there was another voice on the line.

"Hawk One to base do you read me, I repeat Hawk One to base do you read me?"

Rice recognized Aiden's voice, "Base to Hawk One, I read you loud and clear."

"Base I am going back in," Aiden said above the din of the rotors. "Get the bear in the air and wait for my signal. Do you copy?"

"The bear is in the air, compadre," Rice replied, with joy in his voice. "Will await your signal. Good hunting."

Minutes later, the Huey gunship sat in the field next to the farmhouse, flight checked and engines warmed, awaiting Aiden's signal.

Chapter 28

Jeremy's eyes had finally adapted to the light, just in time to see one of Kamal's henchmen about to kick his wounded leg again. Physically weakened, but with his adrenaline high, he rolled over onto the wounded side and, with his good leg, kicked the legs out from under his assailant. As the man landed next to Jeremy, Jeremy grabbed his head, and twisting it, broke the assailant's neck.

Kamal's men descended on Jeremy, and he would have been dead immediately if not for Francois and his men's appearance.

"Stop. What are you doing!" Francois yelled.

To make Francois' point, and get their attention, one of his bodyguards fired his gun in the air.

When the men pulled back, Francois could see that though Jeremy had made a gallant effort, successful as it was, it had compromised his already deteriorating condition.

"Are you crazy?" Francois said to Kamal, who had remained standing against the cell's wall during the attack. "If you kill him, you will have nothing."

"We will have your friend, Miss Reynolds, to supply the information," Kamal said, as if to rub in the treachery she committed.

"She is not here," Francois lied. "The security guard at the gate said she went into town this morning, and planned to take a taxi to the airport."

"And not say goodbye?" Kamal said, almost laughing. "How cruel."

"She left a note with Phillip," Francois said, and offered the note, which had been written by a previous lover with the same initial as Alanna's, to Kamal,

It said:

My dearest,
Sorry to leave without saying goodbye. You were busy. Will call when I reach home.
Love, A.

Jeremy could not believe his ears. He knew there was no such plan and that Alanna had not left the chateau. Francois was covering for her. Maybe he had gotten her out.

"You are a liar, Francois," Kamal again laughed, as did his men, "But, I give you this, your heart is in the right place, if your brains are not."

For a moment, he turned his attention back to Jeremy, then swiftly turned back in Francois' direction. In turning, he pulled a gun from under his cloak and firing point blank, killing Francois instantly. Followed, in the confusion, by Kamal shooting Francois' two bodyguards.

"Hakeem!" Kamal called. "Hakeem!"

But Hakeem did not reply.

"He is gone," Mohammed said. "He left when Francois arrived."

"Where has he gone?" Kamal asked angrily

"He said to find the woman."

"Yes, find the woman, Mohammed," Kamal said. "Take this place apart, but find that women. And in the meantime, I will see what I can get from our clever friend here before all of his blood is spent."

* * *

As the helicopter lifted off, Aiden set the black satchel on the ground. He released the lock, yanked it opened, and removed its contents.

Before abandoning the car, he'd retrieved and donned his bulletproof vest. Now, he inserted the side-by-side magazine loaded with 9mm BAT rounds into the H&K MP-5SD submachinegun that had been in the bag. Then, he strapped on a belt to which he attached a pouch of stun and fragmentation grenades, and additional magazines for the H&K and the Beretta 92SPF he wore in the holster under his arm.

Just for good measure, Russo had included a LAW rocket.

Aiden disposed of the satchel in the church dumpster, slung the LAW over his left shoulder, and the H&K over his right. Then, he checked the meter on his right wrist. It was the one that would read the signals from the transmitters he hoped Jeremy and Alanna had swallowed. The good news was there were two blips on the screen. The bad news was one was stationary, the other was moving toward the first, and neither was moving in a direction that would get them out!

He picked up the last piece of equipment, a small, but powerful secure satellite communication radio, set to Rice's frequency.

He pressed the call button.

"This is POPPA BEAR to MAMA BEAR, do you read? Come in MAMA BEAR."

"This is MAMA BEAR, you are loud and clear." Rice's cool, professional response was immediate. "By the way, you should know the mole is out of the hole, and is headed your way by taxi."

"I ten four that. I'm going in!" Aiden said, as he moved off in the direction of the chateau.

"Acknowledged. Good luck, Sir!"

* * *

"This is the all-time best day of my life." Rakeland said, to the taxi driver from the back seat. "How far are we from the chateau?"

"It is just around the bend, Monsieur," the driver replied.

"Hey, then stop for a minute." Rakeland said. "You know, I always wanted to know what it felt like to drive a cab. How about letting me drive yours to the chateau."

"Oh, I couldn't do that, monsieur." The driver replied. "It is against regulations. I could lose my license."

"Hey, no one out here is going to say anything." Rakeland said jovially. "They're going to think it's a great joke. Who's to know? I have 500,000 francs here that says you'll go along with my joke. What say you, friend?"

"Just to the chateau, monsieur," the driver said, hesitantly.

"Just to the chateau, that's all friend." Rakeland said. Already out the door, and waiting for the driver to change places, money in hand.

"Oh, and I've got to wear the hat," Rakeland said, lifting it from the man's head before the driver could object, while holding open the door for him to get in the back seat.

Rakeland got behind the wheel, and drove toward the chateau. He had been there once before, undercover, on a guided tour. Then, there had been at least four guards on the gate. As he approached, he saw only one, the glass enclosed guardhouse not revealing any other personnel on duty, a strange practice for such a sensitive time.

He slowed the car as he approached the guardhouse. The guard had his hand on his weapon, not unusual given the circumstances. Rakeland rolled down both the front and back windows as he pulled to a stop and the guard came alongside.

"Monsieur Rakeland, to see Comte de La Croix." Rakeland said, in his best, unaccented French.

As the guard moved toward the rear window, Rakeland saw him cock the pistol, lift it, and fire at the taxi driver, who died immediately.

Before the guard could turn to him, Rakeland had drawn his own gun, and shot the guard.

Rakeland sat for a moment. His better instincts told him to get the hell out of there, but he wanted his money. Who ever had ordered him killed would think he was dead, and that it was just some frightened taxi driver headed their way.

He put the car in gear and headed for the chateau. He had people to take out, and money to collect, and he was going to get it done.

* * *

Mohammed took his men, and headed for the passageway entrance. He had no idea what had happened to the men he'd left there. Hopefully, they had gotten the old man to talk, and were in pursuit of the woman.

He hurried through the passageway to the spot he'd left the men. Aiming his flashlight slightly high and to the front into the passageway before him, he never saw Salem's body until he fell over it.

"What, what is this," he said, picking himself up and shining his light around, suddenly realizing both his men were dead, and the Frenchman was nowhere to be seen.

"They are dead," said one of his men, "but how? There is no blood, no marks, nothing broken on them."

"I do not know," replied Mohammed, for his man's observations had not escaped his attention.

"Come. We are wasting time," he said, stepping over Ahmed's body and continuing down the passageway, now more slowly. His men following hesitantly, now knowing the dark harbored mortal danger.

* * *

As she moved through the passageways toward the dungeons, Alanna could hear the sound of gunfire. She knew it was not just Jeremy holding a one-man, running battle with the enemy, for there were too many guns firing from every direction. She hoped it was Aiden and the US Cavalry, but that, she knew, was unlikely.

Finally, she reached the dungeon area. She saw a tiny beam of light coming through the wall near one of the ledges. She removed her goggles, and climbing onto the ledge, looked through what was a hole in the mouth of a gargoyle mounted on the wall, and aimed down at the cells below.

She could hear Kamal's angry voice and Jeremy's anguished cries as they continued to try to torture information out of him. The sound of gunfire was getting closer, and it caught Kamal's attention. He emerged from the cell, spattered with blood.

An overwhelming sense of anger and loathing filled Alanna. So many people have died because of you and your treachery, she thought. It must end here.

But, there were many armed men, and despite her many skills, she found herself outnumbered, outgunned, and helpless to rescue Jeremy without going through them, risking both their lives.

Suddenly, there was the sound of men approaching. She laid still on the ledge, huddled against the wall of the passageway, her back blocking the light from the hole.

She could hear Mohammed's voice as he gave orders to, what by the sound of their footsteps appeared to be, three other men. Mohammed moved confidently, but the three other men came skulking along, their eyes darting in all directions.

And then the reality of their fear struck her, and she knew what to do.

First the science, she thought as she let them pass. On a panel she wore on her chest was a button. Cautiously, she moved her hand and pressed it. It sent out a radio wave that interrupted the circuitry in the batteries in the flashlights the men carried, draining them of power. Slowly the lights went out.

And now for the magic, and she tossed two balls made of a thin soft rubber. They hit the ground without making a sound, bursting on impact. The powder they released mixed with the dampness in the air. Soon, a thick mist began to rise behind the men. A small, battery-operated fan ensured that the mist moved in the men's direction.

The men stopped in their tracks, unsure of what was happening.

When the mist had filled the tunnel to the ceiling, Alanna dropped several more balls. These were also silent, but solid, and upon their impacting the ground, triggered a mechanical response that produced a hissing sound much like that of a snake.

"What is that?" the last man in line said, turning at hearing the hissing sound, and seeing the white floating cloud in the darkness.

The other men turned to look, and for a moment stood in stunned silence.

The cloud had moved out of the fan's range, and now just hung in the air, the hissing sounds continuing to emanate from it.

Mohammed said nothing, for he had no answer. This panicked the men further. One fired at it, and Alanna had to duck her head to avoid the ricocheting bullets.

"Stop," Mohammed commanded, as he flicked on his cigarette lighter, which did little to explain the cloud and sounds, but did illuminate what appeared to be a passageway off to the side. By now the men were so unnerved that, seeing the passageway, two of them ran for safety, rather than face the unknown.

"Come back," Mohammed ordered, but they did not obey him.

He and the other man held their ground. Mohammed searched the area with what light his lighter offered, and said, "I know you are here Miss Reynolds. You can come out now. I am not frightened by your slight of hand."

"That's too bad for you and your friend, Mohammed," Alanna said, then silently dropped to the ground and flattened herself to it, as she knew Mohammed's first reaction to her voice would be to fire his gun in her direction.

Which he did, the bullets whizzed harmless above her. The flash from the muzzle revealed the location of Mohammed's right arm, which held the weapon.

From her prone position, Alanna let fly a circular metal blade, which caught Mohammed in the forearm slicing into his flesh, causing him to cry out in pain and drop his weapon.

Before he could recover, Alanna back somersaulted twice, which covered the distance between them, and on the third somersault, she kicked him under the chin knocking him into the wall, and his lighter to the ground, dousing its light.

Before total darkness enveloped them, she grabbed the second man by the arm. Distracted by Mohammed's cries, he was caught off balance; she pulled as if to pull him past her, putting herself behind him. Then, she struck him with a sharp blow to the back of his head, forcing his head downward, while her leg came up sharply under his arm, resulting in her toe connecting with his face at the bridge of his nose, killing him instantly

She dropped the arm of the man she had just disposed of letting him fall to the floor, and turned to finish Mohammed off.

Suddenly, a bright light filled the passageway.

"Hakeem!" Mohammed said, holding his bleeding arm, the relief in his voice evident.

443

She turned to see Hakeem standing several yards behind her, a powerful flashlight in one hand, and a pistol in the other.

"Shoot her, shoot her," Mohammed yelled.

Swiftly, Hakeem raised the pistol, and before Alanna had time to react, fired one shot. There was silence, and when Alanna looked in Mohammed's direction, she saw him slide down the wall dead, a bullet hole right through his forehead.

Not knowing what to expect next, she turned to face Hakeem.

"Bad shot, was it?" Alanna said, indicating the dead Mohammed with a toss of her head.

"Perfect shot." Hakeem replied, as he put the gun on safety, and tossed it in her direction. "Remember Alanna, take care of the girls, and they will take care of you."

She caught the 9mm Beretta, and immediately recognized it as the one Jake had named Gloria, the one missing from Jake's gun case.

She looked at Hakeem at first unbelieving, but his and Jake's words echoed in her mind. "Take care of the girls and they will take care of you."

"You were Jake's contact?" She said, and suddenly all the little unexplainable events -- the tour of the pavilion, the escorting her on her jog -- were all clear.

"We met at Mossad headquarters when I was a recruit and were friends for many years," Hakeem replied, his stance relaxing as he spoke "All the time it took me to get where I have gotten. I commend you, Alanna. You were successful, as Jake knew you would be. But, it's Jeremy that's important now, and he is in serious trouble."

"It takes many years to develop a valuable cover like yours, Hakeem," Alanna said. "Helping me will blow it."

"Be that as it may, you will need my help to get Jeremy out." Hakeem replied.

"Then, let's do it," she said.

* * *

Rakeland drove determinedly towards the chateau, his only thoughts, those of his newfound wealth, and finally to take out Jeremy Slade, and the real prize, Alanna Reynolds.

"I have you now, Slade," he said, out loud to himself. "It's taken a long time, but now you're mine."

* * *

Aiden crossed the road between the church, and a line of shops that backed up to the perimeter of the chateau. He could now hear gunfire.

To his amazement, there were no guards at the narrow gate that led to the moat surrounding the chateau. As he started towards the entrance to the underground storage area that had once been the north dam of the moat, he heard a car approaching quickly. Needing a diversion to allow him to cross the open ground of the moat, he decided to put the LAW to use.

As he slipped along the curved stairs that led from the lower ground, he readied the missile launcher. Squatting down, so as not to be seen, he sighted on the approaching vehicle, which just happened to be a Paris taxi.

Well Rakeland, looks like you made it just in time to join the party, Aiden smiled at the thought. In fact, I'm going to see to it that you get to see the fireworks up front and personal.

The sound of the 66mm rocket firing drowned out the other gunfire. There was a tremendous back-blast as it left the tube.

While at the receiving end of the missile's trajectory, the sharp eyes of the soldier Rakeland had once been, spotted the man with the missile launcher aimed at him. He reached for the door to bail out, but the end came swiftly.

A second later, the taxi disintegrated in a pillar of flames.

* * *

Aiden dropped the rocket tube, and ran down the steps. There were men fighting everywhere, Francois' against the Arab force. The explosion startled them, causing them to dive for cover.

Aiden moved quickly over the grass, to the door at the base of the underground storage area, his submachinegun at the ready. Reaching the door, he allowed a fragmentation grenade to precede him in. There were cries of pain from within. Exposed as he was, he followed it in, hoping it had taken care of any opposition. The two guards inside were dead.

Aiden made his way through a door to a stairwell that led to the main level.

The sound of gunfire was ear splitting. What the hell was going on, he wondered. He made his way up the stairs, checking his wrist meter as he went to make sure he was headed in the direction of his receiver's readings. Now, both indicators were on the move, but not together. He was aware that just because the transmitters were still emitting signals, and were moving, was no assurance Alanna and Jeremy were still alive. He shook the thought.

He worked his way down a corridor, diving for cover as three Arabs rounded the far corner. They opened fire on four of Francois' men who had unexpectedly come around the opposite corner. Bullets ricocheted around the long hallway, some finding their mark. When the survivors took off in opposite directions, he continued on his way.

He had overheard one of the Arabs say something about the dungeons. He knew he was headed in the right direction, but with so many levels in the chateau, they could be on any one of them. Which one they were on was something his device could not tell him.

Aiden heard the sound of footsteps coming up the stairway he was approaching. He hid against the wall of a grotto, and waited for them. When they came into view, he stepped from the grotto, and as the red beam from the laser sight on his gun appeared on the first man's chest, he fired. Quickly, he moved the beam to the second man, who froze in his tracks. The man he was with having crumpled without a sound to the ground next to him, dead.

"Where are the Americans?" Aiden asked, the gun in his hand the incentive to talk.

At first there was no reply, but then the Arab said, "The man is in the dungeon." And he gestured in the direction he had come. We do not know where the woman is."

"Thank you," Aiden said, as he pulled the trigger, sending the second man to his death.

"That was for all the innocent lives you and your kind have taken, ass hole." Aiden said, stepping over their bodies and heading down the steps.

* * *

Alanna and Hakeem made their way to a passageway entrance that led to the dungeons. Twice they had avoided trouble by pretending Hakeem had taken her prisoner, and they were on their way to Kamal. But, when they got to the cell Jeremy had been in, it was empty, save for Francois' dead body.

"He tried to help me," Alanna said sadly, as she bent down and closed his eyes that still held a look of surprise in them. "A change for the better, too late do him any good."

Hakeem did not comment. Death was part and parcel of what he did. To him there were no regrets.

"Did he have Jake killed?'

"No."

"Was it Kamal?"

"Yes."

Alanna moved past Hakeem and into the hallway.

"Where would they have taken Jeremy, Hakeem?"

"I do not know, but they had to have gone this way." And he started in the opposite direction they had come.

Alanna passed him, in a hurry to save Jeremy if he were still alive, and keep her promise to Jake to make sure Kamal did not leave there alive.

She didn't go far before she saw fresh bloodstains on the floor. The pattern suggested something bleeding was being dragged over its surface.

"Oh, God," was all she said as she broke into a run, Hakeem right behind her.

As they rounded a corner, they could see men dragging a body by one leg, weak cries of pain coming from the person being dragged.

It was Jeremy they were dragging.

Never had Alanna been filled with such anger. Before Hakeem could say a word, she took off after them. As she ran, she scooped up a crooked wooden staff that lie along the wall, and, in one ferocious move, pillared the last man in line with it.

The suddenness and the ferocity of the attack caught the six other men off guard. She used the forward falling motion of the impaled man to knock over the next man in line, who did not have time to recover before Hakeem took him out with his gun.

In a second, she leaped in the air and delivered a fatal kick to the sternum of the man dragging Jeremy.

"Down," yelled Hakeem.

And as she fell across Jeremy's body to protect him, Hakeem felled the remainder of the men, who were set to fire on her, with a burst of fire from his gun.

"Oh, Jeremy," Alanna said, cradling her gravely wounded friend's body in her arms.

"Hi, beautiful," he said weakly. "I never thought you'd get here."

Then Jeremy caught sight of Hakeem, and cried out, "Alanna, look out behind you."

Looking but only seeing Hakeem, she said, "It's all right, Jeremy, he was Jake's contact. He's helped me, and we're going to get you out of here."

Jeremy closed his eyes.

He is too weak for me to leave and go after Kamal, she thought.

"Come on Hakeem, help me, Kamal can wait."

Hakeem put his gun down, as he bent over to pick up Jeremy, Aiden came rushing around the corner.

Seeing only Hakeem, and Jeremy and concluding the worst, he yelled, "Hakeem!"

Alanna seeing Aiden, and sensing what was about to happen, screamed out a warning, but it was too late.

Aiden had already fired. The bullet struck Hakeem, who had turned to face the calling voice, knocking him to the ground. Too late, Aiden realized his mistake.

Alanna set Jeremy's head gently on the ground, and went to Hakeem. She helped him to a place where he could rest his back against a wall.

Before she could say anything, Hakeem said, "Go, Alanna. It is better this way. Now my cover is preserved and the agents I trained are still of value. My wound is not serious. Go. Go. Now, you have Aiden to help you,"

"What is this, Alanna," Aiden said, from where he knelt beside Jeremy.

"Hakeem was Jake's contact, he was helping me get Jeremy out of here." Alanna said. "We've got to go Aiden, Jeremy's dying. Is there anyone who can help us get Jeremy to a hospital before it's too late?

"We'll know soon enough," Aiden said, taking out the secure transmission device and radioing Rice.

"Base do you read?" he said. "Base come in, do you read me?"

"Loud and clear, boss," came Rice's reply. "What is your status?"

"We have wounded," Aiden said. "I repeat, we have wounded, need immediate evacuation. Area is hot, repeat area is hot."

"We're on our way." Rice said, as they lifted off. "Our ETA on target is 12 minutes. I repeat ETA 12 minutes."

"I copy you ETA at 12 minutes." Aiden replied. "We are on our way to the recovery zone."

Aiden put away his radio, and with Alanna's help, lifted Jeremy and rested him over his shoulder in a fireman's carry.

Turning to Hakeem, she said, "Come with us Hakeem"

Before he could answer two of Kamal's men came around the corner. They were about to open fire.

"Get down," Hakeem yelled, and firing over their heads as they dropped to the floor, he took out both men.

"Waste no more time, Alanna….. Go!" Hakeem shouted.

"There is a passageway a short distance up, Aiden," Alanna said, "that will take us directly to ground level of the north wall. Rice will be able to see us, and land there and pick us up. If they keep busy fighting one another up top, no one should bother us there."

"Thank you, Hakeem," she said.

"Israel thanks you, Alanna." Hakeem replied. "We will meet again."

Without a backward glance, Alanna and Aiden, carrying Jeremy, started toward the passageway entrance. A short distance from it they suddenly heard anxious Arab voices.

"How will we get out of here? Where is Kamal?" A voice asked.

"He has gone to get the bomb," another responded.

"Come, this is the way out," a third man said, his voice trailing off as they departed the area

Aiden looked at Alanna.

"Just a bit farther," she whispered, and then they were there.

She touched a panel and it opened.

"Take the flashlight, Aiden, and go."

"No, Alanna, forget Kamal."

"Don't argue, Aiden, there isn't time, just go," she said, as she moved off back the way they had come. "When you pass through the door, it will close on its own. Follow the passageway to the end. The levers to open any of the doors from the inside are on the walls, just to the right of where a doorknob would be."

She disappeared around a corner, leaving Aiden no choice but to do as she said.

"No arguing with that one, is there?" A weak voice from over his shoulder said.

"That's for sure," Aiden replied. "Now let's get you out of here."

* * *

Flying nap of the earth, they would be approaching the target with the setting sun at their backs. The Huey was fast approaching a narrow stand of trees that marked the westernmost boundary of the La Croix property, on the other side lay a wide expanse of lawn and gardens, and then the chateau.

Rice reached to the overhead panel between him and Clark. Snapping the toggle switch, he armed the rockets.

Directly in front of him, he illuminated the screen of the ultra-sensitive receiving unit, which bore a scaled down electronic blueprint of the chateau's interior and exterior. It was already picking up the signals from the Alanna and Jeremy's transmitters.

One was headed in the direction of the pickup zone, but the other was headed deep into the interior of the chateau, and upwards toward one of the pavilions. Why had they split up, he wondered, and who was who?

"This is it," Rice said to Clark. "Ready?"

"Ready," Clark replied.

"Ready back there, Russo?"

"Ready.' Came Russo's reply over the intercom in his helmet.

Working the cyclic and the collective pitch, his feet busy on the pedals, Rice maneuvered the aircraft over the trees. Approaching at an angle from the southwest, he fired the first round of rockets at the turret on the right side of the west wall.

Before the Arabs and Francois' men knew what was happening, the first rocket burst through the chateau wall, exploding with fiery fury.

Rice let the Huey drift to the left just long enough to get a bead on the next target. A split second later, with a resounding swoosh, a second round fired. On impact, the left turret was engulfed in flames.

Clark was busy strafing the windows of the second and third floors with the M-60's.

They cleared the rooftop, and Clark focused his attention on the large turret on the left of the east wall, while Russo, swinging his gun into position, blasted away at its mate on the right.

"Receiving Fire!" shouted Clark, as he saw the muzzle blast from the Arabs' AK 47's. The warning was followed by two thuds that sounded like golf balls hitting a metal building.

The Huey took a hit in the tail boom, and one that came through the cargo area, barely missing Russo, and exiting through the roof.

The copter dropped down to take advantage of the lower roof of the east wing. As Rice cleared out, and banked to his right, Russo took aim at the men at the gate, and on the moat bridge, which came up quickly below him. Those, who escaped his sweeping barrage of bullets, dove for what little cover was available. Some attempted to return fire, and were mowed down in the process.

As Rice leveled the craft, Clark opened up on the main guardhouse, which was now manned by the Arabs. Glass and wood splinters filled the air.

They were beyond it by now.

Russo's voice came over the intercom. "We didn't take them out. They have what looks like a RPG-7 in there. We better finish the job."

Heading the aircraft around for another run, Rice again used the landscape for cover as long as possible. Allowing enough room so as not to be caught in the explosion, he fired off two sets of rockets. The air filled with a shower of wood, glass, bodies, smoke and flames. Veering off to the right slightly, he avoided the fallout and swung back to the chateau, the M-60's laying down additional covering fire.

The ground fire on the return trip was heavier, and they took several more hits, including one to the main rotor. That was evident by the high pitched whistle emitting from it.

"MAMA BEAR do you copy," Aiden's voice came over the radio. "We're in position at ground level of the north wing."

"Copy that boss," Rice replied. Turning to Clark, he said, "let's go get 'em."

Rice button-holed the copter over the west wing, and allowed the helicopter to hover just above the ground.

"We still have rockets,' Clark announced. "We need to dump 'em."

"No problem," Rice said, as he squeezed off the remaining two sets into the wooded area along the perimeter. They hit the trees and exploded with ear splitting splendor.

Meanwhile, Russo kicked out the spent ammo cans.

There was gunfire from inside the chateau. Rice landed the Huey so that Russo's gun would offer some cover.

At the sight of the Huey, Aiden ran forward awkwardly, Jeremy slumped over his shoulder. Russo laying down a hail of bullets, driving two pursuing Arabs back into the building.

"Get us the hell out of here!" Aiden yelled, while handing Jeremy over to Russo, then whirling his hand at Rice in the classic take off signal.

Russo laid down additional cover fire as Rice took them over the trees to safety.

"That's far enough," Aiden said, using Russo's helmet to talk to Rice. "Alanna's still in there."

While he did so, Russo took the first aid kit and bandaged Jeremy's leg, covered him with a blanket, and administered a dose of morphine for his pain.

"Where is she?"

"Kamal went to get the bomb, and she went after him," Aiden said.

"Does she have some way to communicate with us?" Rice asked.

"No," Aiden replied.

"Then we'll just have to spot her the old fashioned way," Rice said, as he took the Huey up just high enough above treetop level for Clark, using high power binoculars, to keep a lookout for her.

* * *

The passageway that Alanna had taken put her at the base of the pavilion that housed Francois' safe. She could hear gunfire, but it appeared to be coming from some distance. Still, she was very careful to check all directions as she emerged from the passageway door.

There was an eerie quiet that pervaded the area.

Carefully, Alanna made her way up the steps. On reaching the top, she noticed that the door to the room stood open, the alarm system inactive. A visual search told her there was no one in the immediate area. Looking into the room, she saw that the door to the safe was also open. It was from there that the first sounds came, warning her that someone was present.

To the left of the desk that sat across the room from the safe's entrance, was a full length, standing mirror. Just for an instant it showed a reflection of the person in the safe. It was Kamal.

A moment later, he came out into the room, the soccer ball box in his hands. When he turned his back to the door, Alanna stepped inside, Jake's gun in her hand.

"Pity it's worthless, isn't it?" Alanna said.

Kamal turned to face her, but with the heavy box in his hands and her gun already on him, he had no choice but to stand his ground.

"What do you mean, it is worthless?"

"Just what I said, and I should know, because I made it worthless."

"You are lying!"

"I'm afraid not, Kamal," Alanna said.

He started to move.

"Don't do it Kamal, I am an excellent shot and it would give me great pleasure to shoot you with this particular weapon as it belonged to my good friend, Jake Carter, who you murdered, remember?"

452

"What do you intend to do?"

"Well, since you also killed Francois here in his very own home, while his guest, I think that I will let Francois exact the retribution."

"What are you talking about?"

"Well, I know that you are familiar with the security system in this room, or at least you think you know it," Alanna said pushing the door to the room open wide so the security panel was in view. "But, I'll bet you don't know that if I raise the level of the power of the laser beams to maximum, they are no longer the benign guardians of this room, but a killer force. And since, without special equipment to negotiate through their path, you become their target."

As she said this, she began to turn up the power switch on the wall.

"So," she said, "I suggest you stay right where you are, otherwise you are toast, literally."

"Goodbye, Kamal, may hell be yours for all eternity." And with that parting remark, she stepped back, and closed and locked the door.

"No, wait." Came the shout from inside, and then the sound of a blast and a horrendous scream.

* * *

"I see her, I see her!" Clark shouted, pointing to the roof of the chateau, just beyond the pavilion.

"Let's go get her," Rice said, taking the Huey up and over the trees.

Alanna heard them coming. She braced herself for the rotor wash, and, as the Huey's skid came within her reach, she grabbed it. And the Huey lifted off.

Epilogue

Alanna and Granton sat in the surgical waiting room of the US Air Force base hospital in Britain. Jeremy had been in surgery for hours, his life hanging in the balance.

"Any news?" Aiden said, coming through the waiting room door, Rice right behind him.

Alanna just shook her head.

"You should have left without me," she said to Rice.

"He wouldn't let us go without you, Alanna," Aiden said.

More hours passed. Finally, a man in surgical garb came into the room. They all rose and faced him.

"I'm LTC Holmes, Mr. Slade's surgeon." He paused for a moment, leaving everyone breathless, then said, "Mr. Slade's head wound was not serious, but it became a medical necessity to amputate his leg just below the knee."

"Oh, God," Alanna said, out loud, knowing what that would mean to his career and his emotional state, as Jeremy always prided himself on his physical fitness, his masculine image. Then, not able to wait for him to say, she asked. "Will he live?"

"Yes, but his recovery time, physically and mentally, will be considerable."

* * *

It had been six months since the conclusion of Operation SABRE. Alanna followed Jeremy as he piloted his mechanized wheelchair through the lobby of CIA headquarters. She stopped at the wall of stars, commemorating those who had given their lives in the course of their CIA work. There was a new one. Though there was no name next to the star's number in the book that rested on a pedestal in front of the wall, she and Jeremy knew it was Jake's.

"If it weren't for you, mine would have been right up there beside his," Jeremy said, pulling up beside her. "Despite the inconvenience," he continued, looking down at his partially missing limb, "I guess I'm lucky, they get to hand me my award."

It was a bittersweet moment for Jeremy, who, they both knew, because of his injury, would never do his old job again.

They made their way up to the director's office, where Aiden stood waiting, just outside the door.

He smiled in way of greeting to Alanna, and she returned the smile. To Jeremy, he said, "How have you been doing, Jeremy?"

"Good. Real good. A man couldn't do much better with all the tender, loving care I've been getting," Jeremy replied, while glancing over his shoulder at Alanna. His answer meant to indicate his close relationship with Alanna, and to irritate Aiden

He caught the cross look she gave him, and added, in a friendlier tone, "Thanks for helping me out of there."

"Don't give it a thought,' Aiden replied, "I'd have done the same for anyone."

"We better go on in," Alanna said, breaking the strained silence that followed Aiden's cool reply. It had been her decision, that if Jeremy were to convalesce anywhere it would be at her farm, and in her care. But, while Jeremy might have liked his relationship with her during that time to be more intimate, they were all aware that convalescing there was all he had done.

Inside, Hawthorne, Taylor, Rice, and Clark were already assembled.

They greeted one another upon entering, and Hawthorne welcomed them in.

"Come in, come in, good to have you back, Jeremy," he said. "How are you feeling?

"Good, sir, I have had a great nurse," he said smiling, indicating Alanna standing behind him.

"And it shows," Hawthorne said in agreement. Then, offering his hand to Alanna, he welcomed her by saying. "It is a great pleasure to finally meet you, Alanna. We all owe you a tremendous debt of gratitude. This operation could not have succeeded without your courage and determination against some frightful odds."

"Thank you, sir." Alanna said, while accepting his outstretched hand.

"Isn't is amazing. Whoever would have thought Hakeem would turn out to be an Israeli, working for Mossad? The intelligence business is always full of surprises, is it not?" Hawthorne remarked.

"Hakeem lives his cover very well, almost too well. But then, Jake only dealt with the best in the business. Hakeem was invaluable to the success of this mission," Alanna replied, "and, thankfully, because he survived, will continue to be a valuable asset in the future. We haven't heard the last from these terrorist groups, and, I'm afraid, won't for the foreseeable future.

"Unfortunately, I know you are right, Alanna." Then turning to Aiden, Hawthorne said," It's good to see you again, Aiden. Thank you for coming aboard when we needed you. I hope you will consider signing on as a regular. We could use a man like you."

"Thank you, sir, I'll consider the offer," Aiden replied.

Finally, turning to the others, he said, as he moved behind his desk, "Well, we're all here, so gather round, people. I am going to make this ceremony short, because I know it is still difficult for Jeremy to sit up for any length of time. Someone close the door, please."

Clark did so.

They gathered in front of the desk, and Hawthorne said, "First, I would like to say that you people are first class in every way, and we at The Agency are more than proud of you. We consider it an honor and privilege to count you among us. It is because of the dedication and proficiency of people like yourself that we are able to accomplish the enormously difficult job this organization is tasked with.

"I offer you the heartfelt thanks of your country, the President and myself and your peers. And it gives me great pleasure to present each of you with this Intelligence Star, which is awarded to you for your heroism in the face of existing danger. Notwithstanding the hazards inherent in the operation, each of you carried out his or her assignment in such a manner as to reflect most favorably on his or her courage and determination, and with selfless consideration for the lives and safety of one another. God bless you all."

They each in turn came forward to receive their award.

"Before we partake of the refreshments," Hawthorne said, indicating a table full of food set to the side. "I have an announcement, which you will be the first to hear.

"The President has asked me to step down as director of the CIA, and become his Secretary of the State. He asked if I had any recommendations as to who should succeed me, and I did. Granton Taylor will make a great CIA director.

Everyone applauded his choice, and began congratulating Granton and shaking his hand.

"And," Hawthorne once again summoned their attention, "it is my suggestion to Granton, that if he is smart, he will appoint Jeremy Slade as his director of operations."

There was stunned silence in the room, and then a renewed shaking of hands all around.

"Good," said Hawthorne. "Then, now that we have the awards, and the change of command out of the way, let's eat."

Later, he approached Alanna, who stood looking out the window.

She turned to face him as he said, "I heard some disappointing news. Granton said you're leaving us again. I heard that you're going to Ireland to help Aiden set up his new horse farm. Is that true?"

Smiling, she said, "Yes, it's true. Now that the dust from the French affair has settled, and my cover is reestablished sufficiently, I think I'll take a short vacation."

Then, looking in Jeremy's direction, she added, "but now, the man in charge knows I'm only a phone call away."

"That is most reassuring to know both for me and our country," Hawthorne replied, "and, I'm sure, for our new director of operations as well. The best to you, Alanna, stay safe."

"Thank you, and to you, sir."

The room began to empty.

Aiden said his goodbyes. Then turning in Alanna's direction, he pointed to his watch, and said, "Better get a move on or we'll miss our flight."

"Give me a minute," she said, and he headed for the door.

In route, he stopped in front of Jeremy. Offering his hand, he said, "Congratulations, Jeremy, you are definitely the man to fill Granton's shoes. Take care of yourself."

Jeremy shook his hand.

"Thanks, I will," Jeremy replied. Then glancing in Alanna's direction, he said, "And you take care of our friend."

"I'll do my best," Aiden replied, and left the room, closing the door behind him.

Only Alanna and Jeremy remained.

She crossed to where Jeremy sat, his gaze expressionless. As she approached, he smiled a half-smile.

She came around behind him, and bending down. put her arms around him, and placed a soft kiss on his cheek.

"I'm going to miss you, Carida," he said, sadly, his hands caressing the arms that enfolded him. "You mean everything to me, and yet I've managed to botch every opportunity I've had to make you mine.

"And now this..." he said, pointing to his leg. "Aiden's the right man to make you happy, Alanna. He loves you. That's obvious. And he has everything to offer you, and none of the baggage to live down. But, I want you to know that I will never stop loving you."

Alanna stood, letting her hands glide up his arms and rest on his shoulder.

"It seems that where our personal lives are concerned, we always come to the same end," she replied, gently. "You have a lot to sort out in your life now, Jeremy. When you know how you really feel, and can accept how things are, and be content with them, that is when we can consider if there is a future for us. Until then, we need to live our separate lives."

She came around to face him, took his hands in hers, and said, "My heart and my love are mine to give. For now, I haven't given them to anyone. That doesn't mean I don't long to be loved. I do. But, I need to be loved by the right man. Be the right man, Jeremy."

THE END

About the Author

Karen A. Lynch spent her entire life in the horse business. First as an equestrian and riding instructor, then as a breeder for clients of champion Thoroughbred racehorses on her Kentucky farm, and most recently, as the owner and breeder of classic Spanish Andalusian horses. She is married to former CIA Intelligence Officer Grayston L. Lynch, recipient of the CIA's Intelligence Star. Karen holds a BA in creative writing and political science from the University of Tampa. She was the ghostwriter for her husband's book *Decision for Disaster; Betrayal at the Bay of Pigs,* and authored the stage production *Cat Scanned.* Karen is the mother of geologist Elizabeth Ann Haynes, and grandmother of future equestrian star, Amy Elizabeth Haynes.

Printed in the United States
1370700002B/202